CS 3451

marker on pgs 25-27

CHILDREN OF THE SERPENT GATE

Also by Sarah Ash

LORD OF SNOW AND SHADOWS
Book One of the Tears of Artamon

PRISONER OF THE IRON TOWER
Book Two of the Tears of Artamon

CHILDREN
of the
SERPENT
GATE

Book Three of the Tears of Artamon

Sarah Ash

BANTAM BOOKS

CHILDREN OF THE SERPENT GATE
A Bantam Spectra Book / October 2005

Published by Bantam Dell
A Division of Random House, Inc.
New York, New York

Library of Congress Cataloging-in-Publication Data

Ash, Sarah.
    Children of the serpent gate / Sarah Ash.
      p. cm. — (The tears of Artamon ; bk. 3)
    ISBN-13: 978-0-553-38212-9
    ISBN-10: 0-553-38212-8
    I. Title.

    PS3601.S523C48 2005
    813'.6—dc22

                                                    2005047237

Printed in the United States of America
Published simultaneously in Canada

www.bantamdell.com

BVG   10 9 8 7 6 5 4 3 2 1

For Catherine

ACKNOWLEDGMENTS

As the curtain comes down on the third and final act of the Tears of Artamon, the author expresses her heartfelt thanks to all those people who have stood in the wings and now deserve to take a bow.

First, the highly talented directors and their teams: editors Anne Groell (Bantam US) and Simon Taylor (Transworld UK) who deserve big bouquets for their energy, endless patience, and perspicacity!

And also the agents, Merrilee Heifetz of Writer's House and John Richard Parker at MBA, for getting the whole project off the ground and into print.

Then, the artists: Steve Youll for his brilliantly evocative covers and Jamie S. Warren Youll for the wonderful jacket designs.

Not forgetting Neil Gower for bringing New Rossiya to cartographic life in his map, and Ariel, editor of The Alien Online, and also my webmaster, for designing and maintaining www.sarah-ash.com.

Senior Management at Oak Lodge Primary School, especially Paul Guy, Mike Totterdell, and Elsa Thompson for giving me time when I most needed it! And not forgetting all my colleagues (past and present) for their support and encouragement.

Last, and in no way least, my husband, Michael!

THE ROSSIYAN EMPIRE

Gower '05

KHITAI

St Sergius's Monastery

The WHITE SEA

Arkhelskoye

Lake Taigal

Arkhel Waste

The Arkhel MOORS

KHENDIR

Kastel Drakhaon

Llimin

AZHKENDIR

Narvazh

Azhgorod

SALTYK SEA

Mirom

River Nieva

Erinaskoe

MUSCOBAR

Vermeille Bay

Vermeille

Colchise

SMARNA

Bichvinta Point

SOUTHERN OCEAN

DJIHAN DJIHAR

Desert

TIELEN

Rosenholm

Swanholm

Tielborg

Haeven

The STRAITS

Lapwing Spar

The IRON SEA

Arnskammar

Holborg

Fenez Tyr

Belle Garde

FRANZ VICA

To Provença

Lutèce

PROLOGUE

Red as heart's blood, the five rubies glowed in the golden casket, as if a spark of light burned at their innermost core.

Enguerrand, King of Francia, stared at his trophies. The fabled Tears of Artamon were his now, and in taking ownership of them, he had laid claim to the Empire of New Rossiya.

He laid the casket on the little altar and knelt, head bowed in prayer.

"I never asked for these earthly treasures," he murmured. "But if it be Your will that I use them for the good of Your earthly empire, then Your will be done. Only show me what I must do."

A quiet knock at the cabin door interrupted his reverie. "Enter."

Ruaud de Lanvaux, Grand Maistre of the Francian Commanderie, came in, ducking beneath the low lintel to avoid hitting his head. Grizzled and lean-faced, the soldier-priest had been spiritual adviser and confessor to the young king since Enguerrand's early years.

"Disturbing portents, majesty. Look at the angelstone."

He drew a crystal pendant from around his neck and held it up for the king to see. Enguerrand adjusted his spectacles and peered at the pendant. The clear crystal was filled with swirls of darkness that pulsed and churned.

"What does this mean?"

"Daemonic activity. I've never seen anything like this in my whole life, sire. It's almost as if someone has breached the gateway to the Realm of Shadows and let loose the fiends of hell."

Enguerrand peered more closely at the angelstone. Now he could see little traces of phosphorescent color glinting in the dark: blue, green, scarlet, violet, and gold . . .

"And before there was only the one. Now there are five."

"Five daemon-warriors from the Realm of Shadows?"

"I fear so."

Enguerrand clenched his fists. "Who summoned them? Who is so eager to bring about the end of the world? Haven't they read the Book of Eliazar? Once they are loose, others will follow."

"If only the monks at Sergius's Shrine had agreed to our request and given us their holy relic, we could have reforged Sergius's Staff by now and armed ourselves against these daemons."

"If we can find someone as pure in heart as Sergius to wield the Staff."

The Grand Maistre's lean face softened in a brief smile. "The Commanderie has always believed you to be Sergius's heir, sire. You have led a blameless life and dedicated yourself selflessly to our cause."

Heir to Saint Sergius? A Holy Warrior battling on earth against the powers of evil? Enguerrand felt a blush of pleasure warming his face at the glorious images these words conjured up. But wasn't it a sin of pride to feel so pleased? He willed the thought away, concentrating on other concerns.

"We must impress on Abbot Yephimy the urgent need to hand over Sergius's golden crook," continued the Grand Maistre.

"And if he and the brothers refuse?"

"Then the Commanderie will employ more forceful means." The Grand Maistre's grim expression left Enguerrand in no doubt as to his intentions. "We can delay no longer."

"But we still know so little of the enemy. Could this be the work of the Nagarian clan?"

"Lord Gavril Nagarian died in Arnskammar, sire. Our agents gleaned the intelligence from sources in Tielen. But his daemon is still abroad and—"

A sudden sickening sensation swept through Enguerrand's body. He swayed on his feet. At the same time, the cabin grew dark, as though stormclouds had blotted out the sun. And a shout of terror came from the deck above.

The Grand Maistre grabbed hold of the young king, steadying him. "Sire! Are you all right?"

In the murky darkness, the Tears of Artamon gave off a sudden flicker of crimson fire.

"The—the Tears," babbled Enguerrand, trying to form words. "L—look."

A shimmer of sapphire radiated through the inky black of the angelstone, pulsing in rhythm with the flickering of the rubies.

Enguerrand pushed the Grand Maistre aside and staggered toward the cabin door. He felt impelled to go up on deck, to see what had caused the sudden darkness. But even as he clambered up the stair, the sky outside had cleared and was once again cloudless and blue.

The Grand Maistre followed close behind him.

"Captain Gilduin!" Enguerrand called. All the ship's officers and men were gazing up into the heavens, shading their eyes against the glare of the sun. "What in the name of God was that?"

On hearing the king's voice, the sailors dropped back, bowing. But Enguerrand could not help noticing that they still kept stealing sidelong glances at the sky.

"There it goes, sire." The captain pointed out across the sea.

Enguerrand lifted his hand to his brow, peering through the sundazzle reflected off the waves. There, in the far distance, he could just make out a dark, winged creature—too large, surely, for a bird— skimming away toward the horizon.

Captain Gilduin handed him his own eyeglass and, in his haste, Enguerrand banged it against his spectacle lens as he put it to one eye. In the glass's magnification, cloaked in a shimmer of dark smoke, he spied a creature plucked from the books of legends he had devoured as a child: a great hook-winged dragon, daemon-eyed and daemon-clawed.

A foul fiend from the Realm of Shadows.

"It's not possible," he whispered. A shiver of mortal terror ran through him, even though the sun was burning down. So this was the adversary. He felt his hands shaking as he lowered the eyeglass. Saint Sergius had died battling the Drakhaoul of Azhkendir. Even with the help of the Heavenly Warriors, he had died. And now that Enguerrand had seen one of these daemon-warriors, he knew from the churning in his bowels that it would take extraordinary courage and faith to challenge such an opponent. More courage, perhaps, than he could summon. He felt weak and demoralized, and all too aware of his own mortality.

"Sire," said a quiet voice behind him. He turned and saw Ruaud de Lanvaux holding out a paper. "I think this may interest you."

Enguerrand fiddled with his spectacles, trying to hide the tremor in his hands as he peered at the new dispatch.

"We have intercepted intelligence within the Tielen network confirming that Gavril Nagarian, Drakhaon of Azhkendir, is not dead, as reported earlier, but alive and believed to be at large in Smarna."

"Alive?" His eyes met those of the Grand Maistre over the rim of the paper. "Was that—?" He gestured to the empty sky where, but a minute or so ago, he had seen the daemon-dragon overflying his fleet.

"Very likely, sire." The Grand Maistre's expression was severe.

"And yet he didn't attack us." Enguerrand leaned on the rail, gazing out over the waters.

"Our duty, as devout believers, sire, is to cast the daemons from this world."

"And Gavril Nagarian?"

Enguerrand suddenly saw himself standing alone and vulnerable, raising the Staff of the saint against a snarling dark-winged dragon that breathed searing fire to annihilate him. He swallowed hard. "What can we do? Suppose he attacks us before we're properly armed?"

"We need Sergius's crook to reforge the Staff."

"Then we must send the Commanderie to Saint Sergius's Monastery." Enguerrand heard his own voice issuing the command in such a forthright tone that he surprised himself. "And if Abbot Yephimy refuses to comply, we'll be obliged to seize the relic by force." He saw the stern line of the Grand Maistre's mouth relax as a look of approval warmed his eyes.

Enguerrand could not sleep. Ever since the Drakhaon had flown overhead, he felt that his mind had been touched by darkness.

"Polluted," he murmured, filled with self-disgust. And although he had performed a rigorous cleansing ritual, beating his body with a flail until it bled, the daemonic taint still remained, like the hangover from a nightmare, tarnishing the cheerful promise of a new day.

All he had read in the ancient scriptures warned of the coming of a time when the prince of darkness would burst from his prison in the Realm of Shadows and take dominion over the world of mortal men. In the ensuing battle, the world would be consumed in fire—and all those possessed by the daemons would be condemned to eternal torment.

Enguerrand rose from the cramped bed and crossed the cabin to open the little window and gaze out at the limpid moonlit sea. Tomorrow they would land in Smarna. He had been promised a warm welcome by the Smarnans, who were overjoyed at being freed from the tyranny of the Emperor's rule.

The moonlight traced a gilded trail across the black waters.

"Like an angel pathway to the heavens," Enguerrand murmured, resting his head on his arms. A warm breeze still blew off the distant coast of Djihan-Djihar, dry as the burning sands of the desert. And the moon, a great burnished disc hanging low over the waves, looked as if it were forged from the beaten metal of Djihari prayer-gongs.

Glimmer of golden wings across the face of the moon . . .

Enguerrand stared. He rubbed his heavy eyes. He must have dozed off for a moment, lulled by the gentle onward motion of the ship. Then he stared again, for it seemed to him that a creature, golden-winged, was flying directly toward him along that angel pathway, the moonlight shimmering through its translucent form.

He blinked, took off his spectacles, rubbed them on his nightshirt, replaced them, and looked again.

It was gaining on them swiftly, its radiance brighter than the moonlight, so bright he could scarcely look at it.

"Who are you?" he whispered. "And what do you want?"

"*Enguerrand . . .*" The voice rang sweetly, softly, like a chime of sweet-tongued bells.

"I am Enguerrand."

"*You have been chosen, Enguerrand. Chosen to be a warrior in the wars to come . . .*"

"Me? A warrior?" Had his prayers been answered? Was this one of the Heavenly Warriors coming to his aid?

"*Join with me, Enguerrand.*"

"I will do all I can and more to defeat—"

"*What can you, a mortal man, hope to achieve alone against such forces?*" The gold-winged spirit hovered over the waves; its light was so dazzling that Enguerrand had to look away. "*Join with me and I will give you my powers.*"

"J—join?" Enguerrand did not understand what the Heavenly Warrior meant. But his heart thrummed with emotion. He had been chosen. It was just as he had always dreamed. "You know I am with you, heart and soul. My armies are at your disposal—"

"Heart, soul—and body."

"Yes." And almost before the reckless affirmation was spoken, the spirit rose above the waves, its wings beating so fast that Enguerrand found himself swept up in a glittering whirlwind. He tried to cry out—but his voice was smothered. He fell back, crashing to the floor of the cabin, as a spinning cloud of dazzling light enclosed him.

Caught in a storm of whirling star-shards, Enguerrand sees a figure walking toward him, its arms outspread, as though to embrace him.

"My angel. My guardian angel." He runs to meet it gladly, arms wide-open. For one instant he glimpses a face, golden-eyed, framed by a lion's mane of flaming hair—and then he is consumed in the bright one's burning embrace. Shuddering, ecstatic, he cries out, certain he will be destroyed by its cleansing fire—

"Majesty!"

Enguerrand opened his eyes and saw his valet Fragan bending over him.

"Thank God, majesty, you're all right!"

Enguerrand allowed Fragan to help him up into a sitting position. He blinked. The cabin was bright with early-morning sun. How long had he been unconscious?

"Shall I call the physician?"

"No." Enguerrand raised his hand. "No. A glass of mineral water and I'll be fine."

"But majesty, your mother insisted that if—"

"I said *no*." Enguerrand pulled himself to his feet, one hand gripping the side of his bunk.

"Water, then." Fragan scurried away, leaving behind the tray of shaving materials. Enguerrand picked up the shaving mirror and studied his reflection in it. He looked exactly the same as he had the night before, except for a dark morning shadow of stubble. One hand traced the contours of his face questioningly.

"Was it only a dream?" he asked his reflection. It had all seemed so vivid, so viscerally real. And yet there was no difference in the outward appearance that peered shortsightedly back at him in the mirror. And how he wished that Fragan had not mentioned his mother Aliénor; ever since his brother Aubrey died, she had been insufferably overprotective, surrounding him with physicians, so alarmed at the slightest cough or sneeze that he lived in a constant state of dread.

"*No dream, my chosen one,*" whispered a voice deep within him. "*Soon we shall begin the glorious fight together.*" And to Enguerrand's astonishment, he saw in the mirror a glint of angel-gold radiate from his dark brown eyes, flickering as the voice spoke.

"Thank you," Enguerrand said, falling on his knees at his prie-dieu, hands clasped together in fervent prayer. "Now I know what I must do. I must destroy Gavril Nagarian and the Drakhaoul that possesses him."

CHAPTER 1

"I'm old." Kiukiu stared in disbelief at her reflection. "I'm an old woman." Her fingertips moved over her lined face, lifting her wild, dry locks of greying hair, searching in vain for a thread of gold. She was so shocked she could only stare at the aging stranger in the mirror glass. "How long was I gone?"

"Many days, my dear." Malusha had never called her "my dear" before. That in itself made Kiukiu fearful. "Too many days."

"There's a remedy, isn't there, Grandma?" She turned to Malusha. "Tell me what to do, I'll do it. No matter what it is."

Malusha sat a moment, thinking. "I'll go put the kettle on," she said, easing herself up from Kiukiu's side. Making tea was Malusha's remedy for all ills, great and small.

"Grandma, what do you know?" Kiukiu persisted.

"I know that you wouldn't be still in this world if Lord Gavril hadn't flown to Swanholm to rescue you."

"Lord Gavril?" The glass dropped from her fingers. She looked up and found herself staring into the deep blue of Gavril's eyes. "You're *alive*?" She forgot her own distress and just gazed up at him. "But they said you were dead. They showed me the tower, they showed me where the lightning struck—"

And then she realized that he must be able to see every wrinkle, each strand of dull grey hair. She covered her face with her hands, turning away from him, not wanting him to see her like this.

"Kiukiu?" he said. He said her name so gently—and yet she could detect the bewilderment in his tone.

"Don't look at me. Please." This was the reunion she had dreamed of for so long. But in her dreams, she had been unchanged by the Ways Beyond. She had run to greet him, her arms outstretched, her golden hair loose about her shoulders. "That evil old man," she muttered. "He lied to me. He made me think you were dead, and all to trick me into his trap."

"What old man?"

"Kaspar Linnaius. He sent me into the Ways Beyond to look for you. And then, when I couldn't find you, he spun me some foolish story. And I believed him! Why didn't I trust my own instincts?" She was so angry with herself that she began to shake. "Why did I let him use me?"

"So you got lost in the Ways Beyond, searching for me?"

She nodded. Though even as she did so, she was aware that this was not the whole tale. There was more, much more, and she could not remember what it was, only that it made her shudder even more to think of it.

"Don't cry, Kiukiu." He put his arms around her and held her close, stroking her hair.

"I'm not crying!" *How could he bear to hold her, to touch those dry, faded locks?* Tears spurted, hot against her fingers. She wanted to bury her face in his shoulder and feel safe, comforted and cherished. But all she could think of was the haggard, faded creature she had seen reflected in the mirror.

"It wasn't lightning that struck the Iron Tower, Kiukiu. It was the Drakhaoul."

Her sobs subsided a little. So he also had something to confess.

"I was dying. And it rescued me." His lips hardly moved against her hair, as if he were whispering to prevent the Drakhaoul hearing what he said.

"Dying? So the story was in part true?" She felt another shiver run through her. He had suffered, she could sense it now, and he was not entirely healed. And there was something different, disturbing, about him, almost as if the Drakhaoul had begun to leach its darkness into his soul.

"In part."

"Oh, Gavril," she whispered. One hand, wet with her own tears, crept out to touch his face. *What cruel things had they done to him in that asylum? What damage had they inflicted?*

"Tea's ready," announced Malusha, bringing over three brimming mugs. "You get this hot drink down you, my girl."

Kiukiu tried to take a sip of the fragrant liquid but her hands were shaking so much that she could hardly raise the mug to her lips. She managed a little but then the sides of her mouth begin to sag as the sense of loss welled up from deep within her again. *Old. I'm old before I've lived my life.* She sobbed helplessly into her tea, unable to stop herself, even though she knew that Gavril and her grandmother were watching her.

"Drink your tea." Even though Malusha spoke quietly, Kiukiu heard a note of brisk command in her voice. She shakily lifted the mug again, slopping tea over the top. She still couldn't stop the tears and now she no longer knew who she was crying for: for Gavril, damaged by the asylum; for herself; for their uncertain future . . . The tea tasted salty—though even the taint of her tears could not disguise another richer flavor. There was a potency in the dark, sweet liquid that spread heat throughout her whole body, right to the tips of her fingers.

"What's in this?" she asked suspiciously.

"Something to restore you," said Malusha. "You're all skin and bone. There's moorland honey from my bees, for one."

"Honey, Grandma?" Kiukiu said muzzily. "It tastes like mead to me."

Malusha shrugged. "Mead's made from honey."

The warmth of the heather mead spread into Kiukiu's mind, seeping through the bitter thoughts, numbing the pain. She yawned and tried to force her lids to stay open. She mustn't drift back into sleep. If she fell asleep, she could find herself back wandering those vast halls among the wan, confused spirits of the Newly Dead—or, worse still, gusted far from those she loved by the whirlwinds into that nightmare realm of dust and shadows.

"That's right," Malusha whispered, gently prising the mug from her fingers. "Just lie back. You're safe here."

"How can I be sure?" Kiukiu murmured.

"Be sure of what?" Drakhaoul-blue eyes gazed piercingly into hers.

"That this isn't a dream?"

She felt his hand close around hers, his grip firm and warm. "Does this feel like a dream, Kiukiu?"

"No . . ." The orange glow of the firelight was receding as her eyelids drooped but still she could see the intense blue of his eyes burning into hers through the gathering mists of sleep.

✳   ✳   ✳

Kiukiu's eyes closed at last and her breathing came slowly, regularly. Gavril let go of her hand and rose to his feet.

"She should sleep soundly now," Malusha said. She shook her head as she watched over her granddaughter, her wild locks wispy as an old man's beard against the glow of firelight.

A burning shiver of nausea speared through Gavril's whole body. He tried to conceal it, turning away from Malusha so that she should not see it in his face. He had overspent himself. He had used up the last of his strength in his desperation to save Kiukiu, and now the terrible cravings had begun in earnest. He crouched by the fireside, hugging the hunger in, hoping he could try to stave off the worst of the pangs for a little longer.

"It's never been done. Not without cost." Malusha seemed to be talking to herself, shaking her head and twisting a tassel of her brightly colored shawl between her fingers.

Gavril glanced over at Kiukiu—at the faded, shrunken shadow of the girl he loved so much—and another tremor of anger throbbed through him. He was not used to feeling so helpless.

"Malusha." He took hold of the old woman by the shoulders, forcing her to look into his face. "Tell me all you know."

"Is that you or your daemon talking?"

"Does it matter?"

"First you will let go of me, Drakhaon," Malusha said in an icy voice.

His hands fell away. "Forgive me."

"Yes," she said, staring searchingly into his face. "It is growing stronger. I am not sure that I could cast it out now as I did before. It has meshed itself far deeper into you, and it is drawing strength from some distant source of power. I sense others of its kin at large in our world."

He could hide nothing from those disapproving dark eyes. "Eugene and the Magus set them free. There are five—and now that the Serpent Gate has been breached, more could follow."

" '*Only the Emperor's Tears will unlock the Gate,*' that's what the Blessed Serzhei said," Malusha muttered. "Kaspar Linnaius." She swore and spat onto the flagstone floor. "Do you know how old he is?"

Gavril shrugged. "He looks about eighty . . . maybe eighty-five."

"Guess again."

"Ninety?"

"Kaspar Linnaius was born one hundred and sixty years ago."

Was Malusha playing games with him? He had never heard of any-one living beyond a hundred years, let alone a hundred and sixty. "But how——?"

"An alchymical elixir. A little dose of that could do my poor Kiukiu a world of good right now."

"Then I'll go back to Swanholm and find Linnaius and his elixir."

Malusha tapped his arm. "You've already flown far. A journey to Tielen and back will use up the last of your resources. How long be-fore you need to feed again, Drakhaon?"

Another shiver of nausea burned through his body. He bit back a groan, hoping she had not noticed.

"Is there any alternative?" The words came out in a snarl. "Would you prefer to fly there yourself?"

"The alternatives?" She ignored his gibe. "I've heard tales of shamans in Khitari, north over the mountains. It's just as far, if not farther."

"Khitari?" The name made him think of the exotic, dusty scent of black and green tea in the kitchen at the Villa Andara, and the black-and-gold lacquer boxes his mother kept her precious teas in, deco-rated with pictures of dragons and lion dogs. "What's so unique about these Khitari shamans?"

"They're said to live very long lives. There's a legend of a secret healing spring."

Gavril shook his head impatiently. "I haven't time to search all Khitari for some legendary spring." His throat and mouth were so dry it was becoming hard to speak, in spite of the tea he had drunk. And the cravings had begun to affect his mind. The coolness of pure water, miraculous healing water, rushed through his fevered thoughts, promising a cure for the waves of nausea. As a stronger pang wracked his body, he dropped to his knees, hugging his burning stomach, trying not to cry out.

Malusha just stood there, looking down at him.

"You're no use to her like this," she said.

"Why—is there—no other—way?" Each word came out on a gasp of pain.

"Because mortal men are too weak to bear such a powerful daemon for long," she said dispassionately. "It's killing you, Gavril Nagarian, just as it killed your forebears."

"It—told me—I could set it free by sending it home through the Serpent Gate. But it lied," he whispered, between pangs. "It used me." Now he remembered—and the bitterness of remembering enhanced the sense of betrayal that had haunted him since Ty Nagar.

"And how long can you last in this condition? Before you attack some defenseless child?"

He shook his head, no longer able to speak. He had expended too much of his power in the duel with the Emperor.

"There's fresh water in the well outside," said Malusha.

Outside, the eerie twilight of the long summer evenings had crept over the moors. In the courtyard, he began to wind the bucket down into the well, only to double up again with the griping pain. He let go of the handle and slid down, his back against the mossy stones of the well wall. The bucket splashed into the water far below with a hollow clank. Next moment, he was retching and a dark slime came up. He lay back when the first spasm was over, feeling the heave and ache of his tortured rib cage. He had used up the last of his strength bringing Kiukiu from Swanholm.

"*There is nothing to restore you here.*" The Drakhaoul Khezef spoke through the receding waves of nausea. "*You must hunt while you still have the strength.*"

Gavril heard the Drakhaoul's words as if through drifting smoke. "Don't make me," he begged, his voice hoarse with retching.

"*The summer nights are short in Azhkendir. And you are far from the nearest village.*"

Gavril closed his eyes, seeing little flickers like firesparks fizzing across the darkness. "No," he said.

"*What use will you be to Kiukiu if you die?*"

Gavril felt a wry, mirthless smile curling his lips. The Drakhaoul always knew how to compel him to do what it wished, at the same time making him believe he was acting in his own interests.

"*And you will die, Gavril, if you don't feed soon. Listen to the beat of your heart. Feel how it strains and judders.*"

"At least let me take a drink of water." Gavril set about drawing up the bucket. He plunged his head into the cold, peaty, moorland water, as if he could drown out the daemon-voice in his head. Then he gulped down as much liquid as he could before the vomiting began again.

A soft flutter of wings startled him. On the crooked tiles of the roof perched a row of Arkhel's Owls, white as ghosts against the dusky sky. Fierce golden eyes stared curiously at him. Malusha's lords and ladies were preparing to flit off across the darkening banks of heather to hunt for their prey.

"I'm not so different from you now, am I, my lords and ladies?" he whispered. "A predator of the night . . ."

Scarlet fire scored his mind. A wordless cry of fury and frustration shivered across the moors, and the sky turned black as smoke.

The cry pierced Gavril's mind like a spear of flame. He dropped to his knees, clutching his temples, as the old wound from Baltzar's botched surgery throbbed and burned.

"What—was—*that*?" he gasped as the flames died down.

"*Sahariel*," Khezef cried, ignoring Gavril. "*Sahariel, wait!*"

"Who is Sahariel? Another Drakhaoul? Where was it going?"

"*He is searching. Searching for one of the Blood. Artamon's blood.*"

"I must find Kaspar Linnaius." Gavril stubbornly repeated the words under his breath as he forced himself back toward the coast and the Saltyk Sea. But with each labored wingstroke he felt himself grow weaker. It seemed that he had been flying over rugged moorland for hours without number—and still there was no sign of the sea. And the pounding blood in his ears and temples was like the thud of an ominous drum.

"*What use will you be to Kiukirilya if you die?*"

What angered him the most was that he knew that Khezef was right. He was pushing his body to the limit of its capabilities.

And then he saw the spires and bell towers of a great cathedral dark against the grey dawn sky.

"This isn't Narvazh. This is Azhgorod!" In his exhaustion, he had flown directly south, not west to the coast and was approaching the capital. "How could I have been so stupid . . . ?" And then he lost control, spiraling raggedly down, helplessly trying to right himself before he hit the ground.

He crashed into bushes on the stony scrubland just outside the city walls. And there he lay, one hand weakly clawing at the raw earth, trying to find the strength to push himself up. He was so spent that he closed his eyes, no longer caring whether he died or no.

"Gone? What d'you mean gone?" Kiukiu cried.

"Well, there was little point in him staying moping about here, was there?"

Kiukiu felt a stab of anguish, cold as a splinter of ice in her heart. "You've driven him away. You and your plain speaking, Grandma!"

"He's gone where he can be of some use to you. Nothing salves a guilty conscience better than a little productive activity."

"And if he fails?" Dire possibilities began to occur to Kiukiu. "Am I to be this way for the rest of my life?"

"Now, now." Malusha took hold of Kiukiu's hands in her own and pressed them firmly between her gnarled fingers. "Let's have none of that kind of talk."

"But why couldn't he stay a little longer? Was it that he couldn't bear to look at me?" Kiukiu had sustained herself for the long months they were parted with the hope that somehow everything would turn out for the best and they would be happily reunited. But all that had happened only served to drive them further apart.

Suppose we're not meant to be together? For the first time she glimpsed quite another future from the one she had so often imagined, the drab prospect of a life lived apart from Lord Gavril. *What hope is there for us now? Every time he looks at me, he'll see the old woman I've become and know that somehow it was his fault.*

"Child, I need to ask you some questions."

"Child, Grandma?" Kiukiu said. She could not hide the bitterness in her voice. "I look as old as you."

For once, Malusha did not rise to her barbed response. "Your memory's still hazy. But I want you to try to remember what errand the Magus had sent you on when you strayed into . . . *you know where.*"

"Why? Will it help?" Kiukiu said doubtfully.

"It might. What were you doing? Think, Kiukiu, think hard."

Kiukiu screwed her eyes tight shut and tried to concentrate. But every time she remembered the desolation of the place of whirling winds and dust, she could only shudder and clutch her arms to herself.

"After all the training I've given you, it was very careless of you to let yourself wander that way."

The criticism stung. "I didn't go there on purpose! I would never have—"

"And yet, there you were. And there you would have stayed if Lady Iceflower and I—"

"Yes and I'm very grateful," snapped Kiukiu. "I'm not so gullible as to go marching back into the Realm of Shadows just for my own amusement. And I remember nothing, so it's no use questioning me further."

Little Zlata, the youngest servant in Lady Stoyan's household, was up before the rest of the household. Her first task of the day, winter and summer alike, was to clean out the tiled kitchen stove and light a fresh fire.

Yawning, her head full of sleep, she went out into the backyard to empty her heavy bucket of ash and cinders. Then she opened the door to the shack where chopped firewood was stacked. She had just begun to fill her bucket when she thought she heard a faint groan.

"Who's there?" Her voice quivered. She hated the shack because of the spiders that lurked in the woodpile; only last week one had dropped into her hair and she had screamed, shaking her head like a madwoman to dislodge it. And hadn't Cook warned her to beware of beggars who liked to steal in at night to shelter?

"Help me . . ."

Now that her sight was better accustomed to the gloom, she caught a glimmer of blue as a shadowy form turned to gaze at her.

"Keep away," she said, backing toward the open door. "Or I'll call Yegor. He's very strong."

"Water . . ."

She could see him more clearly now, a dark-haired young man, well-favored, with blue eyes that gazed so appealingly into hers that she felt her suspicions melting away. He didn't look like a beggar, but then . . .

"What are you doing in here?" she demanded. "You're trespassing."

"Just . . . water. Then I'll go."

From the droop of his head and the faintness of his voice, he looked as if he couldn't go anywhere.

"Are you hurt? Were you robbed?"

He nodded weakly.

"Cook says there's a gang of cutthroats lying in wait for people coming out of the taverns. Looks like they stole everything—even your clothes!"

He raised one hand pleadingly but the effort obviously cost him dear for he suddenly slumped forward, as if he had fainted.

Alarmed, she ran out into the yard to draw water from the well.

"Here," she said, kneeling beside him. She dipped a corner of her apron into the cold well water and dabbed at his head and neck. She could not resist running her fingers through his long, thick dark hair; it was so soft to the touch. It was difficult to be certain in the dim light, but she thought she could make out blue bruises on his body. He must have taken a bad beating, for as she wiped his skin with the wet cloth, he drew in his breath between his teeth, moaning softly.

"I'm sorry," she said, afraid she had made matters worse. "I'll go and call for help. You should see a surgeon."

"No." His hand shot out and gripped her wrist. "Don't go. Don't leave me." There was such urgency in his voice that a surge of fear shot through her. She tried to pull free but he only gripped her more tightly. "I need you." His blue eyes burned with hunger. "Don't be afraid." But she was afraid, mortally afraid, as he drew her down to him on the dusty, spider-ridden floor in the darkness behind the high-piled logs. Hadn't Cook warned her about young men and their importunate needs?

"P—please don't—"

"You touched me with such kindness, such tenderness." He stroked her face, her throat, slowly, gently, as he spoke. "Will you let me—"

"Don't hurt me." She could feel his breath on her neck and it was hot as smoke. But when his mouth sought hers, she began to realize that he had some other, darker intent—and that what he wanted was more than she was willing to give.

"Forgive me," he murmured, cupping her face in his hands. She found herself staring into his eyes, and it was as if she was gazing into a brilliant midnight sky. Everything, the fear and pain, receded, until she felt herself drowning, drowning deep in starlight . . .

Gavril awoke from a confused dream of savage ecstasy to find he was holding a girl in his arms. There were dark red stains on her linen apron and there was a warm, metallic taste in his mouth. He touched her pale cheek and she murmured something inaudible. Her head fell back against his shoulder and he saw with rising horror the bloody lacerations in her throat and breast.

"Why? *Why*, Khezef?" He tried to staunch the blood that was still leaking from her wounds.

"*Go. Leave her,*" urged the Drakhaoul. "*Do you want to be found? You haven't time to waste.*"

Gavril laid the girl down and edged away, a step at a time, unable to take his eyes from her. She was only a servant, he saw now, and a kindhearted one who had taken pity on a stranger.

"She deserves better than this." Tears filled his eyes, blinding him.

"*She was naïve. Gullible. Now, go before we're discovered!*"

Gavril went out into the yard. The city was stirring to life; he could hear horses' hooves and carts rolling past in the street outside. Someone had begun to open the shutters that overlooked the yard.

He felt Khezef unfurl his wings and lift him effortlessly into the air. His great shadow cast the house and yard beneath into darkness as he wheeled around and turned his back on the rising sun.

Yet as he flew away over the city, his tears still fell, hot tears of shame and remorse that scalded his eyes as they dropped onto the wooden roofs of Azhgorod. Her blood had restored his strength and his health—but nothing would clean the stain from his conscience.

Kiukiu drowsed by the fire, afraid to fall asleep in case she found that Malusha's cottage was only a dream and she was still trapped in that dark prison realm of dust and shadows.

Why was I there? she asked herself. *Why can't I remember?*

"Help us, Kiukirilya." The children came clustering about her again, the dead children with their dark, imploring eyes and their terrible wounds. Behind them, a white shore stretched into the distance, washed by a clear azure sea.

"Help us." A girl with hair as sleek as black silk reached out to her. The long, black silk was blown by the sea breeze as she moved closer, to reveal the gaping slit marring her slender throat.

"*Tilua?*" Now Kiukiu gasped as the memories came rushing back, like the frothing tide on the shore. And with them, came the terror. This was Tilua, the wraith-child who had taken possession of little Princess Karila, the very spirit she had been sent to exorcise.

"I tried to help you. But you tricked me, all of you. You trapped me in the shadows." And they must have planned to trap her again. "Because of you, I've grown old before my time."

"Please, Kiukirilya." Tilua seized hold of her hands. "You're our only hope."

"Let me go." Kiukiu snatched her hands away from the wraith-child's grasp. She could feel the panic rising within her. "Let me go back while I can."

"We didn't want to do it." Tilua began to shiver, wrapping her arms about her thin body as if she were cold. "*He* made us. *He* is always listening."

"It's no use." Kiukiu tried to back away. "I can't risk staying here. Don't you understand?"

"He's a prisoner like us. He plans to escape . . . and he believes you will try to stop him." Tilua began to glance around uneasily, as if fearing she would be overheard. "He was very angry with us when he found out we'd been talking to you."

"He's coming," one of the boys cried. "Hide!"

The children scattered. Tilua pulled Kiukiu down into the bushes. They crouched behind huge, fleshy green leaves that reminded Kiukiu of rhubarb leaves in the kastel kitchen garden. And suddenly she felt sick and chilled, overpowered by a sense of black foreboding. The sensation was so strong that she wanted to shrink away—and yet she felt compelled to see who was coming. Peeping out beneath the underside of one of the giant leaves, wide as a parasol, she saw that clouds of a dark vapor were drifting across the white sands, tainting the clear air.

A figure moved within the darkness, preternaturally tall, turning its head slowly from left to right, as though searching. And as it came closer, Kiukiu felt an irresistible urge to rise from her hiding place for a clearer view.

"Don't look at him," hissed Tilua. "Whatever you do, don't look in his eyes."

And yet the temptation was so strong that she could not endure it. One glance, one little glance, that was all she needed so that she might know her adversary . . .

Dull glitter of scales as black as jet, flecked with streaks of moonsilver, furled wings, a shadow-creature that stalks the starlit night.

"Drakhaoul," Kiukiu murmured. Though this one was so much more powerful than Gavril's daemon.

As the questing head swiveled around toward her, Kiukiu felt the penetrating gaze of deep-slanted eyes settle on her hiding place—not two, but three, red as blood rubies, the third set deep in the creature's forehead.

"So it's *you*," she whispered. For she recognized him. He had appeared to her once before, the winter's night that the beacon had first awakened the children. Had they been connected since that day?

The dark Drakhaoul fixed its burning gaze upon her.

"*Did you think you had escaped me, Spirit Singer?*" His voice, darkly seductive, stirred fragments of memories that made her shudder. "*You tried to steal my children away from me. Now you will serve me, Nagazdiel, prince of this wasted realm.*"

"*Your* children?" In spite of her terror, Kiukiu could not help challenging the arrogant claim. "In what possible way can they be yours?"

"*Their blood was shed in my name. They were sacrificed to me and they bring me what I need most of all: the life force of Artamon's children so that I can grow strong again. Strong enough to break free.*"

"You're feeding on children? Live children?"

"*I fed on your life force too.*" And now she remembered—and the memory made her feel faint with nausea.

Leathery coils enwrap her body. "*The more you struggle, the more tightly I will embrace you,*" *whispers a soft voice. The breath is slowly being crushed out of her as the coils tighten around her. A tongue flickers out of the darkness and slithers between her lips, into her mouth . . .*

"Ahh!" Kiukiu opened her eyes and saw it was only Malusha bending over her, not the dark Drakhaoul. "I never really escaped, Grandma," she said, hearing her own voice speaking as if from far away. "He let me think I was free . . . but he's still using me."

"What's all this nonsense?" Malusha demanded. She squatted beside Kiukiu and, placing one hand on her forehead, gazed searchingly into her eyes. "Don't you think I'd have noticed if you'd been careless enough to let yourself be possessed? And who is this 'he,' if you please?"

"A Drakhaoul. But far more powerful than Lord Gavril's daemon. His name is Nagazdiel."

"Nagazdiel? Is that what he calls himself now?" Malusha passed her hands over Kiukiu's body. "Well, I can't sense any Drakhaoul in you now. And I sensed nothing when I found you."

"He said . . . he said he'd been feeding on my life force." Even admitting it made Kiukiu feel so guilty, as if it were her fault that he had preyed on her.

Malusha sat back on her haunches. "Well, he must be a sly, subtle one, for I can't detect a trace. Unless he's only preying on you while you sleep."

"Ugh." Even the thought made Kiukiu feel queasy. "Now I won't dare close my eyes."

"But you're still not telling me everything, child, are you?" Malusha's shrewd gaze made Kiukiu glance away, ashamed.

"They call themselves the Drakhaouls' children. They were sacrificed to bring the Drakhaouls into this world. Their spirits are trapped in the Realm of Shadows. And he—Nagazdiel—forces them to gather life force from living children to make him strong enough to break free.

"Just how did you discover all this?"

"Little Princess Karila has been very sick. So Linnaius asked me to discover what was wrong with her and I—I found that she was possessed."

"But these children were sacrificed centuries ago. What woke them?"

"All I know for sure," said Kiukiu, who was becoming more agitated as each of her grandmother's questions raised another fear in her mind, "is that it's to do with the ruby that belonged to Emperor Artamon. The ruby that can open a gateway between our world and the Realm of Shadows."

"The ruby that the Blessed Serzhei warned us about." Malusha's voice was quiet now.

"It has to be the same one. Because Nagazdiel said—he said five are now at large in our world. *Five* Drakhaouls, Grandma. Someone opened the Serpent Gate and let them in."

CHAPTER 2

"Spy. Tielen spy."

Pavel Velemir felt the muzzle of Iovan Korneli's pistol press against his skull.

So this is it. The inglorious end of my career in the Emperor's secret service. Shot in cold blood by a fanatical insurgent.

He waited, his body tensed, his stomach sick and cold, for Iovan to pull the trigger.

"Stop, Iovan! Put down your weapon," cried Minister Vashteli.

"Why? We've caught him in the act," came back Iovan's sneering reply. The muzzle pressed harder against Pavel's head. "Talking to his Tielen masters."

"Do you dare to disobey me, Iovan Korneli?" The minister's voice cut like a knife. Pavel stood frozen, not daring even to breathe. "Put down your pistol now."

Why couldn't he think of anything right now but Raïsa? Wasn't his whole life supposed to flash before his eyes?

"*Now.*"

Iovan let out a grunt of frustration and slowly lowered his arm. Pavel felt a chill of sweat break out all over his body, in spite of the heat of the day. He had tried not to flinch, not wanting to give Iovan the satisfaction of seeing his fear.

"Don't you think he might be useful to us?" demanded Nina Vashteli. "Have you no sense at all?"

"We shot the others."

"We executed certain Tielen prisoners," she said tersely. "Soldiers, all. But I will not sanction the execution of this man. Not yet. He might have information that we could use."

Oh wonderful. Spared from summary execution, only to be put to the question.

The sound of cannon fire echoed outside, followed by distant shouting.

"What now?" Nina Vashteli hurried to the window to gaze out over the rooftops.

Pavel eyed Iovan, wondering if this was his chance to make a run for it.

"Stay where you are, spy." Iovan brandished the pistol. "Don't even think of it."

"Minister!" One of the citadel militia burst in. "King Enguerrand's flagship has just sailed into the harbor. Everyone's out in the streets to welcome him. Your presence is requested straightaway."

"King Enguerrand has come himself?" Pavel saw a look of surprise in Nina Vashteli's eyes, swiftly concealed. "You were in Francia, weren't you, Pavel? The Francians are not fond of using the common tongue, I understand."

Is she giving me the chance to redeem myself? Pavel swallowed; his throat had gone dry with fear. "I speak fluent Francian, Minister. I would be happy to act as your interpreter."

"Bring him along then, Iovan."

Iovan stared at her. "There must be others in the university, Minister, students of Francian literature and culture—"

"I need an interpreter right now," she said. "Pavel, I want you to listen for me. Not to the official speeches of welcome, but to the other background conversations. Do you understand?"

He nodded. "I do."

"Serve me well in this, and we may be lenient. Iovan?"

"I'm right behind him, Minister." Iovan glowered at Pavel. "And if he tries any tricks . . ."

Pavel could not help but reflect, as he was manhandled down the stairs, that Iovan might achieve far more in life if he learned how to be charming.

The harbor at Colchise was filled with white-sailed ships. The Francian fleet had formed a barrier across the entrance, trapping the merchantmen and fishing boats inside. Francian soldiers, resplendent in surcoats of royal blue and scarlet, marched briskly through the winding streets to the lively beat of snare and kettledrums. Behind them came the standard-bearers, waving the embroidered banners of the Francian royal house to the swaggering lilt of a marching song. The emblems of the golden salamander and the silver rose of the Poet-Prophet Mhir could be seen on every flag and livery. And the inhabitants of Colchise ran out to greet them, or leaned out of open windows to wave and cheer their deliverers. Girls threw flowers and blew kisses, children ran alongside the marching soldiers, and dogs barked, adding to the uproar. Last of all came Enguerrand and his senior officers, riding purebred white-maned Enhirran horses whose silky coats shone like silvered sand.

Curious for a first glimpse of the King of Francia, Elysia Andar strained far forward from her place on the balcony of Lukan's house as the royal party rode into view.

"Careful, you could fall," cautioned Palmyre, grabbing hold of her.

"He's so young. Younger than Gavril. Young . . . and rather charmingly shy, I would guess," Elysia said. She turned to Rafael Lukan, who stood watching, arms folded.

"What do you make of this, Lukan? Were you consulted?"

"This is all Nina's doing." He still stared at the Francians, not meeting Elysia's gaze. "And no, the revolutionary council was not consulted. If we had been, I would have opposed it."

"Why?" Elysia asked, masking a stirring of unease.

"When was the last time you were in Francia, Elysia? The Commanderie has been conducting a brutal campaign against anyone who dares to challenge their ideas. I've no doubt they'll pursue it here."

"On the other hand, this could bring wealthy Francian families to spend their summers in Vermeille," mused Elysia, who was sorely in need of new clients. There had been little call for portrait painters in Smarna of late, and she had expended most of her life's savings in her search for Gavril last year.

"Have you no scruples, Elysia?" said Lukan reprovingly.

"We all have to eat," she replied with a shrug.

Pavel scanned the reception. Iovan Korneli had been at his side during the formal introductions, a surly shadow, deprived of his pistols by King Enguerrand's bodyguard.

Then, Iovan was no longer there. Pavel had been acting as translator for the Smarnan ministers, most of whom had no more than a rudimentary grasp of the Francian tongue. And after the conventional diplomatic platitudes had been exchanged, the formidable Ruaud de Lanvaux had suddenly steered the conversation into a far more sensitive area.

"It has not escaped our attention in Francia that you harbor some dangerous and controversial intellectuals here in Smarna."

The Smarnan Minister of Finance blinked in surprise as Pavel translated the Grand Maistre's words. "Dangerous to whom, precisely, Grand Maistre? We like to encourage a spirit of rigorous debate in our universities. We believe it makes our students into rational, well-balanced individuals who can be of use to Smarna."

Pavel saw the Grand Maistre's eyes hardening.

"All this only encourages lax morals and social unrest," de Lanvaux said coldly. "And without the disciplines of the church's teachings, your society will soon decay into a mire of decadence."

Nina Vashteli swept up, her face set in a wide, gracious smile. She must have sensed the rising tension for she said briskly, "Maistre de Lanvaux, you must come and meet our patriarch, Father Zenon." As she led the frowning Maistre away, Pavel took the opportunity to ask one of the Smarnan guards what had become of Iovan.

"A message came from his home. Something to do with his brother Miran."

Miran, Raïsa, and Iovan Korneli's younger brother, had been the first to fall in the siege of Colchise, gravely wounded by a Tielen bullet. Pavel paused, wondering whether he should slip away to find out how the young student was faring.

"Pavel!" Nina Vashteli had spotted him and was beckoning imperiously.

He heaved a sigh of resignation. This was going to be a long evening.

From the crowds of students gathered at the gates of the walled cemetery, it seemed to Pavel as if the whole university had come to pay their respects to young Miran Korneli.

A young woman went up to the open grave, sinking down beside it in a billow of black silk skirts. She cast in a bunch of sweet herbs and white roses.

"Sleep well, little brother," she said, her voice breaking.

Only then did Pavel realize it was Raïsa—whom he had never seen in skirts before—wearing a mourning dress and wide-brimmed veiled hat. As she raised the veil, he saw how pale she was in the drab funeral black, how red her eyes and nose from weeping.

One of the students at the graveside began to sing softly. Others joined in and soon the singing was swelled by the voices of the hundreds of mourners outside. The song throbbed defiantly, triumphantly, into the sky. Pavel did not know the tune or the words but he recognized the fervent spirit and power of a national anthem and felt a sympathetic ache at the back of his throat.

What's happening to me? Why am I so moved? I never even knew the boy.

Beside Raïsa, his arm protectively tight around her shoulders, was her elder brother Iovan, dashing the tears from his eyes with the back of his hand.

I should cut my losses and vanish now, while Iovan is distracted. I could already be on board ship for Tielen or Muscobar.

Yet still Pavel stood there, his eyes fixed on Raïsa Korneli.

CHAPTER 3

Kaspar Linnaius awoke in darkness, feeling the bed on which he lay swaying to and fro. From the slapping sound of water outside, he guessed he must be on board a ship. He tried to raise his head and found he was bound securely to the bed, with ropes securing him at wrists, waist, and ankles. And he, who had never experienced sea-sickness in his whole life, felt queasy and faint as the vessel pitched, his heart thudding erratically against his ribs, and a vile, billious taste fouling his mouth and throat.

How could he have been so foolish as to let his guard down? He had underestimated Celestine de Maunoir's cunning—and her desire for revenge. The ship crested a wave and he groaned as the motion shuddered through his body.

Celestine must be taking him back to Francia to stand trial. Though he was as good as condemned to burn at the stake already; the trial would be a sham, a warning to others who dared to pursue the study of alchymy, or other darker arts. He must escape. He knew the Emperor would do all he could to free him, but even Eugene had never had to face the Inquisitors of the Francian Commanderie.

Hervé de Maunoir, Celestine's father, had been Linnaius's most promising student at the Thaumaturgical College in Francia, before the Commanderie had begun its ruthless campaign of persecution. The youngest Magus in the College, Hervé had been assisting him with the development of the Vox Aethyria when the agents of the Commanderie had raided his house, carried off documents and plans, and encouraged his God-fearing neighbor to publicly accuse him of communing with evil spirits. She had heard them, she said, speaking through magic crystals.

Linnaius had escaped with the crystals; Hervé had not been so fortunate.

The ship split a great wave, sending another shudder through Linnaius's body. He must warn Eugene. And he was close to the one element he could control without recourse to books or alchymical potions: the wind. He struggled to move his hands, straining against the rough cords that bound his wrists. The effort all but exhausted him and he groaned aloud again, ashamed that he should prove so weak in adversity.

"My powers. My powers . . ." He closed his eyes, listening to the sounds outside the ship's creaking hull, seeking with his sixth magesense for the currents of air that filled the ship's sails, moving it across the sea toward the shores of Francia. But he was so enfeebled that he could scarcely detect the wild breath that drove them onward.

Still, he'd be damned if he would let himself be beaten by a woman, even if she was de Maunoir's child. He could almost smell the wind gusting outside, a strong, briny scent, charged with rain and grey cloud: a storm wind. Another effort of will would bring it under his control. His mind sought it, merged with it, was one.

Linnaius felt the wind surge straight through his body and twirl out again through his fingertips.

The timbers of the ship trembled. Distant cries came from up on deck. Linnaius lay back, his heart pounding. He had broken out in a cold, clammy sweat. He had no idea how long he could control this wind, but he had to try.

Drenching rain blew in gusts across the deck of the beleaguered Francian ship. The wind battered her sails and whipped the waves into great rolling breakers so that she pitched and tossed helplessly. Up on deck, the sailors battled to regain control of the vessel.

Below, Celestine struggled toward the Magus's cabin. Every lurch of the vessel flung her against the wooden walls, but she fought on until she reached the cabin door and unlocked it. The door flew open and she stumbled inside.

The Magus lay bound to the bunk as they had left him. But one finger, his right index finger, was moving slowly. And though his eyes were closed, she saw a faint smile on his pallid lips by the light of the flickering lantern.

"This is your doing." Another great wave threw her against the wall of the cabin. She grabbed hold of the bunk head to try to steady herself. "Make it stop!"

"Release me," he murmured, his voice barely audible above the roar of the storm, "and I will do as you ask."

"But what good will it do if you sink the ship?"

"Release me . . . and no one will be harmed."

Celestine had dedicated her life to tracking down Kaspar Linnaius and bringing him to justice. She was not prepared to let him go.

A sound of splitting timber came from above deck—followed by a great shout and a terrifying crash.

There was a spell she had read in her father's grimoire, a binding spell. She would risk her own reputation as a member of the Commanderie in using such a powerful trick of the forbidden art, but as the ship shuddered, helpless in the blast of the storm, she had little alternative but to try.

She closed her eyes, concentrating with all her heart and will, seeking deep within her for the gift she had inherited from her dead father. She found its source and raised one hand, pointing at the Magus.

"In bonds invisible, I bind thee," she whispered. She could feel the coils of power slowly unraveling and rolling down the length of her arm into her wreathing fingertips, wrapping themselves about him. And she sensed that Linnaius could feel them too. She heard him whisper, "No!" even against the groaning and creaking of the timbers of the ship.

"Now, sleep." She dipped into the little bag of dustlike granules she had found in his laboratory, and softly blew on her fingertips, sending the dust to settle over him in a powdery cloud.

His lids began to close and his finger ceased to move as the protest died on his lips. The wind suddenly dropped and the waves stilled. The sickening pitching and rolling stopped and the ship lay becalmed.

Celestine let out a long, slow breath. She had meshed him in a web of his own making; the sleepdust had worked on him, just as it had when he had used it on her at Swanholm. She had feared he might have made himself immune to his own devices. Just as long as no one from the Commanderie had witnessed what she had done . . .

It was only then that she realized the cabin door hung open and Jagu was standing in the doorway.

"How could you, Celestine?" Jagu's eyes burned dark in his pale face. He was soaked, wet locks of black hair plastered across his forehead. "Our order is dedicated to the eradication of the occult arts."

Jagu had been her loyal partner and companion in the hunt for Kaspar Linnaius. Now she saw the unspoken accusation in his face. *How could you keep your powers a secret from me?*

"You took a vow to abjure all such practices. A holy vow."

She gave a little shrug. "There was no other way to subdue him. If I hadn't stopped him then, we could all have drowned."

"But if Maistre de Lanvaux hears what you have done—" Jagu broke off. He seemed to be searching for a reason that might sway her to his point of view. "Remember what they did to your father, Celestine."

"No one will know if you say nothing, Jagu," she said lightly. Could she still trust him? "No one knows what happened here but you."

CHAPTER 4

The Emperor of New Rossiya adjusted the collar of his uniform. Then he turned to check his appearance in the mirror, and caught his breath. He had forgotten, in the heat of the moment, the changes wrought in him by the Drakhaoul Belberith. The face that gazed back at him was that of his younger self: smooth-skinned, clear-eyed, with not a trace of scar tissue. And his hair had regrown, regaining its original softness, with a wayward wave if not kept short in a regular military trim. Even the color had returned, a rich shade of gold, just as it had been when he was a boy.

"The Francian ambassador's here, highness." Gustave hurried in—and when did he not appear out of breath, to impart some new setback these days?

As Eugene turned away from the mirror, he caught the hint of a grim smile of satisfaction on his own lips. "Good. I hope he's ready to grovel. Or that he has a plausible explanation for the appearance of the Francian war fleet in the Straits so close to our shores." He set out at his usual brisk stride, Gustave at his heels.

"He doesn't have the air of a chastened man. And he's brought his own bodyguard, this time. They're waiting in the courtyard, armed to the teeth."

"Now, isn't that revealing?" Eugene halted. "They anticipate a hostile response." Although it would not be productive to be moved to anger by anything the ambassador might do or say, Eugene was forced to admit that he felt insulted. "Do they think me little better than some savage tyrant? Do they think us incapable of negotiating like rational men?"

The Francian ambassador, Fabien d'Abrissard, was waiting in the library, attended by two plain-suited men carrying dispatch bags; all three bowed as Eugene entered. As the Francian raised his head, Eugene noted with silent delight an expression of astonishment flicker across the ambassador's dark eyes. If nothing else, his altered appearance had momentarily distracted Abrissard from his mission and given him something new to wonder about.

"Who are these gentlemen?" Eugene gestured to the attendants. "I understood this to be a private meeting."

"To which I see you have brought your secretary," d'Abrissard said, all traces of his earlier astonishment expertly concealed.

"So you have come, Ambassador, to explain to me the presence of the Francian war fleet off our shores?" They sat either side of a vast and ornate marble-topped desk, the attendants standing silently behind d'Abrissard's chair. "How do you justify this?" Eugene pushed Enguerrand's letter across the desk to the ambassador, who cast a cursory glance over its contents.

"Know also that we have in our possession the five rubies known as the Tears of Artamon. Ancient law decrees that whosoever holds all five stones is entitled to govern all five princedoms of Rossiya. We therefore assert our right to be called Emperor and impose our holy law upon all five princedoms as well as Francia."

"What is there to explain?" D'Abrissard's slight curl of the lip could have been interpreted as a smile of condescension.

"I left the Tears of Artamon in Kaspar Linnaius's keeping. Kaspar Linnaius, who was forcibly abducted from this palace by your agents." Eugene leaned back in his chair, not once taking his eyes from d'Abrissard's face. "It follows, therefore, that your agents stole my rubies from Linnaius. I would appreciate it if they could be returned. Then I could find it in my heart to forget the whole unfortunate incident."

"Your rubies, imperial highness?" d'Abrissard said haughtily. "The Smarnans maintain that they never made Tielen a gift of the Smarnan Tear."

"I had no idea you were here to represent Smarna as well as Francia,

Seigneur d'Abrissard." Eugene allowed himself a slight raising of one eyebrow at d'Abrissard's allegation. He was damned if he was going to let the Francians distract him with such petty insinuations. He suddenly leaned forward across the desk. "The rubies belong to me, d'Abrissard. I want them back. If your master returns them, I am willing to forget that this whole sorry incident ever occurred."

D'Abrissard—to his credit, Eugene grudgingly allowed—did not falter.

"That," he said, "is out of the question."

"I see." Eugene said. "So this means war."

"Why incur such an unnecessary loss of life? King Enguerrand is ready to talk terms."

"Terms?" Eugene echoed, unable to keep the contempt he felt from coloring his voice. "You mean my capitulation? Does Enguerrand truly believe I will sign my empire over to him so easily?"

Gustave leaned forward and murmured in his ear, "Chancellor Maltheus is standing by to enter into negotiations with the Francians to buy you a little more time."

Eugene nodded. He had absolute faith in Maltheus. "I understand that Chancellor Maltheus is prepared to meet with your First Minister to discuss the situation."

D'Abrissard frowned. "His majesty the king wishes to talk with you, face-to-face."

"I will not talk with King Enguerrand until the Francian war fleet withdraws to neutral waters." Eugene rose, knowing that this would oblige the ambassador to rise too. He had heard all he needed to hear for now.

"And that is your imperial highness's final word?"

"Good-day to you, Ambassador."

Fabien d'Abrissard and his bodyguards bowed stiffly and withdrew. Eugene sat down again and unrolled a map of the western hemisphere on the desk, securing the outer corners with the heavy inkwells of gold and agate and a paperweight in the shape of the Swan of Tielen.

"So much for diplomacy," he said with a sigh. He had played his next move in this game of empire Enguerrand had initiated. It was a gamble, one calculated to call Enguerrand's bluff. He moved one of the inkwells, placing it at the opening of the River Tilälven, then another swan paperweight at Haeven, opposing it.

"Why were we not made aware of Enguerrand's ambitions sooner?" he muttered. "Or was I so obsessed with Gavril Nagarian that I ignored the warnings?"

Marta, Karila's governess, and Lieutenant Petter stood before Eugene, their eyes downcast, as though expecting an imperial reprimand. Eugene saw Marta steal a glance at the young lieutenant, then color and look swiftly away. So the chaste Marta had fallen for dashing Fredrik Petter? He could think of worse matches. And the strength of their feelings for each other could work to his advantage in the current situation.

"At ease, Lieutenant. I don't know what you imagined I had summoned you here to explain," he said, "but as long as it didn't endanger my daughter, then I have no interest in it."

The little sigh of relief that issued from Marta's lips did not escape him. And Petter's stiff shoulders relaxed.

"There are difficult times ahead," Eugene said, "and I think in the circumstances, it would be better to send my daughter farther north to stay with her great-aunt at Rosenholm."

Another glance, questioning this time, flew between the two.

"Marta, you must travel swiftly, so please select only those members of our household here who are essential to her well-being to accompany you. And, Lieutenant Petter, I'm placing you in charge of the princess's security. I want you to take a small platoon of the Imperial Household Cavalry with you to defend Dowager Duchess Greta's manor, if need be."

"Can I select the men, highness?" asked Petter eagerly.

"I trust you to choose the very best men for this assignment. It will ease my mind to know that my daughter is safe." *Safe and as far away from the Francian fleet as possible—and from Belberith's hunger for innocent blood . . .*

"And the Empress?" asked Marta.

Eugene answered the question with as little emotion as possible. "My wife will remain with her parents at Erinaskoe. The Francians appear to be on amicable terms with Muscobar." It was a fiction to preserve his dignity, but even so, he hated to lie to his own household. He had already been obliged to weave an elaborate story involving the masked ball to explain away his daemonic appearance when he returned from Ty Nagar. If the truth of Astasia's flight leaked out, yet more invention would become a necessity to cover the humiliating fact that his wife had left him.

At the first news of the Francian threat, Eugene had ordered that the Vox Aethyriae and the trained staff who manned them should be moved to a suite of rooms in the very heart of the palace. Now he hurried there to check on one or two points that were puzzling him.

"Get me Chancellor Maltheus."

The pastoral tapestries in their soft shades of gold and summer green had been covered with unrolled maps of the empire. And the room was filled with the murmur of voices and the dry scratch of pen nibs.

"The Chancellor, highness." The secretary operating the Vox linked to Tielborg and the Tielen Council rose from his place in front of the device so that Eugene could speak with Maltheus.

"It doesn't look good, Maltheus. Our friends seem very determined to press their case. I've called Enguerrand's bluff. Now all we can do is wait."

There was a pause, then Maltheus's voice came through, crackling and indistinct. *"There's some concern here about the current state of our munitions."*

"What do you mean?"

"The council urgently request your presence at the Fastness, highness. It seems we are not as well prepared to repel an attack as we would wish."

Maltheus's words puzzled Eugene. The armed forces of New Rossiya had no equal; they were better fed, better clothed, and better equipped than any others in the quadrant. He could only assume that the councillors had been thrown into panic by this unanticipated threat from the Francians.

"Please reassure the council that I'll be with them as soon as all is made secure here at Swanholm."

Gustave placed a leather folder on the desk beside him. "The dossier on Enguerrand of Francia that you requested, highness."

Eugene leafed through the carefully scribed pages.

"Enguerrand, second son of Gobain II . . . sickly child, much influenced by his mentor and confessor Ruaud de Lanvaux, Grand Maistre of the Commanderie. Raised to dedicate his life to the church, he found himself heir to the throne when his older and more vigorous brother, Aubrey, died unexpectedly in a hunting accident. Enguerrand was anointed king three years later on the death of his father."

Eugene remembered Prince Aubrey, a tall, well-favored young man, with the strong chin and straightforward manner of his father, Gobain. But Enguerrand? Had Enguerrand been the pale, bespectacled boy he had at first taken for a young cleric or confessor, hovering shyly behind his confident brother? And what had wrought this extraordinary change in him?

Eugene closed the folder and beckoned Gustave to his side. "If there is no further communication from the Francians by the morning, then we must stand ready to defend the empire. After meeting with the council, I will ride to Haeven and join the Northern Fleet there."

"I will see that the appropriate arrangements are made," said Gustave.

"And," Eugene lowered his voice, "is there any news on that *other* matter of significance we spoke of?"

Gustave slowly shook his head.

So there was still no word of Astasia.

Eugene found himself back in her rooms, obsessively searching for any clues among her abandoned possessions, any little scrap of note or scribbling that might hint at where she had gone.

As yet, the news of her disappearance had been skillfully suppressed. The official story he had put out was that she had gone to Erinaskoe to visit her ailing father. Thus far, no one had questioned or checked the truth of the tale. The scandal that would inevitably follow when the news broke had merely been postponed. There would be whispers of illicit affairs and secret lovers, trysts and betrayals. The fact that Lieutenant Valery Vassian had deserted his post at the same time had not yet been commented upon, but it would not be long before some court gossip began to circulate. Ironic, then, that the appearance of the Francian fleet had proved a distraction.

A frown creased Eugene's brow. He had put young Vassian in a position of trust and responsibility at Astasia's request. Damn it all, he had even grown to like the young man, had begun to look for ways to promote him. And now he had betrayed his trust. Was it possible that there had been some illicit liaison between the two? They had known each other since childhood; they had danced together at Astasia's first ball.

Eugene went to the window and gazed out over the gardens, as she must have done many times when he had neglected to return as promised to take supper with her. The green of the parterres, the pleasant gravel walks among beds of scented roses and herbs stretched out below, all bathed in the milky evening radiance of the White Nights.

How desperately lonely she must have felt to be driven to flee the summer delights of Swanholm. Was it loneliness that had made her spend so much time in the company of the Francian singer, Celestine de Joyeuse? Far too much time, Lovisa had commented disapprovingly. Then he had merely been pleased to hear that Astasia was amusing herself making music, one of her greatest pleasures. Preoccupied as he was with his search for Ty Nagar, he had brushed aside Lovisa's concerns. Now he began to wonder if the singer had been sent on another mission to spy on the court, or worse, to poison his young wife's affection for him, to fill her impressionable mind with rumors and slander.

But as he stood in her bedchamber, surrounded by her discarded clothes, her romantic novels, even the pretty little shoes of powder blue leather that she loved to wear even though they pinched her feet, he felt an aching emptiness sweep through him. This was not injured pride, as he had tried to pretend to himself when he first learned of her flight. He had not realized how much she meant to him until now.

"And I never knew," he murmured. "I never knew how much I loved you, Tasia."

He had not intended to fall in love with her. Now he began to think of all he wanted to show her in Tielen, the secret places he had played in as a boy when Swanholm was just a royal hunting lodge: the little trout stream beyond the northern birch woods; the heathlands where the sweetest, juiciest cloudberries grew in summer; the goatkeeper's hut, where old Anneke would give visitors crumbly, creamy goat's cheese to eat. There was so much to share with her, all the little pleasures he should have made time for but had told himself he would attend to later, when he had defeated Gavril Nagarian and tamed the Smarnan rebels.

And now she was gone.

Eugene sat on the bed and let his head sink into his hands.

Was it too late now to persuade her back? Would there be anything to come back to if the Francians defeated the Northern Fleet and took Tielborg? Would Enguerrand force him to abdicate—or worse?

Even when he held the dying Jaromir in his arms, even when he crawled, horribly injured, from the charred remains of his army outside Kastel Drakhaon, he had not once given in to despair or doubted himself. But faced with the very real possibility of defeat, he felt all the certainties on which he had built his life melt away. He knew for the first time in his life how vulnerable he was, and the weight of responsibility for his people weighed so heavily on him that he sat slumped, crushed by the enormity of the burden.

"You can easily defeat Enguerrand's fleet."

He started, glancing around as if the voice had come from someone in the room, not his own head. Belberith had not spoken for a long while—and now the shock of hearing the Drakhaoul whisper deep within him left him speechless.

"Use my powers, Eugene. Protect your empire, make your people safe."

It was a temptation that he had resolved to resist.

"No. Do you think I have forgotten what such an attack would do to me?"

"A small price to pay for the security of your empire."

Seductive words, seductive promises. For a moment he saw the Francian fleet in flames, sinking in the Straits as he swooped low overhead, breathing lethal fire on his enemies.

"How many men are you prepared to lose before you change your mind? I have seen how much you care for the warriors who serve you."

"No!" Eugene said again. The temptation was strong, but so was his command of strategy. He and his generals had fought many successful campaigns together. Only when all else failed . . .

"Then why did you summon me, Emperor? I am the most powerful weapon you possess in your armory."

Something in Belberith's persuasive tone made Eugene remember Gavril Nagarian's warning. *"It winds itself into your will, your consciousness, until you no longer know who is in control."*

CHAPTER 5

"I can sense him. My brother Khezef."

Belberith's voice penetrated Eugene's sleep. In an instant the Emperor was awake, sitting upright, gazing around the bedchamber.

"What do you mean?"

"He is approaching."

"Khezef? Gavril Nagarian's Drakhaoul?" Eugene wondered if he were still dreaming. Wasn't it only in nightmares that such things could happen? He remembered one terrifying recurring dream from childhood in which he was pursued through a warren of dark tunnels by a faceless warrior. Each time he turned and vanquished his pursuer, he would turn a corner and there was his nemesis again, indestructible and relentless. "How can that be? I destroyed Gavril Nagarian. I saw him fall in flames into the sea at Ty Nagar."

"He burned, he fell, but he is still alive. Khezef, my brother, restored him."

Eugene leaped out of bed and grabbed his *robe de chambre*. "Then why is he coming to Swanholm?"

"I cannot tell. I did not summon him."

Eugene went to the window and flung open the shutters, leaning out over the wide stone sill to scan the park. The soft air of the light summer night was enriched with the creamy scent of roses in the gardens below. The waters in the lake lay like a smooth sheen of dark glass beneath the pale sky. Wisps of mist hazed the distant woods.

There was no sign of a winged shadow. Was Belberith merely playing with him?

"He is here."

"Where?" The tension was beginning to grow. He had vowed never to use his powers again, for fear of what harm he might do to his own people while Belberith still controlled him. "And what does he want?"

Even now Gavril Nagarian could be lying in wait. Eugene took out a pistol, loaded shot, and primed it.

"Such puny weapons are no use against a Drakhaoul." The scorn in Belberith's voice rankled.

"Just find me this Drakhaoul," Eugene said, "then we'll see."

A sudden sensation of surprise splashed like a drop of cold rain in his mind. *"He is in the courtyard below."*

It was as brief as a shiver, but it left Eugene's nerves twitching. He just could not get used to sharing his most private emotions and thoughts, or to the eerie feeling that he was never alone. Was it this that drove the Drakhaons of Azhkendir to retreat to their dark, lonely kastel?

If Gavril Nagarian had come to attack the palace, he could already have destroyed the whole building with Drakhaon's Fire. The invisible wards were no longer protecting his palace as Kaspar Linnaius was not there to maintain them. Swanholm was vulnerable.

If Nagarian intended to strike at him here, Eugene would have no choice but to call on Belberith's powers again—at whatever cost— to defend Swanholm. And this time he would make sure Gavril Nagarian did not leave the battleground alive.

As Eugene made his way down the main stair, the thought occurred to him that perhaps it was as well Astasia was not here after all. But that did little to lessen the ache in his heart.

In the hall, he encountered Lieutenant Petter.

"There's an intruder in the palace," Eugene said, keeping his voice low. Petter's eyes widened. "Tell your men: No one is to challenge him. Shadow him, by all means, but keep a good distance away."

"But highness—"

"Leave this one to me, Lieutenant."

He saw Petter open his mouth to object, then snap it shut again. Petter knew better than to question his word.

God knows, I have no time for this, with Enguerrand of Francia's war fleet in the Straits. Still in *robe de chambre* and slippers, Eugene padded on across the courtyard. *Unless Nagarian is in league with the Francians.* That disturbing possibility had not occurred to him before.

And then when he saw where Belberith was leading him, his suspicions increased: Linnaius's rooms.

The sun was still high in the sky. Gavril had been in the air since morning and from his growing weariness he knew it must be evening.

"How can it still be so light?"

"*Don't you remember your childhood in Azhkendir? Here, in the north, the sun never sets in high summer. Your grandfather Zakhar told me they call this time the White Nights.*"

"I remember nothing of my early years." Gavril was scanning the parkland groves for somewhere to land unobserved. Only later, as he made his way on bare feet toward the palace, did he realize that Khezef had not only remembered Zakhar, but had spoken to him with almost human sensibility.

A clock in the stables struck eleven.

There were sentries patrolling the palace grounds and guarding the doors. Gavril slipped through the formal gardens and went through the stables to the servants' quarters without once being challenged. There he borrowed a servant's livery left on top of an overspilling laundry basket.

Disguised in the imperial colors of Swanholm's household staff, Gavril moved silently through courtyard after courtyard toward the Magus's stair. Head down, he hoped he would look to any sentry who challenged him as if he were on an errand.

This was where he had encountered Princess Karila and Khezef had spoken to the little girl, calling her "his child." To Gavril's astonishment, she had seemed utterly unafraid of him. Since then, Khezef had not once mentioned their mysterious connection or sought to explain it. And Gavril had been so obsessed with his search for Kiukiu that he had put it from his mind.

But other memories returned. He had found the Magus's rooms in utter disorder, turned over as if they had been ransacked by thieves. Were others after the Magus's life-prolonging elixir too?

Gavril reached the archway that led to the Magus's stair. Still no one challenged him. The place seemed deserted. Was it a trap? He had expected to encounter a guard or two already.

Gavril hurried up the stone stair and found himself in front of the Magus's apartments. Temporary repairs had already been carried out and the shattered door had been replaced with a sturdy new one. He tested the handle of rope-twisted iron; it was locked. That was only to be expected; he would have been even more suspicious of a trap if the door had swung open to admit him.

Gavril extended his right hand, fingers pointing at the lock. He closed his eyes, concentrating his energy, sending it down the length of his arm to crackle blue in the gloom at his fingertips. Just enough, not too *much* . . . The metal began to glow, red then white-hot. The singed wood smoked, giving off an acrid smell of burning, and the lock melted away. Gavril nudged the door open with his foot.

Inside, the outer room looked much as it had when he had come for Kiukiu. The broken glass had been swept into a corner. The many scattered ancient volumes torn from the shelves had been stacked in piles.

"Where do I begin?" Gavril muttered to himself, picking up a book and examining it in the fading light. "And where's the Magus?"

"I was hoping you might be able to enlighten me on that point."

Gavril dropped the book and spun around. Too late he sensed the distinctive aura of Drakhaoul-glamour—and found himself staring into the eyes of Emperor Eugene.

"Are you indestructible, Gavril Nagarian?" the Emperor asked, almost as if amused at the thought, yet the grim line of his mouth suggested otherwise. And little glints of energy, green as emerald, flickered about his fingertips.

Gavril said nothing. Every muscle of his body was taut, ready to defend himself. *Why didn't you warn me, Khezef?*

"Have you come to give yourself up?" Still the blue-grey eyes stared at him. And still Gavril said nothing, though all the while, his mind was whirling with plans of escape. "You broke out of Arnskammar. You're a fugitive. A condemned criminal."

Gavril gave the slightest of shrugs, assessing the chances of making a break for it.

Eugene took a step toward him. The aura of emerald energy crackled more intensely. Gavril stood his ground although it took all his nerve not to back away. The last time they had met, Eugene had bested him in a vicious aerial duel of fire and sent him tumbling into the depths of the Azure Ocean. Every sinew, every nerve in his arm and shoulder ached at the memory of the fiery breath that had seared his flesh to the bone.

"Why are you in the Magus's rooms?" Eugene's tone of voice was deep, almost intimate. "What exactly is your purpose?"

"My purpose is to find Kaspar Linnaius." Gavril kept his eyes fixed on the Emperor's.

"You come too late. He's been abducted."

"Abducted?" Gavril could not hide his surprise. "By—by whom?"

"By Francian agents."

"*Francian* agents?" Slowly Gavril began to understand that Eugene was in earnest. "So all this mess in here . . ."

Eugene kicked a fragment of shattered glass aside. "They ransacked the place. They seemed to know what they were looking for." He came closer to Gavril. Only then did Gavril register that the Emperor was wearing nothing but *robe de chambre* and slippers. "What are *you* looking for, Nagarian?"

"Your Magus abducted one of my household. He sent her on a dangerous mission. So dangerous that she almost died. He left her here—alone, unconscious, slowly wasting away—in these very rooms. If I had not come for her—" He stopped, trying to get his emotions under control. "He has an elixir that could restore her. If she doesn't get the elixir, she will die."

"And what were you going to bargain with?" Eugene's expression was unreadable. "Your freedom? *Your* life?"

"There was to be no bargain." Did the Emperor believe he was crazed enough to give himself up to Tielen justice a second time? "I've vowed to do everything in my power to find Kaspar Linnaius and his elixir."

"She means much to you then, this Kiukirilya?"

How could Eugene know her name? "Yes," Gavril answered, the fierceness of his tone masking his surprise. "Let me go, and I will bring your Magus back."

"You'd go to Francia and snatch him from his captors? From the dungeons of the Francian Commanderie?" Eugene seemed to be considering the implications of his suggestion.

"I have some extensive experience of prisons, as you may recall."

Eugene took another step toward him. Gavril still stood his ground, although there was barely a foot between them. And he caught the subtlest glint of greenish light in the Emperor's eyes: *Belberith*.

Gavril was so close to his enemy that he could see clearly the miraculous changes wrought in him by the daemon. Eugene's damaged face was restored, all traces of the terrible burns Gavril had inflicted on him gone.

But did Eugene know what else had happened on Ty Nagar after he had flown away in triumph? Did he have any idea what his overweening desire for power had unleashed?

"And if I let you go . . . what guarantee do I have that you will bring Linnaius back to me?"

"My word."

"Your word?" Again a flicker of green lit the Emperor's eyes in the gathering dusk. "You gave me your word once before, Gavril Nagarian. You swore to me in Mirom that you had cast out your daemon."

It was a deliberate challenge.

"Do you think that I would have let myself be arrested if I had still had my powers when your men came to Kastel Drakhaon?"

A clatter of running feet on the stair broke the growing tension.

"Ensign Anckstrom, with urgent intelligence for his imperial highness!"

Gavril glanced questioningly at the Emperor and saw uncertainty in his eyes, a look all too vulnerably human.

"Enter, Ensign," Eugene called, and Gavril saw how skillfully he concealed that brief lapse as he turned to greet the message-bearer.

Ensign Anckstrom saluted the Emperor, handed over the folded paper, and stepped back. His eyes flickered toward Gavril, then he stared straight ahead, as if on the parade ground.

"I see." The Emperor looked up from the paper. "I believe we may have stalled them for a little while. Tell the Admiral I will speak with him shortly."

"Very good, highness." The ensign hurried away.

"It seems," said the Emperor, "that we both have too much invested in Linnaius's survival to let the Francians keep him."

Eugene looked at the young man he called his enemy, the only man ever to have defeated him in battle. He had gone there determined to destroy Gavril Nagarian once and for all. But he began to see that doing so might not be the best course of action in the circumstances. Yet the possibility that Nagarian was party to Minister Vashteli's Francian pact could not be ignored.

Extraordinary situations call for extraordinary solutions.

"You may not be aware," he said, "that in our absence, Enguerrand of Francia has invaded Smarna."

Gavril Nagarian stared at him, wide-eyed.

"The Smarnan rebels called on their Francian allies for help. They're all out in the streets cheering the liberating Francian army to the skies. As yet they have no idea that Enguerrand has laid claim to the five princedoms, asserting his right to be Emperor over mine."

"The Francians are in Smarna?" At last Gavril Nagarian spoke. He seemed bewildered by the news. Either he was an accomplished actor—or, as Eugene had begun to suspect, Minister Vashteli had not bothered to consult him.

"And Enguerrand has the Tears of Artamon to substantiate his claim."

A glimmer, like distant lightning, briefly lit Gavril Nagarian's eyes. Eugene remembered that he was negotiating not just with the young Clan Lord, but with his daemon as well.

"Your mother Elysia is still in Vermeille, I believe?"

Nagarian glared at him. "Are you proposing that we become allies to fight against Francia?"

A large moth blundered against the windowpane. Eugene, nerves on edge, glanced up and saw Gavril Nagarian make the same startled reaction.

A plan had been forming in Eugene's mind. He would make Gavril Nagarian a gesture of good faith. A gesture that he would find hard to refuse.

"Bring the Magus back alive from Francia, Nagarian, and I will pardon you."

Gavril wondered if he had heard the Emperor aright.

"I consider myself a man of honor." The blue-grey eyes gazed back intently into his. This time there was no trace of Belberith's malign glimmer. Eugene was speaking from the heart. "And I do not break my word."

"Kaspar Linnaius's life for mine?"

"You heard aright."

"And my *druzhina*?"

"If that's what it takes, then yes, your *druzhina* too."

The magnanimity of the gesture astounded Gavril. Eugene had played a complex double game with him before. He could not believe that there was not a catch.

"Why is the Magus so important to you? You have Belberith. You have no need of alchymical weapons." Gavril could not let this fact go. "You could swoop down on Smarna and defeat this Francian pretender to your throne with one blast of Drakhaon's Fire."

"You know why, Nagarian. You know all too well."

It gave Gavril a grim kind of satisfaction to hear Eugene make this admission. So he too had experienced the terrible thirst that could only be quenched by innocent blood. Had he killed to satisfy the cravings? Did he now know the guilt and shame that came all too soon afterward to sear the soul?

"In all faith," Eugene said slowly, as though sharing a truth so intimate that he hardly dared speak it aloud, "I believed myself a rational man, a man of science. It was only when science failed me that I was impelled to seek forbidden powers. Now I am sickened by what this daemon has driven me to do. How do *you* live with it?"

Gavril had not expected this. It was a question that demanded the utmost honesty. "Between us, we could scorch the Francian invaders from Smarnan soil," he said slowly, choosing each word with care. "But I know—and you do too, now—that such a huge expense of power would drain us utterly. And then we would be driven to seek out innocent blood. More innocent blood. Each time, the daemon restores the outward appearance but eats away at the soul. That's what drove my father to seek out a way of subduing the Drakhaoul within him."

"By using Altan Kazimir's experiments?"

"Which you then used against me." It still angered Gavril to think he had agreed in good faith to submit to Kazimir's elixir, little knowing that the Magus had laced the doctor's potion with a debilitating alchymical poison.

Eugene shrugged. "In my place, you would have done the same."

"In your place, I would have requested negotiations."

Eugene made a little shake of the head, as if dismissing Gavril's words as naïve and inexperienced. "Altan Kazimir," he repeated. The doctor's name seemed to have given him an idea.

The clock in the stable courtyard struck midnight in a slow, measured chime.

"And how do you plan to infiltrate Enguerrand's Commanderie?" asked Eugene. "I've no firm intelligence yet as to where they are holding Linnaius."

"I was not planning a direct assault by Drakhaon's Fire," Gavril said dryly, "for fear I might fry the Magus along with his captors."

"So what exactly did you have in mind?"

"I'll go as a painter, in search of new commissions."

Eugene nodded. "That might work. But how will you finance yourself? How will you furnish yourself with paints, brushes . . . ?"

Gavril had come to Swanholm to consult Kaspar Linnaius; he had not anticipated he might have to undertake a hazardous journey to Francia to find him. He was, he now realized, utterly unprepared for such an enterprise. And he did not like Eugene's pointing that out to him.

"My secretary will provide you with a purse of Francian coins that you can wear on a chain around your neck," said Eugene. "Then all you need do is invent some story to explain your ragged state."

Only a short while ago they had faced each other in a bitter duel to the death. Now they stood side by side, partners in an uneasy alliance against an unexpected enemy.

"Imperial highness!" Ensign Anckstrom had returned. "The Francian fleet is on the move. Admiral Berger thinks it is making for Haeven."

Gavril glanced questioningly at Eugene.

"I've idled here long enough." There was a suggestion of barely restrained excitement in Eugene's voice, as if he could not wait to meet the Francians in battle. "Wait in the courtyard below," he said to Gavril. "I'll send Gustave to you."

Gavril nodded and as he made to leave, Eugene stopped him, one hand resting on his arm. "Bring Linnaius back, Nagarian. He is a scientist of rare genius. And my friend. He deserves better than to die at the stake."

Yet even as Eugene spoke, Gavril felt as though Belberith's glittering malachite eyes were staring directly at him, penetrating through flesh and bone, to where Khezef lurked, hidden deep within the core of his being. And though he had heard no words, he was certain the Drakhaouls had been in silent communication with each other.

Gavril waited, as bidden, in the courtyard. Through the archway he saw soldiers of the Imperial Household Cavalry making their preparations to escort the Emperor into battle. Everything was achieved with a quiet efficiency that did not fail to impress Gavril. And he found himself almost beginning to feel a grudging admiration for the man he only knew as his enemy. Faced with this unexpected threat, Eugene was calmly getting ready to protect his country. His men needed no blood oath to bind them to him; they followed him because they loved and admired him.

"Lord Nagarian?" A grey-suited official of Eugene's court came toward him from the palace. "His imperial highness asked me to deliver these to you." Without the slightest evidence of surprise at this unusual transaction, he presented Gavril with a leather purse and a chain.

"Thank you." Gavril weighed the purse in his hand.

"And he thought this map might prove useful too."

Useful? Gavril, shamed to think that he had not once considered to plan the route from Tielen to Francia, nodded his thanks.

"Khezef!"

Gavril turned to see a little girl limping toward him. She was dressed only in a thin white nightdress and her feet were bare.

"Princess?" said the official. "What are you doing out of your bed so late at night?"

Princess Karila seemed not to hear him, her eyes fixed only on Gavril. But when she spoke again, it was in a tongue he did not recognize, unfamiliar words pouring out of her mouth.

He felt a shudder deep inside him, then Khezef began to speak in the same alien tongue. Glancing at the princess, Gavril saw that she was in a trancelike state, her clear blue eyes darkened as though by shadow.

"Princess?" said the official again, in tones of concern.

"Don't try to wake her," Gavril said softly. "She's sleepwalking." He went down on one knee before her, gazing into the shadowed eyes that stared right through him, seeing only the Drakhaoul within. *What hold does she have over you, Khezef?* Eugene's little daughter looked so pale and fragile that he feared for her. *What is the connection between you?*

The princess suddenly let out a little cry and sank toward the cobblestones. Gavril caught her before she reached the ground.

"I'll take her back to her bed," said the official, kneeling beside Gavril. "How she got past the guards, I have no idea."

The little girl's fair head drooped against Gavril's shoulder. She weighed so light in his arms . . . and she looked so thin and sickly. He found himself suddenly overwhelmed by a surge of fiercely protective feelings. Were Khezef's emotions overspilling and merging with his own?

"Don't forget me!" Karila whispered as the official gathered her up in his arms and carried her away.

"Don't make me go away, Papa." Karila stared imploringly up at Eugene. "Please don't. I'll be safe as long as you are here—"

"I've made my decision, Karila." This parting was going to be difficult for the both of them. He forced a smile onto his lips. "Besides, you know how fond Great-Aunt Greta is of you."

"And what about my pets? Marta says I can't take Pippi with me. Who's going to look after Pippi while I'm away?" Her lower lip had begun to tremble. He swept her up in his arms and kissed her tenderly.

"Listen, Kari, I promise you that the servants will take good care of your animals. Now I want you to go straight back to Marta to get ready for the journey."

He put her gently down but still she clung to him. "Come back safely," she said in a muffled voice.

Although it was nearly one in the morning, Gavril could still read the map in the soft, pearly light of the White Nights. The most direct route to Francia was to cut down across Tielen on a southwesterly bearing, and cross the Northern Sea toward the more temperate countries of Allegonde, Tourmalise, and Francia.

Just before he folded the map and slid it into the purse, he spotted a little footnote in the margin in neat secretarial handwriting: "We suspect that our friend may be held at the Commanderie Forteresse in Lutèce."

As Gavril sped away from Swanholm through the pale night, he was almost tempted to veer off course to see for himself the bold Francian war fleet that was threatening the security of the New Rossiyan Empire.

Only as he flew doggedly on, the grey waters of the Northern Sea far beneath him, did he begin to reflect on the cursedness of his luck. He had gone to Swanholm for Linnaius's elixir, thinking his greatest problem would be to enter the palace grounds undetected. Persuading the Magus to help restore Kiukiu had seemed the lesser challenge. And then to find such a reversal of his expectations: the Magus abducted and the Emperor offering to talk terms in the face of this unexpected situation . . .

Until that night he had felt nothing but bitter hatred for Eugene. How could he forget the long months he had been confined in the Arnskammar Asylum, and all at the Emperor's command? Now, he found himself prey to conflicting emotions. Could he trust Eugene to keep his word? Could he trust him at all? His manner had been brusque but that brusqueness was more credible than if he had made some effusive show of friendship.

Or had Belberith wrought this change in Eugene? Belberith and Khezef were kindred; had the link between the Drakhaouls also woven some invisible connection between their mortal masters? This thought was so disturbing that he put it from his mind.

Sunlight glittered on the rippling waves below. Gavril had been in the air for many hours. He was tiring and tiring fast. The steady beat of his powerful wings began to slow and there was still no sign of land.

The children had been out gathering mushrooms in the woods and they were late getting home for their supper.

"Look," said little Loic suddenly, pointing up at the sky. "There's an angel!"

"Don't be so stupid," said his sister Kristell, dragging him onward by one hot, sticky, resisting hand. But she looked nonetheless, and stopped, her mouth gaping open. Loic was always seeing things that were not there, but this time he was not telling tales. A great, winged creature flew slowly toward them, its shadow scarring the twilit sky. And a faint shimmer seemed to emanate from its body, blue as the uncertain starlight of early evening.

By now the other children were staring. Kristell could see from the creature's faltering, ragged wingstrokes that it was in trouble. She had never heard of such a thing. Weren't angels beings of might and power, defenders of all that was good? When she looked at this creature, she saw nothing but shadow.

"The angel's falling!" said Loic.

"That's never an angel," said fair-haired Melle.

And as the children stood watching in the meadow, they felt a dry, hot wind from the creature's wings fan their hair as it passed overhead. A dark whirlwind whipped across the long grass, tossing the long-stemmed daisies this way and that. When Kristell looked up again, the sky was empty.

"Where's it gone?" She gazed around, bewildered.

"There!" Loic started out across the meadow.

"Come back, Loic." She ran after him, the others following, and came to a sudden halt when she saw what he had found.

A man lay facedown in the long grass, as if he had fallen from the sky. But there were no wings sprouting from his shoulders and no golden halo shimmered around his head. He was near-naked, clothed only in shreds and tatters. Kristell drew back, tugging Loic with her.

"Where are his wings?" whispered Melle.

Kristell risked another glance. She gave a little cry. The man was unlike any other she had ever seen. His wild dark hair glimmered, streaked with the dark blue of the night sky. *Could he be Loic's angel?*

"Come away," Kristell ordered. She was the oldest; she must take charge. "We're late. Maman will be angry." Loic seemed not to hear her. "She'll send us to bed without supper again."

"Is he dead?" Melle quavered.

"Angels don't die, stupid," put in Brice, who was standing, arms crossed, affecting an indifference Kristell suspected he did not feel. Loic had picked up a stick and was creeping toward the man.

"Come away!" Kristell said again, stamping her foot.

Loic reached out and poked the man with his stick. The man gave a low groan.

All the children shrieked.

"See? He's not dead," Loic said and stuck out his tongue at Melle.

"We should go and get help." A shiver of apprehension ran through Kristell's body. "He may be hurt."

The man let out another groan and tried to lift his head but the effort was too great and he dropped back.

"Father Herblon says we must help people in need," said Melle piously.

"Where are your wings?" Loic asked, squatting down beside the man's head. "Did they burn up when you fell from the sky?"

The man muttered something in a tongue Kristell did not recognize. He began to cough, a horrible retching sound. She started to back away. And then as he lifted his head, she saw his eyes. Eyes glittering blue as the distant stars. Staring at her.

"Brice, you're the fastest. Run to the village and fetch help."

Brice nodded. He seemed glad of the excuse to get away.

"You two, pick up your baskets, and follow Brice. I'll stay here."

Gavril slowly returned to consciousness from a dark place of searing heat.

When he tried to move, he felt every muscle in his exhausted body protest. Once again, he had overreached himself, and now he must pay the price. He had forced himself to fly farther than ever before, and there was no strength left in him.

He could feel his heart beating too fast, too loud, straining against his ribs.

A clear, high voice spoke to him. He opened his eyes to see a girl bending over him. Her face betrayed a mixture of emotions: fear, compassion, and strangest of all, curiosity. He could not understand what she was saying, but she seemed to be asking him a question. He tried to speak but all that issued from his dry mouth was a dragging groan.

A pure white aura surrounded the girl, soft as evening mist. A breath of fragrance wafted over him every time she moved, a fresh, alluring scent that made his body crave to breathe in more. He tried to raise his hand to touch her face but the effort was too much and his arm dropped limply back.

She spoke to him again, rapidly, breathlessly. And now, between surges of nausea, he began to decipher a little of what she was saying. He had not used the Francian language since traveling abroad as a young art student, visiting churches and museums.

"Are you . . . an angel?"

If he had not felt so sick and wretched, he would have laughed aloud at the bitter irony of her question. What kind of angel would see through her translucent skin to the pulsing of her life's blood? What kind of angel would crave the sweet taste, the warmth, of that blood? Only one of the fallen.

"*Now,*" whispered the Drakhaoul, "*while no one else is nearby.*"

"She thinks I'm an angel."

"*Feed,*" Khezef urged.

"She's little more than a child . . ." And yet, even as the Drakhaoul whispered in his mind, he felt his resistance begin to melt. A blaze of blue daemonfire seared through his mind. And driven by a will stronger than his own, Gavril found himself reaching toward the girl. He caught hold of her by the wrist, pulling her down.

She began to scream—but he clamped one hand across her mouth, smothering her cries. And once her struggling body was so close to his own, he felt another hunger, fiercer, darker than his own—a desperate thirst for mortal blood that could never be fully assuaged.

"*Use my power,*" breathed Khezef, his voice suddenly darkly sweet and smooth as honey.

"Why do you fight me?" The honeyed words issuing from Gavril's mouth were no longer his own. "You called me angel. Help me to fly again." He could feel Khezef speaking through him, and, although he fought to resist, his will was overmastered.

Kristell gazed up into the face of her wounded angel. His eyes glimmered blue as starfire.

"Help me," whispered the angel. He bent closer toward her, until she felt herself drowning in the midnight blue of his eyes. She felt his lips brush hers, soft as the touch of feathers. *Kissed by an angel* . . .

"Yes, yes, I'll help you, angel," she whispered back.

And then she felt his lips on her throat. No longer feather-soft, but scorchingly hot, sending shivers of fear and delight through her body.

She was rising into the dark of the night sky, toward the dazzle of the evening stars, slowly at first then dizzyingly fast. Her little world of village and meadows dropped away and was soon so far below and so insignificant that all she could see was the pure white light of the stars . . .

Gavril heard distant voices through the ecstasy of clean, pure blood that had flooded his whole body with warmth and pleasure. He looked up and saw lanterns and torches, bright splashes of light in the darkness.

"Kristell! *Kristell!*"

They were searching for the girl. And when they found her . . .

Kristell lay in his arms, her head lolling back against his shoulder. Flecks of blood stained her fair hair. Her eyes flickered upward. "Angel," she murmured.

Gavril blinked. He was himself again. Khezef, sated, had withdrawn into that dark shadowplace in his mind, leaving him staring in horror and disgust at what his daemon had made him do.

"Kristell!" The search party was drawing nearer.

"Don't die, Kristell." Gavril could only stare at the damage he had inflicted on the girl. How white her skin looked in the starlight, deathly white. He felt tears trickling down his cheeks, tears of bitter remorse. He laid her down gently on the crushed grass where he had taken his fill of her and rose to his feet. Slowly, he began to back away from his prey.

The voices grew louder, more frantic. He could hear hounds, panting and baying.

Blinded by tears, he turned on his heel and ran. Just before he leaped into the air, he heard a wailing cry from far below. They had found her.

As he skimmed away into the night, he knew that he could not always run from the scene of his crimes. One day he would be judged for what he had done—and he would have to pay the penalty.

CHAPTER 6

King Enguerrand's château at Belle Garde revealed itself through the morning mists, a delicate confection of pepper-pot towers and turrets, each topped with a weather vane forged as a gilded salamander or a full-sailed galleon. A fairy-tale castle, Astasia thought, or an extravagant illustration from one of Karila's storybooks.

She alighted from the carriage and stood beside her brother Andrei in the *cour d'honneur*, as a troop of royal guardsmen assembled, pikes on shoulders, to escort them to the sweeping central stair.

"For us?" she said to Andrei, bewildered.

"So it seems." He was glancing around under frowning brows, his eyes wary, shadowed. She did not know this new Andrei at all; ever since they left Tielen, she had begun to realize how altered he was by his terrible experiences. The laughing, devil-may-care boy she remembered with such affection had drowned with his men off the rocky coast of southern Muscobar. The Andrei who had been washed ashore was very different indeed. And since that moment of utter terror when they had seen the Drakhaon flying low over Haeven as they were about to embark, he had become even more withdrawn. She could only suppose that he was preoccupied with worries about the alliance he had forged with Francia. And she had preoccupations enough of her own.

"Empress. Prince Andrei." A grey-haired palace official came forward and bowed. "May I welcome you on behalf of his majesty, King Enguerrand, to Francia? I am the steward of Belle Garde. His majesty is still away on pilgrimage and has asked me to make you welcome in his absence."

The suite of rooms the king's steward allocated to Astasia was situated on the first floor in one of the many towers; Andrei and Valery Vassian were to be accommodated in an adjacent tower.

Astasia stood at the window and gazed down at the formal garden below. She and Andrei had been invited to dine that night with Queen Aliénor, Enguerrand's mother, whose formidable reputation had traveled even as far as the Winter Palace in Mirom.

"What am I doing here?" Astasia whispered. She had been sick for the second time that day and still felt queasy. She could only suppose that the strain of her flight from Tielen was affecting her. On board the *Melusine* she had pretended she was seasick, even though the weather was calm. On land she had blamed the meal they had eaten in port, even though no one else had been affected. But soon Andrei would ask her what was ailing her. And she had told no one but Nadezhda of her condition, not even her husband.

Another pang of nausea overwhelmed her and she gripped her stomach. "My unfaithful husband," she said. Each word tasted bitter as the bile burning her throat. She had seen Eugene alone with Lovisa at the ball. She had seen them talking intimately together. "My deceitful, scheming husband."

Astasia opened a window, hoping that a fresh breeze might help dispel the nausea.

Another new court, with different customs and etiquette to learn, another language to struggle with . . .

"If only I weren't so tired." She had fled Swanholm, but in fleeing she had merely substituted one unfamiliar set of circumstances with another. And in Swanholm, she had been the mistress of the palace, the highest in rank in the land, whereas here she was merely a guest, an exile . . . a fugitive.

An embarrassment.

She sank down in a little *fauteuil*.

What have I done?

"You're looking rather pale, my dear," said Queen Aliénor. The endearment held no warmth and the dry brush of the queen's lips on

Astasia's cheek felt more like the peck of some predatory bird than a welcoming kiss.

"My sister found the long journey tiring," Andrei said gallantly and Astasia glanced gratefully at him.

"We are delighted to entertain Aleksei Orlov's children at Belle Garde," said Aliénor, still without the trace of a smile. Astasia felt as if the Queen Mother's eyes were boring into her, laying bare all the secrets she was concealing from the world.

"We are most grateful for your generous hospitality," said Andrei with a hint of his old charm.

When Astasia saw the long dining table laid out for dinner, and the glint of fine silver cutlery and crystal glasses, she began to feel faint again. There would be many wearisome courses, endless toasts, and the necessity of making polite conversation in the Francian tongue.

I must go through with this somehow. She was angry with herself for such weakness. *If only for Andrei's sake . . .*

"Empress, you will sit on my right hand," ordered Queen Aliénor, "next to the Comte de Pouzauges."

Astasia saw an elderly gentleman smiling at her through a pair of pince-nez precariously balanced on the tip of a long, thin nose.

"I was last in Mirom when your grandfather was Grand Duke, my dear," said the comte nodding.

"Really? How interesting." Astasia was finding it hard to keep a smile on her face. All she wanted was something plain to eat, a little soup perhaps, and some grilled fish . . .

The Queen Mother proceeded to request her chaplain to say grace. Astasia bowed her head, expecting a short blessing. *I must be feeling faint from lack of food. If only I could just eat a little bread . . .*

But the chaplain was still praying, invoking the blessing of holy saints Astasia had never even heard of. She felt herself swaying and gripped the sides of her chair, making her own silent prayer that this ordeal would soon be over.

Then silver covers were lifted from the dishes with a flourish by the servants, revealing piles of tiny roast birds, little feet and beaks intact.

"Ortolans!" exclaimed Astasia's neighbor with relish. "Let me serve you, imperial highness."

Astasia tried to look away, feeling another surge of nausea. "No, no thank you," she said faintly. Savory smells assaulted her from all sides; odors that a few weeks ago she would have found delicious and appetizing now filled her with disgust. Glancing around her, she saw the courtiers eating with enthusiasm, crunching the tiny birds whole—bones, beaks, and all.

"And how is your mother, Sofia?" inquired the Queen Mother, fixing Astasia with her gimlet stare. "It must be at least ten years since we met."

"Mama has retired to our country estate at Erinaskoe," Astasia said, moving her fork around the untasted food on her plate. "Papa has not been well and she felt the air would be good for his health."

"Quite so," said Queen Aliénor. "And you, my dear? You're still looking very pale. You should take some red wine." She raised her hand, beckoning to a servant to fill Astasia's glass.

Astasia watched helplessly as the wine, dark as blood, was poured.

"I had hoped," said Queen Aliénor, in a confiding tone pitched loud enough for all around her to hear, "that you might have proved a suitable bride for my son. But events have overtaken us."

"Me?" Astasia felt a deep blush suffusing her face and neck. She had never been aware that Enguerrand, bookish and fanatically devout, was a prospective suitor. Now she sensed that the Queen Mother was openly criticizing her for making an unsuitable match.

"A toast," continued Queen Aliénor, raising her glass, "to my son Enguerrand and our brave men accompanying him on his new venture!"

Astasia raised the glass to her lips and pretended to drink, barely moistening her lips. She became aware that Andrei was looking at her over the rim of his glass as he drank. What exactly was this new venture of King Enguerrand's they were celebrating?

A court official appeared and approached the Queen Mother, bowing and presenting her with a sealed letter. She broke the seal and, fishing out a little pair of spectacles on a golden chain about her neck, perched them on the bridge of her nose to read.

"I have news from the king," she said, gazing severely at the diners. Instantly the table fell silent, all the guests looking at her, as if they had been reprimanded by a strict teacher. "He is pleased to announce that, following the liberation of the republic of Smarna from the Tielen occupation, our ships are now pressing on toward Tielen."

A round of applause greeted this news.

"Toward Tielen?" whispered Astasia to Andrei across the table. "What's happening? I thought Enguerrand was on a pilgrimage."

"It was a wise move to leave Tielen, my dear," said Queen Aliénor, who had overheard. "Enguerrand has challenged your husband's claim to the empire. I suspect there will be war—and very soon."

For a moment the candlelight and the glittering silver dimmed. Then Astasia blinked and found the Comte de Pouzauges and Andrei were supporting her.

"I'm so sorry," she whispered.

"Your sister is unwell, Prince Andrei," said Queen Aliénor accusingly. "She must see a physician."

"My sister is fatigued after our long journey. Please excuse her, majesty."

"Fatigued or no, I will send my physician to her." The Queen Mother was still staring at her.

"Oh no, no, I thank you," whispered Astasia, horrified at the thought. A physician would know within a few moments exactly what her condition was, and she wanted to keep her secret to herself. It seemed wrong to tell the whole world when the one who should have known first was still ignorant that he was to become a father again.

As Andrei escorted her up the dark stairs to her rooms, a figure suddenly slid out from the shadows. Astasia bit back a cry.

"I didn't mean to startle you, altessa," said a familiar voice in their home tongue.

"Valery! What are you doing here?" demanded Andrei.

"Just making sure your sister can sleep safe and undisturbed."

"So you've been keeping guard, Valery?" Astasia was touched by this show of solicitude. "That's very kind. But I'm sure there's no need . . ."

Astasia heard the astrological clock in the courtyard strike two as she lay, sleepless, in the rose-canopied bed. The mattress was lumpy and instead of soft feather pillows, there was a hard and unyielding bolster on which to rest her head. And she was tired, exhausted by the traveling and the strain of the past few days.

But she could not sleep for thinking of Eugene. Ever since Queen Aliénor had read King Enguerrand's letter, she had felt overwhelmed by a feeling so strong that it was like a physical ache.

It must be guilt. I feel guilty at running away from my duties as Empress. And so I should. What will become of Karila? How could I leave my little stepdaughter at such a time? There was certainly plenty to feel guilty about. Now it would look to the world as if she was the betrayer, running to the court of her husband's enemy. "But I had no idea," she said into the bolster, over and over again. "No idea!"

In the darkness of the unfamiliar bedchamber she imagined again Eugene's expression, stricken, uncomprehending, as he entered their rooms and realized she was gone. At first, during the flight from Swanholm, this thought had given her a bitter kind of satisfaction. But now she remembered how awkward he looked at the start of the Dievona's Night Ball, when she had guided him through the obligatory steps of the opening dance. She had glimpsed a hint of vulnerability then and had found it strangely endearing. None might be Eugene's equal on the field of battle, but in the ballroom, he would have been hopelessly lost without her.

But what about Lovisa, hateful, ice-blond Lovisa, with her perfect manners and her perfect appearance, meeting secretly with Eugene? What was her hold over him? Was she experienced in the arts of love? Did she know how to please Eugene in ways that Astasia had heard hinted at court, in little whispered conversations between the women courtiers behind fast-fluttering fans? The very thought made Astasia feel uncomfortably hot beneath the linen sheets. *He must think me so ignorant.*

And most shocking of all, there had been Celestine de Joyeuse's revelation. Astasia knew Kaspar Linnaius to be Eugene's most trusted servant. If it was true that Kaspar Linnaius had sent a storm to sink the Muscobite fleet, then surely only one man could have given the order.

How could she live with a man who had plotted her brother's death to clear his way to the throne of Muscobar?

But now, in the oppressive darkness, doubts began to assail Astasia. Would Eugene have stooped to such underhanded tactics to achieve his aims? He was ruthlessly ambitious, true, but he was also a man of honor.

"A man of honor with a mistress," she complained, turning restlessly onto her other side, smoothing out the creases in the sheet covering the bolster.

And then she heard again Eugene's words of warning wreathing through her mind: "*Now you are Empress, there are many who will seek to insinuate their way into your affections . . . Be careful, my dear.*"

Had she been careless? Had Celestine swayed her mind and heart, with her sweet smile and friendly, confiding manner? There had been such a delicious thrill in conspiring together that Astasia had never once asked herself what Celestine's true motives might be.

If Tielen and Francia are now at war, what am I doing here in the enemy's court?

Astasia sat up and rang the little bell for Nadezhda. Her maid came in yawning and rubbing her eyes.

"I can't sleep, Nadezhda."

Nadezhda plumped up the bolster and smoothed the sheet over the top.

"I'll see if I can find some proper pillows for you tomorrow. These Francian maids are very hoity-toity, looking down their noses at me as if I were beneath their contempt, so I might have to flutter my eyelashes at the footmen."

Astasia almost managed a smile at Nadezhda's vexed tones.

"I just can't settle. I keep thinking of . . ."

"A cup of lime flower tea will help you sleep. Though heaven knows where I can find somewhere to boil water in this drafty old castle—"

"Nadezhda," Astasia said, "have I made a terrible mistake?"

Nadezhda stopped on her way to the door. "I'm sure it's not my place to say."

"Have I been too hasty? Should I have stayed?"

"It's a little late now for regrets, altessa. Here we are, in Francia."

"I wish we'd gone to Erinaskoe."

Nadezhda turned around. Even in the flickering light of the candle she was carrying, Astasia saw the relief in her eyes.

"That could still be arranged, altessa. At least in our own country, I can make myself understood."

"We have so little money." Even as she spoke, Astasia realized that the thought of staying at Erinaskoe with Mama was infinitely preferable to staying at Belle Garde. Especially as her secret would soon become more difficult to conceal. "I might have to sell some of my jewelry."

Nadezhda shrugged one shoulder. "Needs must, altessa."

"There was so little regard for me at Swanholm that no one even tried to prevent me leaving!"

"Ah." Nadezhda came back toward the bed. "But have you considered the extraordinary events that took place the day we left, altessa? The Emperor was nowhere to be found."

"Gone hunting, indeed! Did he think I was so naïve as to believe his feeble little alibi?"

"And then that *creature* flew over when we were about to embark. Remember the panic, the confusion?"

Only then did another horrible possibility occur to Astasia. She had been so wrapped up in her own hurt feelings that she had not thought through the implications of what she had seen. Had the Drakhaon been winging its way to Swanholm to take a final revenge on Eugene? A feeling of dread crawled through her whole body. She had seen what the Drakhaoul had done to Feodor Velemir. Suppose Gavril had attacked the palace? Suppose he had seared Eugene to a charred, smoldering corpse—

"Is there *any* news from Tielen yet?"

"The old man is still asleep," Jagu said to Celestine as he emerged from Linnaius's prison cell. He lowered his voice. "What did you do to him? You'll need a story to cover yourself for the Inquisitors. They'll ask. You know they'll ask."

Celestine tossed her head impatiently. Since they had arrived at the Commanderie Forteresse to deliver their prisoner, Jagu had become increasingly edgy. And in their working partnership, she had always relied on him to be the levelheaded one.

"I only used his own magic to subdue him. A little sleepdust—what possible harm could there be in that?"

Men's voices could be heard farther along the dark stone passage. Jagu took hold of her arm and hurried her in the other direction. "As agents of the Commanderie, we took a vow. We vowed to abjure all kinds of alchymy."

She shook his hand from her arm. "Only you know what happened on board ship. Only you know what he intended to do. If I hadn't stopped him, we'd all have drowned."

They came to a halt halfway along the passageway in the uncertain light of a guttering lantern.

"They won't see it that way." He was staring at her so intensely that she drew back a step. "They haven't forgotten that you are de Maunoir's daughter. Take off the spell you placed on him, Celestine. Before they guess who is responsible—and put you on trial too." Was it true then, as she had begun to suspect, that he had begun to harbor feelings of a less than professional kind for her? She felt a dark, exultant thrill at the possibility. It was seductively gratifying to be desired by the austere, ascetic Jagu—and to anticipate the power such desire might bring her.

"If your vow is so important to you, Jagu, why don't you tell them yourself?"

Jagu still stared at her, his pale face twisted in an expression of anguish.

"Why, Jagu," she said, reaching out to stroke one fingertip across his pale cheek, "I do believe you would put my well-being before your loyalty to the order."

Andrei sat alone in his turret bedchamber. He kept staring at his reflection in the dusty mirror by the flickering light of a single candle.

"I know you're there," he muttered to the haggard face that stared back at him, red-eyed from lack of sleep. "Reveal yourself. Reveal yourself to me!"

Again, he relived the moment of possession. Again, he stood on the jetty at Haeven, gazing out over the sea as the stormclouds came rolling in across the Straits. But these stormclouds did not bring rain and wind; they flickered with unearthly lightning, streaking the sky with violet, scarlet, and gold.

They were kindred to the spirit who had healed his injuries and restored his lost memory. The spirit who had promised him a great future—before fleeing. And as he stood on the jetty transfixed by their dark aura of power, he knew that they saw him. Suddenly he knew their names, crying them aloud over the wind and rumbling thunder.

The stormclouds whirled about him and in the roaring darkness, he saw the glitter of eyes staring at him, amethyst, like a dusky evening pinpricked with stars.

"Adramelech," he stammered before the darkness overwhelmed him and he fell forward into a place of shadows.

When he next opened his eyes, it was to see sailors peering down at him. As they helped him to his feet, he found a new strength, a new vigor pulsing through his body. He felt charged. Renewed. His senses were sharpened; he saw more clearly and heard the smallest sound.

But since that reawakening, he had been troubled by flashes of visions, and voices had whispered in his head. Whenever he had tried to sleep, he experienced the unsettling sensation that he was no longer alone with his own thoughts. As a little child he had been terrified by a ghost story his nanny told him . . . and now he felt echoes of that same nameless terror, as though he were being haunted by some vengeful revenant.

"Adramelech," he said to his candlelit reflection. Was it a trick of his sleep-starved mind, or had a violet-hued light flickered in his eyes as he spoke the name aloud? "Show yourself. I'm not afraid of you!"

"*Andrei,*" whispered a voice, soft as sleep.

"Where are you?" He rose to his feet, staring into the shadows in the darkest corner of his turret room.

"*Here.*" Was that a shiver of laughter, malicious and mocking? "*I have been with you since we left Tielen.*"

"Stop playing games with me!"

"*This is no game, Prince Andrei. I am yours to command.*"

"What do you mean, command?" That voice—was it really coming from within him? Or had he gone mad? The first healing spirit had spoken to him in this manner.

"*I can tell you secrets. Do you want to know a secret about your sister?*"

"My sister keeps no secrets from me," Andrei said loyally.

"*So she's told you she is carrying the Emperor's child?*"

Astasia was pregnant? This was one complication that had not occurred to Andrei at all. He was so surprised that he could not speak.

"*So she hasn't told you,*" Adramelech continued. "*Nor anyone else, it seems. She's quite secretive, your little sister. What else is she hiding from you, I wonder? Can you really trust her?*"

"Why shouldn't I trust her?" Andrei said hotly.

"*I can make you powerful. Do you want to learn to fly? Do you want to learn how to destroy your enemies with fire? You have only to command me.*"

"To fly?" Andrei echoed, torn between skepticism and longing.

"*Go to the window. Open it.*"

"What—now?"

"*It's dark. No one will see us.*"

Andrei hesitated. Madmen leaped off ledges, claiming they could fly. Madmen also heard voices in their heads. Was he mad too? And yet he found himself moving toward the casement, reaching for the latch of the diamond-paned window, opening it. A soft breath of warm night air touched his face, faintly perfumed with the scent of the yellow roses climbing about the base of the tower. Moonlight touched the turrets and weather vanes of the château with antique silver. Far below lay the grey waters of the moat. If he fell from this height, if his body didn't smash onto the graveled path, it would cleave the cloudy waters of the moat and he would drown.

"Don't you trust me?"

"Why should I?" But now he had swung his legs out over the sill, as if his body was no longer in his own control, but maneuvered by the spirit to do its bidding. And a memory stirred in his mind, a memory he had later dismissed as an impossible dream.

The warship plows on toward him, carving its foaming furrow through the waves.

Deep within him, he feels something stir. His heart twists, then cracks open within his breast. Stars explode across his vision. A wordless cry bursts from his mouth as a dark whirlwind envelops him. And suddenly they are rising, water cascading from their sodden clothes, rising from the sea . . .

"So you have flown before, Prince Andrei?"

"I remember—I remember crashing back into the sea." Till then he had suppressed the memory; now the feeling of terror almost overwhelmed him. The spirit—his spirit—had suddenly let him crash back into the waves, abandoning him and old Kuzko. He had survived, but Kuzko had not.

"You were remade by one of my kin. I can detect traces of his presence. But then he deserted you?"

Andrei clutched his hands to his head. The memory of being abandoned by his guardian spirit came back to him, raw as an unhealed wound.

"How do I know you won't desert me too? How can I trust you?"

The spirit did not answer immediately. Then it said, its voice low, urgent, *"Let go, Prince Andrei. Let go of your fears, and become one with me."*

Let go? Andrei tensed, willing himself to do as the spirit commanded him, but somehow he could not obey. He felt the rough stone of the sill to which he clung, his fingertips digging in, his knuckles clenched. He was not ready to die.

"*You know my name, my secret name. You called me and I came to you. Call my name again and put your trust in me.*"

Something of the old, reckless Andrei awoke at this challenge.

"Adramelech!" he cried aloud—and a fast-rushing wind tore him from the window ledge and hurled him far out into the night. His body was shaken by a convulsive shudder that seemed to rip his flesh and sinews apart. A mist of whirling stars melted before his eyes— and he was flying. His shout of terror transformed into a whoop of elation. He was skimming through the air above the dark trees in the grounds of the château on wide shadow-wings.

"*I will not desert you as my brother Khezef did.*"

Andrei abandoned himself to the thrill of flight. The sensation of swooping like an eagle through the night was utterly intoxicating. He could taste the air, the woody, earthy tang drifting up from the ancient oak forests far below.

He flew on until the moon had set. Soon he could see the distant glimmer of a wide river winding through hills and meadows, grey in the starlight. And on the far horizon he glimpsed the looming shadow of a great, ancient city. *Lutèce.*

His emotions were more intense than with anything he had ever experienced before. He felt powerful. He felt invincible.

Then a thought entered his mind. Lutèce was far from Belle Garde, at least five days' ride. Why was he flying straight toward the city? Was Adramelech carrying him aimlessly through the night to accustom him to the sensation—or was there some other purpose to their journey?

"It must be time to turn back," he said.

"*Can't you sense his presence? He is here.*"

"Who is here?" Andrei did not understand.

"*Khezef.*"

"The spirit who healed me is here, in Francia?"

A shimmer of vivid emotion flickered through Andrei's mind. "*I have unfinished business to settle with him. And so do you.*"

"Wait." Andrei felt as if he were being sucked into a whirlpool. Adramelech was taking control of him and he did not like the sensation at all. "I'm not ready. Not yet. And I have many urgent matters to sort out at Belle Garde that cannot wait. I must be back before dawn breaks."

For a moment, Andrei felt the spirit's strong will resist his. And then a calmer feeling seeped into his mind.

"*Of course, Prince Andrei, you are not yet used to the rigors of flight.*" Was that a slight hint of condescension tainting the spirit's placating words? "*My powers are yours to command.*"

Andrei looped around in the air, turning away from the crowded chimneys, towers, and spires of Lutèce. To know he could fly was enough for one night. He wanted to wash his mind clean of every petty earthbound concern and just relish the feel of the wind on his body.

A brassy braying of horns woke Astasia. She pushed back the rose-pink hangings around her bed and stumbled sleepily to the window. She could hear hounds yapping and barking as she opened the casement and gazed down to see what all the noise was about.

A hunting party was assembling in the courtyard below. Not just the young noblemen of the court were riding to the hunt; Astasia could see several noblewomen dressed for the occasion with elegant little feathered hats perched on their crimped hair and dainty boots showing beneath daringly slashed riding skirts. Crops and gloves in one hand, they sipped glasses of sparkling wine and chattered with the men as grooms led out their horses from the stables.

The Master of the Hunt took up his horn and blew three short blasts; and, still chattering and laughing, the courtiers climbed into the saddle and rode away, the hounds frolicking eagerly about. Servants followed after on a cart, with food hampers and bottles of wine.

Astasia watched them go, squinting into the gleam of the rising sun. The great green forests surrounding Belle Garde would be so cool and refreshing at that hour of the day, smelling of moss and ferns and summer dew. It looked such an enjoyable excursion that even though she loathed hunting, and especially the shooting of deer, she felt left out.

Was Andrei one of the party? She had not spotted him from up here—but the sunlight was so bright, it had not been easy to identify individual faces.

Nadezhda popped her head around the door.

"I can see there'll be no idling in bed here with all that racket below," she said tartly. "Are you ready to rise, altessa, or would you rather take your ease this morning?"

"I might as well get dressed." The truth was, Astasia thought as she drifted listlessly around the bedchamber, that she had no idea what to do or where to go in this foreign court. The thought of spending time with the formidable Queen Aliénor was not in the least appealing. Yet she was not certain how long she could keep to her room under the pretense of being fatigued before the queen sent her physician to examine her.

I need to talk with Andrei and soon. We cannot stay as guests of the Francian court indefinitely. And then what shall we do, where shall we go? The prospect made her head ache.

Sipping a cup of green tea, she penned a swift note to her brother and asked Nadezhda to see it was delivered.

"And ask if there's any further news about Tielen," she added. Nadezhda rolled her eyes.

Hunting horns sounded in the far distance, one answering another.

Andrei turned over on his side. This mattress was damnably uncomfortable. It felt just as if he was lying on rough ground, with dry moss, twigs, and stones for his pillow.

Green daylight filtered down onto Andrei, penetrating his closed lids. He opened his eyes and found he was staring up at a high canopy of interlaced branches overhead: oak, sycamore, and beech.

The hunting horns blew again, closer this time.

"What in God's name?" Andrei stared down at himself in alarm. He was nearly naked, his body barely covered by a few remaining shreds of clothing. He scrambled to his knees in alarm, grabbing a handful of dock leaves for modesty's sake. He could hear the breathy clamor of hunting hounds in the distance and by the sound, he guessed they were coming his way. Too late he remembered that the Comte de Pouzauges had invited him to a day's hunting in the forest. The last thing he wanted was to be discovered lurking, like a wild man, in the woods. Or worse still, for the hounds to pick up his scent and pursue him like a wild boar. "Why didn't you warn me this could happen, Adramelech?" he hissed. "And why did you let me sleep so long?"

"*You were exhausted by the flight. You needed to sleep.*"

"And what do I do now?" Angry and still half-asleep, Andrei stumbled in bare feet over twisted roots and dry leaves. "Get me out of this, Adramelech!"

"*Do you wish to fly back to the château?*"

"Damn it, how can I fly in broad daylight? It's not as if dragons are often seen around here, is it?"

After a half hour or so's slow and painful progress, through brambles and stinging nettles, Andrei spotted a shimmer of water ahead. And more of the comte's conversation from the night before began to return to him.

"If you tire of hunting, there's a well-stocked lake in the forest. The king has a little lodge on the shore; we'll rendezvous there for lunch."

He began to improvise a desperate scenario as he approached the lake; he could already hear voices, and as he crept closer to the edge of the trees, he saw servants busy setting up tables in front of the rustic lodge. He heard the clink of glasses being unpacked and smelled the delicious odor of roasting fowl. They had built a fire and were already spit-roasting duck over the blazing logs. Andrei's empty stomach rumbled like a drum.

"This had better work," he muttered as, shaded by the thick rushes, he slipped into the cold, viscous lake water, trying to repress the shiver of disgust that rippled through his body. Midges hovered over his head. Wading farther through the slimy mud between the rushes, he steeled himself and dived.

A few seconds later he came up, spitting out the foul-tasting water, wreathed in waterweed. Then he hauled himself out onto the bank. Dripping, he waited a minute or two, out of sight of the lodge. Then he began to shout in Francian.

"Where the devil are my clothes?"

Two servants were lowering wine bottles into the lake to cool them. They looked up when they heard Andrei's cries. After a while, one of the men ventured toward him.

"What is wrong, sieur?"

"My clothes have been stolen! I left them here while I was swimming." Andrei pointed to the mossy boulder, improvising recklessly. "Some damned thief must have been watching and sneaked off with them when no one was looking."

The other servant had joined the first; both exchanged blank looks.

"There's nothing in the lodge to wear, sieur, but some old clothes his majesty keeps for his fishing trips," said the first. "I could bring those to you . . ."

Not long after Andrei had dressed, the hunting party arrived at the lodge. Andrei gazed down at himself in dismay. The leathern breeches were made for a much shorter man, and the effect, combined with an itchy woollen jerkin and a pair of clogs, had transformed him into a peasant.

He watched the courtiers dismounting and heard the animated chatter as the men compared their hunting prowess and held up bloodied trophies, and the women gossiped in the shade. How could he mingle, dressed in these ludicrous garments? And then he spotted a lone figure hovering on the edge of the chattering courtiers, evidently a little ill at ease.

"Vassian." Andrei called to him from the lodge doorway, beneath a massive pair of red deer antlers. "Over here, Vassian!"

Vassian stared at him—and then burst out laughing. "Good God! What happened to you, Andrei?"

"I went for a swim, left my clothes on the bank," Andrei explained, "and when I came back, everything was gone!"

The Comte de Pouzauges came up, a glass of red wine trembling in his palsied hand. "*Bon Dieu*, is that really you, Prince Andrei? I thought Jerome had taken on a new groundsman."

Andrei forced a smile. He had been humiliated enough already and his patience was fast running out.

"All your clothes stolen, eh? I'll send one of the grooms back to Belle Garde to fetch an outfit from your rooms."

"Why did they lodge Andrei in a turret room?" Astasia puffed as she slowly climbed the steep winding stair, Nadezhda following behind. "And why didn't he come to see me when I sent a message?"

"I'm sure he's just sleeping late, altessa, you know what young men are like . . ."

"But I need to speak with him." Astasia reached Andrei's door and tapped. There was no reply.

"Perhaps he's gone hunting with the other courtiers after all?" Nadezhda was out of breath too.

"My brother was never that fond of hunting, unless there was a wager involved." Astasia knocked again, more forcefully this time. When there was still no reply, she tried the door handle and, with a wailing creak, the ancient-timbered door slowly opened inward.

"Andrei?" she called, stepping inside. The lime-washed walls of the turret room were painted in the fashion of a century ago: quaintly stylized patterns of gillyflowers and marigolds wound in garlands around the arched windows. Even the arched ceiling was painted; little suns, moons, and stars glimmered gold against a wash of blue. Astasia, who had become accustomed to Eugene's restrained tastes, found herself wondering if she had stepped back into her great-grandparents' time.

"It looks as if your brother isn't here, either," said Nadezhda, picking up Astasia's note from where it lay, unopened, on the floor.

Astasia was still trying to catch her breath. "All that climb for nothing." It was too bad. Just when she had summoned enough resolve to act, he was nowhere to be found. She went to the open window, fanning the fresh air onto her glistening face with her hand.

Clothes had been carelessly discarded around the room, a sock here, a shirt there. Nadezhda began to pick them up and shake them out, folding and tidying as she went.

"Andrei must employ a valet," said Astasia, unable to hide her disapproval of her brother's slovenly habits. "It's not seemly for a man of his rank to travel without servants."

"Looks like his bed's not even been slept in," said Nadezhda, drawing back the heavy curtains around the four-poster. "Perhaps he found some pleasant company last night," she added with a lewd little chuckle.

"Nadezhda!" said Astasia. "Even Andrei can't have had time to . . ." Although Nadezhda could well be right; Andrei's appearance had excited much whispering and coquettish giggling behind fans among the young Francian ladies of the court.

"Well," she said with a sigh, "we will have to go ahead and make our own plans without benefit of Andrei's advice."

"There is always Lieutenant Vassian," said Nadezhda slyly.

"Valery Vassian? Oh no, I can't be seen to be conferring with him unchaperoned. Tongues would wag and my reputation would be in ruins." As soon as the words were out of her mouth, Astasia realized how foolish they sounded; she was a runaway wife and her reputation had been ruined the day she fled Swanholm.

"Even though he's ruined *his* good name to follow you and your brother to Francia?"

Astasia winced. Valery Vassian had deserted a promising career in the New Rossiyan army to accompany them. And desertion was a capital offense in Tielen, especially in time of war. Even if she were to plead on his behalf, a military court would be unlikely to take her evidence into consideration. "All the more reason for not making matters worse," she said firmly.

"But he's our best hope." Nadezhda turned to her, her face set in a determined expression that Astasia recognized well. "He can come and go freely. He could sell your jewelry and arrange passage for us to Mirom."

"Well . . ." Astasia could see the merits of Nadezhda's plan. "All right, then. But any conversation that takes place between us must be seen to be well within the bounds of propriety—and yet not easily overheard."

"Who round here speaks our home tongue?" Nadezhda's expression was triumphant.

"Of course. It must be the summer heat that's making me so stupid and slow."

"It's the baby, altessa," said Nadezhda soothingly. "It's the baby."

The hunting party eventually returned as the sun was setting behind the forest, crimsoning the tops of the trees. Astasia went to look for Andrei among the courtiers and spotted him in the stables, talking and laughing with two demure young noblewomen.

"There you are!" she cried, hastening toward him across the straw-strewn cobbles.

He turned his head.

"Andrei?" Astasia drew back from her brother. It must have been a trick of the fading light, for she caught an unnatural glimmer in his dark-lidded eyes. "Andrei, are you all right? You look . . ."

"I'm fine." His reply was abrupt. "Just a late night, that's all."

"Yes," she said. She could not keep a tone of reproval from her voice. "I know. Nadezhda and I went to find you this morning."

He laughed but the laughter sounded forced. She was sure he was hiding something from her. "A heavy night's drinking. Francian brandy is powerful stuff."

"*Au revoir, cher prince.*" The Francian girls entwined arms and moved away, whispering together. One blew him a kiss, Astasia noticed.

"Who was she, Andrei?"

He gave a shrug.

"You must be careful. We're guests here; it wouldn't do for you to seduce some Francian duke's daughter."

"You never used to be so prudish, sister."

"And you never used to keep secrets from me."

"Are you sure," he said, turning to stare deep into her eyes, "that there aren't some secrets you've been keeping from me? One in particular?"

She found herself backing away. There was that glint again, strange and unsettling. How could he know? Had Nadezhda let drop some little hint?

"Congratulations, sister," he said. "When is the happy event expected?" He was smiling at her now but she did not feel in any way reassured.

"Who told you?"

"Let's just say . . . I guessed."

"Is it that obvious?" Astasia's hands hastily covered her stomach. Dear God, if Andrei had noticed, then how many others had too?

"Don't you think I should have been told?" His tone of voice was light and playful now. "After all, I am to become an uncle."

"Stop teasing, Andrei."

"But it's happy news, Tasia." He opened his arms to her.

"You mustn't tell anyone. Least of all Queen Aliénor."

Once she would have run into his arms to hug him. Now she hesitated.

CHAPTER 7

A hasty council of war had been summoned in Tielborg Fastness, the ancient stronghold that stood on a rocky island in the center of the River Tilälven. Once the home of Eugene's ancestors, the House of Helmar, the drafty old castle had been neglected by Prince Karl in favor of his hunting lodge at Swanholm in summer, or the winter palace on the banks of the Tilälven.

Once a year, Eugene rode through the streets of the city to perform the ancient ceremony (which dated back to Prince Helmar's time) of opening the new session of parliament. But that day there were neither cheering crowds waving flags nor military bands to greet him; the city was in a somber mood, chastened by rumors of imminent war.

"Our situation is critical," said Eugene. "I have rejected King Enguerrand's claim to New Rossiya. It is certain that he will now send in his troops." He surveyed his ministers, seeing a variety of expressions around the table, ranging from angry bewilderment to glum determination. "And now I come to ask you: how ready are we to meet this threat?" His gaze rested on Axel Boden, Chief Minister of the Admiralty. Boden had been an unusual choice for the post, as he was a naval architect, not a retired admiral. Although Eugene had approved the appointment, he was aware that Boden was ill at ease in the formidable company assembled in the council chamber.

"As you know, imperial highness, Admiral Janssen has sailed on the *Dievona* to join Admiral Berger with the Northern Fleet in the Straits. They are our first line of defense against the Francians."

"And how are they armed?"

The minister stuttered a little. "W—with the standard supplies, as stipulated by your highness, for all warships patrolling the Straits."

"Powder, shot, cannons? Alchymical weapons?"

Sweat glistened on Boden's forehead. "Our alchymical stores are greatly depleted. We deployed a considerable amount in the bombardment of Colchise. Then we lost valuable munitions when so many of our vessels were sunk by Lord Nagarian." He reached for his handkerchief to wipe his brow.

"And we lost more supplies when Froding's Light Infantry were decimated in Smarna," added Colonel Soderham, whom Eugene had newly promoted to chief of staff.

"Lord Nagarian again."

Eugene sat staring at the map of his empire spread on the table in front of him, rolling a pencil between finger and thumb. The news was not entirely unexpected, but no less unwelcome.

"But surely we have reserve stocks?"

An embarrassed silence followed.

"No reserves?" Eugene repeated.

Boden cleared his throat. "We requested Magus Linnaius to manufacture fresh supplies. But he has often been away on your highness's business of late and . . ."

It was true and Eugene did not need to be reminded of the fact. He had sent Linnaius out to research the fabled land of Ty Nagar, leaving him little time to work in his laboratory. He looked up from the map. "Until the Magus is returned to us, we must use our remaining supplies as sparingly as possible."

"Then we must face the genuine possibility," said Boden, "that the Francians may defeat us."

Around the table, Eugene saw his ministers shaking their heads at this grim prediction. He could not remember a council meeting more subdued.

"Come now, Boden," he said, forcing an optimism that he did not feel, "what's this talk of defeat? Our men have been put through the best training any soldier or sailor could hope for. Our military academies are the envy of the western quadrant. Our officers are selected for their exceptional skills in leadership and strategy. They will drive back the Francians without recourse to alchymical weapons."

"Even so, highness," said Colonel Soderham, "we must devise an alternative plan to put into practice if the Francians break through our defenses and take Haeven."

"Chancellor Maltheus and the council have called up the Tielborg Militia to help defend the capital," said Baron Sylvius, who had remained silent until then.

Soderham let out a bark of laughter. "A hundred doddering veterans and a gaggle of spotty boys wielding pikes and muskets?"

"With respect, Colonel, you could be called a veteran yourself," said Sylvius, a little aggrieved.

"Where's the Northern Army?" Soderham called, ignoring this last comment. "Where's Field Marshal Karonen? Let's send in the crack troops."

"Karonen is in Muscobar, on the Azhkendi borders," said Eugene, "training the Muscobar Army."

"Then bring back our Northern boys, highness!" Soderham thumped the table with his fist. "Bring 'em where they're needed!"

"And leave the Azhkendi borders undefended?"

"We need not concern ourselves about Azhkendir." Eugene had some sympathy with Soderham's point of view. But to call back the Northern Army from Muscobar across the Straits would require a massive deployment of troop ships. And it would take time. They needed reinforcements immediately. He turned to Ekman, the Minister for Munitions, a pallid Northerner with thinning gingery hair. "This new munitions factory we opened outside Haeven to supply the fleets. Who is in charge overall?"

"Well, I am, highness, but—"

"We still have the Magus's notes at Swanholm, though they are in a state of considerable disorder. Could the ingenieurs manufacture fresh supplies using the Magus's formulae?"

The minister slowly shook his head. "The Magus was very secretive about his methods. And we are talking of highly volatile ingredients . . ."

In the ensuing pause, Eugene could hear Soderham tutting disapprovingly. His ministers seemed defeated already by the Francian threat. Sylvius was doodling abstractedly.

"*Why are you wasting your time with these fools?*" breathed a dry, subtle voice in his mind. "*You have no need of your Magus now. Together we can wreak as much havoc on the Francians as Gavril Nagarian wrought on your Southern Fleet.*"

"No!" said Eugene aloud, striking the table with clenched fist as he willed himself to ignore the daemon's words. Then, seeing the startled glances from his ministers, he continued, trying to cover his outburst, "There is one man, a doctor of science, who might be able to decipher the Magus's notes, or analyze the components of the remaining powder."

"D'you mean that bespectacled Muscobite fellow you appointed last year to the new chair of chymical studies at Saint Ansgar's College, highness?" said Sylvius in his quiet drawl. "He's caused quite a stir among our academics, I hear, with his . . . erm . . . unconventional lectures."

"Altan Kazimir?" said Ekman doubtfully.

"Isn't that exactly what we need right now? An unconventional, original thinker?" said Eugene. "Gentlemen, what other options do we have?" He had not forgotten that this same Altan Kazimir had achieved where all other magi and daemon-hunters had failed; he had developed an elixir to subdue the Drakhaoul's powers. "Have Professor Kazimir sent to me. Straightaway."

When the ministers had departed, Eugene took out his handkerchief and wiped his brow. It was his fault that the empire was in such a predicament. His obsession had made him blind to the rapidly changing situation in Francia. He had concentrated all his energy into seeking a Drakhaoul of his own, in the belief he would then be invincible.

"*Use me,*" whispered Belberith.

"This battle must be won by human forces alone."

"*And when you see your men lie bleeding, dying at your feet, will you still be so stubborn? When your enemy sets Haeven afire and you hear the screams of defenseless women and children burning in their own homes, what will you do then, Eugene?*"

The temptation was strong. He could so easily use his powers to obliterate the Francians. Eugene, who all his life had been so sure of his own mind, was suddenly pitifully indecisive.

"No," he said slowly. "The price is too high." He had killed once already to replenish his daemon-tainted blood. He could remember nothing of the kill itself, but the evidence had been discovered in the parklands at Swanholm, the bloodied and torn body of a young servant girl. No one had suspected him. Why should they? No one knew of Belberith's unseen, malign presence, save the Magus, Gavril Nagarian, and his own daughter, Karila.

"The life of one innocent, sacrificed to save so many? Only one, one who will die anyway if the Francian forces break through your defenses."

"Have you so little faith in my strategic skills, Belberith?" Eugene was unable to restrain a wry smile at the daemon's assumption he would lose.

"You cannot win this battle without great loss of life. Use me and only your enemies will fall."

"No!" Eugene was determined to remain resolute, no matter what blandishments the daemon used. How could he have been so deluded? His search for Ty Nagar now seemed a kind of madness. But there was no time for the luxury of self-recrimination. The enemy was sailing closer to the shores of Tielen by the minute, and he must be with his men to defend his homeland.

"As you wish . . ." said Belberith, but there was no tinge of acquiescence to Belberith's words. More, Eugene detected, a tinge of amusement, as though the daemon from the Realm of Shadows knew him better than he knew himself.

"Still no new information from our agents in Francia?" Eugene paced the Communications Room, hands clasped behind his back. He had transferred most of his intelligence team from Swanholm to Tielborg Fastness, where the delicate Vox Aethyriae could be more successfully defended. Swanholm had been designed as a country seat, a palace to delight the senses, not a fortified bastion against invaders.

Gustave rose from the Vox tuned to the New Rossiyan Embassy in Lutèce; another secretary discreetly slipped in to take his place.

"No word. I can't help wondering, highness, if some of our communications have been intercepted—and our agents arrested or forced to go to ground."

"Intercepted? How?"

"Pavel Velemir took a great risk in revealing the workings of the Vox to the Smarnans. And now they have used it against us."

It was the nearest Gustave had ever come to criticizing one of his decisions.

"And what of diplomatic immunity?" demanded Eugene, noting

the criticism, but not rising to it. "We have made no move against Abrissard and his household."

"I have been in touch with our embassies in Allegonde and Tourmalise. They have heard little more than us. It seems that the Francians have acted alone. The official bulletins announced that Smarna has broken away from New Rossiya and has welcomed its Francian liberators."

"We need news from *inside* Francia, not this official pap," Eugene burst out. Several of the secretaries flinched at this uncharacteristic display of frustration.

Who was fueling his anger? Was it the daemon Belberith speaking through him, urging him to act? Eugene's soldierly instincts told him that it was not yet time to strike back at the enemy; self-restraint was essential until the situation became clearer.

"We still have other means at our disposal." Gustave beckoned him to the window. "Slower, and a little vulnerable to aerial attack."

Plump grey-and-white feathered birds sat preening and cooing on the ledge outside.

"Carrier pigeons?"

"When all else fails . . ."

"Don't forget that the Francians are fond of their food. Our messengers could end up in a fricassée or a casserole."

"Oh, these are tough old birds," said Gustave, with the hint of a smile hovering about his lips. "I doubt the Francians would find them palatable, even after several hours' stewing."

Professor Altan Kazimir settled back in his comfortably upholstered leather chair with a glass of good red wine and adjusted his spectacles to read the minutes of the Imperial Chymical Society's last meeting. The insistent tolling of the college bell in the quadrangle outside reminded him it would soon be time for dinner.

He set down the papers and rubbed his hands in anticipation of the good meal to come; Saint Ansgar's College treated its academic staff well and the food at high table was delicious.

"Professor Kazimir?" A loud voice called his name. He looked up over the rim of his spectacles, frowning. Was this some undergraduate prank, designed to lure him out into the cloisters where he would be pelted with flour or whitewash? Best to ignore the pranksters; they would soon tire and go in search of some other victim.

The door burst open. Kazimir leaped up, spilling his wine. Two tall, uniformed soldiers loomed in the doorway.

"Wh—what is the meaning of this?" Kazimir tried to disguise the quiver in his voice.

"We come on the Emperor's business." One thrust a letter into his hands. It bore the imperial seal, and Kazimir seemed all fingers and thumbs as he tried to break the seal and open it. The message was brief:

> To Professor Altan Kazimir:
> Your presence is urgently required. Please be so good as to
> accompany these officers directly.
> > Eugene.

"Directly?" Kazimir could hear the dinner bell ringing again. "But I was just about to dine—"

"We have a carriage waiting at the college gate."

"I see." Kazimir stifled a sigh. There was roast goose on the menu and strawberry meringue for dessert.

"The Emperor is waiting, Professor."

There was obviously to be no arguing with his escorts. As the guardsmen hurried him through the cloisters, he caught a faint whiff of sage, apple, and onion stuffing wafting tantalizingly from the college kitchens.

Eugene paced the Knights' Hall, pausing every now and then to gaze out the narrow window at his capital city below. A portrait of his father Karl, painted several years before his decisive victory over the Francian fleet, hung on the wall. Eugene swung around on his heel to gaze at the portrait. It showed Prince Karl gazing out with a young man's optimism and pride. He was dressed in the uniform of the Household Cavalry, his hair still golden and crisp, his face fresh-complexioned, showing no sign of the debilitating heart condition that would shorten his life.

"What would you have done, I wonder?" Eugene asked the portrait. But the situation would never have arisen. His mother, Eleanora, had been devoted to his father. She had retired from public life after her husband's death, afflicted by grief. And Eugene was sure that Prince Karl had never once given her cause to mistrust him.

"Professor Kazimir, highness," announced Eugene's new adjutant, Anckstrom's youngest son, Rolf.

"I—imperial highness." Professor Kazimir bowed low. "How may I be of assistance to you?"

College life evidently suited Altan Kazimir, for his hollow face had filled out and Eugene noted that the gold buttons on his waistcoat of damson velvet were undone to accommodate a swelling waistline.

"You may have heard, Professor, that Tielen is under attack. The Francians are threatening to invade."

"The *Francians*?" Kazimir repeated, his eyes glazing over.

"They were also inconsiderate enough to abduct Kaspar Linnaius, leaving us with inadequate supplies of alchymical powder to defend ourselves. That's why I've summoned you here tonight."

"Me?" said Kazimir warily.

"At the time of Linnaius's abduction he was working on a new, volatile material mined in Azhkendir."

At the mention of Azhkendir, Kazimir blanched. He began to shake his head. "I'm very flattered that you should consider me, imperial highness, but I don't really think I'm suitably qualified to undertake such an important project—"

"All the material is here in Tielen, Professor." Eugene cut in across Kazimir's babbling. "Unfortunately, the Magus's notes are in considerable disorder. I believe you are the only scientist experienced enough in the field to help us."

"Here in Tielen?" Kazimir seemed only to be concerned that he should not be forced to have anything more to do with Azhkendir. "Well then, I—I will do all I can to help you."

Eugene nodded. "I have arranged for you to be transported to the munitions factory at first light. All the Magus's remaining papers have been collected and brought here from his laboratory; I'd like you to look them over tonight and compile a list of what equipment you'll need to start work."

"Yes, yes, of course." Kazimir kept rubbing his hands together nervously.

"So that's settled, Professor?"

A strange rumbling issued from Kazimir's direction. "Er—there was just one thing."

Eugene nodded indulgently.

"I missed hall this evening. A little food would set me up for the night's work."

"This is hopeless," muttered Kazimir as he turned over page after page scribed in the Magus's faint, spidery handwriting. All the pages were torn and crumpled; on some the ink had run into great blotches and the words and diagrams were indecipherable. There were fascinating yet frustrating glimpses into failed experiments. By midnight he had come to the conclusion that these random scraps had been gathered from Linnaius's wastepaper basket, and he was looking at ideas the Magus had tried and rejected.

"Pods of soap beans to make the smoke black; arsenic oxide and arsenic sulfide; wolfsbane and aconite," read Kazimir aloud. "Mix with croton oil to bind . . ." He shook his head. "But this is lethal stuff, even for those who are preparing it. I trust the workers at the factory are wearing masks and gloves; if they inhale the fumes, they'll start to bleed from the mouth and nose."

In the distance outside his little chamber, he was constantly aware of the sound of activity, even so late into the night: horses clattering over the drawbridge; soldiers mustering in the courtyard; large pieces of ordnance being dragged over the cobbles and loaded onto barges. Preparations for war.

"There is of course one other possibility." Kazimir picked up one of the papers and held it to the lamp to see if there was any hint of invisible ink. "Ahh . . ." He fumbled in his capacious pockets and brought out a little stoppered phial. There were many ways to hide writing from curious and prying eyes; he himself used a special invisible ink occasionally, an ink whose formula he had deciphered from an ancient Djihari alchymical manuscript in Saint Ansgar's College.

Sure enough, his hunch was correct. As he sprinkled a little of the liquid onto the paper, faint letters and symbols began to appear. Swiftly he held the paper to the flame again to seal them with heat before they wavered and vanished again.

He was flattered that the Emperor had chosen him for this vital project, but he was also apprehensive. How would Eugene react if he failed? It was tempting to pretend he knew more than he did. It would be only too easy to set up fake experiments.

He pulled off his spectacles to wipe his tired eyes. There was simply not enough information to work with, only tantalizing fragments of some greater experiment.

"Surely his assistants must know something of his processes," he muttered.

The flame in the lamp wavered as the door silently opened. Kazimir looked up to see the Emperor standing behind him.

"Don't get up," the Emperor said quietly.

Kazimir wound his spectacle wires securely back around his ears and refocused on the crumpled papers. "I confess I'm not making much progress here, imperial highness."

Eugene sat on the opposite side of the desk. His eyes glinted with a fevered intensity in the lamplight. "Our time is running out."

"If I could speak with the Magus's assistants . . . surely he left formulae for his alchymical explosive powders behind?"

"Formulae? Oh yes," said the Emperor with a wry lift of the brows. "But formulae that require the inclusion of rare alchymical compounds. They are attempting to analyze and duplicate them at the factory laboratories as we speak."

"Duplicate them?" Kazimir looked up, alarmed. "Some of the ingredients mentioned here are not only volatile in certain combinations, they can prove lethal."

"I understand from Minister Ekman that all his scientists are experienced in the use of volatile materials."

"Highness, I really must advise that you send an urgent message ordering them to cease work. Immediately."

The Emperor's carriage rattled through the cobbled streets of Tielborg, throwing its occupants from side to side as it negotiated the narrow corners.

Eugene would have preferred to have ridden on ahead to the munitions factory with his messenger, but he wanted to continue to interrogate Altan Kazimir who, for all his apparent lack of self-confidence, seemed to be the only scientist in Tielborg to understand how the Magus's mind worked.

"Linnaius's books were stolen when he was kidnapped by Francian spies," Eugene said. "My agents have no idea why these few papers were left behind. I can only assume that the Francians were careless—or in a hurry."

Kazimir grabbed hold of the swaying cord grip as the carriage slewed wildly to the left as it took another bend. "And no one else thought to check for hidden texts?"

"No one else was clever enough to discover them."

And then the ground shook with a terrifying rumble. The sky flashed with a lurid and dazzling brilliance as deafening thunderclaps made the city tremble. But the night was fine and there was not a rain cloud in the sky.

"We're too late." Kazimir pulled down the window and stuck his head out as the coach slowed down. "We're too late."

Eugene opened the door and jumped down into the street. The coachman was trying to settle the startled horses. Shutters were flung open in the houses and shops on either side and heads poked out. Everyone was talking at once.

"Are the Francians attacking?"

"What's all that smoke?"

"Is the city on fire?"

All Eugene could see was a fiery glow lighting the sky and clouds of pale smoke. It looked as if his warning had come too late.

"*Let me take you there,*" urged Belberith.

"Drive on, coachman," said Eugene, ignoring him and clambering back inside.

Not much remained of the munitions factory. The second explosion had blown the roof off and the ensuing fire was sweeping through the buildings with vicious intensity. The broken walls were silhouetted against the flames which still leaped and roared into the sky, giving off clouds of foul, choking smoke.

Attempts were being made to pump water from the River Tilälven but each time the rescuers ventured close, they were beaten back by the ferocity of the flames.

"No one could survive such a conflagration," Eugene said. "Poor devils."

At his side Kazimir kept shaking his head. He seemed dumbstruck; the glow of the flames was reflected in the glass of his spectacles.

Another carriage rolled up to stop close by and Minister Ekman stumbled out. He had obviously been woken from his bed as he had pulled a jacket over his nightshirt and had carpet slippers on his feet.

"This is a disaster," he said, staring as though hypnotized by the sight of the burning factory.

"Our warning came too late," Kazimir said in a whisper.

A sudden series of loud retorts went off from within the flames, spewing out fragments of brick and metal.

"We must move everyone farther away," said Kazimir agitatedly. "There may be more explosions still to come."

"How many workers would be employed at this hour?" Eugene asked Ekman.

"We run two shifts in summer; the second shift finishes at eight in the evening. But the chemists have been staying here late into the night, analyzing the Magus's powders, as your highness requested."

"And now we have lost them all," said Eugene. It was a bitter blow. In one ill-charged experiment, the main munitions factory had been destroyed—and with it all their scientific expertise.

A third carriage came rattling over the stony ground and stopped to let Chancellor Maltheus descend. The heat from the burning buildings was intense and Maltheus was mopping his face with a handkerchief.

"Fortunate that the wind is blowing the fumes away from the city," he observed. "Could it have been Francian saboteurs? Do we have any eyewitnesses?"

Ekman was conferring with one of his clerks. "It seems that we have one survivor; the night watchman was blown clear. His leg's broken, his hair's singed, but he's alive."

"How can we keep news of this one quiet?" Maltheus caught Eugene's eye. "A blast that loud must have been heard out in the Straits! Once the Francians realize we've lost our main munitions factory, they'll launch a full-scale attack."

Eugene had been thinking the same. "There's nothing we can do. Francian sabotage, or unfortunate laboratory accident, we must make do with what we have."

Another imperial carriage rolled up and Gustave clambered out, clutching a dispatch. One look at his secretary's face told Eugene that the news he bore was not good. He opened the dispatch, reading by the light of the burning factory.

"Well, gentlemen," he said. "This news comes from Admiral Berger. The Francians have made their move. It has begun."

Eugene gave the order to evacuate the streets closest to the waterfront in Haeven. If the Francians started firing on the port, the houses and taverns on the quays would be the first to be hit. All able-bodied men of fighting age were to be issued with weapons to defend the town. And all the elderly, women, and children were to be given temporary shelter in the churches beyond the harbor.

A swift sloop was awaiting the Emperor, ready to transport him down the River Tilälven to Haeven and the Northern Fleet. But there was still one thought troubling Eugene. He hesitated, scanning the assembled dignitaries and troops of the Imperial Guard lining the river quay. Where was Gustave? He was itching to get to the action, yet at the same time, reluctant to embark without any fresh news of Astasia's whereabouts.

He paced his study.

Now he was about to engage the enemy forces—and, even though he was protected by Belberith's powers, he knew he was not invincible. He had kissed Karila farewell in Swanholm, but Astasia's flight had deprived him of the chance of saying any kind of good-bye, should he fall in battle. There was so much he wanted to say to her, so much he wanted to put right between them, and he knew he might never have the chance.

He seized pen and ink and started to scribble a hasty note, scratching out, blotting words in his desperate eagerness to express his feelings.

> My dearest wife,
> I write this on the eve of battle in case I do not return. Of late, I realize that I have neglected you—and I want you to know how deeply I regret this. Our brief months together have truly been the happiest of my life. Can you ever find it in your heart to forgive me, Astasia?
> Your devoted husband, Eugene.

He was just folding the letter and sealing it with his signet ring, when Gustave came in. On seeing the name inscribed on the letter, Gustave raised one eyebrow inquiringly.

"Is there any new intelligence yet?"

"A young woman closely resembling the Empress was seen disembarking from the *Melusine* at Fenez-Tyr in Francia, highness. The same *Melusine* that sailed from Haeven not long after her disappearance from Swanholm. But that's all our agents have been able to report so far."

"Francia." What on earth had possessed Astasia to go to Francia? Was she there as a guest of Enguerrand's court? There had always been strong links between the royal houses of Francia and Muscobar.

Or had she been abducted?

"In the circumstances, how am I to deliver this, highness?"

"Your ingenuity has never let me down in the past, Gustave," Eugene said, smiling at him. "You'll find a way."

"Godspeed, highness," said Gustave with more fervor than Eugene had ever heard before in his voice.

Eugene laid a hand on his shoulder. "Farewell, Gustave."

And if we all come through this alive, I will see to it that Gustave is suitably rewarded for his services to the crown. A country estate and a title . . . But not too far from Swanholm—for what would I do without him at my side?

CHAPTER 8

Blood. There was dried blood on the shreds of Gavril's clothes, blood spattering his hands and body, the taste of blood on his lips.

Clean. Must wash myself clean.

He had flown farther inland under cover of night, following the course of a wide river. But now the bright dawn of early summer was lightening the horizon.

The girl's blood that he had gulped down with the desperation of a starving man burned into his skin. He felt sure that the bloodstains must gleam fiery red in the daylight, marking him for the monster he was. All he wanted was to try to scrub the tainting marks of guilt from his body.

He landed in a rushy meadow by the river and walked along through morning mists rising like clouds of thistledown, searching for a sheltered place to bathe. Soon he came to a bend in the river, where the water had carved out a shelving pebbled shore, and plunged in.

The cold of the rippling water took Gavril's breath away. He surfaced with a shout, spitting out a mouthful, then shaking his head like a dog. He tugged up a handful of waterweed and started to scrub at the bloodstains, scrubbing until his skin was sore.

But no matter how clean his skin was, he could not rid himself of the black shadow of remorse shrouding his soul. He had killed again. Or Khezef had killed, taking control of him, forcing him to do a deed so abhorrent to his own nature that just thinking of it made him loathe himself.

As Gavril pulled himself up onto the stony shore, he forced himself to walk barefoot over the sharpest pebbles, wincing at the acute pain they caused. But he found no relief from the guilt in this self-inflicted penance.

Still dripping, he limped on until he found firmer ground, a grassy field, warmed by the morning sun. There he flung himself down on the turf and let the sun dry his body. The river had left the taste of mud and green duckweed in his mouth and throat.

Lying staring up at the fresh summer blue of the sky, Gavril was forced to acknowledge that Khezef was growing stronger. With each kill, the Drakhaoul's hold over him increased. He had tried to impose his will on Khezef, but Khezef had overmastered him. Even now, he wondered how much longer he could shield his innermost thoughts from the daemon. There were times when he sensed that his own identity was slowly disintegrating and merging with the Drakhaoul's.

How can I stop it? Before I become his slave, forced to do his bidding against my will?

The diligence bound for Lutèce jogged onward through the stifling afternoon heat.

Gavril had been reduced to stealing clothes from a washing line. He had left coins on the window of the farm cottage before two large dogs came snarling after him and chased him into a nearby spinney.

Now, attired like a peasant farmer, he had paid his passage to the capital city and, wedged between a priest and a smartly dressed apothecary, was on his way at last. Sitting opposite him was a bourgeois family: the husband reading a newspaper, his harassed-looking wife attempting to amuse their two young daughters by reading them a story.

Lulled by the rocking of the coach, Gavril fell into a deep sleep.

"*Adramelech,*" Khezef whispered, his voice searing through Gavril's dreams. "*One of my kindred is near at hand.*"

Gavril started awake. The other passengers in the coach were staring at him. He must have cried out in his sleep. The man next to him drew his coattails closer to him.

"Excuse me." Gavril coughed, hoping they might excuse his cry as a cough. The matronly woman opposite him stared pointedly out of the window. Her husband hid behind his newspaper. Their pigtailed daughters giggled behind their hands and kicked each other.

Gavril gazed uneasily out of the window. All he could see was the dusty green of fields and tall trees. "*Near at hand.*" How near? Was there a winged shadow pursuing them, high overhead?

"Where are we, if you please?" he asked stiltedly in his schoolboy Francian.

The black-garbed priest was the only one to reply. "We are approaching the city of Lutèce," he said, enunciating each word slowly so that Gavril could understand.

"Thank you."

Still the Drakhaoul's warning whispered through Gavril's mind as he gazed out of the window at the passing countryside. *Adramelech.* Khezef had greeted one of the Drakhaouls from the Serpent Gate on Ty Nagar with the same name. Had Adramelech come in search of Khezef? Or was the daemon-spirit at large in Francia?

By now Gavril could make out the towers and church spires of Lutèce on the horizon. They passed windmills, their sails clacking and whirring in the dry summer breeze. The diligence passed through a massive stone archway and entered the city. Soon the driver steered it into the courtyard of a coaching inn and jumped down to let his passengers out.

The bourgeois and his wife hurried their daughters away, shooting suspicious glances back at Gavril over their shoulders, as if to make sure he was not following them.

Gavril was stiff after sitting so long on the hard seats. He was hot too, and the coarse material of the shirt and trousers he had appropriated was proving unbearably itchy. Worst of all were the thick brown woollen socks, which rubbed his heels and made his feet sweat. He looked like a farm laborer. He hoped that he had not acquired any extra livestock of the biting kind with the clothes. Besides, if he was to make a convincing portrait painter, he would have to find an outfit that was far less homespun. And, most important of all, some paints.

He wandered aimlessly for a while until he caught a familiar smell seeping from a shop doorway. It was a nostalgic smell, reminding him of his mother's studio. Inside the shop, he stood, eyes closed, breathing in the potent blend of turpentine, white spirit, and oils. It was like finding a little pocket of home in this unfamiliar city.

Gazing around, Gavril saw shelves lined with jars with gold and black lettering, much like those in an apothecary's, except that these were filled with pigments, ready for grinding, or sold by the gram for artists to prepare by their own methods. There were tall cabinets with drawers containing a rainbow selection of pastels and different thicknesses of charcoals. Other cabinets were devoted to papers for watercolorists. Canvases had been stacked in height order against a back wall, from the smallest square to the greatest expanse, fit to paint a royal banqueting scene or a dramatic sea battle . . .

Smoke, fire, and deafening explosions flickered through his mind.

Why had the thought of a battle at sea come to him so vividly at that precise moment? He had left the Emperor preparing to defend Tielen from the Francian war fleet; even at that moment they could be engaged in a desperate struggle for the empire. Gavril glanced around the shop. All he could hear was the quiet murmur of conversation: the relative merits of sable and squirrel brushes were being debated in one corner; in another, a woman was examining a boxed set of pastels, holding each stick up to the light to examine it while the shop assistant hovered nearby. There was no hint of war to be sensed in here. Even on the streets he had seen no sign of marching troops.

"Can I help you?" A stooped old man stood at his elbow, staring at him suspiciously.

Gavril remembered his peasant clothes; he must look an unlikely artist, even an impoverished one. "Yes," he said. "I want to buy paints." His command of Francian was barely adequate for the task, so he jingled the coins in the purse loudly and began to point out the articles he wanted to purchase.

As he left the shop, he checked how much money he had left. He needed new clothes and a bed for the night. And above all, he needed a well-fitting pair of shoes. He was not sure if the remaining coins would cover all these necessities.

The sound of shouting and jeering caught his attention. At the end of the street he could see people gathering on the broad avenue. Uneasy, yet curious, he went closer to see what had caused the uproar.

Soldiers in black uniforms had surrounded a tall house. The front door was wide-open and the sound of terrified screams and protests came from inside. Just as Gavril arrived, he saw more soldiers emerge, dragging a man along with them.

"Lucien! *Lucien!*" A woman flew after, crying out at the top of her voice, her hands extended, as if to claw back the man who was being arrested. The man shouted to her as the soldiers bundled him down the steps, his voice breaking.

For Gavril, the scene brought back memories, still raw and painful, of his own arrest by the Emperor's troops. And when he saw a black carriage with barred windows driven up and the man flung inside, the memories became even more vivid. He knew only too well what it was to be forcibly taken prisoner, to lose everything that mattered to him—even his own name.

Now the soldiers were carrying out crates and boxes overflowing with books and papers. The crowd began to taunt the prisoner and shake their fists at him. Amid the jeering, Gavril could distinguish one word, shouted again and again. *Heretic.*

The woman sank down and began to sob as the sealed coach drove slowly away, followed by the soldiers carrying their spoils. Several of the crowd ran after, still shouting abuse.

"What is happening?" Gavril asked in his broken Francian. "Where are they taking him?"

A soberly dressed man in front turned around and began to speak. Gavril understood every third word or so.

"Forbidden . . . dangerous . . . scientific . . ."

"May I ask, friend, what you are carrying in that bag?" said another voice in the common tongue. A man stood beside him, dressed in the same funeral black as the soldiers. He pointed to Gavril's newly purchased art case. "Would you be so good as to open it up for me?"

"I am an artist, newly arrived from Smarna," Gavril said. He did not like the smooth tones of his interrogator but he was not going to argue and draw attention to himself. He opened the case and displayed his paints and pastels.

The man cast an eye over the contents and nodded. "You seemed remarkably interested in what you witnessed here." His smooth tone had not altered but Gavril knew he was being cautioned. "Let me give you a little advice, my Smarnan friend. Don't involve yourself with these heretical dissidents. The so-called freethinking favored by some of your Smarnan compatriots is not in favor here. The Commanderie is dedicated to the eradication of such dangerous and seditious ideas—and those who promulgate them."

"Thank you," Gavril said, forcing himself to keep his face a mask. "I will remember."

"Now move along," said the Commanderie official, turning to the other onlookers. "There's nothing more to see."

As the crowd broke up, Gavril walked slowly in the direction the coach had taken. If the Commanderie were taking the man they had arrested to a prison for heretics, then it was possible Kaspar Linnaius could be confined there too. It could even be the Forteresse that the Emperor's secretary had mentioned.

But the black coach was gathering speed and by the time Gavril reached the busy square at the end of the avenue, he had lost sight of it among the many other carriages and carts crossing and crisscrossing.

And now he could not think of anything but the official's warning. If Smarna had welcomed in the Francian fleet as its liberators, the rebels would realize their mistake all too soon—especially the students and their professors who had fought on the barricades at Colchise.

"Rafael," he murmured, "take care." For Rafael Lukan was exactly the kind of radical philosopher whose writings the Commanderie would describe as seditious and heretical. The freethinking professor could be in far more danger now than under the Rossiyan occupation.

"Psst! Over here!"

Gavril glanced around and saw a hand frantically beckoning to him from a side alley. He hesitated. But what had he to lose? A tiny glimmer of blue fire crackled at his fingertips. If this was a footpad, he had picked the wrong victim in Gavril Nagarian.

The narrow alley was rank with the stink of rotting refuse and cats. The one who had beckoned Gavril went ahead, slipping into a shadowed doorway.

"What is this about?"

The stranger turned to face him. Even in the dim light, Gavril could see that he was of middle years, stockily built, with thick chestnut-brown hair and beard, speckled with grey.

"I heard what you said to Inquisitor Méloir. You're one of us, friend."

"Of us?" Gavril still suspected a trap.

The stranger pointed to Gavril's case. "You're an artist." He held up his hands, grinning. "See?" Close up, Gavril could make out the engrained paint residue staining his fingernails. He looked down at his own hands, the claw-nails glinting Drakhaoul-blue. In this half-light, the unnatural color could easily be mistaken for paint.

"The name's Lavret. Budoc Lavret."

"Not *the* Lavret?" Gavril stared at him, amazed—then took the outstretched, paint-stained hand and shook it warmly. "Lavret of the *Young Girl Spinning*? And *The Dice Players*? The intensity of light in those canvases—"

"Stop, you'll embarrass me," said Lavret, grinning wider. "And we can't stay here. You've just seen what they do with freethinkers who dare to oppose the Commanderie. Unless you're interested in religious painting, you've made a wasted journey to Francia."

"I'm a portrait painter. The name's . . ." Gavril longed to tell Lavret his real Smarnan name but dared not risk such a revelation. Instead, another name came into his mind, authentically Smarnan, yet unlikely to raise any suspicions if they were overheard, "Korneli. Miran Korneli."

"Well, young Miran, all I can offer you is a safe haven overnight with fellow artists."

"I'd like that." It felt strange to be addressed by another's name. "Thank you."

Budoc Lavret led Gavril up flights of steps and through winding alleys before emerging on a windy hilltop ridge with an impressive view of the river and the more fashionable and prosperous quarters laid out below.

"My studio," Lavret said, gesturing to a ramshackle building, more an abandoned warehouse than what Gavril had imagined as a successful artist's residence. "Come in."

Gavril sniffed the air; there was a strong whiff of turpentine that reminded him poignantly of home. He followed Lavret down a narrow, ill-lit passageway that opened into a great, airy space beyond, which rose five stories up to exposed timber roof struts. Canvases of all sizes lay stacked against the lime-rendered walls; a work in progress was propped on an easel and the worn flagstone floor beneath was splattered with splashes of bright colored paints, as if some fabulous bird were roosting in the rafters above. The tall, lozenge-paned windows were grimy and matted with cobwebs, yet light streamed in, all the more interesting to Gavril's painterly eye for being filtered through the dirt.

"In my grandfather's time it used to be a silk factory," Lavret said. "Then all the mulberry trees caught blight and died . . ." Gavril nodded absently, drawn to the half-finished painting on the easel. It showed an angel appearing to the prophet Mhir in a vineyard, a scene much favored by religious painters in the previous century. He turned questioningly to Lavret, who gave an apologetic shrug.

"Not quite the Lavret you know, hm? When I go out, I always leave this pious work on show, in case any uninvited visitors happen by."

A door at the far end of the studio opened and a delicious smell wafted in.

"Papa? We're in the kitchen."

Gavril saw a young woman in the doorway. And to his dismay, he sensed Khezef wake at the sight of her.

"Come and meet my daughter Trifine." Lavret, beaming, was hugging his daughter. He beckoned Gavril toward them. "This young painter is from Smarna, Trifine. His name is Miran Korneli."

"Demoiselle." Gavril went up to Trifine and bowed. Trifine burst into giggles at this which, to his shame, made the color rise in his cheeks.

"No need to be so formal, Miran," she said, reaching out and pressing his hand between her own. "All artists are welcome here, especially those out of favor with the Commanderie."

"*Ahhh,*" breathed Khezef in a voice laced with desire.

Gavril forced a smile at Trifine and nodded. She was the model for the angel in the unfinished canvas; thick, chestnut hair of the same rich shade as her father's, cascaded down her back, barely restrained by tortoiseshell combs. And though her nose was tip-tilted, giving her face a charmingly homely air, her deep-set brown eyes had a disturbingly sensual luster.

"We can eat now, if you like," Trifine said, going ahead into the kitchen.

"I'll bet you're famished, Miran," Lavret said. "I was always hungry when I was your age."

A savory steam rose from a cooking pot bubbling on an ancient range set in a wide fireplace. Gavril realized, as he sniffed the enticing smell, perfumed with bay leaves, thyme, and rosemary, that Lavret was right; he was starving.

Three men were seated around the long kitchen table, drinking red wine. They rose as Lavret and Gavril came in.

"Meet Miran Korneli, a fellow painter," Lavret said. "Introduce yourselves, gentlemen."

"Herbot, watercolorist," said the first, tall and stooped, with a lugubrious expression.

His companion, grey-haired with a neatly trimmed beard, bowed to Gavril with the precision of a military man. "Similien, specialist in engraving."

"And I'm Bastian." The third, young and good-looking, had already sat down again. He greeted Gavril with a lazy wave. "Budoc's apprentice."

"Who's for *coq au vin*?" called Trifine from the range.

Gavril wiped the last of the gravy with a corner of crusty bread and pushed away his empty plate.

"More chicken, Miran?" asked Trifine, ladle in hand.

"It was excellent, but I'm full, thank you."

Standing at the range, her cheeks flushed with the heat and soft tendrils of her chestnut hair framing her face, Trifine looked like a goddess of the kitchen.

"*So desirable,*" whispered Khezef.

"You cook very well, Trifine," Gavril added, willing the daemon to be silent. "It was delicious."

"More wine?" said Bastian. Gavril shook his head; he had drunk only a mouthful or so, but already felt strangely light-headed. *Perhaps I'm tired after the journey . . .*

"You're very abstemious," said Bastian. "Unusual for an artist!"

"So what brings you to Francia, Miran?" asked Herbot, turning his long, melancholy face toward Gavril.

"There's not much work for a portrait painter in Smarna these days. All the rich families who used to spend their summers in Vermeille have been scared away by the fighting."

"Miran arrives in Lutèce and who does he run into?" Lavret said, lighting up a long-stemmed pipe. "Inquisitor Méloir, no less."

"Méloir!" Trifine set down the plates she was clearing away with a bang. "Papa, you were careful, weren't you? You didn't risk—"

"No, no," said Lavret, drawing on his pipe. "But Professor Sekondel was rather less fortunate."

"Ah!" said Similien. "So the rumors I heard are true."

"They took him and they took all his books and papers too."

"This Professor Sekondel," Gavril said, "what did the Commanderie want with him? What was his crime?"

"No crime, except to pursue his scientific research, like any learned man," said Lavret.

"Research that is forbidden by the Commanderie," added Similien. Herbot said nothing but slowly shook his head. Bastian left the table to help Trifine clear away the dinner dishes.

"Where were they taking him?" asked Gavril. This was his only lead so far as to where Linnaius might be held prisoner. "And what will become of him?"

Herbot pulled a grimace. "There's an old fortress outside the city walls that the king gave the Commanderie as their new headquarters. They'll interrogate him there and hold a trial."

"A trial? A trial that anyone can attend?" When Gavril had stood trial for crimes of war in Mirom, it had seemed that half the city was there, crammed into the courtroom.

Lavret let out a shout of laughter. "You Smarnans have no idea, have you? The Commanderie are judge, jury, and executioners. And why is that? Because they have a holy right to do so. Oh—and the king is their most fervent acolyte"—the mocking tone in his voice took on a harder edge—"so whatever the king decrees is carried out. And the king decrees whatever the Commanderie tells him to."

"Hush, Papa," said Trifine. "You never know who's listening."

A stout silver tabby sauntered in, sniffing the air. It brushed up against Trifine's skirts, mewing plaintively.

"Go and catch mice, Madame Mistigri, and earn your dinner," Trifine said, shooing the cat away.

Gavril was assessing the information, scant though it was, wanting to learn more yet not daring to risk too great an interest in case his hosts began to suspect his motives. "But will your friend, Sekondel, be allowed visitors? I saw a woman at his house—his wife?" Mistigri started out toward the table, winding herself around chair legs, tail high—until she came to Gavril.

"Surely the Commanderie are not so coldhearted that they would deny his family—" Suddenly, Mistigri drew back from him, hissing and showing her teeth, fur bristling. Startled, Gavril looked into her opal yellow eyes and saw feral fear and loathing.

This has never happened before. Is it you, Khezef, can it sense you?

Trifine knelt and stroked the cat, trying to calm her, but Mistigri would have none of her soothing and shot away, squeezing under the kitchen door.

"I—I'm not much good with cats," Gavril said, trying to laugh it off, aware that they were all staring at him.

"Well, you'll have to keep the mice from gnawing my canvases in the studio tonight, Miran," said Lavret, laughing too. "And I'll bet you'd make a better job of it than poor Mistigri. She's getting lazy in her old age."

"Trifine spoils her with tidbits," said Bastian, but Gavril did not miss the sidelong look he gave him.

The studio was silvered blue with moonlight; Lavret's canvases glimmered in the soft light. Gavril paused, hearing the faintest scuttling of tiny paws from the farthest corner.

Trifine came in, carrying a rolled mattress and a blanket. "I hope you don't mind sleeping in here. It's a bit drafty, and . . ."

"And there are the mice." Gavril finished her sentence, unable to restrain a grin. "Believe me, Trifine, I'm just grateful that your father took me in. I would have been sleeping under a bridge tonight. Sharing with a few mice is a small price to pay for shelter and a good supper."

"Shall I bring you a candle?"

"No; the moonlight is all I need." Gavril took the bedroll from her and laid it down on the flagstones in a lozenged patch of moonlight. When he straightened up, she was still there, picking up a handful of discarded brushes. "Papa is so untidy. Whenever his work isn't going well, he just throws his brush down. And brushes are so expensive."

"*She is attracted to you,*" whispered Khezef. "*She could be of use to us . . .*"

The silvered shafts of moonlight filtering down from the tall windows had turned Trifine's rich brown hair to bronze.

"Let me clean those brushes for you." And when she hesitated, Gavril held out his hand. "I am an artist, remember. I could grind pigments for your father, prepare canvases—"

"That's my job," came a voice from the doorway. Surprised, Trifine dropped the brushes. Bastian stood there in the shadows, arms folded across his chest, watching them.

"Don't worry. I'll be moving on soon." Gavril knelt and picked up some of the scattered brushes, handing them to Trifine.

"Just as well," said Bastian, with a smile in his voice as if he were making a jest of it.

*   *   *

Gavril wakes to starlit darkness. As he lies drowsing between sleep and waking, he sees the pale figures on the great canvas slowly detach themselves and come floating across the studio toward him.

Lavret's angel bends over him, her long, dark hair brushing his face. Her white robes slip slowly from her shoulders . . . and he sees terrible wounds, encrusted black with dried blood, in her throat and breasts.

"Remember me, Drakhaon?" she whispers from pallid lips. "It was days before they found my broken body in the gorge."

He clutches his hands to his face, trying not to look, but through his fingers, he sees her white skin is blotched and discolored with decay.

"Gulvardi?"

"Remember how we kissed?" She leans closer still. "I thought you loved me. But all you wanted was my blood."

"I called you my angel." A small, slender figure glides to Gavril's side. "I saw you fall from heaven. I only wanted to help you."

"Kristell." Her name tears from his throat in an agony of self-loathing.

"Why did you kill me?" asks Kristell.

"I didn't mean to. I didn't want to." He begins to sob uncontrollably. "It made me. It took control. I wanted to die."

"My mother cried too. I whispered to her to stop crying but she couldn't hear me."

There are so many more pale figures gathering in the shadows, their eyes hollow, their moonlit bodies gashed with wounds that leak stains of darkness.

"But who are you?" he asks, bewildered. They are coming closer now, clustering about his bed. "Why are you here? I don't recognize any of you."

"We are the Drakhaon's Brides. You took our blood so that you could live." Fingers, thin as bone, reach out to stroke his face, his body. "Now we want yours, Drakhaon."

Their long threads of faded hair are soft and sticky as spidersilk. Their lips have shriveled away, revealing yellowing teeth in blackened gums . . .

*   *   *

"You were shouting out in your sleep."

"I was?" Gavril gazed up at Trifine uncertainly.

She sat down beside him on the floor, hugging her knees, like a schoolgirl. He began to wonder if she was younger than she affected to be. "You've been in a battle, haven't you, Miran?"

He looked away, no longer able to hold her gaze. "I have." *Dear God, what did she hear me say?*

"It must have been terrible."

He nodded and felt her hand on his arm, a tentative gesture of comfort.

"We heard about the uprising in Smarna. You were with the students, weren't you? How brave to take on the Emperor's army."

"Not brave," he muttered. "Rash. Foolhardy." If he were to tell her the true substance of his nightmare, she would snatch her hand away, recoiling from him in revulsion. Though he had seen enough horrors in the field to give sane men nightmares. "So . . . what did I cry out?"

Her brown eyes grew wide. "Blood," she whispered.

Gavril tried to sit up but felt the studio tilt alarmingly as dizziness swept through him. Suddenly his whole body was soaked with sweat. Heat sizzled from his skin. And then he began to shiver as the drenching sweat gave way to fever chills and the aching began.

Faces appeared in the darkness. He saw the hollow eyes of the Drakhaon's Brides hovering above him and flung up his arms to protect himself.

"Leave me be!" he cried out.

"Must be a touch of summer river fever," said a man's voice. "Best give him a draft of willow bark."

Gavril woke again in the night. The fever had abated but he felt so dizzy he could hardly lift his head from the mattress.

"What's wrong with me?" he whispered to Khezef. "Why am I so weak? You've healed me before, Khezef; why can't you heal me now? I haven't the time to be ill."

"*Maybe the blood is no longer enough.*"

"Not enough? But I—you—took so much that the girl died. She died, Khezef!"

"*Yes, I have mended your body and your mind too. But these injuries have taken their toll. You have been without rest—and your body needs time to recover. And even then, I fear the blood may still not be enough."*

"What are you saying?" Gavril heard the Drakhaoul's words with growing alarm. "That I'm dying? But there's still so much to be done, Khezef. So many people are depending on me—"

"*All the more reason for you to give yourself time to heal from this sickness.*"

Was Khezef playing him false again? Or was the Drakhaoul telling him plainly what he had refused to acknowledge: that he had over-stretched himself and was paying the price? He had believed himself indestructible—but it seemed he had reached the limits of his capabilities.

"*You are only mortal,*" whispered Khezef. "*Even gifted with my powers, you are not invincible. And I must cherish you, for you have given me life in this world.*"

"Papa, my foot's gone to sleep," Trifine said plaintively.

"Just a moment or two longer, Trifi," muttered Lavret through the brush he held between his teeth as he dabbed at the canvas. "Just hold the pose—"

"*Papa!*" Trifine hopped off the dais where she had been standing and sat down to rub her foot.

Lavret let out a grunt of frustration and threw down both brushes. "I said only a moment longer, Trifi. Now a cloud's come over the sun and the light's altered." Muttering under his breath, he stomped away toward the kitchen.

"Don't forget I'm modeling for free!" Trifine called after him. "Madelon La Brune charges double if you don't allow her a proper break. And Véronique said she'd never come back after the last time, remember?" She tried to put her weight on her foot. "Ow!" she cried, hopping. "Now I've got cramp."

Gavril put down his sketchbook and went over. Too weak still to leave the studio, he had tried to while away the time in drawing. "Here," he said. "Let me help you."

Trifine pulled a grimace as he helped her onto a stool. He knelt and prised the rope sandal off her foot. Then he began to massage her cramp-distorted toes. Her feet were small but strong, with high arches, just as he had drawn them. And in spite of the summer sunshine outside, they were cold.

"Thank you," she said, her face relaxing. "Can I see now?"

"See what?" he said, sitting back.

"I know what you've been doing. Sketching me." She darted up from the stool and snatched the sketchbook before he could stop her.

"They're only sketches."

She was gazing at his pastel drawings intently, leafing over page after page. He had concentrated on little details: the drape of the fabric, her hand, the tilt of her chin. He had limited himself to ochre and umber, highlighted with touches of white.

"But they're good. They're very good."

It pleased him beyond words to hear her praise his work. It was so long since he had used his craft that he feared he had lost the skill.

"We must show Papa."

He reached out and gently caught her by the arm. "No," he said. Lavret would ask too many questions. "They're only sketches. Later, maybe, when I've had the chance to work on them."

"What must we show Papa?" Bastian was standing in the doorway watching them. There was a raw edge to his voice that belied the smile on his lips.

Gavril's hand dropped away from Trifine's arm.

"Miran's been drawing me."

"Oh, has he indeed?" Bastian came over and snatched the book from Trifine. "I don't like this. Not at all."

As Bastian flicked dismissively through the pages, Gavril watched, arms crossed.

"Why are you so angry, Bastian?" Trifine asked. "What's the harm of a few sketches?"

"A few sketches of you wearing nothing but a flimsy sheet?"

"Why, I do believe you're jealous." Trifine walked up to Bastian, her sheet trailing over the dusty floor, and poked him in the chest, grinning.

"First he's mixing paint for your father, then he's using you like some cheap ten-sous model for his sordid drawings—"

Bells began to chime, ringing out until the walls of the old factory seemed to tremble with the din.

This was no ordinary call to prayer; it sounded more like a warning.

"What's going on?" Lavret Bastian and Trifine hurried outside and Gavril followed, slowly.

Had Eugene, impatient and under attack, ignored their pact and flown to rescue Linnaius himself? Gavril shaded his eyes and looked up into the bright summer sky, searching in vain for a winged shadow.

"I'll go and find out." Bastian hurried away, disappearing down the little alleyway opposite.

"Take care, Bastian!" Trifine called anxiously after him.

"I'll go too." Gavril started out in pursuit of Bastian over the weed-choked cobbles but Lavret stopped him.

"You'll never catch up in your condition; young Bastian runs like a hare. And then how will you find your way?"

Gavril turned back with a shrug as the bells dinned on.

"Coffee, Miran?" called Lavret.

But Gavril lingered outside the studio, gazing down over the city. He thought he could hear the faintest sound of cheering voices carrying upward on the clear air. What were they celebrating? Another victory for Enguerrand's armies?

He heard a grunt of exasperation from the studio. "That damned cat! She's only gone and walked across my palette. Look—rainbow paw prints all over the floor . . ."

Gavril went in and found Lavret scratching his head over his sullied paints. "And now I'm out of flake white—and that ochre I was using for highlights."

"I'll be happy to help," Gavril said. "Tell me what kind of consistency you prefer—and I'll grind fresh pigment and mix up what you need."

"Ruaud de Lanvaux has returned from Smarna," Bastian announced. The bells were still ringing in the city below.

Gavril, pestle in hand, looked up from the white lead he was grinding into a fine powder. "Smarna?" he said. He did not like to be reminded of the unexpected alliance Smarna had made with King Enguerrand. He had begun to wonder if the world had gone mad.

"What are you doing?" Bastian demanded, coming over to where Gavril was working. He picked up the mortar and stared into it, sniffing suspiciously and moving it from side to side to check the consistency. "You've put in too much turpentine."

"He's put in just the right amount," came Lavret's calm voice from behind the easel. "Tell us more, Bastian." He came out from behind the canvas, wiping his brush on a rag. "Why is de Lanvaux back?"

Bastian put the mortar down. "There's talk of an execution. A sorcerer they've been hunting for years."

"A sorcerer?" said Gavril. "Or a man of science?"

"They usually don't make much distinction between the two. They say he's the last of the mages; they've been hunting him for years."

It had to be Kaspar Linnaius.

"But is there any news of Professor Sekondel?" Trifine called from the kitchen. "Is there any date for a trial?"

"Who says they'll bother with a trial? In their eyes, he's guilty and they have his writings to prove their case. It'll be the scaffold for him—or worse."

"There must be something we can do to save him," she said. "Isn't there an influential patron you could ask, Papa?"

Lavret slowly shook his head. "We're powerless. De Lanvaux has informers everywhere."

"Where do they hold these executions?" Gavril asked.

Bastian gazed at him curiously. "Why would you want to know, Miran Korneli?"

Gavril realized, too late, that he should not have asked such a leading question. "Do you think me such a ghoul, Bastian, that I would want to go and watch?"

"They call it the Place du Trahoir," said Trifine quietly. "And I pray to God that the professor is spared the horrors inflicted on the other poor souls condemned to die there."

"Why so?"

"Because that's where they burn people at the stake."

CHAPTER 9

"Why couldn't we bring Pippi, Marta?" Karila asked yet again and saw her governess raise her eyes heavenward.

"You know very well why. There was no room for a pet deer in the coach. There was precious little room enough for us and Doctor Amandel."

"But who will look after Pippi and the others while we're away?"

"The servants have their instructions. They'll feed the animals in your menagerie."

"I miss Pippi," said Karila, heaving a sigh. "I wish someone could bring her here to Great-Aunt Greta's." But she knew that there was not the slightest chance that anyone would respond to her wish.

"Now finish your handwriting practice, highness. We have still some arithmetic exercises to complete before lunch."

Karila let out another sigh. Laboriously she began to trace a line of looping l's. "Is there no word from Papa?"

"No word today."

Karila sighed again and made a small blot.

"Repeat the line, please," said Marta crisply.

"Suppose the Francians ride into Swanholm." The thought struck Karila suddenly as she dipped her pen nib in the inkwell. "Suppose they kill my menagerie for food? Papa says that an army needs lots of food. All the fighting makes men hungry."

Marta said nothing but pointed sternly to the page.

Karila repeated the line and began to copy out a verse about the virtues of being a well-behaved child.

"And I miss Tasia," she said. "Why couldn't she come with us to Rosenholm?"

Marta hesitated. "You know the Empress has gone to Muscobar," she said, but a slight flush had darkened the governess's cheeks and Karila suspected she was not telling the whole truth.

After lunch, Karila accompanied her great-aunt for a stroll in the gardens. Rosenholm Manor was much farther north than Swanholm and, in the brief summer, the gardens bloomed with sweet-scented roses.

"Yellow roses are quite my favorites," said Great-Aunt Greta, stopping to sniff at a cascade of apricot-gold blooms. "Which ones do you like best, Karila?"

"The crimson ones." Karila was stroking the petals of a dark red rose, dark as blood. It felt like the softest, silkiest velvet. And then she experienced the most curious sensation: someone was watching her. She looked up, staring out across the rose garden. There was a man, standing in the archway. Servants usually hurried from one task to another and did not stop to smell the sweet-scented roses or gaze idly at the gardens. So he could not be a servant. "Why is that man watching us?" she asked.

Marta looked too, as did Great-Aunt Greta, raising her lorgnette to her eyes to peer at the stranger.

"Oh, you mustn't mind him," she said. "Poor fellow, he's still re-covering from his injuries. Your father sent him here to recover."

"Papa sent him?"

"His mother owned the neighboring estate. Countess Ulla Alvborg."

"Wasn't she a famous beauty at Prince Karl's court?" Marta said. "I remember hearing my mother speak of her. Bewitching, she said, with white-blond hair."

"Poor Ulla." Great-Aunt Greta seemed to be talking to Marta now, the conversation passing to and fro, like a shuttlecock, above Karila's head. "Driven to an early grave by her husband's shockingly licentious behavior."

"And her son?"

"Injured on active service in Azhkendir." Great-Aunt Greta's voice dropped to a confidential whisper. "Lost his wits. Battle-shock. The Emperor took pity on him and restored his mother's estate and title.

But he's"—and she mouthed the words—"not really right in the head."

"Doesn't it bother you, Duchess?" said Marta. Karila heard the unease in her governess's voice. "Does he just stand and stare—like that—very often?"

"Oh, Oskar's harmless," said Great-Aunt Greta with a little laugh. "The muttering, the staring, it can be disconcerting at first. But for poor Ulla's sake, I give him dinner once in a while and ensure his valet has enough funds to clothe his master in a manner befitting his station."

Karila, half-hearing the adults' conversation, peeked out over the bloodred roses at the injured man. From what she could see, his injuries reminded her of Papa's after he had fought the Drakhaon in Azhkendir. That red, burned skin, with its silvered gleam, was just the way Papa's face and hand had looked.

Had he also been wounded by the Drakhaon in battle?

Marta and Great-Aunt Greta were still absorbed in their discussion. Much against her will, Karila found herself turning to look again—and saw to her alarm that the man was slowly making his way along the path toward them.

"Marta." She tugged at Marta's hand, wanting to go before he reached them. "Marta, let's move on."

"Don't interrupt your great-aunt, highness, it's very rude."

"But Marta—"

"Daemon's child!" Oskar reared up from behind a rosebush, his burned face contorted, his finger stabbing toward Karila. "The damned fiend has laid his mark on you. Now we will all burn!"

Karila gave a scream and hid behind Marta.

"Oskar!" cried Great-Aunt Greta. "How *dare* you shout at the little princess. Make your apologies at once."

But Karila didn't want the man to apologize, she just wanted him to go away. His pale eyes terrified her; they blazed with a virulent and unreasoning hatred.

She heard the man mumble a few words. "S—sorry, Greta. D—did it happen again?"

"Yes, and it must stop." Great-Aunt Greta's voice was crisp with disapproval. "Or I shall be obliged to have you confined to your room while there are other guests here."

"J—just can't c—control it. S—sorry." And Oskar lurched away.

One of the servants came out of the house and hurried toward the dowager duchess. "He gave me the slip again, your excellence," he said. Karila, peeping out again, saw that the man's cheeks were almost as red as the roses with the exertion of running.

"Yes," said Great-Aunt Greta icily. "We know. And it must not happen again, Benno. You must keep him in his rooms. These outbursts are getting more frequent by the day. I would not want to have him confined in Arnskammar, but . . ."

"I understand." Benno was bowing and backing down the gravel path in Oskar's direction as he spoke.

"You're very generous toward this unfortunate young man," observed Marta. Karila watched as Benno caught up with Oskar and tried to persuade his master to leave the rose garden. Oskar did not seem very eager to go.

"My dear brother Karl was once very fond of his mother. Of course, nothing could come of such an attachment, you understand." Great-Aunt Greta's voice had dropped to a confidential whisper, Karila noticed, the tone that adults adopted when they were discussing matters unsuitable for young ears. And yet young ears were much keener at picking up these little wisps of gossip and conjecture. "It was hard for Ulla, left alone up here for months, while her husband was away fighting in the Francian Wars. Count Alvborg was a jealous man, and rather too keen on his liquor. He treated the boy very harshly. Is it any wonder Oskar has lost his wits?"

"No! *No!*" Oskar was resisting Benno's attempts to lead him away. "*She* is one of them." He flung his arm out toward Karila. "Can't you see? She will destroy us all!"

Karila shrank back behind Marta.

"Perhaps the princess's physician could examine him?" suggested Marta.

"A second medical opinion would certainly be appreciated," said Great-Aunt Greta, nodding slowly. Then she seemed to forget all about the disturbance and put her arms around Karila, hugging her. "Poor sweet! You must find this very dull. Would you like me to invite some children to tea?"

Karila tried not to scowl. "Children to tea" always ended with the young guests playing energetic games involving much running around—and Karila sitting, obliged to watch because of her disabilities. "Maybe in a week or two," she said, forcing a smile.

Besides, she had Tilua and the other children to play with.

Oskar Alvborg could not sleep. He was still in pain from the injuries Gavril Nagarian had inflicted upon him. At night, in the moist, humid warmth of the brief northern summer, his damaged skin felt as if a swarm of tiny creatures were crawling across it. He would drop into a doze, then wake, screaming, trying to brush off the milling insects.

Benno came in, lamp in hand, yawning until his jaw cracked.

"Get them off me! Get them off!" Oskar was in a frenzy, rubbing his face on the sheet, clawing at his skin.

Benno knelt beside him and held up the lantern. Oskar blinked, dazzled.

"Look, Oskar. There're no insects. They're all in your mind." He tapped his forehead.

"In my *mind*?" cried Oskar in horror, imagining a horde of minuscule ants burrowing into his skull, nibbling their way through his brain with tiny sharp mandibles.

"No, no, what possessed me to say that?" Oskar felt Benno lay one hand on his trembling shoulders. "What I meant was that you were having a nightmare again. I'll mix a draft to help you sleep."

The image of the little fair-haired girl illumined Oskar's mind, bright as Benno's lampflame. And there was the other child lurking behind her, as he had glimpsed her in the rose gardens, dark-haired, with eyes as dark as death.

"She shouldn't be here," whispered Oskar. "She will draw them to us. She must go."

Scarlet light bathed Oskar's troubled dreams. The sky was afire. But these flames were rich with the dying light of the setting sun, a pure and translucent red.

And as he gazed into the setting sun, he thought he saw a figure coming toward him out of the light, its arms outstretched as if to embrace a long-lost friend. And a voice spoke to him, a soft, consoling voice.

"You have been gravely wounded. Let me heal your wounds."

"Yes," Oskar heard himself say with his whole heart, even though he knew he was dreaming and his wish could never be granted. "Heal me. Make me whole again." He rose from his bed not certain if he was still dreaming.

Still the dazzling figure came on, until Oskar thought he could make out the form of a winged man, with radiant locks of scarlet and golden hair crackling around his shoulders. Most compelling of all were his eyes, eyes that burned with such heat and intensity that Oskar feared he would be consumed by them.

"*Trust me,*" breathed the soft voice. "*Don't flinch. At first you will feel intolerable heat. And then you will come through the flames, reborn and renewed.*"

Oskar gazed into the flaming eyes and found himself transfixed. "I—trust—you," he gasped, and then he was enveloped in the fiery embrace.

All went black. He felt the flames ripple across his body, searing away the damaged skin. A scream of agony tore from his parched throat. He was being flayed by fire. He was burning and no one could hear his cries.

Then the flames flared up so brightly that they became cold, white, purifying. He lay back, bathed in their chill light, floating on a lake of pale fire. After that there was no more pain. Just a feeling of serene tranquillity, as though all the cares that had beset him had melted away . . .

As he floated there, his healer whispered words that puzzled him.

"*Your blood drew me to you, Prince Oskar.*"

"I'm not a prince."

"*The blood of your ancestors burns strongly in your veins. The blood of the Emperor Artamon.*"

"How can that be? My father was Count Alvborg. There's no royal blood in our house."

"*Then perhaps Alvborg was not your true father.*"

"What?"

"*Perhaps your mother hid your true parentage from you. Perhaps she was forced to do so by the reigning House of Helmar.*"

"I will not hear my mother's good name tarnished." Oskar was growing increasingly irritated by this dream. He willed himself to wake up.

"*But you are awake . . .*"

Oskar sat up. He was lying on his bed and from the rumpled state of the sheets, it looked as if he had been struggling with an imaginary assailant in the night. Sunlight poured in through every chink and hole in the shutters.

"*Go and look at yourself in the mirror.*"

Oskar pushed aside the tangled sheets and hurried to the mirror. Even in the shuttered daylight, he could see his reflection clearly. He was just not sure it was his own reflection.

He gazed a long time, gently touching his smooth, flawless skin with trembling fingertips. He ran his fingers over his head, feeling the thick, soft locks of pale fair hair that had regrown overnight. He smiled for the first time in many months—and saw the youthful face that Gavril Nagarian had ruined smile back at him.

"That treatment Doctor Amandel gave me . . ."

"*Let the others believe he worked this miracle. Only you and I will know the truth of the matter.*"

Oskar looked around the room, searching in vain for his miracle-worker. "Where are you? Show yourself."

"*Look in the mirror once more.*"

Oskar obeyed. At first he saw only his healed body with its sleek skin and its fine, pale hair. Then it seemed that another shadowy form superimposed itself, emerging through his reflection as though from deep within him. He glimpsed a cruel, proud face, with deep, slanted eyes that burned like coals in their sockets. And what looked like the silhouette of powerful furled wings protruded from his shoulders.

"Who are you?" stammered Oskar.

"*Some call me Araziel, others Arazyal. But to you alone I confide my true name: Sahariel. Think of Sahariel as your guardian spirit, my prince.*"

"But why choose me?"

"*Your blood called to me. You are descended from the Great Arta-mon. You were born to rule, Prince Oskar.*"

"To rule? What do you mean?"

"*I have been searching for you a long time, Artamon's child. And now that I have found you, we shall fulfill our destiny.*"

" '*Our* destiny'?" Yet even as Oskar gazed at Sahariel, the image swirled like drifting smoke and vanished.

"*It's time to find answers, my prince, answers about your true parentage . . .*" The soft, subtle voice faded into silence and the

sounds of early morning reasserted themselves in Oskar's consciousness: sparrows chirping in the tangle of climbing roses and ivy outside his window; the distant patter of servants' feet as they hurried
down the side stairs from their attic quarters to start work; the regular tread of the sentries Lieutenant Petter had posted around the
manor house to protect the princess in case of a Francian attack.

Benno had left a glass decanter of eau-de-vie on a little table by the
bed. Oskar poured himself a measure to steady his nerves and swallowed it in one swift gulp. The spirits seared a burning path down his
throat but did nothing to calm the turbulence in his mind.

*Born to rule. Descended from the Great Artamon. It's time to find
some answers . . .*

*A flaming comet rushes through the northern sky. All of Great-
Aunt Greta's household run out and gaze upward, chattering excitedly and pointing.*

"It's a meteor, not a comet," Doctor Amandel says pedantically.

*Karila alone stands staring at the "comet." Why can't they see it
for what it truly is? Is she the only one who can make out its great
wings, its fiery scales of scarlet, orange, and gold? Or its dark eyes
that gleam, bright as burning coals? Drakhaoul eyes that fix on her
with sinister and murderous intent.*

Karila sat upright in bed, clutching the sheet to her.

"It's here," she whispered, glancing anxiously around. "It's *here*."

CHAPTER 10

Astasia looked again at the gilt-edged invitation from Queen Aliénor and gave a little shiver of distaste.

"And your reply, highness?" asked the lady-in-waiting in haughty tones.

"Must I reply now?"

"It is a great honor to be invited to play cards with her majesty after dinner."

Astasia hated to play cards; she would much rather have walked in the cool of the gardens or danced. She had no head for the cunning little strategies employed in the card games her mother enjoyed, and she had no taste for the petty squabbles such games provoked among the older ladies of the Mirom court. Yet she could sense the disapproving stare of the queen's attendant as she hesitated, longing to think of an excuse and failing. It would not do to offend her royal hostess.

"Why then," she said, forcing a smile, "I accept."

"Deep breath, altessa," encouraged Nadezhda, tugging hard at the fastenings on Astasia's blue satin evening gown.

Astasia held her breath until she felt she would burst as Nadezhda struggled to do it up.

"It's no good," Nadezhda said as Astasia let the breath go in a rush and the tight bodice sprang open again. "Your waistline is disappearing."

Astasia felt tears pricking at her eyes. She flopped down in a chair, trying not to cry. "There must be another dress I can wear tonight." She looked up at Nadezhda pleadingly, only to see her maid shaking her head. "Then you must let it out."

"There's not enough material to let it out any further."

"Then sew me in."

"Certainly not!" Nadezhda made the sign against evil. "Don't you know the old saying, highness? It's very bad luck—the worst kind— to sew clothes on a living person. It's like sewing them in their shroud."

"Fine. So either I offend Queen Aliénor by not attending her soirée, or I go and set all the ladies whispering behind their fans at my ill-fitting, unfashionable dress."

Nadezhda was already on her knees, riffling through the contents of Astasia's little traveling trunk. "Aha!" Astasia heard her say in triumph. She rose, holding out a fine lace stole.

"*No one* is wearing those this year—" began Astasia, then as Nadezhda bustled about her, folding and pinning the stole with expert fingers, she stared at her reflection in the mirror. "Why, Nadezhda, you're so clever." She turned around once, smoothing down the dress over her thickening waist.

"Now dry those tears," said Nadezhda, observing her with a critical eye, "and enjoy yourself."

Queen Aliénor's intimate soirée, which Astasia had imagined to include a dozen guests at most, turned out to be a lavish affair. A little band played in one corner of the hall, sweetening the air with popular *airs de cour*. Servants moved among the guests, offering glasses of sparkling wine.

The queen, who missed nothing, glanced up the moment Astasia entered and fixed her with a piercing stare.

"Come and join me, child." It was a command, not to be disobeyed. Astasia felt the eyes of the whole company follow her as she made her way through the cardplayers to the queen's table. "You play *lansquenet*? The Comtesse de Lucé has just lost us this round. You can partner me instead."

Have they noticed my dress? Astasia meekly nodded her thanks to the comtesse, who rose from the marquetry card table with a piqued toss of her flame-colored hair. All the women were exquisitely dressed in somber-hued dresses of taffeta and rich silk, embroidered with little seed pearls and diamonds. Beside them, Astasia's pale blue gown looked insipid—a young girl's dress, more suitable for a first ball than such a distinguished gathering.

She lowered her eyes and cast a quick glance at her cards. It was a weak hand and she could do little with it. After much deliberation, she selected what she hoped was a safe card and placed it on the table.

The queen frowned a little but did not comment, speaking instead to the fourth player at the table, an elegant woman of middle years. "Madame de Romorantin, do you have news of your husband?"

"Indeed I do," said Madame de Romorantin. Astasia became aware that she was glancing at her, toying with the fine pearls around her neck, as though not entirely at ease.

"Then please share it with us."

"Your son has honored my husband with the command of the fleet sailing to Tielen." Madame de Romorantin glanced sidelong at Astasia again.

Astasia only half heard what she said; all her attention was concentrated on playing her next card.

"You need have no concerns about speaking in front of the Empress," said Queen Aliénor. "It must be common news now that she has left her husband."

Astasia, who was leaning forward to place another card on the table, dropped it. Her hand shook as she retrieved it and laid it on the others.

"My husband is very confident that Tielen will soon capitulate," Madame de Romorantin said with a smile.

"Capitulate?" Astasia looked up from the card table, not certain that she had heard aright.

"Oh dear." The queen tutted as she saw the card Astasia had played. "How vexing. Young women these days have no head for cards."

"The new Francian fleet will prove more than a match for the Tielens," went on Madame de Romorantin. "Should it come to a battle, that is."

"But why?" Astasia could no longer concentrate on the game.

"I should have thought that you, my dear, would know better than most." Aliénor gave her a severe glance above her spectacles. "The House of Tielen has controlled the trade routes to the south for too long. Your estranged husband, and his father before him, have used practitioners of necromancy and alchymy to achieve their ends. Your own brother nearly died because of their meddling in the dark arts. Now that we have their Magus in our custody, the days of Tielen's supremacy are at an end." The queen paused. Astasia sat there, trying to keep control of herself as the choking feeling of panic grew stronger. "It is fortunate that you have chosen to remove to Francia to raise your child, far from the dangerous influence of its natural father."

"M—my child?" Astasia felt her whole body grow hot. Had the queen guessed her secret?

"Your brother told me. Though I had guessed as much myself, from your sickly demeanor. Which, by the by, has been commented upon at court."

"*Andrei* told you?" Astasia felt betrayed. Her own brother had blabbed her secret to this horrible meddling old woman?

As she was sitting there, burning with humiliation, Andrei strolled over, accompanied by Valery Vassian. He bowed gracefully to the queen and approached the table, gazing over Astasia's shoulder at her cards.

"Andrei," she whispered, "how *could* you?"

"With that hand, I'd admit defeat, if I were you."

She gazed up at him and saw his mouth quirked in a teasing smile. Had he no regard for her feelings?

"As my brother's so good at cards, he should take my place," she said.

"This game is growing tedious," said the queen, casting down her cards. "I think I shall play *tric-trac* instead. Would you care to join me, Madame de Romorantin?"

When the queen rose, the others at her table were obliged to rise too. Astasia stood up, glaring at Andrei. She had been publicly humiliated, then snubbed by Aliénor, and it was all his fault. As soon as the queen had moved away, Astasia gathered her skirts and marched toward the door.

"Tasia?" Andrei called after her, causing both courtiers and liveried servants alike to stare. Was her ordeal never going to end? She swept on, head held high, not once turning back, ignoring him as she entered the lofty tapestried passageway that led back to the tower where she was lodged.

How dare he treat her in this fashion! The old Andrei had loved to tease her—but he had been sensitive enough to know when to stop. It had been bad enough having to undergo the queen's disapproving scrutiny, but to be lectured on her husband's crimes was doubly mortifying. She felt as if all her clothes had been stripped away, revealing her swelling breasts and belly to the whole court.

The great tapestries Astasia passed depicted armored horsemen from ancient legend, trampling their enemies underfoot and carrying off their women. Abandoned infants lifted their chubby hands in vain for pity. She shuddered, averting her gaze.

And what was this talk of Francian ships and Tielen capitulating? All this while she had been worrying in case Gavril had attacked Swanholm, when the real threat had come from an entirely unexpected quarter.

"Come back, Tasia." She could still hear Andrei calling, his voice still tinged with that new, unpleasant note. "What's the harm? How long was it to be before someone noticed?"

She turned then. "What's the harm, Andrei? Have you lost your mind?" She spoke in their home tongue, afraid that someone might overhear them and report back to the queen. "Didn't you hear the admiral's wife? Her husband is sailing to attack Tielen. And—or have you forgotten—I'm the wife of the Prince of Tielen. They could use me against Eugene."

"But you hate Eugene. You told me so yourself. Why else would you run away?" That odious drawling tone grated on her nerves. "Don't tell me, little sister, that you're regretting your decision?"

"Don't 'little sister' me, Andrei." Astasia turned and walked swiftly on, her fists clenched at her side, only too aware already of the damage he had done.

Again he caught up with her, neatly stepping in front of her to block her way. "I'm sorry, Tasia. I didn't mean to upset you." His eyes brimmed with concern and the mocking tone was gone.

"Let me pass."

"I was only concerned for your safety—and that of your child."

"You have a strange way of showing it."

"You're upset. That's natural in your condition. But you must think of your health—and the baby's." He reached out to take her hands in his.

By then Astasia was utterly confused. A few moments ago, she had hardly recognized her own brother.

"I'm only glad that you agreed to come with me." He pressed her hands between his own, a gesture of reconciliation from childhood days. "The thought of you cut off in Tielen, with the Francians invading . . ."

Astasia gazed searchingly into Andrei's face, trying to discern whether he was in earnest or merely dissembling. She had always adored her dashing big brother, and she found this unpredictable behavior disturbing.

"You would never hide anything from me, would you, Andrei?" she said softly, gazing up into his eyes.

"Listen, Tasia. Events have overtaken us. I had no idea the Francians were planning—" He glanced round. Slipping her hand under his arm, he began to stroll along the corridor, obliging her to accompany him.

"Andrei?"

"I thought I saw one of those tapestries move. We may well be observed." He was silent until they reached the shallow stone stair that wound upward to Astasia's rooms. "At least here you are far from any fighting. And the queen has generously arranged for her physician to attend you."

"I'm not ill!" she said sharply. "And what fighting are you talking about?"

"You don't imagine your husband will just hand over his country to his oldest enemy without a struggle? We're talking about Eugene of Tielen here, Astasia. He's probably on board his flagship already, training his cannons on the Francians."

But Astasia had been baited enough for one evening. "I have a headache, Andrei. I'm going to lie down. Good night."

Astasia tore off the carefully pinned lace stole and flung it on the floor. What was the point in dissembling anymore? Now her secret was common knowledge.

Why did you do it, Andrei? Desperate for fresh air, she opened the casement window and leaned out, breathing in the sweet fragrances of the summer night rising from the flower beds below: heliotrope with its cherried perfume, and clove-scented pinks.

His excuses did not ring true. She sensed that there was more to this than he was prepared to tell her. Perhaps—and the thought made her hug her arms about herself in apprehension—he had entered into some covert agreement with Enguerrand, an agreement that involved her.

As Andrei entered the Great Hall at Belle Garde, he saw the gold-framed portraits of generations of the Francian royal house staring haughtily down at him. Each stern face exuded an aura of power and authority. And, sternest of all was the black-robed woman who sat awaiting him, stiff-backed, one hand resting on an ebony walking cane. A great painted globe had been placed beside her. He saw why the queen had chosen this place for their meeting. Here, her will was reinforced by the presence of her many royal ancestors.

"So, Prince Andrei," said Queen Aliénor, "now that you have had time to reflect on my son's proposed alliance, what is your decision? Are you with Francia?"

"I am with Francia," said Andrei without hesitation. "But as for my countrymen . . ." He ended in a shrug. Both the army and navy had undergone significant reforms under Eugene's leadership. He had no idea where their loyalties would lie if put to the test.

"We are aware of your father's enforced abdication. We are also aware that, even without an army behind you, your presence here is of considerable significance. It only serves to emphasize Eugene's isolation. One by one, his former allies are deserting him."

"*Would her pious son be so eager to welcome you if he knew your secret, I wonder?*" Adramelech's mischievous question startled Andrei; he glanced at the queen, wondering if she had noticed his discomfiture.

"Even now, my son's fleet is sailing to challenge Eugene in the Straits," Queen Aliénor pushed herself up, leaning on her cane, and beckoned Andrei closer. She tapped with one nail on the globe. "Smarna welcomed Enguerrand with open arms; I suspect he may encounter more resistance in Tielen. But with you and your naval experience at his side . . ." She scrutinized him, her cold eyes narrowed as though trying to read what he was thinking. "We have more ships ready to sail from Fenez-Tyr, Prince Andrei. We would like you to take command of the *Aquilon*; she's a fast frigate, with thirty-eight guns. What do you say?"

To command his own ship again? This possibility had not occurred to Andrei and the queen's proposal took him by surprise. For a brief moment, the memory of the wreck of the *Sirin* arose like a cresting wave, threatening to overwhelm him. Had he lost his confidence, let alone his ability to command, in that terrible storm?

And then a voice, dark as the smoke of battle, whispered deep within him. "*With me to guide you, you will prove invincible.*"

"The *Aquilon*?" Andrei drew himself to his full height. "I'd be proud to accept."

"If you ride tonight, you can be aboard the *Aquilon* at Fenez-Tyr by tomorrow evening."

"*If you take to the skies, you can be there much sooner.*" Again that maliciously playful tone had crept into Adramelech's voice. Andrei frowned. How could he arrive tonight when he was not expected until the following day? It would not be the best way to take up his new command.

"And how will your sister fare while you are away at sea?" The queen was gazing out at the gardens below.

Andrei saw Astasia walking slowly through the rose gardens, Nadezhda trotting alongside, holding up a lace parasol over her mistress's head to keep off the sun. There was a distinct air of dejection about the way Astasia moved; Andrei hardly recognized his lively, graceful sister in this sad, drooping figure.

He had been so intent on pursuing his own ambitions that he had neglected to think of her. Now he felt guilty that he would be leaving her so soon.

"It's very warm today," he said, as if that would excuse her listless demeanor.

"Your sister is unhappy here," observed Aliénor.

Andrei's mind was already far away, excited at the thought of assuming his own command again. He racked his brain to think what might lift Astasia's spirits. "She enjoys music. She much values the friendship of Celestine de Joyeuse—"

"Mademoiselle de Joyeuse is very busy at present."

Andrei wondered why he had not seen Celestine since they landed. Disappointed, he tried to think of another idea. "Astasia loves to dance. A ball, perhaps or—"

"In her condition, vigorous exercise is not to be encouraged. Besides, the Commanderie have banned all public performances of ballet. Those girls' flimsy costumes were a disgrace, inflaming unsuitable passions!" The queen spoke so severely that Andrei did not venture another suggestion.

"Just as I thought," continued Aliénor. "Like so many young women these days, she has nothing of value to occupy her mind. But before we set about improving her spiritual life, I would like my physician to examine her. You may tell her to expect a visit."

Andrei hurried down the *grand escalier*. His own command again! And, at last, the chance to strike back at Eugene.

"The chance to avenge your drowned crew."

Courtiers were coming up the stair past him. As he passed them, he recognized eager Nikifor, his youngest midshipman; dour-faced Ship's Master Daniil, who had taught him more about the sea than any of his naval academy tutors; his friend and right-hand man, Lieutenant Dmitri Borisov, grinning lopsidedly—

Even as he stared the familiar faces blurred, as though seawater were washing over them, and began to decay before his eyes, until nothing remained but hollow-eyed skulls, wreathed with squirming lugworms.

Andrei stopped, grasping at the smooth, marble rail.

Faces from the *Sirin*. His crew, his shipmates, his first command.

The ghastly vision faded and there were Enguerrand's courtiers, all looking askance at him and whispering to one another.

He stumbled down to the hall, still feeling sick and shaken.

"*Adramelech? What kind of cruel trick was that?*" He leaned against a painted pillar.

"Are you all right, highness?" inquired a servant.

"Fetch me a glass of wine. No—brandy." When the servant returned, Andrei took the glass and raised it. "To the crew of the *Sirin*," he cried, not caring who heard. "Rest in peace, lads," and swallowed it down in one gulp.

"Your own command, Andrei? And a Francian ship?" Astasia gazed at her brother warily. Here was another unexpected development and one that was not at all welcome. Once Andrei had left Aliénor's court, who would be there to protect and defend her?

"I must leave as soon as possible."

"Why the haste? Are you going into battle? With Eugene?"

He gave an awkward little laugh. "Now, Tasia, do you really expect me to answer such a question?"

"But with you gone, Andrei, I shall know no one here." It came out rather more plaintively than she had intended, but the truth was that she felt more isolated as each day passed. She found Queen Aliénor intimidating and the young Francian noblewomen ignored her.

"Vassian is staying. Good old Valery—you know you can rely on him to protect you."

The chance meeting between Astasia and Valery Vassian was carefully stage-managed by Nadezhda.

Astasia went into the gardens to feed the royal carp, whose prodigious size and appetites were famous throughout Francia. As she threw little morsels of bread into the limpid green waters of the moat, she was astonished to see the great whiskered fish swarm to the surface and fight fiercely over the food.

"Look at the size of that one, all black and gold." Nadezhda pointed excitedly. "He'd feed a family for a week!"

"He's quite the bully. Look how he pushes all the others aside." Astasia glanced up to see Valery Vassian coming to join them on the wooden bridge, the sun catching ambered glints in his dark hair. He bowed formally to her.

"Would you care to visit the royal aviary?"

"I've given all my bread to the carp," said Astasia, brushing the crumbs from her fingers, "but yes, I think I would like to see the birds. I hear there's a parrot that mimics Queen Aliénor."

There were courtiers strolling in the gardens, so they said little of consequence to each other, talking of the weather and the game of *jeu de paume* which Valery had played against a Francian vicomte and won.

When they reached the aviary, they found themselves alone among the great ironwork cages. Only the whistles and whooping cries of the brightly plumaged birds could be heard, and would make their conversation hard to follow for any Francian spy shadowing them.

"Ooh, look at that one with the blue feathers," said Nadezhda, tapping on the wire. "Here, pretty, pretty . . ."

"How can I be of service to you, altessa?" Valery said softly.

"Valery, you've always been a good and faithful friend to me and my family." Astasia suspected he would read far more into her words than she intended. But what choice did she have? His devotion to her would be well rewarded when she reached Mama and Papa at Erinaskoe. And if he was still prepared to look on her so adoringly in her current condition, then she need feel no shame in appealing to him for help. "I miss my parents, Valery. And I'm worried about Papa's health. I wondered"—and she held out the necklace in both hands—"if you could sell this for me and use the proceeds to arrange passage for us to Muscobar?"

"You know I'd do anything for you." He took the necklace from her and as he gazed at it, his eyes widened. "But this is one of your betrothal gifts from the Emperor. It's a unique piece, specially commissioned for you. Amethysts and diamonds. I remember hearing him remark on it once—and how pleased he was to see you wearing it at the reception for the Allegondan ambassador."

"Really? I had not thought that Eugene took any notice of such trivial matters." Although the words came out coldly, Astasia felt a little pang at Valery's words. Eugene rarely complimented her on her appearance, so it was a surprise to hear that he had not only noticed but appreciated the way she was dressed. "I can't afford to be sentimental, Valery. And I really do want to leave as soon as possible."

"And your brother is accompanying us?"

"No!" Astasia tried to calm the note of panic that crept into her voice. "He has business to attend to here in Francia. I'm sure he'll join us soon. It will," and she improvised wildly, "it will give me the chance to break the news of his survival gently to our parents. Given the poor state of Papa's health . . ."

Valery nodded; to her relief, he seemed perfectly satisfied with this explanation. "It may take me a little time to find a jeweler, let alone a good price, highness. My command of the Francian language is less than perfect and many don't—or won't—speak the common tongue."

"I know I can trust you to do what's best, Valery," she said, smiling at him with genuine affection.

But when Valery had gone, she sank down onto a bench, her heart beating fast.

"Altessa?" Nadezhda produced a handkerchief scented with orange water and dabbed her forehead.

"I'm all right, Nadezhda." The mingled smell of bird droppings and overripe fruit in the food troughs was becoming overwhelming in the afternoon heat. "Let's go and walk in the rose gardens, where the air is sweeter."

"If your highness would be so good as to raise his right arm," said the tailor. It was Andrei's final fitting for his captain's uniform and the dapper little naval tailor was making the last adjustments to the royal blue coat. Andrei was impatient to be on his way; his few belongings were already packed and now this perfectionist of a tailor was fussing over a few extra stitches.

One of the queen's female attendants appeared in the open doorway. "If you please, Prince Andrei, the queen wishes to speak with you."

"What, now?" Andrei gestured irritably at the tailor, who, his mouth full of pins, made a helpless gesture.

"When the queen sends for you," said the lady-in-waiting sternly, "it is inadvisable to keep her majesty waiting."

"Were you aware, Prince Andrei," asked Queen Aliénor, "that your sister has been selling her jewelry?"

Andrei shook his head.

"Your friend, Lieutenant Vassian, was seen visiting a number of jewelers in Lanthenay today on her behalf. He then booked passage on a post-chaise for three travelers." Aliénor leaned forward and sharply tapped him on the arm. "I really do not think we can let a woman in her condition travel post-chaise. And certainly not alone with such a handsome young companion as Lieutenant Vassian. The scandal would be difficult to live down. It could tarnish your whole family—and at such a delicate time, when you are preparing to reclaim your right to the throne."

Andrei paced his turret room. Now, just as the Francians had shown proof of their confidence in him by giving him his own command, Astasia's irrational behavior was threatening to place his career in jeopardy.

"But then she's always been unpredictable . . ." Only a year ago she had been foolish enough to let Gavril Nagarian kiss her in public, at a soirée, where anyone, even the servants, could see.

"*If she leaves Francia, she will be beyond our control.*"

"Control?" It was an odd word to use and it made Andrei stop pacing.

There was the slightest of pauses. Then Adramelech said softly, gently, "*I can see into your heart, Andrei, and I know how much Astasia means to you. How can you allow your only sister to undertake the long and arduous journey to Muscobar in her delicate condition? If she were to miscarry at this stage in her pregnancy, it would seriously endanger her health . . .*"

"Why are you so concerned about my sister's health?"

"*Because I only want what you want, Andrei. And you want to be certain that she is safe.*"

It annoyed Andrei to admit it, but Adramelech was right. "Of course. If there's a big sea battle brewing in the Straits, the last place she should be is on a ship going to Muscobar. And to travel overland from Smarna in the heat would soon exhaust her."

"*You know what's best for her and her child. Even if she cannot yet see it is the best solution, she will come to understand.*"

Put in such simple terms, it made perfect sense. Any mother-to-be would make the baby's health her first priority. Adramelech had named himself Andrei's guardian spirit and now it seemed he was taking care of Astasia as well.

"Yes. Even if she protests, she'll soon realize how dangerous such a long journey could be."

"Is everything packed?" Astasia whispered, even though no one was close by to hear what they were saying.

"Yes," puffed Nadezhda, struggling to force the clasps shut on the bulging traveling trunk. "Although I could swear we've more than we started out with from Swanholm."

"Impossible!" Astasia was jittery with excitement; she flitted about the room, checking under cushions, opening and closing drawers to make certain she had left nothing behind.

"That's done." Nadezhda sat down on top of the trunk and wiped her shiny brow on her sleeve.

"So we're ready?" Astasia turned to her maid, breathless with excitement. "We can escape this horrible place?"

"Just as soon as Lieutenant Vassian comes with the barouche to take us to the town."

"Oh, I can't wait for us to be on our way!" Astasia clasped her hands tightly together to try to stop them trembling. "Just think; we'll see Mama again, and Papa—"

There came a discreet tap at the door and Nadezhda went to open it. Valery Vassian stood in the doorway. "All's ready, altessa," he said with a smile.

"Thank you, Valery," she cried, hurrying to the open door.

Nadezhda waited for Valery's man to remove the bulging trunk. "Mind you're careful with that and don't you dare drop it, or I'll box your ears."

Astasia was already halfway down the stairs with Valery following close behind.

"The barouche is waiting for us in the stable courtyard. It's less conspicuous there."

"You think of everything, Valery." A new energy drove Astasia; after dreary days of inaction and aimlessness, she felt as if she were floating down the stairs and away from the dour presence of Queen Aliénor.

The sticky heat of late afternoon had been tempered by a cool breeze. Evening sunlight warmed the slate tiles of the turrets and the twisted barley-sugar chimneys of Enguerrand's château with a rich golden light.

As Astasia took Valery's hand to step up into the barouche, she gazed back up at the little tower that had been her refuge in Francia. She felt nothing but relief that she was no longer to be a guest at Queen Aliénor's court.

"What have you arranged, Valery?" she asked. Nadezhda, who had been making sure that the trunk was firmly secured with rope, climbed up to sit beside her.

"I've booked us rooms at the coaching inn in Lanthenay; we leave at dawn tomorrow for the port. A light supper awaits us."

The coachman shook the reins and turned the horses' heads toward the wide archway and the little bridge across the moat.

Astasia sat back as the barouche rattled slowly forward over the gravel. Then a line of the Francian Royal Guard appeared, marching to block the archway. The driver called to the horses and the barouche slowed to a stop.

"What is the meaning of this?" Astasia rose and glared at the guards. "Let us through."

"I'm sorry, altessa, but I can't do that." An officer approached the barouche.

Astasia glanced at Valery and saw from his bewildered expression that he was as confused as she. Why was her perfect plan falling apart? And just as everything was going so smoothly?

"What's wrong with taking a pleasant little drive on a summer's evening?" She used her sweetest tone, favoring the officer with one of her most appealing smiles.

"A little drive?" said a drawling voice. "All the way to Fenez-Tyr—and beyond?"

"Andrei?" Astasia saw the line of armed guards part to let her brother through. He was wearing a royal blue uniform.

"Let me help you down, Astasia." He raised his hand to her.

"I'm going home, Andrei," she said, ignoring his outstretched hand. "And you can't stop me."

He laughed then, just as he used to when she was small and wanting her own way. "Do you think I would let you risk such a hazardous journey in your condition? Besides, Tasia, there's a war on." He looked over to Valery Vassian, his indulgent expression fading. "And you, Valery, I'm surprised you agreed to put my sister in danger."

Valery blushed and stared at the floor of the barouche. Astasia found herself wishing that he would draw his sabre, grab the barouche reins, and charge the soldiers blocking the archway, knocking them off the bridge into the moat . . . But Valery was not made from the same valiant mold as the heroes of her favorite novels.

"Andrei," she said, her eyes filling with tears, "I just want to go home. To Mama. Don't you understand?"

"This matter is beyond your brother's control, Empress." Queen Aliénor entered the courtyard, flanked by two dark-robed priests. "I must insist that you remain here as our guest until hostilities have ceased between our two countries."

"Guest?" Astasia's legs no longer seemed strong enough to support her. *I will not faint. Not in front of that woman.* She gripped at the side of the barouche to stop herself from falling. "You mean prisoner, Queen Aliénor."

"See that the Empress is escorted back to her rooms." Aliénor turned on her heel and went back into the château. The priests came directly toward the barouche and waited for Astasia to descend.

"Valery," whispered Astasia in one last, desperate appeal, "help me."

He gazed at her helplessly, his brown eyes dark with distress.

One of the priests put out a hand to help Astasia down.

"Don't you dare touch me!" She glared at him with such fury that he hastily withdrew his hand. Head held high, almost blinded by tears, she began to walk back across the courtyard, which had begun to darken with the first evening shadows.

"Andrei? Is this your doing?" Astasia challenged her brother.

"I only wanted to ensure you were safe. Queen Aliénor seemed so concerned for your health. I had no idea they were planning on using you. The queen spoke only of the dangers of sailing to Muscobar when there was fighting in the Straits—"

"Using me?" The full implications of what he had said began to sink in. They had manipulated her, played on her trusting nature and her gullibility, and fool that she was, she had fallen into their trap. "Using me—to force Eugene to surrender?"

"That seems to be the idea."

Anger welled up inside her. "How could you, Andrei?" She lashed out at him.

He caught her hand before it struck. "I had no idea what they intended, Tasia, believe me." His voice was harsh, his tone intense. "You've got to believe me."

"I will not be held to ransom. You have to get me out of here."

He released her hand. "Since when have you become such a loyal, loving wife? It can't be more than a year since you were loudly protesting that you would rather die than marry Eugene of Tielen. A year since I came upon you kissing Gavril Nagarian in the gardens of the Villa Orlova."

Astasia's hand burned; he had gripped it so hard he had left a red mark. "That's unfair, Andrei."

"You begged Papa not to marry you to Eugene. What's caused this change?"

Astasia was rubbing her crushed fingers. "I didn't know Eugene then."

"Remember the Orangery? Just a few weeks ago?" His tone softened. "You wept, Tasia. Was that the reaction of a happily married woman?"

"I was weeping because of you, Andrei." Astasia gazed defiantly into his eyes. "Is that so hard to understand? I hadn't seen you since the day you sailed away on the *Sirin*." It wasn't entirely the truth, but in the circumstances, it was more than he deserved.

"Aren't you forgetting that Eugene invaded Muscobar?"

"And aren't *you* forgetting that Eugene's army rescued our parents and servants from the rioters? If Field Marshal Karonen hadn't come to our aid, Mama and Papa would have been murdered and the Winter Palace burned down."

"Eugene has no right to my throne, Tasia."

"*Your* throne?" So was this what it was all about? Before the sinking of the *Sirin*, Andrei had never seemed much concerned about his birthright. He had been happiest squandering his money on horseracing, gambling, and beautiful mistresses. "What have the Francians promised you, Andrei?"

"What is rightfully mine."

Again she caught that dark glint in his eyes. It was a glint of longing, of greed and desire, mingled. "Muscobar? But it's not theirs to give."

He looked at her, one eyebrow quirked.

"So that's the deal you've brokered? And all this cosy little brother and sister talk is meaningless blather." She drew herself up to her full height. "You've betrayed me, Andrei."

"You'll come to see things differently soon, Tasia. You'll thank me."

She did not answer. He did not deserve an answer.

She heard him turn on his heel and leave the room. There was a chink of keys as the guard outside locked the door again.

CHAPTER 11

The *Kirstina*, flagship of the Northern Fleet, was engaged in close combat with the Francian invaders.

Eugene leaned on the rail of the *Dievona*'s observation deck, assessing the situation. Admiral Berger had positioned the Northern Fleet in a defensive position across the wide mouth of the River Tilälven. Behind them lay the port of Haeven.

"It's too dangerous for you to be on deck, imperial highness!" yelled Admiral Janssen. Another broadside from the Francian men-o'-war thundered out across the sea toward the New Rossiyan fleet and hit the mainmast of the *Kirstina*. The great mast split with a shuddering creak and crashed down onto the deck. Faint cries came to them as fleeing sailors were crushed beneath. Both men watched, helpless, as the falling sails and rigging swept many more into the churning sea.

Eugene swore under his breath.

"This defensive strategy isn't working, Janssen."

If Linnaius had not been kidnapped by the Francians, he could have twisted the winds with his fingertips to give the New Rossiyan fleet the advantage, sending the Francians broadside to their own ships, creating chaos and destruction.

"We still have enough alchymical firepower to hold our own," said the admiral, scanning the scene with his glass.

"But for how much longer?"

"*Why do you let the enemy destroy your men and your ships?*" A voice whispered in his mind, a daemon-voice scorched and dry as smoke.

Eugene tried to ignore the Drakhaoul, concentrating all his attention on the enemy ships. "*Use me. Use my power. Your power, Eugene.*"

"If we could only get a direct hit on their magazine." The temptation to give in to Belberith was growing stronger by the minute.

"They're closing on the *Kirstina*." Janssen trained his eyeglass on the ships in the vanguard of the Francian fleet. "By God, that man-o'-war's moving fast. They're going to board her."

"And my orders, in such an event, were to save those last alchymical mortars and grenades until such an eventuality."

"Berger issued your orders to all our captains, highness. They know their duty. But it's risky. If the wind turns, the fumes will blow back toward our men, disabling them."

If the wind turns. Linnaius would have prevented this whole catastrophe.

"Can't we move another vessel to plug *Kirstina*'s place in the line?" Eugene was growing more restless by the moment. "Wasn't that the strategy we agreed?"

"I'm more concerned, highness, about that little squadron that's moving off toward shore." Janssen handed him the eyeglass.

Sure enough, five frigates had broken away from the main Francian fleet and were boldly sailing directly toward Haeven.

"They're going straight for the port. Block them. Block them!"

Janssen spoke to a lieutenant hovering nearby, who sped away.

A thunder of guns rang out, echoing and reechoing across the sea. Cloudy smoke besmirched the clear blue of the summer's day, drifting across the water, thick as sea fog.

"They're firing on the port."

This was not going at all the way Eugene had planned.

"Don't forget the cannon we positioned on the jetty. They have orders to return fire."

"But have they the range, highness? These little Francian frigates are fast and deadly. They can cause much damage, yet stay clear of the guns onshore."

"We're not yet outgunned—or outmaneuvered." Eugene heard the defiant words issuing from his mouth, yet in his heart he knew they were merely playing a defensive game when they should be on the attack, driving the Francians back across the Straits.

Another round rumbled out as the breakaway Francian squadron fired on Haeven again. In the rolling clouds of smoke, Eugene saw the bright flicker of flames.

"They've hit the customs houses," said Janssen, squinting into his glass. "If the wind turns, it'll fan the flames and set the quay alight."

"*Make your move now,*" urged Belberith. "*Before it is too late.*"

Eugene was not used to adopting a defensive strategy and the worsening situation was making him feel decidedly insecure. What if the Francians broke through their line? What then? How long could they hold them off until Karonen brought the Northern Army across from Muscobar?

"I will *not* let Enguerrand take Haeven."

A deafening rumble from the Northern Fleet cannons was answered by the Francian attackers. A swift Francian man-o'-war was making toward the *Dievona,* coming about, the wind filling her great sails. Eugene could see the Francian standard clearly, the golden salamanders of Enguerrand's house overlaid on a background of blue lilies. He could even read her name, *Tonnerre,* the Thunderer, emblazoned in gilt alongside her fierce-eyed goddess figurehead.

"*Raise your arm. Even from here you can disable her.*"

Janssen was yelling orders to the helmsman. "About! About! Bring her about!"

The wind was still all in the Francians' favor. Eugene watched, fascinated, as the gun ports opened and the cannons' mouths opened on the *Dievona.*

Slowly he raised his arm. A faint flicker of green fire crackled at his fingertips.

"*The smoke onshore from the burning houses will conceal us. Make an excuse.*"

The temptation was growing too strong.

The timbers of the *Dievona* shuddered as cannonballs thudded into the hull of the *Gunilla* astern.

Orders were bellowed from one officer to another, voices cracking as the men strove to make themselves heard above the boom of the cannons.

At Eugene's side, Janssen swore and struck the rail with his fist.

"Too close, highness." Janssen turned his sun-reddened face to Eugene, his blue eyes watering with the drifting smoke. "For the empire's sake, I beg you to leave on my barge. I don't want to be recorded in the history books as the admiral who allowed his emperor to be blown to bits."

"Your men cheered me when I came aboard. They'll have a pretty poor opinion of an emperor who leaves the ship at the first sign of an enemy cannonball."

A lieutenant appeared and saluted. "She's holed belowdecks, Admiral. We're taking in water." His uniform was drenched. "The carpenters are on to it, but she's listing."

"Lieutenant Tapper, I place the Emperor in your care."

The young man's face flushed and he straightened, saluting again with a smart flick of the wrist. "Please follow me, imperial highness."

"Godspeed, Janssen," said Eugene. "And confusion to Francia."

"And I'll keelhaul you myself, Lieutenant, if the Emperor arrives onshore with a single drop of water on him," added Janssen.

Tapper grinned as he hurried Eugene across the flooded deck, his shoes squeaking on the wet planks. They climbed swiftly down the little stair to the main deck and the smoky air, bitter with the tang of gunpowder, enveloped them. The fug was filled with the shouts of the officers. Some of the sailors put their backs into the capstan; others nimbly climbed the rigging, all striving against the wind to maneuver the *Dievona* into a more advantageous position.

And just beyond the smoke, Eugene was all too aware of the shadow of the *Tonnerre* looming closer, close enough soon to put out grappling irons.

A sudden volley cracked out and a deadly hail of shot whizzed from the Francian deck, rattling into the rigging, severing ropes that whiplashed into sailors' faces. Eugene instinctively ducked, pulling Tapper down with him behind the capstan.

"Chainshot! Take cover!"

"Return fire!" A party of marines was stationed farther up the deck, ready to repel boarders.

From the sound of their returning volley, Eugene recognized the hiss of Linnaius's alchymical canisters as they exploded.

"At last," he whispered. This would buy the *Dievona* the time she badly needed to defend herself. Wisps of alchymical smoke began to drift across from the *Tonnerre*. "Come, Lieutenant."

But Tapper did not reply. And now Eugene saw that the young lieutenant was clutching his shoulder, his lips pressed firmly together to suppress a groan of pain. Blood oozed between his fingers, bright red against the damp grey cloth of his uniform.

"Let's get you below to the surgeon." Eugene put an arm around Tapper's waist and hoisted him up.

"No—highness—" Tapper began to protest.

"Save your strength, lad." Eugene began to help the stumbling lieutenant across the deck, past other fallen crewmen, over boards already slippery with blood.

Another blast from the *Tonnerre* made the whole ship judder. A sailor, shot from the rigging, came crashing down onto the deck. Eugene, accustomed as he was to the carnage of battle, grimly pressed onward. But Tapper was dragging his feet, leaning more and more heavily against Eugene's shoulder. The lieutenant was losing blood fast. The alchymical canisters had only bought them a little time to reload.

"*The Francians are winning. Your men are tiring, they are outnumbered and outmaneuvered. If you don't make your move soon, it will be too late . . .*"

They reached the companionway. Two midshipmen popped up out of the smoke, their faces smeared with oil and smuts.

"We'll take the lieutenant, highness."

The sound of frantic hammering came from below as the carpenters labored to plug the hole in the *Dievona*'s side. In the darkness, sailors hurried to and fro, supplying the carpenters with wood and nails. Powder monkeys scampered past, carrying fresh cartridges of powder for the guns. *Ordered disorder*, Eugene thought, which would suit his purpose well.

"I'll follow you below."

"But my orders—" said Tapper faintly.

"Your orders are to report to the surgeon, Lieutenant."

This was the moment. The midshipmen had seen him; with luck they would report back to Janssen that the Emperor had gone belowdecks. It would be madness to launch a jolly boat under such heavy fire. Now he saw there was no other way to protect his people. There was no need for a significant expenditure of power. A few subtly aimed blasts would cripple the Francian ships and give them the advantage they so desperately needed.

Tapper was lifted down the companionway and carried below. Eugene, resolute now, hurried back up the steep stair and scanned the deck. The marines were reloading their carbines for a second volley. But the holed mainsail drooped dangerously low overhead, obstructing half the main deck, as the sailmaker's crew tried to mend the damaged rigging. And the shouted orders from the quarterdeck could hardly be heard now for the constant din of the Francian guns.

Eugene could just make out the jolly boat intended for his escape, dangling from the davits on the poop deck. In spite of the repeated retorts from the enemy guns, the little crew was still intent on lowering the craft; several oarsmen already sat on their benches, oars raised.

One of them spotted him through the smoke and cried out, "The Emperor. Prepare to launch!"

"Belay that order!" Eugene bellowed, his voice cracking with the strain of making himself heard. "Belay—"

Another Francian broadside blasted out and the impact flung Eugene onto his hands and knees as the flagship rocked. A broadside from the New Rossiyan cannons answered them. His ears rang with the sound as he staggered to his feet.

The jolly boat had disappeared from sight. He could hear nothing but cries of distress from all quarters.

The *Dievona* was in trouble.

Belberith guided him across the bloodied deck, into the gusting yellow smoke of the battle, where the hot air tasted of saltpeter and sulfur.

Eugene found himself at the rail, high over the churning sea, a sea that was stained crimson and littered with splintered wood and broken bodies.

He lifted his arms wide to the sky and closed his eyes. For a fleeting moment he remembered the promise he had made to himself. Was this how Gavril Nagarian had felt when he stood on the cliffs above Vermeille and had seen the New Rossiyan ships bombarding Colchise? Had he felt this same cold, incisive anger that burned like chill fire in his heart?

"*Now*, Belberith!" he cried, his voice ringing out above the bellow of the guns.

Admiral Janssen agitatedly paced the deck, pausing at each crossing to lean out and peer into the swirling smoke.

One of the lieutenants came running up, his once-immaculate waistcoat smeared with blood and powder.

"Any news of the Emperor? Well?"

"He was last seen"—the lieutenant bent double, gasping for breath—"taking Lieutenant Tapper to the surgeon."

"But was he in the jolly boat? When the davit tackle jammed and she tipped the crew into the water?"

"No one—can be—sure. We're still—picking up survivors."

"You'd damned better be sure." If the Emperor were lost overboard, drowned while in his care . . . Janssen felt a cold sweat dampen his whole body. How would he be able to live with the shame?

"Incoming!" yelled the lookout. "Take cover!"

Janssen heard the hissing shriek of the cannonballs as they roared from the Francian guns. He grabbed at the lieutenant, pulling him down, as the broadside struck.

A sickening creak rent the air. The mainmast had taken a direct hit. Splinters of shattered timber flew everywhere, a lethal rain, as the shattered mast began to topple.

"Prepare to repel boarders," yelled Janssen, struggling to his feet and reaching for his pistols.

The Drakhaon Eugene hovered high above the battling ships. From here he could see that Haeven was alight. The Francian cannon had set fire to the customs house and the flames had spread to the warehouses behind. One, filled with barrels of spirits, was blazing fiercely with pure blue flames, like a brandysnap pudding. Although the guns in the Swan Tower at the head of the quay were still thundering back at the invaders, Eugene could see a detachment of Francian soldiers disembarking, preparing to rush the Tower.

I must be careful. I must not expend all my power, no matter how tempting . . .

He wavered, torn between defending the port and the listing flagship.

Another explosion boomed out below, the whizzing hiss of cannonballs, followed by the crack of shattering timbers.

"My *Dievona*!" Eugene hurtled down through the hot rush of air, exulting in his daemon-driven speed, plunging into the rising fumes. The flagship had taken another direct hit to the mainmast; from the numbers of men massing on the deck of the *Tonnerre*, he guessed that they were preparing to board the disabled *Dievona*.

He had lost one flagship to Gavril Nagarian; he was damned if he would lose another—and to Enguerrand of Francia!

As he swooped low over the *Tonnerre*, he could tell that the crew were too intent on their prize to notice the shadow above them, darkening the sky. At this range, he could sear them all with Drakhaon's Fire and—

No. He must not lose self-control. He would distract them.

He drew in a breath and hissed a lightning bolt of green fire into their topsails. Cries and shouts rose from the deck below; as fragments of blazing sail began to drop onto the crew, he saw them scatter, confused, running for buckets and pumps.

The *Tonnerre* was still too close to the *Dievona* for him to risk a major conflagration. Fire in the hold, near the powder room, would not only blast the Francians apart but would catch his own men and ships. But if she limped out to the open sea, he would make matchwood of her.

He swirled around in the smoke-fouled air and darted back to spit another jet of fire.

"*Why stop there?*" Belberith urged. "*You have the Francian fleet at your mercy. Destroy it now and be done with it.*"

Tempting words. Eugene could feel Belberith's power pulsing through his whole body until he was sure he must glow like a falling star. But he had made a promise to himself, and he was a man of his word. He wheeled high above Haeven, scenting the stink of burning flesh mingled with the flames and rising smoke from the decks of the *Tonnerre*.

"Enough," he said.

"*How can it ever be enough? Make Enguerrand pay for his arrogance. Make him pay for what he has done to your people.*"

The tactician in Eugene had nearly been overruled by the daemon's wiles. But he had fought enough campaigns to know when to hold back. The Francians were confused; they had not yet looked to the skies to see what had set the *Tonnerre* alight. He had bought Janssen enough time to steer his disabled ship into the shelter of the port while another, smaller warship sailed to fill her place in the defensive line.

He circled slowly overhead, watching to see what the Francian admiral would do next.

Veiled from sight by the thick fug of rising powder fumes and smoke, it was a while before Eugene noticed that the *Tonnerre* was running up signal flags. Winging closer, he began to decipher the message. The royal blue Francian colors still flew from the topmast, albeit holed and tattered, so this was by no means an admission of defeat.

Pull back, Eugene read, *and regroup.*

From his vantage point he surveyed his Northern Fleet. The *Kirstina* was in a sorry state. All masts shot away, she was burning and many of her men were in the water, clinging to floating rigging and timbers. The flaming hull of the *Gunilla* was slowly sinking.

And the five frigates he had spotted making for Haeven were no longer in view.

"*Can you be sure that your ships have driven them off?*" Belberith, as always, was playing on his deepest misgivings.

"How can I be sure?" Eugene was looking in vain for the frigates. "They've retreated for the moment."

"*Oh, there is one way,*" and the daemon's voice was suffused with a dark, teasing humor, "*but you still refuse to accept my aid. You're proud, Eugene, but you're stubborn too. And your stubbornness is blinding you to the fact that the Francians have the advantage in this battle. They still intend to destroy you.*"

"Highness, thank God you're safe!" cried Admiral Janssen. "When we took that second broadside, I knew you and Tapper were making for the jolly boat. Then when the davit tackle failed and the boat tipped over, I feared . . ."

"I fell overboard." Eugene pulled the borrowed greatcoat closer about his wet, naked body. "But there was plenty of driftwood to cling to. And here I am, thanks to our good sailors. It'll take more than a few Francian broadsides to fell me, Janssen!" And then seeing that Janssen's bright blue eyes were moist with tears, he laid his hand on the admiral's shoulder in reassurance. "You and your crew did an outstanding job." Janssen's unexpected show of emotion touched his heart; such loyalty was beyond price. "But the battle is far from won. They'll be back. The question is when. And can we rout them this time?"

"*Dievona*'s in urgent need of repairs. With your permission, highness, I suggest we make for the Imperial Dockyards."

"Do whatever you judge best, Janssen."

"Highness—there are clean, dry clothes in my cabin. My man will furnish you with whatever you need."

Eugene nodded his thanks. As he left the poop deck, he saw a party of sailors laboring to lift a broken section of yardarm that lay across the main deck. One of the top-men had fallen from the rigging and lay trapped beneath. And from the moan of pain that he let out, Eugene realized that he was still conscious.

"Poor wretch," he muttered, hurrying to join the rescue party. As he put his shoulder to the heavy timber and heaved with the other men, he felt Belberith flood his body with a surge of power. With a grunt of effort, he felt the timber move, and the injured man was dragged clear.

Eugene bent over him and put his hand on his shoulder while his shipmates tended his wounds.

"My brave boys," he said. "We've got the Francians on the run now."

"God save the Emperor," the man whispered through blood-stained lips.

In the Admiral's cabin, Eugene hastily put on dry clothes. Janssen's valet, respectfully averting his eyes, stood by to assist him. The stockily built Janssen was at least a head shorter than Eugene and much broader in girth, so the clothes were far from a perfect fit. He took the shaving mirror from the taciturn valet and checked his reflection. And then checked it again, holding the glass to the light by the cabin window to be sure.

His hair had grown. When he had embarked, it had been short-cropped, military-fashion. Now the longer locks at the back touched his collar. And—though maybe it was a reflection off the waves—his natural shade of gold seemed to radiate an unnatural greenish tinge. He put the mirror down abruptly and, in doing so, saw that his fingernails glinted in the daylight like chips of emerald.

Gavril Nagarian's warning words whispered through his mind once more.

"It refashions its host, body and mind, to resemble the being it once was."

Eugene stared fixedly at the sea, no longer seeing the wreckage from the battle floating past, or the smoke still rising from the burning port. A sick, cold feeling of foreboding overwhelmed him.

And I used so little power . . . He grasped at the little table to steady himself.

"You look exhausted, highness," said Janssen's valet, in the soft burr of Northern Tielen. "A glass of hot grog will soon restore you."

"Thank you," Eugene said absently.

While the valet disappeared to warm up the rum, Eugene slowly lowered himself into Janssen's chair and rested his head in his hands.

How long before others notice? And how can I explain it away?

The Imperial Dockyards lay to the west of Haeven. Eugene's father had established a school there twenty years ago, bringing in many young apprentices from all over Tielen to learn the shipwright's trade.

"Something's amiss." Janssen had been training his eyeglass on the coast for the past ten minutes or so. "That smoke's not blowing across from Haeven. The wind's in the wrong direction."

Now Eugene began to feel even more uneasy. Had all this fire and fury been meant to distract them from the Francians' real target: the heart of Tielen's shipbuilding industry? It was vital to keep the Francians from attacking the yards where essential refitting work was being carried out on the remaining vessels of the Southern Fleet.

A whistling sound interrupted his troubled thoughts. Broadshot and cannonballs splashed into the water just short of the *Dievona*'s damaged prow.

"Bring her about!" yelled Janssen. "Who the deuce is firing on us now? Our own men? Can't they see our colors?"

Eugene peered through the drifting smoke and fog. There were colors flying from the flag post, certainly, but they were a brilliant royal blue. He swore under his breath. "It looks as if those Francian frigates reached the dockyards before we did. They've turned our own guns on us." It was a strategy both audacious and cunning. Whoever had planned it, he felt a grudging admiration for his daring.

Another cannon volley whizzed dangerously close to the *Dievona*, so close that the spray soaked Eugene and Janssen.

"What now, Admiral?" Eugene asked, beating the water from his jacket.

"We're running low on munitions. We're in no position to deal with fire from land as well as sea."

"Then we have no other choice but to retreat."

The *Dievona* put into port at Haeven and Eugene disembarked to the cheers of his men and those citizens brave enough to venture back into the town. There was little to cheer about. Many buildings around the harbor were still smoldering; others were charred shells. The air was still filled with smoke and the acrid smell of burning. The grim legacy of the sea battle was being washed up on the beaches downriver: broken bodies, both Francian and Tielen, from the damaged warships.

Tired though he was, Eugene insisted on visiting a makeshift hospital where many of the casualties, townspeople and sailors, had been moved. Admiral Berger joined him soon afterward, his face still smeared with smoke from the battle.

"Any word from the dockyards?" Eugene asked him quietly. Berger shook his head.

One of Janssen's lieutenants came hurrying up. "We're receiving a communication from one of the Francians through Vox Aethyria, highness. He says it's urgent."

Admiral Janssen had established a temporary command headquarters in the naval recruiting office which, fortunately, had escaped the worst of the bombardment with only a few shattered windows.

Eugene and Admiral Berger were shown to the Admiral's office, where one of the lieutenants was operating a Vox.

"Who is it?" Eugene asked Janssen.

"He says he will only speak with you, highness," said Janssen.

"Very well."

"The Emperor is here and ready for your message, Francia," said the lieutenant. Eugene settled himself beside the lieutenant at the desk and adjusted the Vox so that he could communicate with the Francians.

"*My name is Ruaud de Lanvaux, Grand Maistre of the Francian Commanderie. King Enguerrand has instructed me to speak to you on his behalf.*"

"I prefer to conduct any business concerning the empire face-to-face, Maistre de Lanvaux," replied Eugene coldly. He knew the name well enough already; his agents had documented too many of the Commanderie's ruthless purges of intellectuals in the name of their religion.

"*Were you aware, Emperor, that your wife Astasia is currently in Francia?*"

"What of it?" Eugene felt a rising sense of apprehension. What game were the Francians playing now? "Are you holding my wife hostage? Answer me!" Had she been abducted? All this time he believed she had left Swanholm of her own accord, angered and bewildered by his neglect.

Naïve, trusting Astasia. Why had she not gone home to her parents in Muscobar? What had made her run to Francia, straight into the arms of the enemy?

"*In the circumstances, we suggest that it would be inadvisable for you to use any more unconventional weapons against our ships.*"

"Inadvisable?"

"*I refer to the attack on the* Tonnerre."

Was this a reference to the alchymical weapons? Or—and the thought brought a cold sweat to his brow—had he been glimpsed, in Drakhaon form, hovering high above the Francian fleet?

"*The safety of your wife and unborn child must be of the utmost importance to you, Emperor.*"

So they knew Astasia was with child. And his assumption—based on the little marked calendar he had found in her dressing room after she had fled—was correct. "Where is my wife?" he asked and in spite of all his self-control, he heard his voice tremble. And at a time when it was essential to stay calm. "Let me speak with her."

"*Your wife is in a place of safety . . . for the time being.*"

Eugene glanced up at the waiting officers. From the stunned looks on their faces, he saw they were as shocked and confused as he. "What are you saying, de Lanvaux?" His growing anxiety for Astasia's safety had given him a rank, dry taste in his mouth. He swallowed hard, wishing there were a glass of water or aquavit to hand to moisten his lips.

"*King Enguerrand wishes to propose negotiations.*"

So that was the crux of the matter. Negotiations—or terms of surrender? Eugene gave another glance to Janssen, who raised his eyes wearily to heaven. Then he replied, his voice firm again, "Your warships entered our waters and fired on my fleet and on the innocent citizens of Haeven. I am not willing to negotiate until the Francian fleet withdraws."

"*I see. Perhaps I did not make our terms clear.*" Ruaud de Lanvaux's cool arrogance was growing increasingly infuriating. "*I will leave you a little time to consider his majesty's offer. Until noon tomorrow. Perhaps you will look on it more sympathetically after consulting with your ministers. I am sure they will agree that there is no need for any more bloodshed.*"

The hissing crackle that underlaid the Grand Maistre's words ceased abruptly before Eugene could reply. He looked up and saw his officers staring at him.

"They abducted the Empress?" said Janssen.

"The Empress is with child?" said Berger.

Eugene had no adequate answer to their questions. He could only nod.

"Perhaps Enguerrand wants to propose a ransom, highness?"

"The man's acting more like a damned pirate than a head of state!" spluttered Janssen. "Holding a pregnant woman against her will."

"They wouldn't dare touch a hair on her head. It would be unthinkable."

"They seem willing enough to fire on innocent civilians in Haeven," said Eugene.

A cry went up in the street outside. "The dockyards! The dockyards are on fire!"

"Goddammit!" cried Janssen, throwing up the window and leaning out. "Is it true?"

A group of shipwrights had arrived, all jostling and talking at once.

"The Francians spiked our guns and threw them into the sea."

"Then they set the workshops alight."

"The caulking vats went up like torches."

"Did you catch the name of the frigate leading the raid?"

"*Achille*—no, wait, it was *Aquilon*. The *Aquilon*."

Eugene saw that Berger and his officers were gazing at him expectantly. He sensed they were hoping that he would come up with a new and ingenious solution to their dilemma. But all he could think of at that moment was Astasia.

The Francians had outmaneuvered him.

Eugene could not sleep. He stood at his window, staring out at the dying glow reddening the western horizon that was not a glorious sunset but his blazing Imperial Dockyards.

"Oh Astasia, Astasia," he whispered. "Why did you go to Francia? How did they entice you there? And as for our child . . ." He felt a hollow ache in the pit of his stomach at the thought that any harm might come to them. Had she been rash enough to let the news slip out? Or was her condition obvious to all around her?

"And where are you, Gavril Nagarian? What about our pact? Or have you abandoned me too?"

CHAPTER 12

Slowly Linnaius raised his eyes to scan the great vaulted chamber. His vision was no longer clear, as though the mists of age and time, held at bay for so long by the elixir, were clouding his sight. Black banners hung from the roof timbers high above his head. Tall, arched, lead-paned windows let in a grey daylight, filtered through lozenges of cloudy glass.

Linnaius became aware that a great many men, all robed in black, had filed in and were watching him from the benches around the walls; the murmur of their voices echoed dully around the chamber. To his left he could just make out a heavy table at which sat three scribes, pens poised over open ledgers. And in the center of the chamber in a tall-backed chair, sat one man to whom they all deferred, one man who was addressing him now in a cold, dry voice that made his aging heart flutter with agitation. It was Ruaud de Lanvaux, Grand Maistre of the Commanderie. The one who, over twenty years ago, had made it his life's mission to hunt down and destroy all who practiced the science of alchymy.

"Kaspar Linnaius, you stand before this Commanderie court accused of the most heinous crimes. We will furnish proof that you have practiced heretical and forbidden arts. And we have the evidence to confirm your guilt, taken from your laboratory in Swanholm."

Linnaius closed his eyes as the Grand Maistre continued to speak, listing the many heretical crimes of which he was accused. He had expected no less from his captors. The trap had been cleverly sprung and must have been long in the planning. If only he had not become so involved in the Emperor's obsessive search for the lost island of Ty Nagar, he might have been less careless of his own safety. But when the five Tears of Artamon had pulsed to life in the imperial crown, radiating a column of rubied light toward the stars, he too had become obsessed with unraveling their mystery . . .

"Your fellow magi and students from the College of Thaumaturgy were condemned to death at the stake some twenty years ago. You fled, leaving them to face the justice of the Commanderie."

Faces flickered before Linnaius's failing vision, accusing eyes stared into his, as they had many times in waking dreams: wise old Magister Gonery, his tutor and mentor; Goustan de Rhuys; his own students: enigmatic Rieuk, quirky genius Deniel, and, most gifted of them all, Celestine's father, young Hervé de Maunoir. And then he heard the dying cries of the condemned as they burned on the Commanderie's pyres, all their invaluable scientific knowledge and scholarly mage wisdom brutally eradicated in the name of religion.

"But now the time has come for you to be judged, just as they were. Have you anything to say to the court?"

Wearily, Linnaius opened his eyes. "I can see little point, as by your own words, I know you have already condemned me to death."

The Grand Maistre slowly nodded, as if Linnaius had merely confirmed an earlier assumption. "I am sorry to hear that you show such contempt for our legal process. Nevertheless, it is my wish that the evidence against you is produced here in the court, so that all may see that justice has been done in the name of the Commanderie."

"I ask the court, then, that I may be allowed to sit down." Linnaius could feel his withered legs buckling under the strain of standing. "I am, as you can see," he added dryly, "no longer in the first flower of youth."

The Grand Maistre raised one hand. A wooden chair was brought for Linnaius by two of the Guerriers.

"Thank you." Linnaius slowly lowered himself into the chair, hearing his sinews creak and wincing at the strain this simple movement placed on his bent spine. *How ludicrously old and feeble I have become in such a short time. I don't believe I have the strength to summon the smallest breeze to my assistance. And yet . . . they still seem afraid of me.*

*   *   *

Jagu and Celestine waited in the antechamber outside the court-room to be called to testify against Kaspar Linnaius. Both were dressed in full Commanderie uniform.

A little window was half-open, like a porthole, into the court-room, and Jagu had listened to the testimonies given to the court with an increasing sense of unease. Their turn would be next. And from the way the Inquisitor had been framing his questions, he was certain that their motives would be minutely examined and any weaknesses exposed. It was not just Linnaius who was on trial here; the whole system of ethics underpinning the Commanderie was being revealed to public view. If a cankered shoot were to be discovered, it would be ruthlessly excised.

"Let me testify, Celestine. For us both."

Celestine stared at Jagu in surprise. "But I've waited a long time for this, Jagu. I *have* to do this. For my father."

"Your father? That's precisely the reason you have to let me speak."

Her blue eyes widened, then narrowed. He found himself thinking irrationally that they were exactly the color of the little speedwell flow-ers that starred the fields in spring on the *manoir* where he grew up.

"Don't you see? They will use your evidence to condemn Lin-naius—and then they will condemn you too. You know too much. And you are your father's child."

"Ruaud de Lanvaux will protect me," she said stubbornly.

"Ruaud de Lanvaux doesn't care about you—or me, Celestine. He cares only for the reputation of the Commanderie." Why couldn't she see the danger? "We've been of use to the cause. But now the world has changed. Has it ever occurred to you that we know far too much?"

She turned from him toward the window overlooking the court-room so that he could no longer see her face, like a wayward child who still wants her own way but knows she is losing the battle.

"They're calling our names," she said distantly.

A Guerrier opened the sturdy door to the courtroom and she moved forward slowly, almost as if in a trance.

Had she heard a single word of what he had been saying? Take care, Celestine, Jagu prayed as he followed her inside. *I couldn't live with myself if anything were to happen to you . . .*

*   *   *

"Your name is Lieutenant Jagu de Rustéphan?" asked Inquisitor Visant, checking his notes.

"It is."

"Can you tell the court, Lieutenant, why you visited Saint Sergius's Shrine in Azhkendir this year?"

Why did such a simple question make him feel so uneasy? "I and my companion went to request the return of the saint's golden crook from Abbot Yephimy."

"But while you were at the shrine, you learned that Kaspar Linnaius had been there before you?"

"Yes." Jagu cleared his throat. "It seems he had been sent by the Emperor Eugene to research the life of Saint Sergius."

"Rather an unlikely project for one who has dedicated his life to the black arts, don't you think?" The Inquisitor glanced at Kaspar Linnaius, who sat hunched in his chair, head drooping forward, almost as though it weighed too much to lift.

"That was precisely my thought as well." Jagu was puzzled. The Inquisitor's line of questioning seemed to be concerned with their earlier unsuccessful mission to Azhkendir, whereas he had been expecting to be interrogated about their investigations in Swanholm. Was Visant hoping to trick him into some revelation by this diversion?

"And what did you learn about the accused's researches?"

"Abbot Yephimy was unaware that *The Life of the Blessed Sergius* contained a hidden text. When I attempted to reveal the contents, it became apparent that its secrets had recently been accessed. My guess is that Kaspar Linnaius had already unlocked the cypher."

"Please tell the court the nature of the hidden text," said Visant smoothly.

"It—" and Jagu hesitated, wondering how much of what he had read there was forbidden information. "It was about the five sons of Artamon; it told how they came to acquire daemonic powers."

This provoked a mutter of disapproval in the courtroom.

"Silence," ordered the Grand Maistre. He turned to the Magus. "So your imperial master has been conferring with daemons, Kaspar Linnaius?"

Linnaius slowly raised his head, revealing his wizened features. Jagu stared in shock. The Magus had aged greatly in the days since his arrest, and even the lively, malicious gleam in his eyes had dulled.

He looked so frail and ancient that Jagu imagined he might crumble to dust if roughly treated.

"Answer me, Linnaius. Did Eugene of Tielen employ you to summon daemons? The kind they call 'Drakhaoul' in Azhkendir?"

Linnaius mumbled something inaudible. The two Guerriers beside him grabbed hold of his shoulders and forced his lolling head upward.

"Old man," said Visant, going over to stare into his face, "it's useless to lie. We have evidence that daemons have entered our world. Before Dievona's Night in Tielen there was just one abroad. Now there are five."

"I—did not—summon them," said Linnaius slowly, thickly, as if his tongue were swollen. "It was the—Eye."

"What Eye? Don't prevaricate. We need the truth."

"The Eye of Nagar," whispered Linnaius and fainted.

"Nagar?" echoed de Lanvaux. "The Prince of Shadows? I think we have heard enough, Inquisitor."

"Stand down, Lieutenant," said Visant to Jagu, closing his book.

"We will resume this afternoon," said de Lanvaux, "to allow the accused time to recover."

"Celestine de Joyeuse," said Inquisitor Visant, pronouncing each syllable of her name with exaggerated care. "How long have you been a member of the Commanderie?"

"Since childhood," answered Celestine in her clear voice. "I was orphaned at the age of five and taken into the convent of Sainte Azilia."

Jagu gazed at her standing before the court in her plain black robe, her golden hair drawn back under a simple linen coif, and thought how beautiful—and vulnerable—she looked. He no longer had any idea whether such thoughts were impure, only that he would run through fire rather than see her harmed.

"You have showed great zeal in your quest to track down Kaspar Linnaius," continued Visant.

Be careful. Jagu leaned forward. *He's out to trap you.*

"I acted only as any member of our order would in the circumstances," replied Celestine coolly. "I was given my orders and I carried them out."

Jagu relaxed a little. She had not fallen for Visant's first snare. But there would be more traps, and each one more subtle than the first.

Visant was consulting a sheaf of notes. "Considerable zeal," he said at last, looking up. "I see from the ship's log that the ship bringing the prisoner to Francia nearly foundered in a sudden, violent storm. Can you explain to the court what happened?"

"Linnaius used his arts to summon a stormwind and blow us off course, back to Tielen."

"You witnessed him performing this rite?"

"I did."

Jagu tensed. He alone knew what Celestine had done to ensure Kaspar Linnaius did not work his dark arts. If anyone else had observed what had happened in the cabin and whispered the truth to the Inquisitor, they were both doomed.

"And if the accused is so powerful a magus, why did he not succeed in his endeavor?"

"He was weak," said Celestine with a little shrug. "The effort exhausted him. I saw his hand drop back and his eyes close. I believe he may have suffered some kind of stroke."

"I see," said Visant. "And as a member of our order, you took certain vows?"

"Yes."

"Including a vow to abjure the use of the forbidden arts?"

Jagu closed his eyes, dreading the next question Visant would surely ask her.

"Yes."

Visant paused, as though going to ask another question, then suddenly turned away, returning to his desk. "I have no more questions for Guerrier de Joyeuse," he said, then added, "at the present time."

"Stand up, Magister Linnaius."

Linnaius had been drifting in a daze of disconnected thoughts. Without the elixir to keep his wits sharp, he found it hard to concentrate. Or had he just nodded off to sleep for a few moments? He had the impression that he might have said more than he intended, blurting something out that would finally condemn him.

His guards took hold of him by the arms and brought him forward, step by shambling step, to stand before the Grand Maistre.

"The court has heard enough." Ruaud de Lanvaux's figure was a blur of darkness towering over him. "It is time, Kaspar Linnaius, that you pay the ultimate price for those crimes you have committed against God and mankind. Tomorrow at dawn you will be taken to the Place du Trahoir and burned at the stake. And may God have mercy on your soul."

So they were going to burn him, just as they had burned his fellow mages years before. His long years in exile now seemed but a postponement of the inevitable. He had gambled and cheated death many times. This time, his luck had finally run out.

"Guerrier de Joyeuse," Ruaud de Lanvaux said, gazing intently at Celestine, "there were moments in the courtroom yesterday when I began to have doubts about your loyalty to our cause."

Jagu felt his heart stutter a beat or two.

"I can assure you, Maistre, that you need have no worries on my account," said Celestine without the slightest hesitation.

"Is that so?" Ruaud de Lanvaux still gazed at her, almost as though he sought to penetrate those wide blue eyes and read the secrets she hid so artfully behind her frank and innocent expression. Jagu's anxiety grew. "Well, I am about to offer you the opportunity to prove yourself, Guerrier. I'm sending you both back to the monastery of Saint Sergius in Azhkendir."

"To Abbot Yephimy?" Jagu had not expected this.

The Grand Maistre took out a pendant that hung on a golden chain about his neck and held it up to the light. The purity of the crystal was sullied by swirls and surges of darkness, as if ink had leaked into clear water.

"*They* are here," he said softly. "Here, in Francia. I do not know what they intend, but they walk among us, and we must arm ourselves against them. Before it is too late."

"Too late?" Celestine echoed, glancing at Jagu.

Jagu had been examining the angelstone. "There are two close by," he said. "See? There are streaks of blue—and purple—in the darkness."

"And there are others still, farther off." Ruaud de Lanvaux replaced the pendant around his neck. "And if we don't make a stand against them, they will open the Gate to the Realm of Shadows and lay waste to our world. That is their nature; they are angels of destruction. Since Nagar corrupted their minds and their wills, they have forgotten they were once creatures of light."

"If you intend to reforge Sergius's Staff," Jagu said, remembering

Abbot Yephimy's polite but firm refusal of the Commanderie's request, "the abbot and his brothers were most reluctant to hand over the golden crook."

"He even asked us to give them *our* part of the staff," added Celestine.

"I'm sending a detachment of experienced Guerriers with you," said Ruaud. "The good brothers won't refuse this time."

Celestine had already left the room when de Lanvaux beckoned Jagu back. "You'll be in the Drakhaon's demesne," he said quietly. "Don't neglect to gather any intelligence that could be of use to us in the war to come."

The bells of Lutèce began to ring again. But this was no paean of welcome; they were all tolling together, making an ominous, doleful clangor. Gavril threw down his sketchbook and came out of the studio.

"What's happening? Who's died?"

"No one," called back a weaver who was hurrying past, "yet. They're burning a heretic in the Place du Trahoir."

Gavril fell in beside the man. "Lucien Sekondel?"

"Much worse! One of the old mages, condemned for using the black arts. A soul-stealer, by all accounts."

It had to be Linnaius. But why had there been no public announcement of the execution? Did the Commanderie suspect there might be a rescue attempt?

Everyone in Lutèce seemed to be going in the same direction as Gavril: to the Place du Trahoir. Why were they all so eager to see an old man burned to death? They were just ordinary citizens: clerks, seamstresses, tradesmen; some were even carrying little children as if it were a carnival outing or a fair, not an execution.

Do the resentments still run so deep, twenty years and more after the sinking of the Francian fleet? Are they here to see justice done for the drowning of their sons and fathers?

As they approached the place of execution, the pace slowed and the narrow streets became choked with people.

"What's the problem?" Gavril heard the tension in his voice. He was beginning to fear he had left it too late to snatch Linnaius from his captors.

Squashed too close to his neighbors, oppressed by the smell of sweating bodies in the summer's heat, he drew himself up to his full height, straining to see what was causing the holdup. He could just make out a line of black-uniformed Commanderie guards; they seemed to be checking each onlooker's identity before they let them through into the square.

"Hey, stop shoving!" A heavy-jowled man right in front of him turned around and glared. "Wait your turn, like everyone else."

Damn. What had seemed a straightforward plan was beginning to fall apart. Gavril dropped back, lurking in a doorway, out of the press of people.

This was as close as he was going to get to the Place du Trahoir. He had planned to survey the lay of the land before making his move. The Commanderie were obviously nervous about the possibility of a last-minute rescue attempt.

I can't let him burn. Not while Kiukiu's future depends on him.

He felt jittery. Khezef was fully alert, sharpening every sense.

"What are you waiting for, Lord Drakhaon?"

A deep, muffled bell began to toll close by; Gavril could feel the dull vibrations of its iron tongue through his whole body. A great roar arose from the Place du Trahoir. Beyond the dense press of people ahead, the black-robed Guerriers of the Commanderie must be leading the old Magus to the stake.

Have I left it too late?

Gavril looked up and saw people leaning out from the upper stories of the houses and shops. He spotted a narrow alley to the left. And behind loomed the twin bell towers of an ancient grey-stoned church, its carved saints and gargoyles blackened with age and soot.

He forced his way through the crowd to the opposite side of the street, ignoring the indignant cries. The dingy, refuse-strewn alley must lead to the church. He sniffed the air as he ran; was that the smell of burning? As he stumbled up the church steps toward the door that led into the church, past the blind beggars rattling their alms cups, he felt the whole building shudder as the deep-throated bell began to toll again.

Too late, it dinned. *Too late.*

There was no time left to survey the place of execution from high up on one of the bell towers.

"Khezef!" he cried with all the force of his lungs, flinging his arms wide. The air about him shivered. The pale blue of the sky turned thunder black. His mind was riven with jagged lightning.

Then he was rising, rising high above the bell tower to swoop across the Place du Trahoir, far below.

Kaspar Linnaius heard a great roar as he wandered, lost in a trance, caught between memory and dreaming.

He stood on the shores of Ty Nagar, the lost island, and saw the fire cone of the volcano glow red. Beneath his feet, the sands trembled with the roar from deep within the volcano's core . . .

"Linnaius," the Drakhaon Eugene cried to him. "Climb up on my back and I'll carry you to safety."

"Linnaius?"

He opened his eyes, blinking in the bright daylight. The cart in which he had been traveling had jolted to a stop. He gazed around dazedly. So many people. Nothing but faces, all staring up at him.

"Stand up, Linnaius." He tried to obey his guards' command but, with his hands bound, he had not the strength to push himself to his feet. They lifted him and another great roar assaulted his ears. It was the crowd. They were shouting at him, their faces contorted and ugly with hatred. Some spat; others pelted him with rotten fruit.

"Heretic!"

"Murderer!"

"Burn him. Burn him!"

"It's time, old man," said one of the guards, prodding him.

He tottered across the boards of the cart and onto the platform beyond. He lost his balance once but they yanked on his ropes, steadying him. His vision wavered in the clear light. Somewhere close by a bell was tolling, a dark, funeral dirge, not just for him, but for all the mages burned to death by the Commanderie. And there was the pyre, a wooden stake to which they would tie him as they had tied his fellow mages years before. It was banked high with bundles of kindling; from the strong smell, they had impregnated the wood with pitch to make it burn well.

If I'm fortunate, the smoke will suffocate me before the flames even reach my feet.

A tall figure stepped forward; Linnaius squinted into the sunlight, trying to make out who it was.

"Kaspar Linnaius, you have been condemned to die at the stake for your many heresies and crimes against the Francian state. Recant now and receive the consolation of the church." Linnaius recognized the cold and measured tones of Ruaud de Lanvaux, and a tiny spark of pride awoke. If he was to die, he would not go to his grave without one last attack on his enemies.

"I have no interest in consolation," Linnaius said. "I have dedicated my life to the pursuance of my craft—and to science. You can kill me, but others will follow, others fired by the same desire to decipher the secrets of nature. You cannot stifle us forever. Call us what you will: magus, alchymist, scientist—"

"So be it." Ruaud de Lanvaux struck the tip of his staff onto the scaffold, making the boards tremble. "Die then, unshriven, without consolation, or absolution for your sins."

Linnaius tried to hold his head high as the guards lifted him onto the pyre and tied him to the stake. This was not how he had planned to end his days. He had lived for so long that he knew there were few to mourn his death. But one remained dear to his heart.

"Karila," he whispered. "Little Kari, will you remember me? You were to be my last apprentice. There's so much I wanted to teach you."

He tried to fix the image of the princess in his mind, to remember her eager blue eyes, her questing, curious expression. So like her father Eugene in her incessant desire for knowledge . . .

Pale flames flared in the sunlight. The guards were torching the pyre. They began to toss extra kindling onto the bales of wood at his feet. To his horror, he saw books, his lifetime's work, thrown into the blaze. Pages of experiments, observations, formulae, all in his intricate, meticulous handwriting, began to blacken and burn.

"No!" he cried. "Not my books—" The clear air was suddenly tainted with rising smoke and tears began trickle from his eyes. Cindered fragments of text flew up past his face, disintegrating as he watched.

So there would be nothing left.

And I had dared to hope that you might come to rescue your loyal servant, imperial highness . . . It was becoming hard to breathe; each breath stung his throat and lungs. And he could hear the flames crackling at his feet.

So this is the end of it all . . . consumed in the flames of my own lifetime's work . . .

The air trembled. Screams came from the crowd.

Linnaius raised his smoke-stung eyes. Through the rising smoke he saw a vast hook-winged shadow darkening the hazy sky like a thundercloud as it came swooping down toward him.

"My Emperor," he murmured, "is it you, at last?"

Gavril swooped down over the Place du Trahoir and heard the terrified screams of the crowd below. He had only one aim: to free the frail old man before he suffocated.

Linnaius was already drooping in his bonds as the flames licked at the bundles of wood about his feet.

Too late, tolled the bell. *Too late.*

Gavril heard a shout of command and, with a loud retort, musket balls came whizzing toward him from a line of armed guards. If they hit him, they did no more damage than the glancing sting of a cloud of midges.

"Reload!"

Gavril felt a cruel, vengeful laughter welling up within him. With a flick of his powerful tail, he knocked the men over like so many ninepins, and darted toward the Magus, claws outstretched.

There was no time to untie the old man. Dark wings beating fast, Gavril hovered over the searing flames and tugged at the stake with his claws. Choking black smoke billowed up into his eyes but still he strained until the stake came loose and he lifted it free of the pyre.

Laboring with the weight of the sturdy wood stake and the limp body bound to it, he rose slowly into the air.

Below, the people were in panic, running into one another, as they tried to flee, crushing several unfortunates underfoot. The smoky air was rank with the smell of fear.

"Stop, daemon!" Ruaud de Lanvaux still stood, one hand raised, pointing directly at him. "I command you—stop!"

"*Kill him!*" Khezef hissed. Gavril felt the daemon's hatred bright as a searing flame. "*Kill him now.*"

Gavril hesitated, conflicted. There were so many people below. If he destroyed the Grand Maistre with Drakhaon's Fire, he could harm many innocent bystanders.

The weight of the stake was slowing him down. He winged doggedly onward, up and away from the Place du Trahoir, wheeling high over the city.

"*You didn't hesitate over Feodor Velemir.*"

"I thought he was going to kill my mother!" Gavril turned northward, heading toward open country and the rugged coast far beyond.

"*We should have destroyed him while we had the chance.*"

"My mission was to rescue Linnaius." Gavril was tiring already, weighed down by his burden. He was looking for shelter below, a secluded valley or coppice where he could land without being seen.

Soon he was descending slowly, awkwardly, toward the glimmer of water. He landed by a little lake, fringed by tall reeds and bulrushes, and laid the stake down. With two strokes of his sapphire-sharp claws, he cut Linnaius's ropes. The old man rolled over onto the grassy bank and lay without moving.

Gavril prodded Linnaius gently, questioningly, with one wing tip.

"Magus," he said.

There was no response. Trying to subdue the rising sense of alarm, he tried again, more forcefully this time.

He had not planned on transforming back to human form until they were back in Azhkendir. Now he had no choice.

"Damn it all!" he cried aloud. He pitched forward onto the grass. He felt his shadow-glamour slip from his body and knew himself a man again, naked and vulnerable.

The old man lay faceup to the sky, his robe scorched at the hem. His toes were red and burned. His skin was greyish yellow beneath the smuts and cinder stains.

"Magus! Can you hear me? You're safe now."

Linnaius still lay inert. There was only the faintest hint of a pulse. Gavril laid his head on the old man's chest, listening for a heartbeat.

So many hopes were depending on the successful outcome of this mission. Had he left it too late to come to the Magus's rescue?

CHAPTER 13

"Kiukiu? Come and give me a hand here, will you?"

Kiukiu heard her grandmother's voice as if from far away. She was standing gazing out across the moors, as she had done every day since Gavril left. The crags of the Kharzhgyll Mountains blurred into a misty haze in the afternoon heat and the brightness of the summer sun hurt her weak eyes. Even her sight had lost its keenness.

"Kiukiu!"

Malusha sat on the cottage doorstep shelling peas, a battered straw hat shading her face from the sun.

"Go and pick me some spinach, will you? Peas and young spinach will make us a nice omelette."

"He's not coming back," Kiukiu said flatly.

"And what makes you think that?"

"He's been gone too long. All he had to do was return to Swanholm and fetch the Magus. Now it's been days and days . . ."

"And had you not thought that the Magus might have been off on his travels again? Wind mages are notoriously difficult to track down."

But all Kiukiu could think of was the sad, wrinkled face she had glimpsed in the mirror and the aching tiredness in her bones that seemed to emanate from the despair in her heart.

Malusha put the bowl of peas down on the step and rose, putting her hands on Kiukiu's shoulders.

"Have a little faith, child," she said. "It's too early to give up hope just yet."

*   *   *

Kaspar Linnaius lay, as one dead, on the mossy bank beside the lake.

Gavril tore a strip of cloth from the hem of Linnaius's robe and went to dip it in the cool water of the lake. Mallards were swimming farther out; a pair of moorhens, startled by his sudden approach, flapped off into the reeds with sharp, stuttering cries of protest.

He returned and began to dab at the Magus's temples, hoping the cold water would revive him. Linnaius's skin looked almost translucent in daylight, as if worn thin by the passage of so many years.

"Don't die on me now, old man." It was a command. This decrepit body held the key to the secret elixir that could restore Kiukiu.

Linnaius let out a long, wheezing sigh. He murmured something so faint that Gavril had to lean close to his lips to catch what it was.

"My books . . ."

The sound of distant voices calling out across the water startled Gavril. He glanced round. Two little boats were sailing toward them from the far side; he could hear the splash of oar strokes already. Fishermen, in all likelihood.

"You're safe for now, Magus," Gavril said. "But we can't stay here."

Linnaius reached out an emaciated hand, plucking at Gavril's arm.

"Gavril Nagarian?" he whispered. "Why you? You have every reason . . . to hate me."

"Let's just say that I want a favor in return." His relief at finding the Magus still alive was tempered by the fact that the old man looked so frail and ill.

"Ohé!" One of the oarsmen stood up, shouting and gesticulating. Gavril could not understand what he was saying but he understood the gist of it. They were trespassers. It was time to be moving on.

"We've a long journey ahead of us," he said to Linnaius, raising him and propping him against one knee. "Can you cling to my back?"

Linnaius's eyelids fluttered closed; he was still drifting in and out of consciousness.

"No," said Gavril. "You're too weak. I'm going to have to carry you."

He braced himself and lifted the Magus in his arms just as one of the fishermen jumped out into the shallows and came striding toward them, sending moorhens scattering in panic.

"Khezef!" Gavril cried. The air about him whipped into a whirling kaleidoscope of glittering smoke. Gavril burst into flight, toppling the fishermen into the water, his wing tips scraping the drooping branches of the nearest willows. Then he was powering upward into the summer blue of the sky, climbing in a steep ascending spiral, almost drunk with the delirious joy of flight. The shouts of the astonished fishermen dwindled until all he could hear was the singing of the wind.

He felt he could fly forever onward through the clear air, free of the constraints and complications of his life below.

Gavril was tiring. He flew on through the eerie grey light that was neither night nor day. All the while he was above the Saltyk Sea, the air tasted of brine. But now he detected a moister, greener flavor that smelled of peat and mossy streams. The moorlands of Azhkendir.

The grey half-light was melting into the pale brilliance of early dawn and he could hear the whistling calls of birds wading in the moorland bogs. He scanned the lonely expanse far beneath for Malusha's cottage until, at last, he sensed her presence. She might be able to conceal her home from passing travelers, but with Khezef to sharpen his senses, Gavril could see through the illusion her clever cantrips had created.

And now that he was within sight of his destination, he found himself gripped with apprehension that at some time during the journey, the old man's spirit had quietly fled.

He spiraled slowly down and landed on a bank covered with honey-scented heather a little way from the cottage. He had just laid the Magus gently on the soft purpled bank when the air was filled with flapping wings and all the owls rose from the roof of the cottage, screeching in alarm.

"Whatever's the matter?" cried a tetchy voice from inside the hidden cottage. Malusha appeared through the mists. "Oh. It's you," she said, squinting at him, in the morning sun. "Dear me. We can't have Kiukiu seeing you like that, can we?" Tutting, she disappeared into the cottage, reemerging with an old blanket. "Cover yourself up, Drakhaon."

He was too tired to argue. Wrapping the blanket around his

nakedness, he crouched down in the heather beside the Magus, checking for a pulse.

"You'd better bring him inside."

He lifted the old man again. As he walked slowly past her, she put out one hand and touched his shoulder. "Look at you," she said disapprovingly, shaking her head.

He gazed down at himself then and saw that, in the bright sunlight, the skin on his arms and shoulders was stippled with tiny specks of copper and blue. Scales.

Inside the shuttered cottage, Gavril blinked, trying to accustom his eyes to the darkness.

"Lay him on my bed."

Linnaius's arm drooped limply over the side of the wooden bed as Malusha sat beside him and listened for a heartbeat.

"What's going on?" asked a voice, slurred with sleep. Gavril glimpsed Kiukiu sitting up in her narrow bed on the far side of the fireplace.

"Oh!" She snatched up her blanket, her eyes peeping over the top. "Gavril?" she said uncertainly, as if she was not certain it was really he.

"The same." He went over to her but she shrank away, hiding her face.

"Open the shutters, Kiukiu," ordered Malusha. "And give the Lord Drakhaon one of my old shirts before he dazzles us."

Kiukiu scuttled out of bed and unlatched the shutters, letting the daylight stream into the cottage. She stared at Gavril as the light illumined his glittering skin.

"It's . . . beautiful," she said softly. She tentatively touched his shoulder, stroking the jeweled blue scales. "Like a dragonfly."

He covered her hand with his own. Yet when he gazed into her eyes, he saw the shadow of other ghostly eyes gazing back: dead Gulvardi, Kristell . . .

His hand dropped.

"You'd forgotten," she said. "You'd forgotten how old I look."

"No, Kiukiu." How could he ever begin to explain? All the strength suddenly drained from him and he sank onto a chair.

"Fetch the Lord Drakhaon a drink, Kiukiu," called Malusha.

Gavril forced himself to look around the cottage for familiar objects to focus his thoughts on. Nearest to him, he spotted a bowl of brown-speckled hens' eggs, freshly collected. Malusha and Kiukiu must have been making bilberry jam, for several glass pots filled with the dark, rich preserve stood on the dresser. And someone had been busy with a needle: a pair of stockings lay over the side of a chair with one heel and toe neatly darned.

"Here." Kiukiu handed Gavril an earthenware beaker filled with tea, avoiding his gaze. He drank, raising the beaker with both hands to still the trembling in his hands.

"How is Linnaius?" he asked Malusha.

"He's very weak," she said, her eyes clouded, "and he seems to have lost his powers. What happened to him?"

"And why did you take so long?" put in Kiukiu.

"He's been in a Francian prison. They were about to execute him when I found him."

Malusha touched the charred hem of Linnaius's robe. "It looks as if you were just in time, Drakhaon."

"Yes; but was I, Malusha? They burned all his books. Suppose he doesn't remember how to make his elixir of eternal youth?"

"Lord Gavril needs clothes," Kiukiu muttered. She was searching, as Malusha had bidden her, for one of her old chemises. There was a battered wood traveling trunk in the cottage that Malusha sometimes delved into for odds and ends of materials; it smelled strongly of dried moth herbs, artemisia, and lavender cotton. Kiukiu slowly lowered herself onto one knee, hearing her joints creak, and unfastened the big metal clasp.

The smell of the bitter herbs made her eyes water but, undeterred, she plunged her hands in and began to rummage through the layers of old clothes.

"There must be something here he could wear."

Her searching fingers encountered a barrier. A sheet of leather, which, when prised off after much fumbling, revealed another layer of clothes, compressed by the weight of the contents on top.

"What's this?" Kiukiu lifted out some linen shirts, faded from white to yellowed ivory with age. Then came a couple of pairs of breeches and a jacket. A little decorative seam of embroidery in blue-and-gold thread outlined the stand collar and cuffs on the shirt. The breeches and jacket were cut from a soft indigo, light-woven wool.

They were fine clothes, Azhkendi-style, and she could only wonder to whom they had belonged.

And hidden beneath lay a gusly, with rusting strings, its plain, polished wood still brown and glossy, like the shell of a freshly peeled conker.

"You want me to wear *these*?" Gavril pulled a face as he held up the old clothes Kiukiu had dug out from the bottom of the trunk. Then he saw her crestfallen expression and immediately felt ashamed. She was doing all she could to help him. And he couldn't go to see the Emperor wrapped in an old blanket.

"Forgive me. They'll be fine."

"How does he look, Grandma?" Kiukiu led Gavril back toward the fireplace. Malusha, who was pouring more tea, looked up and stared. She set the pot down with a bang, spilling tea on the table. Her mouth dropped open, slack with surprise, and she let out a strange, soft cry.

"Whatever's wrong, Grandma?"

"My boy. My poor boy." Malusha kept shaking her head.

"These were my *father's* clothes?" Kiukiu had never once imagined that Malusha had kept any mementoes of her murdered son. And she had unknowingly given them to Lord Volkh's son, Volkh who had ordered Malkh's death.

"I'll take them off at once," said Gavril.

"No," said Malusha. She wiped her eyes on a corner of her apron. "What's the point of keeping them for the moths to nibble? My boy doesn't need them anymore, and you do." She picked up the teapot again and continued filling the mugs. "You're much of a height, you and Malkh. And when I saw you in the doorway, I . . . It was just an old woman's foolishness, that's all."

"I'm so, so sorry." Kiukiu was utterly mortified that she had managed to upset her grandmother and embarrass Lord Gavril at the same time.

"So I'm wearing a dead man's clothes . . ." A small, wry smile appeared on his lips and vanished again.

The sudden twang of untuned gusly strings distracted them both.

Malusha appeared, carrying her son's instrument, and put it down on the table.

"There's little point leaving this to rust away any longer. It needs work. Much work! Find me my pliers, Kiukiu. Let's put some new strings on and see how it sounds."

Kaspar Linnaius was floating in a chill grey sea, bathed in mist. Numb with cold, he sensed that he was beginning to drift slowly and inevitably into oblivion. So that when he heard a voice calling his name, he was reluctant to summon the energy to reply.

"Let me be," he murmured.

But the insistent calling continued; and through the mists, he thought he saw a brown-haired shaman woman wading toward him, her dark eyes burning bright with life.

"I said let me be."

"Oh no, Kaspar Linnaius, you don't slip away from me that easily! You have work to do."

"Too tired . . ."

"Take my hand." Before he could protest, she had grabbed hold of his hand and—

Linnaius opened his eyes and saw the shaman woman bending over him, still holding his hand in hers . . . only now she was crooked with age and the fingers that clutched his were knotted with rheumatism.

"At last!" she said triumphantly, releasing his hand. "I thought we'd lost you."

"Where am I?" he asked and heard only a hoarse whisper issue from his throat. Every word cost him great effort; the inside of his mouth and tongue were so parched he could hardly speak.

"At my cottage. And you don't deserve to be, for what you did to my granddaughter."

"Malusha?" He knew her now. "But how did you—?"

"You have my lord Drakhaon to thank for rescuing you," she said.

In the gloom behind Malusha, Linnaius could just make out the faintest glimmer of dark sapphire: two eyes, daemon-blue, watching him.

"You snatched me from the pyre." Now Linnaius began to remember and as he did, the memories came rushing back in a firelit dazzle. "But my books—they're gone, all gone." Linnaius rocked to and fro in grief, mourning his lost writings. Not just all his life's work burned, but that of his teachers before him. So much precious knowledge painstakingly collected had been eradicated in that one brief blaze. So many experiments meticulously recorded, even the unsuccessful ones, and annotated so that others might learn from his mistakes.

Tears squeezed out from his dry eyes and trickled down his cheeks. "They burned my books."

"Now what shall we do?"

Gavril could feel Malusha staring tensely at him in the gloom of the cottage. Kaspar Linnaius had lapsed back into deep sleep, lulled by one of Malusha's sedative teas.

"You think he won't be able to remember how to make the elixir?" He glanced across at Kiukiu's silver head, nodding as she dozed by the fire. The thought that his journey had been in vain was almost too hard to bear.

"He's a ghost of his old self. Without the elixir, he's sliding fast into senility. Did you see how he wept for his books? The old Kaspar Linnaius would never have allowed himself such a sign of weakness."

"I promised the Emperor I would bring him back alive."

"Well, he's alive, I'll grant you, but not much more. The Emperor will be sorely disappointed if he was relying on him to use his old skills."

Gavril could hear Linnaius's breath wheezing and rattling as he slept. "Is there anything you can do for him, Malusha?"

"I'll prepare some ginseng tea." Malusha turned to the jars on her dresser and pulled down a little wooden caddy. "It's good for a failing memory."

"Let me take him back to Swanholm. There may be some papers left in his laboratory to jog his memory. Anything." A sudden spasm twisted Gavril's body and he doubled up, clutching his stomach.

"How long can you continue in this fashion, Drakhaon?" She was standing watching him.

"It'll pass," he said, gasping.

"Have you taken a look at yourself? A really good look?" She knelt to open an old chest of tooled leather and took out a bronze-framed mirror, holding it out. When he hesitated, she thrust it into his hands. "Go on. Do it."

"Is this a trick mirror?" Gavril heard the edge to his voice as he stared in disbelief at his reflection. "Is this another of your illusions, Malusha?"

Even in the dull light inside the cottage he could see that his eyes gleamed unnaturally, luminously blue. And his hair had grown overnight, the long dark locks streaked with sapphire and cobalt. His cheekbones had become more prominent, his nose sharper, his nostrils flared. When he looked at himself, he began to see the Drakhaoul he had glimpsed in his dreams made flesh. And again he remembered his father's warning, the warning he had repeated to Eugene:

It refashions its host, body and mind, to resemble the being it once was.

"How can I go among people looking like this?" he whispered.

"Don't ask me, ask your daemon," Malusha said, pouring water into the kettle.

But before Gavril could reply, he felt a tremor go through him.

"*Khezef . . .*"

Someone else—far distant—had called his daemon's name. And Gavril found himself making for the cottage door, his limbs moving, though not by his own volition, controlled by a will far stronger than his own.

CHAPTER 14

The air was heavy, laden with sticky moisture, and swarms of black flies hovered over the boggy pools. Little birds whistled and called from the gorse bushes and high overhead a pair of buzzards wheeled in lazy circles. Gavril stumbled over grassy tussocks, through banks of curling fern and honey-scented heather, until he could feel a whisper of mountain breeze on his face. It blew keen and fresh from the Kharzgylls even though the upper crags were shrouded in afternoon haze.

"What are you doing to me, Khezef?" he cried aloud.

"*Silence! Can't you hear my brother calling to me?*" There was a harsh tone of authority in the Drakhaoul's voice that Gavril had never heard before.

"No—you listen to *me*, Khezef!"

"*Khezef . . .*"

Was that an echo? Gavril heard—or felt—someone else call the Drakhaoul's name once again.

"*But this concerns you, Gavril.*" Khezef softened his tone a little.

"*Khezef.*" There it was again, the briefest shimmer of sound, like the whining drone of a bee. As Gavril stood still, eyes closed to listen, he realized that all the moorland birds had fallen silent. "*Join me. Together we can take back the Eye of Nagar.*"

"*I cannot join you, Belberith. Not yet. There is work to be done here.*" Khezef's reply was guarded.

"*Other forces are moving to conspire against us. If we don't work together soon, all may come to nothing . . .*" Belberith's voice faded until all Gavril could hear was the breeze stirring the purple heather at his feet. The little birds began to twitter again in the gorse but Gavril still felt a looming sense of unease, as though a storm were building far away.

"I thought you and Belberith were at odds with one another."

"*You and Eugene have been at odds,*" Khezef made the subtle correction. "*We are only here to do your bidding. Isn't it natural that Belberith should wish to aid his master Eugene take back what has been stolen from him? The rubies that adorn his emperor's crown? The symbols of his imperial power?*"

Gavril did not feel reassured by Khezef's words. How long had the Drakhaouls been in communication? And what was their true intent? A great boulder lay across Gavril's path; he propped himself against the moss-covered stone. "Tell me who you really are, Khezef, you and your kindred."

At first Khezef did not answer. But images began to flicker rapidly through Gavril's mind; fleetingly he saw a battalion of winged warriors swoop past, each one as dazzling as a falling star.

"*Nilaihah the golden-tongued, the Poet,*" said Khezef. "*Belberith, the Warrior, of the Malachite Armor.*"

"The Warrior," echoed Gavril.

"*Adramelech, the Dreamer, Weaver of Twilight; Za'afiel, the Spinner of Winds; Nagazdiel, Ruler of the Night.*"

"And you?"

"*Seven,*" Khezef said, ignoring his question, "*we were Seven. Once, we were free, spirits of the aethyr. And then the ones you call the Warriors of Heaven enslaved us. They gave us powers, terrible powers of destruction. We were altered to be the instruments of their justice. But our prince, Nagazdiel, rebelled. We fought for our freedom and we lost. For that rebellion we were condemned to the Realm of Shadows.*

"*We never asked to be brought through the Gate into your world. But now we are here, we have no wish to go back to the Realm of Shadows. Would you want to return to that lonely prison cell in Arnskammar? For all eternity?*"

"No. But if all Seven return, you'll bring about the end of my world!"

"*And had you never thought that maybe this was meant to be? That nothing you say or do can stop it happening?*" Gavril recognized the subtle, persuasive tone that he had heard Khezef use before. "*Why are you still tormenting yourself, Gavril? Surrender your will to mine. Be one with me, and this mental anguish will cease. Forever."*

Peace of mind. To abandon this increasingly futile struggle against impossible odds, to give in and let his identity merge with the daemon's . . .

And then he thought of Kiukiu. "How can I forget those I love, who love me?"

"One mind, one purpose," continued Khezef, as if Gavril's questions were irrelevant. *"We can change you. We can make you indestructible. Immortal."*

"You call this immortality? You use us—and as we age and die, you just cast us aside and take new bodies. You can't exist in this world long without flesh and blood to clothe and protect yourselves."

"You misunderstand me. My prince—whose name you bear—has powers far greater than my own. Set him free, and he will remake your mortal body. I have begun the process, but only he can finish it."

"Wait." Gavril had only just begun to understand what Khezef was suggesting. "You mean I would become a daemon. An angel of destruction. Gavril Nagarian would be gone."

"Not gone, but altered. Translated."

The Drakhaoul had never spoken so bluntly before and Gavril could only wonder what had prompted this frankness. "Khezef," he said at length, "you came back to me when I was dying and gave me life again. But I can't accept what you're offering."

Kiukiu watched as Linnaius sipped his ginseng tea and saw how a little trickle dribbled out down one side of his mouth. His palsied hands shook as he put the mug down.

Am I looking at myself? she wondered. *Is this how I shall be soon, if he doesn't regain his wits and remember the recipe for the elixir?*

"Magus," she said, "do you recall anything about how to make the elixir?"

"Eh?" Linnaius cupped one hand over his ear, leaning toward her. *Now his hearing's failing as well.*

She knelt beside his chair, feeling the stiffness in her knees, hearing the joints crack. "The elixir, Magus," she said loudly. "You need it— and so do I." She wondered if she would be able to get to her feet again without assistance. "Tell me what ingredients you need and I will find them."

He looked at her blankly. There was a milky cloudiness veiling his eyes. Then he bared his teeth in a skull-like grin. "Ha! Wouldn't you like to know? You don't steal my secrets from me that easily."

Kiukiu stifled a sigh of frustration. "The Emperor needs you, Magus. But what use are you to him like this?"

Malusha whispered into Kiukiu's ear, "I slipped something in his tea; it should soon loosen his tongue a little."

"Grandma!" Kiukiu said, shocked.

"Don't tell me your elixir contained agrimony." Malusha continued in a loud, provocative tone.

"Agrimony? Pah," said Linnaius dismissively. "Any true magister knows that's inefficacious."

"Then it has to be the plant they call ephedra, from the east."

Linnaius began to giggle, as if she had said something extraordinarily amusing.

"If he doesn't rally soon, we'll have to risk a Summoning," Malusha said to Kiukiu as tears of laughter ran down the Magus's cheeks.

"But who would we summon?"

"See if you can charm the name of his master out of him."

"Me?" Kiukiu wondered if she could charm anyone ever again with her wizened face and faded hair. But if the Magus's sight was as weak as hers, then maybe she might succeed. She remembered times at Kastel Drakhaon when she had tried to coax old Guaram to tell her about Lord Gavril, little intimate details that a man might share with his valet.

"Gulvardi—no, *no*!"

Kiukiu started, hearing Gavril cry out in his sleep.

"Bad dreams, guilty conscience," said Malusha, shaking her head.

"Wake up."

Gavril started awake to find Kiukiu kneeling over him, one hand on his shoulder, shaking him. In the half-light, he could not see the wrinkles on her face, or the grey of her faded hair, only the blue of her eyes, which still shone clear as a spring sky.

"What's wrong?"

"You were shouting out in your sleep."

"What did I say?"

"It sounded like names."

"Names." The horror of the dream still polluted his mind.

"Gavril," she said, "tell me what you were dreaming about."

"I can't."

"Tell me."

"Innocent blood," he whispered. He put his hands over his face. "*They* come back to me whenever I try to sleep, Kiukiu."

"Ah," she said. She sat back on her heels. "Drakhaon's Brides."

"It made me do it," he said through his fingers. "It took me over. Now I can't always tell who's in control. I know I have to put things to rights, but I don't know how."

She said nothing.

Silence hung between them—where there had never been silence before. At length he said, "I've killed, Kiukiu. The first one—"

"The *first*? How many were there?"

"She was running away from me. I tried to stop her, but she fell before I could catch her. She fell down a ravine. There was nothing I could—"

"And the next?"

"I was all but spent after I brought you back here." How pathetic the excuse sounded—and yet it was the truth. "Without her, I would never have reached Francia."

"Was she the last?"

He shook his head. The words would not come. He saw a young girl's face, sweet and trusting. *Kristell.*

"You killed her?"

"I tried to fight it. But it made me. It forced me. When I came back to myself, it was too late." Burning tears trickled down his cheeks at the memory and he felt no release in them. "I'm beginning to lose my human face, Kiukiu," he said, his voice choked. "In spite of the . . . the blood, I'm changing."

She put out one hand and tentatively touched the glitter of scales on his cheekbones.

"And if my outward form is Drakhaoul, I can't be sure how long I can still be"—he hesitated—"myself." He gazed at her, wanting her to forgive him. "Help me, Kiukiu. Please help me."

"So it's growing stronger." Her voice was expressionless, as if she were deliberately holding back from telling him her true feelings.

"Ever since the Serpent Gate was breached and its kindred let loose, it's been growing stronger. They seem to draw strength from one another."

She just looked down at her hand, as if at a loss for words. He pushed back the blanket and, slinging the shirt over his bare shoulders, padded across the worn flagstones toward the door.

Kiukiu made no move to follow him. And was it so surprising, considering the crimes he had just confessed to? He pushed open the cottage door and went out to the well.

Kiukiu had supported him unquestioningly throughout the long months of transformation and exile. But if she rejected him now, then he would be utterly alone. Was this the same feeling of black despair that had overwhelmed his father when Elysia fled Kastel Drakhaon?

Better to have said nothing.

Kiukiu's fingers were damp with Lord Gavril's tears. She slowly raised her hand and pressed it against her withered cheek. She no longer knew what to feel. His confession had shocked her beyond words. Now she knew that he had attacked three innocent girls and that those glittering blue claw-nails had torn into young flesh. She knew that the sensitive mouth that had kissed her so tenderly had been stained with warm human blood. Worst of all, she had learned that three lives full of promise had been extinguished to satiate the Drakhaoul's obscene hunger.

And yet he had wept. And they were bitter tears, tears of remorse and despair. If she rejected him now, he might lose all hope and let the daemon possess him utterly. Even now, the Drakhaoul might be working its malign influence on him, seeping its dark poison into his heart and soul, destroying the last vestiges of his humanity.

"But how can I help you, Gavril, *how*?"

Gavril sat on a lichened boulder, staring out across the moorlands, at the distant grey wasteland that lay beyond at the foot of the mountains. The grey scar created by his father's fury, where nothing grew and no birds sang.

The Drakhaouls were instruments of destruction. Their poisonous breath seared the earth and turned it to dust and cinders. If Khezef's kindred were allowed to remain at large, all New Rossiya could soon become one empty, polluted waste.

"*What point is there in staying here?*" Khezef seemed restless, eager to move on. "*You have unfinished business in Tielen.*"

Gavril thought of Kaspar Linnaius and the promise he had made to Eugene. He shook his head. "The old man is too weak to survive another journey. He needs to rest and regain his strength."

He heard a finch give a startled cry. Kiukiu was making her way toward him through the misty banks of heather, shading her eyes with one hand against the sunlight.

"They were never meant to be in this world, were they?" she said. A soft breeze stirred her ash-grey hair. "Innocent blood brought them through."

Fragments of half-forgotten Drakhaoul-dreams were stirred up from Gavril's memory. She knew. Yet how?

"Linnaius took me to Swanholm to heal Princess Karila. But she wasn't sick. She was possessed by the spirit of a dead child. This child—Tilua—is linked by blood to your Drakhaoul, Gavril."

"*Tilua . . .*" Gavril heard Khezef echo the name. "*For one moment in the dark between worlds, we were one. And then we were torn apart.*"

"Tilua was the sacrifice?"

Kiukiu nodded. "I tried to send her spirit to the Ways Beyond, but it can't leave this world. Not while your Drakhaoul is still here."

"What are you saying, Kiukiu?"

"I think," she said slowly as though working the idea through as she spoke, "that if I could somehow charm Tilua away from the princess and reunite her with your Drakhaoul—*her* Drakhaoul—then it would be made whole again and both could leave our world in peace."

Her words kindled a fresh spark of hope in Gavril's heart. Malusha's exorcism had left him damaged in mind and soul, and had only sent the Drakhaoul raging through the world, a vengeful, turbulent spirit. But if there could be a final peaceful separation . . .

"No one has ever thought of that before!"

"No one?" She looked up at him, her eyes uncertain, wary.

The idea excited him so much that the words came tumbling out. "Don't you see, Kiukiu? There are other Drakhaouls. So there must be other children."

"Oh, but there are," she said, shivering as if the memory chilled her to the bone. "Ever since the night of the fiery beacon, there have been *other* children."

Gavril sensed a rapid burst of violent emotions tremble through him, as though Kiukiu had awakened something long buried.

"*Help us, Khezef,*" he pleaded. "*How do we find these children? Why won't you answer me? Is she right?*" But Gavril's pleas were only met with silence.

"Can you trace them, Kiukiu?"

"I don't know if I have the strength," she said sadly, "or the courage, to go back to that terrible place."

He saw then how worn and tired she was, her head bent, weighed down by the burden of all the lost souls that haunted her.

"I have no right to ask such a thing of you. I'm sorry." He reached out to stroke her faded hair, but she flinched at his touch.

So that was how it was between them. His hand fell away.

"The sun's too bright," she said, turning and walking slowly back toward the cottage. He watched her go, his heart twisted with grief.

When Gavril returned to the cottage, he found Malusha sitting bent over Malkh's gusly, gnawing her underlip in concentration. She was twisting a new string into place and testing the pitch with one thumbnail, wielding her pliers like a skilled craftswoman. She did not even glance up as he came in but said, "Well, and what did you expect? She heard you crying out in your sleep."

"But how can I make things right again?" Gavril's sense of desperation was rising within him like a choking tide. From the chair by the fireside, Linnaius let out a long, wheezing snore. "I used up too much of my strength bringing the Magus here from Francia. And now look at him! He's no use to us—or to his emperor."

"My old skin may be tough as leather, but gusly wire'll slice right through a fingertip if I don't give this job my full attention." Malusha laid down her pliers. "What's really bothering you, Drakhaon?"

Gavril stared down at Linnaius, who was dozing with his mouth open. "Eugene promised a pardon for me and my men if I returned Kaspar Linnaius to him."

"So that's it, is it? You want the Magus cured so that you and your band of *druzhina* thugs can go free? Do you think you deserve that freedom?"

"I made them a promise." He spoke more forcefully than he had intended.

"This was my son's first gusly. My son Malkh, murdered by *your* father's men. For years I haven't been able to bear to look at it. Now she's found it and I'm restoring it for her to use. Why should I help you, Drakhaon?"

Gavril had no answer. How could he make reparation for his father's crimes? He had enough of his own to atone for.

"I'm going to speak plain, Lord Drakhaon. She's all I've got left and I'd give the last drop of blood in my body rather than see her hurt."

Gavril opened his mouth to protest but she raised one hand. "Yes, I know, you traveled all that way to bring back the old man. But he's too far gone to be any use to her and I have to find a way to get her to Khitari."

"Let me take her."

"You?" Malusha gave him a contemptuous look. "What makes you think she'd want to go with you?"

Gavril stared at her.

"I warned her. But would she listen? You're all the same, you Nagarians." Her eyes hardened. "Sooner or later, the daemon takes control and the hunger drives you."

"But I did it to save her—"

"You're polluted, Lord Drakhaon, tainted with your victims' blood. You cannot walk the shaman paths she must follow. You'd only hinder her chances."

He felt the despair rising within him again. "Then tell me how I can be of use to her. Tell me, Malusha!"

"You already know the answer." Her eyes were now so dark and deep that he felt as if he were gazing into the Ways Beyond.

CHAPTER 15

The last barrel of firedust was being rolled—with extreme caution—onto the waiting wagon. Captain Nils Lindgren stood by, supervising the operation.

The message from Tielen had been curt:

"All remaining supplies urgently required. A merchant ship will be waiting off Narvazh."

Lindgren had been planning to accompany the wagon across the moors to Narvazh to ensure that the highly volatile material was transported safely. But another dispatch had come an hour ago from the customs post at Arkhelskoye on the eastern coast, one that had awakened his suspicions:

Unusually large number of pilgrims disembarking. Destination:
Monastery of Saint Sergius in Kerjhenezh Forest.

"Is that barrel secured?" Lindgren called up to his lieutenant, who was on the wagon.

"Secured and ready to go, Captain!"

"Then you'd better be on your way. And don't relax your guard for a moment. The Emperor wants that cargo delivered safe and sound."

The moment the wagon was rumbling off down the dirt track from the mine workings, Lindgren was hurrying back to Kastel Drakhaon.

"Sosia!" he called, entering the hall.

The kastel housekeeper came out of the dining hall, a cloth in one hand, a pot of beeswax in the other. "How can I help you, Captain?"

Since the night when he and Gavril Nagarian had worked side by side to rescue the men trapped in the mine workings, she had treated him very differently. Once, he had even glimpsed the glimmer of a smile on her worn face when he had complimented her on the food at dinner.

"Tell me, Sosia, is there a festival held in honor of Saint Sergius at this time?"

Sosia looked puzzled. "Blessed Serzhei's Day falls toward the end of the year. Long after the first snows. My mother, God rest her, used to make us all wrap up warmly, with rags round our boots to stop us slipping on the ice. Then we'd trudge off through the forest in the early-morning dark with our lanterns to the shrine, and the good brothers would give us hot mulled ale to drink . . ."

"Then why would pilgrims be coming to the shrine in high summer?"

Sosia shrugged. "There's always a few, when the weather's at its best. Nothing unusual in that."

"This is considerably more than a few, Sosia."

She gave him a quizzical glance. "Best consult the Bogatyr, then."

Lindgren nodded resignedly. This was not going to be the easiest of meetings, but he needed the *druzhina*'s local knowledge. It was always possible that this "pilgrimage" was an Azhkendi ruse to drive him and his men out. Except that the ships bringing the pilgrims were from Francia . . .

Lindgren had housed the *druzhina* casualties from the mine workings in one of the restored watchtowers. He had sent his regimental surgeon to tend to their injuries. The older soldiers seemed to have fared least well in the accident. Bogatyr Askold's crushed leg was taking a while to mend, and one of his lieutenants, Gorian, his face already seamed with fearsome battle scars, had lost an eye.

As Lindgren approached the watchtower, he noticed that Askold had posted two of the younger men outside as guards. Tattooed in blue and crimson with Nagarian clanmarks on foreheads, right cheeks, and bared forearms, they scowled at Lindgren, moving to block the doorway. It occurred to him that he was possibly risking his neck in coming alone into the enemy stronghold. He had no guarantee that the *druzhina* would not seize him and hold him hostage; he could only trust that his gesture of good faith would earn him safe passage out.

"Take me to the Bogatyr," he ordered curtly. He had learned soon enough that the *druzhina* had little respect for the disciplines of the New Rossiyan Army. Wild as a horde of marauding wolves, they only responded to the snarling of a pack leader. He recognized Dunai, Askold's eldest son, by his fair braids and the insolent glint in his narrowed blue eyes.

"Now, Dunai!"

After a moment's hesitation Dunai nodded, his face still a mask of hostility. "Follow me."

Lindgren followed Dunai into the watchtower; other *druzhina* sprang up as they passed, abandoning their game of knucklestones. Lindgren walked by them with what he hoped passed for a confident, purposeful stride.

Askold was seated in a wooden chair; his broken leg, splinted and bandaged, was supported on a stool.

"You'll excuse me if I don't get up, Captain Lindgren," he said, with a wry curl of the lip. Dunai moved to stand behind his father's chair, arms folded.

"An unusually large number of pilgrims are making their way to the monastery in the forest," Lindgren said. "Does that strike you as odd, Bogatyr?"

"We don't have much to do with the monks of Saint Serzhei. Their allegiances lay with the House of Arkhel in the Clan Wars." Askold's face was closed. One of the older *druzhina* spat at the mention of Arkhel.

Everything always came down to the old clan rivalries in Azhkendir. Lindgren tried another tack. "And these pilgrims have arrived by ship. They're not Azhkendi."

This time he saw Dunai glance at his father.

"Surely the all-powerful New Rossiyan Army is not intimidated by a few religious fanatics, Captain?"

Lindgren ignored the barbed taunt and decided to risk all. "I need your help, Bogatyr. Your men know the terrain; they know how to move unseen through the forest—"

"You want to use the *druzhina* to spy on these pilgrims?"

"Yes."

"Unarmed?"

Lindgren had always suspected this was where his plan would founder. Rearm the *druzhina* and they'll slaughter you all in your beds, Field Marshal Karonen had warned him.

"You can't expect my men to go out against an unknown enemy unarmed. You wouldn't do it to your own lads."

"Enemy?" So Askold acknowledged that the arrival of so many pilgrims was unusual.

"I'll take you to reconnoiter, Captain," said Dunai suddenly. "I know ways through Kerjhenezh that no pilgrim has ever discovered."

"I'll come with you, Dunai." Young Semyon came to stand beside him.

Askold's clenched fist crashed down on the arm of his chair. "I'm not sending my son—or any of my men—into danger unless they can defend themselves."

What would the Emperor have done in such circumstances? Lindgren decided it was a risk worth taking.

"Meet me in the kastel armory. Any man that accompanies me on this mission may reclaim his weapons."

And then, just to cover his back, he sent out reinforcements to Lieutenant Palmgren in charge of the New Rossiyan detachment guarding the port.

"Detain anyone acting suspiciously. Use force, if necessary. Stay in touch with the kastel by Vox at all times."

"Another textual anomaly," muttered Doctor Frieda Hildegarde, delighted to have unearthed an intriguing variant in the ancient Azhkendi manuscript she was translating:

Artamon, weakened by grief, lay in a fever . . .
"My sons fight over my empire even before I am dead, like mad dogs."
Archimandrite Serzhei of Azhkendir was brought to the Emperor's sickbed to offer the consolation of faith to the dying man.
"My sons are possessed by powerful daemons, Serzhei. In God's name, I beg you to exorcise them."
"I fear it may be too late," said the wise archimandrite. "Your sons have become mere puppets. Not only do they resemble their daemonic masters, they behave like them."

"Puppets? Can that be right?" The scholar leafed through her notebook, opened her dictionary, and pushed her spectacles farther up her thin nose to distinguish the tiny print more clearly.

Doctor Hildegarde had dedicated her life to writing a definitive biography of Artamon the Great, though she had never expected it would excite much interest beyond the close academic circles in which she moved. Her researches had led her to libraries in lonely and distant monasteries. She had disguised herself as a man and traveled deep into the red deserts of Djihan-Djihar, seeking out ancient texts. She had joined a silk caravan and ridden for weeks on a camel across the vast steppes of Khitari, searching for the ruins of Khan Konchak's palace, sacked by Artamon as his armies swept across the continent. She had even risked the wrath of the Drakhaon of Azhkendir. Her first illicit visit to the Monastery of Saint Sergius had been all too brief; Lord Volkh had sent his barbarous *druzhina* to escort her to the nearest port and put her on the first ship out. That had only excited Hildegarde's scholarly curiosity even more. What lay hidden in the monastery library that the Drakhaon was so eager to keep secret?

When, years later, an unexpected summons had come from the Emperor, she felt gratified, though also a little mystified. She had rationalized to herself that Eugene, the first ruler to reunite Artamon's fractured empire, must be keen to ensure that her work was dedicated to him. Imperial patronage would greatly enhance her reputation; it surely was to be welcomed. And yet . . .

Their meeting in Tielborg Fastness had been brief. The whole city seemed to be in turmoil, with the militia massing in every square. And when the Emperor greeted her, he was in uniform, as if about to ride off to war.

"It may have escaped your notice, shut away in the university library, Doctor," said the Emperor, "but the empire is under threat of attack from King Enguerrand." He then proceeded, to Hildegarde's bemusement, to quiz her about Artamon's sons.

Hildegarde's attention was immediately engaged. She was impressed. The Emperor was well-informed about Artamon's life; he had obviously read her manuscript. "But when it comes to Artamon's sons," she was forced to confess, "there is a sad paucity of material. The Rossiyan Empire was in such disarray at the time that many chronicles were burned. Or lost."

"Except in Azhkendir." The Emperor handed her a purse of money and a sealed letter. "I want you to return to the Monastery of Saint Sergius, Doctor, and resume your researches. Abbot Yephimy will grant you access to any manuscript you wish to consult. Uncover every fact you can about the sons of Artamon, no matter how insignificant you think it may be, and report back to me regularly by courier."

How could she refuse? And yet she was puzzled as to why the Emperor was so interested in these shadowy historical figures. Was it anything to do with the Francian threat? As an imperial carriage swiftly conveyed her to the port, she began to wonder if she had been employed to supply ancient legal ammunition to defend Eugene's right to the empire, should King Enguerrand issue a challenge.

Abbot Yephimy had raised an eyebrow when he realized the visiting scholar from Tielen was a woman. But he had said nothing. She supposed that, seeing her practical traveling clothes, her sandy hair pulled back into a tight knot so that strands would not dangle in her eyes as she worked, he judged that such a plain woman was unlikely to distract the younger monks from their devotions. Since then she had been utterly lost in the glorious past, reading, translating, puzzling, in the little library cell. The whitewashed walls receded and in her imagination she rode at Artamon's side as he led his armies into the steppes of Khitari to face the murderous hordes of Khan Konchak.

Frieda Hildegarde had grown up in a little village near the overgrown ruins of one of Artamon's summer palaces. When the other children were playing ball around the crumbling stones, she found herself pushing back the layers of ivy and creeper, curious to see what lay beneath. And there, choked with the dust and dirt of hundreds of years, she had spotted a fragment of carving. Her grimy fingers traced the faded outline of a warrior-king's face, hawk-nosed, strong-chinned, proud, and handsome. Enthralled since that childhood discovery, she had developed an obsession with unraveling the truth that lay behind the ancient legends.

Artamon . . .

That's not quite the whole story, she admitted to herself with a little grin. *I fell in love with him.* And the little Monastery of Saint Sergius, tucked away in the forests of Azhkendir, held treasures she had only dreamed of: murals as old as Artamon himself in the crypt to restore and obscure incunabula in the library with hidden texts to discover. It was a scholar's paradise on earth.

She carefully turned the vellum page with silk-gloved fingers.

Puppets. There seemed no other way to render the word in the modern tongue.

Tears glistened in the Emperor's eyes but his voice, though faint, was firm. "If my faithful hound were to foam at the mouth and go mad, I would not hesitate to kill him. These daemons must be sent back to the Realm of Shadows that spawned them. Even if it means my sons must perish too."

Doctor Hildegarde raised her head. "So Artamon ordered Serzhei to kill his sons to exorcise the daemons," she whispered. "What must that decision have cost him? And to go into the darkness, believing that all of his children were dead and his empire in ruins . . ."

Abbot Yephimy lifted the lid from a vat and inhaled the fumes of the liqueur Brother Gleb was distilling. He blinked, as the strong odor made his eyes water, and felt his nasal passages clear. The liqueur ex-uded an aroma as cold as a bitter wind off the mountains in midwinter.

"I've added gentian, as you suggested," said Brother Gleb. "Would you like to taste?"

"Not until after evening prayers," said Yephimy. He suspected that the spirit was strong enough to strip the paint from the frescoes in the shrine. "And a little more of Brother Beekeeper's honey, Brother Gleb, might make it acceptable to more sensitive palates?"

Brother Gleb's round, pleasant face darkened at the mention of Brother Lyashko. Yephimy had hoped that the keen rivalry between the two monks could be mitigated by encouraging them to work to-gether. Selling this liqueur could raise much-needed money for the monastery. The heavy snows of the last winter had brought down the guesthouse roof and two of the stained-glass windows in the shrine were badly in need of restoration. But his suggestion had only wors-ened the rift between Gleb and Lyashko. They seemed to regard it as more of a competition than a joint project.

"Abbot! Abbot!"

Yephimy had just opened his mouth to rebuke Gleb when the dis-tillery door was flung open and one of the acolytes rushed in.

"Pilgrims. And Brother Cosmas says where are we going to ac-commodate them all?"

Yephimy raised his hand to silence the breathless flow. "I'll come and greet our visitors." He followed the boy, turning back once to say to Brother Gleb, "Don't forget, more honey." But in the court-yard, Yephimy stopped and stared in bewilderment. There were black-robed pilgrims everywhere he looked, as if the monastery had been invaded by a flock of giant crows. And he had seen robes like these some months earlier.

"The Francian Commanderie," he muttered, quickening his stride as he made for the shrine. "They've come for Serzhei's Staff."

Little clouds of midges hovered in the clearing, tiny dancing stars in a single shaft of sunlight that had penetrated the green gloom of Kerjhenezh.

Since dawn Lindgren had been following Dunai and Semyon through the ancient trees, beneath the great boughs of fir and pine. They traveled on horseback at first; now they were to continue on foot. The plan was to leave the horses by a mossy-banked trickle of a stream, under the watchful eyes of two of Lindgren's troopers.

Semyon returned from filling the water bottles in the stream.

Lindgren gulped down a long, cold draft of mountain water; he was hot and sweating already and the midges kept whining in his face. He slapped them away and asked the question that had been mystifying him since the previous day. "What is there at the monastery that would draw so many pilgrims?"

"The relics of the holy saint," said Semyon, recorking the bottles.

"I think we're agreed, Semyon," said Dunai dryly, "that we're not talking relics here."

"I knew that," said Semyon, coloring bright red.

"What's this?" said Doctor Hildegarde aloud. The copy of *The Life of the Blessed Sergius* had been made on fresh vellum—except for the final two pages. If she held them up to the light, it was just possible to discern that the copyist, having run out of new vellum, had scraped clean an old page or two. Due to his haste or lack of skill, the original text was still mostly discernible to the trained eye—albeit upside down. And the more she squinted at the faint letters, the more she was certain it was a letter. A letter in code.

To Volkhar, Prince of Azhkendir . . . our brother Prince Rostevan still holds to life by a thread. Since the daemon was cast out, madness has gripped him . . . judged unfit to rule . . . Vakhtang has seized the imperial throne . . . fear he has murdered Rostevan's children . . .

"I want you to uncover every fact you can about the sons of Artamon," the Emperor had said, "no matter how insignificant you think it may be."

And now Doctor Hildegarde was so excited at what she had unearthed, she could hardly breathe. She tugged at the pearl button of her constricting chemise collar to give herself air; she fanned herself with a scrap of loose paper; she stared again at the encoded text, a cleverly contrived cypher devised by some anonymous scribe. In the current empire, such ingenuity would have made him rise high in the Emperor's secret service. Why, she mused, had he felt it necessary to conceal this particular information? So few people in Artamon's time would have been able to read anyway . . .

But it was those simple words "our brother." This could only be a letter from one of Artamon's sons. But which one? The next line gave her the clue: "Vakhtang . . . has banished Teimur to the wastes of Khitari. Now only we can stand against him."

"Helmar," she said triumphantly as she scribbled in her notebook. "This is a letter written by the Emperor's ancestor, no less! And yet more proof of the terrible strife between the sons that brought down their father's empire."

Slowly Doctor Hildegarde began to realize that the library had emptied and she was alone. Yet she had not heard the bells ring to summon the monks to prayers; neither was it time for the evening meal. She shrugged and turned back to her deciphering.

"Good-day to you, Abbot." The leader of the pilgrims shook off his hood and Yephimy recognized the pale face and dark eyes of Jagu de Rustéphan of the Francian Commanderie. "I think you can guess why we are here."

Had it come to this? Yephimy surveyed the Guerriers massing in the courtyard. The odds were not in their favor. But the brothers were ready to defend their sacred relic to the death. The few weapons they had kept hidden in the crypt since the Clan Wars had been hastily brought out.

"I gave you my answer once before, Lieutenant." Yephimy placed himself on the steps in front of the shrine. The monks were assembling on either side of him, forming a human barrier between the Commanderie and their goal. "The crook stays here. With the Blessed Serzhei's bones."

"It's very peaceful here in Kerjhenezh, isn't it?" said a clear voice. Yephimy sensed a stir among the brothers as they realized that the speaker was the young and beautiful woman who stood at Jagu's side. "But the situation beyond your walls has changed, Abbot. There are now five Drakhaouls at large. We must reforge the staff and defeat them or they will tear our world apart."

"Then let us repair the staff here," said Yephimy equably. He would not be forced into handing over the monastery's greatest treasure, one that he had vowed to protect with his life. "We have a forge."

The young woman's lips curled in a disdainful smile. "This task requires the most delicate craftsmanship."

"I must ask you again, Abbot," said Jagu, "to hand over the crook."

"And I tell you again, Lieutenant, that I cannot do that."

"We have no wish to harm you or any of the brothers here. But we have our orders from the Grand Maistre."

Yephimy cast a hasty glance over the pilgrim-warriors filling the courtyard. There seemed to be more arriving by the minute. And he caught the glint of weapons half-concealed by their robes. No, the odds did not look good. It was some years since he had been forced to take up arms to defend the monastery. Then it had been to beat back Lord Volkh's ransacking *druzhina* on the search for Arkhel sympathizers. But this was different . . .

"Abbot." Brother Lyashko nudged him. "Here's your broadsword."

Yephimy took the heavy sword and weighed it in his hand. The roughness of the grip, worn with use, was reassuring. He had taken a vow to abjure his old warrior ways, but defending the shrine and its sacred treasures was an exception.

"You'll have to kill us first, Lieutenant de Rustéphan," he said.

Abbot Yephimy took up his sword and placed himself in front of the shrine doors. Jagu saw at once from the abbot's stance that he had used that sword before—and probably to lethal effect. Beside him, the brothers brandished their weapons: woodcutters' axes; ancient, rusty pikes; Azhkendi sabres. But many of the monks were white-bearded and stooped; their heavy blades wavered in palsied hands.

This was not going as Jagu had planned. He took Celestine by the arm and drew her to one side. "I don't want any bloodshed if we can avoid it. But they seem determined to put up a fight."

"Leave it to me," she said.

"Listen!" Dunai raised his hand for silence. Lindgren frowned. He outranked Dunai; he should be giving the orders. "A fight!"

"At the monastery?" Semyon said, wide-eyed.

Dunai had remarkably keen ears, Lindgren concluded; he could hear nothing yet but the caw of crows in the green boughs of the giant firs overhead. They passed an ancient stone shrine, covered with ochre lichen.

"Down!" hissed Dunai suddenly, crouching low in the bracken and gesturing to them to copy him. Lindgren bit back a retort and did as he was bidden. Now he could hear sounds he recognized: the clash of blades and the guttural grunts and cries of men fighting.

"Why are they attacking the monks? They're only old men!" Semyon's outraged outburst was smothered as Dunai clapped a hand over his mouth.

"Have you forgotten everything my father taught you, Sem?"

Semyon, face bright red again, shook his head, and Dunai released him.

"It's too late to send for reinforcements." Lindgren spoke in an undertone. "But we could create a diversion."

"How?" Now it was Dunai who frowned, as though suspecting Lindgren of some ruse.

Lindgren reached into the leather bag he wore slung across one shoulder and carefully removed the single grenade he had brought for just such an emergency.

Dunai swore under his breath. "You could have blown us all to pieces!"

Lindgren ignored him and began to move forward, keeping his head and body low, until he could see the monastery walls. The din of hand-to-hand combat grew louder. If they were to prevent a massacre, he must act immediately.

He pulled the pin from the grenade and, rearing up, lobbed it with all his strength. Not over the monastery walls, but just beneath, on the forest side. He ducked down, hands cupped over his ears, and waited.

The ground shook as the grenade exploded, releasing a thin cloud of white alchymical gas into the air. If he had judged the wind direction correctly, the released gas cloud would drift away from them, luring their unknown foe in the opposite direction.

Dunai swore again. Lindgren, knowing that the Bogatyr's son was glaring at him, kept his eyes on the open monastery gates, waiting. Sure enough, a number of armed men, garbed in black, soon came running out, gazing all round them. One pointed toward the drifting white smoke and they set off, calling to each other in a tongue Lindgren did not recognize.

"Now," he said quietly, beckoning the two *druzhina* to follow him. He drew his pistol, primed it, and ran toward the gateway. Dunai and Semyon followed, darting into the shadow of the gatehouse, Semyon gripping his crossbow.

An extraordinary sight was revealed. The monastery swarmed with black-robed pilgrims. The monks had gathered together on the steps of the shrine, attempting to beat back the intruders with pitchforks, hoes, and rusty swords. One brother had fallen already, hands clutched to his throat. Only one among them wielded his weapon like a warrior, a tall, broad-shouldered man, who swung his ancient sword about him with all the skill of a *druzhina*. Before the dazzle of his scything blade, the intruders dropped back.

"Look at Abbot Yephimy!" whispered Semyon in admiring tones, fitting a bolt into his crossbow and winding the mechanism. "Who'd have thought he was a fighting man?"

"If we ever get back to Kastel Drakhaon, ask my dad for tales of Yephimy Two-Blades. He wasn't always a monk." Dunai drew his sabre.

Lindgren only half heard the exchange. He was watching two figures, standing a little apart from the main assault force. One of them, slim and golden-haired, was, he suddenly realized, a young woman. And then, before he had recovered from his astonishment, she was on the move, zigzagging through the fighters, straight toward the abbot.

He raised his pistol, supporting his wrist on his forearm, closing one eye to improve his aim. He had no wish to kill a woman. But if she attacked the abbot, he would have no choice.

"What the—" he heard Dunai gasp as the young woman opened her hand and with a dextrous flick of the wrist, cast a fine glittering powder into the air about the abbot's head. As the abbot's broadsword came slicing down, she neatly sidestepped the blow and darted clear.

The broadsword dropped from Abbot Yephimy's grip with a sonorous clang. The abbot fell to his knees—then crashed forward onto his face, his big body slowly rolling down the steps. The brothers nearest to Yephimy began to sway, to collapse to their knees.

"Magic," whispered Semyon, making the old country sign against evil.

"Na," said Dunai, skeptically, "some kind of sleeping powder. Crafty."

Lindgren was still watching the young woman and her companion. The instant the abbot fell, she was beckoning to him, darting up the steps.

The brothers crowded around their fallen leader. A few elderly monks still tried to block the door, but they were knocked aside and trampled as a surge of black-robed pilgrims charged into the shrine. Half a dozen stayed outside at the top of the steps, glancing all around, tensed and ready to repel any further assault.

"Are they brigands, come to rob the shrine?" asked Semyon, his face a mask of confusion.

If only I'd brought more men. Lindgren was cursing his lack of foresight. His troopers waiting back at the stream might have heard the grenade explode. But two would not be enough to make a successful stand against so many armed men. Although every soldierly instinct was telling him to retreat, he could not stand idly by and see the venerable old men so callously cut down.

One of the fallen monks tried to raise himself, one hand waving feebly, as if calling for help. The nearest lookout turned and struck the old man with the flat of his blade.

"Let's get the wounded to safety," Lindgren said to the two *druzhina*.

But Semyon, pale with rage, had not heard him. He aimed his crossbow at the lookout and fired.

"No!" cried Lindgren, too late. The lookout let out a gurgling cry as the bolt transpierced his throat—and fell.

"Good shot, Sem!" cried Dunai as Semyon reloaded and aimed again.

"You young fool!" Lindgren could see the other lookouts turning around, scanning the area to see where the shot had come from. He knew their confusion would not last long; it was obvious that they were highly trained and well disciplined.

Semyon loosed another shot. But this time the bolt missed its target and four of the lookouts came hurtling down the steps, leaping over the bodies of the monks, making straight toward them.

Dunai gave a bloodcurdling whoop and ran out, whirling his sabre. "Let's show 'em what the *druzhina* are made of!"

"Drakhaon! Drakhaon!" yelled Semyon, throwing down the crossbow and drawing his sabre.

This was a disaster. Lindgren watched for a moment, open-mouthed. Had the sight and smell of blood sent the *druzhina* mad? Blades clashed and sparks flew. Dunai fought like one possessed, his fair braids flying round his head. Semyon wielded his sabre with dogged determination, his freckled face set in a grim scowl of defiance. Already one of the lookouts had fallen back, clutching a slashed forearm, blood dripping through his fingers.

Lindgren rose, pistols primed, wondering how he could pick off his targets without harming either of the young *druzhina*.

But before he could fire, the shrine doors opened and the young woman appeared, surrounded by her companions. One of them was carrying a plain wooden casket. Was this what they had come for? And what treasure did it contain that merited all this bloodshed?

He saw the woman take a swift look at the skirmish in the courtyard below.

"Drakhaon!" shouted Semyon again at the top of his lungs.

The woman said a few words to her companion and he nodded.

"Put down your weapons," she ordered in the common tongue. "You're surrounded."

It was only then that Lindgren realized that the group who had gone to investigate the grenade explosion had returned and had crept up behind him.

There was nowhere to run. They were trapped.

CHAPTER 16

Malusha was late back from the market. Kiukiu fretted, unable to settle to any useful task, wandering from the cottage to the garden to gaze anxiously across the moors and back again. Grandma was not getting any younger, and if there were robbers lying in wait for unwary travelers on the moors, she might not be quick enough to outwit them.

Inside the cottage, Linnaius still slept, snoring faintly, a little spittle trailing down his chin.

What happens to me, Magus, if you don't regain your memory? Kiukiu felt a chill little shudder go through her. With every day that passed, she was growing older. All her cherished dreams might never come true.

Dreams of the two of them keeping house here together . . .

Gavril with easel and brushes, painting the moorlands; Kiukiu tending the kitchen garden, scattering seeds for the greedy hens; Kiukiu stirring a pot of savory soup over the fire, Gavril coming up and putting his arms around her waist, kissing the nape of her neck . . .

She hugged her arms tight around herself, trying to stop hope from leaking away. *It could still happen.* "Mustn't give up," she muttered to herself. "Mustn't . . ."

"Is that kettle on the boil, Kiukiu?" demanded a voice petulantly. "I need my tea."

"Grandma!" Kiukiu leaped up as guiltily as if Malusha had tapped into her daydreams. Her withered bones creaked and she winced, grabbing hold of the table to support herself. For a moment she had forgotten her predicament—and her body had reminded her in the cruelest way possible.

"And get out an extra cup. We've got company."

"Company?" Kiukiu looked up to see Malusha ushering a stranger into the cottage. A stockily built man with a broad, weathered face stood there, bowing his head, and smiling.

"This is Chinua, the tea merchant," Malusha said. "Chinua, this is my granddaughter Kiukirilya."

Chinua pressed his palms together and bowed again. "I am honored."

"M—me too." Kiukiu flashed a glance at Malusha, wondering what eccentric whim had made her invite the tea merchant back to the cottage. "Please sit down."

On their rafter perch, high above, the snow owls awoke and shifted, huddling together, as though sensing the presence of a stranger.

Linnaius let out a long, wheezing snore. Chinua raised one grey eyebrow inquiringly. "Is this the one you call the Magus?"

"That's him," said Malusha, taking out her purchases from the woven basket, "or what's left of him."

Chinua knelt beside Linnaius and laid his hand on the Magus's pale forehead. Kiukiu watched, intrigued. Chinua was obviously no ordinary tea merchant.

"He's in a very deep sleep. What did you give him?"

Malusha looked up from her unpacking. "Valerian tincture, mixed with balm to restore his nerves, and a little mountain gentian from above the snow line."

Chinua nodded, as though approving her choice of remedies. "He's not far away. I think we may reach him if we go now."

"Go now?" Kiukiu looked up to see Malusha carrying over little bowls of a strange-fragranced steaming tea.

Chinua untied his plain, dark jacket and removed it, folding it neatly. Beneath, Kiukiu saw he wore a necklace of jagged teeth. From his belt hung a little double-sided drum. "Let me be your guide," he said, smiling at her again. Kiukiu felt the little hairs rise on the back of her neck.

"Chinua is taking us to consult Master Oyugun, his teacher." Malusha handed her a little bowl of the dark-scented tea. Kiukiu sniffed it suspiciously; it smelled odd, musky and fusty, reminding her of the old oak casks in the wine cellars at Kastel Drakhaon.

"I take it this journey is not in this world," she said, raising the little bowl to her lips and taking a sip. "Ugh." She pulled a face. "What is this stuff? It's disgusting."

"A Khitari shaman draft. Drink it down in one gulp," said Malusha, pinching her nose shut as she swallowed the tea.

"*Now* you tell me!" Kiukiu copied her, grimacing as the vile-tasting tea slid down her throat.

Beside her, Chinua had softly begun to beat on his drum with his fingertips, murmuring a repetitive, one-note chant. Kiukiu sat back on her heels, listening. The drumbeats became louder, like the steady pad of soft paws, and the monotonous chanting drowsier. Her eyelids felt heavy; she strove to keep them open, but they kept drooping shut.

And then she saw the pathway, a long, dark road winding away into the distance. Ahead of her, a creature was loping along the road, its nose to the ground as if scenting a trail. It turned its head, and she saw that it was a black-and-silver wolf, its orange eyes bright with intelligence.

"Follow me," said the wolf in Chinua's voice. "I think I've found him."

"You're a *wolf*?" But even as she asked the question, Chinua had bounded away and she had to hurry to keep up with his fleet feet.

It was the strangest of strange gatherings, Kiukiu reflected, here in the desolate hinterlands of the Ways Beyond, where only shamans and spirit singers who walked the paths of the dead strayed. And strangest of all was the young man standing beside her. Tall and slender, with long, straight hair of alder-bark brown, he had an unnatural silver gleam in his grey eyes that helped her recognize him: their own Magus.

"Well now, Kaspar Linnaius," said Malusha, a slight smile playing around her lips. "Who'd have thought you were once such a handsome man? You must have broken a few hearts in your time."

Kaspar Linnaius looked down at his spirit form, then at Malusha.

"Malusha?" he said bemusedly.

"Who else?" she said. "Old in body, but young in spirit." And then she turned to Kiukiu and the smile froze on her lips. "But we must move fast, Kiukiu, if we're to save you."

"Why?" Kiukiu wavered, wondering why they were all staring at her.

"My dear child, you're fading. You must have lost so much spirit energy in the Realm of Shadows that you're all but a shade here yourself."

Kiukiu gazed down at herself and saw to her horror that Malusha was right. Her spirit-form was pale and insubstantial, as if it had been sketched on gauze.

"Lead on, Chinua," commanded Malusha, taking control.

The wolf Chinua sniffed the air and set off at a fast lope, calling, "Follow me."

I'm fading . . . Kiukiu glided forlornly after her grandmother. As if it wasn't bad enough to have woken up to find herself a grey-haired old woman, now her spirit energy was failing too. If she hadn't felt so oddly detached, she would have started to rail at Kaspar Linnaius for getting her into this wretched state.

"Why did you abandon your shaman skills, Kaspar?" Malusha asked. "What made you turn away?"

Kaspar Linnaius stared into the far distance. "In the village where I was born, it was considered a curse to be born with the silver eyes."

"Not all shamans have silver eyes," put in Malusha.

"When the people of my village discovered I could twist a wind with my fingers, they threw me out."

And as he spoke, Kiukiu glimpsed a young brown-haired boy, no more than nine or ten, standing alone in a green mountain pasture, gazing down on a village filled with neat timbered houses. Children played in the meadow below, sledging down the grassy slopes on pieces of wood. The sound of their carefree voices carried up to the boy who stood watching, knowing he would no longer be allowed to join in their games. She saw him shoulder his pack and turn away, trudging slowly off up the stony track.

Why? she wanted to ask. Why did they turn you out? Was it because of some terrible thing that you did? But the question remained unasked, for she suspected he would resist any probing that dug too deep.

"I went in search of a place where I would not be rejected. Where I could be trained to control my talents. It was well over a year till I found my way across the sea to Maistre Gonéry and the College of Thaumaturgy in Francia."

"So he took you in?"

"On the sole condition that I renounced my shaman heritage and learned to control and subdue my natural gifts. The college taught me that there were other routes to power and knowledge. I thought if I learned the secrets of alchymy and became a magus, I could start anew."

"Ha!" said Malusha. "So attending a college and changing your title made you somehow . . . respectable."

Kaspar Linnaius bridled at this. "You misunderstand me. The years of study I spent working in the laboratories of the college gave me scientific knowledge I could never have achieved as a simple village shaman." Kiukiu caught a glint in his silver-grey eyes. "And combining my natural talents with alchymical science gave me advantages I hadn't even dreamed of."

She had almost forgotten that this young magus was the same Kaspar Linnaius who had stolen her soul, then abandoned her to a living death in the Realm of Shadows. But that brief glint reminded her how dangerous Kaspar Linnaius had been before he lost his wits. Even now he had seduced them with his tale of a lonely child, rejected for his special gifts. And he had still not told them what had caused the people of his village to cast him out.

Chinua came bounding back. "My master is near," he called.

Kiukiu had learned the hard way not to trust the evidence of her eyes in the Ways Beyond; a lush green landscape could swiftly dissolve and leave the unwary spirit traveler lost in a dark forest, or stranded on a vast, empty plain. She had begun to understand how to see with her other senses.

The misty wasteland through which they had been traveling for so long was slowly melting away to reveal the sparkling water of a lake. And on a little curved wooden bridge spanning the lake stood a man, leaning on the rail to watch the water that flowed beneath. Kiukiu caught a flash of gilded scales and saw there were carp in the lake.

Chinua rushed eagerly up to the man, his plumed tail wagging; more a faithful dog, Kiukiu thought, than a wolf.

"Gently now, Chinua, you'll frighten the fish," said the man, straightening up and absently patting the wolf's head.

"This is Master Oyugun," said Chinua, frisking back toward them. His master had long mustaches, just like the whiskers of the gold and silver carp that swam in the clear waters.

Kiukiu found herself bowing to Master Oyugun as he approached. There was something about him that commanded respect.

"You have lived long beyond your natural span of years, Kaspar Linnaius," said Master Oyugun. "Only those who have bathed in the Jade Springs of Khitari can live so long—or, perhaps you once dared to pass through the Phoenix Fires?" The master's broad cheekbones and calm, benign smile reminded Kiukiu a little of Chinua in his human form.

"The Jade Springs," repeated Kaspar Linnaius slowly, memory lighting his silver eyes. "Yes, that was the place."

"Where are these Jade Springs?" demanded Malusha. "And will they do my Kiukiu any good?"

Master Oyugun's smile had faded. "There is a price to pay if you wish to bathe in the Jade Springs. Was this a choice you made willingly, Magus?"

"A price?" repeated Malusha. "What price?"

But Master Oyugun had turned from Kiukiu and was gazing intently into Kaspar Linnaius's eyes. Suddenly, the Magus lowered his head, as though the master had looked too deeply into his soul.

"You must examine your motives very closely before you seek out the Jade Springs," said Master Oyugun, "for no one who enters the waters comes out unchanged."

Kiukiu wondered what he could mean. She wanted more than anything to be changed.

"It's not easy to be gifted with the silver eyes. I can see that you have suffered much in your long life. And you have also done much harm." Master Oyugun reached out to touch the Magus's face, tipping his chin upward so that he could not glance away. "Yet you will have one chance to make reparation, Kaspar, child of the North Wind. There are many who depend on you—and in a perilous time yet to come, they will rely on you and you alone, to make a choice."

"One chance?" Linnaius seemed puzzled.

"And now I must feed my carp." Master Oyugun turned away and shuffled back toward the wooden bridge.

"Master—" began Linnaius. Chinua shook his thick coat and nudged the Magus.

"No more questions," he said. "Time for you to find your own answers."

"This is an old herd trail I follow sometimes on my way back from the tea traders," said Chinua. "It leads across the eastern steppes to the shores of Lake Taigal. There you will be able to buy a passage across the lake to the northern shores."

"That's quite a grueling journey for these two old ones," Malusha said, jerking her thumb toward the Magus and Kiukiu as they sat in the back of the pony cart. They had hitched Chinua's sturdy sorrel-and-white gelding Alagh, alongside Harim, and the two ponies jogged along side by side quite companionably.

"Grandma!" Kiukiu said, outraged to be called an "old one" by her own grandmother. And then she said again, more to herself than the others, "I shouldn't be going away without telling Gavril."

This journey had forced Kiukiu to confront her unspoken fear, the one she hardly dared admit, even to herself, the fear that haunted her uneasy sleep, that her fast-aging body might wear out before they reached Khitari—and she would die without ever seeing Gavril again.

CHAPTER 17

The Imperial Household Cavalry had pitched camp on the cliffs outside Haeven, directly overlooking the Straits. Eugene, unable to sleep, had ordered that the Vox Aethyria be placed in his tent, so that he could receive any further communication from Ruaud de Lanvaux firsthand. And while he sat there waiting, staring at the crystal Vox glittering dully in the lamplight, he tried to jot down all the arguments that occurred to him, for use in the coming negotiations. And yet all he could think of was Astasia, held against her will by the Francians. He hoped they had not put her in a cell, like a criminal. Surely they would not treat a pregnant woman with such insensitivity!

Eugene sensed Belberith suddenly stir within him, as though awakening with a start. He laid down his pen. The flame in the lamp flickered and nearly went out. Eugene glanced up.

"*Ahhh . . .*" whispered Belberith. "*There you are.*"

Half-clothed in shadow, a man stood in the tent doorway. An old soldier's instinct made Eugene's hand reach for the hilt of his sheathed sabre.

"Nagarian?" he said uncertainly.

"The same." Gavril Nagarian came in. There was an aura of smoky darkness about him, as if the shadows of night still clung to him.

"And my guards?" Eugene's hand still hovered near the sabre.

"It seems they heard a suspicious noise and went to investigate."

"Leaving their Emperor unprotected?" Eugene could not help but smile at the irony. He would reprimand them when Nagarian was gone. "So," he said, recovering from his initial surprise, "where is Linnaius?"

"In Azhkendir."

What game was Nagarian playing? "That was not part of our original bargain."

"He's only just clinging on to life. So I took him to Malusha; she's caring for him as best she can."

"I see." This was not what Eugene had hoped to hear at all; only now did he begin to realize how much he had been counting on Linnaius's wisdom to rescue them from their predicament.

"He was already on the pyre when I found him."

"So the rumors are true?" Eugene could not conceal another smile. "You snatched him from right under the Commanderie's nose?"

"There was no other way."

Eugene sat back in his chair. "I wish I could have seen it."

"He won't be much use to you—or me—in his present condition. Malusha plans to try to heal him with her spirit-singing skills."

So there was little point in looking to Linnaius for help. But how far could the young Drakhaon be trusted? Eugene decided to put him to the test. "The situation has changed since we last met. The Francians have Astasia."

"What's that to me?" Gavril Nagarian cast him a long, hard look.

"I know she was . . . important to you once. Don't deny it. I have the betrothal portrait you painted. Every brushstroke speaks of your feelings for her."

"What of it?" Nagarian shrugged. "She married *you*."

"The crux of the matter is—" Now that Nagarian was there in front of him, Eugene found it difficult to put his dilemma into words without losing face. "They're holding her hostage. And their terms—"

"Her life for your empire?"

"Her life—and the life of our unborn child."

Eugene saw genuine surprise in Gavril Nagarian's eyes. "Now you understand why I can't just swoop down on Enguerrand's château and carry her off, as you did with Linnaius. The shock could make her miscarry. I can't risk it."

"And so you plan to give in to the Francians' requests?"

Was Nagarian deliberately out to goad him? Every question was barbed.

"What choice do I have?"

"You'd sacrifice your empire for one woman?"

"I seem to remember a certain Azhkendi lord who gave himself up to his enemy to save the lives of his household."

Nagarian gave a brief nod, acknowledging that Eugene had scored a point. And then he looked up, fixing Eugene with the full power of his Drakhaoul-blue eyes. "*They* won't let you." His voice was barely a whisper. "You know that, don't you? They are scheming together. Haven't you heard them? Talking to one another?"

For one disconcerting moment, Eugene remembered the wild-eyed, distraught prisoner he had visited in the cells in Mirom. Then he believed that the loss of the Drakhaoul had driven Gavril Nagarian mad. Now he began to wonder if that madness had ever been fully exorcised.

"There are *others* at large. You set them free from the Serpent Gate when you summoned Belberith." Nagarian's voice was still low, desperately intense. "I don't know what they intend. I don't know where they are. But they are growing stronger."

"Other Drakhaouls?" Eugene regarded Gavril with some skepticism. Belberith had never alerted him to such a possibility.

"And look at me." Nagarian pulled open the neck of his shirt and Eugene saw that the stippling of metallic blue spots extended down from his face to his throat and shoulders.

"You used your powers."

"Not since we fought together. But there have been times of late when I have not been responsible for my own actions. Do you understand what I'm saying? Even now I can't be certain that I'm acting alone. That there isn't some motive other than my own driving me to come here. Or why I'm being allowed to speak to you. Be on your guard, my lord Emperor." The blue eyes burned into his with such passion that Eugene felt a terrible sense of foreboding overwhelm him. "The Francians may prove the least of your worries in the days to come—" He broke off with a sudden sharp indrawing of breath, as though in pain. The luminous shimmer in his eyes dimmed. Eugene watched, puzzled. Was it the cravings that were affecting him and causing such a dramatic reaction?

"What's wrong, Nagarian?"

"My *druzhina*," he said, a strange, stricken look on his face. And he turned on his heel and hurried from the tent.

"Wait a moment!" Eugene strode after him but he had already taken to the air, melting into the gathering clouds.

Jagu stared from the shrine door at the carnage below. Bodies lay sprawled across the entrance: both monks and his own Guerriers. He could see blood trickling slowly down the steps. The air stank of gunpowder.

"Drakhaon!" yelled a defiant voice.

There, surrounded by his Guerriers, stood three strangers; one wore a Tielen uniform, the other two looked like barbarian warriors from an earlier age, with their tattooed faces and war braids.

And Jagu remembered the enigmatic words that the Grand Maistre had whispered to him before they set sail for Azhkendir. *"You'll be in the Drakhaon's demesne; don't neglect to gather any information that could be of use to us in the war to come."*

"The war to come," he repeated under his breath. He looked at the two warriors and saw that, in spite of their ferocious appearance, they were very young, one scarcely more than a boy.

What better way to learn about the Drakhaon than from his own men?

"Take those two alive."

"Are you mad, Jagu?" Celestine cried, aghast. "Let's just get out of here before reinforcements arrive."

"I'm merely obeying instructions."

"You'll never take us alive!" yelled the taller of the two Azhkendi warriors, whirling his sabre about his head as he rushed toward the steps.

"No, Dunai!"

Jagu saw the Tielen raise his hand in a vain gesture, as if to stop the boy. He heard the dull thud of pistol-stock blows on flesh and bone. The two Azhkendi warriors toppled and fell at the feet of their attackers. The Tielen slumped to the ground, unconscious.

"Bind them, hand and foot," Jagu ordered. "But leave the Tielen."

"They'll only slow us down." Celestine pushed past him, daintily lifting the hem of her robes to avoid soiling them in the spilled blood. She turned at the gateway and said, "Well, what are you waiting for, Jagu? The Drakhaon? Didn't you hear? They called for him."

*   *   *

Gavril flew high above the Saltyk Sea.

"*Drakhaon . . .*"

Many weeks had passed since he had left Kastel Drakhaon, and in all that time he had had no communication with his *druzhina*. He had even begun to wonder if the connection between them had been severed when Eugene bested him and he had plunged, burned and defeated, into the sea off Ty Nagar.

Why were his men in danger? Captain Lindgren had given his word that the mine works would be shut down. And he felt in his heart that he could trust Nils Lindgren to keep his word. The Tielen captain had shown genuine concern for the *druzhina*'s safety when the rockfall had trapped them below ground.

"*Drakhaon . . . help us . . .*"

The distant appeal for help came again. His blood responded to it even before his mind had fully registered what was happening. His wingbeats quickened. His senses sizzled alert as he crossed the western mountains and turned his head toward Kastel Drakhaon.

Eugene stared desultorily at a map of New Rossiya and its neighboring countries. He traced again with one finger the rocky outline of Smarna, lingering over the wide Bay of Vermeille.

"No other alternative," he muttered.

Negotiations were still in progress on board the Francian ambassador's ship. He could do nothing but wait to hear the outcome. And he did not like being made to wait.

The enforced inactivity was almost more than he could endure. He had sent for a fresh uniform and had his valet Jakob trim his unruly hair. Jakob, who had been in Eugene's service since his first military campaign, was both reserved and discreet, qualities that Eugene valued greatly in one who was obliged to deal with his most intimate needs. But he was certain he heard the usually taciturn Jakob tutting quietly as he swept up the glittering clippings even though the valet had made no comment as he snipped away.

"The Chancellor has returned," Gustave announced.

Eugene started up from his desk as Maltheus entered. "What news?"

"It could be better, highness."

Suddenly all Eugene's pent-up frustration burst out. "I will not negotiate with Enguerrand's lackeys! Let Enguerrand meet with me, face-to-face. Why must he hide behind his ministers?"

"They were at pains to remind me that the Empress is in their custody."

"So now they mean to humiliate me! To make me beg for my wife's life!"

Maltheus listened patiently. When Eugene had calmed down a little, he said, "I've done as you requested." He accepted the little glass of aquavit silently offered by Gustave. "King Enguerrand and his ministers will meet with us in the most neutral territory we could arrange: on board the barque of the Allegondan ambassador, some twenty miles offshore."

"Well, let us thank God for Allegonde's impartiality." Eugene could not hide a certain bitterness from his tone; Maltheus had attempted to woo Allegonde to the New Rossiyan point of view but the prudent Allegondans had elected not to be drawn into the conflict.

Maltheus downed his aquavit and held out his glass to Gustave for more. He looked tired, and one of his eyelids had developed a slight twitch.

"What does Enguerrand really want, Maltheus?" Eugene asked softly.

"Your empire, highness. He wants New Rossiya."

"Yes, but *why*? Do you really believe this story about opening up trade routes to Djihan-Djihar and beyond? I want to know who's manipulating him—and to what ends. Is it his mother, Aliénor? Or is it Grand Maistre de Lanvaux?"

"God help us if de Lanvaux's set him on some divinely inspired mission to convert us all." Maltheus beckoned Gustave over to refill his glass again.

"We need better intelligence. If only young Velemir hadn't come to grief in Smarna."

"We're not entirely certain that he's out of the game, highness."

"Oh?" Eugene looked at Maltheus with renewed interest.

"We 'intercepted' a communication from Smarna to Francia. We think the Smarnans may be using him as an interpreter. It's thanks to him that we are aware what's really happening in Colchise."

Eugene nodded, unable to prevent himself from smiling. "A triple agent. How long can he survive before the Francians smell a rat?"

"He may yet prove as resourceful as his uncle," said Maltheus with a chuckle, "if he can extricate himself from his present predicament."

This was the best news Eugene had heard in a long while. And in that moment, he saw clearly what his next move would be. A move that would not prove popular with his council but which might yet surprise his enemy.

"I can see no alternative, Maltheus, but to cede Smarna."

Maltheus's eyebrows shot up. "And let the Francians control the trade routes?"

"Smarna has been nothing but trouble. The Francians have no idea what they've taken on. I could take great pleasure in sitting back and watching Grand Maistre de Lanvaux and his Commanderie crows attempting to tame the rebels. Let's see if they fare any better than we did."

"But to sacrifice one fifth of the empire—"

"One fifth which cost us most of the Southern Fleet."

"Then there's the border with Muscobar—"

"We need to be seen to be making concessions."

Maltheus fell silent a moment, digesting what Eugene had said. "We'll have a hard time justifying this to the council. Many lives were lost fighting the Smarnan rebels. Many families lost a son, a brother, a father there . . ."

Eugene had already anticipated this argument. "And many more lives will be lost if we don't buy ourselves a little time to rearm and regroup."

"But it will be seen as a defeat. Your first significant defeat."

Eugene leaned forward across the map to gaze into the Chancellor's eyes with all the conviction he could muster. "Trust me in this, Maltheus."

CHAPTER 18

Nils Lindgren became aware of a roaring sound in his ears. Then the roaring intensified, changing to a slow, intense pounding that vibrated through his whole skull.

He opened his eyes and winced as daylight blinded him.

"I think he's coming round." The voice was a woman's, brisk and cheerful. Her face loomed over his. "Well, officer, how are you feeling?" she asked in Tielen.

"Ahh." Lindgren slowly put one hand to his head. Little tingles of pain radiated out from beneath what felt like a bandage, and he let his hand drop back again. "What happened?"

"You took a nasty blow to the side of the head. But we've bound you up. What's your name, officer?"

He tried to remember. "Lindgren . . . Nils Lindgren. Captain."

"So your memory's unaffected. Good! I think you'll live. Would you like some tea?"

"My memory . . ." Lindgren's last recollection was of a chaos of shouting voices. Then there had come a blow like a thunderclap and blackness, nothing but blackness. He gazed around, slowly taking in his surroundings. He was lying in a long, low, lime-washed room filled with makeshift beds, every one occupied. Monks in grey robes moved between the beds, speaking in hushed voices as they tended to the wounded. The sharp smell of wound salve barely hid the rank taint of blood.

"The *druzhina*!" He tried to sit up, and the room spun. "Where are the boys?" Determined to find them, he staggered to his feet and stood there, swaying, having overestimated his strength.

The woman who had gone to get him tea came hurrying back. She set down the mug and took hold of him, helping him lie back. "You must rest, Captain."

"My two Azhkendi lads." He felt responsible for them even though they had disobeyed his orders. "Where are they? Are they alive?" How would he break the news to Askold if Dunai, his eldest son, had fallen defending the monastery?

"There were no boys among the casualties," she said. "Two of the monks were killed and half a dozen more seriously injured. The others are walking wounded, like yourself."

Only then did he take a good look at her. She was sturdily built, with sandy hair peppered with silver strands pulled back in a no-nonsense knot. But her brown eyes belied her severe appearance: shrewd and sparkling with wry amusement beneath pale lashes. She reminded him a little of his formidable aunt Tilde who ran an academy for young gentlewomen in Tielborg.

"What are you doing in an Azhkendi monastery?" he asked, raising his mug unsteadily to his lips.

"The Emperor sent me."

Lindgren, surprised, slopped his tea down his front.

"My name is Hildegarde. Doctor Frieda Hildegarde." She leaned forward and dabbed the spilled tea from his shirt. "I have some urgent information for his imperial highness which I believe you may be able to transmit to him."

Nils Lindgren felt his head begin to throb again. What was going on? He had not expected to encounter one of the Emperor's agents in this lonely monastery.

"Let me take that for you," she said, firmly prising the mug from his hands.

"The pilgrims," he said, "what did they want? What did they steal?"

"They were no pilgrims, Captain," she said and the twinkle faded from her eyes. "They were our enemies, the Francian Commanderie. And they stole the monastery's treasure, Saint Serzhei's golden crook. The monks are utterly distraught. It's been kept safe here for hundreds of years."

"Any enemy casualties?" Lindgren hoped there might be an opportunity for interrogation.

"They took their wounded away with them. The operation was well planned and ruthlessly executed."

"We must blockade the port," Lindgren struggled up again. "I must get word to my men—"

A shadow darkened the sun and plunged the little hospital into sudden darkness. Shouts of terror came from outside.

"What's that?" demanded Doctor Hildegarde, marching across to the window to gaze out as the daylight returned. And then she let out a loud whistle. "I never thought I'd live to see the day." Lindgren thought she sounded impressed. "So it's all true. What a magnificent sight!"

Lindgren stumbled toward the window and looked out. There, glimmering dully in the cloudy evening light, crouched a creature torn from the pages of his boyhood storybooks—a great winged dragon, whose wild blue eyes burned fiercely as it slowly scanned the courtyard. A group of terrified monks cowered in a corner.

"Lord Nagarian," said Lindgren softly. "What brings you here, I wonder?"

And even as they stared at the Drakhaon, the air around him shimmered. A fine, dark mist arose in a fast-spinning spiral, and just as swiftly melted away, revealing a man standing where the dragon had been. But no ordinary man; a torrent of wild dark hair, more blue than black, cascaded down his back. His skin still shimmered, as though covered in a fine dust of sparkling scales. And the nails on his hands were long, curved, cruel talons, glinting like shards of blue glass.

"Where's Abbot Yephimy?" he cried. "And where are my *druzhina*?"

"It was a good ruse." Jagu felt pleased with himself. Their earlier journey to Azhkendir had afforded him the opportunity to map the remote and rugged coastline that lay beyond the monastery, to spy out little bays and inlets where a small vessel could hide, unremarked by the few local boats that fished this stretch of water.

"It was messy." Celestine had said nothing till then.

"Yes. That was unfortunate. But who would have guessed that the monks would take up arms against us?"

"And those boys." He could tell she was still displeased from the little frown creasing her forehead. "Was it really necessary to bring them along with us?"

"The Maistre wanted more intelligence about the Drakhaon. Who better to supply it than the Drakhaon's own men?"

The little frown deepened. "What better way to bring the Drakhaon storming after us?"

Why didn't Celestine understand? He sensed a rift opening between them. Was it because she had always led and he had followed unquestioningly?

They led their horses along the steep, stony track that zigzagged down the side of the cliff toward the cutter that lay waiting for them in the sheltered cove below. Jagu stopped halfway down to signal to the captain to send out a rowboat to pick them up.

As they reached the beach, a few grey gulls, disturbed from the rock pools, flapped away.

A ragged girl, skirts tucked up immodestly high, revealing the sunburned brown of her thin legs, was wading in the rock pools, dragging a net through the sandy water. Farther off, a grey-bearded man was emptying crab pots.

"Now we've been seen." And Jagu had hoped they could slip quietly away, so that if the Drakhaon came after them, they would be impossible to trace.

"Shall we silence them, Lieutenant?" asked Viaud, his souslieutenant.

"No. There's been bloodletting enough today."

"Are you sure that's wise?" Celestine gave him a pointed look.

In response to their signal, a rowboat had set out from the cutter and was drawing near. Jagu led his horse out into the lacy tide.

"It'll take two trips with these prisoners," Celestine complained. "And that will only delay our escape."

"You take the crook and get on board first." Jagu lifted her down from her horse and carried her out through the lapping waves to the waiting rowboat. For a moment he felt the warmth and softness of her slender body in his arms, close to his heart, and a surge of forbidden love and desire washed through him. He hastily set her down and let the sailors steady her. "If the Drakhaon appears before we've joined you, just set sail. I'll try to hold him off. Save yourself."

Jagu strode back through the frothing tide. He noticed that the young girl was watching them, her mouth open, as she leaned on her net. The grey-bearded man straightened up from his catch and shouted at her. She flinched at the sound of his voice and, hitching up her trailing skirts, lowered her head and began sifting through the sediment again with her net.

Perhaps Viaud was right. Perhaps the witnesses should be eliminated.

Jagu peered out into the cloudy light reflecting off the waves. The rowboat was returning. There was no time to waste on silencing a few impoverished fisherfolk.

"Viaud, let's split the men between us; four will go with you and the other four will come with me to guard the prisoners. As soon as we've cast off, I want you to take the horses back through the forest to Arkhelskoye."

"Very good, Lieutenant."

As Jagu was rowed out to the cutter, he found himself scanning the sky and the headland. He wished he was still in possession of the angelstone so that they could have some warning if a Drakhaoul were near. The two prisoners lay half-conscious in the bottom of the rowboat. One let out a soft, low moan and then lay still again. He was little more than a boy with the faintest shadow of ginger hair darkening his upper lip. And for a moment Jagu's conscience pricked him, knowing what they would be subjected to at the hands of the inquisitors.

"But this is the price you pay for following a corrupt and evil master," Jagu murmured as the sailors hauled the prisoners one by one up into the cutter.

"What do you want, Drakhaon?" Abbot Yephimy, supported by two of the brothers, confronted Gavril. The abbot's voice was slurred, his eyes slid from side to side as if not focusing correctly and his powerful frame sagged against the monks holding him upright.

Gavril stood, slowly taking in the scene of carnage. He could see bodies covered by bloodstained sheets. A sandaled foot protruding from beneath one of the sheets told him that there had been monks among the casualties.

"What happened?"

"We were attacked." Yephimy's strong voice trembled. "Attacked and the shrine violated. Our most precious relic has been stolen."

"Who attacked you?"

"The Francian Commanderie."

Gavril swung around and saw Nils Lindgren, white-faced, propping himself up against a door frame. His head had been bandaged and there was a small stain of blood leaking through, staining the dressing.

"They took two of your *druzhina*, Lord Drakhaon: Dunai and Semyon. They put up a brave fight, but we were outnumbered."

"Dunai and Semyon?" Gavril repeated, not yet taking in all the implications of this act.

"And they stole our most precious relic: Serzhei's golden crook," said the abbot.

"The crook Saint Serzhei used against the Drakhaouls?" Was this what the Commanderie were planning? To find a second Sergius to turn them all to stone again?

"I beg you, Lord Drakhaon," Yephimy tottered a step or two toward him. "Go after the thieves."

"You want *me* to get the crook back?"

"The Drakhaon is in no fit state to go after anyone just yet, Abbot." It was a woman of middle years, her voice strong and forthright. "Captain Lindgren has sent orders to his men to blockade the port. Those relic thieves won't get far."

"I've two frigates standing by in Arkhelskoye," said Nils Lindgren. "They'll intercept the Francians and free your men."

Without the slightest hesitation or embarrassment, the woman marched over and draped a monk's grey robe around Gavril's naked body. "Frieda Hildegarde's the name," she said briskly. "I'm here on the Emperor's business. And I've made a discovery or two that may be of interest to you too."

Gavril sat shivering, still clutching his empty mug. Frieda Hildegarde had brought him hot herbal tea laced with the monastery's aromatic liqueur, and he was wishing he had not drunk it.

Outside, a detachment of Tielen soldiers had finally arrived from Lindgren's regiment. Gavril could hear him issuing orders, sending some in pursuit of the Guerriers, setting others to help the monks dig graves for the dead.

"They'll never catch them now," he muttered. *But if I take to the air again, I can track them down.*

"Did you know, Lord Drakhaon," said Doctor Hildegarde brightly, "that your ancestor, Prince Volkhar, was forced to ally himself with his older brother Helmar against his other brothers? It's all here, in this manuscript! Vakhtang and Teimur planned to murder them."

"Helmar?" Gavril, struggling to quell the rising nausea, found it hard to concentrate on what she was saying. He knew nothing of the legends of Artamon's time.

"The Emperor Eugene's bloodline can be traced right back to Prince Helmar. Don't you see, my lord," Doctor Hildegarde was getting more and more excited as she spoke, "that at one time your country and Tielen were allies? Your ancestors were allies!"

He began to grasp the gist of what she was saying. "Volkhar and Helmar fought the others together? But why? I thought they all hated each other."

"It seems from this account that these two agreed to bury their differences."

So Belberith and Khezef had once allied themselves against their kindred. Did they still remember their old allegiance?

"*Drakhaon . . .*"

Gavril's head jerked up, listening intently. His captured *druzhina* were calling for his help. And now the blood-oath scar on his wrist began to throb, the scar of the wound from which they had drunk his blood, the burning blood of the Nagarians.

"*Drakhaon . . .*" Only then did he begin to wonder why the Guerriers had taken his men hostage. Did they mean to torture them? What did they think they could learn from them? There was so much more he wanted to ask Doctor Hildegarde, but his questions would have to go unanswered for the time being.

"I must go after my *druzhina*." Gavril stood up; the white walls of the room wavered and he clutched at the back of his chair to support himself.

"You should rest a little longer, my lord," said Doctor Hildegarde sternly. "Let Captain Lindgren's men take care of this."

Gavril hardly heard what she said; he was already on his way to the courtyard.

"Promise me you'll come back," she called after him. "I've more to show you—so much more!"

"*Drakhaon . . .*"

Gavril spotted the Francian ship below him, a cutter, fast and trim, making good speed on the evening tide with a fair wind in her sails. He had followed the faint, despairing cry for help; as he hovered far above, he heard it again and knew he had traced Semyon and Dunai.

He circled slowly, too weary to think clearly. If he attacked the ship, everyone on board would either burn or drown and Serzhei's golden crook would be lost in the fathomless depths of the White Sea. Yet every time he heard the *druzhina* calling to him, his frustration grew harder to bear. He was Drakhaon, and yet he could do nothing to save them.

What would he tell Askold? That he had let the Francians take Dunai, his eldest son? He knew how fiercely proud the Bogatyr was of his handsome boy.

Gavril's strength was fast failing. He sought out the prevailing wind and let himself rest and glide a while.

Why had he tarried so long at the monastery? If only he had arrived before they embarked, he could have snatched them from their captors on the beach.

"*Blood . . .*" whispered Khezef. Suddenly Gavril found himself dropping toward the dark sea, tumbling over and over in the air. His tail thrashed the water; his wing tips grazed the caps of the waves. Then he was in the sea and it was so icy cold it stole his breath away, leaving him gasping with shock. The strong pull of the shoretide caught him, and washed him back toward the land.

The daylight was fading as the samphire-gatherers returned to the cove in ones and twos. Dotya, weary and desperately hungry, wiped one dripping hand across her forehead. Father was coming toward her and he would not be pleased with these meager pickings. Sure enough, he stared down at the basket, then hit her across the mouth. She was too slow, too tired to dodge the blow, and fell back onto the sand.

"How are we supposed to survive on this?"

Dotya put one hand to her mouth; she could taste blood, warm and salty, on her sore, swelling lip.

"Useless. Just like your mother." He was already tramping away up the beach, the sack containing the day's catch slung over one shoulder.

She struggled to her feet. "Wait, Father—"

He ignored her, trudging after the others as they made their way through the twilight, head down.

One of the older women called sharply to her from farther up the beach.

"Hurry along now, Avdotya. Night's coming."

Dotya turned her back on them. She did not reply. She was swallowing the sobs that kept trying to heave their way out. She stared at the sea, watching the ship, a tiny speck on the horizon. She had wanted to run after the strangers, to beg them to take her with them. She would have done anything to get away from the drudgery and misery of her life with Father, scrubbed decks, mended sails, *anything . . .*

She had felt sorry for him when he broke his leg. He said he needed the drink to numb the pain. But the leg had mended, after a fashion, over a year ago, and still he went on drinking. And when she tried to stop him, he hit her, swore at her, and called her "useless."

Well, she'd had enough of it. If she was useless, he would do better without her to hinder him! She stared out across the sea, seeing the single evening star, bright as a glittering raindrop against the thinning clouds.

"Avdotya . . ." They were still calling her name, their voices faint as the cries of distant gulls skimming over the waves. Let them call. She didn't care.

A chill little breeze shivered across the sea. She glanced around, suddenly ill at ease.

"Is anyone there?"

Now Dotya remembered the stories told around the fireside of the savage beast that stalked the forest, the dragon with eyes of blue fire that snatched and devoured young girls, tearing their tender flesh with its sapphire claws. Suddenly her skin went cold and prickly with goose bumps. Because she had the strangest feeling that something was crawling out of the sea, dragging itself up the beach behind her.

"Help me . . ."

She dropped her damp bundle, samphire spilling out. Turning again, she saw a figure slumped on its face in the sand.

A drowned man. Or half-drowned, for he had life enough in him yet to call out to her for help.

She wavered. Should she go back to the village? Her father was as like to strip him of his valuables and leave him to die.

"Please help me . . ."

He sounded so desperate. And he was speaking her own tongue,

Azhkendi. If she saved his life, he was sure to reward her. She turned and went down the beach toward him.

Kneeling in the wet sand beside him, she put out one shaking hand and touched his wet hair, long and dark as strands of seaweed. His eyes were closed, yet he let out a shuddering moan at her touch.

"Are you hurt?" she whispered. She had nothing with her to bind up his wounds but the damp folds of her ragged skirt. Gently she raised his head onto her lap and saw that he was young and good-looking. His dark-lashed lids fluttered open, revealing eyes that glimmered blue as the evening star overhead.

"Thank you," he said and his voice was soft as the wash of the waves on the sand behind them. His hands moved, shakily at first, to touch her face, her neck, her shoulders.

Dotya wanted to look away, but found she could not; she could only gaze into his eyes, until she was drowning in deep, blue waters.

She was a scrawny girl, all long legs and tangled, unkempt hair that smelled of the sea, a fishergirl.

Gavril raised his head from his prey. He wiped one razor-taloned hand across his mouth and knew from the warm stickiness that it was stained with her blood.

"No," he said, backing away across the damp sand. "I said no more, Khezef. *No more!*"

The frenzy of hunger was gone. And in its place came the bitterness of self-revulsion. He touched the girl's face. There was no response. She lay limp, her fixed eyes staring at him, through him, at the stars.

Gavril threw back his head and let out a shivering howl of remorse.

I never meant to take your life. I never wanted you to die.

"How can I go on living with myself?" All the pent-up bitterness of the past weeks came flooding out. "How can I go back to Kiukiu with more innocent blood on my conscience?"

"Kiukirilya knows you are Drakhaon. She knows you do what you must to survive in this world."

"But I should be strong, strong enough to resist the urge to kill."

The tide was coming in, gently washing over the girl's body, as if reclaiming its own.

Gavril rose. He felt stronger. But this renewed strength had come at too high a cost. He stood looking down at the girl's body until he could no longer see it for the tears blinding his eyes. "If I can't resist, the reason's all too clear: I must have lost what little humanity was left to me."

"*If you had lost your mortal conscience, you would not still be here, grieving,*" said Khezef, and his tone was strangely gentle.

"And I never even knew her name."

Suddenly Gavril felt a deep sadness welling up within him.

"*What is this strange sensation?*" Khezef sounded confused. "*When I look at her . . . I feel . . . an emotion that is unfamiliar to me.*"

Slowly Gavril began to realize that a change was taking place in Khezef.

"*What's happening to me? I don't understand. It was just another death. One of so many. And yet, and yet . . .*"

"You're feeling remorse. And grief."

"*I had forgotten what it was like to experience mortal feelings like these. I can't let myself become weak.*" Khezef seemed to be struggling with himself.

"Why is it a weakness to feel compassion for others?"

"*Because I was made to destroy. An instrument of destruction cannot afford to feel compassion.*"

"An instrument of destruction? But you are so much more than that, Khezef."

There was a pause. But when Khezef spoke again, Gavril knew the daemon had managed to control the feelings that had threatened to overwhelm him.

"*Give her back to the sea. Let the sea take her.*"

Gavril hovered above the little cove, gazing out across the empty sea. He listened for voices calling to him, but all that he heard now was the sound of the waves and the wind.

He had wanted to play the hero, winging to his *druzhina*'s rescue. But he could still feel the rawness of Khezef's self-revelation resonating within him. Lindgren had told him that there were two frigates standing by at Arkhelskoye. The Drakhaon would just have to admit that he was fallible and rely on the efficiency of Eugene's navy to bring his lads back.

A yearning rose within him to be with Kiukiu again, a yearning so strong that it overmastered all other concerns. He needed to know she was still alive. He needed to be with her.

No tendril of woodsmoke rose into the sky from the crooked chimney of Malusha's cottage. And although a few hens were scratching around in the little yard, the place looked deserted.

Gavril alighted on a patch of springy moorland turf. He checked around the outside of the cottage and saw that the door had not been forced and the shutters were still barred.

He was tired. And to find that Kiukiu was not there made him feel more dispirited than he could have imagined. He leaned one hand against the doorpost and rested his forehead on the silvered wood.

The hens clucked expectantly around his bare feet. Left to forage for grubs and seeds by themselves, they had come hurrying up the instant he entered the courtyard. Now he remembered that Malusha kept the key under an old flowerpot in Harim's stable . . .

The stable was empty of both pony and cart. Perhaps they had gone to market in Azhgorod. He found the key and, hens still fussing at his heels, returned and unlocked the cottage door. Inside, the cottage smelled stale, of cinders and owl droppings; a single shaft of daylight filtered in through the owl hole in the roof. There was only the faintest shuffling from the beam where the snow owls roosted. He could make out three or four hunched, pale shapes high above his head.

Gavril found an open sack of grain in the corner and filled a bowl. The hens had followed him into the cottage, so he led them outside again and sprinkled grain around. This led to a greedy rush, with much vicious pecking and squawking.

"There's plenty for all," he called to them, scattering more grain as the speckled feathers began to fly.

He went back inside and unbarred the shutters to let in fresh air. Then he opened up Malusha's leather trunk and took out another of Malkh's shirts and the second pair of breeches.

"Dead man's clothes." The crumpled linen was redolent of old moth herbs and lavender. Yet Gavril could not help remembering that Malkh had been about the same age as he was now when the *druzhina* had tortured him to death.

Then he began to search around the cottage for any sign of a message. Kiukiu could barely write her own name but Malusha or Linnaius might have left him some clue as to their destination.

Crouching beside the hearth, he sifted the cold ashes through his fingers. So they had been gone some time. But where?

He rubbed his hands on his arms to try to warm them. He had been hoping for the comfort of a fire and food—and above all, he had been wanting to see Kiukiu. *Even if she's still angry with me—and God knows, she has every right to be.* There was not just the need to warn her, to protect her; there was his own aching need to be with her. They had parted badly and he wanted to make things right between them again.

But there was little point kneeling in the cinders feeling sorry for himself. He would light a fire and brew himself some tea.

Gavril shoveled up the ashes and cleaned the grate and as he did so, he remembered how every day Kiukiu had performed this service for him in Kastel Drakhaon, with never a murmur of complaint. Then he drew water from the well, laid a fire, and found the tinderbox to strike a spark for the kindling.

It was only then that, in the fire's flickering light, he noticed a tea caddy on the table. It reminded him of one that his mother had always treasured, a little black-lacquered jar, whose decorations, depicting white cranes and golden chrysanthemums, had faded over the years with frequent use. He opened the jar and the delicate, aromatic scent of dry jasmine tea wafted out, transporting him back to the Villa Andara. There he stood, six, maybe seven years old, guiltily looking down at the jar he had knocked over when playing with his ball in the kitchen.

"*It's only tea,*" he had protested. "*Only dry old leaves.*"

"*But, Gavril,*" he heard his mother saying as she swept up the precious leaves, "*this tea is special. It's come all the way from Khitari, carried by merchants across the mountains and then by tea clipper all the way to us here in Smarna . . .*"

"Khitari!" he cried, striking the table. "They've gone to Khitari!"

Gavril felt a sharp little nip on his shoulder. He found himself gazing into the round, ambered eyes of a snow owl sitting beside him. It took all his self-control not to cry out and startle it.

"Lady Iceflower?" he said. The snow owl nodded. "Why haven't you gone with your mistress?"

She turned her head right around and, following her line of vision, Gavril saw two young owls, nearly fully grown, perched on the top of Malusha's chair, solemnly regarding him.

"You have chicks. I understand."

She picked something up in her beak and dropped it on his chest. It was a dead mouse.

"Well, thank you," Gavril said, picking it up by its tail, not certain whether to feel honoured or repelled by the offering. "I *am* hungry . . . but I hope you won't be offended if I don't eat this. Perhaps your chicks would like it?"

Lady Iceflower hopped off and he sat up, wondering how long he had slept. The young owls were eyeing the mouse greedily. He tossed it to them and one caught it in his beak. An undignified tug-of-war ensued between the two which their mother watched.

Gavril searched among the jars on Malusha's dresser and found dried oats and honey. The fire he had made had gone out. It would take a while to light a new one, boil water, and make porridge. There were eggs in plenty from the hens and herbs in the vegetable garden so he would not starve.

But after he had eaten, and soaked the porridge pot with well water to loosen the crust around the rim, he went out onto the moors again, Lady Iceflower flitting after him, like a white shadow. Even though he had slept, he still felt oddly listless and drained.

Thank God Nils Lindgren has the situation in hand.

Gavril took the path up through the browning heather to the place where he and Kiukiu had last walked together. He had glimpsed in her eyes the steadfast, true courage that had first made him fall in love with her. But how old and frail she had looked, as if each tottering step drained a little more of her ebbing life force.

"I must go to her, Khezef!" he cried aloud. He flung his arms wide to the sky. He waited. A grinding, visceral sensation twisted through his body. It felt as though Khezef was struggling to wrench his wings out from inside him. Gavril toppled forward into the heather in agony. "Khezef, what's wrong? Why can't I transform?" Dark mists, the color of blood, swathed his vision.

The Drakhaoul's reply came haltingly. "*It's—as I warned you in*

Lutèce. You need to rest. You have pushed yourself far beyond your physical limits."

"But I fed. You made me feed." Gavril saw again the fishergirl's lifeless eyes staring up at the stars. "Was that innocent death for nothing?"

"*Each time your body takes longer to heal.*"

"And Kiukiu?" The question came out a sob of utter frustration.

"*You must be patient, Gavril.*"

CHAPTER 19

The lush grasslands of Khitari stretched on into the distant horizon, bright with summer flowers. On the moorlands in Azhkendir, Kiukiu had grown used to the muted shades of purple heather and yellow gorse, but here she saw blue poppies, wild delphiniums, drifts of white asphodel and nodding scabiosa.

"It's so pretty," she cried out in delight.

All that day, the next and the next, they traveled onward under a light, sunny sky without ever seeing another human. The air was warm, freshened by a light breeze, and smelled faintly of honeyed pollen. Little golden bees were busy among the flowers, and bright green grasshoppers whirred in the long grass. Once they glimpsed a herd of gazelles, their white tails bobbing as they skipped away.

"It's like the top of the world," Kiukiu mused aloud. "Empty. Unspoiled."

"We're no longer alone," said Chinua softly, pointing to a ridge in the distance. And there was the solitary figure of a horseman, sitting very still, watching them. "He's been shadowing us for some while now."

"Who is he?" Kiukiu could not see clearly but she thought she made out the outline of a bow strapped across the horseman's back. And as she shaded her eyes, the horseman turned his steed around and vanished over the far side of the ridge. She felt the peaceful, protected feeling vanish, replaced by a troubling sense of unease.

"Who was he?" she asked Chinua. "A lookout for bandits?"

"We've poor pickings," Malusha said.

Chinua said nothing but shook the reins and clicked his teeth to make the horses move faster. But soon a sound, like the rumble of distant thunder, disturbed the birds' song.

"What's that?" Kiukiu gazed around behind them and saw a troop of armed horsemen riding swiftly toward them, their horses' hooves scuffing up a cloud of pale, chalky dust. Old tales, whispered around the kitchen fire in Kastel Drakhaon, came back to her now, of unwary travelers crossing the steppes, robbed and strung up by their thumbs and left to die, or forced to eat their own flesh until they choked . . .

The horsemen were gaining on them and soon the cart was surrounded. Kiukiu gazed fearfully at their captors, seeing spears and slender, barbed arrows aimed at them, and dark eyes regarding them suspiciously from underneath metal helmets.

"Trespassers," said the foremost among them in the common tongue. "Identify yourselves." Kiukiu noticed the long, thin scar that ran from his right cheekbone to his jaw.

"We mean no harm," said Chinua, smiling back.

How can he be so calm at a time like this? worried Kiukiu. Her heart was thudding wildly.

"I'm Chinua, the tea merchant. This is Malusha—"

"Chinua?" interrupted the leader. He glanced at the other warriors. "Chinua the shaman?"

Chinua nodded.

"Come with us." One of the riders leaned down from the saddle and took hold of the reins.

"Come where?" Malusha demanded, rearing up from her seat.

"Sit down, old woman," said the leader.

"Grandma, please don't make a fuss." Kiukiu grabbed hold of her arm, pulling her back down.

"I won't be ordered about!"

Chinua spoke rapidly in the Khitari tongue to the horsemen. Another look passed between them. Then the leader replied and, snatching the reins back, tossed them to Chinua and rode to the head of the troop. One rider was dispatched to go on ahead; his horse sped away so speedily that he was soon lost to sight, hidden in the dust cloud scuffed up by his horse's hooves.

They set off, the riders forming an escort around them, so that Chinua was obliged to steer the cart in the direction they chose.

"You're not giving in to these bandits, are you?" Malusha's voice was shrill above the thud of the horses' hooves on the turf. "What have we got that they could possibly want to steal?"

"They are Khan Vachir's men," said Chinua. "His son is sick. They were on their way to find a shaman to cure him. I said to Captain Cheren that now they have three for the price of one." His broad face crinkled in a smile.

Malusha let out a snort of exasperation. "So now we must waste time, valuable time—"

"You do not say no to Khan Vachir."

Kiukiu, glancing warily up at their armed escort, could only silently pray that her grandmother would not offend the khan and get them all executed.

An hour or so later, Kiukiu spotted thin wisps of smoke on the horizon. The little cavalcade climbed one of the long, low, undulating hills and, on the other side, the khan's encampment was revealed.

Many large, round tents had been pitched on the grass where sturdy horses and ponies grazed. Brightly colored war banners and flags flapped in the breeze at all corners of the vast encampment. The smoke of cooking fires twisted in thin ribbons up into the blue sky.

"Don't they have proper houses?" Kiukiu whispered to Malusha.

"This is how the warlords live in Khitari," Malusha said with a shrug.

Beyond the tents, young riders practiced their archery, galloping at breakneck speed toward the targets, leaning dangerously far out to aim and loose their arrows.

Kiukiu watched, openmouthed at their daring. Not one of the *druzhina* was so skilled in horsemanship.

"I will bring you to Khan Vachir," said Captain Cheren.

One large tent was pitched apart from the others, with armored guards standing outside. The captain raised the door flap and ushered them inside.

A stern-faced man was sitting cross-legged on a cushioned dais. Although he was dressed in soft robes of the finest sky-blue silk, his bearing was that of a warrior, and his every gesture was lithe and precise. His weapons lay beside him on a cushion.

"These are the old women, mighty Khan," announced Captain Cheren.

Old women, indeed? How dare he! Kiukiu glared at the captain.

"You must show respect to Khan Vachir," he said in disapproving tones.

"Bow. Bow down, like this," said Chinua. He went down on his knees and leaned forward until his forehead rested on the carpet.

"You expect me to do that? With my rheumatics?" Malusha slowly copied him, muttering and groaning, as she knelt. Kiukiu followed, wishing she was not so stiff and slow.

"We will speak in the common tongue," said Khan Vachir. "Rise."

As she slowly raised her head, Kiukiu could not help staring in amazement at the rugs and hangings decorating the great tent. As her eyes became accustomed to the muted light, she noticed the gorgeous colors of the carpets on which they knelt. They showed intricate patterns in grass green, poppy blue, and saffron yellow, interwoven with stylized images: birds, camels, and flowers.

"My only son is very sick," said the khan. "And my shaman, Unegen, has failed to drive the illness from his body. He says the spirit that is causing his sickness is too powerful."

"So the child may be possessed?" Malusha glanced at Kiukiu. "I can make no promises, my lord Khan. But take us to the child and we'll see what we can do."

Captain Cheren led them from the khan's tent. A sturdy pony was tethered close by, cropping the stubbly grass. Although his coat was a rich chestnut red, with a distinctive white star on his muzzle, there was something about his stocky build and thick mane that reminded Kiukiu of Harim. She reached out to pat him, but he gave a disdainful toss of his head and moved away to a fresh patch of grass.

"Qulan is proud, just like his young master," said the captain. "But he's growing fat and lazy with no exercise." He stopped before another great tent. "The prince used to ride him all the time. Before his illness . . ."

He held open the fringed flap for Malusha, Kiukiu, and Chinua to enter. Inside, a group of women were seated on a couch. All were richly dressed, with their sleek black hair looped into intricate coils, interwoven with silken ribbons. They carried fans of painted paper with which they were stirring the air.

"Bow," whispered Malusha, nudging Kiukiu sharply. Still painfully stiff, Kiukiu managed to lower her head in what she hoped would pass for a gesture of respect. Chinua was already on his knees.

Incense smoke hazed the air. The smell was not unpleasant but reminded Kiukiu of the camphor crystals Sosia used to fumigate the kastel latrines. Little rocks of perfumed incense glowed like live coals in a dish of enameled metal placed before a small shrine.

"Where is the child?" asked Malusha.

The women all rose, moving aside in a swish of heavy brocade gowns to reveal a little bed lined with woven rugs and cushions of soft fur. On the bed lay a boy of nine or ten years. His black, silky hair was stuck in damp strands to his glistening forehead and his eyes were closed. But the instant Kiukiu saw him, she experienced a strange jolt of recognition.

"I think I know him, Grandma," she said under her breath to Malusha. "But how is that possible?"

Malusha glanced at the silent women, who were still gently waving their fans to cool the child.

"What's his name?" she asked, reverting to the common tongue.

"Bayar," said the youngest of the women. A little girl-child was clinging to her skirts, sucking her thumb. "He is my son."

"This is Orqina-Khatun, first wife to Khan Vachir," said another woman. "You may call her Lady Orqina."

"May I touch him?" Kiukiu asked. But as she extended her hand toward Bayar, a vicious growling sound began, and what she had taken to be a furry cushion uncurled itself, showing little yellow teeth. She snatched her hand away as the woman reached down and scooped up the fierce little creature and popped it inside her voluminous sleeve.

"Hush, Chagan!" she said.

"Is that really a dog?" Kiukiu asked, amazed that a dog could be small enough to be carried in a sleeve. She could just see the little black snub nose poking out from the green-and-gold brocade. And suddenly she knew she wanted a little sleeve dog of her own, to guard her pillow and lick her hand with its rough, pink tongue . . .

"Kiukiu!" said Malusha sharply. "What was it you sensed just now?"

Kiukiu laid her hand on the boy's forehead and closed her eyes.

Whisper of blue waves on a white seashore . . . distant laughter of children at play . . .

"No." Kiukiu opened her eyes. "Oh no." She did not want to visit that place ever again. Its dreamlike beauty was deceptive, the purity of the soft, pale sand, the deep, translucent blue of the sea. She knew too well that it concealed a terrible secret, like the shiny scarlet skin of an apple that hides black, worm-eaten decay at its core. The tranquil seascape was merely an illusion.

"What is it?" Malusha knelt beside her. "What did you see?"

Kiukiu slid her hand off the boy's hot, sticky fingers. "He's one of them," she said slowly. "One of the children of the Serpent God."

CHAPTER 20

Prince Bayar still lay without moving, little pearls of sweat dewing his upper lip. He seemed to be unaware that Kiukiu and Malusha were gently touching his face, his hands.

"Children of the Serpent God?" Malusha scratched her grey head in confusion. "Whatever do you mean, child?"

Kiukiu sighed. "He's *not alone,* Grandma." They had lapsed into the Azhkendi tongue and now she became aware that the watching women were glancing at each other uneasily over the tops of their fans.

"Spirit possession? A simple exorcism, then."

"No, Grandma!" Kiukiu lowered her voice. "Don't you remember? The last time I tried that—with Princess Karila—that was when I was tricked and trapped in the Realm of Shadows."

"But this spirit is slowly draining the little one's life force. Look how debilitated he is. He should be running around chasing his puppy and riding that fat little pony we saw outside."

"I know," Kiukiu said unhappily. "But these spirit children aren't like any others we've encountered. They won't—or can't—be exorcised, remember, Grandma? Not until their Drakhaouls have been banished from our world for good."

"Is there any hope for my son?" asked Bayar's mother anxiously.

Instantly Malusha altered her manner, bowing her head and adopting a reverent tone of voice. "Forgive us, my lady. We were debating the best way to heal your son—"

A man thrust his way into the tent and, pointing first at Kiukiu, then Malusha, began to shout out in the Khitari tongue, his face contorted with rage.

Chinua, who had been sitting cross-legged, patiently watching the proceedings, got to his feet and began to speak to the newcomer in quiet, reassuring tones.

"Witchwomen!" spat out the man, changing to the common tongue. His thin face was twisted with hatred. "Go home. This is no place for you."

"Who is this rude man, Chinua?" asked Malusha. "And can he be persuaded to leave?"

"This is Unegen, the khan's shaman," said Chinua.

"Ah. I see. He doesn't like competition."

Unegen had turned to Lady Orqina and was gabbling to her, emphasizing his words with furious gestures. Kiukiu began to feel more and more uncomfortable as the tirade continued. Unegen's eyes, as they flickered in her direction, flashed with malice. He looked like a wild man, with necklaces of yellowed animal teeth and a belt of foxes' tails. His unkempt hair and face had been smeared with streaks of a bright red paste, giving him a distinct air of malevolence. And his dirty clothing exuded a strange, feral odor; Kiukiu wrinkled her nose as she realized he smelled strongly of . . . *fox*.

Lady Orqina suddenly interrupted the shaman. Even though Kiukiu could not understand a word of what she said, the sharpness of her voice was unmistakable in any language. Unegen stopped shouting and dropped to his knees, bowing his head to the ground.

Two of the khan's men entered the tent and the women all turned away, hiding their faces behind their fans. Unegen was roughly hauled to his feet and dragged away.

"What was he saying?" Malusha whispered to Chinua.

"He was making threats. Against you, against me," said Chinua affably.

"Threats?" Kiukiu felt alarmed; the man's wild eyes had been filled with resentment.

"Don't worry. He is fox," Chinua said, sitting down again, "but I am wolf and wolf can defeat fox any time."

"Right, now where were we?" Malusha took up Malkh's gusly and settled herself into a comfortable position.

But Kiukiu had lost too much in that terrible place of dust and despair. *I can't. Don't make me go back, Grandma.*

"You'll be with me." Malusha squeezed her arm reassuringly. "Don't forget, child, I've rather more experience of the Ways than you." She unwrapped the gusly and tested the strings.

"But we can't send the children back. Back to where they should be." Kiukiu was jittery with apprehension now. "It can't be done. I've tried." Why couldn't Malusha understand?

"I'm ready. Are you?" Malusha began to pluck the slow, somber notes of the Sending Song and Kiukiu felt a shiver of revulsion at the sound. Then as her grandmother's strong voice rang out, she reluctantly joined in, ashamed to hear how feeble and quavery her own singing sounded.

The bright weavings in the tent blurred together, faded, and began to recede into wave upon wave of dark, drifting mist. Kiukiu heard the sound of the sea. And as the mists melted away, revealing the all-too-familiar seashore, the old, sick feeling of panic returned.

"I don't want to be here, Grandma."

"Look," breathed Malusha. There was Bayar, wandering along the edge of the white sands, letting the clear tide wash over his bare feet and picking up pebbles to skim across the waves.

"But where's *the other*?" Kiukiu kept glancing anxiously up and down the shore.

"Bayar," sang Malusha, "Bayar, come back home with us now. Your mother is waiting for you. And your little dog, Chagan, wants you to play with him."

Bayar turned and saw them. His black eyes, bright as polished onyx, rested on them with a look both proud and willful. "I don't want to come home."

"He's his father's son all right," murmured Malusha. But Kiukiu only half heard her. She was fearfully scanning the beach, remembering how swiftly the illusion had shattered last time. And she thought she had caught a glimpse of another child hiding from them between the trunks of the tall trees fringing the shore.

"I see you!" she cried. "Come out here and show yourself!"

"Why are you spoiling our game?" Bayar stamped his foot. "*I* was supposed to find him."

"Your mother will be sad if you don't come home." Malusha moved toward him, her voice honey-smooth. "And you don't want to make your mother upset, do you, Bayar?"

Bayar crossed his arms and turned his back on her.

This isn't going at all well, Kiukiu thought, as the chill, sick feeling grew stronger. She forced herself to concentrate. *When I was Bayar's age—which wasn't that long ago—what made me do as I was told? Apart from a sharp slap from Auntie Sosia?*

Memories of taunting games returned, of her much-loved doll snatched away, dangled just out of reach, then casually tossed into the muck of the pigpen by Ninusha, a year older and a head taller. And then there was the pretty little bone comb which Uncle Yuri had brought her back from a fair in Klim. Sosia had taken it away from her when she had neglected her housework tasks, threatening to give it to Ninusha instead.

"You'd better hurry back with us, Prince Bayar," she said, crossing the fine white sands toward him. "If you don't come now, your father is going to give your pony to"—she improvised desperately—"to your little sister." The bright, warm light seemed to be fading, as though distant clouds were gathering.

"He wouldn't dare." Bayar still stood, arms crossed, head turned away. But she had heard the slight waver of uncertainty in his voice.

Malusha nodded her approval to Kiukiu. "Come back with us now. That's the only way to be certain." She edged closer to Bayar.

"I'll bet your little sister's always wanted your pony. Hasn't she?" Kiukiu glanced behind her again and saw long shadows creeping across the shore toward them, turning the white sands grey as ash. And it was rapidly growing darker. A cold, sepulchral wind stirred the waves and rattled through the leaves. This was just as it had happened before. Kiukiu could taste the dust in her mouth and throat, the dead, dry dust of the Realm of Shadows.

"Grandma!" she cried in terror.

Malusha grabbed hold of Bayar by one arm; Kiukiu grabbed the other. The only way to escape the rising clouds of dust was to run straight into the sea, dragging the struggling boy with them. A last, brief glimmer of blue sky between the looming clouds promised escape. And as they leaped up into the darkening air, pulling Bayar with them, Kiukiu heard him yell above the moaning of the wind, "Koropanga! Cling on!"

There he was, Bayar's soul-child, the same wiry, dark-eyed, dark-skinned boy who had once implored her, *"Help us."* He had gripped hold of Bayar's foot and was being swept up and through the closing sky-portal by Malusha's spirit-powers.

"Koropanga," she said. "Your name is Koropanga!"

And then she was blinking in the incense-fumed light of the tent.

Bayar opened his eyes. "I want to see Qulan," he said in a voice that, although faint from fever, had lost nothing of its imperious tone.

Lady Orqina gave a little cry and rushed to her son's side, sweeping him up in her arms, hugging him and kissing him. The little dog tumbled out of her sleeve, righted itself, and started jumping about over the rugs yapping angrily. All the other women began to laugh and weep, clustering around the bed, while Bayar endured their attentions with a sullen expression.

Malusha's head was drooping over the gusly. She gave a start as all the commotion began and looked up at Kiukiu. Kiukiu saw exhaustion in her grandmother's eyes.

"That was close," Malusha said quietly. "And we did little enough; the boy is still possessed. This respite will only last a short while."

"But now we know *the other's* name," said Kiukiu.

"You've returned our son to us." Lady Orqina rose from her son's bedside and, pressing her palms together, bowed low. Malusha bowed back, nudging Kiukiu to copy her. "How can I thank you?"

"A bowl of tea would be very welcome," said Malusha, giving a little dry cough. "All this singing dries the throat."

The Khitari summer night was fragrant with the scents of grasses and wildflowers. Kiukiu lay awake, staring up at the stars, which spread like drifts of tiny white daisies in a dark meadow above her. Nearby she could hear Harim and Alagh contentedly chomping the rich grass and giving the occasional breathy snort.

"I have to go back," she said to the stars.

"What's that?" Malusha half heard her and opened one eye.

"I have to go back to find those children."

"It's far too dangerous. I won't hear of it. Besides, we have to get you to the Jade Springs first, or had you forgotten?"

But Kiukiu could not stop thinking about Koropanga and Tilua: young lives pitilessly destroyed to fulfill the dark dreams of ambitious and ruthless princes.

"It's bad enough that they were murdered," she said softly, "but to be trapped in the Realm of Shadows, to be kept from their rightful place in the Ways Beyond . . . Is there no way we can make things right again, Grandma? No way to stop Princess Karila or Prince Bayar slowly fading away, just as I've done?"

But the only reply she had was a gentle snore; Malusha was sound asleep.

Kiukiu opened her eyes to a bustle of activity. All around them, the khan's men were busy dismantling the tents and loading them onto carts. The early light from the sun, just rising over the eastern steppes, dazzled her so that when a shadow fell across her and she glanced up, she could not make out who the tall man was at first. When she saw it was Khan Vachir, she tried to bow, only tangling herself up in her blanket and embarrassing herself even more.

"We break camp today," said Khan Vachir. "Now that my son is well again, we travel to Lake Taigal. You will travel with us."

"I—we will?" Malusha was awake now, knuckling the sleepdust from her eyes.

"Chinua has told me of your quest. I offer you my protection in thanks for your healing skills."

"Thank you, my lord Khan," said Kiukiu, surprised at the generosity of this unexpected gesture.

"And you will watch over my son. You will ensure that he does not fall sick again." With this brusque command, the khan turned and walked away.

Chinua approached, smiling and nodding.

"You must eat now, before we break camp," he said. "There is tea to drink, yogurt, and mare's milk. I could get you some whey cakes, if you like. Or freshly roasted marmot?"

Kiukiu pulled a face. "Just tea for me, thank you."

Malusha whispered, "We've still got a little rye bread left. We can dip it in the tea when no one's looking."

"Let's face it, Grandma," said Kiukiu, looking regretfully down at their last loaf, "we're going to have to learn to like Khitari food soon—or starve."

Chinua's cart set off, following the winding caravan, behind a herd of long-haired yaks. Harim seemed to be thriving on the diet of Khitari grass and trotted on amiably enough beside Chinua's red-and-white-dappled pony. The Magus stared at the sky and muttered from time to time under his breath in a foreign tongue that Kiukiu did not recognize. The motion of the cart and the warmth of the afternoon sun lulled her into a doze . . .

It was growing hotter. She fanned her hand across her face, wondering why the sunlight was so strong. Then she heard the whisper of waves close by and realized that she was back on the children's imaginary island, with the lacy tide lapping at her toes.

Who's called me back? Why am I here?

"Kiukirilya!" Farther up the beach, a dark-haired boy was waving at her teasingly, jumping up and down.

"Koropanga?" she called out.

"Catch me if you can!" The boy darted away, lithe as a young hare, plunging into the forest.

"Wait." Kiukiu went after him, in among the swaying trees.

"Catch me!" Koropanga was swinging upside down from a branch above her head.

"Oh! You startled me, Koro—" she began but he was already on the move again. At least it was shady out of the hot sun under the great, glossy green leaves.

"I want answers," called Kiukiu sternly. "Where are the other children?"

Dark eyes gazed at her warily from the curling fronds. "Some are here. Others . . ."

"All this is illusion, isn't it?" Kiukiu spread out her arms, encompassing the shore, the sea, and the jungle. "Your illusion?"

"This is all we remember of our home." The boy rose from his hiding place and Kiukiu winced as she saw the dark, jagged wound gaping across his throat. "But as our memories fade, so it fades too. Set us free."

"Why me?"

"You are special. You are strong. You've been touched by a Drakhaoul—and lived."

"But how can I set you free if I don't know who you all are? You've got to help me. Tell me more."

"Koropanga." The air shimmered and Kiukiu saw the boy freeze in terror as a shadow materialized directly behind him. *"Do you dare to disobey me?"* With one blow of the back of his hand, the shadow sent the child crashing to the ground.

Kiukiu let out a cry of outrage.

"And you, Spirit Singer. Why are you here again?"

Nagazdiel came toward her. Suddenly reaching out, he cupped her face in one clawed hand, drawing her close. She tried to twist away but the dark brilliance of his blazing eyes seemed to burn through to her soul.

"I am growing stronger, as you can see, with the life essence that these children bring me. Soon I shall be strong enough to break free of this place."

"But if you break down the gateway into my world, you'll only let the darkness in with you." Kiukiu struggled to speak. "You'll make my world another prison. Another Realm of Shadows. Is that what you want?"

"You dare to question my will, Spirit Singer? I, who was a prince of the Heavenly Warriors?"

She glimpsed for the briefest blink of an eye a ruined majesty beneath the darkly glittering Drakhaoul carapace, the shadow of a being once noble and proud, eaten away by anger and despair.

"What can you do to stop me? You are nothing." He flung her down, turned, and continued on his way.

When he had gone, she just lay there, shaking. Corrupted by the emptiness she had glimpsed at the core of its being, she felt a numbing sense of hopelessness. The children were trapped there for eternity and nothing she could do would ever set them free.

"Nothing," she repeated. "I am nothing . . ."

"Kiukirilya. Wake up."

Kiukiu started awake to see Malusha's face close to her own. It was dusk and the khan's men were lighting torches. The cart had stopped.

"You were back there again, weren't you?" Malusha said. A sharp breeze was blowing the torchflames.

"He said I was nothing," whispered Kiukiu. She could still feel the black aura of despair infecting her mind.

"Why did you go back?" Malusha clicked her tongue against her teeth disapprovingly.

"I—I couldn't help myself. I heard Koro calling to me. He called me and I had to go."

Malusha gently placed her hands on either side of Kiukiu's face. "You mustn't go back again. Not until you've regained your strength. This presence you've met, this Nagazdiel, is draining you too much, Kiukiu."

"But the children need me—"

"They've waited years without number, my love. They can wait a little longer."

CHAPTER 21

The *Halcyon*, Ambassador Valamas's ship, rocked at anchor off the coast of Tielen in an unseasonably choppy sea. Even in the heat of midsummer the weather in the Straits could be unpredictable.

Because of the cramped accommodation offered by the ship, each country had elected to limit its representatives to a party of five, excluding translators and secretaries.

Eugene, flanked by his ministers, entered the ship's stateroom to find several eminent Francian nobles, elegantly attired in dark brocades, already waiting to greet them. All bowed with elaborate and old-fashioned flourishes as Eugene appeared.

"Where is King Enguerrand?" demanded Eugene.

"His majesty is suffering from a bout of summer fever. So he has nominated his uncle Josselin, Duc de Craon, to represent him," said Ambassador Valamas. A grey-bearded Francian minister came forward and bowed stiffly.

"I see." Eugene exchanged a glance with Maltheus. Was this a snub? Or was the young king genuinely indisposed? Whichever, it rankled that he was not going to meet his adversary face-to-face.

Now Eugene saw that on the richly fringed velvet cloth covering the table lay the five Tears of Artamon. And he sensed Belberith awaken within him. A crackle of energy pulsed through the air. "*Nagar's Eye*," hissed Belberith, his voice heavy with desire.

"So you have returned my rubies to me," Eugene said, unable to resist the challenge.

"It is our contention, Emperor," said Josselin de Craon, "that you gained four of these rubies unlawfully."

So this was the way the Francians planned to play the game.

"Imperial highness, please be seated so that we can begin," said Ambassador Valamas, evidently sensing the growing tension. "Wine?"

Eugene shook his head and took his seat to the left of the ambassador. The rubies glowed dully in the muted daylight filtering into the stateroom and Eugene's fingers itched to touch them once more, to feel their latent energy pulsing through him.

"The Emperor is not prepared to barter for what is rightfully his," said Maltheus.

"What is in dispute here is a legal matter, Chancellor. Is the owner of the five Tears of Artamon entitled to rule the five princedoms? Or is the title of 'emperor' merely an anachronism?"

Eugene had not come to be insulted and felt strongly tempted to say so.

"And your contention?"

"I call Minister Vashteli of the Smarnan council to speak." Josselin de Craon beckoned and a smartly dressed woman of middle years moved to stand beside him.

"The Smarnan council was never consulted," she said. "We awoke one winter's morning to find Smarna occupied by Tielen troops. We had been annexed by New Rossiya." Her stiff stance, the proud tilt of the head, all betrayed that fierce, fanatical national pride that Eugene and his ministers had utterly underestimated.

But while Minister Vashteli was speaking, one of the Smarnan delegation caught Eugene's attention. A young fair-haired secretary was conferring in hushed tones with his opposite number in the Francian contingent. It was when a lock of honey-gold hair flopped down over his eyes and he flicked it back with a careless toss of the head, that Eugene was sure he knew him. So Maltheus's intelligence was correct! Eugene felt a distinct admiration that Pavel Velemir had extricated himself from such a tricky situation.

"We made several offers to negotiate," Maltheus was saying, "and each time you refused. You then had the governor, Colonel Armfeld, executed, along with many of his men."

"We are not here to enumerate past grievances," Ambassador Valamas intervened. "We are here to bring about a peaceful conclusion to the present stalemate."

"I find it hard to talk peace when my wife is being held to ransom," said Eugene.

"Ransom?" Josselin de Craon repeated in offended tones. "The Empress Astasia came to Francia of her own accord, in company with her brother."

"Andrei Orlov again," Maltheus murmured in Eugene's ear. "Is he the mastermind behind all this? Is he playing us against Francia?"

"So why is the Empress still in Francia?" Eugene persisted.

"It was deemed inadvisable to allow her to travel in the current unstable situation."

"How considerate." Eugene beckoned Gustave to his side. "Gustave, would you be so good as to read us the transcription of our most recent conversation with Grand Maistre de Lanvaux?"

"Maistre de Lanvaux: 'The safety of your wife and unborn child must be of the utmost importance to you, Emperor,' " read Gustave. "The Emperor: 'Let me speak with her.' De Lanvaux: 'Your wife is in a place of safety,' and here the Grand Maistre paused, 'for the time being.' "

"There you have it. An overt threat to the Empress's life," said Maltheus.

"With respect, Chancellor," said Josselin de Craon, "you are misinterpreting the Grand Maistre's words."

"Misinterpreting? Note the pause. That pause was of the utmost significance." Maltheus leaned toward the duc. "And was the Empress once allowed to speak or write to her husband, to reassure him that she was in good health? No, not once. I put it to you that the Empress is being held against her will as a hostage."

Josselin de Craon gave a dry, drawling little laugh. "This allegation is ridiculous, Chancellor. As ridiculous as it is pernicious."

Eugene's patience was exhausted. "What are Francia's terms, de Craon? What do you want in exchange for my wife's freedom? Smarna?"

His question provoked the reaction he had hoped for. The scratching of the secretaries' pen nibs ceased. The Francian ministers were staring at one another. Minister Vashteli stood, her neatly coiffured head held high, her painted lips pressed firmly together, as though to stifle a cry of triumph.

"Perhaps I didn't express myself clearly enough?" Eugene said in the silence. "I am prepared to cede Smarna. But on the understanding that my wife and her entourage are allowed to leave Francia."

"*Cede* Smarna?" repeated Minister Vashteli, the look of triumph fading from her face. "Smarna has never been yours to cede, Emperor!"

Josselin de Craon was conferring with the other ministers.

"I do not for one moment believe," continued Eugene, ignoring Minister Vashteli, "that you would seek to tarnish Francia's reputation by harming a pregnant woman."

The duc turned back to face Eugene. "We are prepared to consider your offer. The well-being of your wife and unborn child must be ensured. And though I assure you, Emperor, that the Empress has not been maltreated in any way—in fact, the king's own mother has taken care of her. We are willing to ensure that she is safely transported from Belle Garde to a place of her own choosing."

Eugene gave a curt nod of assent. He did not wish to be seen to be overgrateful; damn it, he was ceding one fifth of his hard-won empire. "Then Smarna is yours. As soon as I am assured that the Empress is safe. Ambassador"—and he turned to Valamas—"I would be obliged if you could act as witness to this agreement."

"Pavel!" Minister Vashteli swept over to Pavel Velemir. "Is there some fine point or legal technicality I've missed here? Is Smarna not to be consulted in this?"

"I would like to reassure Minister Vashteli of Francia's good faith," began Josselin de Craon. "We look on this as the beginning of a long and fruitful partnership that will benefit both our countries . . ."

Eugene leaned toward Maltheus, as Minister Vashteli expressed her feelings in a forthright manner. "Now the Smarnans may begin to wish they had not been so hasty to judge us."

"Out of the pot and into the fire," said Maltheus, nodding sagely.

But Eugene was distracted by the sight of Josselin de Craon placing the rubies—*his* rubies—into a golden casket. He could feel Belberith's longing as powerfully as if it were a fever burning through his whole body.

"*Take back what is rightfully yours.*"

Eugene felt the Drakhaoul's power begin to tingle at the tips of his fingers.

"No," he said silently to his daemon, though it cost him dear. "*I must endure this humiliation for Astasia's sake. We must bide our time.*"

*   *   *

"Free to go?" Astasia gazed in astonishment at the Comte de Pouzauges, who had brought the news. Behind her she heard Nadezhda smother a cry of exultation. "To go where?"

The comte consulted the document he had brought. " 'To a place of your own choosing.' "

"But—but why?" Astasia was sure there must be a catch.

"The king and the Emperor Eugene have signed a treaty."

"A peace treaty?" Hope swelled within her. No more bloodshed, no more fighting—

He hesitated. "Not precisely. The Emperor has ceded Smarna to King Enguerrand."

The comte began to read the articles of the agreement to her but as he read, all she could think was that Eugene had sacrificed part of his empire to win her freedom. *He's done this for me. He's given up Smarna for me. How can I ever make it up to him?*

"And his majesty has put a ship, the *Aquilon*, at your disposal."

"The *Aquilon*? Isn't that my brother's command?"

"His majesty thought it appropriate that your brother should escort you home. I understand that the *Aquilon* has already set out for Fenez-Tyr."

"Home . . ." Astasia had risen to receive her guest; now she found herself dizzy, swaying, reaching out for something to support herself. "Where is home?" she asked stupidly as Nadezhda rushed forward to catch her.

"Sit down, altessa." Nadezhda helped her into her chair and propped a cushion behind her.

"Please excuse me," Astasia said, annoyed with herself for showing such weakness in front of one of Enguerrand's courtiers. "When can we leave?"

"Why, as soon as your imperial highness wishes." The comte bowed and withdrew.

"Free to go!" Nadezhda chuckled to herself as she brought Astasia a glass of barley water. "Free to go home, to Muscobar!"

"Home to Mama," whispered Astasia, tears of relief blurring her eyes as she sipped her barley water.

*   *   *

"So the Emperor has ceded Smarna to Enguerrand, has he?" Muttering to himself, Andrei began to fling the few personal items he possessed into his trunk. "What a fool. He must care for Tasia much more than I ever imagined . . ."

"*Everything has a purpose. Now I understand why I was sent to you,*" whispered Adramelech. "*It was to protect your bloodline, the line of the Orlovs that stretches back to Artamon's eldest son, Prince Rostevan. It runs in the blood of your sister's unborn child too.*"

"But she's going back to Muscobar."

"*And that is all to the good.*"

"Now wait a moment!" Andrei stopped in front of the old, dust-speckled mirror on the cabin wall. "At first you said the journey to Muscobar would put her health at risk. You said it was safer for her to stay here. Why have you changed your tune?"

"*The situation was unstable. Now she will be able to travel by sea without risk of being caught up in the hostilities.*" The spirit's words spread like a soothing balm through Andrei's agitated thoughts. "*Why do you still doubt me, Andrei? I was sent to guard and guide you.*"

As Andrei gazed at his reflection in the cloudy mirror, it seemed that he caught a glimpse again of his shadowy guardian. "*But it would be best if your sister knew nothing about me, Andrei. I do not wish to frighten her.*" Eyes, dark purple as a smoky twilit sky in autumn, gazed calmly back into his, then faded away like drifting mist.

Eugene and his ministers stood on the Water Gate quay in Mirom, waiting to receive the Empress and her little entourage. The *Aquilon* had been sighted over an hour ago at the mouth of the Nieva and the wind was favorable for sea traffic sailing toward the capital. The sky was a delectable summer blue, dotted with tender white clouds. Although it was warm, the breeze off the river kept the strong odors from the tanneries and the smokeries from tainting the air. Brown swifts swooped low over the river to catch flies, letting out a chorus of thin, high cries. Herring gulls floated on the water, bobbing up and down with each passing vessel.

"Sign of fine weather," said Maltheus gruffly as Eugene consulted his pocket watch for the tenth time.

Eugene tucked the watch away and started to pace the quay again, hands locked behind his back. He was more apprehensive about seeing his wife again than he had imagined. Would she cut him dead in front of all the dignitaries? Or would she give him a dutiful peck on the cheek before getting into the waiting carriage and driving away without any further greeting?

"I would remind your highness that you are showing extraordinary magnanimity toward the Empress," Maltheus murmured, almost as if he had read Eugene's thoughts.

Eugene rounded on him. "But we must not, on all accounts, remind the Empress of that fact!"

"Quite so," Maltheus said, diplomatically retreating.

"The *Aquilon*!" announced an officer on lookout.

"Attention!" shouted the captain of the Muscobar Imperial Bodyguard, and the two lines of men making up the guard of honor clicked heels and straightened shoulders. "Present arms!"

Eugene gazed into the brilliant sunlight, frowning as he saw a fine frigate slowly approaching, proudly flaunting Francian colors.

Was Astasia on deck? He strained to catch a glimpse of her—and felt his stomach give a lurch.

What's the matter with me? I'm as nervous as a schoolboy.

The truth was that he would rather have been preparing to engage the Francians in battle than greet his estranged wife. He adopted what he hoped would seem like a casual, yet neutral, stance. Yet he could not stop rehearsing in his mind what to say, what to do when she disembarked. How should he greet her? Should he kiss her on the cheek—or would she think that too formal and cold? But then to kiss her full on the lips in front of so many dignitaries might embarrass her. And, if she were still angry with him, she might turn her head away and he would look even more ridiculous, snubbed in public by his own wife.

And at the last moment as Eugene moved out toward the approaching vessel, a horrible thought occurred to him. If the Francians had wanted to catch him when he was most vulnerable, they could have deceived him, using an actress to portray Astasia, luring him out, unprotected, onto the quay so that a concealed marksman could easily eliminate him with one well-aimed shot . . .

Eugene glanced around uneasily, wondering why this unpleasantly devious scenario should occur to him precisely then.

He could see Astasia clearly, standing with her chin defiantly raised, the faithful Nadezhda in attendance. And he felt his heart beat faster at the sight of her, even though from the haughty tilt of her head he guessed that she was not yet ready to forgive him.

A tall young man stood protectively at her side, smartly dressed in a Francian naval officer's uniform of royal blue and gold. Eugene recognized Valery Vassian. But where was the elusive Andrei, her brother?

The feeling of unease was growing stronger. And it was not connected with Astasia. There was something else approaching, something that made Eugene's skin crawl. He checked the sky for thunderclouds—but there was no hint of rain. The swifts still darted and swooped overhead. And yet the unsettling sensation felt like the distant tingle of an electrical storm.

Several Francian sailors leaped ashore to secure the frigate with ropes; others began to lower a companionway. Eugene saw Astasia turn to Vassian, who offered her his hand to help her along the companionway and onto the quay.

Eugene felt a tightening in his chest as she approached. He wanted to rush forward and sweep her up in his arms. But protocol demanded that he stand there and greet her as formally as if she were some visiting foreign dignitary.

Astasia was still feeling queasy after a rough crossing from Fenez-Tyr. Or so she told herself as they sailed down the Nieva. She was reluctant to admit that these last twinges of nausea had little to do with rough seas and everything to do with the prospect of seeing Eugene again. She had hoped they might be able to slip quietly into the port and drive off to Erinaskoe without any fuss. Then a message had been received warning that an official welcoming party was waiting to greet her and any hope of a quick escape was lost.

And the sight of the Emperor, standing waiting for her on the quay, impeccably dressed in his favorite Colonel-in-Chief's uniform (which must be unbearably hot and uncomfortable), provoked another pang. Her heart began to flutter with apprehension.

It wasn't until Valery Vassian offered her his hand to lead her to the quay that she remembered that he was risking a great deal in returning to New Rossiya. He was a deserter and would certainly be court-martialed.

"Go back on board, Valery," she whispered as he helped her down onto the cobbled quay. "While you're on a Francian ship, they can't arrest you."

He stared at her in surprise and nodded, retreating as the sailors carried down Astasia's trunk.

"The Empress Astasia!" shouted an officer. "Present arms!"

Astasia looked at Eugene. And to her surprise, he came running toward her and gathered her close in his arms, so that she was crushed against the gold buttons and braid of his uniform. And for a moment, she forgot all her anxieties and just let herself rest against him. For the first time in many weeks she felt cherished, protected . . . loved.

"Thank God you're safe," he murmured into her hair. Then, as though a little embarrassed by this public show of emotion, he drew back, gazing at her intently. Dazzled by the brilliant sunshine, she looked up into his face.

"Oh!" she said, shocked. There was not a single trace of the disfiguring scarring. His hair had grown back, his brows and lashes were golden again, just as in the portrait painted before he had fought Gavril Nagarian. He looked years younger. "You—you're healed." She could not stop herself from raising her hand to touch his face, to feel the smoothness of the new skin. But as she did so, she noticed an unfamiliar glint of malachite green in his blue eyes. And at the same time, she sensed that same unpleasant prickle of fear she had first felt in Swanholm when the Drakhaon had swooped down to rescue Elysia.

Drakhaoul.

She snatched her hand away, as if she had singed her fingers.

"Astasia?" he said, puzzled.

No, not you too, my dearest. For a moment the shock was so great she could not speak. And when she did, her voice had dwindled to an anguished whisper.

"What have you done to yourself, Eugene?"

CHAPTER 22

Astasia drew away from Eugene, her dark eyes blazing with shock.

And at first he could not understand why. She had fallen quite naturally into his embrace, she had nestled up against him, as if all the intervening weeks of misunderstanding and heartache had never been. And now she was backing away from him, one hand raised to keep him at arm's length.

"Why?" she asked, her voice low, hard. "Why did you do it, Eugene?"

"*She knows*," whispered Belberith.

How could she know? Eugene was utterly bewildered. What had given his secret away? Unless Belberith had revealed his presence to her by some sly, subtle trick. And if that were so, what malign motive had prompted the Drakhaoul to do so?

The regimental band struck up the New Rossiyan anthem for the third time and he remembered that the guard of honor was still waiting to escort them into the palace.

"Let's talk, Astasia," Eugene said quietly. "But not out here, not in public."

She was silent a while, not meeting his gaze but staring fixedly out beyond him at the rooftops and spires of the city. "Very well," she said at last.

Eugene quietly closed the doors of the Blue Morning Room. Astasia sat down on a rosebud-patterned couch—a little more slowly and carefully than of old, he noticed. A servant brought a tray of tea and he dismissed her, saying they would serve themselves.

He poured tea into one of the delicate porcelain cups and placed it on a little table beside Astasia.

"Lemon? Sugar?"

"Thank you," she said, still not meeting his eyes.

Silence followed, broken only by the tinkling of teaspoons on porcelain as he and Astasia each stirred their tea. He gazed at her over the rim of his cup as he drank and thought he had never seen her look more beautiful. The pregnancy had brought a soft bloom to her pale cheeks.

Yet still she said nothing.

He set down his cup and saucer, knowing he must make the first move. "Astasia, we need to talk."

There was another silence. Eventually she said, "What is there to discuss?"

"It doesn't change how I feel about you."

"Has it never occurred to you it might change the way *I* feel about *you*?"

"I knew you hated to look at me, to see, to touch the scars, so I—"

"Do you expect me to believe that?"

"Yes, though there were other reasons too." He went over to sit beside her. "I did it to protect the empire. To protect you."

She moved away to the far end of the couch. "And our child?"

Eugene suppressed the urge to remind her that she had neglected to tell him, the father, that she was pregnant. "Your safety—and the safety of our child—is of the utmost importance to me, Astasia."

"Then," she said in a distant tone, "you will understand me when I say that I can't risk your coming near us. Not until you are rid of that—that *thing* inside you."

Now it was he who fell silent. What she was asking—no, demanding—of him was all but impossible. She was right, of course. But he sensed that Belberith was listening and would fight any attempt he made at exorcism.

Only one man had ever succeeded in ridding himself of the Drakhaoul.

And even if I succeed, will the exorcism leave me weakened, prey to delusions? Or utterly insane?

"I'd like to go and stay with my parents." Astasia's voice broke in upon his thoughts. She spoke in a formal, detached voice, as if he were a stranger.

"Of course," he said, equally formally. "I'll make the arrangements."

"Thank you."

But when he looked at her, he saw such sadness darkening her eyes
that it was all he could do not to take her in his arms and kiss her
fears away.

"How is Karila?" she asked. "Is she safe?"

Safe. The little insinuation did not escape his notice. "She is with
her great-aunt at the Manor of Rosenholm. She is well protected
there."

"I'm glad to hear it."

There was so much Eugene yearned to ask her; how was her health,
her appetite, had she felt the baby kick yet? Yet one glance at her tight-
pressed lips and downcast eyes told him that on this occasion, she was
not prepared to enter into any further discussion with him.

"Well, then." He reached for the bellpull to ring for a servant.
"There's nothing more to be said."

The imperial barouche drove through the streets of Mirom, with
its mounted escort of the Imperial Household Cavalry trotting along
behind, harnesses and spurs jingling.

Astasia sat back on the slippery seat of buttoned leather and gazed
out as she glimpsed familiar landmarks.

How could Eugene have done such a dangerous thing? She was
still so angry, she could think of nothing else. She had been more than
ready to forgive Eugene his past faults. She had come to Mirom with
her speech prepared. And then she had seen him waiting for her on
the quay, and her heart had melted. She had wanted nothing more
than to run to him and forget all the heartache of the past weeks.

They were crossing Saint Simeon's Square, where the brightly
painted domes of the great cathedral towered above the houses. Astasia had a sudden vivid recollection of her wedding, a grey winter's day
of bitter cold. Then the branches of the tall plane trees lining the square
had been stark and leafless; now they made a shady canopy of dusty
green leaves. And it came back to her that when she had driven away
from the cathedral seated beside Eugene, the waiting crowds who had
stood so silently when she arrived with her father, suddenly broke into
cheers as all the city bells dinned out to welcome them. They hadn't
cared about his injuries; they had seen him as their liberator.

A flower seller on the corner of the square recognized her and tossed her a little bunch of white roses, calling out, "Welcome home, Empress!"

Now other passersby noticed her and stopped to wave and cheer. Astasia sat up and forced a smile onto her lips, acknowledging them with a gracious nod and a gesture of her lace-gloved hand.

Is it my fault? Was I so squeamish that I drove him to such drastic measures? The little cavalcade turned into the Southern Parade, and as their pace quickened, Astasia caught her first glimpse of the woodlands beyond the city walls. The smile faded. *Or is it nothing to do with me at all and all to do with revenge? For how else could he take on the Drakhaon of Azhkendir?*

Andrei lay brooding in his cabin on board the *Aquilon*.

The glimpse of the Emperor standing in front of the Orlov family residence with such a self-assured and proprietorial air had maddened him. Damn it, this was *his* ancestral home; there had been Orlovs living in the Winter Palace by the Nieva for centuries. And at the same time, he had felt a surge of violent emotion from Adramelech, sharp as a lightning shock.

"Stand back, Prince Andrei. Don't let the Emperor see you."

Andrei was so astonished by the unexpectedness of Adramelech's warning that he had obeyed without question, going below. And lying there, in his narrow bunk, he had begun to fantasize again about ousting Eugene and winning back Muscobar.

"This truce cannot last forever. The Rossiyan navy will take months to recover from the blow you dealt them."

Andrei's first successful mission in command of the *Aquilon* had earned him and his crew a considerable sum from the king and his ministers. Astasia need never know that he had led the squadron that destroyed Prince Karl's famous dockyards and the ships inside.

"Would it please you to create a little more havoc in Eugene's crumbling empire?" Adramelech whispered slyly. *"With me to guide you, you can inflict far more damage than you can possibly imagine . . .*

Masts crack and burn like matchwood. Sails fall in flaming shreds onto the panicking sailors beneath. The black sky lights up with a lurid, amethyst light—and then a fog of blinding, choking smoke covers the sea. Men, set alight, roll on the tilting deck in agony—or fling themselves into the churning waters.

Andrei swung his legs over the side of his bunk, intrigued. "Tell me more." He began to pull on his boots.

"*The Emperor is already smarting from the losses in his navy. Let's see if we can destroy the few remaining ships.*"

"But the truce—"

"*Did I say you would need to take the* Aquilon? *No, this is a solo mission. Order shore leave for the crew. Tell them you're going to pay a visit to your family.*"

"My family." Andrei halted; a sense of yearning for familiar places and people overwhelmed him. He had not seen his parents since that ill-fated day when they had stood on that very quay, shivering in the bitter cold, to watch him sail out to his first command, the *Sirin*.

In that one moment, Andrei decided to make his way to Erinaskoe, just to catch a glimpse of his parents and reassure himself that they were well. He knew several unobserved ways in and out of the grounds. As a young boy, he had often sneaked away from his tutor to go hunting rabbits with the gamekeeper's son.

He flung open his cabin door. "Vassian!" he called. "I'm going to Erinaskoe. Shore leave for the crew."

"*As you wish, my prince,*" said Adramelech.

Eugene sat staring at the sofa where Astasia had been sitting.

Why did I think that she wouldn't notice? And why did I ever believe that she wouldn't care?

A numbing despair had descended upon him; since she had left for Erinaskoe, he had stayed in the Blue Morning Room, immobile, no longer certain, for the first time in his adult life, what to do.

She was right, of course; he saw it at last. For with the despair had come a horrible clarity of vision. And only on seeing her was he beginning to understand the implications of what he had done to himself on Ty Nagar.

The look of loathing and fear in Astasia's eyes had seared him to the depths of his soul.

He could see no other course of action but to make Altan Kazimir replicate the experimental treatment he had used on Gavril Nagarian and Lord Volkh.

There was a tap at the door and Chancellor Maltheus came in.

"There's a delegation from the council here to speak with you, highness. They're worried about the Francian situation."

Eugene rose to his feet. "As am I, Maltheus. As am I. And to that end, I'm returning to Tielen on the evening tide." There was no point lingering in Muscobar any longer.

Maltheus's bushy brows rose. "Aren't you going to join the Empress at Erinaskoe? I'd have thought—"

"I'm content to know she's safe with her family." Eugene tried to temper the brusqueness in his voice. Maltheus knew him well enough to know when he was dissembling; he just hoped that the Chancellor might attribute his curt manner to his preoccupation with the current international situation. "I'm off to Saint Ansgar's to see how Professor Kazimir is progressing."

"Ah." Maltheus beamed. "Our chemist. Our new munitions."

Eugene let his hand rest on Maltheus's sturdy shoulder a moment. "We can but hope."

The vile smell emanating from Professor Kazimir's laboratory made Eugene wrinkle his nose. And yet there was something oddly nostalgic about the odor; it reminded him of the Magus's experiments. And that could only be a good sign. Eugene reckoned he could put up with any amount of unpleasant chymical stinks if the end result was a decisive victory over Enguerrand and his armies.

He turned to his adjutant, young Rolf Anckstrom, and saw from the pained expression on his face that he found the chymical odors equally offensive.

"I want you to keep watch outside, Lieutenant."

The lieutenant saluted with alacrity—and, Eugene suspected, considerable relief.

The laboratory was hazy with yellowish vapors and Eugene peered into the fug, trying to determine where the professor was. He could hear muttering nearby.

"Professor Kazimir?"

Kazimir appeared, a glass phial in hand. "Imperial highness?" he said, blinking.

"Is there somewhere we could talk?" The fumes were beginning to irritate Eugene's eyes.

Kazimir set down the phial on a metal support and opened a side door.

Eugene ducked down to avoid hitting his head and found himself in a scholar's cabinet. Papers littered the desk, scribbled equations, formulae, and scientific diagrams, all as meaningless as the pictograms of Khitari to Eugene.

"Please sit down," said Kazimir, absentmindedly wiping his spectacle lenses on his shirttails.

Eugene lifted a pile of books from a chair and sat. "You're making progress?"

"With the Azhkendi firedust? Yes; though it's highly volatile stuff." Kazimir pointed, a little ruefully, to where Eugene now saw his eyebrows had been. "I've been experimenting with a way to combine it with conventional gunpowder. Of course, our initial supplies have been exhausted, but I hear that a new shipment is expected soon from Azhkendir. I've been working closely with Minister Ekman and I think we may have some promising results for you by next week. The minister has put a small team of bombardiers to work, running tests at the firing range in the quarry upriver—"

"That was not the reason I came."

"Oh?"

"Look at me, Professor. Look at me closely." Eugene had tied his wild hair back with a black velvet ribbon; he pulled the ribbon undone, letting the gold-green locks loose about his shoulders.

"Dear God." Kazimir peered through his spectacles and then started back in alarm. "You're—you're—"

"Drakhaon. And I want you to change that for me. So here I am. Do you need to take blood?" Eugene started to roll up his sleeve.

"I—I can't!" Kazimir seemed aghast at the suggestion; his hands had begun to shake.

"Of course you can." Since Eugene had made up his mind to pursue this course of action, he was impatient to get on with it. "I made you, Professor Kazimir. I established this Chair of Chymical Science so that you could pursue your researches. And is this how you repay my trust?"

"N—no," stammered Kazimir, backing away. "It's just that it's a very risky procedure."

"But your elixir worked in the case of Lord Volkh." Eugene lowered his voice, even though he knew that the creature within him could read his innermost thoughts. "It worked with Lord Gavril."

"It's dangerous, imperial highness. And I left all my research, all my notes at Kastel Drakhaon. You may remember I was obliged to extricate myself from the kastel after the bombardment."

"It is a risk I'm prepared to take."

"Even if I can't be certain I remember the process correctly?"

"You're a highly intelligent man. Surely where your memory fails, scientific logic will dictate how you proceed."

"But the new firepowder—"

"You just told me yourself you were close to a breakthrough."

Kazimir threw up his hands in a gesture of panic. "But if I make an error and you—you succumb, I'll be tried for regicide."

Eugene looked at him with astonishment. He could not understand how a scientist as brilliant as Altan Kazimir could prove so spineless when faced with a challenge.

"Then might I—erm—make a suggestion?" Kazimir cleared his throat. "I should like to prepare an antidote as well, just in case you change your mind . . ."

"I can assure you that there will be no need. Bring me paper, pen, and ink," Eugene ordered. Then, as Kazimir looked on anxiously, rubbing his trembling hands together, Eugene wrote:

I, Eugene of New Rossiya, agree to a course of treatment prescribed
by Professor Altan Kazimir. The professor is not to be held
responsible in any way, should there be any unforeseen consequences.

When he glanced up from the page to request sealing wax and candle to set his seal on the document, Kazimir had reappeared with a phial of clear alcohol with which he was cleaning the tip of a syringe.

Just as Kazimir tightened the tourniquet around his arm to make the vein stand out, Eugene heard Belberith speaking to him. Only now there was a new pleading tone in the Drakhaoul's voice. "*I have sought only to serve and please you, Lord Emperor. Tell me how I may amend my faults and serve you better. But please don't do this!*"

For a moment, Eugene's resolve faltered and he raised his hand to hold Kazimir off.

Then he felt the needle's sharp graze and saw the blood, no longer crimson but tinged with a shimmer of malachite green, trickle into the glass phial. It was too late to turn back.

CHAPTER 23

"So this is Smarna." Jagu gazed at the broken walls of the old citadel. The sun was burning down from a cloudless sky and he took off his broad-brimmed hat to fan his face. They had just disembarked, handing over their Azhkendi prisoners to a fast man-o'-war that was waiting to transport them to the Forteresse for interrogation.

"Why do you suppose the Maistre asked us to meet him here?" Celestine was darting suspicious little glances around as they followed their escort party, armed Guerriers, from the harbor.

Jagu shrugged. "Perhaps he has a new mission for us." He could not help noticing as they passed Smarnans in the dusty winding streets that all turned away, as though silently refusing to acknowledge their new masters. Could these be the same townspeople who had welcomed King Enguerrand so warmly only a few weeks ago?

The Guerriers led them to a balconied mansion built of golden stone. It had once been the Colchise residence of the princes of Smarna, hastily abandoned in the uprising when the deposed royal family fled into exile. Inside, the lofty hall was refreshingly cool, and Jagu could glimpse a green courtyard garden beyond and hear the splash of a fountain. But the antechamber in which they were left to await the Maistre's summons had a sad air of faded grandeur: the gilding on the ornate cornices had all but flaked away and cracks marred the painted plaster.

*　　*　　*

"Well done, my children." Ruaud de Lanvaux held up Saint Sergius's golden crook, caressing it with reverent fingers.

Considering that the mission to Azhkendir had not gone according to plan, Jagu was relieved to hear the Maistre's approving words.

"This more than compensates for the blow struck against us in Lutèce. While you were in Azhkendir, the Magus was snatched from us."

"What do you mean, Maistre? The Magus escaped?" said Celestine. Jagu glanced at her anxiously, knowing that she had spent many months planning, then laying the trap for Kaspar Linnaius.

"I saw the foul creature myself." De Lanvaux's voice was hushed. "I was knocked to the ground by its beating wings. It was a beast of darkness, one of the daemon Drakhaouls from the Realm of Shadows. It swooped down into the Place du Trahoir and snatched the Magus from the burning pyre."

"The Drakhaon? Why did we not hear anything of this?" Jagu demanded.

"There was a stampede." De Lanvaux laid the golden crook carefully down on its velvet covering. "Many onlookers were crushed in the panic. I felt it would not reflect well on the Commanderie's reputation if such a story were broadcast abroad." He looked up and Jagu saw a ruthless gleam in his eyes. "So I suppressed it."

"The Magus escaped," repeated Celestine. She hardly seemed to have heard the rest of the conversation.

"Our agents have not been idle in your absence. Inquisitor Méloir has been particularly industrious in his investigations." The Grand Maistre carefully placed the relic in a cedarwood box and locked the box with a gilded key from a chain around his neck. "He's already on the trail of a young Smarnan painter who was asking a few too many questions in Lutèce a few days before the trial took place." He placed his hands protectively on top of the box and Jagu noticed—not for the first time—how smooth and pale the skin was, how well manicured the nails. "Now whether this so-called painter was a spy, or the Drakhaon of Azhkendir himself in disguise, we have yet to determine. We can only be sure of two facts: Lord Nagariàn grew up here in Smarna—and he trained as an artist."

"But what would Lord Nagarian want with the Magus?" burst out Celestine.

"As yet we can discern no obvious motive. The Emperor is the one most disadvantaged by the loss of his chief alchymist—but it's highly unlikely, in the light of recent events, that Lord Nagarian would risk such a hazardous enterprise to help his enemy." Ruaud de Lanvaux glanced up, and Jagu saw a look of obdurate determination in his eyes. "No; the motive is irrelevant. Our duty as Guerriers is clear. We must destroy the Drakhaon. And now we have the means to do it." He stroked the cedarwood box. "While our finest craftsmen are at work reforging the Staff, we will be laying our trap for the Drakhaon."

Jagu nodded. It seemed that all their efforts to destroy the daemon were finally to bear fruit. "So what is our next mission?"

"Send me after Kaspar Linnaius, Maistre," Celestine said, and though her voice was quiet, it burned with fierce intent. "I won't let him escape me a second time."

De Lanvaux passed her a printed bill and Jagu read over her shoulder:

Reputed Portrait Painter seeks new commissions. Illustrious recent clients: her imperial highness, Astasia, Empress of Rossiya; the Grand Duchess Sofia; his Excellency, Ambassador Garsevani. Please address all inquiries to Elysia Andar at the Villa Andara, Vermeille.

"You want me to have my portrait painted?"

"We have already made arrangements for you to give a concert at the ambassador's residence. A little villa has been reserved for you overlooking Vermeille Bay. Your nearest neighbor will be Madame Andar and you will commission her to paint your portrait. It seems that the Drakhys of Azhkendir has fallen on hard times."

"The Drakhys?" echoed Celestine.

"She is Gavril Nagarian's mother."

"Maistre—isn't this a highly dangerous mission?" Jagu protested. "If you mean to bring Lord Nagarian to heel by holding his mother hostage—"

"I'm well aware of the dangers involved, Jagu," said Celestine, flashing him a defiant look.

"We've learned much from the intelligence you gathered from the servants at Swanholm," said Ruaud de Lanvaux. "Mistakes were made that day, which gave the Drakhaon a significant advantage. We won't allow ourselves to be so careless."

Jagu shook his head. Ruaud de Lanvaux was hazarding Celestine's life by using her in this way.

"And you will be joining Mademoiselle de Joyeuse as her accompanist, Jagu."

"I shall need a maid if I am to play my part convincingly. Staff to run the villa." Celestine ticked off each item on her fingers. "A decent fortepiano, not some worm-eaten, out-of-tune, neglected instrument. And new gowns and jewelery, if I am to impress fashionable society here in Colchise—"

"All this has been anticipated. The treasurer is awaiting you, Mademoiselle." The Maistre turned his attentions to the relic in the cedarwood box; they had been dismissed.

Jagu was about to follow Celestine out when de Lanvaux called quietly, "A moment more of your time, Lieutenant."

Jagu paused, wondering what the Maistre wanted with him.

"You've proved your loyalty to the cause often enough, Jagu. I think I can confide in you." The Maistre put his hand on Jagu's shoulder. Jagu was shocked at first by this unexpectedly familiar gesture, then immensely gratified. De Lanvaux's voice dropped to a more intimate level. "I have great hopes for your future within the Commanderie. I see potential in you, and that is why I'm going to share my thoughts with you." Jagu glanced questioningly into his leader's eyes. "I know you hold *her* in great regard. But you must be on your guard. She is driven more by her own desires than the greater good of the order."

"Celest—" Jagu began and then broke off, hearing the note of warning coloring de Lanvaux's words.

"I have serious concerns about her, Jagu. I know you would come to me—in confidence, of course—if you suspected that she was no longer acting in our best interests. Or if she allowed herself to stray too far from her mission. Do you understand me?"

Jagu felt the pressure of the Grand Maistre's hand on his shoulder. Was he being forced to make a choice?

"I understand," he said slowly, wondering as he spoke the words aloud if he were already betraying her *"for the greater good of the order . . ."*

Jagu met Celestine in the old palace's shady courtyard garden. As they walked toward the entrance, Celestine was silent and subdued.

Jagu matched his pace to hers. Sparrows chirped shrilly, balancing on the rim of the fountain to drink.

Celestine suddenly stopped. "How come Kaspar Linnaius was rescued from the pyre, and my own father burned?" She gazed up into Jagu's face and he saw tears glittering in the tender blue of her eyes.

"Why are you working for the Commanderie, Celestine?" Jagu asked softly. He felt, to his alarm, a sudden melting ache around his heart to see her so distressed. He could not afford to harbor such feelings for her, especially after Ruaud de Lanvaux's warning. "Surely if you're out to avenge your father's death, the Commanderie should be your target."

"It's . . . complicated," she said, angrily blinking the tears away. "I made a vow of allegiance to the Commanderie. And besides, they took me in and they brought me up, when they could have abandoned me to a life on the streets. But now . . ."

"If we can entrap Lord Nagarian, he may reveal to us where the Magus is hiding."

"Or fry us all with his fiery breath!" she said with a harsh little laugh.

"Well, well, Budoc Lavret," said Inquisitor Méloir, as his men pulled out canvas after canvas and threw them onto the floor of the studio, "these paintings have a stink of sedition about them." He sniffed the air loudly. "In truth, this whole place reeks of heresy— and conspiracy."

Budoc Lavret, held firmly by the arms by two Guerriers, could only stand and watch helplessly as Ruaud de Lanvaux's men trampled over his work, the heels of their boots ruining months of labor. And all he could think was, *Keep away from the studio, Trifine. Keep well away till all this is over.* Mercifully, she had gone with Bastian to the fish market on the Île, and he had been alone with his paints in the studio when the Commanderie had burst in, simultaneously breaking down both front and back doors, so that he found himself trapped, with nowhere to run.

Inquisitor Méloir turned to face the painter, a little smile on his pale lips. "It's not just these paintings, Monsieur Lavret, corrupt and debased though they are." Hyacinthe Méloir, dapper as ever, with his ivory-topped cane and his black leather briefcase filled with tear-stained confessions. "It's the guests you've been inviting to dine."

Lavret had learned long ago to keep an impassive expression on his face when visited unexpectedly by agents of the Commanderie. Yet all the while, his mind was churning with troubled questions, foremost among which was, "*Who are they after this time?*"

"You entertained a stranger here not so long ago. A foreigner."

From the glint in Méloir's eyes, Lavret knew the Inquisitor was playing with him. Well, he could play games too, and stall for a little time to plan exactly how much he could tell without implicating his friends and family. "Is there a law against giving shelter and food to foreigners now?"

"So you don't deny it?"

"Why should I? You seem to know all the facts already."

"And his name?"

"Korneli. Miran Korneli, a student from Smarna."

"Interesting." One thin, dark brow quirked upward as if the Inquisitor were somehow amused by Lavret's reply. "Especially as one Miran Korneli died of a bullet wound received at the uprising in Colchise . . . several weeks ago."

Lavret felt sweat begin to break out on his face. *Stay calm.* "So, unless I was entertaining a ghost, he was an impostor and—"

"And there's no law against being duped by impostors." The amusement suddenly faded from Méloir's eyes. "But you failed in your duty as a citizen, Budoc Lavret. You were harboring a stranger who was asking questions; far too many questions. Didn't that awaken the slightest suspicions? At a time when we are at war with New Rossiya, didn't that strike you as odd? Thank God, there were others in this household more vigilant and loyal than you, others with the courage to come forward with information."

Who betrayed me? Lavret began to turn over the possibilities in his mind: a patron, a rival painter, a friend . . . "Who the hell was this impostor 'Korneli' anyway?"

"We can't be certain," Méloir began to pace slowly in front of Lavret, "but we suspect that your Smarnan visitor was plotting to spring a dangerous heretic from our custody."

"What!" This revelation was not entirely a surprise to Lavret, but he played it for all it was worth.

Méloir stopped suddenly in front of him and stared at him through narrowed lids. "How can I be sure you were not part of his plot?"

"Why would I want to free heretics?" Lavret felt the sweat begin to drip from his forehead.

Méloir pointed at the nearest canvas with the tip of his ivory-topped cane. "Yes, why would you? Unless you're one yourself, Monsieur Lavret. And this daub—this excrescence that you choose to call a painting—would seem to bear witness to that fact."

Lavret reminded himself that these were mere insinuations, with no evidence to back them up. He had eminent friends with Commanderie connections who would vouch for him if Méloir was determined to pursue this further.

"A responsible and conscientious citizen would have reported his 'guest' to his local Commanderie post," continued the Inquisitor. He swung around to gaze sternly at Lavret. "I'm afraid, Monsieur Lavret, that your answers have not been very satisfactory. I must insist that you accompany me to the Forteresse for further examination."

The Guerriers untied the blindfold around Budoc Lavret's eyes and he blinked rapidly, dazzled by the light.

"Was it necessary to bring me here shackled like a criminal?" he asked. "I've done nothing wrong!"

"If that's the case, then you've nothing to fear," said Méloir smoothly. He flicked back his coattails as he seated himself at a desk and opened up a file of papers, scanning the contents, nodding to himself as he read. Lavret watched, trying to suppress his increasing sense of agitation.

"So this is all she's told you so far?" he asked one of the Guerriers standing by, hands behind his back, waiting for orders.

"She's not been very cooperative, Inquisitor," replied the man in an undertone.

"This is a matter of state security," Méloir said, shutting the file with a snap. "Bring her to me."

Lavret had not missed any of this conversation. *She.* He felt a tightening in his throat, his chest. And his fears were confirmed when the Guerrier returned a few minutes later, dragging a young woman along by the arm, her chestnut hair half-unpinned, spilling loose over her shoulders.

"Get your hands off of me!" She was raging so furiously at her guards that she had not even noticed he was there.

"*Trifine!*" he said in despair. And he had believed that she had evaded Méloir's trap.

"Papa?" She stopped abruptly, her mouth dropping open in a little "o" of shock. "Oh, Papa—" She came rushing toward him but was instantly caught and held back by two of the Guerriers.

"I'll answer your questions." Lavret's voice was hoarse with anxiety. He cleared his throat. "I have nothing to hide. But let my daughter go, Inquisitor."

"Just answer me this." Méloir thrust a paper in front of him. "Who is this man?"

"Why—that's Miran Korneli," said Lavret. The likeness was remarkably true; a pencil sketch that with very few lines had captured much of the young man's brooding and intense nature. "But who did this? It's very good."

"An artist with a very promising future in the Commanderie," said the Inquisitor. "Your apprentice, Bastian."

"Bastian?" Trifine echoed, outraged. "Bastian betrayed us?"

Lavret had taken Bastian as his apprentice two years ago and had come to like the young man and respect his talent. He had never once suspected he might be a Commanderie spy.

"You know everything then," he said heavily.

"We already have his sworn statement that the so-called Korneli stayed at your studio and disappeared the very day that the heretic sorcerer Linnaius was rescued from execution."

"I was duped," Lavret said. "Duped by the Smarnan and duped by my own apprentice. But is it a crime to be gullible, Inquisitor? If so, then I'm guilty. But I can't see the slightest reason for you holding me and my daughter here anymore."

"Very well," said Méloir. "This time I shall allow you to go free. But remember, Lavret, that we'll be watching you."

"That rat, Bastian!" said Trifine for the twentieth time as they made their way home. "If I ever catch sight of him again . . ."

It was a long way from the Forteresse to the Quartier des Tisserands; they took a riverboat to the center of the city, where Lavret stopped for a restorative glass of brandy. Then, feeling a little less shaky, he set out with Trifine still ranting about Bastian.

"I'd just found some cod, really cheap, for supper, when the rat disappeared, saying he thought he'd dropped his wallet. Next thing I knew, two Guerriers were either side of me, saying, 'Come with us, Demoiselle,' and I was being hustled away, like a common thief, and all before I could—" She stopped, pointing up the steep lane that led to the top of the ridge. "What's that glow, Papa?"

"I can smell burning," said Lavret, quickening his pace.

"The studio!" cried Trifine, running on ahead.

The night sky was red with flames. The old silk factory was an inferno. A few neighbors had gathered outside, buckets in hand, but the heat was so intense that Lavret knew instantly that there was no hope of rescuing anything inside. All he could do was stand and stare, openmouthed, at the burning factory.

"My paintings," he murmured. "All my paintings . . . gone."

CHAPTER 24

Elysia came into the kitchen where Palmyre was picking over the last windfall of apricots. She feigned a look of utter dejection, although a triumphant smile kept threatening to break through and spoil her little deception.

"Well?" Palmyre looked up at her, her eyes brimming with hope. "Oh, no. Don't say the Francian lady changed her mind." She cut out a wasp-eaten portion from an apricot and put the other half in the bowl. "Well, that just goes to show that they've no taste, these Francians, and we'll just have to tighten our belts another notch—"

"Palmyre," cried Elysia, unable to keep the good news to herself any longer, "she's commissioned a portrait in oils!" She flung a fat little purse onto the table. "And she's paid half the sum in advance." She hugged Palmyre. "Now we can stop living like poor nuns off what grows in the kitchen garden and buy some real food." She waltzed Palmyre around the kitchen floor until they were both giggling and out of breath.

"Tea from Khitari," said Palmyre, with tears of laughter running down her cheeks. "Chocolate."

"And wine, Palmyre. We must have wine to celebrate."

"So, what is she like, our new neighbor?" Palmyre asked when they both recovered a little.

"Exquisitely pretty. A fair complexion and the eyes of an angel. She'll have all the young men fighting over her." Elysia sighed, knowing that the days when she was one of the sought-after young beauties in Vermeille were long gone. "She's a singer. She's to give a recital at the Garsevani residence in a week or so."

"A singer, hm? So who's paying for the portrait?" Palmyre raised one eyebrow meaningfully. "Some rich patron? Or lover?"

"Who knows? Who cares, as long as I get paid!"

"And when do you start?"

"She's arranged a preliminary sitting for tomorrow afternoon so I can do some sketches." Elysia clasped her hands together. "And if the portrait is favorably received, let's hope she tells all her well-to-do friends about me and I'm flooded with commissions!"

"It won't hurt to have something to take your mind off other matters; it's good to be busy."

Palmyre had not referred directly to Gavril but suddenly Elysia felt as if a cloud had drifted across, sullying her good spirits.

"Where *is* he, Palmyre?" She sighed. "It's been so long since we heard from him."

"Back in Azhkendir, like as not. You said he had a girl up there, didn't you?"

"Yes, but it's unlike him to send no word." Another sigh escaped. "He knows I worry."

"These are difficult times." Palmyre shook her head slowly as she chewed on an apricot. "The world keeps changing. First the Tielens invade, then the Francians. Why can't they leave us alone to get on with our lives? Ugh." She made a face and spat out the half-chewed apricot into her palm. "Unripe."

"I'd best go and make sure my brushes are clean." Elysia turned for the door, moving slowly now as her thoughts centered on her son. *I know I must get used to our lives running along different paths now, but it would ease my heart to see you again, dear Gavril, and to know all is well with you.*

Elysia took her wide-brimmed straw hat and purse, and hurried out of the villa into the bright morning. She did not want to be late for her rendezvous with Rafael. For more years than she could remember, they had met on the last day of the month to share their news over a cup of strong coffee and a glass of *karvi*.

It was very hot already and the sea breeze off the bay had dropped, leaving a moist, sultry feel to the air. She gazed up at the sky, wondering if there might be a summer storm on its way. But there were only a few white clouds, soft as thistledown, drifting over the sea. She tied the ribbons on her hat under her chin and set off toward Colchise along the cliff path.

Elysia had always loved to walk along the cliffs for the dramatic views of the bay in all its different moods. She loved the dusty summer scents of mallow, dog rose, and bramble flowers. But since the Tielen assault on the citadel, the familiar view had changed beyond recognition. The citadel walls were in ruins; great boulders still lay at the foot of the gun-battered cliff on which it stood. And even more chilling to Elysia's eyes, was the swathe of grey ash-filled sand that still polluted the beach and the waters that lapped beneath the ruined walls: Gavril's doing.

No. She corrected herself. *The Drakhaoul's doing, although my son must bear his share of the responsibility. Though who knows what would have become of us all if he hadn't stopped the bombardment when he did . . .*

Now she wished she had not begun to think of Gavril. She had tried to dissuade him from going to drive back the Tielens on the northern borders and he had resented her interference. Well, he was a grown man, and she had no right to tell him what to do. But she wished that they could have parted on better terms. She had received news of him, of course, from Raïsa Korneli, but that was many weeks ago, and Elysia could not help but long for a letter written in his own hand, assuring her he was well.

A gust of wind off the sea set the flags fluttering on the citadel walls. Elysia stared, puzzled, wondering if time had turned back. For the crimson and gold of Smarna had disappeared again, to be replaced by the brilliant royal blue of Francia, alternating with the austere black of the Francian Commanderie.

"What does this mean?"

The cliff path meandered downward, away from the shore, toward the Vermeille Gate leading into the citadel. As Elysia approached, she saw a long straggling queue of people waiting to be allowed inside.

"What's happening?" she asked the woman in front of her, a stout henwife carrying a wide basket filled with brown-speckled eggs.

"They're checking identities," the henwife said, raising her eyes heavenward. She was perspiring in the heat, little runnels of sweat trickling down her cheeks. "It's all right for them; they've got plenty of shade."

"But why?"

"Haven't you heard?" A dairyman turned around on his cart seat. "Eugene of Tielen gave us away to Francia. We're part of the Francian empire now."

Elysia was so taken aback that for a moment she couldn't speak.

"And some important Francian dignitary has arrived. So they're making sure we're not smuggling weapons in to assassinate him."

"Which dignitary?" Elysia asked, recovering her voice.

"Some priest."

"What do they think I'm going to do, pelt him with my precious eggs?" grumbled the henwife.

Now that they were in sight of the gate, she could see Francian soldiers, on guard in their scarlet-and-blue uniforms, while two black-robed officials questioned each one in the queue in turn. Thus far, no one had been turned away, but one of the officials was hastily scribbling down details in a large ledger.

If they were checking identities, who were they searching for? Or were they compiling a dossier?

"My cream'll curdle if we have to wait around in this heat much longer," complained the dairyman loudly.

At last Elysia found herself standing before the clerks in the shade beneath the old gatehouse. Patiently, she gave her name and address.

"Madame Andar."

She saw a look pass between the two men and felt a little twinge of apprehension.

"Do you attend worship regularly, Madame?" asked one earnestly.

The question caught her off guard.

"Worship?" she repeated. "What do you mean?"

"King Enguerrand is most anxious to ensure that the people of Smarna observe the teachings of the church."

She stared at them. Whatever next? Were they to be forced to attend regular worship? As they waved her through the gateway, she thought she saw the official put a mark by her name. What did that mean? Nonbeliever? Troublemaker?

Elysia hurried away into the winding cobbled streets, making for the university quarter, where the artists' shop nestled in the shadow of the old college walls.

The heat lingered in the narrow places of the citadel, intensifying the odors of stale cooking, leaky sewers, and the pungently feral scents left by marauding cats.

She made her purchases at the art shop and exchanged a little gossip with the proprietor, who was always gloomy, especially in hot weather.

"Colchise stinks. We could do with some rain to wash the gutters clean."

"Your wish is sure to be answered. There'll be a storm later today," Elysia said as he scooped the granules of cinnabar into cones of paper and twisted them with deft fingers into packets.

"I could wish it'd wash a few other foreign bodies from the streets and back where they came from."

Elysia nodded, understanding all too well what he was implying.

"Rafael?" Elysia knocked again on the door to Lukan's rooms. There was no reply. *Have I come on the wrong day?* she wondered. But she was sure she was not mistaken; the college clock had just chimed eleven. And it was unlike Lukan to forget.

Puzzled, she went to the porter's lodge to check if he had left a message for her.

Galaktion, the porter on duty, beckoned her to one side, and said in a low voice, "The Francians paid him a visit last night."

"What kind of visit?" she said. "I mean—did he leave with his visitors?"

"They said it was a formality. Questions to be answered about the content of his lectures or some such."

Elysia did not like the sound of this at all. "And he hasn't been seen since?"

"The other staff and the students are none too happy about it. They've called a meeting over in the School of Rhetoric. If you hurry, you should make it before they close the doors."

Elysia hurried back around the sides of the quadrangle, not daring to walk over the parched grass lawn—a privilege reserved only for the most eminent scholars. The domed hall of the School of Rhetoric lay ahead, an elegant building over two hundred years old, ornamented with marble busts of antique philosophers and sophists.

She ran up the steps, hearing the buzz of many voices issuing from inside. Two students at the door barred her way. "I'm sorry, madame, this is a private lecture."

Elysia had opened her mouth to protest that she was Professor Lukan's oldest friend and ally, when an auburn-haired girl spotted her and waved, calling out her name. "Elysia! Over here!" It was Raïsa Korneli.

"I'm not allowed in," Elysia called back. Raïsa came over, and stared in annoyance at the two students on the door.

"I said turn away anyone we don't know, not friends of the cause. This is Elysia Andar, you idiots."

The students glanced embarrassedly at each other and stood aside to let her in. The hall was full; every seat was taken.

"How are you, Raïsa?" Elysia exchanged a kiss of greeting with the young woman.

"Well enough." Raïsa had to raise her voice to be heard. She still wore a mourning band around one sleeve of her plain white linen blouse in memory of her brother Miran. Her exuberant hair was confined beneath a white linen kerchief, giving her, Elysia thought, the grave air of a young schoolmistress.

"Look," Raïsa said. "Everyone's here in support of Professor Lukan. Is there any chance the Francians will listen to us and release him?"

Before Elysia could reply, a hush fell as several eminent academics took their place on the platform, all resplendent in their full academic regalia—gowns, hoods, and caps. Foremost among them, she recognized the chancellor of the university, the elderly Professor Petris, who had to be helped up to the lectern to address the crowded hall.

"I have grave news," he said, gripping hold of both sides of the lectern to support himself. "We have just been informed by the Francian authorities that Professor Lukan has been arraigned on two counts: sedition and heresy."

In the ensuing shocked silence, Elysia glanced at Raïsa.

"How dare they do such a thing!" Raïsa whispered.

"Minister Vashteli is currently negotiating with the Francian Commanderie to try to get Professor Lukan released on bail."

Heads began to turn as the doors opened and Minister Vashteli came in, followed by Pavel Velemir. Professor Petris rapped on the lectern for silence as the minister walked to the center of the platform.

"I have just come from a meeting with the officials of the Francian Commanderie."

Raïsa glanced uncertainly at Elysia.

"And I regret to say that they will not make the smallest concession to our requests."

A low, angry grumble of protest had begun among the listening students and the chancellor had to thump on the lectern several times before silence fell again.

"I beg you all"—and Petris's voice trembled—"not to attempt anything rash. We lost many brilliant students in the recent troubles." At Elysia's side, Raïsa was sadly nodding in agreement. "We cannot afford to lose any more. Professor Lukan would not wish a single one of you to risk his life on his account."

"But the Francians burn heretics!" a student shouted out.

"We won't let them burn our professor!" shouted out another.

Suddenly the whole hall erupted into chaos, all the students shouting in support of Lukan and stamping their feet.

At Elysia's side, Raïsa rose to her feet, one clenched fist punching the air as she joined her voice to the chorus.

"Set Lukan free! Set Lukan free!"

Elysia checked the great clock on the wall and saw to her dismay that she was late for the sitting. "I must go," she signed to Raïsa.

She was hurrying through the gatehouse when she saw Minister Vashteli getting into her carriage. The uproar in the School of Rhetoric had settled into rhythmic chanting. The minister paused, as if listening, and as Elysia approached, she turned around.

"My dear Elysia!" They exchanged kisses. "Will you listen to that? There'll be another riot."

"Is there any hope of bail?"

"Dear me, no. These Commanderie officers are utterly fanatical."

"Oh dear." Elysia had hoped for more encouraging news. "And is it really true what they're saying on the streets? That Eugene has ceded us to Francia?"

Nina's eyes flashed. "We have been used as ransom in some extraordinary deal brokered between Enguerrand and Eugene." Another roar of fury rang out from the School of Rhetoric. "I was invited to address the meeting—but I've decided to wait until the students are in a calmer frame of mind. Can I drop you anywhere?"

"Oh, thank you, yes," Elysia said, grateful at the thought she would make up much of the lost time.

"Actually, Elysia, I was planning to ask your opinion on a rather delicate matter," said Nina Vashteli as the little carriage clattered away over the cobbles.

"Me?" Elysia wondered what the self-possessed Nina could possibly wish to consult her about.

"It's about my son Giorgi."

"Has he been unwell again? I remember you said that he's been in indifferent health of late."

"May I confide in you?"

"Of course."

The carriage lurched around a narrow corner and Elysia was obliged to grab hold of the strap to avoid being flung into Nina's lap.

"He's been asking questions. Difficult questions."

"About . . . ?"

"About his father." Nina gazed out of the window as she spoke. "And I'm afraid I lied. It wouldn't have advanced my reputation—let alone my career—to have it generally known that my son's father was of royal blood, would it? Especially as I had espoused the republican cause so fervently."

Elysia was curious, in spite of herself. "I had no idea. But surely, you're not talking about mad old Prince Giorgi?"

Nina Vashteli's green eyes flashed with a look of utter disdain. "Oh, please, Elysia, credit me with a little more taste and discernment than that. Did you never meet Old Giorgi's nephews, Nicoloz and Eduard?"

The carriage slowed as it approached the Vermeille Gate.

"Not Nico Gorgasali, the playwright?" Elysia exclaimed. "Oh, but he was *so* good-looking. I remember one night, after the first performance of his play—" And she broke off, blushing. "It wasn't Nico, was it?"

"It was Eduard, his younger brother," said Nina haughtily. "We met in Allegonde. He was studying architecture, I was doing the 'tour.' We spent a perfect few months together in Bel'Esstar, then went our separate ways."

"Does he know about Giorgi?"

"He does. But he has a wife and family in Allegonde. We agreed to leave things as they are."

"How convenient for him," said Elysia pointedly.

"My late husband was very understanding," replied Nina with a shrug. "We had no children of our own. He was so much older than I; he was pleased to have a son."

The Francian guards on the gate were waving the carriage through.

"But why tell me all this now, Nina?"

"Because you have a son who is . . . *different* too."

"Different?" Elysia stared at Nina Vashteli warily. "How different?"

"It all began back in the winter. One night he woke crying inconsolably. He said he had a horrible dream. He said"—and Nina shuddered as she spoke—"that a wicked man had cut his throat and that he was bleeding to death. He said the sky was colored red with blood. And when I opened the shutters to show him he was only dreaming"—Nina's voice went very quiet—"he was right. There was a fiery glow in the night sky."

"But all children have nightmares," said Elysia. "The glow in the sky must have been a coincidence."

"Since then, the nightmares have grown worse. And he spends so much time sleeping. I'm afraid he's wasting away, Elysia," said Nina, biting her lip, "and yet the doctors tell me they can find nothing wrong with him."

"Did he witness any of the fighting in the citadel? That was a very frightening time. I'm sure all the children in Colchise have been suffering nightmares since then."

"I wish it were that simple."

Elysia was suddenly seized with an unpleasant possibility. "He wasn't anywhere near the bay, was he, when Gavril destroyed the Tielen fleet?"

"No. That had also occurred to me."

"Nina, would you like me to talk with him? I could do some sketches, if you like. Often sitters open their hearts to a portraitist. I've heard many confidences in my time."

"Oh, Elysia, would you? It would relieve me so. Of course you must let me know your fee—"

Elysia raised her hand. "I wouldn't hear of it."

"But I couldn't possibly use your professional skills without some form of remuneration."

"Then," said Elysia, inspired, "would you, in turn, do me a favor? Would you approach the Francian Commanderie again and see if they will drop these ridiculous charges against Rafael Lukan?"

"Ah!" said Nina, eloquently raising one slender dark brow. "I will do what I can. But I make no promises, Elysia. You may well wish you had accepted my first offer."

CHAPTER 25

As Elysia approached the villa, she heard Celestine de Joyeuse's voice issuing from an open window, singing scale after scale, effortlessly rising in pitch. Elysia stopped, enchanted by the ethereal purity of her tone, forgetting for a moment as she listened the turmoil she had left behind at the university.

"I'm so sorry to be late," she said, as Celestine's maid Nanette admitted her to the drawing room where Celestine sat at the fortepiano. "I went into the citadel and got caught up in . . ." She opened her case, taking out pencils and charcoal as she spoke. "Well, you don't want to hear about all that."

"Poor Madame Andar, you look hot. Won't you join me in a glass of iced mint tea?"

Even the words sounded cool and deliciously refreshing. "Mint tea would be heavenly." Elysia pulled off the lace fichu around her neck and fanned herself with a sheet from her sketchbook.

"I heard there was some unrest in the citadel," remarked Celestine, pouring Elysia a glass of tea.

"Dear me, yes. The students are very angry about the arrest of Rafael Lukan." Elysia sipped the tea and let out a little sigh. "Ahh. That's better. It can get stiflingly hot here at the tail end of summer. Tempers rise with the heat. And we Smarnans have a reputation for volatility . . ."

"This Rafael Lukan must be a very charismatic teacher to inspire his students to rebel."

Elysia nodded. "His ideas may seem revolutionary, but they're all well-grounded in the writings of the ancient philosophers."

"I hear he has given some controversial lectures. And hasn't he written a treatise called 'The Decline of Religion in Contemporary Society' or suchlike?"

"Goodness me," said Elysia, going to set up her easel, "you are very well-informed, demoiselle. I had no idea Lukan's writings were known in Francia."

"Lukan," repeated Celestine with a little smile twitching around her lips. "Would I be correct in thinking you know the professor quite . . . intimately?"

"I've known Rafael Lukan for many years." Elysia suddenly felt so hot that she had to fan herself vigorously. Idle tongues must have been wagging again.

"I'm sorry, I didn't mean to pry." Celestine smiled so charmingly that Elysia could not feel offended for long. "Now, where would you like me to sit? At the window, looking out at the sea? Or at the fortepiano?"

Celestine stole a swift glance at Elysia Andar as the painter helped her settle into the pose for the portrait. Thus far, Elysia showed no sign of any adverse reaction to the powder Celestine had slipped into her glass of tea. That was some relief, for she had never concocted anything so powerful from her father's grimoire before and was more than a little apprehensive in case she had inadvertently poisoned her victim. "To draw out the truth from the unsuspecting," read the description of the spell. And it had not been easy to obtain all the ingredients, especially the rare and expensive tincture of purple hellebore, which was said to grow only on the lower mountain slopes behind Lake Taigal. "It loosens the tongues of the unwary, causing them to reveal all manner of secrets."

Elysia gently tipped Celestine's chin a little to the right.

Celestine could not tell yet how successful her ploy had been. "I saw your portrait of the Empress Astasia in Mirom," she said casually. "That decided me; I wanted no other painter but you, Madame Andar."

"Oh, please call me Elysia." Elysia drew back and gazed at her, as though assessing the effect of the pose.

"Then you must call me Celestine. I insist."

Elysia went back to her sketches, which she had propped up on the easel. "Well, Celestine, I must confess that I did little other than complete that portrait. My son Gavril must take the credit for it."

"And where is your son now?" Celestine asked innocently.

Elysia was squinting at her as she held up her pencil and did not answer straightaway. "My son?" She sighed as she picked up her charcoal and began to make marks on the canvas. "I wish I knew."

Was the truth powder working? Or would she have to tempt Elysia to another glass of tea and slip in a second spoonful?

"So there's no chance of commissioning him to do another portrait?"

"I haven't seen Gavril since he rode off with the rebels many weeks ago. Too many weeks . . ." Elysia let out another sigh as she sketched with light, darting little strokes.

"He was with the rebels?"

"They would never have defeated Eugene's men without him. The rebels think he has a secret weapon which he used on the Rossiyans." The charcoal dropped from Elysia's hand. She was staring blankly at the canvas.

The truth herb was working. "So if it wasn't a secret weapon, what was it?" prompted Celestine, leaning forward.

"He is possessed by a daemon called a Drakhaoul." Elysia spoke in a low, expressionless voice, as though unaware she was talking aloud. "It gifts him with terrible destructive powers. He can obliterate an entire army, an entire fleet, a city. But using his powers makes him weak and ill. The only way to restore himself is to drink the blood of innocents."

"How horrible," said Celestine.

"It's slowly destroying him. The same way it destroyed my husband. That was why he employed Doctor Kazimir. To make an antidote to subdue the daemon within him."

"Doctor Kazimir?"

"A Muscobite chymist. A very nervous man—but a genius."

Nanette popped her head around the door. "Your accompanist is here, demoiselle, for the rehearsal."

"Rehearsal?" Elysia blinked, as though waking from a doze. "Dear me, where has the time gone? I had no idea it was so late. The light has altered."

Celestine rose and stretched; she was stiff from holding the pose for so long, but she did not mind in the least. The powder had done its work and although she smiled at the portraitist and agreed to another sitting at the same time the next day, her mind was turning over and over the extraordinary things she had learned from Madame Andar.

"I can't think what we can have found to talk about," said Elysia as she packed away her paints and brushes. She seemed bemused and as she lifted her case, she lost her balance. Celestine hurried over, catching her by the arm and righting her.

"Are you all right?" she asked, not without some anxiety. There was no mention of aftereffects in the grimoire.

"Just a little weary; it's been a long day," said Elysia, one hand pressed to her forehead. "We were talking of my son, weren't we?"

"Yes?" Celestine said warily.

"Sometimes I worry too much about him." Elysia wiped away a tear. "Please excuse me, I had no intention of unburdening myself. It's quite unforgivable."

"It's quite understandable." Celestine patted her arm in what she hoped would seem a gesture of reassurance. "Nanette!" she called. "Madame Andar will go home in my carriage."

"Oh, please don't go to all that trouble on my account. The fresh air will do me good."

"No, no, I insist." Celestine took a firm grip on Elysia's arm and helped her out into the cool of the hall. "The driver will fetch your paints. After all"—and she forced a little laugh—"it's in my best interests to look after my portraitist, isn't it?"

Celestine waved the carriage farewell from the steps and went back into the villa to find Jagu standing in the salon, arms folded, awaiting her.

"How could you?" he said sternly. "How could you risk using your father's grimoire again?"

"What if I have?" she said, pushing past him to seat herself at the fortepiano. "I've learned more this afternoon than de Lanvaux's spies have in a year."

"You promised me, Celestine. And it's so dangerous—for you, as well as your victims. Don't you know how insidiously these forbidden texts work? They deceive you. You think that you are using them, but in reality, they are using *you*."

"I hate it when you preach, Jagu." Why couldn't he understand? The grimoire was only a tool, for her to use when she saw fit. She shuffled through the music on the fortepiano and suddenly threw all the sheets up in the air in her excitement. "She told me so much, Jagu." Jagu was picking up the scattered sheets. "She told me that Professor Lukan was like a second father to Gavril Nagarian. And best of all"—and she knelt beside Jagu—"she told me that there's a Muscobite scientist called Kazimir who knows how to make a potion to subdue the Drakhaoul and rob the Drakhaon of all his powers!"

"And when the Maistre asks how you came by this information, what will you say to him? You'll have to lie. And then one lie will only lead to another—and another." Jagu's eyes burned into hers. "Don't do this to yourself, Celestine. Don't perjure your immortal soul. Destroy the book."

His words hurt her. She had wanted his approval. Well, what had she expected from a Commanderie lackey?

"Or if you are no longer strong enough to do it, let me do it for you."

"No!" Celestine backed away from him. "It's all I have left of my father. I forbid you to touch it. If you really cared for me, Jagu, you'd understand."

He just looked at her.

"I don't feel like rehearsing anymore." She seized the music from his hands and banged it down on top of the fortepiano. "I'll send a report on my findings to the Maistre."

"But the recital—"

"If you want something to do, go and try out the fortepiano at the ambassador's house. You know how these people neglect their instruments." And she turned her back on him, pretending to rearrange the bowl of drooping musk roses Nanette had placed by the window.

Celestine heard him hesitate—then he turned and left the room.

Surely he couldn't be right about the grimoire? A spell was just a spell. How could it work both ways?

"Ow!" She had pricked her finger on the musk rose thorns. She raised her finger to her lips and sucked the tiny bead of blood.

She had never seen Jagu so angry before. And yet she had sensed another emotion underlying his anger. She had always judged him a dedicated Guerrier, ambitious and utterly committed to the Commanderie. He had always treated her with respect and courtesy. But she could not help but notice the way he had looked at her that afternoon. Now she understood that she could wield quite a different influence over him.

"Ah, Jagu," she said softly, "is that the way it goes?" Were his feelings for her strong enough to make him forget his vows?

*   *   *

"Are you feeling all right, Elysia?" Palmyre asked as Elysia tottered into the kitchen.

Elysia sank into a chair, pressing her fingertips to her aching temples. "I must have taken a touch of the sun today. I have a terrible headache."

Palmyre made her a cold compress and poured her some tea. "It's not so surprising, with all the worry about Lukan. So—did you glean any news about the Professor from the Francian lady?"

"What?" Elysia said vaguely. She tried to remember the conversation with Celestine but clouds seemed to be fogging her mind. "Do you know, Palmyre, I don't think we talked of anything of significance . . ." She winced as her head began to throb again.

"You look very pale. Why not go and lie down till the headache wears off?"

For once, Elysia did not argue with Palmyre.

"Where's Gavril Andar?" Raïsa paced Minister Vashteli's antechamber. "One moment, he's fighting the Tielens at our side. The next, he disappears."

"Has Elysia Andar heard any news from her son?" Pavel asked. He noticed that a single lock of auburn hair had come loose from beneath Raïsa's neat kerchief, giving her an endearingly distracted air.

"Not a word. And just when we need his help . . ."

"Yes." Pavel was remembering the heart-stopping moment when he had witnessed the impossible and learned Gavril Andar's terrible secret. It would take a Drakhaon to spring Rafael Lukan from the Commanderie's clutches.

The minister's door opened. Raïsa immediately sat down and raised a book to cover her face, peeping over the top.

"And I trust," a man emerged, dressed all in black, "that you will ensure there are no further demonstrations." He gave a brusque little bow.

"If you insist on pursuing this, then I'm afraid I can give you no guarantee," Minister Vashteli replied in tones of frost. "Good-day to you, Inquisitor."

Pavel rose from his desk to see the visitor out.

"Who was that man?" hissed Raïsa when he returned.

"This doesn't look good for Rafael Lukan. That was one of the Commanderie inquisitors. They're going to try Lukan for heresy."

CHAPTER 26

Day by day, Gavril had been slowly regaining his strength. Malusha's hens had been well fed and the vegetable garden weeded, watered, and hoed. But much of the time, he had slept the hours away, watched over by Lady Iceflower and her brood. Perhaps Khezef was right; he had depleted so much of his natural energy that he was too weak to fly anymore. Perhaps Khezef had reasons of his own for staying hidden in remote Azhkendir . . .

Gavril was at work in the little vegetable garden behind the cottage, kneeling on the raked soil, thinning out a late crop of carrots that Malusha must have planted some time before they left for Khitari. There was something indefinably therapeutic about working in the fresh air, getting his hands dirty in the good, rich earth of Azhkendir. Perhaps he was still healing from the long months of imprisonment in the Iron Tower.

"*Drakhaon . . . help us!*"

The harrowing cry seared through him; he dropped the trowel and clapped his hands to his ears. "Did you hear that, Khezef? It's my *druzhina*! Something must have happened at Kastel Drakhaon."

Khezef hesitated. "*Are you sure you're ready?*"

Gavril was already hurrying back toward the cottage. He tamped down the embers in the grate, shuttered the windows, and locked the door, putting the key back in its hiding place.

"I'm ready," he said quietly. Truth was, he had been dreading this moment, fearing that when it came, he would find he was still too weak to transform into Drakhaon form. He walked up onto the moors. Standing there with the sun warming his upturned face, he closed his eyes and surrendered himself to Khezef's powers.

The air around him turned thunder-blue. A convulsive shuddering racked his body until he thought he would break apart. And just when he feared he was losing consciousness, he felt himself lifting, rising into the air.

"We did it, Khezef!" he shouted, as the daemon bore him upward on outstretched wings and the brown bracken banks dropped away below. "We did it!"

After a hasty scan of the kastel from the air, Gavril was puzzled. He could see no sign of trouble. He decided to approach the old watchtower on foot. A lookout soon spotted him and let out a full-throated shout. "The Lord Drakhaon is here!"

The *druzhina* came running up, crowding around him, jostling to be the first to greet him, foremost amongst them flax-haired Vasili, Dunai's younger brother, grown to full height.

"What news do you bring, my lord?" he cried.

"Take me to the Bogatyr" was all Gavril said.

Askold rose to his feet, leaning heavily on a stick, as Gavril entered the watchtower. His shaggy-haired hounds whined and loped away, their tails between their legs.

"Welcome home, Lord Gavril," he said.

Gavril felt a deep and genuine pleasure to see his Bogatyr. "You're looking well, Askold," he said formally. Then he forgot protocol and went toward the older man, his arms wide, and embraced him.

"I thought for a moment that your father had come to take me to the Ways Beyond," said Askold, gazing intently into his face. "You look a true Drakhaon now, my lord."

So this was how Volkh had appeared when the Drakhaoul's hold over him had grown too strong, when he had ordered his youthful portrait to be burned because he could no longer bear to be reminded of how he had changed.

"And my son?"

"Dunai?" Gavril gazed around, slowly realizing from the *druzhinas'* somber faces that all was far from well. "But Captain Lindgren dispatched ships to intercept the Francian cutter off Arkhelskoye. I assumed—"

"There's been no word."

Gavril touched the blood-oath scar on his wrist, confused.

"But what about the captain?" Lindgren had taken a blow to the head in the fight at the monastery. "Isn't he back yet?"

"The Tielens tell us nothing!" burst out Vasili.

"He must have stayed at the port to direct the operation. The Francians can't have sneaked past the Tielen blockade." Surely the Tielens would have been more than a match for the Francians?

Askold suddenly gripped Gavril's arm tightly. "Bring back my boy, Lord Gavril," he said hoarsely. "That's all I ask of you. Bring him back to me."

Gavril headed east again toward the port. Nils Lindgren had been confident that his ships would intercept the Francian cutter as it rounded the long spit of rocky coastline on the trade route south. Yet Gavril saw no sign of Tielen soldiers making their way back to the kastel.

As he wheeled out across the harbor, he caught sight of two Tielen frigates at anchor off the port, one with the topmast shot clean away, the other listing, her sails in shreds.

"The Francian men-o'-war came out of nowhere, my lord. Must have been lurking off Jhenezh Head." The harbormaster poured Gavril a shot of vodka. "So when Captain Lindgren's ships tried to head off the Francian cutter, out pop the men-o'-war and they start firing. In all the smoke and confusion, the Francian cutter just slips away."

Gavril swallowed the vodka and set the glass down sharply. The harbormaster flinched. The atmosphere in the harbor office was tense; all the sailors and merchants were staring at him, as if expecting him to lose his temper. "What was their heading? Where were they making for?"

"I didn't exactly catch—"

"Smarna," said an old sailor. "I heard Smarna."

"And with a fair wind, how long would it take them to reach Smarna?"

The old man shrugged. "Ten days, two weeks, maybe more."

"And if I sailed after them?"

"You'd find it hard to catch 'em up now, my lord, fair wind or no."

Gavril tossed him a coin as he left the office; the old man caught it, nodding his thanks.

Gavril stopped to lean on the harbor wall and gaze out across the White Sea. The wind was fresh and little waves were whipping up into foam as they crashed against the harbor wall below. Gulls shrieked over the fishermen's catch as open barrels of silvered herring were unloaded. There seemed no choice but to follow the Francians to Smarna.

"We were outnumbered," said a voice behind him, "and outwitted."

Gavril turned to see Nils Lindgren approaching, the sea wind blowing his brown hair back, revealing the half-healed gash on the side of his head.

"I'm relieved to see you alive, Captain."

Lindgren pulled a wry face. "I underestimated the Francians' desire for that relic. We took a severe pounding." Lindgren leaned on the wall beside him. "It was all we could do to limp back to Arkhelskoye. The Emperor will not be pleased."

"And Semyon and Dunai?" Gavril asked, although he had already guessed Lindgren's answer.

"I'm sorry."

"I made a promise to Askold. And the Lord Drakhaon does not break his word. I've got to get them back."

"There's something else." Lindgren withdrew a paper from his uniform pocket. "We've received an enigmatic message by Vox Aethyria. It seems to have come from Smarna."

"Oh?" Gavril took the folded paper from Lindgren, opened it and read:

Rafael Lukan to stand trial in Colchise, charged with heresy.

Gavril crushed the paper in his hand.

"A friend of yours?" Lindgren said. His hazel eyes had darkened with concern.

"A very dear friend." There was no way he could leave Lukan to face the Commanderie court's justice. "In many ways, a second father."

"It could be a trap. A Francian trap."

"And you know, Captain, as well as I, how the Francians punish heretics."

Lindgren nodded. "You must do what you judge best, Lord Drakhaon." He saluted him. "I wish you Godspeed."

Gavril nodded in reply, touched by the warmth in Lindgren's farewell. "Take good care of my kastel till I return, Captain."

The salt wind began to gust more strongly.

"A fair wind to carry us swiftly south to Smarna."

Without looking back, Gavril walked to the end of the quay that jutted out into the open sea. He lifted his arms wide to the wind. He no longer cared who saw him transform, for this was Azhkendir, his own domain, and home to all the Drakhaons before him.

As he rose into the air, he murmured, "Forgive me, Kiukiu." And then there was nothing but the endless expanse of the sky and the dazzle of sunlight on the White Sea below.

CHAPTER 27

"I need to see the duchess now!" Oskar Alvborg had waited an hour in the antechamber for the old lady to finish her primping and preening.

"But she's still at her *toilette*," insisted the maidservant as he walked toward the door. "You can't go in—"

"And you can't stop me." He pushed her aside and opened the door.

The dowager duchess, still in her silken *peignoir*, was seated at her dressing table, her back to the door, while her maid teased and twisted her thinning grey locks into an elaborate, ringleted style.

"Who is so rude as to invade my privacy without even the courtesy of a knock?" demanded the dowager duchess. And then she saw Oskar's reflection in the oval mirror and let out a little cry. "Oskar?" she whispered, turning around, one grey curl still dangling awry. "Oskar, what's happened to you?" He could not help but feel gratified by her reaction. "Come here and let me look at you."

He decided to indulge her just this once. He didn't really want to be pawed by the old woman but it might prove a useful way to coax the information he needed out of her. So he went down on one knee beside her chair and let her rheumatic fingers touch his face and hair.

"This is nothing short of a miracle," she said. "Has Doctor Amandel seen the results of his treatments?"

"Not yet." Close to, he could see how yellow and stained her few remaining teeth were and could smell the decay on her breath, even though she had tried to sweeten it with aniseed pearls. As a boy he had hated being fussed over by the old aunts in his mother's household, had loathed the way they could never resist patting and stroking his hair, as if he were a lapdog.

"Even your hair has regrown. And it's just the same shade as your poor mother's, that wonderfully distinctive white-blond."

"My mother," repeated Oskar, hoping to prompt the dowager duchess into one of her reminiscences.

"Would you like some coffee?" The dowager duchess nodded to her maid, who brought him a delicate little cup and saucer. But as she proceeded to pour coffee into the cup, only a thin black trickle emerged.

"I'll go and fetch a fresh pot," the maid said, excusing herself with a little curtsy.

They were alone.

"There's something I've been meaning to ask you," Oskar said. The dowager duchess was gazing critically at herself, twisting the errant curl back into place. "There was gossip at court about my mother. Was any of it true?"

"Poor Ulla. It's true that my brother adored her." She dusted her face with a swansdown puff, and little clouds of white powder filled the air.

"Prince Karl?"

"But he had a wife and a healthy son. It was sad, of course, that my sister-in-law, dear Eleanora, suffered so many miscarriages after Eugene was born."

"But what does this have to do with my mother?" Oskar was growing more and more impatient with the old woman's rambling.

"And your father was a proud and intolerant man. It was an ill-made match from the start. I don't like to speak ill of the dead, but he treated your mother very harshly. Was it really necessary to shut her away up here, so far from court? To forbid her to entertain visitors? Oh, I know he made some pretense about her being in a frail state of health, but we guessed otherwise—"

"*Was* he my father?" Oskar demanded. "Was that why he punished her? Because she had betrayed him?"

"Great heavens, you mustn't speak like that of your own mother!" The dowager duchess threw up her hands in horror.

"Someone must know the truth." Oskar rose to his feet, towering over her. "And if I find that you have lied to me—"

The door opened and Greta's maid reappeared, carrying a steaming pot of fresh coffee. Oskar saw the expression of alarm on the dowager duchess's face. He backed away, muttering an excuse, and headed for the door.

"Your coffee—" began the maid but he just pushed past, ignoring her.

"Marta," Karila said as Marta brushed her hair, "is there any word from Papa today?"

"Your Papa's a very busy man," said Marta briskly, "protecting us from the Francians. And you know the old saying, no news is . . ."

"Good news," finished Karila. And then she sighed, a small, sad sigh. "It seems so long since I last saw him."

Shiver of fire-bright wings flecked black as coal . . .

"Stop brushing, Marta!"

Karila went to the window as fast as her twisted frame would allow her and gazed out, scanning the grounds and the sky for a glimpse, any glimpse of what she had sensed was near.

But all she could see was a blue sky with soft fleece-white clouds . . . and a lone horseman riding away down the broad drive.

As Oskar urged his horse down the gravel drive, he felt a sudden certainty that he was being observed.

He turned in the saddle and looked back at the old manor house. The shutters were all open to let in the fresh morning air. And at one window, framed by the yellow blossoms of a climbing rose, he saw Princess Karila standing watching him. Beside her, he could just make out the shadowy form of another child, the dark-eyed girl he had seen in the rose gardens.

Was she an omen of ill luck? Oskar kept asking himself as he rode through the bright morning back to the neighboring Alvborg estate. Or was it just his mind, playing on the morbid fantasies that had plagued him since his encounter with Lord Nagarian? She was probably a little companion of the princess's. But the way they had both just stood there and stared at him . . . it made him shudder to remember it.

"*Forget her,*" whispered his guardian spirit. "*You have greater mysteries to unravel.*"

Countess Ulla Alvborg, Oskar's mother, had spent her last years there in the austere country mansion, far from the court of Prince Karl and the society balls she had loved to attend. The winters were long and harsh with little or no daylight, and she had slowly wasted away, shunned by the nobles of the court who had once feted her beauty. When Ulla died, not long after his twenty-second birthday, he had sold off most of the estate to pay the gambling debts he had incurred. Why, he had reasoned to himself, would he want to live in the house his mother had often called her prison? And then, invalided out of the army after his disastrous encounter with Gavril Nagarian, he had found himself with nowhere else to go. Thanks to the dowager duchess's hospitality, he had spent hardly more than a few nights in the dilapidated house, returning only to collect clothes and papers from time to time.

"Master Oskar, welcome back again." The elderly housekeeper, Hillevi, curtsied as she opened the door. "Will you be eating here tonight?" And then she looked up at him and gasped, raising her apron to her mouth. "Your face! It's a miracle—"

"Give me the keys to my mother's apartments." He snatched the keys from her, leaving her offering praises to the saints for his miraculous recovery. The sound of his booted feet echoed hollowly around the empty hall as he hurried up the stone staircase. There were faded rectangular patches on the walls where fine paintings had once hung. And everywhere, there was an all-pervading stale smell of damp and neglect.

Only his father's portrait remained, and Oskar stopped to look at it with a cold, appraising eye.

Count Gunnar Alvborg, his father, had died in sordid circumstances, from injuries received in a sabre duel with another officer. The whole affair was hushed up at the time, but Oskar later learned that the two men had been drinking heavily in a Tielborg brothel. An argument had erupted over the favors of one of the whores. The sabre cut had not been severe enough to kill the count, but gangrene had soon set in and he had died in agony. Many inferred at the time that the count's dissolute habits had hastened his end. Oskar, forced to visit his father on his deathbed, could only remember the smell of scented candles, burning to cover the stench of the suppurating wound.

"Do something worthwhile with your life, for God's sake, Oskar!"

The count's pain-contorted features had terrified him and he had shrunk away from his father. "Don't fritter it away in cards and liquor like me . . ."

Little details in the portrait hinted at the life of dissolution that would eventually lead to his downfall: the red veins darkening Gunnar's nose, the ruddy complexion, the full, oversensual mouth. Just to look at Gunnar's portrait brought back early memories of the count returning home late at night, staggering blind drunk through the hallway, bellowing like a mad bull for his mother, while the two of them cowered behind the locked door of her bedroom, hoping and praying that he would collapse insensible before he reached them.

Oskar had ordered one room to be preserved exactly as it was when she was alive: his mother's bedchamber. He unlocked the doors and opened all the shutters to let the light in. A thin white film of dust lay over everything: the bed hangings of grey-and-lilac brocade; the little card table by the fireplace; the ebony cabinet inlaid with ivory and tortoiseshell in which she kept her personal treasures and papers . . .

Hillevi had covered the gilt-framed mirrors and portrait with sheets so that, he supposed, Ulla's sad spirit should not find a way back.

"Why would she want to come back here?" he muttered. With one tug, he whipped the sheet from the portrait of his mother, sending up a fine cloud of powdery dust into the sunlit room.

There she was, the society beauty. Her soulful eyes, the tender blue of meadow speedwells, seemed to smile down on her son. The portrait had been commissioned to celebrate her presentation at court. Even though the cut of her white satin court gown was old-fashioned, it was not difficult to see why she had been so admired. Oskar wiped away the wetness leaking from his eyes; the dust must have made them water.

"Mother," he whispered, "is it true? Why didn't you tell me?"

Of course, it was possible that she was a distant descendant of Artamon's line and the imperial blood in his veins came from her side of the family. But the more he gazed at her face, the more that little smile on her pretty lips seemed to tantalize him, hinting at hidden secrets that were there to be found, if only he was astute enough to seek them out.

"Why do you need proof? Don't you trust my word?"

The last time he had seen Ulla, before an inflammation of the lungs carried her off, she had been lying listlessly in this very bed, muffled up in a gossamer shawl of rose pink. He had been given special leave of absence from his regiment to visit his dying mother. And he had been shocked to see how wasted, how pale she looked. Only then had it occurred to him that she might have been lonely.

"How . . . handsome you look in your uniform," she had said, her voice so weak he had to bend close to hear. "How proud your father would have been . . ."

If only she had left a diary, letters, any little clue . . .

"Can't you see?"

"See what?" Oskar gazed at the painting.

"There is something concealed behind the frame."

Oskar gripped hold of the heavy portrait by its carved and gilded frame and carefully lifted it down from the wall. Sure enough, a tiny gilded key had been tucked into the back of the frame and secured there with yellowing gummed paper. And he would never have known if Sahariel hadn't shown him.

Weighing the tiny key in his palm, Oskar glanced around the room, wondering what it might unlock. All his mother's jewels had been sold years ago; even the pearl-and-sapphire necklace in the portrait had gone to cover the cost of her funeral.

His eyes focused on the ebony cabinet. And he heard her voice, from the depths of his childhood:

"My father brought this back all the way from Khitari, Oskar. There's a secret drawer concealed within—I'll wager a barley-sugar stick that even your clever little fingers can't find it."

He must have been no more than seven or eight years old at the time. He could remember her laughter, gently teasing, as he became more and more frustrated, turning and pulling little gold-and-ivory knobs, and all to no avail.

"Look," she had said, guiding his fingers to either side of the open cabinet. "You need to press with both index fingers on the flowers at exactly the same time. There's a trick to it. If one finger is too slow, it won't open."

Now his fingertips sought out the inlaid ivory chrysanthemums and tried a gentle pressure. His fingers were much larger now but his coordination was better. After three attempts, the concealed drawer shot open. And within the drawer lay a plain little wooden box, with a single lock.

"Now we'll see." Oskar inserted the tiny key and turned it. The box contained a miniature portrait, painted with intricate skill, of a handsome, firm-jawed man of middle years, his curling golden hair receding a little at the temples.

Beneath lay faded, folded papers, the writing blotted and smudged, as though with rain or teardrops, and as Oskar opened one, he released the faint, fading scent of pressed rose petals that crumbled to dust as they fell to the floor.

You know only too well, my dearest Ulla, that what you ask of me is impossible. I have done everything in my power to ensure that you are both generously provided for. But it can never be more than that; to acknowledge him as my own would lead to strife and contention in years to come. In these uncertain times, it is vitally important that Tielen remains united to face the threat from Francia. And a scandal could divide the nation. No, better he remain in ignorance and lead a happy and fulfilled life as his father's son.

K

"K for Karl?" muttered Oskar, raising his eyes from the letter to his mother's portrait. And he felt an overpowering sense of resentment that Prince Karl should have treated them both so shabbily. "What you ask of me is impossible." He could only guess how unhappy Ulla must have been when she realized that her charms were no longer so appealing to her royal lover.

And yet, these few intimate letters were hardly verification that he had royal blood in his veins. Eugene's lawyers would soon claim they were forgeries and it would be hard to dispute the case.

"*Haven't you proof enough now, my prince?*" whispered Sahariel.

"No." He needed the testimony of someone who had known Prince Karl, someone who was party to the shameful affair and had been sworn to secrecy all those years ago.

"*Uncover the mirror.*"

Oskar obeyed.

"*Look at yourself. And now look at the miniature.*"

Oskar glanced from his own reflection to the miniature and back several times. There was a likeness; it was undeniable, although it was more in the strong line of the jaw and the sculpted cheekbones than in coloring.

"It's still not enough."

"*Listen to me, Prince Oskar.*" His own reflection shimmered, and there was Sahariel again, etched in fire and smoky shadow, flickering like a windblown flame. "*These are difficult and unstable times. Now you are under my protection, I can make you strong, I can give you powers beyond your wildest imaginings.*"

Oskar gave a dry laugh. There was an echo of old childhood tales in this promise. "Oh yes? And, don't tell me, I have to sign my soul to you in blood?"

"*It's natural for you to be skeptical, my prince. But you were burned by the Drakhaon of Azhkendir. Imagine that he is standing here before you and you have the chance to retaliate. Hold out your hand.*"

Oskar was back on that desolate, icebound shore in Azhkendir. He saw Gavril Nagarian confronting him, he saw the blinding blast of fire, such beautiful azure blue fire, burst from the Drakhaon's fingertips and sear all his men to oblivion . . .

Oskar slowly extended his right hand. And as he did so, he felt an extraordinary energy pulsing through his arm, as though his blood had turned to liquid fire. Five points of scarlet flame flickered at the ends of his fingers, turning his flesh translucent, so that the fine bones were made visible, a skeletal hand enwreathed in fire.

"*Now do you believe?*" breathed Sahariel.

Oskar gazed down at his burning fingers and saw the flames slowly die down. The possibilities of wielding such phenomenal power began to beguile him; he could feel his resistance melting with the dying flames. It felt in some way a seduction, with the soft, caressing voice of Sahariel persuading him to do anything he wished.

"I believe," he said. "Oh yes, I believe."

Karila could not sleep. It was a warm night and Marta had drawn the heavy brocade curtains across the window to keep out the light, making the room feel stuffy and airless.

Downstairs, Great-Aunt Greta was playing cards with friends, entertained by a couple of peasant musicians from the Rosenholm estate who were performing plaintive folk songs on pipe, tabor, and fiddle. Eventually, lulled by the music, Karila drifted into fitful slumber.

"*He is coming,*" Tilua whispered to Karila.

*   *   *

The Dowager Duchess Greta sat in front of her dressing table mirror. She had dismissed her maid for the night; the girl had been yawning as she unlaced the duchess's dress after the card party. Greta had decided she would rather have Jannike alert in the morning than all fingers and thumbs. Greta had always found it difficult to sleep in the light, warm nights of midsummer. She put on a lacy nightcap and opened the casement windows. A cloud of little white moths fluttered in, attracted by her single lampflame. And then a sudden gust of hot, dry wind made the flame flicker wildly, scattering the moths like cinders.

"Who's there?" Greta demanded. She turned around to see Oskar Alvborg standing by the open window. "Oskar? How did you get in?" There was a disconcerting gleam in his eyes that made her feel nervous. "Please leave. Immediately."

"Tell me the truth," he said. "Was Prince Karl my father?"

She had prayed that she would never have to answer this question. Who had told him? Who had broken their vow?

"Let's discuss this in the morning, shall we?" Greta began to edge toward the bellpull. He moved so swiftly that all she saw was a shadowy blur. And there he was, standing in front of her, blocking her way.

"Was he my father?" he repeated in a low, urgent tone.

Her heart began to beat painfully fast. She must try to humor the madman. "Oskar, although Karl was my brother, he didn't share all his secrets with me—"

"I have proof," he said in a voice of deadly quiet. "I have letters. But I want to hear it from you, Duchess."

She stared up into his face. His eyes burned into hers.

"It won't change anything, Oskar," she said. "You were given privileges, money, a title—and you drank and gambled it all away."

He reached out and gripped hold of her shoulders, bringing his face closer to hers. "I want the truth."

Greta was so terrified by now that she could hardly breathe. Did he intend to kill her? Suddenly she began to gabble and out came the secret she had kept for so many years, even from the rest of her family.

"The truth? That my brother was tempted in a moment of weakness that he lived to regret for the rest of his days?" The room seemed to be growing darker. "Yes, you are Karl's illegitimate son. Yes, he chose not to acknowledge you." Each word was harder to say than the last. She was gasping for breath. "Because it would have hurt Eleanora, and Karl could not bear to hurt her. And what good will this knowledge do you, Oskar?" All she could see in the darkness were his eyes: two stars of flame burning in the shadows. And then she was falling into darkness, one hand stretched toward him, though whether for help, or to push him away, she no longer knew . . .

A hot, dry wind fanned the air in slow, rhythmic gusts, ominous as the steady beat of great wings.

"*He is here.*"

Karila limped to the window, tugged back the heavy curtains, and gazed out into the pale sky. An ominous aura of darkness hovered above the manor house, like a stormcloud.

"Who is he?" Karila whispered back. "And what does he want?"

A hoarse scream tore the air. Karila gripped the window frame to steady herself. She heard confused shouts from down below as the guards came running up from their sentry posts.

"He's getting away!"

"Stop him!"

"Fire! *Fire!*" The harsh crack of carbine shots rang out as a fiery streak of shadow burst from the roof and flung itself across the sky, in a dazzle of sparks.

"Another dragon?" Karila's heart was pattering, her head was dizzy with excitement. The guards were pointing up into the sky, aiming their carbines, in vain. But the midnight visitor had gone and all that remained was a trail etched in soot and flame against the eerie light of the midnight sun.

"Help here!" called a woman's voice shrilly. "The duchess is unwell!"

The whole house was in an uproar as Karila made her way through the winding corridors toward her great-aunt's apartments. No one seemed to notice her or to remark on the fact that she was in her nightgown and her feet were bare. Servants ran hither and thither, some in their nightclothes too, and all were calling for Doctor Amandel.

Karila reached the antechamber where several of Great-Aunt Greta's women guests had gathered; they were speaking together in low, agitated voices.

"And he threatened her?"

"How did he get in past the guards?

"We could all be murdered in our own beds!"

Karila continued toward her great-aunt's bedchamber, hoping they might not notice her. Just as she reached the doorway, one of the older women cried out, "You mustn't go in, Princess. Your great-aunt is not well enough to receive visitors."

"Karila?" came a faint voice from within. "Let her come in."

Karila started forward with her ungainly, twisted walk.

Her great-aunt lay in the heliotrope-swagged bed, propped up on many pillows. The old lady's face was unnaturally pale and her lacy nightcap was awry, so that several grey locks had escaped from its confines, giving her a distracted look, quite unlike her usual neat appearance.

"Karila," said Great-Aunt Greta in a rasping whisper, "come closer."

Karila hesitated. She had always known that her great-aunt was very old but the dowager duchess's vivacity of spirit had successfully concealed that fact. Now Karila feared her great-aunt might be dying. Dutifully, she moved to stand at the old lady's bedside.

Great-Aunt Greta reached out one trembling hand and caught hold of hers, squeezing it feebly. "My child, I'm sorry, so very sorry . . ." Her eyes filled with tears. "He made me tell him. And now we are all in danger."

CHAPTER 28

"Your majesty." Ruaud de Lanvaux went down on one knee before King Enguerrand. "We have finally collected all the pieces of Sergius's Staff. Our most skilled craftsmen are already working to reforge it. We . . ." His voice trailed away as he looked up into Enguerrand's face. "Is all well with you, majesty?" he asked more gently. For the young king was gazing at him with a smile that made his eyes shine with warmth. The Grand Maistre slowly rose to his feet, still looking into Enguerrand's radiant face. "Majesty?" he said again, puzzled.

"I have something to confide in you." Even Enguerrand's voice sounded different; there was a new quality of calm assurance that de Lanvaux had never heard before.

Ever since the Grand Maistre entered the king's chamber, he had sensed that the angelstone had begun to glow. Now it was giving off such a dazzling brightness that the light penetrated his black military surcoat.

"What does this mean?" Ruaud de Lanvaux drew out the crystal and held it up. "Is a Drakhaoul-daemon approaching?" The crystal was alive with swirls of liquid gold. De Lanvaux had never witnessed such a phenomenon before. His gaze slid slowly to rest on the king, who was still smiling and nodding.

"You see the gold? Pure gold? It's an *angel*, de Lanvaux. I've been chosen."

"An angel?" repeated de Lanvaux warily. He had never seen Enguerrand like this before.

"It came to me one night, de Lanvaux. And it told me what I have to do. Once Sergius's Staff is reforged, I must use Artamon's rubies to lure the other Drakhaoul-daemons to me. And then I must destroy them."

There was such conviction in the king's voice and such a look of determination in his eyes that Ruaud de Lanvaux was almost tempted to set aside his doubts. Yet what did these pulsing swirls of gold lighting the angelstone mean? The crystal had been passed down from Grand Maistre to Grand Maistre since Lord Argantel had fled Azhkendir, but its true function had been lost over the centuries.

"The Commanderie has used the angelstone to monitor daemonic activity since the order was founded," Ruaud said.

"And if a Drakhaoul is near, the stone turns dark."

"And your point is, majesty?"

"Ask yourself, de Lanvaux, why it's called an angelstone. Because it detects the presence of powerful spirits from beyond our world, powers of good as well as evil!"

Ruaud de Lanvaux slowly nodded. Although Enguerrand's simple reasoning made a kind of sense, there were too many unanswered questions to satisfy his skeptical mind.

"The Heavenly Warriors came to Sergius's aid when he fought the sons of Artamon," continued Enguerrand. "I am to be Sergius's successor."

De Lanvaux was growing increasingly troubled by Enguerrand's fervor. "If you're thinking of challenging Lord Nagarian, please remember that the first Drakhaon of Azhkendir was too strong for Sergius—and slew him."

"This time it will be different." Enguerrand reached out and placed his hand on de Lanvaux's shoulder. "Have faith in me. This is my destiny. I was born to do this."

There was a certain irony in this reversal of roles, de Lanvaux reflected. Since Enguerrand's early years, he had encouraged his student to devote himself to the cult of their patron saint and to lead a devout life. Now Enguerrand was gently rebuking him, as if he was the master, chiding his acolyte for the weakness of his faith.

As Ruaud walked away from the king's chamber, his mind was still dazzled by the golden radiance emanating from the angelstone. Could it be true? Had Enguerrand truly been chosen by unearthly powers to be Sergius's successor? He was so preoccupied that he did not notice that Inquisitor Visant had fallen into step alongside him until he spoke.

"One of your agents has been causing the council some concern, Maistre," said Inquisitor Visant.

"One of *my* agents?" Ruaud de Lanvaux said.

"We've had our suspicions for some time. Mage blood will reveal itself, sooner or later."

"I have no idea to whom you're referring." But Ruaud knew all too well that Visant meant Celestine de Joyeuse.

"One of my men was in the raiding party that went to Saint Sergius. Mademoiselle de Joyeuse was twice observed to use some iridescent dust that caused those who inhaled it to fall instantly into a deep sleep."

"Your man must have a strong imagination. A dust that causes instant sleep?"

"There was a recipe for just such a dust in the books that were burned on Kaspar Linnaius's pyre. And she *is* de Maunoir's daughter."

"Proof. I need proof, Visant, before I can order her arrest."

"If the Commanderie is seen to condone such dangerous arts, our reputation will be tarnished beyond repair. We must make an example of her."

"How can we bring her to trial without firm evidence?" insisted Ruaud.

"One could almost believe that she has bewitched you too, Maistre, with those angelic blue eyes."

"That is a very serious allegation, Inquisitor," said Ruaud coldly.

"Which can be disproved by bringing the young woman before a Commanderie tribunal. If she is innocent, she will walk free. If guilty . . ."

Ruaud stared at Visant, knowing himself outmaneuvered. *What, I wonder, do you really wish to gain from this, Inquisitor? Are you out to discredit me, so that you can become Grand Maistre in your turn?*

"Then recall her. But be prepared. If she is guilty, as I strongly suspect she is, she will try to escape. And she knows far too much to be allowed to go blabbing our secrets to our enemies."

"I think you have misread Celestine de Joyeuse's character," said Ruaud. It grieved him to think that Celestine, his protégé, might have been tempted to use those same dark arts that had corrupted her father. "But I will have her brought back from Smarna. And then she is yours for questioning."

When Visant had gone, Ruaud found himself reflecting on Visant's irritating punctiliousness. A merchant's son, Visant had compensated for his lack of noble blood by using his considerable intelligence to study law, advancing to the high rank of Inquisitor. He was ambitious and Ruaud suspected he had been cultivating several members of the Commanderie council who were not in sympathy with Ruaud's opinions.

So, with some reluctance, he summoned a Guerrier. "I need to bring one of our number back from Smarna. Ask the Admiralty which Francian ships are in the area."

The Guerrier returned a little while later. "The *Aquilon* is making fast for Colchise, Maistre, and is at your disposal."

Ruaud hastily wrote out an order, sealed it, and handed it to the Guerrier:

Demoiselle de Joyeuse is ordered to return to the Forteresse as soon as possible.

Hot air gusted out from the dark forge, stinking of molten metal. Ruaud de Lanvaux followed Enguerrand into the Commanderie workshops, where his ears were assaulted by the ringing clang of hammers.

The king was eager to watch the master craftsmen at work on Sergius's Staff and although de Lanvaux had counseled patience, Enguerrand was not to be dissuaded.

At Enguerrand's request, the most skilled craftsmen in metalwork had been brought to work on the sacred relic. Maistre Erwan, a goldsmith trained in the making of reliquaries and devotional treasures, was working on the crook as they entered the forge. In the extreme heat, he had stripped off his shirt and wore only an old leather apron over his sweat-streaked chest. When he saw the king approaching, he bowed, wiping his hands on the apron.

"Forgive my appearance, your majesty—" he began.

"Is the Staff nearly ready?" The king pulled off his spectacles, which had misted over with the steam, and rubbed them impatiently on his sleeve.

"We're making good progress." Maistre Erwan gestured to the

pieces of the Staff that lay on his workbench. Ruaud listened to the king's eager questions, which the craftsman patiently answered. He was still uneasy about Enguerrand's "angel." Even with the aid of the Heavenly Warriors, Saint Sergius had met a martyr's death in his final battle with the Drakhaoul. As Ruaud watched Enguerrand's enraptured face, eyes bright as the forge fires, he could only think of Sergius's terrible fate. What would become of Francia if Enguerrand fell? Enguerrand had no heir; he had refused to consider marriage until his "mission" was completed. If he were to die, his sister Adèle was next in line to the throne—and as she was married to Ilsevir III of Allegonde, this would bring Francia under Allegonde's control. Francia could slip so swiftly into unrest and civil disorder . . .

In that moment, he knew he must determine the true nature of the aethyrial spirit that had appeared to his royal master.

Ruaud was forced to wait until the evening devotions were at an end and all the other officers and priests had left the Chapel of Saint Sergius before he could talk to the king in private.

He found Enguerrand still kneeling before the saint's statue. When the king eventually rose, Ruaud said to him quietly, "Are you sure, majesty, that you want to go through with this?"

"I know you say you have my best interests at heart. But can *you* be sure, de Lanvaux, of your true motives?"

The king's incisive tone took the Grand Maistre by surprise. "Me, majesty?"

"Examine your heart, and then tell me that there is not a drop—the smallest drop—of envy in your soul."

Ruaud stared back, unable to reply. Enguerrand had never spoken to him so bluntly before.

The king smiled his sweetest, most affectionate smile. "And it's natural for you, the head of the order, to wish that the Heavenly Guardians had chosen *you* to do their will."

Ruaud recovered. "Your angel, majesty. Has it revealed its name to you?"

Enguerrand's expression became beatific as he spoke in soft, reverent tones. "He is called Nilaihah."

"Nilaihah," repeated Ruaud. The name was not familiar, but then he had never devoted himself to the study of the Heavenly Guardians. He would set the angelographers to work to research the name.

"You want to send the Drakhaouls back to the shadows as much as I do, don't you, de Lanvaux?"

The Grand Maistre looked into the king's radiant eyes. "I want Gavril Nagarian first," he said. "But everything we've read in the old annals tells us one fact: The Drakhaon of Azhkendir was too powerful even for Sergius and the Heavenly Warriors to subdue." The young man's confident manner only made Ruaud fear for him the more; he could have no idea of the danger he was courting. "I can't let you risk your life against him, majesty. Not unless . . ."

"Unless?" Enguerrand was listening to him at last.

"Unless we find a way to weaken his defenses. I've sent agents to Azhkendir and Smarna to glean any information about him that they can. If that fails, then we must strike at those he loves and bring him to us that way." And there were the prisoners taken in Azhkendir who were ripe for interrogation as well . . . though Enguerrand need not be troubled with such unpleasant particulars.

"Eugene of Tielen tried that tactic and failed," Enguerrand reminded him.

"Eugene miscalculated. We will not make the same mistake."

CHAPTER 29

As Pavel emerged from the council chambers, Raïsa came running up to greet him.

"How is the trial going?" she asked anxiously. The strain of waiting was showing in the pallor of her face.

"Not well." Pavel rubbed his aching eyes. He had sat through hours of Francian evidence, in which the stern-faced Inquisitor had called witness after witness to testify against Rafael Lukan. All were Francian scholars and priests and many had obstinately refused to use the common tongue. So Pavel had been obliged to translate their lengthy and abstruse testimonies for the Smarnan lawyers representing Lukan.

"They have no right to deny us entry!" Raïsa's eyes blazed defiance. The start of the trial that morning had been delayed by a rowdy student demonstration. The Inquisitor had not hesitated to order his Guerriers to eject the protesters and close the trial to the public. The ejection had been efficiently brutal and several students had been injured. "If only Smarna hadn't ended up as a pawn in Eugene of Tielen's game of empires. Giving us to Francia, when we were never his to give!"

Pavel let out a faint groan. "Don't let's go into all that again."

"Oh, Pavel, forgive me. Here am I ranting on and you've been working so hard on Lukan's case all day." Her tone softened. "It's just that I feel so—helpless." Her eyes, dark amber, met his, and he forgot how tired and irritable he felt. He wanted to make her smile again. He beckoned her into the First Minister's office, knowing that Nina Vashteli was not back. "I sent a message," he said quietly.

"To Gavril Andar?" She had drawn closer to him and he saw that her eyes shone with new hope. "But how did you know where to contact him? Elysia said—"

"I had a hunch."

"You're so clever, Pavel."

"He may not get the message. And even if he does, he may not get here in time—"

A brusque knock at the door made them both jump apart, almost guiltily, Pavel thought, as though something had changed between them, but neither one was ready to admit it yet.

The door opened and Iovan came in. "What are *you* doing here?" He glared suspiciously at them. "Alone, with my sister?"

Pavel sighed. "I work for the minister. What are *you* doing here?"

"I came to invite the minister to a *special lecture* given by Professor Petris," Iovan said, still glowering. He placed a card on her desk. Pavel glanced at it and saw that the lecture was entitled "Free Speech in Ancient Smarna."

"Come with me, Raïsa," Iovan said, grabbing her arm and steering her toward the door. "There's much to be done."

"Pavel?" she said, shaking herself free. "Will you be there?"

"I have to work tonight," he said, unable to stop a note of regret creeping into his voice. "I'll be manning the Vox again up at the Villa Vashteli."

As Pavel rode back to the villa, he felt restless, unable to stop thinking of Raïsa Korneli.

What was the matter with him? He had fallen in and out of love so easily before—and he had always been the one to end the affair. But this was different. Raïsa was unlike any of the other girls he had known. If he had any sense, he would quietly disappear on the next ship out to Muscobar. But he could not bear to leave her, even though he knew that the longer he stayed, the deeper she would draw him into the rebels' machinations.

I'll never earn back my father's lands and title now. Somehow this thought did not disturb him as much as it should. Maybe he had fallen in love with Smarna too, its sun-warmed vineyards and its passionate, good-hearted people, all so much more spontaneous than the snobbish, self-centered aristocratic circles of Muscobar in which he had been raised.

Perhaps I am not so like my father as I thought after all . . .

Jagu played a rippling arpeggio or two on the fortepiano and let out a sigh. The instrument was in fine condition but he was sorely out of practice. The past weeks had left him no time for music. He had traveled from Francia to Azhkendir—and now here he was in Smarna.

A melody began to wreathe around his brain; the fingers of his right hand began to pick it out, the left hand playing an arpeggio figuration to accompany it. The tune became more insistent, forcing itself to the front of his mind. "Shall I never see you again?" Now he could remember her singing it, her sweet, clear voice bringing out each poignant phrase, each subtle nuance . . . And the Grand Maistre had ordered him to spy on her, to report directly to him if her behavior gave rise to any suspicions.

Jagu began to question where his own loyalties lay. Since boyhood he had wanted nothing more than to be a servant of God, a warrior for truth. But then he had met Celestine.

Of course, his fears could be groundless. She would have time in Smarna to reflect on her conduct. He prayed she would soon come to her senses. For he was sure Inquisitor Visant had suspicions about her; he had already tried to force a confession from her in the courtroom. And if her heresy were exposed, he was certain that Ruaud de Lanvaux would not hesitate to make an example of her.

Celestine entered the salon. Startled, he hit a wrong note.

"I hope you're not going to play like this at the soirée," she said. He knew that she had not forgiven him for the frank way he had spoken to her the day before and yet her disdain only made him yearn for her even more. This coldness made her blue eyes glitter, clear and hard like a winter's sky. In the guise of professional musicians, without their somber Commanderie uniforms, he felt less constrained by his vows, as if another Jagu had been liberated by the warm Smarnan sun.

"This has just been delivered for you." She handed him a sealed order and he could sense her watching him as he read.

"I am requested at the citadel," he said, a little surprised. "They're expecting trouble."

"Why you—and not me?"

"Rafael Lukan has been condemned to die. The inquisitors have called him 'a dangerous heretic whose ideas have corrupted the hearts and minds of the Smarnan populace.' "

Pavel poured himself a glass of wine and went out onto the balcony of the Villa Vashteli to watch the moon rise over the bay. It had been a black day for Smarna. The verdict that Lukan was guilty of heresy on all counts and would be executed the next day had shocked the courtroom. His students keeping vigil outside the courtroom had received the news in stunned silence. And Raïsa had run to Minister Vashteli, demanding that the council do something—anything—to grant a stay of execution.

But Pavel had seen the workings of the Francian Commanderie firsthand in Lutèce. They would not be swayed from what they believed to be their God-given mission. He went inside to pour himself a second glass and as he returned, nearly dropped it in surprise.

A figure stood on the balcony, silhouetted against the moonlit sky, long, wild hair stirring in the breeze, slanted blue eyes gleaming with a predatory light.

Pavel felt his heart miss several beats.

"I got your message about Lukan," said the figure. "Tell me what's happened."

"Gavril." Pavel's heart slowly settled back to a more regular rhythm. "The news isn't good. He's condemned to die. And they've posted Guerriers everywhere about the citadel. The Commanderie intend to make an example of him. Come with me—there's a meeting in Professor Petris's rooms in an hour."

"I can't go like *this*." The Drakhaon's voice was hoarse.

"Ah! I remember now. That inconvenient little disadvantage to your gift." Pavel could not help laughing as he went to fetch some clothes.

"Wait." There was something in Gavril's tone that made Pavel stop. "Listen, Pavel, I can guess what you're planning. You and the rebel council want me to attack the citadel and destroy the Commanderie."

"I can't deny that would give us a certain advantage."

Gavril shook his head. "I've done enough damage to Colchise and the bay already. Have you seen the grey sands below the citadel? I can't risk polluting the bay again. But what I can do is create a diversion."

"A diversion to draw the Guerriers away from the citadel?"

"Then you would have to do the rest." Eyes of intense blue seared into Pavel's. "Have you planned an escape route?"

"The idea is to smuggle him out of Colchise by fishing boat. I have . . . useful contacts in Muscobar."

Gavril did not seem surprised by this information. "And before that?"

"A little swapping of clothes, smuggling of weapons, the usual," said Pavel with a shrug. In truth, he had never rescued a condemned man from his jailers before, but he was sure that some of the little tricks Feodor had taught him would come in useful. And might impress Raïsa as well.

"What time is the execution?"

"Midday."

Gavril nodded. "Expect a diversion one hour before midday. You won't have long." He placed one hand on Pavel's shoulder and Pavel could not help but see that it was encrusted with jewel-bright scales. "Rafael Lukan's a good man, Pavel. Don't let them execute him."

"I am in his debt," said Pavel. "He saved my life in the uprising."

Gavril went in through the open balcony window, soundlessly pushing aside the billowing gauzes. There Elysia lay, asleep in her bed, the rumpled sheet thrown back for relief from the sultry heat.

If only he could stay. But there was no time. He just wanted to assure himself that she was all right.

He knelt beside her and put out one hand to stroke her cheek. In the moonlight he saw how the scales glittered.

"Mother," he said softly.

She opened her eyes and stared sleepily at him.

"Gavril?" She blinked. "Is it really you? Or am I dreaming?" She lifted her hand to touch the dark mane of sapphire-streaked hair that tumbled about his blue-scaled shoulders. "Look at you . . ."

He nodded. "I can't stay. But I'll be back when this is over." He bent over her and kissed her cheek. "I promise."

"Take care," she whispered, closing her eyes again.

"Are you sure Gavril said eleven?" whispered Raïsa to Pavel. Outside in the citadel square, the Commanderie had been laboring all night to build a scaffold. Armed Guerriers ringed the platform. It was obvious that they were expecting trouble. Pavel wriggled his shoulders, which were becoming stiff with tension. Now that it had come to it, he wanted the action to start.

The clock on the Cathedral of Saint Saba began to strike the hour. Raïsa glanced tensely up at him. She was dressed as a young legal clerk and was clutching a dispatch bag tightly. She made a handsome boy, he thought fondly, with her collar-length auburn hair and slim, boyish figure. She had even balanced Miran's spectacles on her nose to complete the disguise.

A dark cloud passed swiftly across the sun and the golden light in the square faded. A woman screamed. The Guerriers looked at each other uneasily and some began to prime their muskets.

Raïsa glanced up. "What *is* that?"

Pavel winked at her. "Our signal to go into action." He started out across the square just as the dark shadow swooped low across the citadel again. People scattered. Raïsa ran beside him, head down.

One the far side of the square Pavel saw the students massing, carrying banners, ready to invade the square.

The Guerriers aimed their muskets at the creature as it wheeled about and came back again. Daemon-blue eyes stared coldly down from the smoky glitter of the great hook-winged shadow-dragon. For a moment Pavel glanced back, amazed at the sight.

"I'm glad he's on our side," he muttered.

He heard the sound of musket fire as the Guerriers discharged their weapons. The dragon merely flicked the musket shot aside. Raïsa said, breathless from running, "This is all a dream, isn't it, Pavel?"

A young, dark-haired officer stepped forward to bar their way. His pale face was stern and he seemed not in the least fazed by the appearance of the dragon.

"I have a pass signed by the First Minister."

The officer shook his head. "No one is allowed in to see the condemned man."

Raïsa suddenly said, "But I'm his son." Pavel blinked and stifled a smile.

"I have no record of any wife or son here," said the officer coldly, scanning a record book. As he glanced down, Pavel slipped his pistol out of the dispatch bag.

"His illegitimate son," Raïsa hissed.

Outside there came a sudden uproar as hundreds of students

poured into the square and rushed the Guerriers. And the Guerriers, caught reloading their muskets, were not ready for them.

"Damn!" cried the officer, distracted.

Pavel hit him over the back of the skull with his pistol butt and he crumpled.

"Go!" Pavel shouted to Raïsa but she was already sprinting off down the passageway. He dragged the unconscious officer out of the way as Iovan Korneli came charging in, brandishing his sabre, followed by an excited mob of students and citizens.

Pavel fought his way down to the old dungeon where Lukan was confined. The Guerriers on guard were swept aside by the tide of Smarnans washing through the citadel. But where was Raïsa?

He spotted her kneeling in the dim light frantically trying to unlock the shackles around Lukan's ankles as the fighting raged around her. And then he saw that a Guerrier had also spotted her and was raising his pistol, aiming at her bright head.

Pavel fired. The man crashed forward, his own shot going wide. Raïsa glanced round, unaware till then of the danger that she was in. Pavel dived down to her side.

"I've never been so glad to see my students in my whole life," whispered Lukan as they tugged off the shackles and helped him to stand.

The previous night, Minister Vashteli had shown the rebel council an ancient map of the citadel. An old supply tunnel, used in times of siege, led down to the harbor from the cellars. Now Pavel and Raïsa half dragged, half pushed Lukan along its dark and filthy length.

"This stinks like a midden," complained Raïsa.

"It smells like freedom to me," said Lukan.

Pavel, crawling on hands and knees, could see a chink of daylight ahead. "Do you object to becoming our elderly mother?" he asked Lukan, pulling out a voluminous cloak and skirt from his bag.

"Dear God, I'd willingly turn into any obscure relative you care to name," said Lukan with a spark of his old, wry humor.

As the fishing boat sailed out of the harbor to join the little flotilla heading for Bichvinta, Pavel looked back and saw smoke rising from the citadel. And darker than the smoke itself, a dark-winged dragon lifted high into the air and circled once above them, as though ensuring that no one was pursuing them.

Raïsa shaded her eyes and looked upward.

"You said that Gavril had come back to help us," she said, her eyes wide. "Was that—?"

"It was," said Pavel.

"I owe you all a great debt of gratitude," said Lukan. "And you, Pavel, what will you do now?"

"Let's get you safely to Muscobar first," said Pavel.

Raïsa suddenly flung her arms about his neck and kissed him passionately. The crew of the fishing boat all whistled and cheered.

"I see you already have all the thanks a man could wish for," said Lukan with the hint of a wistful smile.

CHAPTER 30

It amused the Orlovs to call Erinaskoe their dacha but, like the Villa Orlova in Smarna, it was more a large country house than a simple rural retreat. Grand Duke Aleksei was particularly fond of his hothouses, in which he cultivated rare orchids and grew bananas, oranges, and pineapples. There was good fishing on the estate too, with a lake well stocked with carp and perch.

As Andrei made his way between the oaks that screened the western borders of the estate, he caught his first glimpse of the house and felt his heartbeat quicken at the sight. Its stucco walls painted the rich yellow of egg yolk, Erinaskoe was set like a brightly painted box on the green baize of the valley.

He stopped, leaning against a thick oak trunk, surveying the scene. He could see Astasia's barouche in the stableyard. Peasants were working in the fields beyond the park but all was quiet around the house. When his father was still in power, there had always been a steady stream of visitors: local landowners, courtiers, politicians . . .

He started out down the grassy slope, making for the boating pavilion, set amid weeping willows, whose long branches trailed in the waters of the lake.

Andrei had reached the pavilion before he spotted movement on the graveled terraces that surrounded the house. He slipped inside.

Soldiers in the grey and purple of the Imperial Household Cavalry filed out of one of the servants' entrances. Astasia's escort. He watched as they took up positions, each one stationing himself every few feet in front of the house, carbines on shoulders.

"Guarding their Empress well," he muttered. He would have to double back and approach the house by the kitchen gardens to avoid being seen.

The kitchen gardens were sheltered by high hedges of yew and beech. Andrei made his way past spiny gooseberries and red currant bushes whose jeweled berries he had often raided as a boy. Just the memory of the taste of those tart, juicy red currants made his mouth water.

Around the corner lay the great glass span of his father's hothouse, filled with rare ferns and palms from distant, hotter climates.

He peered in through the curling fronds of some giant exotic plant imported, no doubt at great expense, from far away. There was no one in sight. He laid his hand on the door handle, pressed it down, and went inside.

A fug of damp heat enveloped him. He closed the door silently and stood a moment, wondering which way to go. Only a glimpse of Mama and Papa . . .

Andrei set off through the hothouse. The hot, wet air was filled with strong woody, earthy odors that made the lining of his nose prickle. One plant he passed, a cactus with green, fleshy spines, was covered with frilly orange flowers that exuded a ripe, rotting perfume. He clapped one hand over his nose and mouth, trying not to inhale its scent of putrefaction.

"Who's there?" demanded an indignant voice. "Don't lay a finger on that cactus—it only flowers once every twenty years!" And from the other side of the tub appeared Grand Duke Aleksei, dressed in a peasant's gardening smock and wielding a trowel to repel the intruder.

"Papa?" stammered Andrei.

"My dear, dear son." His father, who had never been one to show his emotions, clutched Andrei as if he would never let go. Andrei could hear his mother softly weeping at his side as her hand gently patted his.

"Let me look at you." The Grand Duke held him at arm's length, gazing at him through tear-bright eyes. Andrei rubbed the tears from his own eyes with the palm of his hand. "It's a miracle. A miracle!"

"All that time they were searching for you in all the wrong places," sobbed Sofia into a lace handkerchief. "And you were lying sick in that drafty fisherman's hut, with your memory gone."

Now that his first rush of emotion had calmed a little, Andrei found himself looking at his parents as if through new eyes. He saw that his father was stooped and that his thinning hair had gone grey. His mother's complexion, of which she used to take great care, was pallid, with little worry lines on her forehead. And she was restless with anxious glances and twitches: constantly patting her hair, fiddling with her lace fichu, pulling at her emerald earrings. Could they really have aged so much in such a short time? It was as if he had been away for ten years, not one.

"So Enguerrand's given you your own command," said his father, setting down his glass and gesturing to the servant to refill it.

"The *Aquilon*."

The Grand Duke swallowed another shot of vodka. He looked Andrei in the eye. "A Francian ship? Is that wise, my boy?"

"Wise, Papa?" Andrei felt a stirring of rebellion.

"You've placed yourself in the enemy camp. Muscobar is part of Eugene's empire now. If it comes to all-out war, you could find yourself firing on our own lads. Your countrymen."

This possibility had already occurred to Andrei and he had dismissed it as an unfortunate consequence of the current situation. Besides, when he declared himself, he was confident that his countrymen would defect to his side, as Vassian had done. "It would be equally awkward for me to ally myself with Eugene. After all, it was he who ordered the sinking of the *Sirin*."

"Yes," said his father slowly, "Astasia told me. Or rather she told me that Eugene's Magus called up a storm in which the ship went down. It doesn't sound to me the sort of act Eugene would condone; that man really relishes a good battle!"

"And your point, father?" Andrei asked, rather more cuttingly than he intended. Why was Papa arguing in Eugene's favor? Had his recent illness affected his brain? It was not the kind of reasoning Andrei had expected; it sounded suspiciously like a gesture of appeasement.

"Did you say that Valery Vassian is with you?" broke in Sofia. "Why not invite him here to dinner? It will be just like old times."

"And what are *you* going to do now, young Vassian?" asked the Grand Duke at dinner.

"Have you been to visit your mother?" asked the Grand Duchess. Valery, struggling with a bony mouthful of perch, shook his head.

"You should, you know. Poor Elisaveta has had such worries since the awful shock of your father's death and—"

"Mama, I'm sure Valery will go to visit his family as soon as he can," put in Astasia. Valery glanced gratefully at her for sparing him one of Sofia's little lectures. The Grand Duchess was not known for her sensitivity, and he knew his mother had suffered much social embarrassment at some of Sofia's tactless yet well-intentioned remarks.

"Well, if it were me, I should want to see my firstborn son at the very first opportunity," remarked Sofia, looking pointedly at Andrei.

"And here I am, Mama!" said Andrei. He gestured to the waiting servant to refill his wineglass.

"But you've been in Francia for weeks and never a word!" Sofia kept scraping little traces of soup from her bowl and the repetitive sound of silver on porcelain was becoming irritating.

"I had to wait for the right time." Andrei drank his wine rather too fast, Valery noticed, and there was a distinct edge to his voice.

"To visit your parents? The ones who gave you life?"

Andrei banged his glass down and stormed out of the dining room.

"I'm sorry about dinner tonight, Valery," said Astasia. In the soft summer twilight, her eyes were dark with sadness.

"Will you be all right here, altessa? Things seem a little . . . tense."

"Oh, I'll be fine. You know Mama and Andrei; they both have strong personalities. In the morning, it'll all be smoothed over."

"But the Grand Duchess was right," said Valery. He had been brooding over what she had said all evening. "I should go and see my mother before the *Aquilon* sails."

"Then I mustn't detain you any longer. You've been so kind to me, Valery." Astasia pressed his hand between her own and Valery felt his heart melt. He didn't want to leave her. He had stayed by her side throughout the whole disastrous Francian escapade. He felt responsible for her safety, even back home in Muscobar, doubly so now that he must leave her.

Who would look out for her when he was gone? Who would care as devotedly as he had for her safety?

* * *

Andrei paced the terrace. He stopped beneath a lantern whose glow had attracted many pale, soft-winged moths and gazed out at the darkening valley.

Why had he bothered to come? He had fondly imagined that his parents would be overjoyed to see him, but he had been there but a few hours and already the criticisms had begun. And all the while he was close to Astasia, he felt tense, wondering if by some unconscious gesture or word, he might have betrayed the presence of his guardian spirit.

"*She suspects nothing.*" Adramelech's words floated through his mind like dusky mist.

"How can you be sure?" Andrei reached into his jacket pocket for his little silver hip flask and took a quick mouthful of Francian brandy.

"*You're drinking too much. You need to keep your wits sharp.*"

"There you are, Andrei!" It was Valery Vassian, hailing him from the farther end of the terrace. He hastily pocketed the flask.

"*And be careful how you treat this one.*"

"Look, old man, there's no easy way to say this." Vassian's tone was low, confidential. "I'd follow you to the ends of the world, Andrei, you know that. But the way you've been treating your sister—well, it's harsh and she doesn't deserve it. You've dragged her into some pretty hellish situations. A few kind words from you before we set sail would help to smooth things over."

Andrei stared at his friend coldly. "You've got some nerve, Vassian." Adramelech was whispering again, but he took no notice. "What makes you think this is any of your business? And who are you to give me advice? You've ruined your career, tagging along after a married woman who's pregnant with another man's child. What kind of an idiot does that?"

Vassian took a step back. By the sheen of the lanternlight overhead, Andrei glimpsed the look of hurt in his eyes, like that of a faithful spaniel whose master has struck it. In the silence, the burbling chorus of the little frogs in the reeds around the lake filled the night air.

"You look like Andrei Orlov," said Vassian, "you sound like him, but the Andrei I knew would never have spoken to me like that."

"*I warned you to be careful. He suspects. Make your peace—or dispose of him.*"

Adramelech's blunt warning shocked Andrei. He was not prepared to take such drastic action. "I'm sorry, Vassian," he said stiffly. "Coming home has not been easy for me. I've behaved like a boor to everyone—especially you—and I hope you can forgive me." He put out his hand.

Vassian hesitated a moment, then gripped his hand and shook it warmly. "I understand. But do talk to your sister, Andrei; she's very fond of you, you know. Oh—and what time do we sail tomorrow? It's just that I have a family visit of my own to make."

"If we sail on the afternoon tide, we should make Yamkha by nightfall."

But when Vassian had gone, Andrei set out toward the lake. There he angrily skimmed pebble after pebble across the surface of the water.

"Here I am, back in Muscobar, and nothing has changed. Even my own father accepts the fact that Eugene has taken my place. Enguerrand promised me Muscobar. Why has he reneged on his promise?"

"Enguerrand is distracted at present. He has other concerns. Perhaps it is time to remind him that he has only acquired one of the five princedoms so far; there are four more to conquer."

"And how do you propose we do that?"

"You have already caused considerable damage to the Emperor's war fleet. It would not take much to disable it completely. And then Tielen would be ripe for the picking . . ."

For the first time in his life, Valery Vassian went out and got stinking drunk. This was not the carefree, celebratory drinking that he and his fellow officers sometimes indulged in; this was a dedicated, joyless attempt to blot out the grim and guilty memories that his visit to his widowed mother had dredged up.

And to cap it all, Andrei's taunting comments kept playing over and over in his head like the monotonous refrain of some street corner balladeer:

"You've ruined your career, tagging along after a married woman who's pregnant with another man's child. What kind of an idiot does that?"

"An idiot who's stupidly, hopelessly in love with another man's wife," he told the landlord as he slapped down a handful of coins on the bar for a new bottle. In this dark drinking den by the docks, no one would ask any awkward questions. Then he returned to his corner and grimly downed one shot of vodka after another until the spirit dulled his anguish.

"Valery."

Someone was shaking him. Valery raised his head from his arms and tried to focus on the familiar face looming above his.

"Andrei?"

"Look here," said Andrei, "I said some harsh things to you earlier today. I've been going through some . . . difficult adjustments. I realize it must have been just as hard for you to come back to Mirom as for me."

"You're a good friend, Andrei." Vassian's eyes filled with tears of gratitude. "And I'm shorry I ever doubted you."

"By God, Vassian, you stink of spirits." Andrei let go of him, taking a step back. "We've new orders, fresh in from Francia. We're sailing to Smarna on the morning tide."

"Shmarna?" repeated Vassian stupidly, hearing his own voice thick with drink.

"Go and get yourself cleaned up. We've got to set these Francians some standards. It won't do for my first lieutenant to come rolling back to the *Aquilon*, smelling like a still."

Flying high over the Straits, Andrei felt an immense sense of release. He had left his problems behind in Erinaskoe; up here in the clouds, he need think of nothing but the wind and the sea below.

But Adramelech had other plans. "*You must rejoin your command soon; we haven't long to act.*"

They had left Muscobar far behind and the shores of Tielen were in view.

"What's that vessel?" Andrei had spotted a trim merchant ship flying the New Rossiyan flag, making for Haeven, escorted by three frigates. "Now why does a simple merchantman need a naval escort?"

He circled slowly overhead; the clouds gave him some cover, but not enough to conceal him from view if he launched an attack. And, with his Drakhaoul-enhanced sight, he noticed barrels on deck, hidden beneath a tarpaulin.

"Munitions," he said. "The Tielens must be reduced to importing gunpowder from Khitari or Azhkendir."

Muscobar had little in the way of mineral resources, compared to its mountainous neighbors, and bought most of its powder from Khitari.

"Of course it could be barrels of wine, or beer . . ."

"*There's only one way to find out.*"

Adramelech's malicious sense of humor infected Andrei. Coming about, he felt the spirit's powerful energy begin to flood his veins.

"*And one accurately placed bolt should do it.*"

Hovering, he felt the charge tingling at his fingertips. With a shout, he hurled the bolt of energy toward the deck of the merchantman.

The resulting explosion turned the sky and sea blindingly white. Andrei felt himself hurled through the air by its cataclysmic force. His ears thrummed with the sound.

Breathless, astonished, he righted himself. "What was *that*?" Beneath him, the sea boiled and a fog of white smoke descended, covering everything. "Whatever those barrels contained, it was powerfully dangerous stuff."

As the smoke began to clear, Andrei saw that nothing remained of the four vessels, except for driftwood floating on the churning sea. The massive explosion had destroyed them all.

CHAPTER 31

Eugene left his bed and staggered toward the cheval mirror. Grabbing hold of its sides to keep himself upright, he peered at his reflection, searching for signs that Belberith's influence was waning. His eyes, as bloodshot as if he had been up drinking all night, looked more blue than green. And as he dragged his fingers through his disheveled hair, it was no longer than it had been when he went to bed the night before.

"It's begun to work, then," he muttered. He stretched out one hand to check his nails but swayed, lost his balance, and dropped to one knee.

"What's the matter . . . with me?" His head felt heavy and hot. The room seemed filled with a haze of heat that rippled before his eyes. Dizziness overcame him and he slid to the floor. Lying on the polished boards, he felt his heart thudding wildly, erratically, against his ribs. He seemed to have no strength left; if he tried to raise his head, the room spun and the pounding in his chest grew louder. A cold sweat soaked his body.

"*I'm poisoned . . .*" Belberith's voice was so faint, it sounded like a dying whisper. "*Why did you summon me only to subdue me, Lord Emperor?*"

"I . . . did not fully understand what I was doing. I . . ." Eugene began to shiver. He had not known, in spite of all Gavril Nagarian's warnings, that it would feel like this.

He had not once imagined that he would feel so guilty.

*   *   *

"The cargo exploded?" Eugene was still shivering in spite of the warmth of the day as he scanned the report of the loss of the shipment of Azhkendi firedust. "How?" He looked up at the glum faces of his ministers gathered around his desk. So now they had no fresh supplies for Professor Kazimir to test. And worse still, they were running dangerously low on conventional powder.

"There were no survivors," said Minister Boden, "and so, we can only rely on the reports of witnesses some distance away from the incident."

"No survivors," repeated Eugene, slowly shaking his head. "So many brave men lost . . ."

"It seems," said Minister Ekman, "that there was a flash of lightning, then the whole flotilla went up."

"The explosion was heard in Haeven, some fifty miles away," added Boden.

"Though the lightning explanation is somewhat implausible." Ekman handed Eugene a second report. "It was cloudy, but there was no report of a storm."

"Sabotage, then?"

"If it was the work of a saboteur, he would have gone down with the ship."

Lightning without a storm. Was it possible it was one of the Drakhaouls he had set free from the Serpent Gate? *"They are growing stronger,"* Gavril Nagarian had warned him.

"These witnesses." The writing on the report seemed to blur and writhe like insects crawling across the page. Eugene passed one hand over his eyes and tried to concentrate. "How far off were they? Did they see anything else unusual?"

"We're talking about local fishermen here," Ekman said with a shrug. "They were busy with their catch when the accident happened."

Eugene suddenly realized that they were all looking at him expectantly, waiting for him to tell them what to do.

"It's damnably hot in here," he said. "Could one of you be so kind as to open a window?"

"Are you feeling all right, highness?" ventured Boden nervously as Eugene drank a glass of iced water.

"A touch of summer fever, that's all. I'll be fine by tomorrow." Eugene rose—and his legs buckled beneath him. He crashed to the floor, insensible.

*   *   *

Eugene's bed had become a pyre; he lay on fiery coals, as the smoke-daemons of his fevered brain swirled around him, whispering their malicious plans and caressing him with their burning fingertips.

A while later, he came back to himself and saw daylight beyond the curtains of his bed. Somewhere nearby he could hear Kazimir babbling in a high, terrified voice. "B—but he asked me to do it. He *commanded* me. I have a document to prove it. Here, see . . ."

And another voice, quiet, measured, infinitely patient. "This proves nothing, Professor Kazimir."

"Baron Sylvius," murmured Eugene, recognizing the soft tones of the head of his secret service. Whatever the matter was, it must be of the utmost importance for Sylvius to have come in person.

"Arrest me, and you will be the instrument of his death. I have already administered one dose of the antidote to the elixir." Kazimir seemed to have passed beyond fear to a state of desperate defiance. "At least let me make more—"

"In the circumstances, you seem to have done enough damage already, Professor." That was Maltheus, even more gruff than usual.

Eugene tried to raise his right hand. But it felt heavy as lead and the effort exhausted him.

"I can't understand what went wrong," Kazimir kept repeating. "It worked before; it should have worked this time."

Figures appeared at Eugene's bedside and faces peered down at him, distorted, as though reflected in a silver spoon. He shrank away from them, fearing the return of his shadowy tormentors and their searing touch.

"He's still delirious. It's been five days now. Why doesn't the fever break?"

Someone touched his arm and he cried out as tiny darts of fire exploded in his tender flesh. He bit back a cry of agony.

"See this swelling, and the red tracery of infection in his veins? There is some poison in his blood that must be purged before it reaches the heart."

"The flesh is so inflamed that we'll have to cut away his nightshirt."

Again he felt the agonizing pressure of fingertips on his arm and tried to jerk it away.

"But first we must reduce the fever."

"Imperial highness, can you hear me?"

"Yes . . ." It took such an effort to say just the one word.

"We're going to put you into a cool bath. That will bring down the fever and make you feel better."

"*Remember how swiftly I made your body whole again on Ty Nagar?*" Belberith's voice was faint as the flutter of wings. "*But I am so weak now I can do nothing to help you.*"

"I made her a promise," Eugene whispered. "I can't break my word."

"What did he say?"

"I think he may be referring to the Empress." That calm, steady voice could only be Gustave.

"Should she be called?"

"In her condition? Would it be wise?"

"But if he were to—"

The air began to buzz with flame-winged bees. Eugene could feel them crawling across his skin, he could feel their poisoned stings burning in his blood. He cried out and tried to beat them away, writhing and flailing his arms until his strength suddenly failed and he fell back, exhausted, onto the bed.

"She must be informed."

"Of all the times for him to fall ill!" blustered Maltheus. "Now what are we going to do about Princess Karila?"

"Given the Dowager Duchess's deteriorating state of health, Rosenholm's not the best place for a child." Those soft, subtle tones could only be Sylvius. "Particularly after the recent unpleasantness . . ."

The princess. Were they talking about Karila? Was she in danger? Anxious now, Eugene strove to speak but his tongue was too dry and swollen.

"Should we tell him about Alvborg?"

"That lunatic should have been locked up in Arnskammar for life. Don't worry, Chancellor," said Sylvius. "My agents are already on his trail. We'll ensure he can't do any more harm."

"K—Kari . . ." It took all Eugene's strength to whisper the first syllables of her name.

"Eugene?" Eugene heard the relief in Maltheus's voice as the Chancellor came over to his bedside, Sylvius following. "Thank God; you're lucid again."

"Kari," Eugene repeated. Why didn't Maltheus understand? He needed to know she was safe. He saw Maltheus and Sylvius exchange a wary look.

"Your aunt, highness, has had a seizure. We were wondering if it was wise to leave the princess at Rosenholm, now that the Dowager Duchess is unwell."

Eugene had assumed Karila was being well looked after by Aunt Greta, far from the Francian invasion force, in Northern Tielen. Her safety had been the least of his worries. Now even that certainty was gone.

"Erinaskoe," he murmured.

"Do you want to send the princess to her stepmother in Muscobar? It's a long and tiring journey. And suppose there's fighting in the Straits?"

Maltheus's questions were exhausting; all Eugene wanted was to close his eyes and slide back down into a black pit of sleep.

"He's slipping away from us."

"We should let him rest."

"We'll just have to make the decision for him . . ."

Astasia was sitting reading in the shade of an old lime tree, her feet propped on a footstool to rest her swollen ankles. The day was hot and heavy; the sky, though sunny overhead, was dark with clouds to the west, promising thunder later. Little black flies clustered under the sticky lime leaves and from time to time she was obliged to swat them away with a fan.

She found it hard to concentrate on her reading. For—to her discomfort and extreme delight—the baby was in a frisky mood and had been kicking all afternoon. Each time she felt a prod, she laid down her book and placed her hand on the place, hoping he was aware—for Karila had assured her it was a boy—that she was taking notice. It was a little like a game between them; first the kick, then the response.

But it was too hot, even under the tree, to enjoy the game for long. Her loose dress of sprigged muslin was damp with perspiration.

She reached for her glass of lemonade and took a sip. The cloudy, sour-sweet drink was one of the few savors she still relished. Even mint tea was no longer to her taste.

This time last year, I was sitting in the Villa Orlova for my betrothal portrait.

She felt a little frisson of regret, as she remembered those brief idyllic sessions with Gavril, when she had found herself falling in love with him, before she had learned of his terrible secret . . .

Looking back, she could not remember a single summer not spent in Smarna. Her earliest memories were of running along the sandy bay shore in bare feet, or trying to catch the lizards that liked to sun themselves on the white walls of the villa. And oh, that deliciously refreshing cool breeze off Vermeille Bay that tempered the baking heat . . . if only there were such a breeze today. The late-summer weather around the Nieva plain was always oppressive and muggy, and the afternoon had turned sultry.

Another sharp little prod took Astasia by surprise. "Ow!" she cried. Was that a little elbow, or a knee this time?

And then she noticed that a man was approaching across the lawn, and to her surprise, recognized Gustave. Had Eugene sent him to persuade her to come back to Tielen? She found herself clenching her fists, indignant that he should dispatch his private secretary rather than come himself.

"What brings you to Erinaskoe, Gustave?" she asked, sitting up.

"The Chancellor thought it best I come in person, highness," he said. His voice was grave. "The Emperor is ill. So ill that the doctors are not certain he will make a full recovery."

"Eugene ill?" The news was so unexpected that she could not make sense of it for a few moments. Eugene was never unwell! "But—how?"

"He has been undergoing a course of treatment. It seems that this treatment may have caused a dangerous infection of the blood."

"How dangerous? Is he—" Suddenly she found her voice had dried; she could not bring herself to ask if his life was at risk.

"He is very weak. If he survives the crisis, he will need a long period of recuperation."

Astasia was mechanically asking the questions as they occurred to her and not taking in the full content of Gustave's replies. Yet the phrase "a course of treatment" kept repeating itself in her mind like an ominous refrain. Had Eugene taken drastic measures to try to rid himself of the Drakhaoul after their last disastrous meeting? Was this crisis in some way her fault? "Recuperation," she repeated. "Here? At Erinaskoe?"

"I fear he is not strong enough to make such a long journey."

This sent a little stab of alarm through Astasia's heart. She had thought Eugene invulnerable; to hear that such a strong, vigorous constitution had been so depleted by this illness alarmed her.

"Did *he* send you, Gustave?" Her voice faltered. "Was he asking . . . for me?"

"The Emperor was delirious when I left, highness, and incapable of coherent speech."

"I see." And for a moment, she had deluded herself that her husband cared enough about her to call her name, to want her at his side.

"But we believe he would like you to take care of the princess here for a while."

Astasia blinked, realizing that Gustave was talking about Karila. "I thought Kari was staying with her great-aunt."

"She is still in Rosenholm. But the Dowager Duchess has suffered a seizure."

"Oh no." Astasia's hand flew to her mouth. "How is she? I must write to her. I must send her a gift . . ." She had not known Eugene's aunt Greta for long, but she had formed a distinct affection for the elderly lady, liking her sensible approach to the difficulties of everyday life.

"So may I make the appropriate arrangements for the princess and her entourage to come to Erinaskoe?"

"I'm her stepmother, of course she may stay here." *Mama will make a fuss, and complain that we are not ready to receive royal visitors, but the air here will be good for Karila's lungs.*

"Thank you, highness," Gustave said and she saw his grave expression soften a little. "I will return to Tielen straightaway."

"Oh, please stay and dine, Gustave," said Astasia. "You must be tired after traveling so far." She remembered how highly Eugene regarded his personal secretary. "*Men like Gustave, men of integrity and discretion, are worth more than a hundred fawning courtiers,*" he had remarked to her once.

"It's all part of my job, highness," Gustave said, a little less stiffly. "But I can't pretend that I wouldn't appreciate your offer of hospitality."

"I'll inform my mother." Astasia reached down for the little bell she had placed beneath the garden chair and rang it until its insistent tinkle brought one of the maids hurrying across the lawn toward them.

Astasia watched until Gustave's familiar, grey-suited figure had disappeared after the maid into the house. Then she picked up her book and opened it at the place she had marked with a plait of blue-and-rose silk. But a few minutes later she found she was still staring unseeing at the words on the page, the door that led into that charmed world of make-believe suddenly closed to her as the crises of real life rudely intruded into her dreams.

"Have you heard the latest news from Tielen?" Enguerrand asked Ruaud de Lanvaux. "It seems that the Emperor is very sick. One of our sources says his life is despaired of."

"What is his sickness?" This sudden illness seemed rather too convenient; Eugene could so easily be playing for time, secretly rearming his troops and refitting his damaged ships. For all Ruaud knew, the Magus might already be back in his laboratory at Swanholm, concocting his lethal ammunition for a new assault on the Francian army.

"It's an infection of the blood, contracted from some trivial graze or scratch."

"So how does your majesty suggest we proceed?" Ruaud asked the question out of courtesy to his young master, but he knew exactly what he was going to do: lay a trap for Gavril Nagarian and his Drakhaoul. He was still smarting from losing the Magus, to whose capture and trial he had devoted many years.

"We've also had reports of a devastating explosion in the Straits. Our source believes that a ship bringing munitions to rearm the Tielen navy caught fire and blew up." Ruaud noticed how Enguerrand's eyes glowed as he described the latest misfortune to befall the enemy. "I've already sent my orders to Admiral de Romorantin. My plan is to launch an invasion force into Southern Tielen."

"Is that wise, majesty? Isn't it a little soon to send in our troops? And if I recall, the seas around the south of Tielen are filled with rocks and treacherous currents. Many vessels have foundered there."

"The Tielens are demoralized. Their emperor is sick—what better time to attack?"

*   *   *

Astasia could not sleep. It was a hot, sticky night and the threatening thunderstorm had not broken. With the casement open, she lay behind thin muslin drapes to protect her from the mosquitoes that bred around the lake. But there was not the slightest stir of breeze outside and whichever way she shifted, she could not get comfortable.

Mama had kept commenting throughout dinner that she had taken the news about Eugene's illness extremely well. "If it were your papa lying at death's door, I'm sure I should be beside myself with worry. But then you have the baby's health to consider."

It was just another of Mama's tactless remarks but it had stung because, for once, Mama was quite right. And as the minutes of the airless night ticked slowly past, Astasia tried to stop herself imagining Eugene, pale as death, tossing and turning on his sickbed, calling out her name in his agony. "*Forgive me, my dearest Astasia . . .*" And she had seen herself kissing his fever-damp forehead, clasping his blindly seeking hand between her own, and murmuring tenderly, "*I forgive you, my only love.*"

But such affecting scenes of reconciliation only took place in her novels of romance. The troubled thoughts that kept her awake were so much more confusing.

Astasia pushed open the muslin bed hangings and went slowly, awkwardly, to the open window and sat on the cushioned window seat. The harvest moon hung low over the little valley, warming the dark woods with its amber light. She let her hands rest lightly on her swollen belly.

"I want you to know your father," she whispered to her baby. "He's proud. He's—*complicated*. But he's a good man at heart. So he can't—he mustn't—die before you're born."

Again she felt that strange feeling of emptiness and desolation rising to envelop her like mist over the lake. *I miss him so.* She hugged her arms around herself and wished that he was there to hold her and make her feel safe.

I think I shall write to him.

Karila tried to suppress a cough. She had been ill again and Doctor Amandel had confined her to her bed. This was the first day he had allowed her to get up; she was hoping she might be able to eat some proper food instead of the nourishing broths Marta had been spooning into her.

She was playing with her dolls when Lieutenant Petter came in. He clicked his heels and bowed to her. "Princess." Karila liked the sound his boots made when he saluted, so she smiled at him, even though she knew he had come to talk with Marta, not her.

Marta had been sitting in the window seat, sewing. Karila saw her gaze anxiously into Lieutenant Petter's eyes as her needlework dropped from her fingers.

"Any news?" Marta asked.

"Instructions from Baron Sylvius. The Emperor has decided that we should leave Rosenholm."

"So the Emperor has recovered?"

Recovered? Karila was listening with full attention now. Had Papa been ill too? Or worse still, wounded fighting the Francians?

Petter hesitated. "It's felt that it would be unwise for us to stay here a moment longer." He had not answered Marta's question, Karila noticed.

Marta went to him. "Fredrik," she said, no longer formal, "where are we to go? I thought it wasn't safe to travel—"

"Ever since we ceded Smarna to Francia, the situation has stabilized. In the circumstances, it's better to move farther south."

"Because of Count Alvborg?" said Karila. Both Petter and Marta turned to stare at her. "Why can't I pay Papa a visit? You said that the fighting's over now, Lieutenant Petter."

She heard Petter sigh. "The Emperor has asked me to take you to stay with your stepmother in Muscobar, Princess."

"But that's such a long journey!" Marta said. "By the time we get to Muscobar it will be autumn. And you know how stormy the Straits can be at that time of year."

Karila began to cough again.

"She's not strong enough yet, Fred," said Marta. "Can't we go back to Swanholm?"

CHAPTER 32

Andrei tossed and turned on his narrow bunk. His dreams were disturbed by voices that argued incessantly, until he could bear the discord no longer and woke, to hear the bitter dispute still continuing.

He clutched his hands to his ears, trying to shut them out.

"Be quiet! *Quiet!*" he shouted.

The cabin door opened and Vassian appeared. "I've told the crew to keep the noise down," he said, "and the ship's surgeon is here to see you."

Andrei stared as if Vassian were mad. "Why in God's name do I need to see the surgeon?"

"Because you've been shouting out in your sleep. We thought you were ill."

"I'm not ill. So you can send him away."

"And there are fresh orders in from Francia."

Andrei opened the tiny document, which had come by carrier pigeon, and read:

To Captain Orlov of the *Aquilon*: sail directly to Colchise where you will collect Demoiselle de Joyeuse and take her to Fenez-Tyr.

"Celestine? Celestine is in Smarna?" This was one mission Andrei was keen to pursue. He still dreamed of her. He longed to see her again.

"Set a new course!" He hurried up on deck, buttoning his uniform jacket as he ran. "Colchise."

* * *

"'In the light of recent unfortunate events in the citadel,'" read Celestine,

> I feel it is inadvisable to proceed with your recital. I hope you will understand, Demoiselle. It is with regret that I have decided to postpone the concert until the situation has stabilized.
>
> Yakov Garsevani, Ambassador

"Unfortunate events?" she said aloud, unable to conceal her annoyance. "And if they had paid heed to my report, they would have taken Rafael Lukan to stand trial in Francia! Then they could have lured the Drakhaon there and entrapped him, far from his home. But no, the Commanderie knows best and all my hard work is for nothing!"

Nanette appeared.

"Well?" said Celestine crossly. "Is there any news on Lieutenant de Rustéphan? Is he recovered from his injury?"

Nanette, seeing her mistress's vexed expression, delivered her news in a meek whisper. "There are two Guerriers here to see you, Demoiselle."

She showed in two officers; both wore the discreet emerald insignia on their black uniform jackets that marked them as belonging to the inquisitorial division. Visant's men.

"We have urgent instructions from Maistre de Lanvaux," said the taller of the two. "You are to return to Lutèce with us straightaway."

"With you?" This was not what she had expected. "But I need time to pack—"

"We have orders to take charge of all your luggage."

There was something about his tone that made Celestine feel uneasy. "Let me at least send word to Lieutenant de Rustéphan."

"We must leave straightaway," repeated the first officer.

As they escorted her into a carriage, she saw other Guerriers entering the villa. She had concealed the grimoire inside an old book of *chansons* but the inquisitors were trained to ferret out all manner of hidden secrets.

It was airless and stickily hot inside the carriage. Why were they waiting? And then she had a sudden horrible suspicion. Had Jagu reported her to their Commanderie superiors? He had warned her not to use the grimoire and she had ignored him. For where was he now?

Had he betrayed her? Was his loyalty to the cause stronger than his feelings for her, after all?

A Guerrier came running up. He handed over a package to the officers.

"Demoiselle de Joyeuse," said one, "can you explain why this was found in the villa?"

The other held up her father's grimoire.

"I have no idea," she said, keeping her face a mask.

As the airless carriage drove away beneath the hot Smarnan sun, she stared at the officers, who sat one on either side of her, their faces impassive.

I've risked my life many times for the Commanderie. Surely that will stand me in good stead if it comes to a trial?

As the *Aquilon* sailed out of Colchise harbor, Andrei found himself pacing the upper deck with his mind on matters other than navigating the strong currents in the bay. The sun was setting and the western sky bled crimson light into the sea, hazed by ragged tatters of gauzy cloud.

What was the matter with Celestine? She had not even looked at him when she came on board. Her manner had been subdued, her eyes downcast. The two Commanderie officers acting as her escort had not once left her side. And there was no sign of Jagu de Rustéphan. The more Andrei puzzled over it, the more he became convinced that something was amiss.

He resolved to speak to her alone as soon as he could distract the two officers. He would get Vassian to make them both read and sign a long document of his own devising; "a new precaution, in these troubled times." And while they were busy with pen and ink, he would seek out Celestine.

"Andrei, I fear I may be in terrible danger. I fear"—and her blue eyes glistened with tears—"that someone harbors a grudge against me. These two officers are working for Inquisitor Visant. He hates me. He would do anything to discredit me."

Andrei could not bear to see her so distressed. "I owe you my life," he said in a low voice. "Tell me what I can do."

"Help me escape."

"But where will you be safe? You can't go back to Smarna. And Francia is utterly out of the question."

"Even in Allegonde, the Commanderie has many connections."

"Muscobar," said Andrei without hesitation. "You'll be safe in Muscobar. I have friends who will ensure that you are safe."

"Oh, but that will mean you disobey your orders. I couldn't put you in such a position—"

"I'll invent some excuse or other. New secret orders, or some such."

"You would do such a thing for me?" The glistening tears threatened to brim over. He could not bear to see her in such distress.

"For you, dear Celestine," he said, "anything. You have only to ask."

She smiled at him through her tears. "There is one other small thing . . ."

"Name it," he said gallantly.

"There is a book of my father's. It's all I have left to remind me of him and they have confiscated it."

They had deprived her of her only memento of her dead father? It made him hot with anger even to think of such an outrage. "Why then, you shall have it back."

She leaned over and kissed him. Just the slightest, sweetest brush of her lips against his, but it stirred a yearning that swept through him like a storm wave.

Jagu, still nursing a pounding headache, arrived at the villa to find the windows shuttered and the doors locked. A gardener pruning the roses called out to him, "The young lady's gone. Two gentlemen in black came for her yesterday."

"Gone?" Jagu echoed. "Did they say where?"

The gardener shrugged and turned back to his roses.

Jagu spurred his horse along the chalky cliff road to the harbor, and as he rode, he cursed himself. Two gentlemen in black. Were they Visant's men? If so, he prayed it was not too late to save her.

Vermeille Bay stretched away into the far distance below him, the blue of the sea softened by the first autumn mists. A salty breeze tousled his hair as he approached the broken walls of the citadel. His growing anxiety simmered in his throat until he could hardly breathe.

At the harbor he went from sailor to merchant, asking, and only receiving blank looks. At last a fellow Guerrier told him that the *Aquilon* had sailed from Colchise for Francia yesterday, carrying two of Visant's inquisitors and Demoiselle de Joyeuse.

Jagu tugged his collar open, as he broke out in a sweat at the news.

"Sit down and rest, Lieutenant," said the Guerrier. "You're not yet recovered from your wounds."

But Jagu knew he could not rest until he was certain that Celestine was safe. "My mission here is over." He wiped his glistening face. "When is the next ship back home?"

Andrei tugged his fingers through his hair. It had grown long again overnight—and only yesterday, his servant had cut it. He felt as if he had a hangover; and yet he had drunk nothing but a single glass of wine the day before. He caught sight of his reflection in the round mirror and stared in disbelief. He looked as haggard as if he had been up carousing all night. On closer examination, the dark shadows around his eyes seemed to be made up of minuscule flecks of amethyst, like glittering insect scales. He rubbed them hard; they did not come away.

"What's this? What have you done to me?" he demanded. Adramelech did not answer him.

Just then he heard voices from the deck. "Why are we taking this course?" The Francian officers were remonstrating with Valery. "Why are we sailing north up the Straits?"

"New instructions," Vassian replied, just as Andrei had instructed him. "We may be engaging the Tielens in battle again."

"But there's nothing left of the Tielen fleet to engage! Are they sending fishing smacks against us now?"

The change of course had been enough to draw both officers from their cabin; Andrei slipped inside and frantically began rummaging through their luggage.

"A small, leather-bound journal," Celestine had told him, "inscribed with the name Hervé de Maunoir."

He found it and thrust it inside the breast of his jacket against his fast-beating heart, kicking the chest lid shut, before making a hasty retreat.

Then he went back on deck. A sea fog was blowing in and visibility was rapidly decreasing.

"How far off Lapwing Spar are we?" he asked the ship's master.

"Another half hour or so—unless we become becalmed."

*   *   *

"Tikhon? Is it really you?" Old Irina, surrounded by her chickens, stared at him through rheumy eyes. Then she flung wide her arms and hugged him. "My boy. My boy's come back to me!"

Solitude and age had made her forget his true name. He returned her hug, suddenly ashamed that he had not returned to see her until now that he had a favor to ask of her. He turned to see Celestine, hugging her shawl to her, shivering in the damp of the sea fog rolling in across the dunes. He saw her looking uncertainly at the drab little fisherman's cottage.

"Irina, this is Celestine. Could she keep you company for a few days? Until I return to collect her?"

Irina peered at Celestine and nodded. "Well, you're a pretty one and no mistake. Come in and have some tea, both of you."

Andrei hesitated. "We'll have time to talk when I come back. My ship's waiting."

The last he saw as he went back to the waiting boat was Celestine watching him forlornly. Then she turned and was lost to him as the fog rolled in more thickly.

Back on board, Vassian came up to Andrei in a state of some agitation. "Those two Francians—they're either dead drunk or ill."

Andrei went below to look. The officers lay on their bunks and did not respond to slaps or cold compresses, except for the faintest of groans.

He had only done as Celestine had bidden him; a draft, she had said, that would make them sleep for a day and a night. She had given him her pearl-and-diamond ring, which concealed a fine white powder within the bezel and, when no one was looking, he had added it to their wine, for a toast "to Francia and confusion to all her enemies."

Surely she wouldn't have made him poison her captors—would she?

"My kin are warning us; we are in grave danger."

"Your kin?" Andrei awoke, hearing Adramelech calling him. Now he remembered his vision on the quay at Haeven, the spirits that had streaked the stormy sky with violet, scarlet, and gold.

"Enguerrand plans to lure us to his fortress—and destroy us."

"King Enguerrand?" repeated Andrei in disbelief. "Why would he wish to destroy you?"

"He fears we will become too powerful and overthrow him. He plans to use Saint Sergius's Staff and call the Heavenly Warriors. It is

the same staff that they used to imprison us. The staff that channeled the Warriors' powers and turned us all to stone."

For one stomach-twisting moment, Andrei looked down at his hands, his feet, and saw the color fading to grey, and felt a terrible paralyzing numbness spreading swiftly through his body . . .

He shook his hands and the illusion vanished.

"But Enguerrand is my patron. My ally. He secured this command for me."

"Have you met him yet?"

"Well, no, but . . ." Andrei stopped and thought about what Adramelech was saying. Even though Enguerrand had invited him to Francia, the king had not once deigned to welcome him in person. And here he was, working as captain of a little Francian frigate, when he was Enguerrand's equal in rank and status.

"King Enguerrand is using you, Prince Andrei. He promised to help you win back Muscobar. But now that he has used your sister to gain what he wanted, he has forgotten all about you."

The more Adramelech said, the more Andrei saw it to be true.

"Enguerrand's mind has been poisoned by the Commanderie." Adramelech's voice had become dark and bitter. *"All he can think of is destroying us."*

"Tell your crew the orders you've received contain a secret code that only you know how to decipher. You must leave the Aquilon *immediately. Hand over command to Vassian."*

"Abandon my command?"

"You must go. The danger is real, Andrei."

Andrei had his crew row him ashore in a lonely little bay on the rocky northwestern coast of Smarna.

"But when shall we pick you up from this secret mission?" Vassian asked anxiously.

"You need not concern yourself with that, Vassian," Andrei said. "You are in command in my absence."

"Are you sure it's not a trap?" Vassian asked in their home tongue.

"Stop being such an old woman, Valery. I'll rejoin you soon enough."

Andrei walked up the shingled beach toward the rocks; a clump of bent, stunted sea pines gave him cover so that he could watch the rowboat returning to the *Aquilon*. Soon, his command was sailing out of the bay, making for open water, with a good breeze filling her sails.

As he stood there, the breeze stirring his long hair, he felt a stronger wind blast overhead, tossing the branches of the pine trees. And a shiver of fire ran through his body. Turning, he saw a winged monster bearing down on him, etched in fire against the hot blue of the Smarnan sky.

A dragon.

"*Sahariel!*" cried Adramelech in greeting.

Andrei watched the fire-scaled dragon's form ripple, as if burning white-hot in the scorching summer sun. A man's shadow appeared within the heat haze and, as he walked toward Andrei, the dragon illusion fell away, melting into the sunlight.

"Who the devil are you?" demanded Andrei. For the newcomer was an extraordinary sight, even now that he was no longer clothed in Sahariel's glamour. His hair streamed, white as a snowstorm, down his back, and his strong, well-formed body glittered with scarlet scales.

"Alvborg's the name; Oskar Alvborg," he said in the common tongue. "You must be Andrei Orlov." There was an arrogant drawl to his voice that Andrei took an instant dislike to. "I believe we have a mutual enemy."

"Oh?" Andrei said guardedly.

"Eugene of Tielen"—and Oskar Alvborg smiled as he pronounced the name—"your brother-in-law."

"I thought Enguerrand was plotting to destroy us."

"So it appears," said Alvborg casually. "I believe he plans to lure us to Lutèce with the Tears of Artamon. And then destroy us with Sergius's Staff."

"How did you find out about this?" Andrei asked suspiciously. He had no idea who this Alvborg was, or how he had come to be adopted by one of Adramelech's kindred.

"*Because I told him it was so.*" The fiery words that seared through Andrei's head could only be Sahariel's.

"So, Andrei Orlov," rang out Alvborg's sardonic voice, "are you with us?"

"And what's in it for me?" Andrei was still far from certain he could trust Alvborg.

"The Ruby of Muscobar," said Alvborg, "which your father gave to Eugene as your sister's dowry—and with it, your birthright."

CHAPTER 33

Malusha spotted a crystalline shimmer in the far distance. She rubbed her eyes, wondering if it were a mirage. They had been jogging on for so many days over the endless steppes that she had begun to fear that the fabled Lake Taigal was just a traveler's tale.

She rose up in the pony cart, gripping the rail. "Here, Magus, you hold the reins." She thrust Harim's reins into his hands and shaded her eyes to see more clearly in the late-afternoon haze.

It was no mirage; they were approaching a vast expanse of water.

"And not before time," Malusha muttered under her breath. She turned round and saw that Kiukiu had nodded off to sleep again in the back of the cart. "Look, Kiukiu," she said, "we're here. At last!"

Kiukiu's eyes opened and she managed a faint smile. It pained Malusha to see how pale and cloudy her granddaughter's eyes had become. She lay, wrapped in bright rugs and furs, a skeletal, shrunken shadow of her former youthful self. She was fading away, it seemed to Malusha, with every hour that passed.

The clear waters of the great lake reflected the blue of the sky, but the mountains rising behind were already dusted with fresh snow and there was a distinct hint of chill in the air as the sun moved westward. Summer was dying. And there were little flecks of autumn color tinting the trees on the lower mountain slopes.

Young boys galloped past on their ponies, whooping and laughing. Malusha recognized Prince Bayar among them, joining in the race, his proud face flushed with excitement.

At least the little one is keeping well. But as for my girl . . .

Malusha sat down again and took the reins back from the Magus's rheumatic fingers.

"He hasn't come back," whispered a hoarse voice behind her.

"And how would he know where to find us?" Malusha replied tartly. "We've been on the road for weeks."

"I should have waited for him."

"You had to take your chance when it came." Yet Malusha found herself glancing up whenever a white-tailed eagle or a hawk skimmed high overhead, casting its shadow over them. *Hurry back, Gavril Nagarian, if you want to be sure of seeing my girl alive again. If we don't reach these miraculous waters soon, I fear we shall lose her to the shadows . . .*

Kiukiu wandered in a dim dreamscape between the Ways Beyond and the bright light of the Khitari day. Ever since she had encountered Nagazdiel, she felt herself slipping farther and farther away from the world of the living. She feared he was still slowly draining the life force from her fading body, using her spirit-energy to grow strong. Now she only caught fleeting glimpses of the Drakhaouls' children as they played on the bone-white sands or splashed in and out of the azure sea.

"Come and find us, Spirit Singer!" She would hear the sound of distant laughter and eagerly follow it, only to find that her elusive companions had vanished again into the jungle.

This teasing game of hide-and-seek was becoming frustrating. If only she could learn the names of the other children and their mortal hosts. Why, when they'd begged her to help them, were they playing games with her? Didn't they realize how little time she had left? Or were they so afraid of Nagazdiel that they didn't dare talk to her anymore?

Peeping between the thick-haired trunks of the low-bending palm trees, Kiukiu spied a little cluster of children digging in the damp sand, molding it into shapes with their fingers. They seemed engrossed in their game, chattering to each other.

"What's that funny animal?"

"It's a horse. Can't you tell?"

"What's a horse?"

"Have you never seen a horse, silly?"

"No. And I'm not silly. You are."

There was a little pause. Then she distinctly heard the one who had made the horse reply, "At least I don't have a silly name. Kahukura, what kind of a name is that?"

"Kahukura," murmured Kiukiu.

"It means rainbow. What does your name mean, Giorgi?"

There came another little pause. "I don't really know," said the boy with dignity, "but I know it's not as silly as Kahukura—"

There came the sound of scuffling and suddenly two little boys went rolling over and over in the sand. Kiukiu's first instinct was to go and separate them, but suddenly the fight was over, as swiftly as it had begun, and both boys had flipped over onto their backs, chuckling.

That evening, Chinua came to sit with Malusha and Kaspar Linnaius by their little fire. It was not that they chose to keep themselves apart, but Malusha sensed that the members of the khan's entourage were more than a little in awe of their shamanic powers.

Chinua brought them a bowl of *koumis* as a gift from Khan Vachir. Malusha had come to tolerate—if not exactly relish—the fizzy tang of the fermented mare's milk. She poured a little for herself, then passed it to the Magus, who sucked noisily from the bowl, smacking his lips in appreciation. He had become more and more like a wizened child as the weeks passed, placid and vacant, content to slumber away the days.

"My lord khan has given permission for you to leave the caravan to go in search of the Jade Springs," said Chinua. "He has asked us to rejoin him at Taigazin Bay, where he plans to celebrate the prince's recovery with horse races and games. So, are you prepared?"

Malusha nodded slowly. She had become resigned to the fact that there was no other course of action to be taken to try to save Kiukiu. Yet one thing had been troubling her throughout the long journey. "Master Oyugun warned my granddaughter that there was a price to pay. But he would not tell her what it was."

Chinua's gentle smile faded. "Perhaps for her it will be different. All I know is that the Guardian of the Jade Springs always exacts a payment."

"And the Magus?" Malusha jerked a thumb toward Kaspar Linnaius, who was engrossed in licking the last traces of *koumis* from the bowl. "Sometimes I think he's happier this way. But he's been here before, hasn't he, though he doesn't remember it. What did he forfeit the first time, I wonder?"

"It's not an easy path to the springs. It's rough country. Will Kiukirilya be strong enough to walk, do you think?"

Malusha cast a glance over her shoulder to where Kiukiu lay, wrapped in a shawl of soft yak wool Lady Orqina had given her, asleep again.

"Giorgi . . ." murmured Kiukiu.

"What's that?" Malusha went over to her granddaughter and knelt beside her. "What did you say?"

Kiukiu's cloudy eyes opened a little. "I learned his name, Grandma," she said, trying to push herself up on one elbow. "It's Giorgi. He's another of the Drakhaouls' children."

"Now what did I warn you about going back to that place? You've little enough strength left as it is. Look at you, child." And Malusha put out one hand to touch Kiukiu's hair, which had become as white and wispy as the fluff drifting from the fireweed growing by the lakeshore. It pained her beyond words to see how swiftly Kiukiu was aging. *I should go first, not her; she should have many years left.*

They were entering wild and untamed country; Kiukiu could still catch a glint of blue through the dark pine trunks where Taigal's waters sparkled in the morning sunlight. For a while they could see and hear the carts of Khan Vachir's straggling caravan as it continued on its way along the lakeside; then the voices dwindled and there was only the soft sighing of the wind in the branches of the stone birches and pines.

"Did I mention the bears?" Chinua, who was leading the way, paused, waiting for the others to catch him up.

"Bears?" repeated Malusha in alarm.

To Kiukiu each step required more effort than the last; she leaned on the stout stick Chinua had found her, gasping for breath. The route upward was tortuous, winding between the slender white trunks of the birches; the ground underfoot was muddy and treacherous with knotted tree roots.

There was a cold tang to the air. The birch leaves had turned color and came fluttering down as the wind stirred the branches, like flocks of yellow-winged butterflies.

As it grew dark they made camp in a little clearing. Kiukiu was so tired that she fell asleep even before Chinua had brewed the tea.

On a far-distant shore, the golden sun was setting over the waves. The shadows cast by the palm trees were lengthening, merging into a blue twilit haze.

A cluster of girls knelt in the sand, weaving together strands of palm husk to thread shells on them. Kiukiu recognized Tilua and Karila, their heads close together, one fair, one dark, as they swapped shells and held up their necklaces to compare. She heard a chuckle and saw a baby boy happily patting the sand with his chubby hands.

A baby? She could not remember seeing a baby before. But before Kiukiu could eavesdrop on the girls' chatter to discover who the baby was, Tilua looked up and stared straight at her.

"You shouldn't stay here. You should go."

"You knew I was here?" Kiukiu was so surprised she did not take in what Tilua was saying to her. "How did you know?"

Tilua rose. "*He* is angry. He knows what you are planning to do."

"He? You mean—"

"Ssh. Don't say his name aloud. Never say his name." The girl's dark eyes were wide with concern.

"But how can I help you if I don't come back?"

Clouds of steam billowed from a cleft in the mountain, drifting away like evening mists. The clear air was tainted with an acrid, sulfurous smell that made Kiukiu cough.

"We're nearly there," said Chinua. "The Jade Springs. Can you hear the water gushing out of the rocks?"

Kiukiu sank down on a mossy boulder. She had used up the last of her strength. A numbing lassitude seeped through her, infecting both mind and body. She was too tired to care anymore. Nothing mattered. It was as if she were walking slowly away from herself and all her troubles. She glimpsed a girl called Kiukiu who had loved a dragon-lord more than life itself. And what had that love brought her? Nothing but heartache. All she wanted was to close her eyes and let the darkness take her.

"Just a few steps farther," coaxed Malusha's voice.

"Too . . . tired."

"You come back to me right now."

Kiukiu wished her grandmother's sharp voice would stop nagging. "Leave me be . . ."

"I most certainly will not!"

Suddenly Kiukiu felt a sharp slap to her cheek. She opened her eyes to see Malusha bending over her. "It's not your time to go. I need you. Those children need you. Lord Gavril needs you!"

"No, he doesn't," murmured Kiukiu. "He'd have come back for me by now if he did."

"Has it never entered your mind, child, that he might have battles of his own to fight? That he might be keeping those other Drakhaouls at bay?"

"I don't know, I don't know . . ."

"You're not going to give up now, not so close to your goal. I'll get you to those springs if I have to carry you on my back."

The Magus suddenly wandered over, his rheumy eyes bright. "Look," he said triumphantly, holding out cupped hands, "cran-berries!"

Malusha absently patted his hands, folding his fingers over the berries, as though humoring an infant. "Very nice, Kaspar. Well done." And then she whispered to Kiukiu, "I think I prefer him this way. And he's happier too. He can't remember any of the terrible deeds he's done."

"Don't think I can . . . make it, Grandma . . ." Kiukiu felt herself slipping back into the shadows.

"I'll carry you," offered Chinua.

She felt his arms around her, strong and sinewy. Then he lifted her as easily as if she were a little child, and set off again up the stony track.

Water gushed out of the mountainside into a steaming pool. The air was so moist that droplets hung, like liquid diamonds, from every branch and leaf tip.

Yet this water was not like any other Kiukiu had ever seen before; beneath the rising steam, it was the palest shade of green, like the precious jade from which the springs took their name. And it gave off a faint luminescence, a green glow that shimmered on the mossy boulders surrounding the pool.

"Where is this Guardian then, Chinua?" Malusha asked, gazing around. Rocks rose high on every side and even the little gap through which they had squeezed was no longer visible, as if the bushes and trees had parted to let them in and closed again behind them.

"The Guardian will not appear while we are here. We must leave Kiukirilya here alone."

"Alone?" said Kiukiu. She was not sure now that she wanted to face this ordeal on her own.

"And don't forget to take off your clothes, Kiukirilya."

"But it's freezing." Kiukiu began to shiver at the thought.

"She'll catch a chill!" protested Malusha.

"You will find that the Jade Springs are delightfully warm," said Chinua, smiling encouragingly at her. "May the Guardian bless you with good fortune."

"We'll be waiting for you," said Malusha loudly. "Close by. Just call out if you need us."

Kiukiu stripped off all her clothes, layer by layer, keeping her warm shawl of soft yak wool for modesty. Her teeth began to chatter as she folded her clothes neatly and placed them on a boulder beneath a stunted, stooping larch tree.

"You must enter the water as naked as the day you were born."

Slowly, Kiukiu discarded the woollen shawl she had wrapped around herself for warmth. One unsteady step at a time, she walked forward to the edge of the green pool, feeling the rocks bruising the tender soles of her bare feet.

Suppose the Guardian asks me to give up something so dear to me that I can't go through with this?

She cast anxious glances around her. Where was the Guardian?

"G—Guardian?" she called softly.

The waters stirred and began to ripple and undulate, as though a large and powerful creature was snaking through the pool toward her. Kiukiu bit her lip, wondering if she had been tricked into being the evening meal of some ravenous mountain monster.

As it drew near, the waters swirled and parted, and a giant water snake reared up, its great green coils glistening, to stare directly into her face. Its long forked tongue flicked out to touch her cheek.

Kiukiu gave a little cry and stepped back, almost losing her balance on the slippery algae-sheened rock.

"What do you ask of the Guardian of the Springs?" The Guardian Snake's voice was as sibilant as the hiss of the drifting steam.

Kiukiu swallowed. She felt utterly alone, utterly vulnerable, standing there naked and shivering. "Please, give me back my youth. Give me back the years that were stolen from me in the Realm of Shadows."

"And what do you give to the springs in return?" The Guardian fixed her with its reptilian jade eye.

"Is there a choice?" Kiukiu had thought that the Guardian would tell her what she must sacrifice to the springs; she was so apprehensive now that her mind had gone blank.

"I am lonely here," hissed the Guardian, "and I long for a companion. It is many years since the springs were protected by a priest or a priestess. Give me your firstborn child, be it boy or girl, to tend my shrine here."

"How can you ask me to do that?" cried Kiukiu. The thought of bringing her baby, any baby, to this desolate place and leaving it alone with the snake appalled her beyond words.

The Guardian Snake lowered its head and turned away from her, the luminous waters churning and spraying Kiukiu with fine drops as it dived.

"*Wait!*" Kiukiu dropped to her knees, head bowed, the last of her strength spent. She had traveled so far, pushing her failing body to the point of collapse, sustained only by the hope that the power of the springs would restore her. She knew at that moment she would agree to anything. "I will do it."

The Guardian Snake swam slowly, sinuously back. "Send the child to me when it reaches its seventh year." Gusts of steam rose from the pool, like billowing smoke, growing thicker and thicker, until they drifted in soft waves across the rocks and she could no longer see anything but a faint glow.

"If it was my child, I'd have to stay here with it!" Kiukiu blurted out. "I know too well what it's like to grow up without a mother or father to care for you."

"Come down into the water, Kiukirilya." The Guardian's voice urged her through the smoke.

Trembling with cold, Kiukiu dipped in one foot, searching in vain with her toe for the bottom. "It's warm," she said in surprise.

"Give me your hand," coaxed the voice.

Kiukiu lost her balance, slipped, and fell into the pool with a splash. Panicking, she thrashed about, gasping and spluttering.

Someone grasped hold of her and brought her back up to the

surface, supporting her head. "Lie back. You're quite safe. I won't let you drown."

"I—I can't swim—"

"Don't fight me," said the calm, steady voice. "Trust me."

Kiukiu stopped coughing water and looked up. Through the shifting mists, she saw eyes, green as jade, smiling down at her. She was lying in the warm, fizzing waters, held up by a tall woman, whose long hair floated around them like waterweed.

"My name is Anagini," she said, "and I am the Guardian of the Jade Springs."

"Anagini," repeated Kiukiu, amazed. And whether there were some calming properties in the mineral fumes she was inhaling, or just Anagini's influence, she closed her eyes and surrendered herself to the water's gentle caress.

"That's right," murmured Anagini soothingly, stroking her face. "Whatever happens now, you must remember that I am protecting you."

"Whatever—?" Kiukiu's eyes snapped open and saw a myriad of little flames catch light on the surface of the water. The flames gathered together, surrounding her, burning with a soft hiss until all she could see was their dazzling green phosphorescence and all she could feel was their intense heat.

Fire and water mingled—how can that be possible? Every instinct made her want to flee, to cringe away as ripple upon ripple of fire licked her naked body until she was enveloped in flame.

Green fire seared her mind and she cried out in pain and terror. She was burning. All that was old and sere was being stripped from her, blistered away by the jade fires.

The flames died down until she could only hear the hiss of the steam. Her dazzled sight slowly returned and by the bubbling water's luminescent gleam, she began to make out little details of jagged rock, spiny bush, and overhanging tree. High overhead she could see the black of the night sky, pinpricked by stars.

"Well," she said cautiously, "I still seem to be here. And in one piece." Beneath the luminous waters, her limbs looked pale as water lilies. "Two arms, two legs . . ."

She pulled herself up and out of the pool and saw her shawl lying on the rocks, where she had left it. Dripping, she wrapped the shawl around herself. "It would be silly to catch my death of cold, having come this far," she muttered to herself. It was difficult to see clearly by starlight, but her skin felt smoother and firmer as she rubbed herself dry with the shawl.

"Don't forget, Kiukirilya," hissed a voice, so soft she could hardly distinguish it from the hiss of the steam. "Your firstborn child . . . at seven years." A forked tongue flickered out and touched her bare ankle. Kiukiu gave a little cry of pain. "And you must never tell anyone what passed between us here today or you will find yourself an old woman again. Do you understand me?"

Kiukiu rubbed her sore ankle. "I understand."

She found her clothes, still neatly folded, under the stooping larch tree, and dressed hurriedly. Her hair still hung damp about her shoulders as she made her way from the springs in search of Malusha and Chinua.

She soon spotted the dying light of their fire between the pines. As she made her way carefully down the stony track, she noticed how much easier it was to descend than it had been to climb up. It seemed no distance at all, even in the darkness.

A grey shadow detached itself from the rocks and wolf eyes gleamed at her. She leaped back, heart beating fast.

"Welcome back, Kiukirilya." The wolf-form shivered and out of the shadow, Chinua arose, bowing and smiling.

"Chinua!" she said, one hand trying to calm her pounding heart. "You startled me."

"I was keeping watch," he said. "Would you like some tea to warm you?"

"Oh, yes," Kiukiu said fervently. At that moment, a cup of Chinua's hot, fragrant tea was the thing she desired most in the whole world.

As Kiukiu sipped her tea by the embers of the fire, she saw that the stars were fading overhead. Malusha and Linnaius still slept, and Kiukiu let them be, not ready yet to face the inevitable questions that would follow.

"So the Guardian granted your wish," said Chinua, nodding approvingly.

"Thank you, Chinua, for taking such good care of us." Kiukiu smiled warmly at him. "We would never have found our way here without your help. How can I ever repay your kindness?"

"Your grandmother did me a great service, many years ago," said Chinua enigmatically. "Now the debt is paid."

"Who's talking of debts?" said a sleepy voice. "You know very well, Chinua, that I never expected any payment." Malusha sat up, rubbing her back and groaning. "I'm too old to sleep on such hard ground." Kiukiu waited patiently while the grumbling went on for a while longer. "Well, bless me," said Malusha suddenly, "but who's this pretty young woman, Chinua?"

"Grandma, it's me!"

"Well, of course it is. D'you think I don't recognize my own flesh and blood? Come here and let me look at you properly."

Kiukiu knelt beside her grandmother who flung her arms around her and hugged her hard. Then she took Kiukiu's face gently in her hands and gazed deep into her eyes. "Well, it's a miracle. You don't look a day older than the night Snowcloud found you lost on the moors." She stroked Kiukiu's hair, holding out a strand, so that the rising sun caught it. "Gold as the sunlight." She winked at Chinua over Kiukiu's shoulder. "D'you think the Guardian would make an old one like me young again?"

"Grandma?" said Kiukiu, wondering if Malusha was in earnest.

"I'm only jesting, Kiukiu. I've had a long life, long enough. What's the point in living beyond your natural span? It can be mighty lonely." She jabbed her thumb at the sleeping Magus. "What happiness has it brought him?"

What did you have to give to Anagini, Kaspar Linnaius? Kiukiu wondered. *What will she ask of you this time?* And then she remembered her secret bargain with the Guardian and the clarity of the morning sunlight seemed to dim. *My firstborn child. Whatever was I thinking of?* And a little voice at the back of her mind answered, *Gavril. I wanted to see Gavril again. I wanted him to see me as I was before. Was that too much to ask?*

"Why do I have to bathe?" asked the Magus. He was in a cantankerous mood this morning and seemed reluctant to leave the fire. "It's too chilly. I'll catch cold."

Kiukiu heard them arguing; but did not join in. She was slowly, gently combing her hair and checking that the gold had not faded.

"I'm not looking at that scrawny, skinny old body without its clothes on, thank you," said Malusha vehemently. "You'll have to help him, Chinua."

"But Magus," said Chinua, "these are healing springs."

"Are they good for the rheumatics?"

"Yes, yes," said Malusha, "just go and get it over with." But when Chinua had led the reluctant old man away up the steep path, she turned to Kiukiu. "We must be on our guard from the moment the Magus returns. God only knows what kind of bargain he'll have to make to regain his lost wits, but once he's got them back, he'll be capable of all manner of mischief."

"Why?" Kiukiu had begun to plait her hair; alarmed, she looked up and all the strands unplaited themselves. "What do you think he'll do?"

"My hope is he'll go back to his royal master and leave us in peace."

Kiukiu fell silent, wondering what Anagini would ask the Magus to give her. What did the old man have left to offer? His immortal soul?

My firstborn child . . .

It was dusk and the last light of the sinking sun was warming the grey stone of the mountainside.

"They're still not back," said Kiukiu, unable to quell a nagging feeling of anxiety. "Has something gone wrong?"

"Something's not right," said Malusha, glancing around with beady eyes. "Can you sense it? There's a touch of mischief in the air."

Kiukiu sniffed, wrinkling her nose in distaste. "There's certainly a strong smell of fox."

"Here they are," said a triumphant voice. Suddenly the khan's men surrounded them. "Didn't I say I could track them for you?" Unegen gloated.

The khan's soldiers flung Kiukiu and Malusha down before Khan Vachir.

"Prince Bayar has fallen ill again," said the khan coldly. "And you told me he was cured."

Kiukiu helped Malusha up. She glowered defiantly at the khan's guards who had manhandled Malusha so roughly. "Are you all right, Grandma?" she whispered in Azhkendi.

"I'll do," said Malusha, wheezing.

"My son needs you. And as long as he needs you, you will stay here, at my court."

All Kiukiu's dreams collapsed; she had been planning to leave

Khitari as soon as possible, certainly before the first snows. The leaves were turning, autumn was in the air; once winter set in, they would be trapped at Lake Taigal for the long, dark months until the thaw.

"But I serve Lord Nagarian of Azhkendir," she protested.

"You are my shamans now." The khan turned to his guards. "Take them to Prince Bayar." And before Kiukiu could protest again, the guards grabbed her by the shoulders and removed her from the khan's tent.

"Why is my son still sick?" Lady Orqina rose from Bayar's side. She was agitatedly twisting the tassels of her wide silk belt, knotting and unknotting them. "You said he was cured."

Kiukiu stared at the boy who lay watching her with eyes half-glazed with fever. She was remembering the warnings she had received from the Drakhaouls' children.

"Not quite so, my lady," said Malusha. "We know the cause of his illness. But it's not so simple to effect a cure."

"Let me try again," offered Kiukiu.

Malusha took her face in her hands and gently stroked her cheek. "You're only just restored, child. Let me go in your stead."

"*As our memories fade, so it fades too.*" Koropanga's words still haunted Kiukiu. She could not bear to think that the Drakhaouls' children were in thrall to that dark, corrupt spirit. Or that young Bayar's life force was steadily seeping away, drained by his connection to Koropanga.

In spite of Malusha's warning, she knew she had to find out more.

"Koro," said Kiukiu, "you asked me to help you. Tell me the name of your Drakhaoul."

"My Drakhaoul?" Koro looked at her with doubting eyes.

"Your blood gave a Drakhaoul life in my world. You are linked, whether you like it or not."

"But if I tell you his name, horrible things will happen to me."

"How can anything more horrible happen to you?" she asked gently. Had the Drakhaoul prince threatened the children with tortures just to amuse himself? Or was he genuinely afraid that the sharing of his kindred's names might lessen their power?

"*He* can let the dust and the whirling winds back in."

"And increase his own suffering as well as yours? I don't think so."

Koropanga gave a little one-sided shrug. He beckoned her close and cupped one hand over his mouth as he leaned to whisper in her ear, "Adramelech. Adramelech is my Drakhaoul." And then he glanced around fearfully as if expecting the sky to collapse in on them.

Kiukiu heard the name and repeated it silently to herself.

And suddenly she was surrounded by the murdered children, all gazing at her with desperate longing in their death-dark eyes. Tilua clung to her hand as if she would never let go.

"We're tired of this place."

"Send us home, Spirit Singer."

Her heart was twisted with pain, thinking how long, how very long they had been imprisoned here in this illusion of their own making.

They had created a little paradise where the sun gilded the soft sands and warmed clear blue water, but the reality it masked was a place of eternal punishment.

CHAPTER 34

Enguerrand rode to Belle Garde. Though he was not of a morbid disposition, he felt he should visit his mother. He was certain he would not fail in his glorious endeavor . . . but some deeper instinct, filial duty or love, maybe, drove him there.

Or the hope that, for once, she might show him a little motherly affection.

Gardeners were sweeping up fallen leaves and piling them into heaps for burning. The air was smokily sweet with the smell of bonfires. Aliénor was a great believer in the virtues of fresh air and, in spite of the first touch of autumnal chill, she was sitting in an arbour with her companion, Madame de Romorantin, both busy with their embroidery needles. She looked up from her frame as he approached and presented her cheek for him to kiss. Madame de Romorantin curtsied and discreetly withdrew, leaving them alone together; as her skirts brushed against the pruned lavender bushes, he caught a sharp waft of their stringent scent.

"Your hair's grown very long," Aliénor said, looking him over with a critical eye. "It needs a good trim."

Enguerrand had been too preoccupied with other matters of late to bother much about his appearance. One hand rose to check his hair and found, to his surprise, that his usually neat locks had reached his shoulders.

"So, to what do we owe the honor of this visit?" she said. He wished she wouldn't speak to him so formally.

"I just wanted to see you, Maman," he said, smiling at her as he sat down beside her.

"Don't tell me you've decided at last to get married. Francia needs an heir!" She leaned across and flicked a speck of dirt from his jacket. "And I wish you wouldn't call me Maman. You're a grown man now, Enguerrand."

"No, *madame*," he said patiently, laying emphasis on the form of address she preferred.

"Just as I thought. And there is a dearth of eligible princesses at present. Little Karila of Tielen is only a child still and horribly deformed, from all we have heard. Of course, you could consider your cousin, Esclairmonde . . ."

La Belle Esclairmonde. Enguerrand's heartbeat quickened at the mere mention of her name. But he could not allow himself to be distracted by matters of the flesh. "All in good time, madame," he heard himself saying and saw her expression freeze. "By which I mean," he added hastily, "that I'll put my mind to it as soon as I return."

"Return? Where are you going?"

Enguerrand reminded himself that it was probably a sign of motherly concern that she still treated him like an errant schoolboy.

"If I succeed in this enterprise," he said, "then I promise you, madame, I will choose a bride."

"Enguerrand, explain yourself!"

If he stayed any longer, she would make him tell her what he intended to do. And she would never understand. He leaned forward and kissed her dry cheek a second time. "Adieu, madame."

"Adieu? What do you mean?" He heard her calling after him, but kept walking along the lavender-bordered path, determined not to turn back. "Are you going into battle?"

I am, dearest mother. The serene smile still lit his face. *A battle more glorious and dangerous than you could possibly imagine.*

Ruaud de Lanvaux had given instructions that the young Azhkendi prisoners be kept in solitary confinement in one of the cells in the Forteresse. Now he was ready to interrogate them.

Following his instructions, the Guerriers had shackled the youngest one to a punishment post in full view of the other, who was still confined behind the bars of the cell.

The prisoner looked like a savage; stripped to his breeches, the blue-and-crimson tattoos marking his face, neck, and right arm from shoulder to hand, were all too visible. The young man—barely more than a boy, with the merest shadow of a reddish beard on his chin—stared defiantly back, but the Grand Maistre could tell that, for all his show of bravado, he was terrified.

If you think those primitive tattoos will protect you from harm, Ruaud thought, staring at the clanmarks, *then you are about to be sorely disappointed.*

"I ask you once again," said Inquisitor Visant in his smoothest tones. "Is it true that your Lord Drakhaon will come if you call him?"

Ruaud de Lanvaux focused all his attention on the younger of the two Azhkendi warriors. He was certain that he would break the first under questioning.

"What if it is?" said the one called Dunai. Sweat glistened on his face—a good sign, Ruaud knew from experience. Beneath his bravado, the young man was terrified. And well he might be; one sight of the devices arrayed in the little room to aid the inquisitor in his questioning was often enough to loosen stubborn tongues. But these two were proving remarkably resistant; he could only conclude that their upbringing in the mountains had accustomed them to hardship.

"Use the boot," he said to Visant; they were running out of time. Even if Dunai refused to speak, Semyon might well break when faced with the sight of his friend being tortured.

Visant nodded to his two assistants, who brought out the device. Fashioned from iron to resemble an artificial limb, it opened up to enclose the victim's leg. When the bolts that secured it in place were tightened, they caused a slow crushing of the flesh and bone encased within. The results proved excruciating to the prisoner and extremely rewarding to the inquisitor.

"Do what you like," said Dunai defiantly as the Guerriers went to work. "I won't betray Lord Gavril."

"Of course you won't," murmured Ruaud, "but your young friend will . . ."

"Let me ask you one more time," said Visant in his most weary tones, "have you the power to call the Drakhaon?"

Dunai said nothing. Visant signed to his assistants, who proceeded to twist the bolts a notch tighter. Ruaud saw Dunai wince but, to his credit, not even the slightest sound escaped his lips.

"I ask you again," said Visant.

Still Dunai said nothing. Again the Guerriers tightened the bolts and this time there came the faint but horrible sound of cracking, as though the metal had begun to penetrate living bone. Dunai turned his face away and let out a slow, agonized moan.

"Dunai!" As Ruaud had predicted, Semyon was close to breaking point. His features twisted in sympathetic agony. Words began to pour out of his mouth in Azhkendi.

"No—Sem—" gasped Dunai.

Visant was at Semyon's side in a second, grabbing him by the hair and jerking his head back. "Go on, my young friend. I am all attention."

Ruaud saw the boy's face begin to crumple.

"Another twist and all the bones in his shin and ankle will be crushed," continued Visant in a soft voice. "He'll be crippled for life—if he survives. Do you want that on your conscience? Answer my question and I will spare him." He let Semyon go and stepped back. "Well? I'm waiting."

Tears began to leak from Semyon's eyes.

Visant again lifted his hand to sign to his assistants. As they gripped the screws to drive the bolts farther into Dunai's leg, Dunai gave a shuddering cry.

"Lord Drakhaon!" screamed out Semyon. "*Help us!*"

"Is that all you had to do?" Visant thrust his face into Semyon's. "Call his name?"

"Damn you, Semyon," gasped Dunai, and his head slumped forward.

"And how can we be sure he will come?" Ruaud asked.

"Oh, he will come," said Semyon. Although tears still coursed down his cheeks, his eyes burned with hatred and defiance. "And he will sear you all to ashes for what you've done to Dunai."

Enguerrand and his entourage stopped at Tessé-les-Bains so that the king could bathe in the hot spa baths.

Enguerrand avoided visiting spas whenever possible. A poor swimmer, he had never properly mastered the technique of breathing underwater without choking. But now he felt daring enough to plunge his head beneath the hot mineral waters, eyes squeezed shut and nose pinched tight between finger and thumb.

"*Don't be afraid,*" whispered Nilaihah. "*I won't let you drown.*"

And to Enguerrand's astonishment, he found that, with the angel's help, not only could he swim and breathe underwater, he could even open his eyes without discomfort.

After this ritual cleansing, Enguerrand had his valet Fragan help him dress in the clothes he had had made especially for the occasion: a monk's robes, of the finest white linen, tied with a silken cord, in which was woven a single thread of crimson to remind him of the fragility of mortal life.

He wished, though, that his mother had not mentioned his cousin, Esclairmonde, for now he found himself thinking of her all the time. He had never really considered her as a potential bride before, especially as the last time they had met, she had spent much of the time giggling with her little sister Aude. Now he remembered how charmed he had been by those mischievous hazel eyes . . .

"*This can only be a trap.*" Khezef was growing increasingly jittery as they flew toward Francia.

"Yes," Gavril said. He was well aware of the odds. "I know."

"*They have the Staff. They may try to use it against me and my kindred.*"

"Dunai and Semyon don't deserve to be caught up in this. They've suffered enough already on my account."

"*They're your bodyguard. They took an oath to protect you.*"

"And I promised Askold I would find his son."

Enguerrand ordered candles of the finest, whitest wax to be lit in every sconce and alcove of the Commanderie chapel. The great rose window behind the altar let in a soft light filtered through the petal-panes of colored glass, which touched the pale stone columns with flecks of blue and gold.

The walls were hung with massive paintings depicting the lives of the saints; scenes of martyrdom and pious acts, whose bright colors had been dimmed by age and the residue from greasy candlesmoke. But a marble statue dominated this end of the chapel; a life-size sculpture of the Blessed Sergius wrestling with one of the Drakhaouls in its dragon-form, his staff raised like a spear, to pierce the snarling daemon's throat. Even if the legend were true, the final heroic battle could never have been like this—and yet this was the single image that had inspired Enguerrand since he was a young boy.

Enguerrand gazed reverently at Sergius's reforged Staff. It lay on a rich tapestry of azure and crimson, the gold crook gleaming in the light filtering through the stained glass.

He had been waiting for this moment for so long. And now he was not sure if he was worthy of the task. Had he been guilty of the sin of pride in assuming that he was the one destined to destroy the Drakhaouls? Only one pure of heart could wield the Staff. Now that it had come to it, he faltered, filled with self-doubt.

"But hasn't this always been your dream?" whispered his guardian angel. *"To be Saint Enguerrand, the Drakhaoul-Slayer?"*

"Saint Enguerrand," repeated the king under his breath, then felt a tremor of guilt at imagining such a prideful thing in this holy place. "Am I really the chosen one?"

"There is only one way to be certain."

"And if I fail?" He dropped to his knees at the altar, still gazing up at the Staff. "I think I'm afraid to die. There's so much I haven't done . . ."

"Courage, Enguerrand." The angel's voice flowed through him with the golden warmth of honey. He felt comforted, invigorated, uplifted. *"No one else has your determination—or your strength of purpose. You have the Tears of Artamon. The Drakhaouls desire those rubies more than anything else in this world."*

"Why do they want them so much?"

"Because they are the key to the Serpent Gate. They are imbued with special powers, the powers to unlock the portal between our world and the Realm of Shadows. The Gate is already unstable. They seek to use the rubies' powers to open it and release their master, Prince Nagar, from his eternal imprisonment."

"Suppose one of them escaped with the rubies while I was battling the others?"

"Do not forget, they are all subservient to their human masters. And that makes them weak."

"But if their human masters have been corrupted, they may do as their Drakhaouls wish—"

Nilaihah laughed, a gentle, reassuring laugh. *"It's understandable,*

Enguerrand, that you have so many doubts and fears. But you have me to guide you. If you are truly as pure of heart and mind as you believe, then nothing can go wrong."

Ruaud de Lanvaux stared at his king. Surrounded by the shimmering light of the candles, Enguerrand looked like a young saint in his pure white robes. For a moment, the Grand Maistre felt a catch in his throat as he gazed at his protégé. There was a radiance about the king; his eyes gleamed gold in the candleglow and a faint glimmer seemed to encircle his head, like a halo.

"Will he come, do you think, Ruaud?" he asked. And the faint tremor in his voice betrayed his fear and his vulnerability.

"Oh yes, sire, he will come." Now Ruaud feared for Enguerrand. He was facing an unimaginably powerful opponent. And his only weapon, Sergius's Staff, was a relic from a bygone age, little more than a symbol of the saint's triumph over the forces of darkness. Sergius had used the Staff to channel the power of the Heavenly Warriors; without their aid, the Drakhaouls would never have been bound in stone.

"And the *others?*"

Ruaud came closer to Enguerrand. "If you have the slightest doubt as to the wisdom of this venture . . ."

Enguerrand gave him an affronted look.

"There would be no dishonor in abandoning the attempt," Ruaud said gently.

"I won't abandon." There was a stubborn glint in Enguerrand's eyes. "I'm no coward, Ruaud. I'm not afraid. I have my guardian to guide and protect me."

"Nilaihah," said Ruaud under his breath.

"And he will summon others to assist him if needs be." Enguerrand seemed to be growing in confidence as he spoke.

The summer daylight outside the chapel began to fade. Clouds must be rolling up fast, Ruaud thought, feeling the hairs prickle on his body; thunderstorms were common at that time of year. Yet he recognized the unsettling feeling. The last time he had experienced it was in the Place du Trahoir as the flames began to take hold on Kaspar Linnaius's pyre.

A turbulent wind began to gust, high about the ornately carved spires of the chapel.

The great door to the chapel suddenly banged open. All the candleflames guttered wildly and blew out.

"Is he here already?" Ruaud swung around. A man stood in the doorway. Even in the dim light, Ruaud could see that his skin glittered as though jeweled with iridescent scales and his wild dark hair tumbled about his shoulders. This was not the terrifying daemon-dragon that had swooped down on the place of execution to carry off the Magus, but neither was it an ordinary man.

"*I am here,*" said the Drakhaon.

Eyes as blue as midnight stars stared at Enguerrand.

"My adversary," whispered the king. His fingers crept out toward Sergius's Staff and gripped it tightly.

"I've kept my part of the bargain, King Enguerrand," said the Drakhaon quietly. "Now it's your turn."

"*Don't hold back,*" urged Nilaihah. Enguerrand's mind had gone blank. "*Point the crook of the Staff toward him.*"

The Drakhaon began to walk down the aisle toward Enguerrand.

"Well?" he said. "You promised that my *druzhina* would be released. Where are they? And where are the rubies?"

"Ruaud," ordered Enguerrand; his voice cracked with the tension. And just when he needed to sound strong and firm of purpose.

The Grand Maistre went to the altar and brought out the golden casket in which the Tears of Artamon had been sealed. He opened the lid and crimson light shone out.

"Your reign of terror is over, Drakhaon!" cried the young king, raising the gold-tipped Staff high, brandishing it like a hunting spear, ready for the kill. "This is Saint Sergius's Staff."

Gavril felt Khezef writhe within him, as though terrified at the sight.

"Daemon, I conjure you," said Enguerrand in a loud voice. "Leave this man's body!"

Gavril braced himself, gripping hold of the carved back of one of the chapel stalls. The golden crook gleamed like a crescent moon as the daylight faded from the chapel.

Gavril's gaze was drawn upward to the great rose window behind Enguerrand. Shadows clustered outside, winged shadows, dark as night.

"You don't understand, Enguerrand!" he cried. "They were once creatures of light too. They deserve better than this. Have you no compassion?"

"Hear how the daemon talks through him," came Ruaud de Lanvaux's voice through the gathering dark. "Pay no attention, sire. He will say anything to sway you."

The golden glow around Enguerrand was becoming brighter, as though he were caught in the beams of the rising sun. He grasped the crook with both hands and pointed it directly at Gavril's breast. Gavril stared, mesmerized, into the king's radiant face. The Heavenly Warriors must be working through him, lending him their powers, as once they had Saint Sergius.

"*Khezef, I'm sorry. I can't do anything to stop him.*"

Enguerrand's eyes gleamed as dazzlingly, unnaturally gold as the crook he wielded. "I call upon my guardian angel to help me." He came toward Gavril. "Nilaihah, work through me—and draw out this daemon."

"*Nilaihah.*" Gavril heard Khezef echo the angel's name. And a powerful burst of violent emotions flooded through Gavril: a riot of kaleidoscopic colors and feelings. Foremost among them, Gavril tasted—amusement. Then dry laughter shook his body; the daemon was laughing and Gavril could do nothing but laugh too, collapsing to his knees, clutching his sides, overcome with mirth.

"Why is nothing happening?" Enguerrand's voice, confused and upset, issued from the golden haze. "Ruaud—"

"*It's been a good ruse, brother,*" Khezef said, and Gavril knew he was not talking to him. "*But it's time to end it.*"

"Nilaihah!" cried Enguerrand again, his voice straining. "Destroy him."

And Gavril heard another voice, rich and commanding, cry out, "*Sahariel, Adramelech—now!*"

The rose window splintered into a million shards of colored glass. Through the deadly rain of splinters burst two dragon-daemons, one scarlet as flame, the other dark as purple twilight.

Enguerrand let out a scream and turned, pointing the Staff at them with trembling hands.

The scarlet Drakhaon reached out one clawed hand and snatched the Staff, snapping it in half as if it were matchwood. The other blew a little burst of flame; the golden crook steamed, bubbled into a puddle of liquid metal, and melted onto the tiles on the chapel floor.

Enguerrand collapsed.

Disjointed words issued from his mouth as he cowered on the floor before the two daemons.

"Why—did you—to your Chosen One? Am I—*unworthy?*"

"*You fool. Have you still not realized what I am?*"

As Gavril watched, the king's body began to tremble, then to twitch and thrash about as though he were in the throes of a violent epileptic fit. A fine gilded mist arose, spinning around him, until the air glittered.

Gavril heard Ruaud de Lanvaux call out, "*No!*" and saw the Grand Maistre reach out, as if to grab hold of Enguerrand. But it was too late. Where the king had lain, there crouched a third dragon-daemon, armored with burnished scales as resplendent as the morning sun. And it was weeping; boiling tears sizzled down its long snout and dripped, steaming onto the floor.

The scarlet Drakhaon thrust its head down toward Gavril, until he could feel the fiery heat issuing from its flared nostrils. It spoke to him directly, its coal-black eyes narrowed.

"*You don't remember me, do you, Nagarian?*"

The hot air shimmered and a man stood before him, a man transformed by his daemon, with long, unnaturally white hair and a powdering of scales, like scarlet-and-black sequins, encrusting his whole body. Yet there was something about his arrogant stance, his folded arms, the proud jut of his jaw that was familiar.

Gavril stared at him. "Should I know you?"

"*You attacked me and my men. At Narvazh. I think we're better matched now.*"

Gavril heard the challenge but chose to ignore it. He remembered the encounter at Narvazh well enough; it was the first time he had used his powers against his fellow men and he had woken up for many nights afterward in a cold sweat, reliving the nightmare.

One clawed finger reached out and tipped Gavril's chin upward until he could not avoid the malicious stare of those black-and-scarlet eyes.

"*My name is Alvborg. Oskar Alvborg. Remember that name, Lord Nagarian.*"

With a contemptuous flick of his clawed fingers beneath Gavril's chin, he turned back to his companion. "*It's not safe to leave the Eye here. We're taking charge of it.*"

Khezef awoke. "*Why should you take charge of the Eye?*"

"*Because, dearest Khezef, we don't trust you.*"

The one who had named himself Alvborg tipped the lid of the golden casket shut and picked it up in his taloned fingers.

"Wait!" Gavril started forward but the silent Drakhaon moved, placing himself between them.

The air whirled in a flicker of fire and shadow as Alvborg transformed.

"*And don't come after us. You're too weak, too slow.*"

The two Drakhaons rose into the air and flew out through the ruined window, the wind from their great wings almost knocking Gavril to the ground.

"We must go after them," he cried to Khezef.

"*You know they're right; we haven't enough strength to catch them up.*"

Fists thudded against the barred wooden doors of the chapel; muffled voices clamored to be let in.

Ruaud de Lanvaux slowly, painfully, pushed himself to his knees, then to his feet. There was no sign of the Drakhaouls. Broken glass and fragments of stone were scattered everywhere. The chapel was cracked open to the sky, a great, jagged hole gaping where the magnificent rose window had been.

And sprawled on the floor, unmoving, lay Enguerrand.

"Sire," Ruaud called, ashamed to hear that his voice trembled. "Sire, are you unharmed?" He tottered toward him and saw that little remained of Enguerrand's white robes; they had been shredded to tatters, leaving the king nearly naked. Yet he could see no bruises or wounds on the king's body.

What would he do if the daemon had killed the king? And how would he explain it to Aliénor? She would blame him. She would have him and his closest advisers executed in the most prolonged and painful way she could devise.

Loud, rhythmic thuds made the locked doors shudder on their hinges. He guessed that his Guerriers must be trying to force them open.

"You young fool," he muttered as he knelt beside Enguerrand. "Why did I listen to you? Why did I doubt the angelstone? All the evidence was there before me—and yet the daemon's lies deceived me too."

The king let out a soft moan, as if he had heard what Ruaud said.

"Sire?" Relieved beyond words, Ruaud leaned forward as Enguerrand tried to lift his head and helped the king to sit up. "Thank God you're alive." He took off his jacket and slipped it over the king's shoulders. Enguerrand was shivering uncontrollably; he seemed in a state of shock.

"Uncl—clean," he stuttered. "D—don't come too close."

The doors crashed open and armed Guerriers came rushing in. They hurried through the chapel with pistols and muskets at the ready, to take up defensive positions at all corners.

"Maistre, the king?" called an officer.

"The king is unharmed," said Ruaud, forcing himself to appear more confident than he felt.

"The Staff." Enguerrand's voice was barely more than a whisper. He was staring fixedly at the scattered splinters.

"It was just wood and metal." Ruaud felt a deep disillusionment pervading his soul. "We were arrogant fools to think that any among us was pure enough to inherit Sergius's powers."

And he heard a muffled sob escape the king's throat.

Enguerrand knelt before Ruaud, his head bent. "Don't look at me, Maistre. I'm corrupted." His voice was heavy with self-loathing. "I'm not worthy to be called one of your Guerriers. Tell me how I can rid myself of this curse."

Ruaud gazed down at Enguerrand's abject posture and knew that he was utterly at a loss. The king was begging him for consolation— and he had none to give. Nagar's daemons had defeated him.

"We will just have to pray for guidance," he said distantly.

"Where is the king?"

Ruaud turned to see a messenger in the russet livery of the House of Provença gazing about him in bewilderment at the wrecked chapel.

"The king is not well," Ruaud said as Enguerrand, still trembling, huddled in Ruaud's jacket. "I will answer for him."

"My master, the Duc de Provença, sent me to . . ." The messenger's voice trailed away as his eyes slid sideways to the shivering figure, ". . . to inform his majesty that he and his daughters have arrived in Lutèce and will be honored to receive his majesty at the Hôtel de Provença whensoever he pleases."

Ruaud frowned. Another unforeseen complication. Was this Aliénor's doing? "And his majesty will be pleased to welcome his cousins to the palace," he replied, "as soon as he has recovered from this touch of . . . summer fever."

The Commanderie Forteresse was filled with running men; Gavril slipped into a doorway and watched as Guerriers, panicked and confused, hurried toward the chapel to aid their king.

He had come to rescue Semyon and Dunai and he would not leave Lutèce without them. Drained as he was, he must get them out of the Commanderie dungeons. Beyond that, he had no idea where he would take them.

It was ironic that the unexpected arrival of Khezef's kindred had created the ideal distraction to allow him access to the prison.

He called out to the *druzhina* silently again. "*Dunai. Semyon. Where are you?*"

And at last a faint answer resonated through his mind. "*Here, Lord Drakhaon . . . below ground.*"

He recognized Semyon's voice. "*Keep talking to me, Sem. Guide me.*"

He set out, following the distant voice trail, hiding in doorways whenever any Guerriers came past.

The trail led down a steep stair into a dark, lanternlit passageway. There was a rank, damp smell lingering here that reminded Gavril of the odor of the dank passageways and cells of Arnskammar. And that memory brought back such powerful feelings of dread and disgust that he sensed a righteous anger reawakening deep within him.

At the end of the passageway he caught sight of a couple of Guerriers on guard duty. Behind them, thick metal bars encaged the prisoners; from Gavril's place of concealment, he could make out several figures, some sitting with their heads bowed, others slumped on the floor, unconscious or asleep.

Two Guerriers.

"*Soon they will come looking for you,*" warned Khezef.

There was nothing for it but to brazen it out.

The stale smell of urine and unwashed flesh grew stronger as he set out down the passageway.

"Halt!" cried one of the Guerriers as he approached. Gavril kept on walking. "Stop!" The Guerriers lifted their muskets, ready to fire. He guessed that, in the flickering lanternlight, they could not see clearly what was walking toward them. He pointed one blue-taloned finger at the muskets and concentrated what little firepower he could still summon. A burst of flame, sapphire-bright, shot out, and both muskets disintegrated with a muffled bang of powder.

One Guerrier fell wounded to the floor. The other turned tail and ran. Gavril cursed silently; he was sure to raise the alarm. He grabbed the keys from the fallen Guerrier's belt and unlocked the door of the cell.

Pallid faces turned to stare at him from the semidarkness. And among them he spotted Dunai and Semyon, barely recognizable under many days' growth of stubble. Haggard, emaciated and dirty, they sat on the dirt floor of the cell in their own filth. The stench, now that he was close, was overpowering and his eyes began to water. How could the Commanderie treat their prisoners with such a lack of respect?

"Lord Drakhaon!" Semyon broke into a ragged smile. "I said you'd come for us . . ." Dunai nodded; he looked so weak he could scarcely move his head.

"We'll have to move fast," said Gavril, glancing uneasily behind him, knowing it was but a matter of minutes before reinforcements arrived. He knelt by each of the *druzhina* in turn and unlocked his shackles. Semyon tried to stand but fell back, weak-legged as a newborn colt.

The other prisoners gazed at Gavril as he put Dunai's arm over his shoulder and hoisted him to his feet. "Free me!" cried out one in the common tongue. "Free us all!" said another.

"*You haven't time,*" Khezef warned him again.

Gavril propped Dunai against the wall and, kneeling, freed the nearest man from his shackles, before tossing him the keys.

"You're on your own now." How he wished he could see they were all safely delivered. But it was already obvious to him that neither Semyon nor Dunai had the strength to walk.

"*How far can we fly, Khezef?*"

"*Not far enough,*" came back the wry reply.

"*I'm not leaving without Semyon and Dunai.*"

"*Then you'll have to bear the consequences,*" said Khezef ominously.

Gavril made slow progress along the corridor, trying to support Dunai's weight. Semyon staggered after them but soon fell to his knees, dragging himself at Gavril's heels over the damp floor. And with every slow step, Gavril's heart was pounding, and the blood rushing in his ears, dreading to hear the Guerriers coming back.

They reached the steeply winding stair.

"Can you make your own way up?" Gavril asked Dunai.

"I can damn well try," said Dunai through gritted teeth.

"I'll go on ahead."

Above ground, the open courtyard was deserted. Was it another trap? Gavril glanced all around, wondering if there were armed Guerriers crouched in waiting, just out of sight. His heart was still beating too fast but now he felt charged, dangerous, elated by the risk he was taking in snatching back his own men from Ruaud de Lanvaux's impregnable stronghold.

"Is the coast clear?" Semyon's dirt-streaked face appeared in the gloom of the stairwell; Dunai had crawled up the stair behind him.

"We'll have to risk it."

The sound of agitated voices filled the stairwell; shouts and cries in the Francian tongue rose from below. It was the other freed prisoners, stumbling over one another in their desperation to escape.

"For God's sake tell them to be quiet!" The commotion must have alerted the whole Forteresse by now. Sure enough, as the prisoners came surging up the stairs, a patrol of armed Guerriers appeared at the far end of the courtyard. "*Khezef—there's no way out of here but up.*"

A wry shimmer of laughter echoed through his mind.

And then the sky turned thunder blue and he was no longer Gavril, he was Drakhaon, flexing his great wings in the cramped courtyard. He heard the distant shouts of the Guerriers as they aimed their muskets at him and fired. Musket balls bounced off his scales harmlessly, like hailstones.

"*Climb onto my back,*" he ordered. Whether Dunai and Semyon heard him above the din of musketry, he had no idea, but they clambered on and he leaped into the air, hoping he had enough strength to clear the high battlements.

The Guerriers would need a little time to reload their weapons; if he could get beyond musket range, then Dunai and Semyon would be less at risk from a stray shot.

Weighed down by the two *druzhina,* he labored hard to keep

climbing into the sky. He could feel them, desperately clinging on, slewing erratically from side to side as he rose slowly, bearing them upward. But the effort was exhausting him. He could sense the strength draining from him, wingstroke by slow wingstroke.

Soon the Drakhaon was high above the island Forteresse and could see the city below, spreading out on either side of the broad river, rising to the heights of the old Silk Quarter where Budoc Lavret had set up his studio.

But each heavy wingstroke jarred his whole body. His burden was too great. Little sparks and florets of fire flickered in front of his vision. Pain burned through his chest. He was losing height. He was falling.

"*I warned you,*" whispered Khezef as they dropped toward the ramshackle rooftops and crooked chimneys below. Up on the heights there were only weavers' cottages, mills, and factories noisy with clacking looms. There was no hope of an easy landing, in grassy fields or the sea.

"Just—a little farther." It was a desperate plea to Khezef. The tip of his tail grazed a tall factory chimney, dislodging a brick or two. He was damned if he was going to give up now. He had risked so much to rescue his *druzhina*. He could not bear to think it might all have been in vain.

"*This is . . . far enough.*"

A windswept ridge topped the heights of the quartier, bare, but for a few ancient mulberry trees. He had stood on this ridge beside Budoc Lavret and gazed down at the bustling city below. He could only hope that Lavret or one of his circle might offer them shelter until he had regained enough strength to continue the journey.

A sound rose from the city above the rushing of the wind, the frenzied clanging of the city's bells, ringing out from every tower and steeple. The din surged up to meet him as he dropped out of the sky. He had heard that clamor before. Then the peals had been joyous, welcoming Ruaud de Lanvaux home from Smarna in triumph. Now they were sounding the alert. And the waste ground, all brambles and nettle patches, was rising all too fast to meet him.

"Why?" Enguerrand asked his golden-eyed reflection. "Why did you lie to me?" He had been used. Betrayed. And most of all, deeply humiliated that he had been so easily deceived by the Drakhaoul.

"*I told you what you wanted to hear,*" said Nilaihah.

"Were you sent to torment me? To punish me for being too proud, too ambitious?" Enguerrand began to cry again, helpless sobs that shook his whole body. He had not cried so bitterly since his brother Aubrey died. "If so, then you couldn't have chosen a crueler punishment."

"*On the contrary. I came to make you great. I can make you Emperor, if that is your wish.*"

Enguerrand clapped his hands over his ears, saying loudly to block out the daemon's words, "No more lies. I'm not listening. I'm not listening to you."

"*I can help you win your cousin's hand in marriage,*" whispered Nilaihah suggestively.

"How can I go near her like this?" The idea was so repugnant that Enguerrand felt nauseated just thinking about it. Unclean. Polluted.

"*I know your most intimate fears and desires, Enguerrand. I know you're too shy to tell your cousin how you truly feel.*" Nilaihah's soft words began to evoke images in Enguerrand's mind. "*But now you have me to aid you, to twist the sweet, persuasive words from your tongue that La Belle Esclairmonde longs to hear.*" Lascivious, forbidden imaginings of amorous encounters with his cousin invaded Enguerrand's mind, as though Nilaihah had unlocked them.

"Stop!" Enguerrand let out an agonized cry and dropped to his knees, hands still covering his ears, swaying to and fro in his distress.

"Lord Drakhaon." Someone was shaking Gavril by the shoulder and every shake sent little tremors of agony knifing through his body. "We can't stay here. They're out searching for us."

Gavril opened his eyes to see Semyon's face looming over his. He tried to raise his head and waves of dizziness washed over him. He rolled over onto his side, feeling stones and gravel grate beneath him. He was grazed and bruised all over from the hard landing. A little farther off lay Dunai. Gavril struggled to sit up, propping himself on one skinned elbow.

"Dunai!" he called. "Are you all right?" Dunai did not respond.

"I think he's just fainted," Semyon said.

Gavril began to shiver. The sun was sinking, and a chill evening breeze had begun to blow. Semyon stripped off his filthy tunic and draped it about Gavril's naked shoulders.

"Lavret's studio," Gavril muttered. "I'm sure it was here, near the edge of the ridge."

He must have lost his bearings. All he could see was the blackened shell of a tall building that had once been a factory or a warehouse. Fire had swept through and the heat of the blaze must have been so fierce that the roof had fallen in and with it, the upper stories.

And then a horrible possibility began to dawn upon him. He had not mistaken where he was at all; this charred ruin was all that remained of the great painter's studio.

"*Someone's coming.*"

"Stay out of sight," warned Gavril. He steeled himself to fight, if need be, to defend his *druzhina*.

The footsteps drew nearer, but they were light and swift.

"*Innocent blood,*" sighed Khezef. Gavril ventured a glance to see who it was and recognized Trifine Lavret, toiling up the narrow lane, carrying a laden basket.

"Miran Korneli?" She came marching up to him. "You—you impostor! How dare you show your face here again?"

CHAPTER 35

"Why did you lie to us?" Trifine Lavret put down her basket in front of Gavril. "Why did you give us a false name? A dead man's name? Who *are* you? No, wait, don't even bother to tell me. It'll only be another lie." She picked up her basket and turned away to walk on.

"Wait, Trifine." Gavril could hardly summon the strength to call her name. "Forget me. But help my friends. They've been tortured by the Commanderie."

"Why should I believe you?" Yet she hesitated and he knew he had caught her attention.

"Dunai's leg is crushed. They used something called 'the boot' on him."

"But you're wanted men. They'll come looking for you. And then we'll be arrested again."

"Again?"

But Trifine was bending over him and he could smell the musky fragrance of her loose hair as it brushed his face. "You look terrible. You can't stay here. I suppose you'd better come back with me. But you'll have to be gone by dawn."

"Back?" Gavril repeated weakly.

"They burned down the studio. We're staying with Similien. You remember? The engraver."

"They burned the studio? With all your father's paintings?" Gavril was so stunned that for the moment he forgot his own troubles. Had the Commanderie been searching for him when they destroyed

Lavret's house and life's work? If so, then it was no wonder that Trifine was so furious at the sight of him.

Similien had established himself in an old tapestry manufactury farther along the ridge, setting up his press where the looms had once stood.

Gavril forced one foot to follow the other as he and Semyon half carried, half dragged the semiconscious Dunai between them.

"Wait here."

They propped Dunai up against the wall as Trifine went inside. Gavril heard a sudden burst of voices, speaking in rapid Francian, too fast and too faint for him to understand. It sounded as if her news was not well received. He closed his eyes. He could fend for himself. He just wanted to be sure Dunai and Semyon were in good hands.

The door suddenly opened and Budoc Lavret appeared in the lamplight.

"You'd better come in."

"We'll be gone in the morning," Gavril said to Lavret.

"None of you look in fit shape to go anywhere," the painter said gruffly.

"It seems I brought you more than enough trouble first time around."

Gavril exchanged Semyon's threadbare tunic for an old shirt and trousers that Madame Similien found for him from her husband's wardrobe. She gave him strong, sweet coffee to drink, laced with brandy. He drank it, then was forced to excuse himself, vomiting it up again in the privy outside. Now his sore stomach felt as if it had been scoured with vitriol, and the cramps were beginning again.

How long can I last? Long enough to get Semyon and Dunai away from Lutèce?

Outside, in the twilight, Trifine had not noticed the changes in him. But in the lamplight indoors, he knew that he could not conceal them so successfully. If challenged, he could say they were splashes of paint or ink. But in an engraver's house, he would soon be offered white spirit to clean the "stains."

While he was outside, a doctor had arrived, sent for by Similien, and was examining Dunai's leg. Semyon had fallen fast asleep on the floor near the fire, like a hound.

"Poor lad," said Madame Similien, covering him over with a blanket. "Let him sleep. I can put salve on those nasty sores on his wrists and ankles when he's awake again."

"I don't know how we can ever repay you," said Gavril. He had not expected to find such kindness and hospitality a second time.

"Tell me who you really are." Lavret lit his pipe with a long paper spill. "Tell me why the Commanderie were hunting you down."

Gavril could not deceive Lavret a second time. "My name is Gavril Nagarian. I'm Azhkendi by birth. I came to rescue my men from the Commanderie." It was by no means the whole story, but it would suffice.

"One of them called you 'my lord.' " Trifine was looking at him suspiciously now. "What kind of a lord? I thought you were a painter."

But Gavril was spared from further questioning by a frantic rapping at the door. He glanced uneasily at Lavret, who gave a shrug and said, "The Commanderie don't bother to knock."

Similien went to see who it was and seconds later, Herbot the miniaturist came in, trembling with excitement, his habitually lugubrious expression transformed. "Have you heard? Someone broke the prisoners out of the Forteresse—" He stopped, seeing Gavril. "What is *he* doing here?"

"I believe you just answered your own question," Lavret said, gesturing with the stem of his pipe to where Semyon lay asleep.

"You?" Herbot came closer to Gavril, extending his long, thin neck, like a tortoise peering out of his shell. "There're all kinds of ridiculous stories going around the city. How *did* you get them out?"

"I and a couple of . . . acquaintances created a little diversion." Gavril's wry smile became a grimace as a black wave of pain washed through him. Lavret caught hold of him, supporting him.

"You're hot. You've got another touch of fever. Let me get the physician to check you over."

"No. All I need is some fresh air."

Gavril had made a supreme effort to master his needs but he could not control himself any longer. It had been almost more than he could bear to be in the same room as Trifine. The scent of her body, her sweet flesh, her young, fresh, life-giving blood, had almost undone him.

On the edge of the ridge he saw the lights of the city glimmering faintly below, as if the myriad stars in the sky above were mirrored in a black lake. If only he could lose himself down there in the darkness . . .

He stumbled down the steep, winding lane between high-walled houses. He was so weak that he soon tripped and fell headlong into the central gutter. And there, a young seamstress found him and took pity on him.

Gavril came back to himself only after he had slaked his thirst. She lay motionless on her attic pallet, her mousy hair spread loose about her pale shoulders. He backed away, wiping one hand over his mouth. The life-giving blood he had craved revolted him now.

"You promised me, Khezef. No more blood. No more killing."

"*She's still breathing.*"

Tears coursed down Gavril's cheeks as he flew away over the rooftops into the night. "It must stop!"

Andrei streaked through the night sky in pursuit of the scarlet Drakhaon.

Had he misunderstood their pact? He thought they had agreed to work together to destroy Sergius's Staff and seize the prized rubies. And then Sahariel had snatched the Tears of Artamon right from under his nose and made off with them.

For a while, Andrei found it hard to keep him in sight, a ribbon of pale fire against the daylight, snaking in and out of the clouds, as though trying to lose his pursuer. But as night fell and they cleared the shores of Francia, the scarlet brilliance of Sahariel's wings flamed out like a beacon.

"Sahariel!" Adramelech hailed him. "*Have you forgotten our agreement?*"

The sound of laughter came back to him, borne on the wind. "*The look on Enguerrand's face! He really believed he was the Chosen One. The Blessed Saint Enguerrand!*"

"*The rubies, Sahariel.*"

"*And now he knows he's doubly damned. Damned by the Heavenly Warriors for his presumption. And damned again, for being host to Nilaihah.*" Sahariel had either not heard—or had not chosen to hear.

"*We agreed we would keep the rubies safe.*"

"We agreed that Khezef couldn't be trusted with them."

Andrei was gaining on Alvborg as he flew on toward Southern Tielen. Now he put on a sudden spurt until he was alongside the scarlet Drakhaon. "And can you be trusted?"

"I have as much right to the empire as you, Prince Andrei. I am Karl of Tielen's illegitimate son."

This was news to Andrei. "But you're a damned Tielen. You invaded Muscobar. You've no more right to rule New Rossiya than Eugene."

"And you, Andrei Orlov? What makes your claim more valid than mine?"

"Don't you trust me, Adramelech?" taunted Sahariel.

"Why should I trust you?"

Gavril had intended to stay alert in case the Commanderie Guerriers came searching for the escaped prisoners. But, exhausted by the day's events, he drifted into an uneasy sleep.

"That mortal woman has been visiting the children again. She is conspiring with them." The gold-hued tones of Nilaihah penetrated Gavril's dreams. *"She must be stopped."*

"Tell me where she is and I will destroy her," said Sahariel.

"Adramelech, you must do it. She has already tracked down your child in Khitari."

"And how will I know where to find her? Khitari is vast."

"Listen to my brother!" taunted Sahariel. *"Is that too difficult for you to accomplish? Are you still the weakling among us, Adramelech?"*

"Use your child. Let him guide you. But be on your guard—he is already under her influence. He may try to deceive you."

Gavril woke with a start. He had heard the Drakhaouls speaking of Kiukiu, there was no doubt about it. They saw her as an impediment to the fulfillment of their plans. Their enemy.

He had to warn her. He had to protect her. Before Adramelech tracked her down in the wilds of Khitari and seared her to ashes.

"I fear I've brought you nothing but trouble," Gavril said to Budoc Lavret. "And now I have to leave my men in your care."

"You stood up to the Commanderie," said Lavret. "Now we've seen that they are not invulnerable. We'll care for your men till you return. If there's danger, we've arranged to ship them out on a timber barge. Go—rest assured we'll take good care of them. Besides, I think my Trifi has taken rather a fancy to young Dunai; she's not going to let the Guerriers take him away!"

The carriage carrying the Duchesse de Provença and her two daughters to the Palais de Plaisance turned out of the Hôtel de Provença and trundled through the dark streets of the city.

"How can you even think of marrying Enguerrand, Esclairmonde?" burst out Aude. "You'll have to spend all your days in church or visiting the sick."

"There's nothing wrong with charitable work," said their mother, Duchesse Anne. "And Aude," she added severely, "you are not to say a word about marriage. Not one! Nothing has been arranged—yet."

Esclairmonde said nothing but stared out of the carriage window. She was thinking how dull the weather was in northern Francia. They had made the long journey from the sun and blue skies of their home in Provença and each day had become cloudier than the last as they approached Lutèce. She was not sure if she would want to live day after day beneath overcast skies.

"Queen Esclairmonde," teased Aude.

"That's enough, Aude!" said her mother sharply.

Esclairmonde wished Aude would not keep reminding her about Enguerrand. The last time they had met, he had proved painfully shy and awkward. She had looked at his unflatteringly short, ecclesiastical haircut and his glasses, and felt she might as well have been trying to make conversation with a young village curé. Even his clothes had been as somber and plain as a priest's. He had stumblingly asked her about her journey and then not seemed to hear her answer at all.

"And he's so boring." Aude had begun again. "He doesn't dance. He doesn't hunt."

"But it seems he's a clever statesman," put in her mother. "To make the Emperor Eugene cede Smarna must have taken considerable skill. Why, your father was only saying . . ."

Esclairmonde was no longer listening. Politics held little interest for her. She was wishing with all her heart that she might meet an eligible and handsome young lord at the palace so that she did not have to marry Enguerrand.

"Miaow . . ."

"What's that?" said the duchesse.

"I didn't hear anything," said Aude innocently. Esclairmonde stared at her sister with narrowed eyes. That sweet expression meant that Aude was up to something.

"Miaaow, miaaow . . ." The plaintive mewing was coming from Aude's reticule.

"Aude, is that your new kitten?" said the duchesse sternly.

"Maybe it is," said Aude.

"Open that reticule straightaway! It's cruel to keep an animal locked up in a case."

Aude gave a sigh and did as her mother told her; two blue eyes peeped out and the tiny tortoiseshell crept onto her lap. "Poor little Minette; I thought she'd be lonely on her own."

"You can't bring a kitten to the queen's reception!" cried the duchesse. "Now the wretched creature will have to stay in the coach."

"How well your majesty is looking," said the Duchesse Anne, dropping into a low curtsy. "May I present my daughters: Esclairmonde and Aude."

Enguerrand took Esclairmonde's slender hand in his and touched it with his lips. Then he dared to look at her. She was even more desirable than he had remembered: tall, with bronze hair, glinting with flecks of gold, flawless creamy skin, clear hazel eyes, and a sweet, placid smile on lips that were more coral than rose-pink.

"Welcome to P—Plaisance," he stammered and, to cover his confusion, turned to Aude. Aude was less conventionally pretty than her older sister; there was a slight dusting of freckles on her tip-tilted nose and the ginger shade of her curly hair reminded Enguerrand of the color of brandysnaps. Of course, at just thirteen years of age, Aude was not strictly eligible as a prospective fiancée. But when he touched her fingers with his own, he felt a sudden shock shoot through him.

"*My child*," breathed Nilaihah.

Aude was staring into his eyes, as though hypnotized. "You," she said softly. "It's *you*."

"Aude?" Esclairmonde said sharply. She tapped her sister on the shoulder but still Aude gazed fixedly into Enguerrand's eyes. "Majesty, I'm very sorry, she hasn't been well."

Enguerrand was so surprised that he had not let go of Aude's hand. Now he gently withdrew his hand from hers.

"Please don't apologize. Perhaps Demoiselle Aude would like a cool drink?" He gestured to the servants who stood by a long marble-topped table, ready to ladle out fruit punch or pour sparkling wine for the guests.

The daemon had spoken to Aude; he had heard it quite distinctly. And she had replied, not to him, but to Nilaihah. What was going on? Was he trapped in some crazed feverish dream? He watched Esclairmonde and the duchesse lead the young girl to a chair near the doors to the terrace.

Esclairmonde was fanning her sister, her sweet face so full of concern that Enguerrand's shy heart was touched by the sight.

"She has been suffering from these 'little turns' since the winter," said the duchesse distractedly, "and the physicians can find no reason for them."

"*Your child, Nilaihah? How can Aude be your child?*"

"*We are connected. But you need not trouble yourself with knowing why or how, my king, when we have other matters of greater urgency.*"

"We?" Enguerrand said aloud and then realized that his guests were staring at him. "Um—we are very glad to welcome you all to Plaisance," he continued loudly. He had made himself appear a fool, and in front of the very person he most wanted to impress. In a panic, he backed away, turning and blundering through the courtiers.

All he wanted now was to find Ruaud de Lanvaux. The Grand Maistre had promised he would put all the considerable resources of the Commanderie into researching how to exorcise the daemon. But there was no sign of him yet.

"*Khezef is close by. I can sense him. He is weak and his host is weaker still. Khezef has betrayed us. What better time to seek him out and punish him for his treachery?*"

Enguerrand clutched his hands to his ears, trying to blot out the sound of the daemon's voice.

"Are you feeling all right, majesty?" A firm hand steadied him as he reeled, disoriented. He looked up and saw Ruaud de Lanvaux.

"Ruaud—thank God you're here," he cried, clinging on to his mentor's arm as if he would never let go. "It keeps talking to me, urging me to do things."

"Let's go and discuss this somewhere more private," said Ruaud calmly. He steered Enguerrand away from the party, making for the king's apartments.

"You will have to return to your guests soon," Ruaud said, opening the door to the king's library and closing it quietly behind them. "Your mother will send for you if you don't make another appearance."

"I don't want anyone to see me like this." Enguerrand sank down into a chair and put his head in his hands.

"If it's any consolation, I heard several guests comment on the fact that you look remarkably well. 'In radiantly good health,' said Madame de Romorantin."

"No," Enguerrand said, more of a groan than a denial.

"I've already called a meeting of the Commanderie High Council. Of course, we find ourselves in a difficult situation, majesty, as one of the enemy is now in our midst. Listening to every word we say, spying on our every action. As if things weren't complicated enough already, with the Smarnan situation."

Enguerrand let out another groan. Ruaud's words wounded him deeply. But he deserved to be blamed. He had allowed himself to be seduced by Nilaihah's flattery; he was the one who had let the daemon in. He felt soiled. Unclean.

"I'm afraid the decision of the High Council is a harsh one. You will be excluded from our meetings until we have found a way to exorcise the daemon."

"It's no more than I deserve."

"And all is not lost, majesty. Our agent in Smarna has learned of a way to subdue the daemon within you."

Enguerrand raised his head. "Is that really so? When can I start? Whatever it is, I'll do it, no matter how difficult."

"There's only one slight obstacle—"

The door opened and Queen Aliénor stood on the threshold, looking sternly from one to the other. Ruaud bowed.

"Whatever are you doing closeted in here, the two of you?" demanded the Queen Mother. "Your guests are waiting, Enguerrand."

She fixed the Grand Maistre with a look of ice. "My son has been spending far too much time in your company, de Lanvaux. He's a little old for a tutor, don't you think?"

The fountain in the atrium excited much comment among the guests; a voluptuous marble nymph proffered a cornucopia out of which poured a torrent of red wine from which they could fill and refill their glasses. Enguerrand averted his eyes; he was ashamed that his mother had permitted such a tasteless object to be displayed. He walked on, forcing a smile and nodding to his mother's guests.

The birdlike notes of a flute floated in from the torchlit gardens, accompanied by a ripple of harp strings. He caught sight of Aude on the terrace, sampling the different flavors of ices, pensively sucking her spoon, as she listened to the musicians.

"Which flavor do you recommend, Demoiselle?" he asked, finding himself drawn to talk to her again.

She slowly withdrew the spoon from her mouth, with a last, lingering lick. "This raspberry water ice is very good," she said, "but the peach is delicious. Though I think my favorite is still vanilla."

"Some more vanilla for Demoiselle Aude." Enguerrand passed her another glass dish.

"Won't you try some?" she said, offering him the first spoonful.

"Thank you." There was something so natural and unaffected about the way she spoke that delighted him. He felt at ease with her, as if they had known each other a very long time.

"*Sahariel and Adramelech are far ahead of us,*" Khezef said as they skimmed across Lutèce. Far below, Gavril could see flambeaux illuminating the wide avenues leading to the royal Palace of Plaisance.

"So where is Nilaihah?"

"*I can sense his presence. He is still here.*"

"That evens the odds a little," said Gavril, smiling grimly at the thought. "Only two to one."

"*But Sahariel has the rubies.*"

"Is he heading for Ty Nagar? Is he planning to open the Serpent Gate already?" Suddenly everything was happening far too fast; within the last hours, all three of Khezef's kindred had revealed themselves. Now Gavril knew what formidable opponents he was facing. And he knew he was far from ready to take them on.

Khezef fell silent, as though listening for his brothers in the dark depths of the starry night. *"He's making for Tielen,"* he said at length.

Oskar was delighted with himself. He had seized the Tears of Artamon from Enguerrand of Francia. He felt as heady as if sparkling wine were fizzing in his veins. But weariness began to set in. He glanced over his shoulder and saw that Andrei Orlov was still doggedly pursuing him, even though he looked as though he was slowing too.

Mustn't let my guard down. Or he'll take advantage and steal the Tears from me. But every wingbeat was taking its toll and he was laboring to stay aloft.

A frisson of anger shivered through his body. *"Khezef is pursuing us,"* hissed Sahariel.

"Then let's get away from him," snapped back Oskar.

"He's gaining on us."

"We're more than a match for Gavril Nagarian. Let him come! We'll be ready for him."

The Drakhaouls were making for the southernmost tip of Tielen. As Gavril approached, he spotted the steep cliffs of Arnskammar, rising sheer and impregnable from the churning Iron Sea. The sight brought back memories he had tried to obliterate from his mind and he faltered.

"There's Adramelech!" cried Khezef suddenly. *"Alone."*

"Are you certain?" Gavril could see that the amethyst-scaled Drakhaon was dropping slowly, exhaustedly down toward the cliff tops.

"He's used up too much of his strength. He needs to feed."

"Then let's detain him here until he's too weak to be a threat to Kiukiu." Gavril pressed on, desperate to make use of this advantage. The new hosts had obviously not yet understood the limits of their powers. And Adramelech looked ready to collapse.

Gavril circled lower until he was hovering right above Adramelech.

Scarlet fire suddenly flashed in his face. Dazzled, he flung up his arms, floundering, off guard. Sahariel darted out from his hiding place and flicked another dart of fire into his eyes.

"Ambush!" Gavril gasped, firing blindly back.

A twilight-winged figure shot up from the cliffs and slammed him back against the cliff face. As he struggled to break free, Gavril realized that Adramelech had as much strength left as he had, if not more.

"*Hold him steady!*"

Flame sizzled again and he found that the Drakhaouls had shackled him with chains of fire to the cliff. He was hanging helpless, high above the pounding sea and jagged-toothed rocks far below.

"*We waited for you.*" Sahariel's fiery eyes smoldered. "*Years beyond number, we waited for you, Khezef, but you never came back to free us.*"

"*It suited you very well to leave us imprisoned, didn't it?*" said Adramelech. "*You've enjoyed supreme power in this little world. You could have forced your mortal host to collect the scattered shards of ruby. Yet you chose not to.*"

"*I was imprisoned too.*" The fiery shackles seared into Gavril's wrists and ankles until he could bear it no longer and cried his pain aloud. "*Imprisoned in a mortal's body. I could do nothing without his flesh and bone to fulfill my wishes.*"

"*Nothing?*" echoed Sahariel scornfully. "*You should have compelled your host to do your will. As you must do now.*"

"*This mortal is different from the others.*"

"*Don't be so naïve, Khezef,*" said Adramelech wearily. "*They're all the same as their ancestors: greedy, selfish, treacherous. They're hungry for power, just like the first sons of Artamon. They understand nothing of our true nature.*"

"*You're wrong,*" insisted Khezef. "*This one understands how it was . . . before. And he believes there's a way to send us back beyond the Realm of Shadows.*"

"*We can never go back.*" The volatile Sahariel pronounced these words with such despair that Gavril glimpsed the noble spirit he must once have been before he was cast down into the Realm of Shadows.

"*The Heavenly Warriors would destroy us first,*" added Adramelech.

"*You're a fool, Khezef, to listen to such nonsense. What can a mere mortal tell us of these matters?*"

"*Being fused with a mortal for centuries has changed you. You have become weak.*"

"*Have you forgotten who you are?*" Eyes of fire stared into Gavril's. "*An Angel of Destruction can have no feelings.*" Sahariel brandished the Eye of Nagar in his face. "*We have more pressing matters to deal with. Come, Adramelech.*"

CHAPTER 36

Eugene opened his eyes and saw Gustave standing at his bedside.

"What time is it, Gustave?"

"Your highness recognizes me," stammered Gustave, his voice breaking.

"What's wrong, Gustave? Why are you—?"

"It's nothing, highness." Gustave produced a snow-white linen handkerchief and hastily blew his nose. "Please pardon me. It's just that I'm—that you're . . ." Eugene could not remember Gustave being so tongue-tied before. "I am delighted to see your highness in better health." Gustave recovered sufficiently to produce a phrase appropriate for the occasion.

"I'm damnably hungry." Eugene tried to raise his head from the pillows and felt the room spin about him. "I must have missed a meal or two; I'm empty as a drum."

"I'll order whatever your highness would like."

Eugene considered this. His mouth felt very dry. "Mineral water. And beef bouillon." For some reason he did not want his usual breakfast fare. But then he had the curious sensation that he had slept late and the day was already half-gone. "What time did you say it was, Gustave?"

"Three in the afternoon."

"And you let me sleep late! Why didn't you wake me?"

Gustave gave him a strange look. "But, highness, don't you remember? You've been very ill."

"Ill?" Eugene could remember nothing. "How long have I been ill?"

Gustave hesitated. "Well over a fortnight. The physicians think it was an infection in the blood, from an insect sting, or a cut or graze."

"But what's been happening?" Eugene pushed himself up on one elbow and then sank back again. "Why am I so weak?"

"Because you've been at death's door!" Eugene recognized Maltheus's blustering tone as the Chancellor entered the bedchamber. "And, by God, you scared us all near to death too. We thought we'd lost you a couple of times."

Eugene's head was spinning, though whether from lack of food or the aftereffects of the illness, he could not be sure. He didn't like to think that he had lost over two weeks of his life. All he could remember was a confusion of dark dreams.

"And the Francians?"

"The Francians have gone remarkably quiet, highness. Perhaps all they ever wanted was Smarna. Though it seems," said Maltheus with a throaty chuckle, "that the Smarnans like them even less than they liked us!"

Gustave reappeared with a silver tray and a bowl from which drifted a deliciously savory, beefy smell.

"Your bouillon, highness."

To Eugene's shame, he found he was too weak to sit up without help. And after Maltheus and Gustave had propped him up with many pillows, and he tried to lift the soup spoon, it dropped from his fingers with a clatter onto the tray.

"If your highness will permit?" Gustave tucked a linen napkin around Eugene's neck and began to spoon the bouillon into him.

"This won't do," muttered Eugene, humiliated that he should need to be fed like a baby. But then he forgot his embarrassment as he swallowed the bouillon; he had never imagined that a simple broth could taste so delicious.

After he had finished, he felt a little less dizzy, and urgent questions began to demand answers.

"How is the Empress?" he asked.

"She is well," Gustave answered, ringing for a servant to take away the tray. "When I left Erinaskoe last week, she was in good health—although very concerned about your condition, highness. She would have returned to Tielen with me, except her physician advised her against travel so near her time."

So Astasia had been concerned about him. He didn't know why, but this news brought tears to his eyes. He nodded. "Good, good . . . and Karila?"

Maltheus cleared his throat. "The princess and her entourage are safely installed in Swanholm, highness."

Eugene's memory was still hazy; something about what Maltheus had said did not sound right. "But my daughter was at Rosenholm."

"But you remember, highness, your aunt was taken ill. And then the princess's health deteriorated, so rather than risk the long journey to Erinaskoe—" A knock interrupted Maltheus. "Excuse me." He rose from Eugene's bedside and went to the door. Eugene heard a murmur of voices, too low and indistinct to make out what was being said.

"Would you like me to send Jakob to wash and shave you?" Gustave asked.

Eugene ran one hand over his cheek and felt the roughness of a stubbly beard. "I must look like a vagrant," he said ruefully. "Or a shipwrecked sailor."

"Great God!" Maltheus let out a sudden oath. "Forgive me, highness," he called back, "but an urgent matter needs my attention." And the Chancellor was gone, the door slamming shut after him.

"A letter has come for you from the Empress, highness."

"From the Empress?" Eugene, propped up on pillows, had still hardly enough strength to lift the letter from the tray that Gustave had brought. He noticed the faintest perfume of orange blossom as he broke the seal and unfolded the paper. He instantly recognized Astasia's handwriting and found himself smiling at her endearing attempt to pen a formal letter:

My dear Eugene,
I am writing in the hope that, by the time you receive this, you will be making a good recovery. I thought you should know that the doctors are pleased with the baby's progress, although I must confess I have found the late-summer heat fatiguing. But the midwife assures me there are only seven weeks or so to go before the birth. So now that cooler autumn air is promised, I hope I shall feel more refreshed.

If you are judged strong enough to travel, then Mama and Papa would be honored if you would care to convalesce at Erinaskoe.
Your devoted wife,
Astasia.

Eugene's hand had begun to tremble with the effort of holding the letter. There was no doubt about it; there was a distinct note of reconciliation in the way the letter was written. There was even a little hint of guilt. And then there was the invitation to Erinaskoe.

Did he dare to hope? He lay back and closed his eyes. For the first time in many weeks, he silently asked, *"Belberith, can you hear me?"*

There was no reply.

He knew the Drakhaoul could not be destroyed. And it had not been exorcised. But had Kazimir's elixir weakened Belberith to the point where he was too feeble to exert any influence over him? And how long would the effect of the elixir last?

And—most perplexing of all—where was Kazimir?

He reached for the little silver bell on his bedside table and rang it. This effort exhausted him and he collapsed back onto the pillows.

I must build up my strength. I must be in Erinaskoe when the baby is born.

Gustave returned.

"The letter brought good news, I trust, highness?"

"Gustave, where's Professor Kazimir?"

"Ah." Gustave looked a little discomfited. "It was none of my doing, highness. But Baron Sylvius feared that you might have been poisoned. So he had the professor locked up."

"Locked up! But what about the munitions? Kazimir was reconstructing the Magus's formulae for us. Do you mean to tell me that the whole time I've been ill, no work has been done?"

"The baron thought it a suitable precaution."

"I want Kazimir out of prison and back at work in his laboratory as soon as possible."

"There isn't the slightest possibility, is there, highness, that the professor might have been in the enemy's pay? You may recall that you used him in just such a way against Lord Nagarian last year."

"So I did." This had not occurred to Eugene until now. Did Kazimir bear him a grudge? "Well, I'll just to have take that risk. We need the munitions. Who knows when Enguerrand will attack us again."

"Now that you mention Enguerrand," said Gustave, "there have been some conflicting and—frankly—perplexing reports from our agent in Lutèce. It seems that there was a 'disturbance' at the Commanderie Forteresse. The official Commanderie version of events states that, 'following a direct lightning strike on the Forteresse in the midst of a terrible storm, many prisoners escaped and are still on the run.' "

"Ah," said Eugene, lying back with a smile, "where have we heard that tale before? It sounds as if Lord Nagarian has not been idle after all."

"I will ensure that Professor Kazimir is released immediately," said Gustave.

When Gustave had gone, Eugene reached out and picked up the little hand mirror that Jakob had left after shaving him. He examined his face in minute detail, peering at his eyes, pulling down the lids, searching for the slightest glint of green. There was none. Neither was there any trace in his hair—and his nails, when he examined them, were normal again. He replaced the mirror. Kazimir's elixir had done its work; Belberith had been subdued.

Eugene was dozing in a chair by the fire when he caught fragments of a muttered conversation taking place.

"Is he strong enough yet? Such news could provoke a relapse. And we can't risk that."

"We have to tell him." That sounded like Maltheus, bullishly insisting on his point of view until everyone else capitulated.

"But he'll want to take action. And he's still so weak. It could kill him."

"He must be told."

"Can't it wait till the morning?"

"I take full responsibility," came back Maltheus's reply.

The door opened. Eugene opened one eye. "What can't wait until morning?"

"The Francians have sneaked an invasion force into Southern Tielen."

"Ah!" Eugene sat up, fully awake by now. "Taking advantage, no doubt, of our reduced naval presence. So what's the current situation?"

"They've taken Holborg."

"Ah," said Eugene again, more pensively. He had invested a considerable sum in reinforcing the old military citadel overlooking the harbor. "So even the citadel at Holborg couldn't hold out against them."

"The Southern Army is already on its way, with Tornberg in command. I'm confident that we can drive them back. We know the terrain."

Eugene was far from pleased to learn that the Francian army had set foot on Tielen soil. Yet there seemed something a little halfhearted about this so-called invasion. Was it merely a diversion, designed to distract them from some other Francian enterprise?

"I'm greatly relieved to see your imperial highness in better health," said Frieda Hildegarde.

"Come now, Doctor Hildegarde," said Eugene, "be frank. I look like a ghost of my former self. I feel much like a ghost too—I seem to have no strength in my legs."

"You mustn't expect too much of yourself!" she said severely. "After a serious fever, one should take each day slowly and not put too much pressure on the heart and other vital organs."

"And I thought you were a Doctor of Ancient History," he said, smiling at her with affection. Her brisk manner amused him; she reminded him of his old nurse, Birgitta, whose strictness hid a heart of gold. "Well, Doctor, what have you discovered?"

She glanced around the chamber, as though fearing they might be overheard. Then she leaned closer in and said in a low, confidential tone, "A lost document."

"Ah," said Eugene, also leaning closer.

"What was fascinating was that there were two layers of hidden text. The first appears to be a missing page from Argantel's *The Life of the Blessed Sergius*." She adjusted her spectacles and began to read aloud:

Then Sergius of Azhkendir arose and came to me, saying that the seraph Galizur, Guardian of the Second Heaven, had appeared to him as he slept, and had pointed to certain words in the Book of Eliazar so that they glowed, as if written in fire.

"Prince Nagar must never be set free. For if this prison is breached, the darkness will cover your world in perpetual night and he and his kindred will lay waste to the earth."

And then the seraph spoke to Sergius, saying, "To that end, the Warriors of Heaven have put a seal on the Door to the Realm of

Shadows, that can only be breached by a crime so horrible that none would dare to undertake it. For only by the sacrifice of the Emperor's children in that far-distant place can that Door ever be opened again and the dread prince Nagar released. And no mortal would dare stoop to such a base and inhuman act."

"The sacrifice of the Emperor Artamon's children?" Eugene repeated aloud, as a strange and unsettling feeling came over him.

"Highness?" Doctor Hildegarde was looking at him with a worried expression. "If you are fatigued, we could continue tomorrow."

"No, no, I was just considering the implications of your discovery. And"—he smiled at her again, hiding his concern—"it's a splendid find."

"Saint Sergius's monastery library is full of such hidden treasures," said Doctor Hildegarde, beaming back.

"You said there was more."

Doctor Hildegarde drew out a second paper. This one was folded and as she passed it to him, he saw that her expression had become somber. "This one was protected by a complex cypher. It took me many weeks to break it. Even now I'm not entirely certain that I've cracked it correctly."

"A cypher?" Eugene unfolded the paper.

"Don't pronounce the names aloud, highness, I beg you."

To the Archimandrite Sergius, greetings.
    . . . fools to have meddled . . . the daemons must be . . . are as yet incomplete . . . for once Za'afiel is summoned, he will slay the Emperor's children and open the Gate to free the dread prince Nagazdiel. Then the Seven will fulfill their destiny. They will lay waste to the world and all within it will be reduced to dust and shadows.

"What does this mean?" Eugene slowly raised his eyes from the paper. "And is it genuine?"

"You're right to doubt its authenticity; there have been many forgeries. The monks in Francia and Azhkendir became quite adept at producing 'relics' of their saint to sell to pilgrims." Doctor Hildegarde had been nodding so vigorously that a lock of hair came loose from her chignon. "But this text was concealed. And the cypher was extremely ingenious. It wasn't until I worked out who had sent it that I was able to break the code."

"So who wrote the letter?" Eugene was intrigued, in spite of the new concerns her discovery had raised.

"A venerable scholar and angelographer of that time, Rebh Zohar. That cypher was peculiar to him; I know only of one other instance of its use. That set me on the right road!"

"And who is this dread prince Nagazdiel?"

"You know of him by another name: Nagar. That is his ancient Djihari title."

The letter could only refer to the Serpent Gate. "But surely these apocalyptic texts were made up by the monks? All this talk of destruction and the end of the world was to scare their errant congregations into better behavior!"

"I have met Lord Nagarian. Our modern interpretation of the legends is wrong, isn't it?" Doctor Hildegarde was looking at him with her keen hazel eyes. He knew then what it must be like to be one of her students, constantly challenged by this formidable intellect. "For years we have taught that the 'daemons' cast out by Sergius were nothing but a metaphor, a symbol representing the intense feelings of hatred and rivalry Artamon's sons felt toward each other. But I know now that the legends were true."

So she knew. And there was no point in keeping up the pretense anymore. "Where is Lord Nagarian now? Is he still in Azhkendir?"

Doctor Hildegarde shrugged.

So Gavril Nagarian had disappeared—and without fulfilling his part of their bargain, for why had Kaspar Linnaius still not returned from Azhkendir?

And this ancient text: was it just another prophecy of doomsday . . . or did it mean that his children, the children of royal blood, were in danger?

I have been ill for far too long.

Astasia gazed out at the grey skies and shivered as another rainstorm burst over Erinaskoe. Layer upon layer of louring clouds passed overhead. Trees tossed and writhed as the fierce autumn wind tore through the valley and sent showers of golden birch and alder leaves tumbling down.

Weather this fierce inland meant storms out in the Straits. Perhaps Eugene's ship had stayed in port in Haeven, rather than risking crossing in such unsettled conditions.

She sighed. Another day gone, another day apart.

Suppose the storms continue and he has to stay in Tielen?

She was growing weary of the enforced inactivity; weary of feeling so fat and ungainly. A steady stream of Mirom gentry had been calling on the Orlovs; Mama had been in her element, organizing card games, musical soirées with charades, and little trips to collect mushrooms. Even Papa had ventured out fishing with Uncle Anton. But so many guests had become tedious, especially as all Mama's friends wanted to regale Astasia with horrific tales of the agonies they had endured during childbirth.

"Men have no idea!" declared Katerina, Duchess of Berestovo. "Why, I was in labor for nearly forty-eight hours with my firstborn. The doctors thought I would die. *I* thought I would die!"

"That's nothing, my dear. After I had Andrei, they said I would never have any more children," declared Sofia, "because I was left in such a sorry state *down there*. The doctors insisted I must not exert myself one jot, I just had to lie still, day after day, in excruciating pain . . ."

Oh, Mama, please don't go on so, prayed Astasia, wishing she could go and walk in the park. But the rain was lashing down against the windows and the servants came to light the lamps early, dashing any hopes she might have had of escape.

The baby had been much less lively recently and that also concerned her. But the midwife, Old Masha, who had delivered her and many other Orlov babies before her, listened with a little glass pressed to her belly and assured her there was nothing to worry about.

"Baby's got less room to move about," she said, patting her shoulder comfortingly. "It won't be long now."

"Masha, does childbirth really hurt so badly?"

"I've got a few little remedies to help you through it. Trust Old Masha."

But when Masha had waddled off to the kitchens, where Astasia had asked cook to give her tea and cake, Astasia felt the anxieties return.

Women died in childbirth. One of her bridesmaids, Larissa, had died while Astasia was in Francia, after giving birth to a son. And she knew that Margret, Eugene's first wife, had not survived the long and difficult birth of Karila, even though Eugene had never once spoken of it directly.

I could die and never even see my own child.

A scatter of crows, blown on a gust of wind, flew cawing over the house. Crows meant ill luck. Astasia hastily made the sign against evil.

Why was she in such a morbid mood? Why did she keep having these gloomy premonitions? She opened the trunk in which she was collecting the little gifts of clothes, bonnets, and lacy shawls that Mama's friends had been bringing for the baby. Such tiny garments, she thought, holding them up. Soon there could be a real baby wearing these clothes. A wriggling, squalling, dribbling baby. *Her* baby.

I'm not ready. I don't know what to do. And then, disloyally, *I certainly don't want to turn into another Mama.*

"Are you there, Astasia?"

She turned, still holding a little white linen robe, to see Papa in the doorway. He gave her a fond look and nodded, seeing the baby clothes spread out on top of the chest.

"I thought you'd want to know that the *Dievona* has docked safely in Mirom. The Emperor will be here in an hour or so."

Astasia dropped the clothes. *He's here at last!* Her heart fluttered with excitement. She forgot about the rain, the crows, the dire childbed stories. "How do I look, Papa?"

He came over and helped her to her feet. "You look radiant, my dear," he said and kissed her forehead.

Rain showered down on Erinaskoe as Eugene climbed down from the carriage, the clouds blotting the last lurid sunlight from the afternoon sky.

"How are you feeling, highness?" murmured Gustave, holding up an umbrella over the Emperor's head.

"Fine, Gustave, fine," said Eugene, faking a confidence he did not feel. He put down the uncertain feeling in his stomach to the lingering effects of the stormy crossing they had endured. Usually an excellent sailor, he was ashamed to have been ill on board ship for the first time since he was a boy. Admiral Berger, concerned for his health, had offered to turn back when the storm broke but he had insisted on continuing with the voyage.

Inside the candlelit hallway, the Grand Duke and Duchess were waiting to welcome him. And after the obligatory greetings had been exchanged and Eugene had taken off his greatcoat, he was ushered into the drawing room.

"Will you take tea?" asked a soft voice.

Astasia was reclining on a sofa near the fireplace. A little fire of clean-scented pine branches and cones crackled in the grate. Her loosely flowing dress of hyacinth blue did not disguise the rounded swell of her belly. But pregnancy had brought a soft, becoming flush of color to her pale cheeks and lips.

"Thank you," he said automatically. He came closer, his hands clasped behind his back. "You look well," he said, watching her pour tea for him. "Very well."

"Lemon? And one lump of sugar?"

"You remembered." He took the cup and saucer from her. Their fingers touched. With shaking hands he set the delicate porcelain down. "Astasia," he said, unable to stop staring at her, "I've missed you so much." And then he was beside her on the sofa. His arms went round her and he was kissing her hair, her eyes, her lips. And she was returning his kisses, clinging to him as if she were drowning.

"I'm so glad you're here at last," she whispered between kisses.

"Nothing would have kept me away." He had forgotten till now that slight, subtle fragrance redolent of spring flowers that clung to her hair.

"You were so ill. So ill that I feared—"

He placed his finger gently on her lips. "Let's not speak of it. It's done. All that matters is you and the baby. Let's make this a new beginning for us both. We'll put the past months behind us and start again."

"Yes," she said, nestling her head against his shoulder. "A new beginning." And then she suddenly sat up. "Your tea! It'll be cold. I'll ring for some more."

"No, no, this is fine." He smiled at her. "Let's make the most of our time alone together."

The autumn storm still gusted around Erinaskoe, sending damp drafts shooting through the halls and corridors, setting doors banging or straining at the catches. Sudden spatters of rain rattled against the panes and came down the chimneys, making the fires in the grate fizz and spit like angry cats.

At dinner, Astasia sat beside her husband. She could not help steal-ing little glances at him, checking that there was no trace left of the daemon that possessed him. His face looked more pale and drawn than she remembered and there were blueish-grey shadows beneath his eyes. But nothing else: Professor Kazimir had done his work well.

"Look at our girl, Sofia," said the Grand Duke, after proposing a toast. "She's so happy she can't stop smiling."

"Oh, Papa!" said Astasia, blushing. But she had to admit he was right. Every time she looked at Eugene and their eyes met, she smiled. "*Let's make this a new beginning*," he had said, and at the moment it was as if all her worries had melted away.

"Have you chosen a name for the baby yet?" asked Sofia.

Astasia caught Eugene's eye. She tried to smother a little giggle. "No, Mama," she said patiently, anticipating what was to come.

"Oh, but you must choose a name! Once the labor pains start, you won't want to be worrying about names. Now, we thought Aleksei would be nice, after your father, if it's a boy, or—"

"*You* thought, Sofia," interrupted her father diplomatically. "I have no feelings on the subject at all."

"Well, really, Aleksei, I'm surprised at you! Showing so little inter-est in your first grandchild."

"I shall show plenty of interest when he—or she—is safely deliv-ered."

"Of course there's some excellent names on my side of the family," said Sofia, ignoring this last comment. "My dear father was called Vasili, and his father . . ."

Astasia shared another secret little glance with Eugene while Sofia enumerated the names of her grandparents and her many aunts, un-cles, and cousins.

All that matters to me is that the baby is healthy and has ten toes and ten fingers. There'll be time enough for name-choosing later.

Each day Eugene walked on the grounds of Erinaskoe, just a turn around the garden at first, accompanied by Astasia, then, as he be-gan to feel stronger, venturing out beyond the lake and into the woods. And, in this lull between autumn storms, the trees glowed with rich colors. The birch thickets were carpeted with rustling yel-low leaves, and yet more drifted down from the silvered branches. But the beech woods were still daubed with vibrant shades of gold and copper, as though a breath of autumn fire had caught them alight.

Astasia walked slowly, trying in vain not to waddle.

She had been observing Eugene and, to her relief, noted that every day his health was improving. He walked with something approaching his old vigor and his eyes were brighter. Even the grey pallor of his skin had improved. Sofia was heard to remark loudly that, "The air here is obviously so much more beneficial than the damp, inclement Tielen climate."

Although affairs of state still occupied him every morning, Eugene spent most afternoons with her. But there was one matter between them that was still troubling her, and she wanted to settle it once and for all before events overtook them. But for days she had been trying to find a way to raise the delicate and painful subject, while wondering in her heart if perhaps it might be better to leave it alone.

So now, here they were, taking a turn together around her mother's little rose garden. Both were well muffled up against the brisk autumn breeze that carried on it the smell of burning leaves from the kitchen gardens, where the gardeners had lit bonfires. A few bright red rosehips still clung to stems and briars, but most of the rosebushes had been pruned back for the winter. And the sound of vigorous hoeing came from behind the walls in the herb garden.

"Lovisa," burst out Astasia, unable to restrain herself any longer.

"Lovisa?" Eugene echoed, a puzzled little frown creasing his brows.

"Tell me now, Eugene, so we can put it behind us."

"But there's nothing to tell."

Was he still concealing something from her? She stopped and faced him. "I saw you together. Twice. Once in the rose gardens before the ball and once during the ball."

"Ah."

"Is she your mistress?" The question was out at last.

"My *mistress*?"

Was he angry with her? "You've known her for so long, much longer than me, and I suppose it's only natural for a man in your situation to—"

Eugene pressed her hands between his own. "Who put these strange ideas in your head, Astasia? Lovisa and I are cousins, true, but as to our being lovers—" He suddenly burst out laughing.

Astasia snatched her hands away. Why did he find this so amusing? He stopped laughing then, all traces of amusement draining from his face.

"My dearest girl, I had no idea you had been so misled. And the error is all on my part. I had asked Lovisa to watch over you, to keep you safe. There were hints, vague rumors around at the time, that you had been targeted by some foreign power. I wanted to tell you— I probably should have told you—but Baron Sylvius advised otherwise. He felt it better that you should not be unduly alarmed. It was only the vaguest of threats."

"Lovisa is one of Sylvius's agents?" Astasia was still not entirely satisfied with this explanation.

"Lovisa and I have known each other many years, that's true. But for years she's been passionately involved with Sylvius. It's a well kept secret at court, because he has an invalid wife and three young sons."

"Lovisa . . . and Sylvius?" She had not expected this. Of course, it was always possible that Eugene was inventing it as well.

"The truth is," he said, putting his hands on her shoulders and gazing into her eyes, "that neither of us was being wholly honest with the other, were we?"

Astasia felt a strange, sudden pain that made her gasp aloud.

"Is it something I ate at dinner?" She clutched her swollen belly, and realized it had become rigid. "Oh no," she whispered, taking little shallow breaths to ease the pain. "Oh no, oh *no*." Supporting herself with one hand on the little ormolu table, she waited until the waves of pain died down. Then she stumbled across the room and rang for Nadezhda.

"It can't be," she said aloud. "I'm not ready."

She could hear Nadezhda coming along the corridor, and never before had that pert, pattering footfall sounded so welcome.

"What can I do for you, altessa?" asked Nadezhda. "Dear me, you look a little off-color. Shall I brew you a cup of fennel tea?"

Astasia pulled a face. "I don't think it's heartburn this time, Nadezhda. I think it's—" She stopped as she felt a rush of warm water flood down between her thighs.

"Your waters have broken!" cried Nadezhda. Astasia was sure the whole household must have heard.

"Help me, Nadezhda." Astasia just stood there helplessly, holding up her dampened skirts, feeling like a small child who has unintentionally wet herself.

Now Nadezhda was frantically ringing the bell. Astasia still stood there, bemused, as Nadezhda sent one maid off to call for the midwife, another to fetch the Grand Duchess, a third to tell the Emperor . . .

"Couldn't you have waited just a little longer?" she whispered, one hand still on her belly.

CHAPTER 37

Cold, sleety rain poured down as Gavril struggled to free himself from his shackles. Hundreds of feet below, the Iron Sea smashed into the jagged rocks.

His imagination kept conjuring up chilling possibilities: Kiukiu, alone and defenseless on the vast grasslands, gazing fearfully up at the sky as the daemons swept down toward her on their shadow-wings; Kiukiu, calling in vain for him to come to rescue her; Kiukiu dying before he could reach her and tell her how much he loved her.

"Help me, Khezef!"

"*I can't sear away these chains without burning you.*"

"Kiukiu needs me." Gavril twisted and turned, trying to direct Khezef's bolts of fire toward the restraints. He felt as if his arms were being tugged farther from their sockets.

"*There's nothing for it,*" said the Drakhaoul, "*but to shatter the whole rock face. But it will use up much energy. Are you ready?*"

"Do it!" Gavril gritted his teeth as he felt Khezef summoning up a burst of power from deep within him. The air around him turned thunder-blue. The explosion made his ears throb. Rocks and fragments of stone rained down in a lethal hailstorm. A convulsive shuddering wracked his body until he thought he would break apart. And just when he feared he was losing consciousness, he felt himself lifting, rising into the air.

*   *   *

This was true Arnskammar weather, Gavril thought, remembering drear skies and perpetual downpours. Strong winds buffeted him, almost as if they were trying to blow him off course. He flew stubbornly on above the grey breakers.

"How can we find her, Khezef? Khitari's such a vast country. She could be anywhere. I have no idea where to start—"

"*I fear my kindred may have tracked her down already.*"

"How can we stop them? Is there any way? Any way at all?"

"*My brothers are unstoppable.*"

"But not their hosts. Kill the host, and drive out the Drakhaoul." Gavril could see no other alternative. "It might buy us a little time."

"*If my kindred don't kill you first.*"

"Just let them try!"

The Drakhaon burst through the billowing stormclouds and saw land far below. Tielen was awash with autumn rain.

The rain was fading to a fine drizzle and the sky darkening into night as he cleared the Tielen coast and pressed on toward Azhkendir.

Unegen the Fox sat cross-legged before his little fire and began to tap a slow, repetitive, hypnotic rhythm on his spirit-drum.

"Firefox, come to me. Come to me now."

He was eaten up with bitter envy. He had tried to discredit the Spirit Singers and failed. And now that Khan Vachir had seen the extent of their powers, his own skills had been shown to be so inadequate by comparison.

There had to be another way to revenge himself on the Azhkendis.

As the sparks from the burning pine branches flew up into the night sky, he felt his consciousness leave his body and rise with them toward the stars. Gazing down on the khan's encampment far below, he sought out the tent where the women slept.

"Firefox, show yourself!"

Two bright vulpine eyes glinted in the undergrowth.

"Go," breathed Unegen, "go and mark that tent. Mark it out."

There was a rustle and a little dark shape slid out of the bushes and darted silently down toward the camp, the tip of its bushy tail white as starlight.

From where Unegen was watching he saw the silvered tip of his fox-familiar's tail painting a phosphorescent trail around the Spirit Singer's tent.

"Good," he muttered. He closed his eyes, seeking out the powers of destruction he had sensed close by. Over the past days, they had streaked the night sky like malign meteors. "The one you are seeking is here. Follow the light of the foxfire and you will find her."

"You're in danger." The children's voices echoed through Kiukiu's sunset dreams. "Wake up. Wake up!"

They surrounded her, the older girls carrying the laughing baby and the four boys: Bayar and Koropanga, Giorgi and Kahukura. Even Tilua and Karila were there, their arms interlinked.

"What do you mean, danger?" Kiukiu looked down at their anxious faces. "This is one of your games, isn't it?"

"It's real," said Tilua. "We've heard them. The Drakhaouls. They want to destroy you."

"But how could they know?" Kiukiu began and then saw the fear in the children's eyes.

"Someone's called them. Someone's told them where you are. Someone who hates you. You've got to—"

Kiukiu woke with the warning still clamoring in her ears. She turned to her grandmother, who was snoring quietly beside her and shook her gently.

"I was *not* snoring!" mumbled Malusha, turning on her other side.

"We've got to get away from here," said Kiukiu in a low voice.

"Eh? Why? It's the middle of the night."

"The children warned me."

"And where are we to go? The khan will only send his men to bring us back again. We won't get far."

Kiukiu's skin prickled as though a storm were approaching. And now she became aware of a strange, feral smell pervading the tent. "Someone's trying to work some kind of mischief on us, Grandma. Let's just go a little way farther off."

Kiukiu put her head out of the tent flap. It was dark outside and only the sentries' watch fires burned around the boundaries of the encampment. It was also bitterly cold and the sky was powdered with stars. The unpleasant feral smell was so much more pungent outside that it made Kiukiu's eyes water.

"Phew. What *is* that stink? Not the yaks, surely."

"Fox," said Malusha, sniffing the air.

"Fox?" The sense of imminent danger was growing stronger. "Unegen, more like." Kiukiu wrapped her blanket round her and set out on hands and knees over the damp grass. "Come on, Grandma."

"I'm not going without the gusly."

She heard Malusha grumbling to herself as they crawled away from the tent. Kiukiu began to doubt her instincts. Was Unegen lurking close by? Perhaps he had sent his fox-familiars to drive them *out* of the tent, and she had stupidly led Malusha into his trap.

Kiukiu reached a little clump of cranberry bushes and stopped in their shelter to look back at the tent. She gave a soft gasp. "Look, Grandma." Her breath smoked on the crisp, dark air.

From the faint glimmer in the grass around their tent, they could see it had been marked out from the others.

"Foxfire," muttered Malusha. "That tricky, mean-spirited shaman. What's he up to now?"

"Didn't you put a ward on our tent?"

"Nothing fancy. Didn't see the need here, surrounded by the khan's warriors. So Unegen still bears us a grudge, does he? I'll give him something to bear a grudge about."

Kiukiu was thinking hard all the time Malusha was complaining. Why would Unegen mark out their tent? If he wanted to put some kind of malice on them, he could have done it without leaving any trace behind. No, these foxfire trails shouted out to some darker, more powerful spirit he had summoned: *Here they are!*

Malusha was sniffing the air again. "Faugh. There's a terrible stink of fox out here too."

Kiukiu turned around. "Look!" Bright, malicious eyes were staring at them from beyond the bushes; fox eyes, charged with craft and cunning. And not one fox, but many, too many to count. And at the tip of each fox tail, there burned a pale little flame.

"Where's that confounded Magus when he's needed?" said Malusha.

"They're only foxes," said Kiukiu. She ventured out a step and leaped back hastily as the nearest fox snapped at her ankles with white needle teeth.

"We're trapped," said Malusha. "These are firefoxes. That nasty little man must have summoned them to keep us right where he wants us."

Kiukiu suddenly became aware that a streak of cloud had briefly extinguished the bright, cold glitter of the stars overhead. Too swift for a cloud, even one driven by a winter wind, the shadow was moving purposefully toward them.

"Drakhaoul," said Malusha under her breath.

The shadow snaked around in the sky, high above, and Kiukiu instinctively ducked, catching the faintest purple shimmer. It was searching for her, she sensed it. And an all-too-familiar feeling of dread awoke within her, the same dread she had first felt on that white shore between the worlds when the dark Drakhaoul prince had fixed her with his terrible third eye.

And yet the children had warned her. There must be a way she could use that warning.

"Bayar," she said. "Prince Bayar will protect us. Come on, Grandma." She grabbed Malusha's arm and pulled her to her feet.

"And how do you propose we get to Prince Bayar, child?"

Kiukiu ventured out a few steps toward the encampment; Malusha followed, muttering some barely audible cantrip. The firefoxes began to growl and snap at their heels, prowling ever closer. All of a sudden, one pounced, catching hold of Kiukiu's blanket, seizing it in its sharp teeth and tugging hard.

"Let go!" she shouted, tugging back.

Am I dreaming? Andrei came back to consciousness to find himself winging high above a vast lake whose black waters reflected the stars above him. It was an oddly disorientating experience, especially as he had no idea why Adramelech had brought him here—or even where "here" was, except that the night air sparkled with frost.

"Why are we here, Adramelech?"

"*Leave this to me, my prince.*"

"Leave what?"

"*Quiet!*" The daemon's command was so harsh that Andrei was shocked into silence. "*We have been summoned. Listen.*"

Andrei could hear nothing but the rush of the wind.

"*There,*" said Adramelech triumphantly, "*on the far shore. He's led us straight to her.*"

Far below Andrei could see a little silvered circle gleaming dully on the lakeshore, like a pale eye glinting in the darkness. Adramelech increased his speed and Andrei felt the daemon's cruel exultation flare through him as it gathered itself, darting down like a lightning bolt toward the target.

One thought dominated all others. One desire drove him, though he had no idea why.

"*Destroy.*"

"Wait, Adramelech—"

He felt the fire kindle within him.

"No, wait!"

But he was hurtling toward his goal. Adramelech loosed a single breath of fire and Andrei felt his throat and mouth aflame. Adramelech pulled steeply upward, and circled to see the effects of his attack.

"A tent? With people inside?"

The burning tent exploded in a ball of flame.

"*No mortal could have survived such a blast.*" The daemon sounded grimly satisfied with its work.

Andrei realized that he was no longer in control of his guardian spirit. Adramelech had used his body to achieve this wanton act of destruction.

Far below he heard cries of shock and fear. Panicked horses screamed and bolted. Children were sobbing. And a thin column of smoke, violet-tinged, began to rise from the smoldering remains.

"This isn't what you promised me, Adramelech! This has nothing to do with my fight with Eugene." He felt sickened—and betrayed. "These are just ordinary people."

"*Don't be deceived, my prince. These ordinary people have been harboring a dangerous shaman woman—and she has been scheming against us. Even now,*" said Adramelech, wheeling around to soar over the encampment a second time, "*I can't be sure that I have destroyed her.*"

"But you've"—Andrei faltered, horrified at the thought—"*I've* destroyed innocent lives."

Bowmen were firing on them; their arrows bounced harmlessly off the Drakhaon's glittering scales as Adramelech zigzagged effortlessly through the air above their heads, bearing down on his prey.

"*Why, there she is!*" breathed Adramelech. "*And this time she won't escape me.*"

*   *   *

A burst of violet flame lit the night, bright as winter lightning. The firefoxes scattered. Kiukiu saw the conflagration that had been their tent and felt the shadow of the Drakhaon pass overhead like a rolling stormcloud.

"Now!" she cried, dragging Malusha along with her. The camp was suddenly full of terrified people, all running about in panic, colliding with each other in the smoky darkness. Some were coughing and it was becoming difficult to see her way to Prince Bayar's tent. She could hear the warriors shouting orders to each other in the fog and several bowmen hurried past.

"Precious use arrows'll be against that monster," puffed Malusha. "You're wasting your time!"

"Halt." Soldiers from the khan's bodyguard blocked their way.

"I have to get to Prince Bayar." Even as she spoke to them, Kiukiu was aware that the winged shadow, hovering high overhead, was seeking her out, scanning the camp for a sight of her.

"I have my orders," said their captain, arms folded across his armored chest. "In case of attack, no one is allowed near the prince or his mother."

"You don't understand!" cried Kiukiu. "The prince is the only one who can stop this creature attacking us again."

The archers had begun to fire at the Drakhaon again as it wheeled around for a second time. Its eyes glinted, two twilit stars of flame, coming nearer and nearer.

Khan Vachir appeared in the doorway of Lady Orqina's tent, flanked by two of his generals. "Bayar can stop this monster? Do you expect me to risk my only son's life?"

"Bayar, *no!*" From within the tent came a woman's heartrending cry. And overhead came the onrush of wind from the Drakhaon's beating wings as it bore down on them. The soldiers braced themselves, looking up.

"Your son's life is already at risk," said Malusha. Kiukiu darted between the bodyguard as they were distracted, and dived into the tent.

Bayar stood rigid in the center of the tent, his eyes rolled up in their sockets so that only the whites showed.

Kiukiu grabbed hold of him by the shoulders and shook him. "Koropanga!" she cried. "Koro, Bayar, tell your Drakhaoul to stop his attack!"

*   *   *

"*Now I've found you.*" Claws extended, Adramelech caught the sewn skins of the tent and ripped them asunder, flinging them aside as if they were shreds of paper.

A young, dark-eyed boy stood revealed beneath, gazing upward directly into Andrei's eyes. Beside him stood a fair-haired young woman, her hands clasped protectively about the boy's shoulders, also gazing at him. But in her eyes he saw nothing but defiance and fury.

"Adramelech," said the boy in a small, clear voice. "Don't you know me? I'm your child."

Andrei felt the Drakhaoul shudder. Adramelech halted, hovering, before the child.

"*Koropanga,*" said Adramelech in tones that were almost tender.

"Don't hurt her," said the boy. "She's my friend. She wants to help us."

"*Stand aside, Koro.*" Adramelech's voice was harsh as though he was struggling with some inner conflict too deep for Andrei to comprehend.

"I won't let you harm her," said the boy stubbornly.

Andrei could feel a tremendous energy building up again within the core of the Drakhaoul's being, almost as if Adramelech were no longer able to stop himself, even though he wanted to.

"No, Adramelech," Andrei urged in desperation. "Don't do it."

But Adramelech was not listening to him. "*Give me the Spirit Singer, Koro.*"

"It doesn't have to be this way, Drakhaoul," cried the young woman. "I can send you home. Not to the place of dust and shadows, but your true home, far beyond the stars."

Adramelech threw back his head and let out a harrowing cry that echoed around the mountains. "*That can never be. We are spirits of destruction. They made us so. We are tied to this world by innocent blood.*"

"You'll have to kill me too," said the boy.

There followed a silence, filled only with the whir of Adramelech's fast-beating wings. To Andrei's surprise, he sensed Adramelech make a supreme effort to dampen down the power surging within him.

"*Koro's saved you this time,*" hissed Adramelech, "*but I'll be waiting for you, Spirit Singer. You can't stay with him forever. And wherever you go, I'll find you. I'll track you down."*

And Andrei knew himself suddenly back in control. He turned away from the child who held so much power over his daemon. He heard the zing of many bowstrings as the archers launched another volley, and tossed their arrows aside with a dismissive flick of his tail. Next moment, he was away, winging upward into the dark sky.

As the dragon lifted and turned away from the encampment, Kiukiu heard Prince Bayar give a little sigh. She caught him in her arms as he crumpled, and lowered him gently to the ground. She was shivering as she knelt in the ruins of the tent, supporting the boy who had unknowingly saved her life.

"I owe you," she whispered to him, stroking his forehead.

Lady Orqina's women gathered around their mistress and began fanning her and patting her face to revive her. Khan Vachir approached and, removing his plumed helmet, went down on his knee beside Kiukiu.

"Your son saved my life," she said. "He's an extraordinary boy, Lord Khan."

"He spoke to the dragon," said Khan Vachir hoarsely. "I never knew he had such courage." He gathered Bayar up in his arms. "But what drew the dragon here?"

"Ask your shaman Unegen," said Malusha. Her eyes glinted in the torchlight. "He summoned it. It seems he's been nursing a little grudge against us."

"Unegen!" repeated Khan Vachir. He beckoned one of his captains over. "Find the Fox and bring him to me." He walked away toward his tent.

"We can't stay here," said Malusha. "That daemon will be back."

"But where can we go?" Kiukiu, now that the crisis was over, suddenly felt weak and shaky. She sat down on the damp grass and rested her forehead on her knees, waiting for the faintness to pass. "It's been sent to destroy me. It'll seek me out, wherever I go. And it doesn't care how many people it has to kill to get to me."

Malusha squatted beside her and put an arm around her shoulders. "But it hasn't come back yet," she said. "I'll wager it's been on the wing a long while searching you out. I'll wager it needs to feed. That'll buy us a little time."

"Who could it be?" Kiukiu still felt cold and shaken. "And how many more are there out there, hunting me down?"

"You know who to ask," said Malusha. "The children."

A sunset sky, a strange, intense rose, besmirched with low-hanging, smoky clouds, had turned the white sands pink.

Kiukiu spied three girls cooing over the baby in the feathery shade of a palm tree. Karila was gently tweaking his toes, which made him laugh. "I wonder if my baby brother will be as adorable as this one," she said to Tilua.

Kiukiu tiptoed closer. There was something familiar about the baby, though whether it was his shock of dark gold hair or his bright eyes, she could not be sure.

"The baby. Who is the baby, Karila?"

"We don't know. He's too little to say his name properly yet. Isn't that right, Mahina?"

The girl who was playing with the baby looked up at Kiukiu.

"Surely you must know." Kiukiu knelt beside Mahina and tickled the baby who chuckled and beamed a gap-toothed smile at her.

"Well," she said, picking him up and bouncing him on her knee, "in dreams, I think I've heard his mother talking to him. And he has such a long, strange name for a baby, so I call him 'little sun.' Because his hair is so golden."

"So, what is this strange name?" persisted Kiukiu.

"It sounds like Sta-yo-mi," said Mahina. The baby let out a squeal of delight as she lifted him high over her head.

"Stayomi?" Kiukiu repeated, staring at the baby with renewed interest. The name sounded eerily familiar. "Or Stavyomir?" Stavyomir, the name given to the last of the Arkhels, after his grandfather Stavyor.

"Maybe. Sta-vyo-mir," repeated Mahina, twisting the unfamiliar syllables around her tongue. "Isn't he adorable?"

"He is," said Kiukiu, "but the longer he stays to play with you here, the shorter his life will be in my world."

"I can't do anything about that," said Mahina, with a regretful shrug. "There were others before him. Other soul-friends. They never stay for long."

"Aude is here!" cried Karila, breaking away and running along the shore, waving; Tilua scampered after her. Kiukiu looked around and saw two older girls, one dark, one fair. They were walking along the sands, bare feet paddling in the warm tide, laughing together, their arms about each other's waists. To Kiukiu, who had always longed for a best friend among the kastel children, they looked as if they had been sharing secrets. And a little sigh of envy escaped her lips for what had never been. She could see how important it was for lonely Karila to escape to this seeming paradise where she and Tilua could play to their hearts' content.

As Karila and Tilua reached the older girls, they greeted them with hugs, all excitedly chattering at once. Kiukiu sat back on her heels and watched. And the bleak thought came to her that while the live children's dream-souls were happily playing here, their physical bodies were slowly deteriorating. For every child who was drawn to the dark Drakhaoul's island, there must be a worried mother or father, sitting watching at a bedside, anxiously consulting doctors, and all in vain . . . What doctor of physic could possibly analyze the true cause of the children's debilitating illness? They weren't suffering from a simple fever that could be cured with powdered willow bark.

And here was another "child," a young woman, whom Kiukiu had never met before. Who was she? Karila had called her "Aude."

Kiukiu rose, brushing the clinging sand from her skirts, and went down the beach. She sensed that every move she made, every question she asked, was being observed.

"Oh, that's not true!" cried Tilua and burst into giggles; Karila joined in.

"What's the joke?" asked Kiukiu.

"Waiola said that I—that I—" Tilua broke off, still laughing helplessly.

"That Tilua loves Kahukura," put in Karila, then gave a little squeak as Tilua bent down and splashed her with seawater. The two girls ran away, still giggling.

"So you're called Aude?" Kiukiu smiled at the young woman. "I don't think I've seen you here before. Where are you from?"

No sooner had she asked the question than the sky began to darken.

Waiola, Aude's friend, stared accusingly at Kiukiu. "Don't make him angry. You know these questions make him angry."

A cold little wind began to whip up the tops of waves into foam.

"I don't care," said Kiukiu. "If we don't stand up to him, you'll never be free."

Aude looked uncertainly at her friend. The wind was blowing stronger now and the warm sunlight was fading.

"Just tell me," begged Kiukiu.

"I'm from Francia. Provença," said Aude.

The wind was stirring the sand, blowing up eddies that stung the skin and the eyes. The touch of the sand and the dry roar of the wind brought back terrifying memories of her imprisonment in the Realm of Shadows. Still she persisted. "And your Drakhaoul, Waiola?" She was determined that she would not be intimidated by the unseen louring presence. "The name of your daemon?"

The waves were rising higher and the seawater had turned freezing cold. Waiola snatched Aude's hand, dragging her up the beach, through the billowing sand, Kiukiu following.

"Nilaihah!" Waiola shouted. Lightning shivered through the dark sky. Thunder cracked and rolled overhead. The girls screamed in fear, clutching each other. "Go away!" Waiola turned on Kiukiu, facing her through the whirling sands. "It's useless trying to fight him. He's just too strong."

"I'm not going to give up!" Kiukiu shouted back. "I'm not going to—" Something was tugging her with a force so powerful that she felt herself sucked right off the storm-tossed shore and hurled into a maelstrom of whirling winds.

"I'm not going to give up!" she shouted again and found she was staring up at her grandmother.

"Easy now," said Malusha.

"Stavyomir's one of them." Kiukiu sat up. "I've seen him there."

"What, our little Clan Lord Stavyomir?" Malusha's face crumpled. "But why Stavyomir?" She began to shake her head. "I should have done the naming ceremony. I could have found some way. I could have protected him—"

Kiukiu covered her grandmother's hand with her own. "Even then it wouldn't have been enough. It's his ancestry, Grandma. He must be descended from the sons of Artamon too. All the children are."

"But I can't just let him waste away. He's the last, Kiukiu, the last of the Arkhels. It's my duty, as Praise Singer to his family."

Kiukiu sighed. It was over twenty years since Malusha had been the Arkhels' Praise Singer and yet she was still fiercely, obsessively loyal to her dead lords. "The khan won't let you go, Grandma."

"I've got to find a way."

Andrei, still in Drakhaon form, hunched on a crag overlooking the lake and watched the encampment far below.

"What does it mean?" he asked Adramelech. "Your child? How can that boy be your child?"

But Adramelech had withdrawn into himself and would not answer him. And as the sun rose and mists drifted across the lake, Andrei felt himself growing steadily angrier that he had been forced to participate in this assassination attempt.

"You promised me so much, Adramelech. But what am I doing in this wilderness? What's so important about destroying this young woman? Let the others deal with her. I want Muscobar."

"*I have not forgotten. But she stands between you and your heart's desire, Prince Andrei.*"

"That one girl?" Andrei could not disguise his skepticism.

"*She has poisoned my child's mind. She has turned him against me.*"

Andrei sensed the Drakhaoul receding farther away from his probing. Its glamour slid from around his body, like the folds of a rich cloak dropping to the ground. He wrapped his arms around his nakedness, shivering in the damp of early morning. Without Adramelech to warm and protect him, he felt ill and exhausted.

"What's the matter with me, Adramelech?"

"*You have depleted your strength.*"

"Sleep. I'll sleep and when I wake, I'll feel refreshed. And then I'll be ready to face what must be done."

Wretched and shivering, Andrei crept into a bracken-filled hollow and curled up, feeling the browning fronds rough against his tender skin.

The hawk flies high over the steppe, searching for its prey.

The young rabbit, with its soft fur and white tail, hasn't seen the hawk's shadow. The hawk swoops, claws extended, sharp beak open. There is a short struggle. Then the prey goes limp and the hawk is tearing at the soft fur, desperate in its hunger to drink the warm, sweet blood . . .

Andrei woke from the dream, the horrible dream of carnage and torn, raw flesh. His mouth felt smeared and sticky. He licked his lips and found they tasted of blood, as if he had bitten his lip as he slept. He sat up and, looking down at his naked body, saw dried stains of blood.

"Am I hurt?" He raised his hands and saw traces of dried blood caked in the amethyst claws. And the dream, still so fresh in his memory, seemed too vivid to have been just a dream. He gazed uneasily around him as the early-morning light slowly flooded the open grasslands.

Something lay slumped in the grass, a few feet away from him.

"No," whispered Andrei. He forced himself to go and look. "Please, no," he said again, backing away. In the dream, the prey had been a rabbit. But this was a young goatherd, he guessed, a girl with hair black as a crow's feather, and skin burned brown by the sun of the steppes. *Just a dream . . .*

But what dream could inflict such vicious injuries? It looked as if a wild animal had savaged her, tearing at her throat.

Andrei dropped to his knees. His whole body trembled uncontrollably. The wind blew cold across the grasses, making them rustle and sing. But the girl lay still, her black eyes fixed, staring into another world.

He turned away and vomited until his throat ached. He did not think he had ever felt so wretched in his life.

"Why? Why did you make me do it?" he cried out to Adramelech.

"You have a long journey ahead of you. You were utterly spent. She gave you what you needed."

"A long journey?"

"Your sister is near her time. You want to be with her when her child is born, don't you?"

Andrei still could not take his eyes from the dead girl. "And why should that matter to you?"

"The Orlov line matters much to me, my prince. Her child will be unique."

"The child, always the child!" cried Andrei. "You've made me abandon my command, you've made me commit all manner of atrocities, and all for the sake of this one child! What about the promises you made to me? What about *my* birthright, *my* bloodline?"

"Still so impatient." Adramelech's soft, dusky voice whispered soothingly, calming him like drifting poppy fumes in a smoking den.

"*Trust me. We will go back to Muscobar now, and soon all your wishes shall be granted.*"

Images began to flicker in Andrei's mind: he saw himself kneeling in the candlelit Cathedral of Saint Simeon as the Patriarch Ilarion placed the heavy imperial crown on his head. He saw himself emerging from the dark of the cathedral to a deafening cheer from his people, crowded into the square, as all the bells of the city clanged and clamored. He glimpsed a veiled woman at his side, radiant in white and gold. "*My Empress . . .*" He turned and with trembling hands, raised her lacy veil. Celestine de Joyeuse gazed back at him, her blue eyes brimming with love and adulation.

"Celestine?" He blinked and found himself still standing on the empty grasslands, with only the whining wind whipping through his hair and the stiffening body of his prey sprawled where he had tossed it aside.

"*I know your most secret desires,*" said Adramelech, "*even those you dare not admit to yourself.*"

"Celestine," Andrei repeated as he flew back toward Muscobar. His mind was filled with his memories of her: that sweet voice, the exquisite blue of her eyes, that last burning touch of her lips on his . . .

"Why, there you are, Tikhon." Irina came out of the cottage and hugged him. She seemed to have become more stooped since he last saw her. "That girl." She peered up at him with eyes that were clouded with cataracts. "She's gone, you know."

"Celestine's gone?" Andrei did not know what to say. He had put his career on the line to rescue her and she hadn't even waited for him to come back! "B—but how?"

"Old Evgeni comes by, as usual, selling fish, and off she goes with him to Yamkha."

"Did she leave any word for me?"

"All she said was to tell you she was off to look for . . . now, who was it? Ah, yes. Kaspar Linnaius."

CHAPTER 38

Kiukiu was shaking out the sleeping rugs, in the new tent the khan had given them, when she heard a great uproar outside. There was much shouting and all the dogs in the encampment were howling and barking. She popped her head out of the tent flap and saw Malusha speaking with Captain Cheren.

"We have caught Unegen," said the captain as Kiukiu hurried toward them.

Kiukiu caught Malusha's eye. "What will happen to him?"

Cheren's face betrayed no emotion. "The khan has ordered his immediate execution."

Kiukiu shuddered as she heard the shaman sobbing and pleading for mercy.

"All his shaman skills were not enough to save him," said Cheren.

The cries grew louder as several of Cheren's men appeared, dragging Unegen with them. When Unegen saw Kiukiu, he began to shout. "She should die, not me! The daemons will be back. As long as she is with you, you are all in danger!"

Kiukiu crept back into their new tent and buried her head in the rugs, trying to blot out Unegen's screams.

"Grandma, did you feel that?" Kiukiu was on her feet and running out of the tent to gaze up into the sky. Flying slowly across the lake toward the khan's encampment came a winged creature too large to be a heron or an eagle. Kiukiu stood watching it, her heart pounding in rhythm with its wingbeats. "Gavril, is it you?" she said softly. "Is it really you, at last?"

"Here it comes again!" The cry went up from the lookouts. Women grabbed their children and fled in terror. Cooking pots were overturned in the panic, hot water sizzling into steam as it dampened the fires.

"No, wait!" Kiukiu began to wave her arms at the khan's men. "Don't shoot! It's not the same one!" But they took no notice and pointed their bows at the sky.

"Gavril! *Gavril!*" She ran down toward the lakeshore, still frantically waving.

The Drakhaon was drawing closer, so close that she could see the shimmer of his wings. His eyes, as piercing as the light of the evening star rising over the lake, sought her out. But he was flying slowly, painfully slowly, and she could sense that he was exhausted.

Behind her she heard the khan's officer give the order to fire.

"Stop!" she screamed at the top of her voice.

Gavril just stood on the lakeshore, staring at Kiukiu. In the twilight, a softly luminous sheen seemed to emanate from her, almost as if she were no longer wholly human.

"Is it—is it really you, Kiukiu?" he stammered. She ran across the turf toward him and flung her arms around him and suddenly he was kissing her hungrily as if he could never stop, touching her face, her hair, and she was kissing him back, both laughing and crying all at once.

For a moment, he held her at arm's length and gazed into her eyes. "Look at you," he said, smiling at her, all his fatigue and despair forgotten. He sifted her thick, fair hair through his fingers, seeing how even in the last of the daylight, it glimmered gold as a harvest moon. He kissed her smooth, soft cheeks. "You're completely restored. You're . . . so beautiful."

"It's been so long," Kiukiu whispered, kissing him again, winding her fingers into his wild hair, "and I've missed you so much."

Gavril became aware that a curious crowd had gathered to stare at them: bowmen, mothers, and little children.

"Is there anywhere we can go? To be alone?"

"There's an island out there." Kiukiu pointed across the lake. "It's said to be haunted, so no one goes."

The last of the sun's light illuminated a shadowy blur of trees against the limpid waters of the lake.

"Hold on tight, then." Gavril swept Kiukiu up in his arms and, as she wound her arms around his neck, launched himself into the air. He heard the murmur of amazement as he flew out across the darkening lake waters toward the island, with her clasped tightly to him.

Kiukiu felt she could go on flying in Gavril's arms forever.

She heard a breeze rustling through the thick beds of sedge and reed below them. Then he was alighting on the island shore, gently setting her down on the grass. From where they stood, they could see the watch fires of the khan's encampment like the glimmer of distant stars through the darkness.

"The moon's rising," said Kiukiu, "and the night is clear."

The trees grew almost down to the lake's edge and it was so still that they could hear the quiet lapping of the water against the stony shore.

Hand in hand, they began to explore. Before long they came upon broken columns, overgrown by brambles, choking ivy, and wild clematis.

"What do you think this was?" Kiukiu asked, gazing up at the vast columns. "A palace? The khan never mentioned such a thing."

"No one's lived here in a century or more. No, I'd guess it was a temple," Gavril said, pulling aside some of the clinging creepers. "Look; there are carvings here."

The moonlight illuminated traces of ancient carvings beneath the roots and tendrils, thick with grime and worn with age. But the silvery light was too faint for them to make out any details.

Kiukiu gave a nervous laugh. "You don't think we're offending the gods of this place, do you?" The temple reminded her of Artamon's Mausoleum in Tielen and she began to wonder if there might be hidden vaults beneath where they stood. Or worse, sentinel grave guardians. She shivered.

"What's wrong?" he asked, putting his arm around her. "I won't let any harm come to you. This place is ours for the night."

She laughed again, touching the blue stippling on his chest and shoulders. "With you to protect me, my daemon lord, I know I'll be safe."

"Safe?" he murmured, pulling her closer, enlacing her tightly in his arms, so that she could feel the heat of his body searing into hers. "With me? Aren't you just a little afraid?"

She slowly let her hands travel over his shoulders, touching the dark, furled wings with terror and delight. She felt another shiver go through her, a burning shiver of joy and anticipation. "My Drakhaon," she whispered, pressing her lips to the glittering scales on his throat, his breast.

And then they were falling back into the dry bracken, and though the night shimmered with frost, she didn't care as he tore away her clothes. She just let herself be consumed in the fire of his kisses, burning with desire, until she felt him melt into her. And for a little while, they were one.

Sometime later, they made a fire on the cracked stones of the temple floor, drank from Kiukiu's little flask, and talked of everything and nothing.

Gavril awoke. For a long while, he just lay with Kiukiu curled up against him, her head nestled against his shoulder. His arm was going numb, but she looked so comfortable that he didn't want to disturb her. A deep sense of contentment stole over him. He had dreamed of this moment so many times—and in his darkest days in Francia, it had begun to seem that his dream would never come true, that they would never be together again. Yet, here she was in his arms and she had whispered, "I love you, Gavril," at the sweetest, fiercest moment of their lovemaking.

He tucked her cloak around them both more tightly; their fire had burned down to glowing embers and the air was bitterly chill. In its dying light, he watched her face as she slept, memorizing every soft contour, each golden lash.

Morning light was slowly penetrating the thick foliage of the ruined temple.

"Were you watching me?"

He had not realized she was awake. "I was remembering an old ghost story Palmyre used to tell me, about the soldier who goes away to the wars, leaving his young wife behind. He returns one winter's night many months later and, although his home looks neglected and the hearth is cold, there is his faithful wife waiting to welcome him. In the morning, he awakes and finds he is alone in their bed and the roof is open to the cold sky. She had died of a fever, yet her ghost had kept watch, waiting to welcome him home . . ."

Kiukiu was staring at him and her eyes suddenly filled with tears. "What a sad story," she said. "And were you afraid, Gavril, that I might vanish away with the morning light?"

"I had no means of knowing what had become of you, all these long weeks," he said, kissing the tears from her lashes. "But somehow, in my heart, I knew you were still in this world."

In the fresh, chill light of dawn, Gavril spotted yellow fruit hanging from the branches of a bent little tree, half-strangled with ivy, growing high in the rear wall of the ruins. He climbed up to pick one; then, to be safe, sniffed it warily. No doubt about it; from the sweet-tart smell, this was definitely an apple. A little past its best, maybe, but hungry as Gavril was, he was not going to complain. He finished it in four bites, then clambered up over the tumbled stones to pick more. That was when he noticed the carved frieze through which the tree had grown, splitting the old stone in two. His hunger forgotten for a moment, he pulled back the clinging foliage. Caked in dust and earth, the carved figures had been eroded by weather and time. Engrossed in his discovery, he brushed away as much of the clinging dirt as he could. A woman's image was emerging from the grime—no, a snake-woman, or goddess, her lower body a series of undulating coils, and her features strikingly beautiful, in spite of her serpent eyes. Once the frieze must have been painted, for there were still tiny flakes of green clinging to the carved scales. Perhaps there had once been jewels in the slanted eye sockets, to catch the light, lending a semblance of life and power to the goddess.

"Where are you, Gavril?"

He heard Kiukiu calling. "Up here!" he replied. "Come and look at this."

She made her way up, moving more carefully than he had, testing the old stones before she put her weight on them.

"Apples," he said, handing her one of his finds.

She took a bite and looked up at him, smiling. "They're really sweet."

"And look at this." He held back the curtain of ivy, which had dropped down again over the frieze. "This must be the goddess of the temple."

Kiukiu bent down to take a look. "A snake-goddess?" Her voice had gone very quiet.

"We should leave an offering to thank her for sheltering us," said Gavril.

"Don't joke about such things, Gavril!"

He looked at her in surprise. He had not expected her to react in such a defensive way. But she was still staring at the frieze as if hypnotized. He could only guess that she knew about the goddess but was not yet prepared to tell him.

"I'm starving," he said. "Where can we find food?"

Kiukiu turned her back on the frieze. "At the khan's camp. Across the water."

"Can I go there . . . like *this*?" He gestured to his Drakhaoul-altered body. "They tried to shoot me out of the sky last night, remember?"

"So you can't change back anymore," she said, stroking the softer scales stippling his throat.

"No." Gavril placed his hands on her shoulders, gazing into her eyes. "There's so much to tell you. We need to talk."

She nodded slowly, regretfully. "If only we could stay here a little longer. Just the two of us."

He felt a bitter aching in his heart when he heard her say those words. One night together was not enough, not nearly enough to make up for the long months apart. He let her head rest against his shoulder, gently stroking her hair. "If only . . ."

CHAPTER 39

"A boat," said the Magus, "I need a boat."

Chinua was heading for Khaltuk, a fishing village on the lakeshore, a couple of miles from the khan's encampment.

The Magus had revealed nothing to Chinua of his encounter with the Guardian of the Springs. And he was gone so long that Chinua had begun to wonder if he might ever return to the land of the living. But the instant Linnaius appeared out of the rising mists, Chinua saw that the Magus's formidable intellect had been restored. No longer the shambling dotard the wolf-shaman had helped down into the steaming waters, this Kaspar Linnaius walked with the ease and confidence of a much younger man and his pale eyes pierced Chinua through with the chill force of a winter's wind.

I will do your bidding a while longer for Malusha's sake, Chinua said silently to the Magus, *but once I have found you your boat, I wash my hands of you.*

As they entered the village, little children ran out from the wooden houses to stare and point at them. Women, busy scraping sealskins, looked up from their work. The air was rank with the stink of animal fat and blood. Chinua called out a greeting to them. "We're looking to hire a boat."

The women pointed to the lakeshore.

With a straggle of children tagging along behind them, they reached the stony shore, where men were mending nets and working on upturned shells of little fishing boats. A vile-smelling oily substance was bubbling glutinously in an old tub.

Linnaius walked among them, looking critically at each boat in turn. Chinua gave as friendly a grin as he could manage and began to explain in his own tongue, "The old man here wants a boat. It must be light, he says, and quick."

"Quick? How fast can he row?" asked one of the younger fishermen, breaking into laughter.

"What is this one made of?" Linnaius had stopped by one boat that lay on its side on the shingle.

"It's made of sealskin," said the young man, still laughing. "Skins from the little grey Taigal seals that live out at the point."

"It sounds expensive," said Linnaius to Chinua. "And I have no money."

"And where's he going to take it?" A grizzled man with a scar seaming one side of his face came over to Linnaius's side. "That boat's too light to carry him to the far side of the lake. The water's deep out beyond Seal Point. And very treacherous once the autumn winds blow."

Chinua translated again. Linnaius gave a little shrug of his shoulders as if that was of little consequence to him. "Does it have a sail?"

The old fisherman looked puzzled. "We can fix a sail, if that's what he wants."

Linnaius was watching the fishermen slapping a steaming oily mixture on to the upturned hulls of their boats.

"Tell them I can make their boats watertight. And if that pleases them, they can give me the sealskin boat in exchange."

Their first night together, Kiukiu had dreamed only of love. But the second, although she lay safe in Gavril's arms, she found herself drawn back against her will to the children's island.

It was dark. She could hear the water softly lapping on the shore nearby, but there was no trace of the children. Something had changed—and not for the better.

"Where are you?" she called, turning round and round on the sands. "Tilua? Koro? Kahukura?"

"Ssh." A little figure rose up from the edge of the jungle, beckoning frantically to her. "*He's* here."

"I can see you, Spirit Singer." Nagar appeared out of the darkness straight in front of her.

Kiukiu felt as if she were shrivelling, drying to dust beneath that chilling gaze of dark fire.

"I warned you to stay away from my children. Yet here you are again."

"They're not your children, Prince Nagar. They don't belong here. They're not your playthings, for you to use and abuse as you please. They've been damaged enough."

"And you're their brave champion, come to rescue them?" Nagar's voice burned cold with derision. "Look, children. Your new friend wants to take you away from me." He made a sudden snatch and caught hold of Tilua. "My darling children." The black-taloned hands stroked Tilua's hair. "I will never let you go." Kiukiu could see that the girl had gone rigid with fear; her mouth was half-open, yet she was too terrified to make a sound.

"Let her go."

The dark-scaled hands continued to stroke and caress the child. "You see, Tilua," Nagar whispered, slowly placing his lips close to her ear, "your mortal friend can do nothing to help you."

Kiukiu felt herself choking with revulsion.

"Your little world will be changed forever, Spirit Singer. You will dance to my tune now."

Kiukiu awoke with a start. She gazed around her fearfully, still expecting to see those bloodred, cruel eyes staring at her, challenging her to defy him.

"What's wrong?" whispered Gavril sleepily.

"Nagar," she said. "I've found out the names of the Drakhaouls' soul-children: Tilua, Koropanga, Kahukura, Waiola, and Mahina. But what's been much harder to find out are the names of their living children. And I fear those children are in great danger, Gavril. I fear that the Drakhaouls plan to use them."

"Use the living children?" Gavril propped himself up on his elbow. "How?"

"As a sacrifice to set Nagar free—" She stopped, clapping one hand over her mouth. "Oh, but I forgot. They can hear us, can't they? Through *you*."

"*Kiukirilya.*"

As she looked at Gavril, she saw the shadow of another being begin to issue from within him.

"D—Drakhaoul?"

"*My name is Khezef.*" The voice was Gavril's—and yet it was overlaid with a darker, deeper resonance. And the scars on Kiukiu's throat and breast began to throb and burn, for Khezef knew her as intimately as Gavril.

"Does Gavril know you're speaking to me? Please don't harm him."

"*He knows. He consents.*"

Like staring at the stars through rising smoke, she could just make out the Drakhaoul's features in the gloom. How like Nagar he was, with the same fierce, alien beauty. Yet she sensed nothing of Nagar's cruel perversion in the glimmering blue of his eyes. She sensed she could trust him.

"Your lord, Prince Nagar—Nagazdiel—is not as you remember him, Khezef. He is changed. Embittered. *Corrupted.*"

There was a pause, as though Khezef was reflecting on what she had told him. Eventually the Drakhaoul said, "*He was once the noblest and proudest of us all.*"

"The long years he's spent in the Realm of Shadows have warped his spirit. I saw nothing noble about him. He's taken your soul-child, Tilua. He's using her. He'll do anything to stop us."

Khezef's image began to fade back into Gavril's body. Kiukiu feared that she had revealed too much to the Drakhaoul; Khezef had played them false before. Could they trust him this time?

Gavril went down to the lake in the chill of early morning to bathe.

"*Look in the water, Gavril.*"

Gavril knelt and gazed into the still waters. At first all he could see was his own face, framed by long, dark daemon locks.

"*My kindred are right. I have changed,*" said Khezef. "*I am different from them.*"

Khezef's glimmering shadow form slowly began to emerge, until it had superimposed itself on Gavril's reflection.

"*I've lived too long among mortals. Inhabiting mortal blood, flesh, and bone for so many years has changed me.*" Gavril found he was staring directly into the blue shimmer of Khezef's eyes. "*I've shared your dreams, Gavril. I've lived your life, and so many other Nagarian lives, right back to Prince Volkhar, my first human host. And now I find I have come . . . to care for you.*"

The Drakhaoul's admission stunned Gavril. "To care for me?" he echoed softly.

"But I'm slowly killing you, Gavril. The mortal body is too frail to sustain an aethyrial spirit for long. It was never meant to fly, or to generate Drakhaon's Fire."

"But you've just healed me from my injuries—"

"And each time I heal you, your body takes longer to recover. You will be dead before your thirtieth year if I stay with you. It is time for me and my kind to leave this world, where we were never meant to be, and return to our own."

"And your brothers? They have other plans. They have the Eye."

But the Drakhaoul just gave a slow sigh, like a dying breath.

"Do you feel that, Kiukiu?" Malusha looked up at the cloudy sky. "He's coming back."

"Who?" cried Kiukiu. "Not Adramelech—"

"Can't you tell by the way the wind is blowing? The Magus, child."

A sudden eddy of wind swirled around the camp, making banners flutter wildly and tent corners flap. The khan's horses stamped and neighed, rearing up, pawing the air, as the wind blew stronger.

From out of the sky came flying a small boat, its sail full. And sitting in its stern, steering it, sat Kaspar Linnaius, with Chinua tightly gripping the sides of the little craft as it bumped to a stop over the grass.

"Magus!" Kiukiu ran to greet him as he climbed out of the boat. One glance from his keen, cold eyes told her that all his faculties were restored.

"Kiukirilya." He acknowledged her with a brief nod.

"So the Jade Springs did their work, eh?" said Malusha, who had been following at a slower, more labored pace.

Chinua clambered out and stood unsteadily on the grass, as if trying to regain his land legs.

"I'm going back to the Emperor," said Linnaius.

"Now wait just one moment," said Malusha, wagging her finger at him. "D'you have any idea what's been happening here, Kaspar Linnaius, while you've been off rejuvenating yourself?"

Kiukiu saw from Malusha's expression that her grandmother was making a great effort to restrain her temper.

"I sensed that Lord Gavril was here," said Linnaius impassively. "And before him, another, darker power."

Malusha lost her hold on her temper. "Those cursed Drakhaouls you and your precious Emperor were so careless as to set loose are planning some terrible mischief!" She marched over to the Magus and glared up into his face. "And my little lord Stavyomir is in danger because of it. The last of the Arkhels."

Kiukiu watched in trepidation, wondering how the Magus would react to such an outburst. "I shall be flying to Swanholm," said the Magus calmly.

"Then you can drop me off in Azhgorod on your way to Tielen," Malusha retorted. "It's the least you can do, seeing as how we've taken such good care of you all these long weeks."

"But while I'm gone, who's going to keep watch over my girl?" The instant Malusha had climbed into the sky craft, she started fretting.

"I will take care of her," said Chinua staunchly.

"You're a good man, Chinua." Malusha smiled at him—a smile of genuine affection, Kiukiu noticed.

"I have never forgotten the great kindness you did me and my family," Chinua replied, with a formal bow of the head. Malusha returned the gesture. And then she turned to Kiukiu. "Come and give your grandmother a good-bye kiss."

Kiukiu ran over and kissed her grandmother; Malusha whispered into her ear, "Take great care, child. Our adversary will play us false at every turn of the way. If I fail, you'll have to continue the fight without me."

"No, Grandma, don't say such a thing." Kiukiu felt her heart fail her as she realized what Malusha was saying, and she clung to her grandmother, hugging her tightly.

"We have a long way to go," said Kaspar Linnaius quietly. Malusha gently unwound Kiukiu's arms from around her neck and sat back in the craft.

A swirl of wind whistled around Kiukiu's legs, filling the sail. As the wind blew stronger, the little craft lifted into the air.

"Good-bye!" she cried above the shriek of the wind, waving until the sky craft disappeared beyond the pale horizon.

Will I ever see her again? she wondered, pulling her shawl tightly around herself in the sudden freezing chill that settled after the mage-wind had dropped.

Malusha prowled up and down outside Lord Stoyan's mansion. She knew that Lilias Arbelian and her son were at home because she could hear little Stavyomir's fretful crying and the plaintive sound made her want to go in and pacify the unhappy baby.

"The poor little mite must be teething." Suddenly she knew how she would charm her way into the household. "And I know an excellent remedy that will soothe those sore gums in no time."

Malkh's gusly strapped across the shoulders, she went to the tradesmen's entrance and knocked.

A surly-looking servant woman opened the door and snapped, "Yes?"

"I've brought some simples for the young master. A salve to soothe his gums."

"Were you sent for?"

"Not in so many words—"

"On your way, then!" And the door was slammed in her face.

Malusha was not so easily deterred. She knocked again. The sound of angry wailing swelled as the door was opened.

"You again? I'll have Aram set the dogs on you."

"I don't want payment," said Malusha, putting one foot inside the door, "but I can tell that *you* could do with something to get rid of that sick headache."

The servant woman hesitated and Malusha knew she had made an accurate diagnosis. In an instant, she had produced a little jar from her bag and was triumphantly waving it in the woman's face. The baby was still yelling. "Take a spoonful of this infused in hot water. Add honey to taste."

"What is it?" said the woman suspiciously.

"Feverfew. Keep the bottle. I can see why you get plenty of headaches." Malusha was in the kitchen by now, talking as she walked, looking all around for the source of the crying. In the great fireplace, she saw a wooden baby minder, and strapped inside it, with tears and dribble streaming down his red face, was a chubby baby boy, chewing on his finger.

"There, there, now." Malusha knelt beside him. "Let Malusha take away the pain in those little gums."

She took out a jar of an ointment she had made and smeared a little on her fingertip. Smoothing it onto his hot and swollen gums was less easy as he kept trying to chew her finger. But as the ointment began to work, his sobs began to calm. "That's better, isn't it, little Stavyomir?" She stroked his soft hair. "The same color as your grandfather, true Arkhel gold," she murmured.

The woman was drinking the infusion of feverfew, grimacing at the taste. "Blessed peace at last," she said, sinking into a chair. She looked exhausted.

"Where's his mother, then? And his nurse?"

The woman shrugged.

"Does his mother often leave the little fellow behind?" Malusha did not bother to hide the tone of disapproval in her voice. This was not the way a young Arkhel lord, the last of his line, should be reared. What was Lilias thinking of, leaving him, tethered like a dog, in the kitchen?

"He's not very robust," said the woman, as if this explained Lilias's neglectful behavior.

These words alarmed Malusha. "He's not been in good health?"

"One illness after another. He seems to be poorly most of the time. Of course if his mother had fed him herself . . ."

Malusha was cooing to Stavyomir and tickling him under the chin. She wanted to get some time alone with him. She started to make loud sniffs. "What a stink," she said. "He badly needs a change."

The woman gave a groan.

"I'll do it for you." Malusha undid the straps confining the baby and lifted him out. "You come with me, my little lord."

"There's clean clothes in the laundry," said the woman.

In the laundry, beneath sheets hanging from the ceiling rack to dry, Malusha laid Stavyomir down and changed his clothes; the baby kicked and cooed, one thumb in his dribble-wet mouth.

Malusha quietly began to chant, invoking the names of his father and grandfather, then all the other Arkhel lords. She whispered his name to his ancestors and called on them to protect him.

"Now we must wait," she said to Stavyomir, picking him up and cuddling him, "and see what your ancestors send you."

The owls began to arrive by night. Just one or two at first, quietly swooping down in the darkness to perch on the roof of Lord Stoyan's mansion, then more and more, until the whole roof was covered with white-feathered snow owls.

Malusha stayed in the kitchen, looking after Stavyomir, while Ulyana, the servant woman left in charge, went to her bed to sleep off her headache.

When she was certain Ulyana was sound asleep, Malusha wrapped Stavyomir in a shawl and went out into the night with him to greet the owls.

A little crowd of curious neighbors had gathered to stare at the owls.

"What's drawn them here from the moors? Is it an omen?"

"Snow owls in the city means a hard winter's coming."

"They're Arkhel's Owls," said an old man. "If there's any of Lord Nagarian's men here, they'll shoot them. Old hatreds still run deep."

"Lady Iceflower," whispered Malusha, "come and meet your new lord."

Out of the darkness, Lady Iceflower came floating down to perch on the nearby gatepost.

"Here he is, little Lord Stavyomir."

Stavyomir stretched his hand out of the shawl, trying to touch the owl's soft white feathers. Lady Iceflower regarded him gravely but did not move away.

"Now, my lady, we have work to do," said Malusha. "We must protect this house against the danger that's coming. It's time to weave a ward—and a powerful one, at that, if we're to stand a chance against the storm to come."

CHAPTER 40

Anxious relatives and courtiers clustering in salons and talking in whispers, servants running to and fro with buckets of coal and clean towels, doctors and yet more doctors arriving to be shooed away by the midwifes . . .

Eugene was reliving one of the most harrowing days of his life. And even though he kept reminding himself that Astasia was not Margret, it was impossible not to remember the day of Karila's birth, which had begun so full of hope and ended so tragically.

After Astasia's waters had broken, there had been a first flurry of activity, in the midst of which he had contrived a few minutes with her alone.

"How do you feel, Tasia?" he had asked tentatively.

She had managed an uncertain smile. "Odd. Excited—and just a little afraid."

Only a little afraid. He had reached out then and folded her close in his arms, stroking her hair. He was terrified. Suppose it was the last time they would be alone together? Suppose it was the last time he could hold her and hear the beat of her heart close to his? But he dared not share his true feelings, for she needed all her courage and stamina for the long hours ahead. "Of course you're feeling apprehensive, my dearest girl, but you're strong, you can do this."

"Only I *can* do this!" She snapped, then broke off, biting her lip. "Where's Masha? I want Masha."

* * *

The day wore on and Eugene went every half hour to Astasia's room to receive a report on his wife's progress from the Orlovs' physician. Sometimes he heard her groaning and crying out, the sound soon drowned by the midwife's vigorous exhortations.

To distract himself, he allowed his father-in-law to show him all the exotic plants he was cultivating in his hothouses and endured a lecture on the difficulties in propagating pineapples. He guessed that the Grand Duke was almost as concerned about Astasia as he was, but somehow neither man managed to put this anxiety into words, although Aleksei produced a bottle of vodka and two glasses, which helped to pass the time.

Toward dusk Eugene left the hothouses and encountered the Grand Duchess coming away from Astasia's room.

"My poor little girl," said Sofia, shaking her head sorrowfully.

Eugene felt the false courage induced by the Grand Duke's vodka fast ebbing away. "How is she? Is all going well? Can I see her?"

"Well, she's not at her best, and what woman would be in her condition? But you're her husband, and Emperor too, so who am I to stop you?"

Eugene went in. Candles had been lit in the bedchamber and Nadezhda was tending the fire. To his surprise, he saw Astasia walking around the chamber, supported by an old woman whom he took to be the midwife.

"Eugene?" said Astasia.

"It's always like this with first births, your highness," said the midwife, giving Eugene a wide, gap-toothed smile. "We'll be a little while longer yet."

"Oh," whispered Astasia in tones of frustration.

"But shouldn't you be lying down?" he said, puzzled.

"If my girl wants to walk about, she can walk about," said the midwife. There was something so authoritative about the way she said it that Eugene did not dare to argue with her. Besides, these old peasant ways might be the best. All the doctors in Tielborg had been unable to save Margret.

About two in the morning, Eugene heard the sound of horses thundering down the carriageway toward the mansion. Sentries on duty outside shouted a challenge, but the late visitors were obviously judged to be friends, not foes, and a short while later, the Orlovs' butler announced, "Prince Andrei is here."

Eugene was playing a halfhearted game of chess with the Grand Duke and he felt Aleksei watching him, wondering, no doubt, how he would react to Andrei's sudden appearance. Eugene steeled himself to keep his face expressionless. This was not the time to raise old grievances. And as Andrei strode into the card room, he slowly raised his eyes from the black-and-white squares of the chessboard and merely looked at the newcomer.

The Grand Duke rose and held out his arms to his son. "Welcome, my boy!" he cried, embracing him. "So good of you to leave your command to be with your sister."

And whatever his own feelings for Andrei Orlov, Eugene could not help but feel moved by the old man's genuine affection for his son. He found himself wishing, as he had often wished before, that his own father had not died so young, leaving him ruler of Tielen at the tender age of twenty-three.

"Forgive me for abandoning our game, highness," said Aleksei, turning back to Eugene, his arm still about Andrei's shoulders. "I think you have the advantage." Andrei stared at Eugene, unsmiling, and Eugene felt a sudden inexplicable sense of warning.

"Let's leave it there, then," said Eugene. He nodded curtly to Andrei. Brother-in-law he might be, but nowhere was it written that he should feel any affection for the arrogant young man who had led Astasia into such danger in Francia.

Eugene soon found himself wishing he could avoid Astasia's relatives; every hour seemed to bring another carriageload from Mirom, even though it was well past midnight. Sofia was holding her own little court in the salon next door, and the sound of sympathetic female voices, cooing like doves, was setting Eugene's nerves on edge.

He paced the card room, stopping by the windows that looked out over the terrace, to gaze at the moonlit grounds. This enforced inactivity was exhausting. He wanted to be with Astasia—and yet he also wanted to be far away.

Someone coughed politely. Eugene swung around and saw Valery Vassian standing in the doorway.

"I know I have no right—" he began.

"Indeed, you have not." Vassian's desertion of his post had been one of the many disappointments that had followed Dievona's Night. "I'm surprised you dare to show your face here."

"May I speak to you in confidence, imperial highness?" Vassian kept glancing around, as if he was afraid he might be overheard.

Eugene was not feeling in the least tolerant; he was worried about Astasia and it was the middle of the night. "Don't waste my time, Vassian," he said.

"I know I don't deserve a hearing. But"—and Vassian lowered his voice—"it's about Prince Andrei."

"What about him?"

"I fear he's not"—and again Vassian paused, as though desperately searching for the right words—"in his right mind."

"How so?" Was Vassian trying to curry favor with him by betraying his friend?

"I don't want to seem disloyal. Doubly disloyal. But I've seen things, overheard things that have made me—"

"Is he plotting some *coup*?" Eugene interrupted. "Is he conspiring against me?"

"It's nothing that straightforward," burst out Vassian, coloring dark red.

"Then what?" Eugene had all but lost patience with Vassian's vagueness.

"He treated the Empress very badly in Francia," burst out Vassian. "And now he's abandoned his command, the *Aquilon*. He's just . . . not the Andrei I knew before. It's almost as if he's . . . *someone else.*"

Eugene had opened his mouth to reply when Nadezhda flung open the door and rushed in in a state of near-hysterical excitement.

"Highness! Come quick!"

Every other concern vanished from Eugene's mind as he hurried after her. The candleflames flickered wildly as he ran down the passageway toward her bedchamber. He was aware that many people, servants and nobles alike, had clustered around open doorways, watching and whispering.

As he neared the room, he heard her agonized cry, filled with exhaustion and effort. He stopped.

I can't—I can't lose her too.

And then he heard another cry, high and wailing—the unmistakable cry of a newborn.

"My son," he said in tones of utter astonishment. "My son!"

*   *   *

Astasia gazed down at the tiny, angry, wrinkle-faced baby in her arms.

"Hallo," she said.

To her amazement, he opened his eyes and stared up at her in the candlelight. *This is my son—and he knows me.* Delight overwhelmed her—and then a fiercer emotion, so strong, so visceral, that it almost took her breath away. She would fight to the death to protect this little one.

"Astasia?" said an unsteady voice from the doorway.

"Eugene," she said, her voice trembling too, "he's looking at me."

"So he is." Eugene put his arms around her and kissed her. "Such blue, blue eyes," he said wonderingly, gazing down at his son.

Astasia had forgotten her own exhaustion. Her body felt torn and bruised by the birth, but somehow it didn't matter. They had washed her and put her in a fresh nightgown, but they had left her hair loose about her shoulders and still damp with sweat. In the morning, she knew she would feel every little tear and strain—but now she felt exultant.

"He looks like you," she said tenderly.

"But he has your eyes," said Eugene. He took the baby in his arms, still gazing at him intently. "What shall we call him?"

"I thought we'd decided on Karl Alexei."

"How about Rostevan? After Artamon the Great's eldest son?"

"Rostevan?" Astasia tried the name. It had an ancient and chivalric ring that appealed to her. Also it would neatly avoid any family resentments between the Orlovs and the Helmars. "Prince Rostevan. I love the name. But how did you come up with it?"

"One of the academics at Saint Ansgar's put the idea in my head. She's dedicating her next book—" Eugene broke off. "Well, look at that! He's gripped my finger. And what a good, strong grip too!"

"Where is he? Where's my grandson?" came Sofia's excited voice from outside the chamber.

Astasia looked at Eugene. She knew that this precious moment alone with their son was over. The heir to the empire of New Rossiya was about to meet his household. Eugene carefully placed little Rostevan back in her arms and kissed her again. And she loved him even more in that moment for the gentle and expert way he handled the baby.

"Are you sure you're ready?" he asked anxiously.

She nodded.

He opened the door and Astasia saw a crowd of faces staring at her and her son.

Sofia advanced toward her with arms wide open. "My little girl's a mother!"

The bells of Muscobar pealed out triumphantly in honor of the new prince's birth. Andrei stood on the terrace at Erinaskoe and heard their faint ringing carrying on the wind, from distant Mirom.

Those bells should be ringing to celebrate my coronation.

And now he could hear the retorts of a twenty-one-gun salute, fired, no doubt, from outside the Admiralty, as was the custom when a new member of the Orlov family was born.

"*And soon they will be, Prince Andrei,*" said Adramelech. "*Your time is nigh.*"

"*Sahariel!*" Karila awoke with a scream, clutching her throat. "Sahariel's here!"

Marta came running in her nightgown. "Whatever's the matter, Princess?"

Lieutenant Petter followed close behind, barefooted, wearing only a nightshirt, pistol in hand. But Karila was so frightened she could only stammer and point.

"Come back to bed now, it's only another nightmare."

Karila felt Marta's arms go around her but she could not move. Why didn't they understand? Sahariel was coming and he meant to do them harm; she could sense it.

Lieutenant Petter was at the window, gazing out over the park. "I can't see anything," he said.

Karila broke free of Marta and went limping to his side, jabbing her index finger at the sky. "There. There!"

A streak of scarlet lit the pale morning sky.

"Dear God," murmured Lieutenant Petter, "she's right."

Karila stood, frozen, staring, as the great dragon circled above the lake, the hot wind from its beating wings making all the trees in the park bend and sway as if caught in a winter's gale. There was an arrogance about the way it flaunted its prowess in flying, skimming the surface of the water in an elegant loop before suddenly gathering itself and darting at full speed toward the palace.

Lieutenant Petter grabbed hold of Karila and pulled her down to the floor as the creature dived straight toward them, its claws grazing the roof slates right above their heads. The sound of its wing-beats throbbed through Karila's mind.

Crouched on the polished floor, Marta on one side of her, Lieutenant Petter on the other, Karila could only think one thing: *"He's come for me."*

Shrieks and shouts arose from the other wing of the palace as Sahariel circled overhead. Lieutenant Petter leaned across and kissed Marta on the mouth. "We'll distract him. Take the princess to a safer place."

"Fredrik—wait!" Marta cried but he was already hurrying out of the door. "Please take care," she whispered, clutching Karila to her, and Karila could feel her shaking as tears spilled down her cheeks.

"It's no use trying to shoot the dragon," Karila said. "It'll only make him more angry."

"Where shall we go?" Marta was gazing around in panic. "Where's safe?"

"Nowhere's safe," said Karila, holding tight to Marta. "He wants me, Marta. He wants me."

CHAPTER 41

"Fire!"

Petter's men let off a second round of mortars at the hovering dragon—and it batted the shot away with one sweep of its powerful wings. They peppered it with carbine bullets. Nothing had any effect. And to make matters worse, Petter was certain he could hear the sound of laughter through the powder smoke, as though the creature was mocking their efforts to harm it as it slowly alighted on the parterre in front of the East Wing.

The laughter suddenly ceased. And in the silence, Petter spotted a smaller detachment dragging one of the great cannon over the gravel, heaving and tugging until it swiveled around to point at the dragon.

"No!" Petter yelled. He leaped from behind the balustrade, waving his arms and shaking his head. Had they not seen that the East Wing lay directly in their line of fire? If they missed the dragon—which was almost a certainty—they would smash into the palace itself.

Too late. Confused, they misread his signal and lit the fuse, jumping back as the cannon went off. There was a deafening boom, followed by the sound of smashing brick, glass, and timber. "No," Petter repeated softly, shaking his head in disbelief. The dragon was unharmed, but a jagged, gaping hole had been blown in the facade of the East Wing, ruining the Empress's Music Room.

And before Petter had time to shout out the order to retreat, the sky darkened. The dragon turned its head toward the cannon party and exhaled a single breath of fire. Before Petter's horrified gaze, the cannon sizzled, turned red, then white hot and, as the powder ignited, exploded with an ear-shattering blast, projecting molten shrapnel fragments in all directions.

Petter was flung to the ground by the force of the explosion. Dazed, he picked himself up, dusting the gravel from his clothes.

The dragon had gone. He gazed up at the sky, bewildered. Had it flown away? Or had it been caught by the exploding cannon?

And then he saw the man. Naked, but for the long strands of ice-white hair that streamed about his shoulders, he stood where the dragon had been. Slowly, the man turned to look at him. Petter stared, mesmerized. The man's skin was dusted with flecks of black and scarlet, the color most intensely concentrated on his cheekbones, throat, and across the shoulders and thighs. Strangest of all were his eyes, the eyes that turned on Petter a look of burning disdain. For they were black as jet, except for a slash of fiery scarlet where the pupils should have been.

"You don't recognize me, Petter, do you?" said the man in an insolent drawl.

"Sh—should I?"

"Considering we were in the same year at the Military Academy, then yes. But you were always such a model cadet, Fredrik—and I was such a drunken wastrel."

"G—good God," stammered Petter. "Alvborg?"

Karila heard the cannon fire and clapped her hands to her ears as the building trembled. But what came next was worse. The single flash of scarlet light was so intense that it burned through her closed lids.

"Fredrik," whispered Marta beside her, her hands clasped together as though in prayer.

"How dare he?" Karila was no longer afraid; she had never felt anger like this before. Oskar Alvborg and his Drakhaoul had no right to attack her people. And if he had hurt Fredrik Petter, he would pay dearly.

"It's gone quiet," said Marta, raising her head to listen. "What does it mean? Has that horrible monster been destroyed?"

"I don't think so," said Karila.

Marta moved warily to the window on her knees, keeping her

head low, and peered out just above the sill. "I can't see any sign of it. But who is that strange man with the white hair?"

"So where is she?" said Alvborg. He turned to walk toward the grand curving stair that led into the palace. Petter raised his pistol.

"Not a step farther, Count Alvborg. I'm arresting you."

Alvborg glanced back over his shoulder. "Oh, please Petter, don't make me do anything you'd regret."

Petter tightened his grip on the pistol. He felt a sudden dryness in his throat. "I'll fire."

"This is no fun. Let's make it more even and duel for the palace, shall we? Sabres at dusk?"

Petter pulled back the trigger, but Oskar Alvborg reacted so swiftly that the pistol was flying out of Petter's hand before he knew what had happened. All he saw was the jet of scarlet flame that had sizzled from the end of Alvborg's finger. With a gasp of pain, Petter dropped to one knee, clutching his seared hand to his breast.

"H—how—?"

"Face it, Petter, you were never a match for me at the Academy. You were too slow then, and you're too slow now." Alvborg turned away and walked on up the steps. When he reached the balustrade at the top, he turned and looked down on Petter. "I've spared you this time because I need you to do something for me. But don't forget—as soon as that deed is done, you're expendable. You and all your men."

Petter, biting his lip so as not to cry out with the pain of his burned hand, could only kneel there, powerless, before his onetime fellow cadet.

Oskar Alvborg was feeling pleased with himself. He walked around the empty state rooms of the palace, tugging the dust sheets off the furniture and paintings with a flourish, while the palace servants tiptoed after him. It amused him to hear their terrified whispers as they shadowed him from room to room.

"How pleasant this palace is. I think I shall like it here."

When he reached the Emperor's bedchamber, he flung open the doors and began to search through Eugene's clothes for something to wear.

At length he found a shirt that did not displease him and some breeches that were not too loose. He pulled on a blue silk *robe de chambre*, letting it drape loosely over the fine cambric shirt.

"C—Count Alvborg," ventured one of the servants, "I don't know that it's right for you to be in the Emperor's rooms—"

Oskar slowly turned around to stare at the insolent fellow. To his delight, he saw the valet cringe away.

"I hold the Tears of Artamon. Therefore that makes me the Emperor of New Rossiya—and your new master. Emperor Oskar I."

This precipitated a burst of frantic whispering.

"Forgive me, but is our Emperor dead?" asked the valet. "The Emperor Eugene, that is?" he added hastily.

"Who knows, who cares?" Oskar was fast becoming bored. "But I'm damnably hungry and that's a fact. Bring me food."

"Wh—what would your highness like to eat?"

"Your *imperial* highness." Oskar was suddenly aware that there was a raging pain in his stomach. He could not remember when he had last eaten. "Just bring me food!"

"Yes, your imperial highness."

The valet backed hastily out of the door and the whispering began again. "And no playing tricks with my food," Oskar snarled.

The valet returned a little while later, with a trayful of silver dishes which gave off a deliciously savory smell. "Fricassée of chicken," he announced, whisking off the lids. "Blanquette of veal."

Oskar felt another pang contort his empty stomach. "You," he said to the valet. "Test them for me."

"Me, imperial highness?" said the valet uncertainly.

"Who else is there in this room besides the two of us?" The burning pain was making Oskar's temper worse. He desperately wanted food—and yet he did not want to find himself drugged or poisoned.

The valet hesitated a moment, then picked up one of the silver forks on the tray and speared a slice of chicken. When he had eaten the chicken, he tried the veal.

"And the bread." Oskar was almost salivating like a hound at the sight and smell of the food, but he dared not touch a crumb until it had all been checked. The valet chewed a little of one of the bread rolls, shrugged and stepped back.

"Well?" Oskar said testily.

"Needs a little more salt."

Oskar could restrain himself no longer. He fell on the chicken, greedily forking it down as fast as he could. Then, his hunger still not satisfied, he turned to the veal, emptying the dish in a matter of minutes, and wiping up the rich sauce with the soft rolls.

But the gnawing pain in his belly was worse than when he started. He stared at the empty dishes in dismay. Voices from the nursery haunted him as he pressed his hands to his swollen stomach, "*Don't bolt your food, Master Oskar, you'll only give yourself a bad tummyache . . .*"

But this was not like a childhood bellyache brought on by eating too many strawberries or too much sweet, sticky marzipan. This was hunger of another kind, all-dominating.

"If you've poisoned me—" A nauseating wave of pain rippled through his body. "By God, you'll pay. You'll all pay dearly!" He raised one trembling hand, pointing his black-clawed nails at the cowering valet, willing the scarlet flames to flicker at his fingertips.

"*You've already used too much power, my prince.*" Sahariel's sudden warning took him by surprise.

"Too much? What do you mean?" Oskar pitched forward onto his knees, clutching his stomach. The burning had crept upward into his throat and suddenly his mouth was dry as ashes.

"*You've flown far. You expended the last of my energy firing on the palace.*"

"Can I get your imperial highness anything else?" asked the valet cautiously.

"It's a plot." Oskar could only speak in a whisper. "A plot to kill me."

"I assure your imperial highness that the food was not tampered with in any way." The valet bent over him, offering a glass of wine. When Oskar vehemently shook his head, he drank from the glass. "Look. No ill effects whatsoever."

Oskar struck the glass from his hand, spilling the wine all over the fine Allegondan carpet. "Water," he begged, collapsing. "*Water . . .*"

And then he became aware that something deliciously soothing and infinitely more desirable was drawing near.

"I've brought the water you asked for, highness."

Oskar felt someone lifting his head and tipping a glass to his lips. He was lying in the lap of one of the young palace maids, and the delectable, intoxicating scent came from her soft skin. He gazed up into her eyes.

"You're so very . . . kind," he said. He raised one hand and gently ran one razor-taloned finger along the line of her jaw, feeling her shiver deliciously at his touch.

"We've got to get the princess out of here," Lieutenant Petter said. Karila saw him wince as Marta put healing salve on his burns. "Now, while he's distracted."

"Surely he'll notice."

"We don't know for sure that she's the reason he came here. He seems to like playing at being emperor."

"He doesn't know about the secret passages," said Karila. Both Marta and Petter turned to stare at her.

"Princess, that's true!" Petter said, managing a smile. "And if we provide a little distraction for him on the opposite side of the palace, that might allow us enough time to slip away."

Oskar held the Tears of Artamon in his clawed hands. Just to touch the burning stones sent tremors through his whole body, as though his daemon-Drakhaoul was drawing power from them. And not just power; they seemed to spark off a series of memories and sensations in his mind that left him dizzied and reeling.

There it was again, the sun-drenched shore he had dreamed of, and there were the children playing on the sands. And the sight of them, so happy and carefree, maddened him.

Sated, he let the maid's lifeless body drop back on the floor.

"*Dip the rubies in her warm blood before it cools.*"

Still in a daze, Oskar obeyed Sahariel.

"Now we will fuse them back together with the mingling of her blood and my power." Energy flooded from his fingers into the stones until they glowed. Five stones had become one again, one powerful ruby, imbued with mortal blood.

Each time Oskar gazed down at the ruby now, it seemed to gaze back at him, as though he was holding a living eye cupped in his hands, a blood-imbued eye that penetrated his soul and laid bare his most secret desires.

Karila crept as quietly as she could along the secret passage. Lieutenant Petter was ahead of her, Marta behind. She tried to pretend that this was all a game, but from time to time she heard Petter stifle a murmur of pain as he knocked his burned and bandaged hand in the darkness.

"You're sure, Princess?" Petter whispered. "This passage comes out near the Magus's rooms?"

"I'm sure." She had used it many times when going to see Linnaius.

A sliver of daylight appeared ahead, filtering in through a grille in the wall.

"Let's go," urged Marta.

"No; we must wait for the signal. My men will let off a cannon on the far side of the palace. Then while Alvborg's investigating, we'll make for the stables."

They crouched in semidarkness, waiting and listening. Karila began to think of spiders, earwigs, and wood lice scuttling around in the passageway beneath their feet. The thoughts made her skin feel crawly and she started to brush her arms and hair, afraid lest a spider had dropped into her curls and was about to run down her face . . .

A dull thud resounded outside.

"That's it," said Lieutenant Petter, opening the little door into the courtyard. Daylight dazzled Karila and she screwed up her eyes. "You first, Marta. I'll carry the princess."

Petter swept Karila up in his arms, Marta gathered her skirts in one hand, and they ran out across the courtyard toward the stables. Another cannon went off and Karila heard the sound echo and re-echo around the valley, like distant thunder. One of the grooms came out to meet them.

"All's ready, Lieutenant," he said. A swift calèche stood waiting for them, drawn by two sturdy greys. Petter bundled Karila inside and Marta climbed up afterward. Petter clambered into the driver's seat, took the reins in his bandaged hand, and released the hand brake.

"Let me come along too," said the groom, climbing up beside him and taking the reins from him.

"Poor Petter," said Karila under her breath as she saw how pale and drawn the lieutenant's face had become. "His hand must hurt very much."

"He needs to see a surgeon," said Marta pointedly.

And then they had cleared the stables and were rattling along the carriageway that led through the park to the East Lodge.

"This is a bad business," said the groom. "First the Francians, and now this."

Karila felt a shiver of fire go through her.

"He knows," she said faintly. "He knows where I am."

"How can he know, damn him?" said Lieutenant Petter.

"Language, Fredrik," Marta cautioned.

"Keep driving," Petter said to the groom. They were going faster as the gravel road wound downward, before climbing up the valley side toward the East Lodge.

The sky overhead darkened and that same hot, dry wind blew across the valley.

"Keep going!"

Karila could hear the beat of Sahariel's wings. The horses began to throw their heads from side to side, showing the whites of their eyes. And out of the sky hurtled the scarlet dragon, landing on the road in front of them, so that their way was blocked. The horses whinnied in terror. One reared up, hooves striking empty air; the other tried to bolt. In spite of the groom's shouts, the panicking horses could not be calmed and the calèche tipped over onto its side.

Karila was thrown clear, landing in the bushes alongside the road. Stunned for a moment, she came back to herself to see two flame-red eyes burning into hers.

"*I don't believe I gave you permission to leave the palace, Princess.*"

"Khezef," whispered Karila, shrinking back, "help me."

"*There's no point calling on my errant brother. He's far away in Francia. Too far to help you.*"

Karila could hear groans from the overturned calèche. "Marta?" she quavered. "P—Petter?" The fallen horses were squealing in pain and thrashing around. The sound made her feel queasy and helpless. They were hurt and she could do nothing to help them.

The scarlet Drakhaon turned toward the injured horses and breathed a single, slender bolt of flame. The squealing stopped. Karila squeezed her eyes shut and turned away. Then she dropped to her knees and was sick.

"*Don't run away,*" said Sahariel with casual cruelty. "*Oh, how could I forget? You can't run anyway, can you, Princess?*" He lifted the calèche and tossed it aside as if it were no heavier than a child's toy cart. Underneath lay Petter and Marta; the groom had crawled a little way off before collapsing.

"Don't hurt them!" cried Karila, wiping the saliva from her fouled mouth. And, seeing how still Marta lay, she began to cry, fearing that she was dead. Petter stirred, tried to raise his head—and then slumped back. "Oh Marta, Marta, don't die," wept Karila. She turned to Sahariel and beat against his black and scarlet scales with her fists until her skin bled. "If you've killed them, I'll make you pay!"

"*You're coming with me, Princess.*" She felt two strong, scaly arms go round her and she was lifted high into the air. Next moment she was sitting on his back.

"*Hold tight—or fall and die,*" he said. The great wings unfurled and he leaped into the air. The jolt nearly made her lose hold but she dug her fingers into the spiny ridge on his shoulders between the wing sockets. Swinging wildly from side to side as he gained height, she hung on with all her strength, feeling the wind gusting through her streaming hair. It was terrifying—and yet weirdly familiar. She had dreamed this dream so often. Only this time it was real—and if she let go, she would tumble to her death, far below.

CHAPTER 42

"Karila held hostage by Alvborg?" repeated Eugene. The suggestion was as preposterous as it was obscene. The thought of his daughter in the clutches of that twisted and embittered man made him feel sick with anger. "How could Petter have let such a thing happen? I trusted him with her safety, with her life. By God, he'd better have a good excuse."

"Lieutenant Petter has been badly wounded, highness. He and Marta were fleeing with the princess when Alvborg sprang his second attack."

"But how? Has he raised an army? Why did we have no warning that he was planning such a *coup*?"

"We believed that the princess would be safe at Swanholm," said Sylvius with quiet dignity. "We had no idea that Alvborg had become so . . . powerful."

"Powerful?" Sylvius, subtle as ever, was not telling all he knew, Eugene was sure of it. "What are you hiding from me, Sylvius?"

Sylvius and Maltheus exchanged glances. "Do you recall a previous intruder at Swanholm?" said Sylvius.

"Lord Nagarian? What has he to do with this?" Eugene did not understand what Sylvius was hinting at. "I've no time to play guessing games! Tell me straight."

"Dragon," said Maltheus bluntly.

Eugene stared at them blankly. *Alvborg was a dragon-lord?* And suddenly he heard Gavril Nagarian's words of warning drifting back to him from the shadowed depths of his memory.

"*There are others at large. You set them free from the Serpent Gate when you summoned Belberith. I don't know what they intend. I don't know where they are. But they are growing stronger.*"

"Dear God," he whispered. "This is all my doing."

"What did you say, highness?"

Eugene looked up at his ministers. "What are Alvborg's demands? What does he want?"

Another significant glance passed between Maltheus and Sylvius.

"He claims he has the Tears, highness," said Maltheus. He drew out a handkerchief and mopped his forehead. "He also claims he has proof that he is your father's illegitimate son."

Eugene heard the words but did not take in their full implications. "I see. He wants my throne."

"He demands that you abdicate in his favor."

"And if I refuse?"

"He will destroy Swanholm and lay waste to the surrounding countryside. And the princess will die. He says—as a curious post-script to his demands—that you will 'understand precisely what I mean.' "

"Oh yes," murmured Eugene, "I understand." His instinct was to try to wake Belberith and fly to Swanholm. He would fight Alvborg and duel for his daughter's life, Drakhaoul to Drakhaoul. But would Astasia ever forgive him if he freed the daemon within him again?

"Frankly, I don't know how long we can stall him, highness," said Sylvius.

"The whole affair is outrageous!" burst out Maltheus. "The man's utterly mad."

"Kari is being held hostage by a madman. Better and better."

"I'm so sorry, Eugene, that was thoughtless of me."

"Is there any way that we can suppress this news?" Sylvius mused. "What with the Francians still holding their own against our men in Holborg, your illness, and the recent losses at sea, morale is very low in Tielen. And this is a very real threat to your throne, highness."

All the time they had been conferring together, the sky had been growing darker as stormclouds rolled in from the Straits. An eerie light leaked from behind the clouds as the trees in the grounds suddenly began to whip this way and that, stirred to frenzy by a crazed wind.

"This storm's blown up out of nowhere," said Maltheus. "Shall I ring for the candles to be lit?"

"Wait." Eugene had sensed the approach of a powerful presence. "This is no ordinary storm." He rose, going to the windows that overlooked the grounds, and gazed up into the maelstrom of wind-whipped cloud overhead. "Friend or foe?" he said under his breath. There was something strangely familiar about the onrushing turmoil of cloud and wind. Had Nagarian fulfilled his promise at last?

Eugene gave a shout and ran out into the hall and onto the steps. The great doors banged shut behind him. Gripping hold of one of the pillars to keep upright in the fierce blast, he saw a craft high in the sky, its sail filled with wind. And he gave a shout of joy, for sitting at the helm, directing the little boat toward him, was Kaspar Linnaius.

Eugene ran down the steps to greet Linnaius—and then stopped. It might have been a trick of the stormy light that pierced the rolling clouds, but the Magus's body seemed to radiate a faint silvery aura.

"Linnaius," he cried. "You're restored!"

Kaspar Linnaius looked at him and Eugene felt as if he were being pierced through to the soul. And then the Magus smiled at him.

"I am glad to see your highness in such good health," he said and there was a new quality of warmth in his voice.

"Welcome back, Magus!" boomed out Maltheus, appearing on the steps behind Eugene. Sylvius nodded his white head in greeting.

"I understand that congratulations are in order, highness," said Linnaius. "May I be allowed to see the young prince?"

"We sorely need your help," said Eugene, ushering him up the steps into the house. "Oskar Alvborg has taken Swanholm, and is holding Karila hostage."

"Why is there no response from Eugene yet?" Oskar prowled about the echoing hallways and empty state rooms of Swanholm. "Doesn't he understand I mean business?"

He caught sight of his reflection in the great, glass mirrors. He stopped, turning from side to side, admiring himself. He was wearing the uniform of Colonel-in-Chief of the Imperial Household Cavalry today, with gold medals and ribbons of the highest military honor pinned to his chest. The Emperor's sabre hung at his side. And he had tied back his wildly exuberant hair with a scarlet ribbon.

Oskar sensed there were servants hiding, just out of sight, terrified that he might call one of them. He enjoyed their terror, relished seeing them cringe when he devised increasingly humiliating and bizarre tasks for them to perform. If one of them hesitated, he would catch hold of him by the throat, thrusting his face into his, snarling, "Who is Emperor here?" and waiting for the terrified, strangled response. "You are, imperial highness."

One of the day's unexpected pleasures had been the discovery of the menagerie, hidden away from the main formal gardens and filled with exotic little creatures: marmosets, rare parakeets, and best of all, tiny deer. They'd been damnably difficult to shoot, skipping and jumping erratically all over the place. But he'd bagged a pair in the end and triumphantly brought them back to the palace. There he'd slung the bloody carcasses down on a kitchen table and told the chef to let them hang a while, as that was the way he preferred his venison. When the chef and his fellow cooks had stared at the meat in horror, he'd said casually, "What? Don't tell me you've never hacked up a whole deer in these kitchens!"

The chef had replied with dignity, "I've never been required to cook the princess's favorite pet before."

And Oskar had wondered why one of the little deer was wearing a gold chain about its slender neck.

"Let me go on ahead to Swanholm, highness," said Linnaius. He accepted the glass of wine one of the servants had brought. "Count Alvborg will not be expecting me. With a subtle use of illusion, I should be able to gain access to the palace without being observed."

"Then I'll come with you," said Eugene as the Magus drank. He was so agitated he could not stop pacing the Orlovs' elegant morning room.

"With respect, highness, if the count is possessed by a Drakhaoul, he will sense you're with me and I'll lose the advantage of surprise."

"Ah. I see." Linnaius, as always, was right. Although Eugene was still tempted to say "to hell with it all" and summon up Belberith.

"I'll go straightaway. You must know, highness, how dear the princess is to me," said Linnaius, "and that I would give my life to ensure her safety."

Leaving Eugene at a loss for words at this unexpected expression of affection, the Magus left the salon.

*   *   *

Karila sat on the darkened shore, pressing her knuckles into her eyes to stop the tears leaking out.

"Don't be afraid, Karila." Tilua sat down beside her and put her thin arm around her shoulders, hugging her close.

"But I am afraid," said Karila, trying not to sob. "He's hurt people. He's killed people. And he'll kill me too."

"Not if we can use Sahariel's soul-child," said Tilua.

"His child is only a b—baby." Karila had tried her best to be brave. But Oskar's unpredictable moods terrified her and her courage was failing. He had destroyed half the palace. He had killed people she loved. He was eaten up inside with resentment and old anger, and Sahariel had been stoking the flames. He and his daemon were two of a kind.

She knew she was his next victim. She knew he would not hesitate to kill her to hurt Papa.

"Papa will come and rescue me," said Karila staunchly. "He'll be here soon. I know he will."

Eugene slowly opened the door to Astasia's bedchamber, trying not to make the slightest sound that might disturb little Rostevan.

He had given strict orders that no one except immediate members of the family were to be admitted, unless Astasia wished it otherwise. He wanted to ensure that she was not overtired by visitors.

Astasia sat, propped up by pillows, with the baby in her arms. She was softly singing him an old lullaby, and the sound of her voice, low and huskily sweet, brought tears to Eugene's eyes. How could he break this terrible news to her? He could still not quite believe that she was recovering so swiftly after the birth, and he did not want to jeopardize her health.

He came softly into the room and she looked up, smiling.

"You don't have to tiptoe," she said. "He's sleeping sound."

Eugene came and sat beside her. He could not take his eyes off Rostevan who lay blissfully asleep, with the careless abandon of all newborns.

"Listen, Astasia," he began, "it's—" He broke off, unable to continue.

"What is it?" Her smile faded. "Oh Eugene, what's wrong?"

He made an effort to control himself. "Kari. She's been taken hostage."

"Hostage?" The baby flung out one arm and squirmed in her

arms, letting out a little grumbling cry. Astasia lowered her voice. "Who would dare do such a horrible thing?"

"Someone I should have had locked away. Or executed. A dangerous and unpredictable madman. Oskar Alvborg."

"But what does he want?"

"The empire. He claims he is my father's illegitimate son. He says he has papers to prove it. And he has the Tears of Artamon." The more Eugene thought about it, the more Alvborg's wild claims enraged him. Until now, he had believed his parents' marriage to be happy and fulfilling, and he could not bear the thought that his father had betrayed his mother and indulged in this scandalous affair.

"Eugene, what are you going to do?" Astasia placed one hand on his. "You can't give in."

Eugene enlaced his fingers with hers. "I have to go to Swanholm," he said. "I have to try to negotiate."

"You're not going to try anything rash, are you?" she said, her eyes dark with concern. "You must think of your health, Eugene. You're still not fully recovered."

He let go of her hand and leaned forward to kiss her, and the baby. Rostevan stirred again and sighed, creasing his little face up.

"Eugene!" Astasia called after him. Eugene left the room without a backward glance, for he knew that if he turned around, he would never want to leave. But Kari needed him, and Astasia was surrounded by family and friends.

Astasia had vowed to be strong. But after Eugene had left Erinaskoe, she burst into tears, hugging the baby so tight that he began to cry in sympathy.

"Poor little Kari," she wept. "If only you had been well enough to make the journey here, then none of this would have happened. And now your papa's gone and he's still not fully recovered . . ." And the more Rostevan wailed, the more she wailed too, unable to stop the tears guttering down her cheeks.

"Dearie me," said Masha, coming in with clean clothes for the baby. "Tell Old Masha what's the matter."

But Astasia couldn't begin to explain what was making her so sad. She just leaned against Masha's ample bosom and sobbed.

"All mothers feel like this after the birth," soothed Masha. "It's quite natural. You'll soon be back to your old self again."

*   *   *

"Why doesn't Papa come? He should be here by now." Karila had curled up in the corner of the little dressing room in which Oskar Alvborg had locked her. He had neglected to feed her and she was beginning to feel faint for lack of sustenance. "Perhaps that horrible man means to leave me here to starve to death."

"Princess," called out Oskar in a strange, singsong voice, "I've brought you some delicious food."

There was something about his tone of voice that made Karila shrink back farther into the corner as the door was unlocked.

"Food for her royal highness." His scarlet eyes glinted as he thrust a silver dish toward her, sweeping off the cover with a flourish. "Venison. The most tender, delicious flesh imaginable."

Karila was staring in horror at the meat on the silver plate. She had recognized the little golden necklet.

"Oh," she whispered, anguished, "*Pippi.*"

The first stones of the Chapelle of Saint Meriadec were said to have been laid by Lord Argantel in the time of Artamon the Great. So when Ruaud de Lanvaux and the Commanderie High Council told the king that the ancient chapel was deemed the most suitable place for the exorcism to take place, Enguerrand had readily agreed to their plans.

The walls were covered with stone carvings and statues, some so worn with age that their features were barely distinguishable. Standing guard over the Sacred Texts towered two massive stone guardian angels, one with an upraised sword, the other, lion-maned, holding the keys to the Realm of Shadows. Enguerrand had known their names from childhood: Dahariel and Nasargiel.

Each pair of massive pillars along the narrow nave was decorated with a different motif, one with vines and grapes, the next with thorny briars and roses, yet another pair with oak leaves and acorns. And as Enguerrand lay prostrate in front of the altar, he tried to keep calm by reciting the verses in the Holy Texts that each pillar represented. But the waves of panic kept rising up and the more he muttered, the more apprehensive he became. *Suppose the exorcism doesn't work? Will the daemon manifest itself again? Will it force me to attack the venerable priests and exorcists who have gathered here to help?*

The daemon had been silent for the last hours, no longer tormenting him with its obscene suggestions and promises. But he feared it would not leave him without a terrible struggle. And in that struggle, it might rend him apart. He had read of such horrific ceremonies in the secret annals of the Commanderie.

Blood spattering the tiles, shreds of flesh, brain and bone defiling the sanctuary . . .

Lying on the worn tiles of black and red, where so many supplicants had prostrated themselves in years gone by, Enguerrand begged the Heavenly Guardians to forgive and protect him.

"Make me clean again. I will do anything you ask!"

He could hear the murmur of voices, and the steady tread of the exorcists approaching. One by one, the candles in the aisles were extinguished until only those on the altar still burned. Shadows filled the chapel, and in the pale light of the last candles, the worn statues seemed to take on a life of their own, as though the winged warriors were hovering in the aisles, ready to do combat with his daemon.

The exorcists, robed in black, their faces masked and hooded, stood on either side of him.

"Are you ready, majesty?" Enguerrand recognized de Lanvaux's voice.

"Yes," whispered Enguerrand. He was terrified.

The ceremony began with a low, intoned chant. Enguerrand squeezed his eyes shut and tried to pray. But he could hear a faint whispering that was growing more and more insistent, superimposing itself over the exorcists' measured chanting. And try as he might, he could not blot it out.

"And what will become of my child Aude, if you drive me out? Her health is already fragile. Such a violent sundering could send her mad."

Enguerrand had not once imagined that this secret ceremony might harm his sweet and innocent Aude; on the contrary, he was certain that it could only be for her own good. And now Nilaihah, golden-tongued Nilaihah, was telling him that she could be irreparably damaged.

"Stop!" he cried. Instantly, he was seized by two of the priests and slammed down onto the hard tiles.

"Don't listen to his cries," urged Ruaud de Lanvaux, "it's the daemon talking."

"No! It's me, your king, Enguerrand. And I order you to stop this ceremony at once!" He struggled to break free but the priests were the stronger and held him down.

"Take no notice. No matter what blandishments he uses, ignore him."

But another voice, in the far distance, was calling to Nilaihah. Enguerrand sensed the daemon was all attention, listening intently.

"*Nilaihah . . . it's beginning. It's time.*"

Enguerrand went limp in the grip of the exorcists. He could feel Nilaihah stirring to full consciousness within him.

"*At last,*" answered Nilaihah. "*We've waited long enough.*"

Energy was flooding through Enguerrand's body; it went pulsing through his veins and sinews, as though his blood had been transmuted to liquid gold.

"*It's time,*" repeated Nilaihah, his voice echoing like a great bell through Enguerrand's mind, "*for our final transformation.*"

CHAPTER 43

Ruaud de Lanvaux paused in the chanting of the ritual of exorcism and looked at the king. He lay utterly still, unresisting. Was it having some effect at last? Ruaud hoped so with all his heart. He took up a bottle of holy water and began to sprinkle it over Enguerrand's limp body.

"Be gone, daemon. In the name of Dahariel and Nasargiel, I command you: return to the Realm of Shadows!"

Now he raised the ceremonial spear of the Dragonslayer, tipped with gold, and held it above the king.

Enguerrand's body began to twitch.

"Ah," said Ruaud, his excitement increasing, "it's working!" He consulted the book of exorcism and invoked more of the Heavenly Warriors. "In the name of Galizur, of Taliahad, and Sehibiel of the Second Heaven, I banish you!" His voice rose, full of confidence, strong in the knowledge that he had the power to drive the daemon from Enguerrand's body.

An extraordinary change was taking place. The king's hair was growing, the short-cropped locks lengthening before his eyes, writhing and curling like serpents, golden and black. Surely this shouldn't be happening.

"Hold him down!" Ruaud ordered the priests restraining the king. Unnerved, he read on in the book of exorcism, stumbling over the words as his eyes kept straying to the king, whose hair now reached below his shoulders.

"Enough!" cried Enguerrand. He flexed his arms and with one

sudden gesture, hurled both priests right across the chapel. Then he leaped to his feet and stared at Ruaud.

The candles blew out.

Enguerrand's eyes glittered in the darkness. No, his whole body glittered, as though powdered in stardust.

Shocked, Ruaud took a step back, holding tight to the book. The stunned exorcists lay groaning in the shadows. All was darkness and confusion in the chapel—except for the light that emanated from the daemon's gilded skin.

For the daemon was beautiful. It had transformed Enguerrand into a creature of unearthly splendor. No longer in dragon-form, it towered above Ruaud, golden-feathered wings furled behind its powerful shoulders.

"A—angel?" stammered Ruaud.

"*Do not call me angel. Never call me by that name again!*" Enguerrand reached out and seized the book of exorcism from Ruaud's hands. He cast it on the floor and flicked one finger at it. A little dart of golden fire sizzled out and the priceless ancient book flared up, then subsided into a pile of cinders.

"Majesty!" Ruaud stared in dismay at the remains of the burned book. "What have you done?" With both book and Sergius's Staff destroyed, he knew himself defeated; he had no resources left.

"*We are Nilaihah,*" answered the daemon. "*You will address us as such.*" The voice was still Enguerrand's, but enriched and distorted by the Drakhaoul.

"Where is Enguerrand?" Ruaud demanded. "What have you done with him?"

"*Enguerrand is no longer under your influence, priest. And you believed you were powerful enough to control me.*" Nilaihah threw back his golden head and laughed.

That cruel, contemptuous sound was more than Ruaud could bear. He had dedicated his life to Enguerrand's education; he had worked hard to shape the young man's beliefs and attitudes. And now to hear his protégé deliberately mocking him—

The Enguerrand he knew was obviously dead. This daemon that dared to masquerade as an angel had inhabited his body. And there was only one way to drive it out. He must kill the king—or what was left of him. Without a mortal body to inhabit, the Drakhaoul would be forced to flee; it would be vulnerable.

Kill the king. In destroying Enguerrand, he knew he was signing his own death warrant. But there was no time to consider. Nilaihah was advancing upon him, golden eyes ablaze in the gloom. Ruaud seized the ceremonial spear of the Dragonslayer. With all his strength, he thrust it at the daemon.

Nilaihah gave a howling cry as the spear pierced his breast. He clutched the shaft with both hands, and tugged.

Out came the spear and the daemon's gilded blood leaked out with it, dripping onto the tiled floor, where it sizzled and steamed.

"Forgive me, my king," whispered Ruaud.

But Nilaihah did not fall. He pressed one taloned hand over the wound to try to staunch the bleeding. The other hand slowly raised the spear, pointing the bloodstained tip at Ruaud.

By now Ruaud could hear voices. His Guerriers had come to the rescue. But the doors to the chapel were locked and bolted. He began to back away down the aisle.

Nilaihah launched the spear at him. It caught him full in the chest, the force of the thrust pinning him to the wooden door.

The daemon strode toward him and pulled out the Dragonslayer's spear and cast it away.

"Enguerrand—" Ruaud tried to say his pupil's name, but a sudden gush of blood choked him. As he slid slowly down, the last thing he saw was the dazzling form of Nilaihah rising on golden wings.

"It's time."

As Oskar Alvborg stared into the ruby's pulsing heart, he became aware that another was staring back at him, with a gaze that pierced his brain like a bolt of dark fire.

He dropped to his knees, transfixed.

"Sahariel." The voice seared his mind, each word glowing like a cold flame. *"Set me free."*

"My prince." Oskar heard his Drakhaoul reply, his usually arrogant tones respectful, awed. *"What is your will?"*

"Bring the Eye to the Gate and release your brother Za'afiel."

"A sacrifice?"

"There is no other way. Then you and your kindred must find the living children and bring them to me. Only when their blood is shed will I finally be free."

"But what about Khezef? He's lived too long among mortal men.

He's been corrupted by them. He even displays some kind of affection for his mortal host. He has forgotten our mission."

"Khezef's rebellious nature must be broken. I will deal with him."

The voices in Oskar's head were becoming a torment almost too hard to bear. He was losing all sense of his own identity. Was he Oskar—or Sahariel?

"What about me?" he burst out. "You promised me I would be Emperor!"

The daemon eyes in the ruby suddenly blazed directly into his. He gasped, as flames crackled through his mind.

"So you would be Emperor, would you, Oskar Alvborg?"

"That is my desire." Oskar felt as if the black eyes were sucking him down into a maelstrom of fire. He was finding it hard to breathe. It must be some kind of test, a trial of his determination.

"And do you want to be powerful, far more powerful than you are now? Are you prepared to undergo the final transformation?"

"Why stop now?" Oskar cried, laughing aloud at the thought.

"Then make me a sacrifice at the Gate. Bring Za'afiel through into your world. And he will make you all infinitely stronger—strong enough to defeat any mortal weapon or army. He will help you open the Gate."

An autumn gale swept across Erinaskoe, rattling the tiles and roaring down the chimneys. The Emperor's ministers summoned carriages and departed in a great hurry. Andrei watched, wondering what new crisis could have occurred to provoke so much activity. But as no one thought he was significant enough to keep him abreast of the news, he retired to his room with a couple of bottles of wine.

Andrei was bored. He lay on his bed and stared up at the ceiling as the wind blew through the valley—and, as swiftly as it had arisen, died down again.

It was disorienting to be back in his own room, as if the intervening years had never happened and he was a boy again. His parents had even kept his little treasures: a wooden frog he had whittled and painted, under the instruction of the head gardener, a couple of battered shuttlecock racquets that needed restringing, and a bag of marbles, swirled with amber, scarlet, and blue.

Was I ever that boy? He weighed the marbles in his palm, hearing them click together. *I carry his memories . . . but the spirit that remade his body must have made some subtle alterations.*

"*Patience, my prince . . .*"
Andrei sighed and poured himself another glass of wine.

"*The time is right.*"
"*We must act.*"
Andrei still lay on his bed, but now there were others in the room, whispering together. And when he tried to move, he found he was paralyzed, unable to stir. Were they assassins? Had they come to murder him? He opened his mouth to call for help, but although he strained every muscle in his throat until it ached, no sound came out. And the shadowy figures were moving closer.

I've got to get away. They must have laced his wine with a poison that dimmed the sight as well as paralyzing the muscles. *Dear God, what do they plan to do to me?*

"*He's strong-willed. He'll fight.*"
"*I am far stronger than he is.*"
"*But you must sustain the illusion a little longer,*" insisted the first. "*She must suspect nothing.*"

They loomed over him now, indistinct, distorted, leaning down, their shadows smothering him, erasing all that was Andrei from his mind.

"No," he screamed aloud, "*no!*"

Valery Vassian heard Andrei's terrified shouts and, grabbing his pistol, rushed to his room. Kicking open the door, he leveled his pistol and cried, "I'm here, Andrei!"

In the dull light of early dawn, he saw a disheveled Andrei, sitting up in bed, his hand clasped to his forehead. He looked haggard and ill. But there was no sign of any intruder.

Valery lowered the pistol and went in. "What the devil was that all about?" he demanded. Andrei's odd moods and outbursts were becoming more difficult to deal with as the days of inaction dragged on. People were talking behind his back.

Valery threw open the shutters and Andrei flinched away from the daylight. When Valery turned around, he saw that servants had appeared at the open door, all staring at their prince. Valery curtly shooed them away and shut the door.

"I must have been dreaming," said Andrei, his words thick with sleep.

Valery saw the empty wine bottle and thrust it in front of Andrei's face. "Drinking, more like. What's happened to you, Andrei? You've really let yourself go."

"If you find my company so offensive," said Andrei, "you know damn well what you can do! But, oh yes, how could I forget? You came here for Astasia's sake." There was an ugly rasp to his voice.

"There's no need to bring Astasia into this," said Valery. He was hurt by Andrei's rudeness but he was determined not to let it show. "I'm going for a ride. If you care to join me, I'll see you in the stables in an hour."

"Frankly, Vassian, you're dull company," said Andrei. "If I want a sermon, I'll go to Saint Simeon's."

Valery opened his mouth to reply, then thought better of it. In his present boorish state, Andrei was best left alone.

Nilaihah was heading for the great oak forest that bordered the city's southern bounds. The mortal that had once owned this body directed him there, insisting that it was his domain and belonged to him.

Nilaihah needed time to repair the damage that Ruaud de Lanvaux had inflicted. Golden blood still dripped from the deep spear wound inflicted by the priest, sizzling onto the roof tiles and chimneys of the city. And each wingbeat used muscles that had been scored by the spear tip, sending a sharp shaft of pain through the mortal's body. Fused into one being they might be, but Enguerrand, his host, was still vulnerable.

Alighting in a sheltered grove, Nilaihah slid to the ground. He was weak from loss of blood. He would have to concentrate all his powers into healing the wound before he could continue with his mission. And it was so long since he had inhabited a mortal body that he had forgotten how complex they were—and how susceptible to damage.

The yellowed leaves were falling from the great branches of the ancient oaks as Nilaihah dropped to his knees on the rustling carpet. The jagged, rending pain in his breast throbbed into his shoulder and wing with every breath. He pressed his fingertips tightly on the torn flesh, closing his eyes, and willing the healing energy to flow from deep within him.

Lutèce was shrouded in gloom and every bell was slowly tolling. A fine drizzle was dampening the grey slates.

Far below Nilaihah, a long funeral procession was wending its way along the wide street; rank upon rank of Guerriers walked slowly behind a horse-drawn catafalque to the somber beat of muffled drums.

He was descending now, diving downward toward a large city mansion surrounded by a walled garden. The russet-and-olive colors of the House of Provença fluttered from the flagpoles.

Aude is here.

There was a girl in the gardens below, looking all around her and calling, "Minette, where are you hiding, naughty kitty? I've brought you some cream. Minette . . ."

She had entered an alley of boxtrees that led to a fountain; Nilaihah landed in front of the fountain. Fog covered the garden; a few dead leaves lay in the fountain basin but no water flowed.

Aude came out of the alley, still calling, carrying a little saucer. She stopped. The saucer dropped from her hand, cream spilling all over the sandy path.

"*I need you, Aude,*" said Nilaihah. "*Come with me.*"

Then when she turned to flee, he was forced to lunge and catch her, leaping into the air before she could struggle free.

"You're coming with me, Princess." Oskar Alvborg's eyes glinted redder than the great blood ruby he held in his clawed hands.

Karila shrank back into the farthest corner of the little room. The expression in his eyes terrified her. "No." All she could see was the Drakhaoul Sahariel staring at her with a deep, disturbing hunger. "I want to stay here."

As she watched in fascinated terror, he took the great ruby and pressed it into his forehead. She heard the flesh sizzle and burn and saw him stagger, drawing in his breath between his clenched teeth in pain.

Could she escape while he was distracted? She lurched forward on hands and knees, dragging herself toward the unlocked door.

Three bloodred eyes pierced her through. Oskar reached down and scooped her up in his scaly arms. She struggled and pummeled him with her fists, but all to no avail; he was too strong. He opened the door and set off at a run along the passageway.

As they reached the great central staircase of the palace, Karila glimpsed frightened faces peering around half-opened doors.

"Help me!" she cried, kicking at Oskar with all her strength.

"That monster's got the princess."

"Stop him. Someone must stop him!"

But though she caught the terrified murmurs, no one ventured out.

Oskar was making for the main doors; he tugged one open and ran down the ceremonial steps. Karila felt fresh air on her face, chill and spiced with the smell of autumn bonfires.

"In the name of the Emperor Eugene, I command you to hand over the princess!"

A young officer of the Imperial Bodyguard had dared to challenge Oskar; he stood on the wide expanse of gravel, leveling his pistol at them.

Karila felt Oskar's body shudder.

"Dragon," she said under her breath, transfixed with wonder and terror. His scarlet wings unfolded and he lifted into the air. Turning his great head, he snarled a searing jet of fire back at the bold young officer.

Karila heard moans and shouts of dismay as the bolt of fire hit the damaged East Wing—then, as they sped away, the unmistakable sizzle of flames.

Queen Aliénor stared around her at the ruined interior of the Chapelle of Saint Meriadec. There were bloodstains on the tiles, and colored glass fragments littered the floor beneath the broken windows.

"Where is my son?" she demanded, leaning heavily on her cane. "Where is the king?"

Captain Friard slowly shook his head. "We have found no trace of the king, majesty."

"No trace?" Aliénor was not sure she had heard the captain correctly. "Your Commanderie will have much to answer for if he's been harmed, Captain! Exorcism ceremony, indeed. I always said de Lanvaux was a bad influence on my son."

"The Maistre was dying when we found him," said Friard, in offended tones. "He said that a winged daemon had attacked him and carried off the king. I believe, majesty, that de Lanvaux died trying to protect your son."

"Winged daemon? Oh please, Captain, don't insult my intelligence." Aliénor struck the tiled floor with her silver-tipped cane in exasperation. "Tielen agents, more likely. Where were your Guerriers when he was kidnapped?"

Friard looked embarrassed.

This abduction was almost certainly a countermove on the part of the Emperor's secret service. And the thought that her son was in the hands of the enemy appalled her. "Eugene of Tielen," she said softly, "if he is harmed, you will pay—and pay dearly." She would never forget the humiliations of defeat that Prince Karl had inflicted on Francia. She had lost her older brother, Aimery, in the conflict over the Straits.

"You will order all your Guerriers to search for my son, do you understand me? All other missions are to be abandoned until Enguerrand is found."

Linnaius approached Swanholm, hidden in scudding clouds. He wanted to survey the palace from the air without being spotted by Alvborg. And, as Alvborg had threatened to kill Karila if anyone tried to enter the grounds without his permission, Linnaius used his most subtle disguise. Yet as he peered down through the shifting layers of cloud, he saw thick smoke rising from the valley in which Swanholm nestled.

"Am I too late?" Below him he glimpsed the encampment of the Northern Army, strung out along the ridge beyond the parkland. Soldiers were running into the park, bayonets fixed, ready to do battle, their shouts rising faintly as he flew overhead.

Linnaius steered the sky craft toward the billowing smoke. As he dipped down into the valley, he saw with a numbed sense of shock that it was rising from the palace itself. The East Wing had been destroyed; the roof had fallen in and the top three floors had collapsed under its weight. Dust was still rising, as well as smoke from a fire that was blazing uncontrolled beneath the rubble.

The pleasing symmetry of the palace that Eugene and his architects had spent many a long hour discussing was already ruined. And if the fires spread, the whole palace would soon be ablaze.

In spite of the efforts of the servants and soldiers beneath him, frantically pumping water from the lake and the palace wells, it would take a torrential downpour to dampen the flames.

Linnaius closed his eyes, seeking out nearby rainclouds. He twisted his fingers, sending a wind to bring them to him.

And where was Alvborg? Why had he not appeared to challenge him? As the clouds gathered and the rain began to pour from the darkening sky, Linnaius landed his craft and set out to investigate the smoke-filled corridors.

Astasia could not rest for worrying about the siege at Swanholm, and the longer she lay in bed, the longer she was sure they would try to keep news from her. So she rang for Nadezhda and asked her to help her dress.

While she sat in front of the mirror, watching Nadezhda expertly curl and arrange her hair, Rostevan slept beside her in his cradle. Nadezhda kept pausing in her work to look at him and let out little cooing noises. "Look at the dear little mite, sleeping so soundly, ah, bless him . . ."

"Is there any news, Nadezhda?" Astasia gazed critically at her reflection in the glass, pinching her cheeks to try to bring a little color to her pale complexion.

"About Swanholm? No news yet."

"I wish I knew what was happening."

"The Emperor went off in a great hurry, didn't he?" Nadezhda spoke through the side of her mouth as she pulled hairpins out from her gritted teeth, one by one.

"If only Gustave could have stayed behind. He'd have kept me informed."

"There we are." Nadezhda stood back to allow Astasia to inspect her handiwork. "Oh—excuse me, altessa, I forgot to collect clean sheets for the baby's cradle. I won't be long."

Astasia rocked the cradle gently, watching Rostevan's face as he slept. An astonishing range of expressions flickered across his little features as he slept.

She heard the door softly open and, looking up, saw that her brother had entered the room. She smiled at him.

"At least you haven't abandoned me, Andrei," she said, holding out her hand. But he hung back, glancing around, as if checking to see they were alone.

"Is all well with you?" He looked as if he had slept badly again, his eyes dark and shadowed. "Where's Nadezhda?" he asked in a hoarse voice.

"She's gone to fetch some clean sheets for the cradle."

Now he was looking down at Rostevan. "May I hold him?"

"Of course!" She was delighted to see Andrei taking an interest at last. "He's your nephew, after all; you'd better start getting to know each other." She slid her hands around Rostevan, and carefully lifted out the warm, damp little bundle. He let out a sleepy yawn and his heavy head bumped against her shoulder.

"Sorry, little one," she whispered, "Mama's still not very good at this." She looked at Andrei over the baby's head with its soft curling wisps of golden hair. "I think he might need changing," she said with an apologetic smile. "Nadezhda will be back soon. Wouldn't you rather hold a clean, dry baby, Andrei?"

He made a helpless gesture. "Whatever you say, Tasia."

Nadezhda trotted in, carrying a tall pile of neatly folded linen that she put down on the bed. "Ooh, Prince Andrei, I didn't see you." She curtsied. "Shall I come back later?"

"No, Rostevan's wet through."

"Come to Nadezhda then," cooed Nadezhda, taking the baby from Astasia. "Who's made himself all wet?"

Andrei, evidently embarrassed by all this baby talk, turned away and stared pointedly out of the window.

"So when do you return to the *Aquilon*?" Astasia inquired.

"I don't know. I may not return."

She had not expected such a curt reply. He had seemed so enthusiastic at Belle Garde at the idea of his own command. "But Andrei—"

"There's not a great deal of point at present, is there? Hostilities have ceased. I'm frankly not interested in being Enguerrand's lackey."

"All done!" said Nadezhda, lifting up Rostevan, all neatly wrapped in a clean shawl and wearing a linen cap with blue ribbon tied under his chin.

"Oh, that looks so sweet," said Astasia, seeing Rostevan's expression beneath the cap, his face puckered in a disgruntled frown. "He looks just like a little old man. But he smells of lavender now."

"And I'll take these to the laundry." Nadezhda hastily piled the wet and smelly garments into a bucket and withdrew.

"Here he is, Uncle Andrei," said Astasia, holding out Rostevan to her brother. "All clean and dry . . . for a little while, that is."

Andrei took the baby in his arms. He looked stiff and awkward, as if he was not sure how to hold him.

"Support his head with this hand, like this." Astasia adjusted his position. "That's better. There you are." She took a step back to look at them.

Andrei's form began to shimmer before her eyes. She grabbed hold of a chair, wondering if she were about to faint. Slanted amethyst eyes glimmered in a face that was no longer human. The hands that held her baby glinted and had become scaled, like a reptile's, with long, cruel claw-nails. Long locks of dark hair streamed down his back and over shoulders that, even as she watched, seemed to be sprouting furled wings.

"Who—who are you?" she whispered. The creature she had taken for Andrei threw back its head and laughed and the sound of its laughter made her shudder.

"What do you want with my baby?" she cried. "Give him back!" She made a wild lunge for Rostevan but the creature merely raised one hand and with a little flick of its clawed finger, she felt herself lifted into the air and flung right across the room.

Bruised and half-stunned, she saw the door burst open. Valery Vassian rushed in.

"Give me the child!" He raised his pistol, aiming it at the creature's forehead. "Give him back."

"No, Valery—" Dazed as she was, Astasia saw the danger that he might hit Rostevan if he fired.

The creature pointed at Valery. A tiny dart of violet flame issued from its fingertip and sizzled straight at him, piercing his chest. Astasia, dumb with horror, saw the pistol drop from Valery's hand, heard his soft, astonished cry. He slowly sagged at the knees, then pitched forward onto his face.

The glittering creature turned and pointed at the windows. Another little flash of fire, and the windows shattered, cold air rushing into the room.

Astasia tried to crawl forwards, one hand vainly stretched out to stop it. But it unfurled its dark wings and leaped out of the window, into the air.

"Come back!" she cried, hearing how weak and pathetic her voice sounded against the whirring beat of its wings. She dragged her bruised body across the floor, and reached the broken windows to see the daemon swiftly dwindling to a dark speck against the cloudy sky—and then it was gone.

CHAPTER 44

"Valery," whispered Astasia, gently touching his face. "Dear Valery, hold on. Please hold on."

But Valery had turned horribly pale and his lips were grey, except for the little trail of blood trickling out of one corner of his mouth. Astasia raised his head a little, cradling him in her arms.

Nadezhda came in to see what had caused the noise.

"Get a doctor!" Astasia screamed and Nadezhda fled. Though she could see hardly any mark on him, except for a dark, burned patch over his left breast.

"Tasia . . ."

Her name. He knew her. Though his voice was so faint she could hardly hear him. She bent closer, stroking his forehead, trying to stop him from slipping away. His lids fluttered a little and opened. He gazed up into her eyes with an expression of such love and longing that she felt shamed for all the times she had snubbed him.

"Dearest Valery," she said, her voice shaking, "you were so brave."

"I . . . failed you."

"No," she insisted, "no, you protected me."

"Forgive . . ." His warm brown eyes were no longer gazing into hers, they were staring through her, and she knew he was gone. Yet still she cried his name, trying to bring him back. "Valery! There's nothing to forgive, Valery." And then there were others in the room.

"Come away, Tasia, there's nothing more to be done for him." It was her father and he had his hands on her shoulders, trying to help her up, to walk her away.

"He tried to save us. He tried," she stammered. "But there was nothing to be done, nothing—" She could not keep herself from looking back at Valery's still, pale face, and even as she saw the lieutenant on duty close his eyes, she could not believe that he was dead.

"That vile monster. Pretending to be Andrei, looking like him, sounding like him—"

"Come away, my dear," urged her father, leading her out of the bedchamber. "We must get the doctor to check you. You look as if you took quite a fall."

"It took my baby, Papa!" Astasia rounded on him. "Don't you understand? My baby's *gone*!"

At first, Karila was utterly terrified—so terrified she thought she would die. And then the terror began to transmute into breathless exhilaration.

She was flying. Flying on a dragon's back, skimming down across the grey waters of the Straits, with the wind whipping her hair all over her face. She gripped the dragon's spiny shoulders as tightly as she could, each powerful wingstroke throbbing through her body until it felt as if she was one with Sahariel. All her life she had been a prisoner in her body, slow, stumbling, and clumsy. Now she felt as if she had been reborn.

If only it were you, Khezef, my own Drakhaoul . . .

Far, far below she saw tiny ships. And then the Straits were behind them and they were flying overland, with villages and towns laid out like miniature models, linked by meandering waterways and rivers.

"Where are you taking me?" she cried but the wind drowned out her shrill voice. "Where are we going?"

Sahariel did not answer her. But Tilua began to whisper, in a high, agitated voice. *"He's heading south. Heading toward my home. Can't you feel the warmth in the air, Kari?"*

"To your island?" Karila began to feel the return of the paralyzing terror as they flew onward. "To where you died?"

"I'm frightened, Kari. Really frightened."

Karila remembered that she was Eugene's daughter. "We mustn't show him that we're afraid, Tilua," she said. "We've got to be strong, you and I."

*   *   *

Eugene leaned on the rail of the *Dievona*, gripping the wood tightly as he willed the wind into her sails. And then he felt as if a bolt of lighting had pierced his forehead. His vision faded and everything was tinged with a mauve dusky light.

"*Adramelech!*" He heard his own voice cry the name out loud.

Something terrible had happened. Something that affected those he loved most.

He opened his eyes and found himself lying on the deck with crewmen bending anxiously over him.

"Highness?" Admiral Janssen knelt beside him and helped him to sit up. "Highness, you're still not well enough to undertake such a long journey. Let Karonen and the Northern Army deal with the Swanholm situation."

Eugene shook his head. How could he abandon Karila to Alvborg's cruel lunacy? And yet every instinct was urging him to turn back and check that all was well with Astasia and the baby.

"I'll ride back to Erinaskoe. Find me a good horse. A fast one!"

"But highness, do you think you—"

Eugene rounded on him. He had had enough of being treated as an invalid. "Just do it!"

Kaspar Linnaius searched room after room in the palace. The rain he had summoned still poured down on the smoldering ruins of the East Wing. But there was no sign of Oskar Alvborg—or the princess. If Alvborg had kept her imprisoned in the East Wing, then there was little hope now of finding her alive.

Utterly dispirited, he was crossing the entrance hall when a bedraggled man hailed him.

"Magus! Is it really you?"

It was Eugene's majordomo. His customarily immaculate livery was drenched and dirtied with soot and his hair was slicked down by the rain.

"Where's Alvborg?" asked Linnaius tersely. "Where's the princess?"

"Gone. He blasted the East Wing and flew away with her." He mopped his face with a wet handkerchief.

I've failed you, Eugene. Linnaius sank down on the first step of the grand staircase. *I came too late to rescue her.*

*   *   *

"I know this place," Karila murmured to herself. There was the long, curving beach below, with its soft sands, lapped by waves more intensely blue than the cold seas around Tielen's shores. There were the fringed leaves of the palm trees in whose shade she and Tilua often played. And there lay the dense jungle, with twisted mangrove trees choking the little streams that wound down to the seashore and the grove where the raucous red-feathered parakeets nested.

"Poo! What is that horrible smell?" Karila wanted to hold her nose but she dared not let go of Sahariel.

Clouds of grey, evil-smelling smoke were rising from the ground far below. As Sahariel swooped down, she saw that the smoke and fumes were issuing from a jagged, broken-topped mountain that dominated the center of the island.

"Is that a volcano?" she asked. She had read of such wonders of nature, where the boiling innards of the earth forced their way upward to spew out molten lava. Now that she was so close that she could feel its heat, and smell its sulfurous stink, she was not so sure she would call it a wonder.

"*This is Nagar's temple,*" Tilua whispered. "*This is where I died, Kari.*"

Sahariel alighted in a clearing in the heart of the jungle. Karila rolled off his back and landed on the ground at his feet, winded and exhausted by the long flight. It was hot. Stiflingly hot. Her mouth was paper-dry. She raised her head and looked around. She lay on an old, paved stone platform, at the top of long, wide steps so cracked by age that creeping plants that had forced their way through.

"I'm thirsty," she said.

"*Hide, Kari,*" urged Tilua. "*Run away and hide.*"

How can I run anywhere? Karila thought wryly. She was hot, tired, and her mouth and throat were parched. She had reached a state beyond fear; she could not run, so she would have to use what Marta called her native wit.

"I'm very thirsty," she said again. She pushed herself up to her hands and knees. Something felt very wrong here. In spite of the intense heat, she could sense a distinct chill emanating from the clearing behind her. Slowly, she managed to turn herself around.

An ancient stone arch rose from the platform, towering above her. It was carved in the shape of a great, hook-winged serpent, its scaly coils wound around the curve of the arch. Its snarling jaws gaped wide open, as if ready to swallow up anyone rash enough to venture too close.

"Prince Nagar," she said, staring up at the daemon's maw. She knew she should feel afraid. "Have you brought me here to kill me?" she asked Sahariel.

"*Perhaps,*" he said. And then in a turbulence of fiery wings, he flew off, leaving her all alone.

Was he going to bring her water to drink? Bewildered and exhausted, she sank back down. The intense, steamy warmth was making her drowsy. And she had not slept properly in a long while. She tried to keep her eyes open but her heavy lids kept drooping . . .

A deep, red sunset infused Karila's dreams. She opened her eyes, hoping with all her heart that she would find herself back home in Swanholm.

A single bloodred flame illumined the night. A shadowy form moved in and out of its crimson beam. Karila began to wonder if she were still dreaming. She thought she heard the distant echo of deep voices chanting. And then—a sound that made her catch her breath in fear, the sound of a child, whimpering.

"Transform me," she heard Oskar Alvborg cry aloud. "Make me stronger, Za'afiel!"

"*Stop him, Kari!*" cried Tilua. "*It's happening again!*"

There was a glinting flash, as if of a blade descending. Tilua screamed and Karila felt a rending stab pierce her. The crimson light dimmed and for a few moments Karila lost consciousness.

And then a great archway shimmered in the darkness. A translucent form appeared, insubstantial as steam at first, yet slowly gaining definition. Karila saw eyes as silvery as a winter's frost as a tall, wraith-pale figure stepped through the archway.

It was another Drakhaoul, one whose chill glance made her tremble as it cast about, searching with a cold, penetrating intensity. And leaking into the jungle glade from the archway, came the shadows, billowing like dark smoke to stifle the light of the stars.

But not before Karila had seen the prone body lying sprawled beneath the Serpent Gate, the body of a boy, dark-skinned, with tumbled black hair, his life's blood staining the ancient stones of the altar.

*   *   *

For a moment, Oskar stared down at the limp body of the boy he had murdered. He saw the child's dead eyes staring up at him. He felt the stickiness of his blood on his shaking hands, his razor-sharp claws with which he had slit the boy's throat.

"Wh—what have I done?" he whispered. He began to gag, sickened to the core of his being.

A tall, glimmering figure materialized before him.

"*Za'afiel. Welcome, my brother,*" cried Sahariel exultantly.

The translucent daemon turned its cold gaze upon Oskar and he felt it pierce him through, searing away all the pain and burning guilt that tormented him until his mind was cleansed of all emotion.

A shiver of storm wind swept through the jungle. When it had passed, Za'afiel was no longer there.

A dazzling creature was winging into the clearing. Karila peeped out and saw that this Drakhaoul had a mane of hair and eyes of lion gold and he was carrying a girl in his arms.

"*Nilaihah!*" Sahariel strode out to greet him.

"Who can she be?" Karila wondered. The girl stared up at the two Drakhaouls; she seemed dazed with fear.

Sahariel stroked the girl's cheek, hooking one clawed fingertip beneath her chin and tipping her face up until he could stare into her eyes. "*So this is Aude,*" he said. "*But where is Giorgi?*"

"*This one fought like a little wildcat,*" said Nilaihah. "*I will return for Giorgi now.*" He took off again, etching a trail of light across the darkness, like a shooting star.

"What's happening?" sobbed Aude. "Why me?"

"Aude!" whispered Karila.

Aude looked up uncertainly and saw her. "I know you," she said. "You're Kari. I've dreamed about you. Is this a dream?"

"I only wish it was."

A crimson spear of light shot through Gavril's dreams and pierced him through.

"*The Eye,*" Khezef said. "*Sahariel has replaced Nagar's Eye.*"

"Are you sure?" This was all happening too soon.

"*Ahh.*" Gavril felt Khezef shudder. "*Za'afiel is free. Can't you feel the chill in the air?*"

Gavril opened his eyes and saw it was dawn. This far to the north, the sun rose late and set early as the winter drew in. Next to him, Kiukiu murmured in her sleep.

"*It's beginning. The Kindred are on the move.*"

Gavril raised himself on one elbow and gazed at Kiukiu drifting deep in sleep. He noted little details that he cherished: the dusting of freckles on her nose and cheekbones, the arching line of her thick, golden brows, the sensuous curve of her wide mouth.

He leaned over and kissed her.

"Good morning," she said, smiling sleepily at him through her disheveled hair.

"I have to go. One of Khezef's kindred has replaced the Eye."

"The Eye?" Her smile disappeared. "Oh, Gavril, why must it be you?" He saw fear in her eyes and knew that he was afraid too. For this parting would be the hardest to bear.

"Why must it be me?" he said, weighing each word, slowly fumbling toward an explanation. "Because I know I will have to pay for what I have done. I know I will have to live with myself and the knowledge of the atrocities I've committed until I die. I can't restore the lives I've taken . . . but I can try to stop it happening again, Kiukiu."

She flung her arms around him, clinging to him as if she would never let go. "Take care. Oh, please take care."

Gently, he unwound her arms from about him and kissed her again, with all the passion and regret that he could not put into words. Then he pushed open the tent flap and launched himself up into the misty Khitari morning.

Gavril let Khezef guide him, steering southward over the mountains of Azhkendir. Khezef was tense now, listening, all his senses alert to the slightest hint of attack.

"*Nilaihah is heading back to Smarna.*" Khezef said suddenly. "*And Belberith's child is in Smarna.*"

"Smarna?" Gavril echoed.

"*Enguerrand has lost all control of Nilaihah. Anyone who stands in his way will be destroyed.*"

Eugene had only left Erinaskoe a few hours ago but he could tell at once that all was far from well. His men were everywhere in the grounds, patrolling.

The ominous feeling growing stronger, he urged his horse up the winding drive toward the great house, leaving his escorts spurring their mounts on in a vain effort to keep pace with him. He had dismounted and was already running up the steps before they even reached the gravel drive.

"What's happened?" he cried, making for Astasia's rooms. "Where's my wife? My son?"

"The Emperor's back!" He heard the servants pronouncing his name in hushed voices. He pushed open the door to Astasia's bedchamber and stopped as a cold wind blew in his face from the gaping hole where the windows had been, setting all the drapes and shredded curtains billowing.

"What in God's name—?" he began, then saw the bloodstains on the blue-and-gold carpet. And an extraordinary feeling overcame him as a cold sweat broke out over his whole body. He just stood there, staring.

"Eugene?"

He turned and saw Astasia running toward him.

She was alive.

He caught her as she flung her arms about him and held her tight.

"Tasia, what's happened?"

"Our baby," she said into his shoulder. Then she looked up at him and he saw that her face was blotched with tears.

"He's not—" He did not want to say the word. Babies were frail creatures, especially in these first perilous weeks of life.

"Gone. *Stolen.*"

"What do you mean?"

"It looked like Andrei. It sounded like Andrei. But it took our baby and k—killed Valery." She started to sob, broken dry sobs that he could not bear to hear. "What will it do with Rostevan? He'll need feeding—and changing."

"*Adramelech.*" He heard Belberith pronounce the name. And he had believed Belberith to be still subdued, weakened by Kazimir's elixir. Eugene gripped his wife by the shoulders.

"Was it a Drakhaoul, Tasia?"

"It was like. But not—not a dragon."

"*Adramelech has assumed his true form.*"

"True form?"

"*He plans to open the Gate. Your child will be a sacrifice.*"

Eugene let out a cry of horror. The Drakhaoul planned to sacrifice Rostevan on Ty Nagar.

"Once Za'afiel is summoned, he will slay the Emperor's children and open the Gate to free the dread prince Nagazdiel . . ."

And if Frieda Hildegarde's interpretations were correct, once Nagar was free, all Seven would bring about the end of the world.

"Who are you talking to? Eugene, speak to me!" Astasia was touching his face, staring at him in alarm. "There's only the two of us here—isn't there?"

He gazed at her. "I'm going after it. But there's only one way I can do it, if I'm to save Rostevan in time." Though even now he could not be sure that his Drakhaoul was not in league with the others.

Astasia gazed back at him, a new, fierce light burning in her dark eyes. "Do what you must, Eugene. But get him back!"

"Belberith. I need your help." Eugene went to the ruined window and stood there with the wind gusting cold into the room.

"I understand." There was not the slightest note of reproach in Belberith's voice.

As Eugene flung his arms to the sky and stepped out into the void, the thought came to him suddenly that if Belberith wanted to punish him, he would let him fall and smash onto the terrace below.

And for an anguished heartbeat, he felt himself plunging helplessly down toward the stone steps. Then he felt Belberith's exultant joy at being released—a whirlwind that tore through his body and bore him upwards.

"I have been waiting, Eugene. Waiting for you to need me."

CHAPTER 45

"Do I have to sit still much longer?" Giorgi Vashteli swung his legs to and fro, kicking the chair legs with his heels.

"Nearly done, Giorgi," promised Elysia, working with swift strokes at the last of her sketches. The truth was, she was frustrated, having elicited little out of Nina's son in three portrait sittings other than the fact that he liked iced gingerbread, hated mathematics, and would rather be out flying his new kite than forced to be indoors.

Giorgi was a delicate-looking boy, pale and slender, with his mother's striking green eyes, framed by thick dark brows and lashes. Elysia was rather pleased with the studies she had done of him; she felt she had captured something of his otherworldly expression and the translucence of his skin.

The windows opened onto the balcony of the minister's villa. The Villa Vashteli perched high on the cliffs at the opposite end of the bay from Elysia's home. The steep rocks dropped away precipitately below the terraced garden and the views of the sea were breathtaking, even on a calm, autumnal day like today, when the horizon was hazed in sea mists.

"I've brought you some gingerbread," Elysia said. "Palmyre made it specially for you. If you just sit still another few minutes, you can have a piece."

"Is it iced?" he asked, frowning.

"Oh, yes. Palmyre makes delicious icing."

"But what flavor?"

Goodness, what a little tyrant, Elysia thought. "It's just plain white sugar icing."

"I hate lemon," said Giorgi vehemently.

"Why is that?" Elysia sensed there was more to this hatred than pure whim.

"Lemon barley water. Ugh. Mama makes me drink it when I'm sick. Lemon barley makes me remember being unwell."

Now we're getting somewhere. "And have you been ill recently, Giorgi?"

Giorgi pulled a face. "Since the winter. They sent me home from school."

"We're done, for now." Elysia laid down her sketching book and handed the gingerbread, wrapped in a clean piece of linen, to Giorgi, who unwrapped it and started munching eagerly. "Why did they send you home?"

"They said I was disturbing the other boys in the dormitory," said Giorgi, his mouth full of gingerbread.

"And how was that? Were you ill in the night?" asked Elysia, pretending to be busy with her charcoals and pencils.

"I had dreams. I shouted out in my sleep."

"They must have been nightmares to make you shout out so," she said softly. She was remembering another boy, with blue, dreamer's eyes, whom she had soothed when he woke, crying out in terror, in the small hours of the night. *Where are you now, dearest Gavril? I wonder what you're doing. You'd laugh if you could hear me, trying to coax out this young boy's hopes and fears. You'd do it so much better than I . . .*

"Nightmares?" Giorgi reached for a second piece of gingerbread and chewed thoughtfully. "Some were the best dreams ever. They were so good, I didn't want to wake up. I'd be playing. Playing with Kahukura on the beach. Kahukura's such a good friend . . ."

An imaginary dream-friend. Not surprising, really, Elysia thought, that a boy who has to spend long hours sick in bed invents a friend with whom he can have fun.

"But then *he* comes and we have to hide. And if *he's* angry, he makes horrible things happen."

"He?" echoed Elysia, beginning to wonder if the child had been abused by a master at the school. "Who is he?"

The gingerbread suddenly dropped from Giorgi's fingers. His face had gone pasty white and he was staring past Elysia's shoulder, out of the window.

"Giorgi?" Suddenly Elysia was worried. Was he having a fit? He seemed not to see or hear her. "Giorgi, what's wrong?" She went to him, putting her arms around his thin shoulders.

"N—no!" Giorgi whispered. He had gone rigid with fear. "Go away. Leave me alone!"

Elysia sensed that the sky was darkening. And it had been such a fine day, with not the slightest hint of clouds in the sky. She turned around to see what he was staring at.

A great, shadow-winged bird was flying swiftly toward the villa across the bay. A golden radiance emanated from its powerful wings.

"It looks just like . . ." murmured Elysia. "But it can't be . . ."

For the briefest of moments, she let herself hope that it was Gavril, home at last. And then she knew in her heart it was not her son.

"Nilaihah," said Giorgi. His eyes rolled upward in their sockets.

"Giorgi, can you hear me?" Elysia was supporting the boy. She tried to lift him in her arms, but he was too heavy for her.

Still the golden Drakhaon came on, alighting on the terrace. With one powerful sweep of its arm, it shattered the windows. Giorgi gave a high-pitched scream of terror. The fresh sea breeze blew in as it stepped into the room.

Elysia turned to face it, spreading her arms wide to shelter Giorgi. It looked like an angel, with its long locks of golden hair and its gilded wings. But its eyes were the slanted, serpent eyes of a Drakhaoul, and they stared at her with an expression of inhuman cruelty.

"*Give me the boy,*" it said.

"He doesn't want to go with you," she said quietly. All she had left was words with which to protect the child. And, although she had been terrified, she felt a sudden extraordinary sense of calm flood through her as she faced the daemon.

"*Out of my way.*" The daemon came toward her.

"Giorgi—run, *run*!" Elysia cried.

"I c—can't," sobbed the boy, clinging to her.

The gilded daemon grabbed Elysia, flinging her aside. She lost her hold on Giorgi as she fell. Winded, bruised, she struggled up to catch hold of the boy once more, clinging to his legs with all her strength.

"Elysia!" screamed the boy. Surely someone must have heard the noise and would be coming to their aid.

"Let him go!"

The daemon pointed his taloned finger at her. The room lit up with the sudden glow of power. A dazzle of golden light blinded her—then a massive force hit her in the chest, lifting her, hurling her right across the room.

The last thing Elysia saw was the daemon sweeping the child up in his arms and unfurling his powerful wings as he launched himself into the air.

Pavel Velemir had returned to Smarna. He suspected that the Francians had put a price on his head but he didn't care. The news he brought for Minister Vashteli from Muscobar heralded an end to the Commanderie's tyranny. For Ruaud de Lanvaux was dead, Enguerrand was rumored to have fled the country, and Queen Aliénor, who had never approved of the Commanderie's influence on her son, had commanded that the order be disbanded. But to be safe, he left Rafael Lukan and the Kornelis at the University of Mirom, as the Chancellor was an old friend of his mother's.

And now, riding Capriole from the Korneli's stables, he was on the high cliff road toward the Villa Vashteli. He was whistling, his head filled with thoughts of Raïsa. The shared danger had drawn them closer together. Walking through the Water Gardens by the Nieva at dusk, he had suddenly confessed his feelings for her, and she had turned to him, kissing him with a fervor that had made his blood sing. The next moment, they were discussing wedding plans.

Pavel had nearly reached the villa when the sky suddenly darkened. And it had been a fine afternoon, the autumn sun muted through a gauzy sea haze, yet still pleasantly mild for the end of the year.

Capriole gave a nervous whinny and began to jitter about, turning his head this way and that, refusing to budge.

"What's the matter?" Pavel dismounted, gripping the reins tightly, and tried to soothe the horse, patting it and whispering reassuringly.

Lightning flashed—and with it came the smash of breaking glass.

Capriole reared up and it took all Pavel's strength to hold on to the reins and stop him from bolting.

"A lightning strike? Without thunder?"

A woman's screams tore the air. Lightning lit up the sky again—and the screams stopped abruptly.

Pavel was not easily alarmed, but he felt his whole body go cold. He let go of Capriole's reins and began to run toward the villa.

Just as he reached the entrance, an inexplicable feeling of terror overwhelmed him. Looking up into the sky, he saw—but no, it couldn't be!—an angel flying away across the bay on great golden wings. And clutched to the angel's breast was a child: Giorgi Vashteli.

A golden lightning bolt shivered through the sky.

"What was that?" Gavril had been flying for so many hours, he had lost track of time.

"*Nilaihah.*"

A second shimmer of gold briefly lit up the sky. And this time Gavril felt the lightning, a shooting pain in his breast, as if it had pierced him to the heart. The steady beating of his wings faltered.

"*We're too late,*" cried Khezef. "*Nilaihah has taken the child.*"

The wide crescent of Vermeille Bay lay ahead in the distance.

"How can we be too late? How can you be so sure?" Did this mean the pursuit must go on? He was tired already; he needed to rest. And then he thought of the Villa Andara. It was so long since he had seen his mother that he had a sudden yearning to go home and rest, even if only for an hour or two. He would sit on the terrace with her and drink tea in the last of the afternoon sun. She would show him her latest painting and ask his opinion. She would chide him affectionately about the length of his hair. She wouldn't stare at his changed body as if he were some fairground curiosity. And he would feel relaxed and at ease, forgetting for a brief while the growing chaos spreading throughout Eugene's empire . . . and beyond.

Pavel ran into the terraced garden and gazed out across the bay. But the angel had already vanished into the rising sea mist. Pavel turned around, utterly bewildered, to look up at the villa and saw the gaping, blackened hole in the wall where the windows of the salon had been.

"That was *not* an angel." And the more he thought about it, the more the creature he had seen reminded him of the Drakhaon of Azhkendir.

He used the thick branches of the wisteria to swing himself up onto the balcony and climbed over the balustrade. From inside he thought he could hear quiet, terrified sobbing.

"Is anyone there? Are you all right?" He stepped over the rubble and shattered glass and went into the salon.

A woman lay motionless on the floor. One of Nina's maidservants stood over her, weeping softly. She looked up fearfully as Pavel appeared and then burst out, "Oh, Secretary Velemir, I think—I think she's dead!"

"Nina?" And then, as Pavel came closer, he saw not the dark hair of Nina Vashteli, but the auburn curls of Elysia Andar. "Oh no. Not Madame Andar." He stared down at her still body, not knowing what to do.

And at that moment, the sky blackened again. Spinning around, he saw the silhouette of a winged figure alighting on the balcony, shadow-dark against the daylight. The maid gave a little cry and fainted away.

But there was no misty golden aura about this angel; it glimmered blue, like a starry night.

"Pavel? Pavel Velemir?" it said and the voice was Gavril Andar's.

Gavril saw his mother lying on the floor and knew in his heart that she was dead. Yet he went to her and gently lifted her in his arms.

"Mother?" he said. His voice began to tremble. "M—mother?" Her head drooped heavily against his shoulder. She would never answer him again. Slowly he laid her back down and kissed her forehead, stroking the errant auburn strands away from her face so that they should not trouble her.

"What were you doing here, Mother?" Tears spilled from his eyes, dropping onto her body. He could see now the black scorch mark staining the cream silk of the dress where Nilaihah's fire bolt had stopped her heart. Such a small mark—but how lethal the power behind it. "Why were you here?"

"She was doing sketches for a portrait." Pavel Velemir picked up the sheets that lay scattered about the room.

Gavril just knelt over Elysia's body, weeping.

"It took Nina's son," Pavel was telling him, and he could not take in what he was saying. "That creature took Giorgi."

"Wh—what?" Gavril slowly raised his head. Khezef had brought him here, following Nilaihah's trail.

"Nilaihah has Belberith's child. And Belberith is coming."

"Belberith is coming here?" Gavril began to understand what Khezef was saying.

"The Emperor wants to speak with you."

"Shall I get you a brandy, Gavril?" Pavel said shakily. "I could do with one myself."

Gavril forced himself to ignore the Drakhaoul voices in his head and answer Pavel. "No brandy, Pavel." He could not take his eyes off his mother's body. She looked so peaceful and so . . . absent. The bright, animated, loving spirit that had nurtured and cherished him had fled.

"Forgive me, Mother." He rose and tried to compose himself. "Pavel," he said, "I have to go after Giorgi. Could you—could you see to it that she is taken home? Palmyre will need help arranging the funeral." He felt ashamed at having to ask Pavel to take over what, by rights, was his filial duty. He wanted to see that Elysia was properly laid to rest, but if he didn't act immediately . . .

Pavel had helped himself to brandy from the crystal decanter; he wiped the back of his hand over his mouth and nodded. "I'll see to it that everything is taken care of. With all the respect that a painter of her talents merits."

"Bichvinta Point." This time Gavril recognized Belberith's powerful voice quite clearly.

"We'll be there."

Gavril launched himself out from the shattered window, powering up into the air. He felt nothing but a blind rage and a burning hunger for revenge. Nilaihah would pay.

CHAPTER 46

"Some fool's gone and opened a door to the Realm of Shadows," Malusha said to Lady Iceflower as the eerie wind moaned around the rooftops of Azhgorod. "Those aren't stormclouds. That's shadow escaping."

The snow owls clustered closer together on the roof of Lord Stoyan's mansion. Malusha hurried back indoors to the kitchen, where Stavyomir lay asleep in his crib, Lady Iceflower following.

"Brace yourself, my lady," she said, placing the strongest ward she knew about the room, one that drained much of her spirit energy. "This could be our hardest battle yet."

The lone figure of a child was wandering along the lightless shore. From time to time he stopped, gazing fearfully around him, clutching his hands across his chest to keep out the cold.

"Where am I?" he whispered. "What is this place? What am I doing here?"

Kiukiu woke with a start. "Who are *you*?" she whispered to the boy she had seen in her dreams. Had there been another sacrifice? Outside she could hear the tethered horses whinnying restlessly.

She wrapped herself in a blanket and poked her head out of the tent flap.

Chinua had been keeping watch by the embers of the fire; she could just see him silhouetted against the pale eastern sky. He was patting Alagh and whispering calming words as the wild-eyed geld-ing tugged at his tether rope, straining to break free.

"Something's coming, Chinua," she said, "isn't it?" Even sturdy Harim was agitated and although she murmured soothingly to him and stroked his shaggy mane, he kept jerking his head away.

"The horses can sense it."

On the far horizon, she thought she glimpsed a shadowy storm-cloud emerging from the darkness, hurtling toward them at tremen-dous speed.

"It can't be Linnaius, can it?"

And then she began to shiver uncontrollably. The temperature dropped. Against the grey dawn sky, the shadowy cloud emanated an icy brilliance. She had felt this intense cold before.

"Za'afiel," she cried. "Why has he come here?"

She felt eyes of silver frost staring at her as the shadowy Drakhaoul came on toward them, flooding her veins with crystals of ice. She grabbed hold of Chinua to stay upright as Za'afiel swept low overhead, making directly for the royal tent at the very heart of the encampment.

"Bayar!" Kiukiu heard terrified cries and, gathering up her blanket around her, ran into the encampment. "He's looking for Bayar!"

"*Look out.*" Chinua pulled her to one side just as the khan's horses broke free from their tethers and came stampeding past in ter-ror. "It's too dangerous here, Kiukirilya," he said as the khan's guards chased after the horses. "They're out of control. You could get crushed."

Kiukiu hardly heard him. "I have to protect Bayar," she insisted, hastening on. She had made a promise. She had no idea how she could honor it, for what she had glimpsed overhead was a Drakhaoul without a host, but she was determined she would try.

The icy wind continued to whirl through the camp, so that she had to put her head down, one arm raised to protect her face, and battle against its force to stay upright.

The khan's great tent, split open like a pomegranate, revealed its rich scarlet hangings within. Khan Vachir rose up before her, one hand extended to fend her off.

"*On your knees, Spirit Singer!*" His once-dark eyes gleamed, pale as frost. His hair, no longer black, streamed behind him like tatters of snow clouds, grey as a winter blizzard. The nails on his outstretched hand glittered like icicle spikes.

She felt herself borne slowly backward by the force of his power, the breath knocked from her lungs. When the khan let his hand drop, she fell to the ground. Beside her, she saw Chinua collapse too, heard him panting for air, as if he too was winded.

"Father, what's happening?" Prince Bayar came out from Lady Orqina's tent, rubbing sleep from his eyes.

"Run, Prince Bayar!" Kiukiu managed to wheeze out a warning. She closed her eyes, silently calling to Koropanga. "*Warn him!*"

"*Come here, my child.*" Khan Vachir turned to Bayar, beckoning.

"No!" Kiukiu began to crawl forward. "Don't touch him, Za'afiel! Let him be!"

But Vachir had already enfolded the boy in his arms. Silvered shadow-wings unfurled from his shoulders. He began to rise into the air, creating a whirling dust storm beneath his feet.

Captain Cheren came running up. At the sight of his royal master ascending on beating wings, with the prince clutched tight in his arms, he let out a yell of astonishment.

"Stop him, Captain!" Kiukiu cried, her mouth clogged with dust, as other soldiers hurried toward them, bows at the ready.

"Fire on our khan?"

"Khan Vachir has been possessed by a powerful daemon." Kiukiu heard herself gabbling in desperation.

"And if we hit Prince Bayar?"

He was right and she knew it; the risk to Bayar was too great. She struck the frost-hard ground with her clenched fist in frustration. She had been utterly powerless to stop Za'afiel. The dark stormcloud that half cloaked the ascending Drakhaoul streaked away southward across the sky, a rippling silver-grey dragon whose slanted eyes glinted like lightning.

Lady Orqina came running out of her tent, her face unpainted, her hair loose about her shoulders. She pointed accusingly at Kiukiu, speaking very fast in a high, strained voice in her own tongue.

"What is she saying?" Kiukiu shrank closer to Chinua.

"She says you failed to protect her son. Captain Cheren must arrest you."

Kiukiu began to back away, shaking her head. The guards

encircled them; she could smell their sweat and their rancid morning breath. She remembered how brutally they had punished Unegen the Fox; she could still recall his dying screams.

"Tell them, Chinua, tell them that I need another chance. One more chance!" Her words sounded so hollow, so foolish, even in her own ears. Tears glittering in her eyes, Lady Orqina shook her head. When she spoke again, her voice was harsh.

"Lady Orqina says that troubles flock to you like crows to carrion. You have brought nothing but ill luck to the encampment. Now she has lost her lord *and* her son."

"Can't you make her understand?" Kiukiu cried. "The trouble was here, long before we came. Khan Vachir is Artamon's descendant. The daemon was drawn to his blood."

Lady Orqina's only response was to turn her back on them and stalk away into her tent. Captain Cheren gripped Kiukiu by the arms; two of his subordinates took hold of Chinua.

"There is a terrible darkness coming!" Kiukiu shouted after Lady Orqina. "Kill us—and who will be left to protect you? Tell them, Chinua!"

Chinua flung back his head and let out a chilling howl. Kiukiu blinked as the two guards suddenly found themselves grappling with a grey-and-white wolf. Sharp teeth snapped; yellow eyes gleamed in the morning light and Chinua went bounding away.

The archers raised their bows and loosed arrows after him but Chinua, fleet of foot, darted from side to side, disappearing among the tents. The soldiers ran after him.

Captain Cheren bound Kiukiu's hands behind her back and pushed her away from the ruins of the royal tent.

What will they do with me? And who will speak for me now that Chinua has gone?

"What in God's name is the meaning of this?" A woman's voice could be heard outside the mansion, rancid with annoyance. "Why is the roof covered with those horrible birds? Tell the men to get rid of them, Ulyana. They'll leave a disgusting mess."

"M—my lady Lilias?" stammered Ulyana. "I didn't expect you back tonight."

"The mother," Malusha muttered to Lady Iceflower, "the negligent mother. Why now?" The owl let out a sharp cry, ruffling her feathers. Her head swiveled around, her golden eyes wild. "You can sense it coming closer, can't you?" Malusha placed herself in front of Stavyomir's cradle.

The cold, dark presence came sweeping across the city of Azhgorod, making straight toward them, as ruthless as a winter blizzard.

The snow owls rose up in a shrieking cloud as it reached the mansion. Malusha braced herself. She felt strangely calm now that it was here.

The timbered kitchen door was torn off its hinges. A tall Drakhaoul with cloudy hair that glittered like frost stood in the doorway. A wind whirled around it, deathly chill, howling into the kitchen and tossing plates, bowls, glasses onto the floor.

In a second the Drakhaoul's snow-silvered eyes had surveyed the scene. It stepped forward, one icicle-clawed hand outstretched toward the cradle. And only then did Malusha see that it already held a child clasped to its breast, a black-haired boy whose face was contorted with terror.

Lady Iceflower let out a high scream of rage and swooped toward the Drakhaoul's face, claws extended.

With one powerful sweep of its hand, the Drakhaoul flung Iceflower to the far side of the kitchen. Malusha flinched as she heard the thud as the owl's body smashed into the wall.

"You've me to deal with now," she said quietly. She raised her hands, weaving the strongest ward she knew, singing it defiantly with all the full force of her guslyar voice.

"Warriors of the House of Arkhel, help me protect this child, the last of your bloodline." Golden eyes glimmered in the night. The owls were massing outside. They were her last hope.

Down they came, in a blizzard of wings. The Drakhaoul hesitated. Then with one dismissive gesture it loosed a single burst of silver fire.

Malusha staggered, feeling the power of the blast like a blade of ice through her own heart. Bloodied feathers came drifting down in a sad snowstorm. She tried to raise her hand to stop the Drakhaoul but it would not move. She tried to cry out but no sound issued from her throat. Paralyzed and dumb, she watched helplessly as the Drakhaoul reached into the cradle and plucked out Stavyomir.

Then it turned for the doorway and launched itself into the

darkness. The last Malusha heard was Stavyomir's bewildered yell fading into the night.

"My . . . little lord. I . . . failed you . . ."

"Grandma!" screamed Kiukiu into the blackness of the Khitari night.

"Silence, witch!" said one of the khan's men who was standing guard over her.

She hardly heard him. She knew only that the bright soul who had cherished her had been suddenly extinguished. She sagged against the ropes that bound her to the post, sobbing her heart out. "Oh, Grandma . . ."

The dogs in the camp heard her and added their howls to hers. Or was that the eerie baying of wolves? Blinking her tears away, she raised her head and listened. The guards were listening too; she could see they were on edge all of a sudden.

Hundreds of yellow eyes gleamed. They were surrounded by wolves. The khan's men seized torches and began to swing them at the wolves. In the confusion, Kiukiu saw a large grey-and-white wolf coming straight toward her.

"Chinua?"

The wolf began to gnaw at her bonds. He tugged at the rope with his teeth and, as it began to unravel, she fell to her knees.

"Hurry," growled Chinua over the shouts of the men as they tried to beat back the wolf pack. "This way."

She stumbled after him in the darkness; he was leading her down to the lakeshore. A little rowboat lay on the shingle.

"To the island," he said. "They'll never dare follow us there."

"What was it? Why did it steal my baby?" Lilias paced the hall of Lord Stoyan's mansion.

Ulyana, grey-faced with shock, could only repeat, "Drakhaon. It was—the Drakhaon."

Lilias stopped and slapped her face. "Are you saying that Lord Gavril took Stavyomir?" Her anxiety turned to anger. So this was how Gavril Nagarian chose to get his revenge on her! "Clan wars have been started for less!" The sound of the servants hammering and cleaning up the ruined kitchen was making Lilias's head throb.

"What in God's name has been going on?" Boris Stoyan had returned from a bear hunt in the mountains. Lilias flew to him, winding her arms about him, stroking his bearded cheek.

"Boris, the Drakhaon has kidnapped Stavyomir."

"What?" Lord Stoyan shook his head in disbelief.

"Please send your men to get him back. For my sake."

"To Kastel Drakhaon in this foul weather?"

"You're not afraid of him, are you, Boris?" asked Lilias slyly.

"It's still as dark as pitch out there. And it's turned bitter cold; the winter blizzards have come too soon." Then he looked into her eyes, relenting. "But if the Drakhaon has stolen a child . . ."

CHAPTER 47

Karila's keen ears caught the approaching beat of wings and, gazing up into the dazzling sun, she saw a new daemon approaching. This one glimmered with the darker colors of twilight. The air around him had a taint of shadow.

He was flying slowly, carefully as though carrying something fragile and, as he alighted, Karila understood why. He was carrying a tiny baby in his arms and the baby was crying, a thin, sobbing cry that wrung her heart.

"Who is that baby? Is it Stavyomir?" she asked, remembering Mahina's mortal child. But this baby was so small it looked almost a newborn. Although Karila had not seen many newborn babies, there was something about the way it cried and flung out its little arms that told her it badly needed its mother.

"*Can't you keep it quiet, Adramelech?*" snapped Sahariel. "*I can't take much more of that damnable racket.*" Karila cringed; she had come to know that tone of voice in the past days only too well. It usually presaged one of Oskar's violent outbursts.

Adramelech gave a shrug. "*It must be hungry,*" he said.

"*Then why didn't you bring its mother as well? Do you want the little runt to starve to death? If heatstroke doesn't carry it off first?*"

Adramelech made a helpless little gesture of his taloned hands.

"Give me the baby," Karila said.

"*Who is this?*" Adramelech demanded over the baby's yells.

"Give me the baby," she said again.

"*Princess Karila,*" said Sahariel. "*Let her hold the baby. Because you're going to go and find it a wet nurse.*"

"And why the deuce should I do that?"

"*You were charged with bringing it here alive. Find a way.*"

"*Very well, then.*" Adramelech approached Karila and handed over the cross, wailing bundle. "*This is your brother,*" he said. "*He's called Rostevan.*"

"M—my brother?" Karila nearly dropped the baby in surprise. She braced herself, putting her back against a large stone for support. He was wet through, he was almost exhausted with crying and hunger. Yet, as she tried to extract his thrashing limbs from the outer confining layers of shawl, she saw him pause in midyell and take a swift look at her. Blue eyes gazed into hers.

"I'm Kari," she said, forgetting her own thirst and fear for a moment. "I'm your sister." And then he began to wail again and she knew that she must do everything she possibly could to keep him alive in this heat. Off came the shawl; next she began to peel off his wet nightgown. Still he yelled, and there was a heartrending tremor in his voice now that betrayed his outrage and desperate neediness. "There, there," she murmured to him, as he banged his heavy head against her shoulder.

As Adramelech flew away, she limped out of the burning sun into the shade of a tree.

"*Stay where I can see you!*" snarled Sahariel. After a while, he began to pace the clearing again, pausing to glance up at the stone serpent wreathed around the archway. Heat shimmered off his scarlet scales.

"I'm very thirsty," Karila said again, trying to make herself heard above her brother's yelling.

"*And where does her little royal highness think I'm going to find her something refreshing to drink in this jungle wilderness?*"

"There must be a stream somewhere nearby." Karila was feeling faint; she had not eaten in many hours and her head was throbbing with the baby's interminable crying.

"*Damn it all!*" Sahariel leaped into the air. "*Don't move,*" he shouted down. "*I can see you from up here.*"

"He's forgotten," Karila whispered to Rostevan, "that I'm crippled." She closed her eyes, leaning back against the tree trunk. Rostevan had exhausted himself with crying and lay back against her, his eyes closed. She must stay strong to protect her little brother. That was what Papa would want her to do.

"Papa, where are you?" she asked softly. "Why don't you come and rescue us?"

Bichvinta Point was a promontory well-known to sailors, farther down the coast from Vermeille Bay. A great grove of black pines stretched down to the edge of the sandy shore and as Gavril approached, he could catch their sharp resinous smell. Eugene must have chosen this meeting place on purpose; the point overlooked the Southern Ocean, facing toward the far south and the uncharted waters of the distant Azure Ocean.

As Gavril descended, he felt Belberith's aura growing stronger. Soon he spotted a tall winged figure standing on the precipitate edge of the point. Now he realized why Belberith had once been called the Warrior of the Seven: proud head raised, wide, muscular shoulders, great wings furled, and an air of watchful stillness, all suggested a lethal killer poised, ready to strike.

"Here I am, Lord Emperor." Gavril landed beside him on the grassy cliff.

The proud head turned to him and Gavril saw that the Emperor's eyes were red with weeping. "They've stolen my children. Both my children."

"Both?" Gavril repeated, not fully taking in what Eugene was telling him. He was still in shock himself.

"My son. My baby son. I have to get him back. If anything happens to him, it—it will kill her."

Astasia's firstborn child. At last the significance of the Emperor's words began to penetrate Gavril's despair. Astasia was a mother; she had a child, a son.

"Help me, Nagarian. This is all my fault. I released these monsters. I have to destroy them, before they—" The Emperor broke off, choking on the words, as if unable to say what he feared the Drakhaouls would do. "I want to put things to rights again, but I don't know where to begin. Tell me what to do."

Gavril gazed at Eugene. Since Elysia's death, his mind had been full of fury and confusion. He had not been able to think of anything but revenge. But now, if he had heard right, the Emperor was asking him for advice. He cleared his throat, trying to steady his voice. "Adramelech, Nilaihah, and Sahariel have been taking children. Nilaihah abducted Giorgi Vashteli and killed my mother when she tried to stop him."

"Your mother? Elysia is dead? I—" Eugene seemed at a loss for words. "I'm so sorry, Nagarian. These daemons have left nothing but a trail of death in their wake." And then he seemed to understand what Gavril had said. "They've been taking other children? Oh, dear God, is that what they intend?"

"What do you know?" Gavril demanded.

" 'Once Za'afiel is summoned, he will slay the Emperor's children and open the Gate to free the dread prince Nagazdiel,' " quoted Eugene. "Doctor Hildegarde's researches unearthed this ancient warning from Artamon's time." And then he looked up, as if making a supreme effort to master his feelings. "Belberith has played me false once before. Is he part of this conspiracy? Dare I trust him? Or will he betray me too? And, damn it all, can I trust you and your daemon?"

Kiukiu patted the wolf's shaggy coat. "You've risked your life for me again, Chinua." She was still shaking and numb from the shock of Malusha's death.

"I was in your grandmother's debt. She did my family a great service, many years ago."

A chill, dry wind shivered across the steppes. Kiukiu shuddered, sensing that it blew from another world. "It's growing darker, Chinua."

"*Kiukirilya . . .*" She started up, certain she had heard the children's voices on the wind, calling her.

"Chinua," she said, "what can I do?"

"Do what you were born to do," he said simply. "You are the last of the Spirit Singers. Now is the time to use your gift. Sing, Kiukirilya, and I will keep guard."

"Why is it so dark?" the Emperor cried to Gavril. "Is there a storm coming?"

Gavril gazed up into the heavens. "This is no storm. Look at the way those clouds are moving." The darkness was uncoiling, like a nest of shadowy serpents spilling out across the sky.

"My God," said Eugene, his voice very quiet, "what does it mean? I've never seen the like before."

But as Gavril watched the coils of dark mist spreading and blotting out the light of day, he remembered that he had seen such a phenomenon once before.

"This is coming from the Serpent Gate," he said. "There's no time to waste."

Eugene turned to look at him, his eyes suddenly alight. He clapped Gavril on the shoulder, and said, "Who'd have thought it? You and I, together against the Kindred!"

And before Gavril could reply, he had leaped into the air and Belberith was wheeling above him on outspread wings of green.

"Khezef!" Gavril followed, bursting into flight as Belberith darted off.

"Do you remember the way?" Gavril shouted after him.

"Just steer into the heart of the darkness!" Eugene shouted back.

"Coconut milk for her royal highness."

Karila opened her eyes. Sahariel was back and he was holding out a large, strange fruit with a hairy husk. She shrank away.

"Don't tell me you've never seen a coconut!"

She shook her head. She did not like the look of the hairy object at all.

He punctured it once, twice, with his sharp talons and tipped it up to his mouth. A pale liquid dripped out and he licked his lips, nodding. "Sweet. Refreshing." He handed it to her.

Karila tried to lift the heavy coconut in her free hand, but she was too weak. He took it back and held it to her lips, letting the milk splash into her dehydrated mouth. And he was right; it was good. So very good that, had her eyes not been dry with heat, she would have cried and not cared that he saw her. After gulping down the sweet milk, she looked into his fiery eyes—and saw that little traces of the man she remembered as Oskar Alvborg had begun to reappear.

"Thank you," she whispered. "Thank you, Oskar."

Then she heard the sound of distant, terrified screams. Sahariel jumped up, ready to attack.

Adramelech flew down into the clearing. He was carrying a dark-skinned young woman. When she saw Sahariel, her screams only grew louder and she dropped to the ground where she lay trembling and speaking very fast in a tongue Karila had never heard before.

Poor woman, Karila thought. *She must think she's going to be sacrificed by the Drakhaouls.*

"Princess," said Sahariel in weary tones, "show her the baby."

Karila limped toward the cowering woman. "I know you can't understand me," she said, "but please help us. My brother's hungry." She held out the squirming baby, now dressed only in his stained vest. The woman ventured a glance at her. Her dark eyes reminded Karila suddenly, poignantly, of Tilua's. "Please," begged Karila again, "or he'll die. I can't let him die."

The woman pointed at the baby, then at herself.

"Yes, yes," said Karila, nodding encouragingly.

The woman looked fearfully at the two daemons, then back at Rostevan, who had begun to whimper again. Was she checking to see he was mortal and not a daemon child? Karila wondered. Then, tentatively, the woman reached out to take him from Karila.

"Oh thank you, thank you," cried Karila. "Come and sit here in the shade." She gestured to the tree where she had been sitting. The woman settled herself beneath the tree and put the hungry baby to her breast. Karila looked over to where Adramelech stood beneath the Serpent Gate, watching them. His expression was unreadable.

"Thank you, Adramelech," she said fervently. She meant it. And it struck her that he looked less like a Drakhaoul now than when she had first seen him; she could almost glimpse the face of a young man emerging from beneath the unearthly glitter of dusky scales.

Who are you? she wondered, but dared not ask aloud. *And why have you stolen my brother?*

A golden light suffused the clearing. Karila realized that she must have dozed off for a few minutes.

A third daemon-Drakhaoul stood before the Serpent Gate. And a boy stood beside him, a boy she thought she recognized, although the dazzling light emanating from the third daemon made it hard to see clearly. She rose unsteadily to her feet.

The boy was gazing around him. She wondered why he had not tried to run away. And then, as she tottered forward, she saw that the golden daemon had one hand clamped on his shoulder, restraining him. He saw her, and cried out, "Karila!"

She recognized him now, by his green eyes and shock of dark hair.

"Giorgi? Is it you?" She had only seen him in dreams and it was so strange to meet him at last. *If only this could be a dream,* she thought.

"What have they done to you, Kari?" he asked in the common tongue as she limped slowly toward him. "Are you hurt?"

"No," she said sadly, "this is how I really am." For he had only met her in dreams, and there she was as fleet-footed and straight-backed as any normal child.

And then a spasm passed across Giorgi's pallid face and he put one hand to his mouth, retching. Nilaihah let go of him as he bent over and vomited. Karila turned her head away. She thought he might feel ashamed to have been sick in front of a girl. She also felt more than a little queasy herself. It would not do for them both to be ill.

"I'm sorry," he whispered, wiping his mouth on his sleeve.

"Come and sit over here," she whispered back, beckoning him under the tree where the woman was nursing Rostevan.

"*Where's the Eye, Sahariel?*" demanded Nilaihah.

"*You prepare the child, I'll replace the Eye.*" Karila heard Sahariel revert to that dismissive, callous tone he had used so often in Swanholm. It made her shiver to remember and she huddled closer to Giorgi, feeling even more afraid.

Adramelech was just standing, staring at them. "*Suppose Khezef was right. Just suppose there is another way—*"

Nilaihah caught hold of him by the throat, dragging his face close to his own. "*Is that your host speaking, Adramelech?*" His golden eyes probed Adramelech's. "*Look at you. You're losing control over him. With every mortal feeling you admit to, every doubt, every fear, you lose a little more of your powers.*"

Adramelech glared back.

"*Why do you take any notice of Khezef?*" said Sahariel. "*He betrayed us once, he'll do it again. That's why we must eliminate him. As we agreed.*"

"*They're planning to hurt you, Khezef.*" Karila closed her eyes, seeking him with her mind, hoping he could somehow hear her warning.

Astasia stood at the broken window, gazing out. She had been standing there for hours, staring at nothing. Her arms ached with emptiness. Her breasts were sore and heavy with milk. And even the sky seemed to mirror her desolate, desperate mood, fast filling with dark clouds.

She could hear the servants hurrying to light the lamps and candles as the light faded. The storm seemed to be sucking the daylight from the sky. All the colors were dimming, turning the rich autumnal colors in the park to ashen grey.

"My baby," she whispered. "Where are you?"

The darkness suddenly rippled in front of Karila and a fourth Drakhaoul appeared in the clearing. Its body was silver, almost translucent, with jagged hair like icicles. In one arm it carried a baby, in the other, a proud-faced, dark-haired boy. And when it turned toward her, she saw with a jolt that its eyes gleamed silver too, like the eyes of Kaspar Linnaius.

"*Za'afiel—at last!*" cried Sahariel.

"*All the royal children are here.*" The silver eyes betrayed no hint of emotion; they were utterly cold and expressionless. "*Now it's time for them to die.*"

CHAPTER 48

The sky seethed with shadows and the Azure Ocean far below had turned as black as ink. All Gavril could see in the darkness was Belberith's phosphorescent shimmer beside him. And when he looked down at the black sea beneath him, he could see a radiant trail, red as blood.

A foul volcanic odor began to drift upward. Another glow, almost as fiery-bright as the beacon cast by Nagar's Eye, appeared in the gloom—a red-hot incandescence, boiling up from a rift in the mountain's crust.

"The fire cones," murmured Gavril, remembering Zakhar's last journey. "We're near."

Eugene suddenly darted ahead. "I'll distract the Kindred; you destroy the Eye."

"But what about your children?" Gavril tried to match his speed, though Belberith, as before, was still the swifter and more powerful of the two Drakhaouls.

"Just take out the Eye, Nagarian."

"Damn it!" Gavril resented the fact that even there, Eugene could not forget he was Emperor and was commanding him to follow his orders, as if he were his subordinate.

"Besides . . . I have a score to settle with Sahariel."

As they approached the source of the darkness, the old enmities had begun to reassert themselves. Belberith's eyes crackled with green fire. This was where they had dueled before and he had nearly died.

"Old scores can wait." Gavril could sense that Nagar's insidious influence had begun to infect his consciousness—and it was taking all his willpower to counter it. "Eugene—can't you feel what's happening to us? Nagar's poison is affecting us, turning us against each other. We must seal the Serpent Gate first. We'll need all our strength to do it—and they'll try every trick they know to stop us."

Eugene fell silent, skimming low across the surface of the inky sea. "Very well," he said at length. "We'll do this together. And if one of us falls, the other must finish it."

There would only be a brief moment to assess the situation below. And if the children were being held hostage, as Gavril suspected, the Kindred might well use them as shields.

"*Where is Karila, Khezef? Can you still sense her?*"

"*Down there!*" cried Khezef suddenly.

Gavril dived, swooping down through layer upon layer of choking dark fog, Eugene swiftly following, heading straight toward the place where the darkness swirled most impenetrably. Thicker than smoke, the snaking tendrils wound about them as they descended. By contrast, the Eye's crimson radiance seemed to be growing more intense, swelling to illuminate the whole clearing.

"Papa, Papa!" It was a child's voice, shrill with fear. A fair-haired girl stumbled into the clearing below them, her arms desperately raised, as though begging them to rescue her.

"No, Kari!"

Gavril heard Eugene's anguished cry as a dazzling flicker of scarlet darted out, scooping up the child in its arms. Next moment, the Drakhaoul was hovering directly above the Serpent Gate, Karila dangling in front of the stone serpent's glowing third eye.

Gavril halted, horrified. How could he destroy the Eye now without harming Karila?

"*Sahariel,*" Khezef said quietly, "*let my child go.*"

"*Is that what you really want, Khezef?*" asked Sahariel, his voice sly and mocking.

"Oskar Alvborg." Eugene's challenge rang out, cutting through the smirched air like a trumpet call. "Leave my daughter out of this. Your quarrel is with me. Let's settle it now."

"The Gate, Eugene!" Gavril cried out. Had the Emperor forgotten their plan so soon? If they didn't work together, they would fail.

"So you want my empire, do you, Alvborg?" Eugene was coming

steadily closer. And he looked every inch the daemon-warrior, tall and muscular, his broad shoulders braced, his body armored with scales of green and copper. "Then fight me for it. Fight me now."

"Papa," said Karila again, so faintly, so imploringly that Gavril could hardly hear her.

"It will be my pleasure," said Oskar Alvborg. He was smiling. "But we have other business to conclude first."

And suddenly he let go of Karila. She fell, with a high, keening scream that stopped suddenly, abruptly, as she hit the stone plinth.

"*Ahh!*" Khezef gave a breathless cry. Gavril felt the Drakhaoul's power faltering, waning. He could see Karila sprawled on the sacrificial stone beneath him, her fair hair and pale skin tinted bloodred by the light of Nagar's Eye that glared down on her.

She wasn't struggling anymore. She lay still, her once-white frock tattered and filthy. And a little thread of blood began to trickle out from beneath her head.

Eugene had flung himself forward in a vain effort to catch his daughter. Now he crouched over her protectively, stroking her hair, saying her name brokenly again and again.

Sahariel slowly descended until he stood over Eugene in front of the Serpent Gate.

"Innocent blood." A golden incandescence lit the clearing as a Drakhaoul with the face of an angel came out of the gloom. "At last. Our waiting is over." His hands were clamped on the shoulders of a boy and a girl; both seemed to be in a trance, staring glazedly ahead, as if they were oblivious to the extraordinary events that were unraveling before him.

"Nilaihah." Gavril recognized the honeyed tones of King Enguerrand's Drakhaoul. Was the boy Giorgi Vashteli, the child his own mother had died trying to protect? And who was the girl?

"It's time." Now he heard the deep, somber voice of Adramelech as the third Drakhaoul appeared, carrying a baby.

"*Khezef, what do they mean to do?*" Gavril's eyes kept straying back to the sacrificial stone—and to Eugene, protectively shielding Karila's broken body.

"*They mean to kill them all.*" Was Khezef weeping? Could a Drakhaoul feel grief, as he did now? "*They all have Artamon's blood, and the seal that holds Nagar in the Realm of Shadows will only be broken with the shedding of that blood.*"

"They mean to kill the children? Even the baby?" Gavril felt sickened to the core of his being at such an obscene plan. The baby could only be Astasia's newborn son. And the feelings he had once cherished for her were stirred up from the depths of his memory. He had loved Astasia. And even though she was Eugene's now, for the sake of that lost love, he would not let them harm her son.

The Sending Song was unlike any other Kiukiu had sung before. She had tried once before to send Tilua's lost spirit back and failed. But as she knelt in the ruined temple where she and Gavril had made love, she sensed there was some ancient magic still trapped within the broken walls, for she felt as if an ancient arcane power was lending its strength to her voice.

The tumbled stones and columns slowly receded and she found herself on the white shore of the children's island. But where were the children?

"You're too late, Spirit Singer." Nagar's voice rang out, exultant.

Whirling around, she saw the verdant darkness of the jungle shimmering around him. The faint outline of a great gateway began to appear, as though etching itself into the insubstantial fabric of the imaginary island.

"No!" She stopped singing. She could glimpse another shadowy world beyond the gateway—her world, in which the jewel-bright figures of the Drakhaoul-possessed princes moved, preparing to sacrifice the royal children. She tried to sing again but despair choked the notes in her throat and her voice died.

In spite of all their striving, Nagar was too strong. They had lost.

Eugene knelt by his daughter, holding her hand, calling her name. Everything else around him had receded into a dim fog; he thought he heard voices, far away, and distant lights flickered through the darkness.

Why was I so slow? Why didn't I see what the daemon intended? Why didn't I catch her in time, my bright, beautiful girl?

She lay so still that at first he had thought her dead; now he could feel there was the tremor of a slight pulse. But he didn't dare move her for fear of making her injuries worse. And all the while, the blood-infused light from the rubies was leaching into his mind, until everything he saw was tainted with its morbid glow and every thought tainted with despair.

My reign is over. I thought I was born to bring enlightenment to my people, but I've brought them nothing but suffering, war, and death. And all because I was too weak to curb my own desires. I'm no longer fit to be Emperor. He slowly raised his eyes to the Serpent Gate and saw the sharp fangs gaping open, etched black against the fiery light. He saw the shadow of Nagar darkening the portal and heard the wailing cry of a baby.

"Rostevan?" In his grief for Karila, Eugene had forgotten his son. Only then did he realize what they intended. His son was to be Nagar's host.

Gavril watched the Drakhaouls move slowly forward, bringing the mortal children toward the sacrificial stone below him. They were distracted by their rite. At any moment, the Gate would open and Nagar would enter the mortal world.

It has to be now.

Gavril gripped hold of the Eye with his talons and tugged.

"*Stop him!*" cried Nilaihah. Sahariel flung himself into the air, making straight toward him.

The crimson light flickered. Eugene blinked, as if he were waking from a dream. He saw shadowy movement high above his head.

Gavril Nagarian was trying to prise the Eye of Nagar from the stone serpent's head. And Sahariel was out to stop him. Sahariel, who had tormented his daughter, then callously let her fall to her death.

"*The Eye's power is waning,*" Belberith said, his voice urgent.

Eugene raised his hand, pointing at Sahariel, and loosed a shaft of malachite fire straight at the Drakhaoul's head. All of his rage and grief were concentrated in that single shot. Sahariel, intent on attacking Gavril, was taken by surprise.

The shaft caught the Drakhaoul as he slewed around in the air, searing into his neck and shoulder, half-severing one of his scarlet wings.

Sahariel let out a rasping hiss of pain. Broken wing alight, he plunged from the top of the Gate to crash onto the ground below.

Fiery pain shot up through Gavril's fingers into his wrists, his arms. It felt as if he had plunged his hand into a pan of scalding water. Yet still he held on, twisting and turning the burning ruby, though his nerves were screaming to him to let go.

Through the flames Gavril saw crimson eyes staring back at him. A feeling of dread overcame him and he knew with sickening certainty that he was in the presence of Nagar. And the daemon face that confronted him glittered with scales of crimson and jet, starkly beautiful, as if carved from living jewel.

"*You are too late, Gavril Nagarian.*"

Too late. He had striven so hard to prevent this happening—and he was too late. Gavril faltered, his grip on the ruby slowly slackening. It had all been in vain. Elysia was dead. Karila was dying. And the Drakhaouls had prevailed.

"*Karila,*" sobbed a child's voice, heartbroken and terrified.

"*My rule in your world is about to begin. And neither you—nor the traitor Khezef—will stop me now.*"

"*Help me, Karila . . .*"

Only then did Gavril see that the Drakhaoul prince's taloned hands rested possessively on the naked shoulders of a small dark-eyed girl. The child was shivering with fear and loathing.

Kiukiu was right. What had once been a noble and proud nature had become warped, corrupted beyond redemption.

"Never," Gavril said. "I shall never let you into my world. Not while I have breath left in my body."

The pain in his hands was so intense that he cried out in agony. And the Eye suddenly came away from the ancient stone that had gripped it so tightly. There he was, hovering, above the Serpent Gate, with the Tears of Artamon clutched in his seared palm.

"Eugene!" he yelled so that every fiber in his throat strained with the effort. "Close the Gate. Close it *now*!"

Eugene heard Gavril Nagarian's voice as if from very far away.

"*He's taken the Eye.*" Nilaihah let go of the boy Giorgi, and launched himself into the air, making straight toward Gavril.

"You and I together, Belberith," Eugene commanded. "Let's make one final effort."

"*Together,*" Belberith echoed.

Eugene lifted his hand toward the snarling stone serpent. In the thickening gloom, he saw that each taloned fingertip was alight, sizzling with flashes of green fire.

"*Stop.*" Adramelech stepped out in front of the Gate. Now that the rubies' maleficent light was extinguished, only his eyes could be seen at first, a glimmer of amethyst in the smoky darkness.

"*Destroy the Gate and you destroy your son.*" Adramelech raised the baby in his arms and Eugene felt his heart fail him as he recognized Rostevan.

Nilaihah came hurtling toward Gavril like a golden meteor, scattering sparks of fire in his trail.

"*Give me back Nagar's Eye!*"

Shafts of gilded flame sizzled through the smoke-choked air. One grazed Gavril's thigh, sending shivers of fire through his body, yet still he flew on.

"*It's not too late, Khezef. Join us.*" Gavril recognized Nilaihah's rich, persuasive tones. "*Give me the rubies, and Nagar will forgive this lapse.*"

"*Nagar. My Lord Nagar.*" Khezef began to slow down, though whether through failing strength or Nilaihah's influence, Gavril could not tell. The Drakhaoul seemed distracted.

"Don't listen to Nilaihah, Khezef," Gavril pleaded. "Remember Karila. Remember Tilua, your soul-child."

Nilaihah was almost upon them, a gilded whirlwind in the murky night.

"*The rubies, Nagarian.*"

It was sheer instinct that made Gavril raise his hands to protect himself from the blast. There was nowhere to shelter; defenseless, he could only close his eyes and wait for annihilation.

Rostevan let out a faint whimper in Adramelech's arms.

"*Destroy the Gate and you destroy your son,*" repeated Adramelech.

And Eugene heard Astasia's distraught voice telling him, "*It looked like Andrei. It sounded like Andrei. But it took our baby.*"

Until that moment he had not been certain. But now he knew for sure. Here was another of the embittered princes, all descendants of Artamon's warring sons—even little Giorgi—all chosen by the Drakhaouls to foment chaos and destruction within the Rossiyan Empire, just as they had, centuries ago.

"Andrei?" he said. "Andrei Orlov? Have you sunk so low that you would kill your own nephew? Your only sister's child? What kind of a monster have you become?"

Andrei was wandering in a dark nightmare, through a lightning-riven wilderness. He was lost.

And then he heard his name as if from a great distance away. His mortal name.

And he heard the plaintive cry of a baby.

He looked down and saw the baby in his arms, as if for the first time. He looked into the baby's blue eyes. Astasia's eyes. His sister Astasia's eyes.

"What am I doing here?" he said, utterly bewildered.

The black night burst into flames of white gold as Nilaihah launched his attack on Gavril.

Instinctively, Gavril raised his hands to shield his eyes.

Khezef awoke. As Nilaihah's dazzling shaft of fire hit the rubies, Khezef's lightning reflexes took over. The Eye of Nagar flew up into the air at the moment of impact—and shattered in a blinding explosion.

Gavril found himself tumbling head over heels, hurled through the sky by the force of the blast.

A dazzle of light illuminated the dark maw of the Serpent Gate. Eugene clutched Karila to him, reeling as the ground shook. In the aftershock, Adramelech swayed, thrown off-balance.

"*Now!*" Belberith's energy surged through Eugene's body. Green fire shot from his outstretched hand and hit the snarling serpent right in the center of the empty eye socket. The stone head burst into a thousand fragments.

Adramelech put his head down and ran.

Eugene fired again and again, pouring all his rage and grief into Belberith's final assault.

First the great wing shafts shattered, then the taloned claws. Stone by ancient stone, the great arch crumbled away beneath his furious attack. Until at last, with a low rumbling as though the ground beneath their feet was about to crack open and swallow them, the Gate fell in on itself, and a dust cloud rose, covering the clearing with pulverized stone.

"It's finished, Nagar!" Eugene cried, with all the force of his lungs. "Yes, I opened the Serpent Gate—but now I've closed it, and it will stay closed forever!"

With a sudden pop, the gateway vanished. And the dark Drakhaoul prince threw back his head and howled aloud his fury and frustration, a sound so desolate and filled with despair that Kiukiu trembled to hear it.

"What's happening?" The children came running back to Kiukiu, crowding around her. "Why is he crying?"

"He has lost all hope now," she said softly. They crept closer to her, seeking comfort, and she opened her arms, trying to hug them all to her.

The sunlight was extinguished. The white sands turned to grey. The blue of the sea faded as the waters swiftly receded, exposing the dry seabed beneath. The nodding palm trees and knotted mangroves vanished. The island illusion, sustained for so long, was disintegrating, and the dust of despair was gusting in from the Realm of Shadows.

"No," whispered Kiukiu, realizing what was happening. "Must we be trapped here with *him*—forever?"

They huddled together as the winds began to blow across the drear landscape.

"Papa . . ."

Eugene's body was still tingling from the tremendous surge of energy that had flowed through him. His brain buzzed and crackled.

"Papa . . ." Only then did he hear her calling him, her voice so feeble, that it was barely a whisper.

"Kari?" He knelt beside her in the darkness. "I'm here. Papa's here now." Was there still a chance for her? He had believed her dead. He stroked her forehead, as he had done so often at home in Tielen, when she lay in her golden swan bed, eagerly awaiting his bedtime visit.

"Tell me a story, Papa . . ."

"My brave girl," he said, his voice unsteady.

"Tell me about the Swan Princess."

"I've been a bad father, Kari, I should have been there for you, but I, I—"

"Once upon a time . . ." she began.

Eugene cleared his throat and continued, "There was a young maiden with hair as bright as the sun."

"As the sun . . ." She whispered, her voice trailing away.

"But a wicked sorcerer turned her into a swan." He choked over the familiar words. "And she flew away to hide from . . ." He touched her cheek, her throat with shaking fingers, feeling for a pulse. "Oh, Kari, Karila, my dearest child." Tears filled his eyes. Her pale, still face, barely visible in the dim light, blurred as he bent over her broken body, sobbing.

CHAPTER 49

Winded, scratched, bruised, but alive—and surprised to be so—Gavril picked himself up. The blast had flung him halfway across the jungle and he had landed in a tangle of branches.

"Khezef," he said, "Khezef, did we succeed?"

"*The Eye has been destroyed.*" The Drakhaoul's voice was subdued. "*And the Gate has been sealed.*"

"You saved my life. If you hadn't reacted so swiftly, I'd have been caught in the blast."

Gavril began to notice that there was a change in the night air. The dark, miasmic fog that had come pouring out of the Serpent Gate was slowly dispersing. The rich indigo of the night sky had begun to appear and, beyond the shreds and tatters of fog, he glimpsed a distant glitter of stars.

He staggered a pace or two, wincing as the burn in his thigh began to bite. Walking was not an option. He had no idea where he was, or which way to go. And the other Drakhaouls might still be lying in wait for him.

"Can we still fly?" he asked.

"*We can try,*" came back the ironic reply.

But it was an effort. Rising through the dense vegetation, pushing through swaths of liana and vine, forcing a way upward toward the clear sky, Gavril sensed Khezef falter.

"What's wrong?"

"*I must go to her.*"

Khezef faltered again, as though his life force was waning.

"*She's dying,*" he gasped, "*and I can feel her pain . . .*"

*   *   *

The Drakhaouls' children huddled together in darkness as the winds whipped up the dust in stinging clouds around them.

Kiukiu felt as though her heart would burst with anger at the injustice. She rose, the children still clinging to her.

"No!" she cried, her voice strong above the whine of the wind. "They don't deserve to be trapped here as well! They are innocent!"

And from far, far away she thought she heard Malusha's voice answering hers, "Then sing them free, child. Use your gift. Sing with all your strength, with all your heart!"

Kiukiu nodded. She closed her eyes and began to sing the Sending Song. At first her voice was weak and shaky and she had to strain to make the notes audible above the wind's desolate wail. But then, to her surprise, she heard a thin voice joining hers, and then another and another. The children were singing. They were singing with her.

Her own voice swelled, growing louder and more confident. And the louder they sang, the more the winds abated.

"Look, Kiukirilya," said Tilua suddenly, pointing excitedly, "I can see Kari!"

One by one, the children turned around, staring.

The faintest outline of a doorway had appeared in the darkness. And there, on the threshold, was Karila.

"Don't stop singing, Kiukirilya!" cried Karila. "Can't you see that your song is working?"

Kiukiu sang on, pouring all her heart and soul into the song, singing for her dead grandmother, for Karila and Tilua, and for all the other children. The winds died down. And while Karila stood in the open doorway to the mortal world, Kiukiu's Sending Song began to trace the filigree outline of a second doorway. A doorway that led to the infinite starry vasts of the Ways Beyond.

By the light of the southern stars, Gavril saw the clearing below them and the ruins of the fallen Gate. With every wingstroke, he had felt Khezef weakening, and they dropped, hurtling out of control, toward the stone pavement.

"*Khezef,*" said a faint voice, "*you came back for me . . .*"

Khezef just managed to right himself. Gavril, shaken and dizzied by the rapid descent, found himself slowly descending.

Eugene knelt over Karila. He was weeping, his tears slowly dropping onto the child's still face and the ancient stones beneath.

"We're too late." Gavril felt his heart near to breaking; he must be experiencing Khezef's grief as well as his own. They had striven so hard to save her. "She's—she's gone."

"*Look,*" whispered Khezef. "*Look there.*"

At first Gavril thought it must be moonlight filtering down through the tall trees, for Karila's fair hair was silvered by a thin, frail radiance. And then he saw that there was a rent, a thin tear in the very fabric of the clearing, leaking light into the dark night, as if a doorway were slowly opening into another world.

"Only the Emperor's Tears will unlock the Gate," he said aloud, remembering Serzhei of Azhkendir's parting words to Kiukiu and Malusha. They had thought he was talking of the Serpent Gate but now Gavril began to see that this was quite another gate. A gate that did not lead to the Realm of Shadows.

"*Karila,*" cried Khezef, and his voice was filled with longing. And then he said, "*Tilua?*"

Adramelech and Nilaihah had begun to walk toward the gate, drawn as if by some unseen force, too strong to resist.

She was gone. Margret's child was gone. And with her, the light had gone from Eugene's life. Knowing he had failed to protect her when she needed him most only increased the bitterness of his despair. And the tears that leaked from his eyes, dropping slowly onto her sweet face, brought no relief.

"*Eugene.*" There was a gentle quality to Belberith's voice that Eugene had never heard before. "*Eugene, look.*"

Eugene slowly raised his eyes and saw the faint contours of a glimmering doorway appearing. How could this be? They had closed the Serpent Gate. "What does it mean, Belberith?"

And now he felt an extraordinary sensation, a heady rush of joy and hope that suddenly infused his whole body, as Belberith cried out triumphantly, "*It means I am leaving you.*"

"But how?" Eugene gazed at the mysterious doorway, not understanding.

"*She has opened the gateway. The gateway that leads to our world.*"

The other Drakhaouls were staring at the opening doorway.

Eugene raised his hand to shade his eyes as a dazzling brilliance began to spill through into the dark clearing. He thought he could just make out a familiar small figure standing on the threshold, gazing out, hands yearningly outstretched.

"K—Kari?" he stammered.

"*I must go to her,*" said Khezef. "*Will you let me go?*"

And there was such love and yearning in his voice that Gavril could not deny his daemon this last wish.

"Go, then," he said.

Gavril felt the Drakhaoul slide out from within him. For the first time they stood side by side: the mortal man, bruised, dirtied, and bleeding; and the wild-haired fallen angel, its dragonfly skin glittering in the starry tropical night.

"*Farewell,*" said Khezef. He put his blue-clawed hands on Gavril's shoulders and, drawing him close, kissed his eyes and then his lips. The touch of his mouth sent one last shiver of glittering energy through Gavril's mind.

"Be at peace," he said softly.

Then Khezef was hastening toward Karila and she was running to meet him, her arms open wide.

"Tilua is waiting for you," she said.

Gavril saw her transfigured in Khezef's tender embrace, her spirit imbued with his brilliant blue radiance, as the two disappeared through the opening doorway into the light.

And then he saw with numbed astonishment the other Drakhaouls moving slowly toward the doorway, following Khezef, leaving their mortal hosts behind, passing through into the brightness of that other world far beyond their own.

The second doorway towered above them, limned in molten silver. And as they gazed, it opened and light poured in, translucent and pure.

"Where does it go?" asked Koropanga, standing up, shading his eyes.

"Can we go through?" said Kahukura, jumping up and down beside his friend with excitement. "Can we?"

"Wait," said Mahina warily, one hand on his shoulder to restrain him. "It might be dangerous . . ."

"No," said Kiukiu, "can't you feel it, children? This is the door that leads to your homes." The beauty of the pure, pale light enchanted her. "This is the end of your imprisonment in the Realm of Shadows."

"Kari!" called Tilua, stretching her hands yearningly. And there was Karila running toward them, her eyes bright with the same aethyrial radiance that streamed through the open doorway.

"What's happening, Kari?" Tilua asked, catching hold of her hand.

"Here she is, Khezef." Karila beckoned, smiling, and Kiukiu saw a tall figure appear, one that her heart recognized before her mind had fully registered that Gavril's Drakhaoul was here. But if Khezef was here, where was Gavril? Was he dead?

Khezef gazed at Tilua with eyes as blue as the summer sea.

"Oh, it *is* you," Tilua said, her voice soft with wonder, reaching out to him.

One by one, the dazzling Drakhaouls appeared—and one by one, each child ran toward them. First Koropanga was reunited with dusky Adramelech, then Waiola with golden-voiced Nilaihah, followed by Kahukura, who hastened, arms wide, to greet the tall warrior Belberith. Even the ice-eyed Za'afiel turned to acknowledge his soul-child. And last of all, Mahina walked, stately and dignified, toward fiery Sahariel, who still lingered behind, almost as if ashamed to be in such company.

Tilua looked back over her shoulder, and called, "Can't you come with me, Kari? Then you and I can play together forever . . ."

"Can't I come with you?" Karila echoed, her voice twisted with longing.

Kiukiu heard Khezef say gently, "*One day, we shall be reunited. But make good use of my last gift to you, Karila. Go back to your father, who loves you. And, for my sake, watch over Gavril. You must go back. There is much for you to do.*"

Karila's outstretched hands slowly dropped back to her sides.

And as Kiukiu watched, it seemed to her that as each Drakhaoul embraced its soul-child, the two spirits merged together, becoming one dazzling power, growing steadily brighter and brighter, until they melted into the pure radiance that was pouring through the doorway . . . and she could see them no more.

CHAPTER 50

There was no sound in the dark clearing but the soft breath of a little breeze stirring the leaves . . . and the distant wash of the tide.

Khezef was gone. And this time Gavril knew in his heart that his Drakhaoul had finally left this world. The first time he had cast him out in Malusha's exorcism, it had been a violent sundering that had left him damaged and incomplete. But this time, Khezef had gone willingly and their parting had been serene.

Unthinking, he raised one hand, trying to summon a little blue flame to his fingertips to lighten the darkness, but no light came. No surge of daemonic energy powered through his veins. He knew then that he was truly alone. Confused and bereft, he sank down on the cracked stones of Nagar's ruined temple and gave himself up to grief.

Eugene cradled his daughter's limp body in his arms, holding her close. They had triumphed over Nagar—but it was a bitter victory and the price he had paid was too high. He thought that his heart would break.

"Papa . . ."

His imagination must be playing tricks on him—and cruel tricks at that. For he thought he had heard her call his name and surely that could not be possible! He had seen her spirit leave her body.

"Papa . . ." came the faint voice again, and in the starlit darkness he saw her fair head move against his shoulder. Her golden lashes fluttered—and she opened her eyes.

"Kari?" How could this be? She had died, he knew it to be so. His voice was hoarse with emotion. "Kari—"

"I want to go home, Papa," she said, quite distinctly. "Back to Swanholm."

Eugene felt his heart swelling: this sudden joy, this hope that had come from a place where all hope was lost, was almost more than he could bear. He could not begin to understand why she was alive; he even wondered if, in losing Belberith, he had gone mad and, in his delusion, was talking to his dead child.

"You shall go home," he heard himself promising, as he kissed her, though he had no idea how he could fulfill that promise. For now that Belberith had left him, he knew himself a mortal man again, with no powers but those of his own kind. He could not bear to think that they had come through such a harrowing battle alive, only to face a slow death from exposure on this remote island.

Gavril heard voices in the gloom. He had no idea how long he had lain in darkness, grieving. He tried to push himself up from the stones on which he lay. Searing pain stabbed through his burned hands and leg. Now he remembered that there was no Drakhaoul to heal his injuries.

He crawled slowly toward the sound of the voices and realized that it was the Emperor, talking softly to his dead daughter.

"Eugene," he said hoarsely. "Eugene, she's—"

"Gavril?" said a faint voice.

"Karila?" How could she still be alive? He had seen her fall, had seen her broken body on the altar, an unwilling sacrifice to Nagar.

"Khezef . . . healed me," she whispered. She put out her hand toward Gavril. Wonderingly, he reached out to take it in his own.

And then a grumbling cry started up close by. A baby's cry, waking from sleep.

"Rostevan is alive," said Eugene. "Thank God. Thank God."

A young woman came hesitantly out from the shelter of the twisted trees. She was carrying the baby. At her side was a boy, wide-eyed with apprehension, clinging to her arm.

"Giorgi Vashteli?" Gavril said. The boy still stared at him in terror. "Don't be afraid," he said in Smarnan. "I'm Gavril Andar; I know your mother Nina. I'll look after you."

Giorgi nodded uncertainly. "You're hurt," he said.

It was true; Gavril looked at the raw burns scarring his leg and looked away again. There he was, offering to protect the boy and he wasn't even sure he could stand.

Light was slowly returning to Ty Nagar, as the last wisps of darkness melted away into the pale dawn sky.

"Can we go home now, Papa?" whispered Karila. "I'm tired."

Eugene looked up at Gavril above her drooping head and Gavril saw the desperation in his eyes.

"I have no idea how we are going to get the children away from here."

"We're castaways," said Gavril with a wry smile. "Don't castaways make shelters out of palm leaves, and survive on fish and coconut milk?"

"That might work for us for a while, but the children?"

The sea was turning from indigo to a rich, clear turquoise.

"Look," Gavril said. "The sun is rising." All about them, the jungle was waking up: insects whirred and buzzed; rainbow-feathered birds whistled and fluttered from branch to branch; and from deeper in the dense tangle of trees, he heard the distant chatter of monkeys.

Suddenly Karila raised her head, as though listening intently.

"Papa," she said, "Linnaius is coming for us."

Gavril gazed out across the empty sea. The waves sparkled in the light of the rising sun. There was no boat in sight, only a lone gull winging over the waters toward them. Then he looked again, seeing it was not a gull at all, but a sky craft, its sail full with wind and the waves beneath stirred to a frenzy of white foam.

"It *is* Kaspar Linnaius!" Eugene cried in astonishment.

Eugene saw the sky craft skim across the silvered sands and shudder to a stop. He let out a shout of exultation.

"Magus! By all that's wonderful . . ."

Kaspar Linnaius came toward him. Eugene would have flung his arms around him and embraced him, had he not been carrying Karila.

"Eugene," said the Magus, "I am glad I could be of service to you one last time." And Eugene saw a glow of emotion briefly light his cold, silvered eyes. "But I can only take you, Lord Emperor, and your children." He turned to Gavril Nagarian. "Lord Nagarian, I have not forgotten how you rescued me from the Commanderie. If his highness permits, I will return for you and the other children."

"Take Stavyomir," said Gavril Nagarian in a failing voice. Eugene could see that he was at the end of his strength.

He placed Karila, Rostevan, and Stavyomir in the sky craft, then went back to the shade of the palm trees where Gavril had dragged himself.

"I have not forgotten my promise, Nagarian," he said. A feeling of genuine warmth for the young man overcame him. As the Magus summoned up a fresh wind, Eugene knelt and placed his hand on Gavril's shoulder. "I pardon you—and your men. I shall withdraw all my occupying forces. And I name you High Steward of Azhkendir."

Gavril slowly looked up into Eugene's eyes.

"Damn it all," Eugene said, "I'd rather have you as my ally than my enemy." Gavril almost managed a grin. He lifted his hand and Eugene took it in his own, gripping it hard.

"Eugene," called the Magus. The sky craft's sail billowed full with a sudden wind that came whirling off the sea. Eugene climbed into the craft and took his baby son in his arms.

Kiukiu heard the roar of a powerful wind gusting toward the island across the steppes. Drawing her thick cloak more closely about her, she gazed at the grey sky, fearing another blizzard.

But she saw a small craft flying toward them at extraordinary speed.

"Magus?" she murmured. She could see four people in the craft. Her heart began to beat faster as she recognized the Magus's passengers: the proud profile of Khan Vachir, one arm around his son Bayar's shoulders. Beside them stood another man, haggard and pale, his blue eyes dark as midnight shadows as he scanned the ground below.

"Gavril!" she cried, "Oh, Gavril!" As the Magus brought the craft to land beside the frozen lake, she sped through the snow to greet them. And before Gavril could climb out of the craft, she flung her arms around him, holding him as if she would never let him go.

Two war canoes, paddled by the strongest men of the tribe, came toward Ty Nagar, the accursed island. They found the woman asleep under the trees. And when she saw them, she wept and shouted with joy. She told them of winged daemons and a child brighter than the sun. She showed them where pale-skinned men lay injured, all hurt in the battle with the daemons.

They discovered the men lying unconscious in the ruins of the old temple to the Serpent God. They gave them water and then took them back to their own island. In time, a ship might come looking for them.

Enguerrand was wandering lost in a red, fever-hot desert, when he felt the soft breath of a cool breeze. He slowly opened his eyes and saw a girl leaning over him, fanning him with a palm leaf.

"Sire, you're alive!" she whispered and began to weep, her teardrops falling on his parched skin like rain. "Thank God."

"Aude?" he said, his voice a dry croak. She was only wearing her shift and it was stained and torn. And then he remembered the terrible crimes he had committed. He gave a groan and turned his head away from her in shame. "How can you ever forgive me?"

A burst of voices chattering in an unfamiliar language startled him. Curious eyes were assessing them.

"They rescued us," said Aude. She shrank closer to Enguerrand, as the islanders came closer, nodding and staring at Enguerrand. "What will become of us? Suppose we have to live here forever?"

Enguerrand reached out and took her hand in his, squeezing it to reassure her. Weak though he was, he felt a new sense of resolve deep within him. There was so much to put to rights.

"A ship will come to rescue us soon." He reached out and wiped the tears from her cheeks with one finger. "And until then, I'll take care of you, Aude."

CHAPTER 51

Eugene opened the carriage door and gave Astasia his hand to help her down. Then he lifted out Karila and set her on the gravel beside him. Last of all, Nadezhda descended, carefully carrying Rostevan in her arms.

All the servants stood waiting to greet them and as Eugene scanned their faces, he saw that many were as moved as he, some openly weeping.

"Long live the Emperor!" shouted a young voice.

"Long live the Emperor!" The response was deafening.

He took Rostevan in his arms and lifted him up so that they could all see him. "Here is Prince Rostevan, my son—and my heir."

The cheers grew louder and Rostevan began to yell lustily.

"He's hungry." Astasia took Rostevan from Eugene. "Let's go inside." She smiled at him over the head of their yelling son.

The blackened East Wing had been demolished; tarpaulins hung over the ruins.

"We have work to do here," said Eugene briskly, rubbing his hands, excited at the prospect of the restoration. "I want to see the chief architect as soon as possible. We shall make it even better than before."

Gustave came hurrying up with a dispatch. "News from Francia, highness," he said. "It seems that a trader in the Azure Ocean has found King Enguerrand and Aude of Provença alive on one of the Spice Islands. There's mention of two other men with him; both in pretty poor shape, but alive."

"You know my orders on that subject," Eugene said quietly.

"When—and if—Count Alvborg returns to Tielen, he is to be taken straight to Arnskammar. As for Prince Andrei . . ." He let out a long, pained sigh. Andrei might be Astasia's only brother, but his actions had been treasonable. "I see no alternative but to exile him on pain of death. He must never return to New Rossiya."

"Understood. I shall alert all the ports." Gustave disappeared toward his office.

"Your imperial highness?" Eugene turned to see a young man balancing himself precariously on crutches.

"Petter!" cried Karila joyously. She ran to greet him and Eugene saw with quiet pride how all the members of his household stared in astonishment. "Is Marta here?"

"She is still in bed, recovering from her injuries," said Petter, recovering his voice, "but she will be overjoyed to see you, Princess. Shall I take you to her?"

Eugene nodded indulgently and the two set off together. It still brought tears of happiness to his eyes to see Karila walking, running, and dancing like any other child, her twisted body remade as Khezef's parting gift.

"No sign of the Magus yet?" he said quietly to his majordomo who stood awaiting his orders.

"No sign."

"I wonder if we shall ever see him again . . ."

Eugene glanced over toward the Magus's empty laboratory.

"The time of magic is over," he said softly. "I must learn to live as a man again."

The daylight was too bright. But the air was fresh and clean. Altan Kazimir breathed in great lungfuls of it. "The air of freedom," he said to himself as he tottered through the quadrangle toward his rooms. After being confined to a single cell, he was a little unsteady on his legs. It was not that Baron Sylvius's agents had maltreated him. He had been well fed and supplied with books. But he could not forgive them for making him fear for his life. Or for damaging his professional reputation.

The unmarked coach had deposited him at the lodge of Saint Ansgar's and driven away as swiftly as it had come.

"Morning, Professor," said the porter, nodding to him. "Good to see you back, sir. I hope the lecture tour went well."

"Lecture tour?" Kazimir goggled. So that was what Sylvius had told the college to explain his sudden absence. His academic reputation was still intact; nothing had leaked out. "Y—yes. It went very well."

"There's a visitor wanting to speak with you, Professor. Says he's a Francian academic. I sent him away, but he's been very persistent."

"Please send him away again." Kazimir just wanted a few stiff drinks and a long sleep in his own bed; he was not interested in visitors. "Tell him I'm ill."

He hurried through the cloisters, head down, hoping he would not be recognized. The last thing he needed now was to have to spin a story to support the "lecture tour" alibi. Fortunately, all he met were a couple of gardeners sweeping up the damp autumn leaves from the immaculate lawns, and he reached his rooms without incident.

"Brandy. Brandy," he muttered, unstoppering the decanter with shaking hands and pouring himself a glass. He had just taken a good mouthful and was standing, eyes closed, relishing the taste, when the inner door opened. Startled, Kazimir choked on the brandy and began to cough and wheeze helplessly.

"I'm so sorry," said the visitor, "did I startle you?"

"M—Magus?" Kazimir stared at Kaspar Linnaius. "B—but I thought—"

"I've been taking a look at your notes on my work. I'm quite impressed. I've taken the liberty of making a few corrections. I think you'll find they make sense."

"But why? Surely you'll be taking up your duties again now that you're recovered—"

"Good-day to you, Professor Kazimir," said the Magus and, a little smile on his lips, walked out into the quad. "You may soon find an invitation from the Emperor to take up residence in the Palace of Swanholm as his Royal Artificier. Please do accept. You have distinct potential."

Kazimir rushed into his laboratory and saw that the Magus had filled in many of the missing links in the equations and had added precise quantities to the lists of chymical ingredients.

He let out a whoop of excitement. He understood now. He saw the connections that had eluded him over the past months.

And then he realized he was alone. He ran into the quad after the

Magus, eager to thank him. But there was no sign of Kaspar Linnaius.

"Never even saw him leave," said the porter.

Eugene leafed through the report from his agent in Azhgorod:

I regret to report that Madame Arbelian has not been comporting herself with the decorum associated with a woman of her status. She has attracted the attentions of several wealthy noblemen, most notably, the Governor, Lord Boris Stoyan, who has installed her in his household as his mistress. It is observed that whilst Madame Arbelian has enjoyed the privileges of her new status to the full, the child Stavyomir is usually left in the care of her maid Dysis and other servants. Whilst this practice is far from uncommon in the wealthy families of Muscobar, it has been noted that the little boy is of a sickly disposition, and since the new year, has been frequently ill.

"So this is how you mourn the father of your child, Madame Arbelian?" Concern had turned to anger. "It's barely a year since his death!"

He heard the sound of children's laughter coming from Karila's room. Softly opening the door, he saw Karila playing peekaboo with a chuckling Stavyomir. He stood watching fondly until Karila glanced up.

"*Must* he go home, Papa?"

"A baby should be with his mother." But even as Eugene said the words, a plan was forming in his mind. He could not put the report from Azhkendir out of his mind. *Jaro's only son deserves better. He should be raised here at court. He'd make a good companion for Rostevan . . .*

"*Please*, Papa."

"There's something I want to show him." Eugene carried little Stavy off into his study, offering up another silent prayer of thanks that the portraits most dear to him had not been destroyed in Alvborg's crazed attack. Karila's mother Margret still bestowed her sweet, serene smile on him. And beside her hung an informal study of his own parents, Karl and Eleanora, with hunting dogs at their feet. They looked so devoted to each other that Eugene still found it hard to imagine that his father could have betrayed his mother with Ulla Alvborg—or that the child of that illicit union, the embittered Oskar, could possibly be his half-brother. He pushed the uncomfortable thought away.

"That's your father." Eugene lifted little Stavyomir up to see the portrait of Jaromir Arkhel. "I promised him I'd take care of you." Stavy stared, then reached out one chubby hand toward the portrait, cooing earnestly. That gesture was confirmation enough for Eugene. "I should have done this long ago," he said, gently stroking the baby's dark gold hair.

"Start packing, Dysis," ordered Lilias briskly. "We're leaving. And not before time too. I've had quite enough of living in this dreary backwater."

"Pardon me, madame, but my instructions are clear. And you, madame, are not included in them. The Emperor has made Stavyomir his ward, thereby freeing you of any parental commitment or rights to influence his upbringing and education."

Lilias heard the words but did not quite take them in. She heard herself give a little laugh of disbelief. "No, there must be some mistake. Surely the Emperor would not separate a son from his mother. Stavy's only a baby."

The officer's face remained impassive.

Lilias rushed forward and grabbed the paper from the officer's hands. "He can't do this to me." But the order confirmed what the officer was saying. Tears pricked at her eyes but she willed herself not to let them flow. She had not been the most doting or attentive of mothers, it was true, but it was not in her nature to spend hours feeding or changing the child; that was a nursemaid's role. But to take her son from her—that was an act of unsurpassed cruelty.

"You will, of course, be allowed to visit the boy once he is well established in his new routine."

Lilias let out a harsh little laugh. "Well, how very generous of his imperial highness."

"Quite frankly, madame, I'm surprised you don't recognize the singular honor the Emperor is conferring upon your son."

"I'm going to fight this," she said eventually, her voice low and hard with the effort of holding back tears. "I'm going to contest this in every court in the empire until I get my son back."

*   *   *

"And so you are all freed men," said Nils Lindgren to the assembled *druzhina*, "pardoned by the Emperor, every one."

Snow glistened on the kastel roofs and the air sparkled with frost. The steam from the soldiers' horses' nostrils fumed the air.

Gavril shook hands with Lindgren.

"Good-bye, then, Captain," said Sosia somewhat gruffly. "We've had our differences, I know, but you've always treated us fairly. I wish you well, wherever your Emperor sends you."

"Home, I hope, to see my wife and family," said Lindgren and Gavril saw a look of longing brighten his eyes. "It must be nearly a year since I last saw them, and little Karl won't remember me; he was only eleven months old when I left for Azhkendir."

"Godspeed, Lindgren," said Gavril. He smiled at the captain with genuine warmth, "One day, I hope, we may meet again—and in happier times."

"Farewell, Lord Drakhaon." Lindgren took a step back and saluted Gavril. "High Steward of Azhkendir." Then he mounted his horse, rode to the front of the waiting column, and raised his hand to signal the order to move off.

Gavril returned to Kiukiu's side and he and his household stood on the steps of the kastel to watch the occupying regiment ride away from his home, cannons and equipment rattling on the laden carts. The grey-uniformed column wound its way up the lane behind the kastel, their regimental banners fluttering in the chill wind, making for the road across the moors that led to Azhgorod and beyond. They had come into Azhkendir over the frozen Saltyk Sea; they would be going home the same way.

But the instant the jingle of spurs and sabres had dwindled into the distance, the *druzhina* let out a great, raw-throated cheer that echoed around the snowy valley and sent all the crows perched on the tower roofs into the sky, cawing noisily.

"Free!" yelled Semyon, punching the air. Dunai brandished one of his wooden crutches like a sabre, whooping in triumph.

Ninusha was sobbing into her apron.

"Overcome with joy, no doubt," said Sosia tartly.

"Anders said he'd take me with him," wept Ninusha. "He *promised*."

"He's a soldier! What did you expect, you silly minx?" said Ilsi. "And now none of the *druzhina* will have anything to do with you."

"Break open those barrels of wine, Oleg!" ordered Gavril. "It's time to celebrate."

After the first toasts had been drunk, Gavril took Kiukiu's arm and led her away into the snowy garden.

"Where are we going?" she asked as the sounds of celebration grew rowdier.

"You'll see."

"The Elysia Summerhouse?" Kiukiu said, remembering, as he pushed aside the frost-furred creepers growing over the doorway.

This was where they had first come to know each other as they nursed the injured Snowcloud back to health. Gavril opened the creaking door and they went inside.

"When the snows have melted, we'll rebuild it, just the way it was when I was a little child. And we'll put some of her paintings in here." He turned around to Kiukiu. "I think she'd have liked that."

She nodded.

"She told me once about her wedding. It was on a snowy day, just like today. They flew over the snow on a horse-drawn sleigh with little silver bells jingling on the harness. And I thought, I thought, Kiukiu—"

Kiukiu caught her breath. "Yes?"

He took her hand in his. "I thought we could do the same. If you would like to." Suddenly he seemed tongue-tied, awkward.

"Ride in a sleigh?" she said.

"Marry me. In Azhgorod. In the cathedral."

Kiukiu stared at him, openmouthed. "What—me?"

And she thought she heard a soft, sibilant voice whisper, "*Give me your firstborn child, be it boy or girl, to tend my shrine . . .*"

Would he ask me if he knew what I have agreed to?

"You. Who else?"

She saw a vulnerable look in his eyes, almost as if he feared that she was about to reject him. She could not bear to see him look so sad. She would find a way, she was sure of it; Chinua would help her. She cupped his face in her hands and kissed him, laughing and crying all at once.

"Yes, of *course* I'll marry you, my dearest Gavril."

ABOUT THE AUTHOR

SARAH ASH is the author of five fantasy novels: *Lord of Snow and Shadows, Prisoner of the Iron Tower, Moths to a Flame, Songspinners,* and *The Lost Child.* She also runs the library in a local primary school. Ash has two grown sons and lives in Beckenham, Kent, with her husband and their mad cat, Molly.